ACCLAIM FOR THE NOVELS OF MARTA PERRY

"Sure to appeal to fans of Beverly Lewis."　　　　　　*—Library Journal*

"A large part of the pleasure of this book is in watching Rachel be Amish, as she sells snapdragons and pansies to both Amish and 'English' at an outdoor market, taking in snatches of Pennsylvania Dutch."　　　　*—The Philadelphia Inquirer*

"A tender novel of second chances, endearing characters, and a can't-put-it-down story."　　　　　　*—Suzanne Woods Fisher, author of The Imposter*

"A born storyteller."　　　　*—Susan Meissner, author of Secrets of a Charmed Life*

"Perry carefully balances the traditional life of the Amish with the contemporary world in an accessible, intriguing fashion."
　　　　　　　　　　　　—Publishers Weekly (starred review)

Don't Miss Marta Perry's Keepers of the Promise Series

The Forgiven
The Rescued
The Rebel

Other Books by Marta Perry

Pleasant Valley

LEAH'S CHOICE

RACHEL'S GARDEN

ANNA'S RETURN

SARAH'S GIFT

KATIE'S WAY

HANNAH'S JOY

NAOMI'S CHRISTMAS

The Lost Sisters of Pleasant Valley

LYDIA'S HOPE

SUSANNA'S DREAM

Keepers of the Promise

THE FORGIVEN

THE RESCUED

At Home
in
Pleasant
Valley

Marta Perry

BERKLEY BOOKS, NEW YORK

BERKLEY

An imprint of Penguin Random House LLC
375 Hudson Street, New York, New York 10014

AT HOME IN PLEASANT VALLEY

ISBN: 978-1-101-98809-1

PUBLISHING HISTORY
Berkley trade paperback edition / October 2015

PRINTED IN THE UNITED STATES OF AMERICA

10 9 8 7 6 5 4 3 2 1

Cover illustration by Shane Rebenschied.

Penguin
Random
House

ACKNOWLEDGMENTS

I'd like to express my gratitude to those whose expertise, patience, and generosity helped me in the writing of this book: to Erik Wesner, whose *Amish America* newsletters are enormously helpful in visualizing aspects of daily life; to Donald Kraybill and John Hostetler, whose books are the definitive works on Amish life; to Louise Stoltzfus, Lovina Eicher, and numerous others who've shared what it means to be Amish; to the unnamed Plain People whose insights have enriched my life; and most of all to my family, for giving me a rich heritage upon which to draw.

CONTENTS

Glossary

ix

Leah's Choice

1

Rachel's Garden

229

Anna's Return

493

Glossary of Pennsylvania Dutch Words and Phrases

ach. oh; used as an exclamation

agasinish. stubborn; self-willed

ain't so. A phrase commonly used at the end of a sentence to invite agreement.

alter. old man

anymore. Used as a substitute for "nowadays."

Ausbund. Amish hymnal. Used in the worship services, it contains traditional hymns, words only, to be sung without accompaniment. Many of the hymns date from the sixteenth century.

befuddled. mixed up

blabbermaul. talkative one

blaid. bashful

boppli. baby

bruder. brother

bu. boy

buwe. boys

daadi. daddy

Da Herr sei mit du. The Lord be with you.

denke. thanks (or *danki*)

Englischer. one who is not Plain

ferhoodled. upset; distracted

ferleicht. perhaps

frau. wife

fress. eat

gross. big

grossdaadi. grandfather

grossdaadi haus. An addition to the farmhouse, built for the grandparents to live in once they've "retired" from actively running the farm.

grossmutter. grandmother

gut. good

hatt. hard; difficult

haus. house

hinnersich. backward

ich. I

ja. yes

kapp. Prayer covering, worn in obedience to the Biblical injunction that women should pray with their heads covered. Kapps are made of Swiss organdy and are white. (In some Amish communities, unmarried girls thirteen and older wear black kapps during worship service.)

kinder. kids (or *kinner*)

komm. come

komm schnell. come quick

Leit. the people; the Amish

lippy. sassy

maidal. old maid; spinster

mamm. mother

middaagesse. lunch

mind. remember

onkel. uncle

Ordnung. The agreed-upon rules by which the Amish community lives. When new practices become an issue, they are discussed at length among the leadership. The decision for or against innovation is generally made on the basis of maintaining the home and family as separate from the world. For instance, a telephone might be necessary in a shop in order to conduct business but would be banned from the home because it would intrude on family time.

Pennsylvania Dutch. The language is actually German in origin and is primarily a spoken language. Most Amish write in English, which results in many variations in spelling when the dialect is put into writing! The language probably originated in the south of Germany but is common also among the Swiss Mennonite and French Huguenot immigrants to Pennsylvania. The language was brought to

America prior to the Revolution and is still in use today. High German is used for Scripture and church documents, while English is the language of commerce.

rumspringa. Running-around time. The late teen years when Amish youth taste some aspects of the outside world before deciding to be baptized into the church.

schnickelfritz. mischievous child

ser gut. very good (or *sehr gut*)

tastes like more. delicious

Was ist letz? What's the matter?

Wie bist du heit. How are you; said in greeting

wilkom. welcome

Wo bist du? Where are you?

LEAH'S CHOICE

This book is dedicated to my grandchildren:
Bjoern, Greta, Ameline, Estella, Georgia, and Tyler,
with much love from Grammy. And, as always, to Brian.

CHAPTER ONE

*K*nowing your proper place was a basic tenet of Amish life. Leah Beiler smiled as she watched her class of thirty-five scholars living out that belief. The number was up by three with the addition of the Glick children just today, and they were all in their assigned seats. Thirty-five heads bent over the work she'd set for her first- to eighth-graders, and not a whisper disturbed the stillness of the one-room school.

Ten years of teaching had given Leah an extra sense where her scholars were concerned. Despite the quiet, excitement rippled through the room, even though no head lifted for a furtive look at the battery clock on her desk. The prospect of a picnic lunch to welcome the newcomers had everyone, including, she had to admit, the teacher, excited. It would be a welcome break in the usual routine, with the Christmas program now in the distant past and their end-of-school-year events not yet begun.

The April weather had cooperated today, bathing Pleasant Valley, Pennsylvania, in sunshine rather than showers. Through the window, she could see the horses and buggies lined up outside that told her the scholars' mothers had arrived with food for the picnic.

She clapped her hands, amused at the alacrity with which pencils were put down. "It's time for our picnic lunch now, scholars. We'll eat first, and then there will be time to play. You may go outside."

It wasn't necessary to add that they should go in an orderly manner. Order was another precept of Amish life, ingrained since birth. Pencils were in their grooves on the desktops and books were closed before the children stood, murmuring quietly among themselves, and filed toward the door.

Leah followed her scholars between the rows of wood and

wrought-iron desks, and out the door at the rear of the classroom that led onto a small porch and then to the schoolyard.

The white school building, looking like every other Amish school she'd ever seen, stood in a grove of trees, its narrow dirt lane leading out to the main road, a good half mile away. The Esch farm lay to their east and the Brand farm to the west, so that the schoolhouse seemed to nestle in their protective, encircling arms.

A trestle table had been set up under the oak tree that sheltered the yard. Her volunteer mothers and grandmothers, probably also happy with the break in routine, had spread it with a bountiful lunch—sandwich fixings of cheese, chicken, cold meat and bread, an array of salads, bowls of fruit, and jars of milk and lemonade. Trays of cupcakes and brownies were covered, reminding the children that dessert came last.

Rachel Brand, Leah's special friend since girlhood, hurried over, apron fluttering, to thrust a well-filled plate into her hands. "Leah, I fixed a plate for you already, ja. If you waited for everyone else to be served, you might miss my macaroni salad."

"Never," she said, her pleasure at the day's treat increased by the presence of the friend who was as dear to her as a sister. "It's wonderful kind of you, Rachel, but we should be seeing to our guest of honor first."

Daniel Glick, the newcomer, stood out in the group, the only adult male in a bevy of women and children. If that bothered him, he didn't show it. He was accepting a heaping plate from Leah's mother, bending over her with courteous attention.

"Your mamm is taking good care of him," Rachel said. "And if she wasn't, someone else would jump at the chance, for sure. A widower just come from Lancaster to join our community—you know every woman in Pleasant Valley will be thinking to match him up with a daughter or sister, they will."

"They'd do better not to matchmake. Daniel Glick looks well able to decide for himself if he needs a wife."

Daniel's firm jaw and the determined set to his broad shoulders under the plain work shirt he wore suggested a man who knew what he wanted and who wouldn't be easily deflected from his course. He was probably a gut hand at avoiding any unwanted matchmaking.

Rachel, her blue eyes dancing with mischief as if they were ten again, nudged her. "You'd best tell that to your mamm, then. I expect she's already inviting him to supper so he can get to know you."

"Me?" Her voice squeaked a bit, so she was glad that she and Rachel stood a little apart from the others. "Rachel, that's foolish. Everyone has known for years that I'm a maidal."

"Years," Rachel scoffed, her rosy cheeks growing rounder with amusement.

Rachel did still look like the girl she'd once been, her kapp strings flying as they'd chased one another in a game in this same schoolyard. Leah couldn't remember a time when Rachel hadn't been part of her life. They'd shared enough joy and sorrow to bond them forever.

"I know very well how old you are, Leah Beiler," Rachel continued, "because we were born within a month of each other. And you are only an old maid if you want to be."

Leah crinkled her nose. "A maidal," she said firmly. "And I'm a schoolteacher with a love of learning besides, which frightens men off."

Rachel's smile slid away suddenly, and her smooth brow furrowed. "Leah, it would break my heart if I thought you meant to stay single all your life because of Johnny."

The name startled her, and it was all she could do to keep dismay from showing on her face. When Johnny Kile left Pleasant Valley, fence-jumping to the English world like too many young men, he'd left behind his family, including his twin sister, Rachel, who'd loved him dearly.

And he'd left Leah, the girl he'd said he'd loved. The girl he'd planned to marry that November, once the harvest season was over.

Many of those young men who left came back, penitent and ready to rejoin the community, after a brief time in the English world. But not Johnny.

She had to speak, or Rachel would think this more serious than it was. Close as they were, she didn't want Rachel to know how Johnny's loss had grieved her. It would only hurt Rachel, to no good end.

"No, of course that's not why. Johnny and I were no more than boy-and-girl sweethearts, you know that."

Rachel's hand closed over hers in a brief, warm grip. "You loved him. That's what I know."

"It was a long time ago," she said firmly, shutting away bittersweet memories. "What has brought on thoughts of him today?"

Rachel had not mentioned Johnny's name since the day she'd run to the Beiler house, tears streaming down her cheeks, to tell Leah that he had gone. It had shamed his family, as well as grieved them, that he'd left in that way, with no word for his betrothed and only a short note for them.

"No reason," Rachel said, but her gaze drifted away from Leah's.

She set down the filled plate on the nearest table so she could grasp her friend's wrist. "Rachel, tell me the truth." It was the warning tone she used with her scholars when they attempted to evade a question.

Rachel shook her head, dashing away a sudden tear. "My birthday is next week. Johnny's birthday, too, of course. It reminds me."

"And it hurts," Leah said softly. She knew about that pain.

"I'm being foolish." Rachel sniffed. "Here come your mamm and Daniel Glick to talk to you. I'd best see if any of those platters need filling." She scurried off, giving no chance for Leah to say a word of comfort, even if she could think of one.

For a moment the scene—the mothers serving food, chattering among themselves, the children eating quickly so they could scatter to swings, seesaw, and ball field—seemed to shimmer before her eyes. She was a girl again, hearing her sweetheart say he loved her.

She took a breath, clenching her hands against the dark green apron that covered her dress. She wasn't that girl in love any longer. She was a grown woman, a teacher, and she had to act like one.

And here came her mother, towing the newcomer along with her. "Leah, here is the father of your new scholars. Daniel Glick, this is my daughter Leah."

He was taller than many Amish men, that was her first thought. She had to tilt her head to look up at him. Piercing blue eyes met hers, their straight brows giving him a bit of a sober look. His beard was the same chestnut brown shade as his hair, and his mouth above the beard firm.

"Wie bist du heit. It's nice to meet you."

"Teacher Leah." He nodded in greeting, fingering the brim of his straw hat. "It's kind of you to take on three new scholars with the school year so near over."

She grasped a firm rein on her scattered thoughts. "I'm happy to have them. I look forward to getting to know Matthew and Elizabeth and Jonah."

"They are glad to be back in class again after the move." He glanced toward the table where the children sat eating, his face serious. "I would like to talk with you about their schooling. Perhaps when they finish today?"

The prompt request took her by surprise a bit. Still, since the Glick family had just moved here, their situation was different from that of her other scholars, most of whom she'd known since birth, seeing them at work frolics and worship services, watching them grow.

Daniel, being a widower, had to be both mother and father to his children, so she was glad to see he was interested in his young ones' education.

"Ser gut," she said. "I'll see you at three, then."

He gave a short nod to her, another to her mamm, and walked off toward the table where the children were having their lunch.

She watched him go, wondering a little. Still, there'd be plenty of time later to think about what changes the addition of the Glick family might make to her familiar classroom.

She turned to her mother, and her heart clenched with a familiar worry. "Mamm, why don't you let the others take care of the cleaning up and go along home after you eat? You look a little tired."

Her mother always insisted that she was well now, completely recovered from the cancer surgery that had worried them all so much a year ago, but even so, anything out of the ordinary seemed to exhaust her, though she hated to admit it.

"I'm not tired," her mother said predictably. "Well, what do you think of Daniel Glick? A strong-looking man, wouldn't you say? And the three children so bright and happy. They're a fine addition to our community. Aren't they?"

Her heart sank at the indication that her mother was, as Rachel had said, embarking on matchmaking. It was hardly surprising, since Mamm had tried her best to pair her eldest daughter up with every eligible man in their central Pennsylvania Amish community.

She had even suggested a visit to distant relatives back in Lancaster County a time or two, in hopes of finding a husband for her stubborn child.

It had taken all Leah's determination to hold out against her mother's loving wishes for her. Mamm thought Leah should forget her disappointment in Johnny and love again. But Mamm didn't know the whole story.

"They seem very nice," she said. Daniel Glick was an unknown quantity. All she could say now was that he appeared interested in his children's education. As for the children—

She had to banish a frown before Mamm saw it. Happy and healthy, Mamm had said. Certainly the children looked sturdy enough, but she was not so sure about the happy part, at least as far as the older two went. Both Matthew and Elizabeth had seemed withdrawn, resisting her efforts to get to know them this morning.

They might just be struggling to get comfortable in a new place. So why did she have this niggling feeling that something was wrong?

Jacob Esch, the eighth-grader she'd appointed to watch the clock, began to ring the bell that signaled it was time for play. She'd found that without a reminder, some of the scholars would skimp on their eating to be first on the swings.

Children ran toward the swings and seesaw, the little girls with their braids and bonnet strings flying in the wind, the boys racing one another as they always did. Some of the older ones grabbed bats and balls.

The Glick children seemed to hesitate. Then Matthew walked toward the ball field, while Elizabeth took her little brother's hand and led him to the swings.

Leah glanced toward Daniel Glick. He stood near the picnic table, arms crossed over his chest in a way that seemed to close him off from the rest of them. And the steady gaze he directed toward his children was so intent it startled her.

Leah had her work cut out for her that afternoon. She should be focused on assessing the Glick children's scholastic status in preparation for her talk with Daniel Glick later. Or else she should concentrate on the model of Pleasant Valley that her older scholars were constructing or the spelling test she'd be giving tomorrow.

Instead, her thoughts kept drifting into the past. It seemed no time at all since she'd been a scholar here, sitting at the row of desks against the right-hand wall, looking out at the blossoms on the apple tree, daydreaming.

Johnny had sat behind her, Rachel in front, making her a buffer between the twins. Johnny had tied her kapp strings together once, and spent the afternoon recess sitting on a stool in the corner as a result. She could still see him looking over his shoulder to make a face at her when the teacher's back was turned.

She pulled her rebellious thoughts into order. This was Rachel's fault, making her think of Johnny again. Making her feel that familiar sense of failure that came each time she remembered how they'd parted.

She moved to the row of first-graders, bending over to check the lined sheets on which they were practicing the letter *L*. They looked up now and then at the capital and lowercase alphabet that marched across the top of the chalkboard.

"Very nice work, Jonah." She smiled at Daniel's youngest, and the boy's chubby face crinkled in a returning smile. She'd already noticed that Jonah was the most open of the three.

"I like to make letters, Teacher Leah."

"I can see that." She patted his shoulder lightly. "Keep up the good work."

At six, Jonah's ease in English was surprising. Most of the first-graders had spoken only the Pennsylvania Dutch dialect at home before they started school, where they were expected to learn English. Jonah must have had a fine teacher at his last school to be so at ease in his second language. Or third, if one counted the High German used for worship.

Toward the back of the room, Matthew seemed contented enough, working on a model of some sort for the display. She hadn't seen him interact with any of the other children in spite of friendly overtures from several boys.

She walked back to check on the boys' progress, pausing by Matthew's desk. And blinked. What she'd taken for a model of a silo certainly wasn't, unless silos had suddenly taken on a substantial tilt.

"What are you making, Matthew?"

He squirmed a little in his seat, not looking at her. "Nothing. I mean, a silo."

She tapped the model. "I think the grain might fall out, don't you? This looks more like the Leaning Tower of Pisa."

His wide blue eyes met hers again, but this time they were lit by enthusiasm. "I'd like to see that someday. How can it lean over but not fall down? Do you know?"

She heard the wonderment in his voice. Heard it, and recognized it. She knew that yearning to see things that were far away and to understand things that seemed inexplicable. For just an instant she wanted to share the boy's curiosity.

No, of course she didn't. She'd stopped longing for the impossible years ago, when she'd put away childish dreams. She was Amish, and Amish didn't fly off to a foreign country to gape at something that had no influence on their lives.

"I don't know. But perhaps you should make a silo. I'm sure Jacob could use one for his farm."

Jacob Esch, hearing his name, looked up and nodded, and the moment passed. Matthew turned toward the other boy, and if there was disappointment in his face, she didn't see it.

She moved away. Matthew's sister, eight-year-old Elizabeth, was practicing spelling words with Rachel's oldest, Becky. She smiled a little when she made a mistake, but she shot an apprehensive glance toward Leah now and then, as if unsure of her approval.

All in all, she found the Glick children a bit of a concern, although there was nothing she could really put her finger on. As their teacher, it was her job to make them feel at home and bring out their best. Perhaps her talk with their father would help her understand them better.

Beyond the side window, the apple tree had begun to put forth its blossoms. Something fluttered inside her, like the apple blossoms trembling in the breeze. She and Johnny had stood under that tree the first time he'd told her that he loved her. And it was there that they'd said their bitter good-byes.

The automatic timer in her mind went off, and she turned to check the clock on her desk.

"It's time to clean up now. Please be sure the paste lids are on tightly." The older boys sometimes skimped on the cleanup, a little overeager to be out the door. "Who would like to wash the chalkboard today?"

Becky's hand went up immediately, and after a glance at her, Elizabeth Glick put her hand up, too.

"Ser gut. You girls may start on the boards. Please leave the spelling words."

The final routine of the day moved swiftly to its conclusion, and soon her scholars were headed toward the door in an even line, saving the running and jumping for the moment they hit the schoolyard. Leah touched Matthew Glick lightly on the arm.

"Your father is coming to talk with me, Matthew. Will you please watch your brother and sister on the playground until we finish?"

Matthew's face was very like his father's. Guarded in a way one didn't often see in an Amish child. He studied her for a moment, blue eyes serious, before he nodded. "I will."

"Ser gut." She glanced up and saw Daniel near the door, moving aside as the line of children passed him. When Matthew reached him, he extended his hand, as if to touch the boy's shoulder, but then he seemed to change his mind, standing where he was until they were all out. The door closed behind the last scholar.

"Komm in. Wilkom to our school." Leah gestured toward the rows of desks. "Matthew's desk is here, and Elizabeth's there. And Jonah is up in front, with the other first-graders."

Daniel followed her without speaking to the front of the classroom, his shoes thudding on the bare wooden floor. Not that she expected him to chatter, but a few words might ease the awkwardness.

He was a stranger, after all, and she thought again how odd that was. Pleasant Valley's Amish community had been established in the 1970s, when the brethren had left Lancaster County for cheaper farmland in the valleys of central Pennsylvania. Since then, the population had been stable, so that she knew every member of the church district as well as she knew her own family. Daniel Glick and his children were the exception.

She pulled over the visitor's chair for him and seated herself behind her desk. "Komm, sit down. I'm glad you're willing to talk with me about the children. I want to make their move here as smooth as possible."

Daniel balanced his straw hat on his knees. He smiled, the frostiness disappearing from his blue eyes as his face relaxed. It was a very appealing smile. She'd been right—if Daniel was in search of a wife, he'd have no trouble finding one by himself.

Not her, of course. She was content with her life the way it was, and she didn't foresee any changes coming her way.

"We've been warmly welcomed here," Daniel said. "It is a change for the young ones, though."

"And for you."

He shrugged. "I don't mind a new place. I'm just glad to have a chance to buy such a fine farm." His eyes narrowed, accentuating the sun lines that fanned out from the corners. "Amish children should be raised on a farm."

"Everyone doesn't have that opportunity." Even here, farms were being lost every year to development. Most Amish parents couldn't manage to provide land for each of their children, no matter how much they wanted to. "One of my brothers has a farm machinery shop, and another is a carpenter."

Daniel's brows drew down. "My children will have that chance. I'll see to that."

It was what every Amish parent wanted, of course, but Daniel's insistence seemed a little intense, and it made her wonder what was behind it.

"They're going to be a gut addition to our class, I know. I notice that Jonah speaks English very well already—better than most of my first- and even second-graders."

For some reason that made his frown deepen. "Ja." The word was so curt that it sounded as if Jonah's skill in English was a fault.

She struggled for something else to say about his children on such short acquaintance. "Elizabeth volunteered to wash the chalkboard already, she and Becky Brand."

"She's a gut helper." He said the words absently, his gaze on the world map she'd pulled down earlier for geography. "Teacher Leah, there is something I want to say. I want to be certain my children are not learning worldly things in your classroom."

Leah stiffened. That was something the parents of her children seldom had occasion to say, knowing it was a given in an Amish school. She remembered Matthew's comments about the leaning tower. Did Daniel assume that the map meant she was encouraging the children to yearn for the outside world?

"Our course of learning is much like that of any Amish school," she said firmly, on sure ground when it came to her teaching. "I'd be happy to show you our textbooks and our course of study. Or perhaps you'd like to meet with the school board members."

He shook his head. "There's no need for that. I'll see their books soon enough when I help the young ones with their homework." He paused for a moment, as if weighing his words. "I meant no disrespect by what I said, Teacher Leah. But I care about my children's education, and it means a great deal to have them in an Amish school."

"I understand." But she didn't, not entirely. She didn't know Daniel, and she didn't know what drove him. She managed a polite smile. "Well, here is a chance to see young Jonah's primer, since he went outside without it." She picked up the ABCs book and handed it to him.

"That boy would forget his head if it weren't attached." He rose as he spoke, and his expression was indulgent at the mention of his youngest. "I'm grateful for your interest in my children, Teacher Leah. If there are any difficulties, you will let me know."

That sounded more like an order than a request, but she nodded. It seemed that, having delivered his opinion, Daniel intended to leave without further ado.

"Have there been any troubles with the children that I should know about? Any health concerns, or anything like that?"

"None." Holding his hat in one hand and the primer in the other, he turned toward the door. It gave her the feeling that if there had been any problems, she wouldn't hear about them from Daniel.

She followed him back through the row of desks and out the door to the porch. He paused on the front step, one hand on the railing, and looked back at her. "Would you want me to wait while you lock up now?"

"That's kind of you, but I have some cleaning to do before I go home." She waved to the children as they came running toward their father.

"I'll be going then." His long stride cleared the steps, but then he paused again, his eyes narrowing as he stared down the lane. "It seems you have another visitor, Teacher Leah."

Dust rose from the dirt road as a car—a bright red car—drew up to the school. The sunlight glittered on the paint and chrome, and then on the fair hair of the man who slid out and stood looking at her.

Her heart thudded to a stop. Johnny Kile had come back.

CHAPTER TWO

*L*eah reached behind her, pressing her hands flat against the door frame for support. A heavy band seemed to tighten around her chest, compressing her ribs until she couldn't take a breath. Certainly she couldn't speak a single word.

But she had to. She had to breathe, had to nod, had to speak and act as if it were an everyday thing to see John Kile after all these years.

Leah managed a shallow breath, inhaling the scent of fresh-cut grass. Rachel had sent her husband over from the farm to mow yesterday, so that all would be in readiness for the picnic. Rachel couldn't have imagined that her twin brother would show up here today, not that Johnny was likely to notice the grass.

John came toward the schoolhouse porch slowly, as if unsure of his welcome now that he was here. She forced herself to raise her eyes, to look at the person he'd become in ten years away among the English.

Odd. She knew it was John. She had recognized him the instant he stepped from the car. But the boy she'd known ten years ago had little in common with the worldly man who stood before her. The clothes, the hair, even the way he stood and the expression on his face were different. She was so used to seeing a beard on adult males that his face looked naked without it.

Then he smiled, lips quirking in the way that showed the dimple at the corner of his mouth, and he was Johnny again.

"It's been a long time, Leah. It's really good to see you."

His gaze moved from her to Daniel Glick, who stood where he'd been when he spotted the car. Daniel stared back, his face stolid, as if he waited for something. An explanation, maybe.

A natural reaction, that was certain sure. An English man coming to call at the Amish school was unusual. Daniel would stay to be sure nothing was wrong. She had no choice but to introduce them.

"Daniel Glick, this is John Kile. John is . . . an old friend." What else could she call him?

Daniel gave a short nod, not offering to shake hands. His expression didn't change, but she sensed his taut figure stiffen. Had he been in Pleasant Valley long enough to have heard of the Kiles' son, who'd broken his engagement, his baptismal vows, and his mother's heart to turn English?

They couldn't stand here staring at one another. Somehow she had to get things back to normal. Daniel shifted his gaze to her, a question in his intent face, and she managed a faint, reassuring smile.

"It was gut of you to come, Daniel. I'll see the children tomorrow."

He didn't move for a moment, and she couldn't imagine what he was thinking. It couldn't be a positive thought, she'd guess.

Finally he nodded. He turned away, walking quickly toward his buggy without a backward glance. In a moment the children had scrambled in. The buggy rolled off down the lane.

"Someone new in the community?" Johnny asked. "I don't recognize him." He stood looking up at her, one hand on the stair railing, sunlight turning his hair to flax.

"He and his family just moved here from Lancaster County." And why were they talking about Daniel when so many other things shouted to be said?

"He wasn't very friendly."

"Do you expect friendship here?" Her words sounded more in control than she felt.

His hand tightened on the railing. "Maybe not. I guess things haven't changed much, have they?"

"They don't. That's the choice we make." The choice he had rejected.

"Look, Leah, can we go inside and talk?" He planted one foot on the porch step, as if he'd come closer to her, and she felt a wave of something that might be panic.

"The porch is a fine place to talk." She kept her voice calm with an effort.

It was bad enough that Daniel had been here to witness a man who was under the meidung come to visit with her. She wouldn't compound the trouble by being inside the schoolhouse alone with someone the community had shunned.

What must Daniel be thinking about the Amish schoolteacher who apparently had a male English friend? The thought flitted through her mind, and she shooed it away. She had more serious concerns than what Daniel thought of her.

Johnny lifted his right eyebrow in a familiar movement. His hazel eyes were unchanged, but both his brows and hair were a little darker now than they'd once been.

"It looked as if you'd invited him inside—Daniel, was that his name?"

"Daniel is the parent of three of my scholars. Naturally we talked in the schoolroom. But you have no reason to be there."

"I spent eight years there. Remember?" His smile teased, the way it had long ago.

"I remember." She had to fight against the memories, just as she'd been doing all afternoon. "But you're not the same person you were then. No one looking at you now would imagine you to be Amish."

"I'm not." He frowned. "Not anymore."

The flip answer hurt her. "Can you deny what you're born so easily?"

"Not easily." His face became set in sudden, harsh lines, and he looked years older than she knew he was. "But it can be done. You know others who've done it and been happy." His tone challenged her.

Did she? Maybe so. Once they were gone, she didn't have much opportunity to judge whether they were satisfied with their choice or not.

"If you're so happy with your decision, why are you here now?"

As soon as the question was out, her heart began to beat in hard, measured thuds, pounding against her rib cage. What if he said he was here because of her? How would she answer that?

"I'm not here to kneel in repentance and ask the church to take me back, if that's what you're thinking." His jaw hardened. "Look, at least we can sit down and talk like civilized people, can't we?"

He even talked differently now, using phrases she'd never heard

from his lips, speaking in a cadence that was so quick it could never be
Amish. He clearly wouldn't go away until she'd heard him out.

"Fine." She sat down on the top step of the porch, smoothing her
long skirt over her legs. "Talk, if you want."

If he wasn't here to repent, then he hadn't come with any idea of
reuniting with his lost love. That should make it easier to deal with him.

She didn't want that relationship anyway, she assured herself. She'd
been over her feelings for Johnny a long time now.

One thing hadn't changed about him, she noticed. He still wore that
mulish expression when he was balked in what he wanted to do. He
stood for a moment, frowning at her, and then he sat down next to her
on the step, stretching out long, jeans-clad legs.

"So, John Kile, why are you back in Pleasant Valley, if not to rejoin
the brethren?" She was satisfied that she sounded perfectly composed.

"Have you seen Rachel lately? Are you and she still close?"

He jumped from thought to thought like a June bug. That hadn't
changed in his years away.

"I saw her today." She hesitated. Say the rest of it? Maybe she should.
"She mentioned you, feeling a little sad because of your birthdays next
week."

She certainly wouldn't mention Rachel's concern that Leah was still
single because of him.

"I'm sorry." He clenched the knees of his jeans, muscles standing
out on the backs of his hands. "I never meant to hurt her."

She could only gape at him. "Never meant to hurt her? Your leaving
hurt everyone in the community." Especially her. "Maybe you've forgotten that in all the time you've been gone."

"No, I haven't forgotten. Anything." His voice softened. "Not you,
Leah."

She laced her fingers together in her lap. It was best, safest, not to
respond to that, but the words echoed in her heart. "Are you going to
see Rachel?"

"I want to." He leaned toward her, his eyes darkening in intensity.
"Please, you talk to her for me, Leah. Tell her I'm here, that I want to
see her."

"Me?" Her throat clutched. "I can't do that."

"You two were always like sisters." His voice went low and coaxing. "She'll listen to you."

Did he have any idea how hurtful it was to remind her that she and Rachel had nearly *been* sisters? It seemed he didn't. Or if he did, he could ignore it in his need to accomplish his goal.

"She's your twin, Johnny. If you want to see her again, then—"

"I'm scared."

The words sent her gaze flying to his face. He gave her a rueful smile.

"Stupid, isn't it? But I'm afraid to walk up to my own sister."

She tried to harden her heart against that smile. Johnny wasn't her responsibility any longer. "I think you'd better. Or else just go away again."

"I can't go away. I'm going to be working here for the next six months, at least. I'm doing research at the medical clinic over in Fostertown."

She could only stare at him. "You are?"

"Hard to believe, isn't it? I just finished a degree in genetics, and I'm going to assist Dr. Brandenmyer in his work. You know about him?" He slanted a questioning look at her.

"Ja, I know."

Everyone in the community knew about the clinic and the doctor. Geneticists wanted to study the Amish because of the hereditary diseases that occurred too often in a community where most folks were descended from the same small group of ancestors.

Dr. Brandenmyer did gut work, so people said, ministering to those who were ill, in addition to conducting his research. That was not always an easy thing in a society as closed as the Amish were.

"Working with him is the opportunity of a lifetime." Johnny stared past her, as if looking at some future she couldn't see.

"Is your background why the doctor hired you? Because you were Amish once?"

Johnny frowned. "I have very good qualifications. But I suppose my heritage didn't hurt."

"And you want to get back in touch with your family for what?"

She was feeling her way. Once, she'd have said that she knew every thought that went through Johnny's mind. Now she feared that what she said to him might determine whether he saw his family or not.

Please, Father. Guide me. I don't know what is best to do or say.

"I want to see them because they're my family." His tone was sharp, but then he smiled, shaking his head. "But it's true. I need to find a way to make contact with the community again if I'm going to be much help to Dr. Brandenmyer. And it's worthwhile work—you must know that. It can save lives."

Children's lives. She thought of the children she'd known throughout the community—the ones afflicted with Crigler-Najjar syndrome, spending half their lives under the special blue lights that helped them survive to grow up. Or those with the other genetic diseases that were too common among the Amish.

She didn't want to be involved, didn't want to risk the hurt that would come with his return.

But if what Johnny talked about could help those children, wasn't it worth at least trying to smooth his path? She couldn't easily turn away from something that might help them.

Her throat tightened, and she had to push out the words. "All right. I'll talk to Rachel. I make no promises. But I'll tell her that you're back and that you want to see her."

Johnny grasped her hand in a quick, warm grip before she sensed what he was about to do. "Thank you, Leah. You're a good friend."

She pulled her hand free, denying the pleasure she felt at his touch, his words.

"I'm making no promises," she said again. She'd made promises to Johnny once, and that had come to nothing.

"Good enough." He stood, as if afraid she'd change her mind if he delayed. "I'll stop by tomorrow after school to see what she said."

"Not tomorrow." He'd turned into a typical Englischer, always in a hurry. "Maybe on Wednesday. I'll have been able to talk to Rachel by then."

He looked as if he wanted to argue, but then he nodded, his lips curving into the smile that was still familiar.

"All right. Take your time. I'll see you Wednesday."

He'd gotten what he'd come for, so he moved away quickly, sliding into the car without a backward glance toward her.

She rose, standing on the top step. Watching until the red car disappeared around the bend in the lane.

Johnny Kile was back. She didn't think she'd quite accepted it yet.

He wasn't the boy she'd loved, that was certain sure. But who he was now—she didn't quite know. Or how it would affect her, affect all of them, having him here.

Any hope Leah had of going to see Rachel that evening disappeared when she got home and discovered that her brother Levi and his family were coming for supper. Her mother was already bustling about the farmhouse kitchen, and whatever tiredness Leah had observed earlier had vanished in her excitement over having a full table for supper.

"I know the boys have big appetites, but you are making twice as much as they will eat. Why don't you just give us the leftovers from the picnic?" She'd noticed that, predictably, nearly as much food had gone home again as Mamm had brought.

Her mother shook her head, looking aghast. "I can't do that. They would think I wasn't happy to see them."

"You see Levi every day." With her oldest brother doing most of the farm chores now, that was inevitable. "And Barbara and the children at least two or three times a week."

"Not for supper," her mother said with unanswerable logic. She thrust a wooden spoon into Leah's hand. "You make the dumplings. You have a lighter hand with them than Anna does."

"Anna just doesn't want to admit how good a cook she is, for fear she'll have to do more." But she couldn't help but be pleased that her mother thought well of her cooking, even if the feeling was a bit prideful.

The Schnitz un Knepp was already steaming on the stove. Leah took the yellow mixing bowl from the shelf. She'd concentrate on getting the soft dough to just the right consistency. Maybe then she could push away thoughts of Johnny, of Rachel's reaction when she heard the news of his return, even of Daniel Glick and his children. Those worries would have to be dealt with later.

An hour later, the substantial array of food Mamm considered appropriate for a family supper was spread on the long table and the house was crowded with people—all, it seemed, talking at once. Mamm sank into her chair.

Leah, taking her place next to her, frowned slightly, her gaze on her mother's face. Even when she closed her eyes as her father began to pray, the image of her mother's face lingered.

Mamm had aged since her bout with cancer, there was no doubt about that. Her brown hair, pulled tightly back into a bun from its center part, seemed to show more gray all the time.

But it was the strained tiredness on her mother's face at the end of a long day that worried Leah. Nothing would convince Mamm that she couldn't do all the things she used to do.

When the prayer ended, Leah leaned across to murmur to her mother under the clatter of cutlery. "Don't you get up again, Mamm. If anything needs fetched for the meal, Anna and I will take care of it." She glanced at her younger sister. "Ain't so?"

Anna's bright blue eyes registered understanding, and she nodded quickly. "Ja, that's right, Mamm. You cooked, so we'll serve and clear."

Leah smiled. The baby of the family, at eighteen Anna could be unpredictable—sweet and happy one moment, distracted and short-tempered the next. That was natural, wasn't it? When she'd been that age, she'd probably been the same.

When she'd been that age, she'd been in love with Johnny.

She shoved that thought away again, trying to focus on her sister. She couldn't help but worry sometimes that Anna's job, working at a Mennonite bakery in town, brought too many temptations into her life.

Still, Anna was gut at heart. She'd soon settle down and turn her flightiness into falling in love with a suitable young man.

"You have some new scholars at the school, Leah, ain't so?" Barbara, her brother Levi's wife, turned from spooning a dumpling into baby Sarah's mouth to look at Leah inquiringly.

"The Glick children started today," she said. "There are three of them—six, eight, and ten. The other children are making them welcome."

"It's gut for all of us to do that," her mother said. "Poor man, a widower alone with three young ones. We must do all we can for them. I've invited them to supper tomorrow night."

Leah's heart sank. Not that her mother wouldn't be welcoming even if she didn't have two unmarried daughters in the house, but still—

"A widower with young children needs a wife. Maybe a fine opportunity for our Leah, ja?" As usual, Barbara burst out with something the others might be thinking but not be ready to say.

"I'm not looking for a husband," she said, with no hope that would end the topic.

"Every woman is looking for a husband," Barbara insisted. Her face beamed with such happiness that Leah couldn't find it in her heart to be annoyed, though she did sometimes wish that Levi had found himself a wife who wasn't quite so eager to run everyone else's life. Mamm's matchmaking intentions were enough to deal with.

I shouldn't think that of Barbara. A quick prayer formed in her mind. *She is a gut soul, I know, and she makes Levi happy.*

Across the table, Anna put her fork down and leaned forward to glare at Barbara around Levi's bulk. "Every woman is not like you, Barbara."

Leah landed a gentle kick on Anna's ankle, and Anna transferred the glare to her. Anna should know by now that the best way to take their sister-in-law's pronouncements was to ignore them.

"Every woman wants a home of her own," Barbara said, her good humor unimpaired. "You'll find that out when you're a little older, Anna." She beamed around the table. "And now is a gut time to tell you that Levi and I will have an addition to the family, come December."

Under cover of the flood of congratulations from Mamm and Daad and brother Mahlon, Leah exchanged glances with Anna. Another young one coming, with Sarah not out of diapers yet and the little boys only two and four.

Children were a blessing to any Amish family, but where were Levi and Barbara going to put them all in the small house they rented on the

Evansville road? She rose, pressing her cheek against Barbara's and murmuring her good wishes.

Daad cleared his throat, and everyone turned toward the head of the table. Daad exchanged glances with Mamm, and Leah saw a faint nod.

"Your mother and I have something to tell you also." Her father's lean, weathered face was as solemn as if he were at prayer. "We feel it is time for us to move into the daadi haus and let Levi and Barbara take over the farm."

Leah felt it like a blow to the stomach. Levi taking over the farm? Was Daad really ready for that now?

But the past two years had been hard on him, too. Though he seemed as strong as ever, his beard was completely white now, and he didn't move as fast as he used to.

She'd known it would come sometime. That was the way things were done. She just hadn't thought it would be so soon.

Still, the daadi haus, connected to the farmhouse by a covered walk, had been ready for new occupants since Grossmutter died five years ago. Levi was already doing much of the farmwork, and everyone in the community knew this was his place.

But what would the change mean for her and Anna?

Mahlon took the news happily enough, as would her brother Joseph. They were already settled in jobs, Joseph with his farm machinery repair and Mahlon as a carpentry apprentice.

Joseph and his wife, Myra, were probably thinking of starting a family soon, too, and everyone knew that Mahlon was courting the youngest Miller girl, with an eye toward a wedding in November, the traditional time for Amish weddings. Their lives would not be changed by this, but Leah's and Anna's—

"What about Leah and me?" Anna's voice rose above the chatter before Leah could administer another kick. "What are we supposed to do? Do you expect us both to crowd into that small spare room in the daadi haus?"

"I'm sure we'll be fine—" Leah began, but Levi was already shaking his head at his youngest sister.

"We would not put you out of your rooms, no. You and Leah must never think that. The boys can share, and the new babe will come in with us for a while."

And she and Anna would live in a house run with relentless cheerfulness by Barbara. Barbara would change things—it was only natural that she'd want to do things her way in her own house. Leah managed to keep a smile on her face, but she feared Anna wouldn't hold on to her temper long in that situation.

"Of course if you did decide to move," Barbara added, "we would put the baby into your room."

Anna drew breath, and Leah managed to connect with her foot.

"I'm sure we can work all the details out later." She picked up the platter of smoked sausage surrounded by dried apples and dumplings, and handed it to Mahlon. "Who is ready for more? Mamm made enough to feed half the county."

Anna subsided, but the dark look she sent her sister declared that she wasn't finished with the subject.

By the time the dishes were washed, Levi and Barbara and their children had gone home. Leah hung up the tea towel and glanced around the kitchen to be sure all was as pristine as her mother expected.

The wooden cabinets had been wiped down, and the countertop and long wooden table shone. The only decoration on the wall, a calendar from the feed store in town, was a bit crooked, so she straightened it.

She frowned slightly. Her parents were in the living room, Mamm knitting and Daadi reading the latest issue of the *Budget* newspaper. Mahlon had hurried off in his courting buggy as soon as the evening chores were done, plainly headed toward the Miller farm and his sweetheart. Where was Anna?

A quick walk through the house didn't turn her up, and her bonnet and cape were missing from their usual place. Leah slung a shawl around her shoulders and stepped outside.

It was dusk, and a damp April chill permeated the air. Soon it would be May, and the lilacs and roses would perfume the night. Even now, the rhubarb in Mamm's garden had begun to unfurl its wide green leaves.

Across the fields, yellow light glowed from Daniel Glick's windows. The farmhouse had stood empty for months, and seeing lights there again felt right.

But that didn't answer the question of where her sister was. If she called out, Mamm would hear and be disturbed.

Standing there, undecided, she heard a faint jingle of metal from the stable. She clutched her shawl around her against the cool air and headed across the yard.

The stable door stood slightly ajar. She slid it open. Sure enough, Anna was there, harnessing Ben to Mamm's buggy. She swung around, startled, at the sound of the door.

"Going someplace with Mamm's horse and buggy tonight, are you?"

Leah kept her voice light, having no wish to get into a squabble. Still, she had to talk some sense into Anna over the changes that were inevitable, and this was a chance to get her sister alone.

Anna flushed guiltily. "Mamm won't mind. She lets me take it every day for work. Tonight I want to meet some of my friends."

"Amish friends or English friends?" Leah crossed the wide planks of the barn floor and stroked Ben's smooth neck. The gelding nuzzled her, as if to complain about this extra excursion in his day.

Anna shrugged impatiently. "Both, I guess. Does it matter? You and the boys did what you liked during your rumspringa, ain't so?"

Somehow she had the feeling that Anna's ideas of what to do during the traditional running-around time of Amish youth were a bit more adventurous than hers had been. But then, she'd had Johnny, with things already settled between them.

"It doesn't matter if you have English friends, I suppose." She could see that Anna was in the mood to take offense at just about anything. "I just think it's late to be setting out."

"It wouldn't be this late if Barbara hadn't insisted on going all over the house, as if she hadn't seen it before." Anger showed in Anna's quick movements as she fastened the harness and gathered the lines. "She even looked in my dower chest, as if that was any of her business."

Barbara had only too obviously been measuring the rooms for her own furniture. "I know she can be a little too enthusiastic at times, but—"

"Is that what you call it? She's a busybody, and why Levi wanted to marry her and be bossed around all of his life, I don't understand."

"None of us ever understands what makes someone fall in love." She touched Anna's shoulder, but her sister shrugged it off. "She is his wife, she makes him happy, and they are moving in. There's nothing you can do about it, so you'd best accept it with good grace."

"And if I don't want to?"

The patience she had with her sister was wearing thin. As the baby of the family, Anna had not been spoiled, exactly, but she'd certainly been treated with more indulgence than the older ones.

"You don't have a choice," she said firmly. "The decision to move into the daadi haus is Mamm and Daadi's, and they've made it. You're not going to make them unhappy over this, are you?"

Anna paused, hand on the buggy rail. "I wouldn't do that." She swung herself onto the buggy seat, the full skirt of her rose-colored dress flaring out. She picked up the lines and then paused, face sobering under the brim of her black bonnet. "Leah—do you think Mamm is really all right?"

"Of course she is." Her response came quickly, and she could only hope she sounded as sure as she'd like to feel. "Go along now and have fun with your friends." She smiled, relieved when Anna smiled back.

"All right then. I won't be late. I promise." She clucked to Ben, and the buggy moved off.

Leah stood watching the battery-operated lantern on the back of the buggy disappear down the lane. What was behind Anna's attitude?

For some reason she saw again Daniel's indulgent look at the mention of his youngest. Maybe it was human nature to be lenient with the last child.

It was too late now to go back and redo anything about Anna's rearing. Leah could only trust her sister's warm heart and common sense to get her through the changes that were coming in their lives.

And she suspected she'd need a measure of common sense and patience for herself, too.

CHAPTER THREE

*D*aniel and his children came for supper the next evening, as her mother had said, and Leah found herself on pins and needles throughout the meal, wondering if Daniel would mention the visit of an Englischer to the schoolhouse the previous afternoon.

He didn't. Because he knew it would make her uncomfortable? She wasn't sure, but she was grateful. Her family would know about John Kile's return soon enough, but it didn't seem right to talk to anyone else before telling Rachel.

By the time everyone went out to the backyard after the meal, her tension had eased. Daniel leaned against the corner of the porch, deep in conversation with her father about planting times in the area. His strong face was intent, and he apparently was soaking up advice.

He showed an appealing deference to the older man's opinion that she appreciated. Daadi might think he was ready to retire, but he still knew more about farming in Pleasant Valley than just about anyone.

Rachel and her family were coming for dessert, so surely she could find an opportunity to talk with Rachel about Johnny. Then perhaps she could stop feeling as if she carried the burden of his return all alone.

She'd have to be careful about the telling of it, though. Rachel's sweet face showed every emotion she felt, and this was going to be difficult news both to give and to receive.

Sunlight still slanted across the yard, making the yellow trumpets of the daffodils at the corner of the house glow as if they were made of gold. She drew in a breath, loving the mingled scents that said spring was here at last. Every season had its own beauty, but this time of rebirth and growth surely must be close to the Creator's heart.

Her brother Mahlon, still as enthusiastic as a kid about games despite his twenty-two years, had put up the croquet set, and the moment Rachel's family arrived, he recruited all the children to play.

Daniel's six-year-old, Jonah, seized a mallet. Mahlon put his big hands over Jonah's small ones to help him hit the red ball through a wicket, and Jonah laughed with pleasure.

"I see that your brother is wonderful gut with children." Daniel's voice startled her, and she swung around to find him behind her.

Had Daniel sought her out to talk about John's visit yesterday? As the parent of children in her care, he certainly had a right to be concerned about who visited the schoolhouse.

"Ja, he is. We tease him that he'd best be sure his intended wants a big family."

She'd spoken lightly, out of nervousness probably, and as she looked up at Daniel, she caught something—a tightening, maybe—in his face. The look disappeared as quickly as it had come, though, so maybe she was imagining it.

Sun lines crinkled at the corners of Daniel's deep blue eyes, as if he dismissed whatever had caused the reaction. The color of his shirt echoed that blue, making his eyes even more vivid.

"Mahlon's bride will be a fortunate woman, it seems. Is he keeping company with someone?"

"He and Esther Miller have it already settled between them, I think. At least, folks say that Esther's father is planting a long row of celery this spring."

"Gut, since they'll want plenty for the wedding feast come November." His eyebrows lifted. "And is your father planting much celery this year?"

The question's implication startled her. "I think our Anna is enjoying her rumspringa too much to settle down just yet."

He glanced toward her sister, who was chasing Jonah around the edge of the croquet lawn, heedless of the way the breeze tossed her hair loose from beneath her kapp.

"Anna is a lively girl. But she is not the only unmarried daughter of the house."

His gaze came back to her face, and the question in his blue eyes startled her. For just an instant her breath seemed to hitch before she got control of herself.

"I don't think Daad will be planting any celery for me. I have no plans to marry."

Then she realized that his intent expression and his words might well refer to John's visit to the school yesterday. He wasn't expressing interest in her. He was wondering if John was courting her. She could hardly deny it without bringing up a subject she had no wish to discuss with him.

"Your family has made us feel so welcome." He changed the subject, perhaps seeing that he'd embarrassed her by his comment. "The children were happy to eat someone else's cooking tonight. I'm not very handy in the kitchen."

He was trying to make it easier for her, but he couldn't. No one could. The timing that had brought Johnny to the schoolhouse when Daniel was there had forced Daniel into the secret, like it or not.

She took a breath, trying to find the right words to acknowledge the situation. She had a quick look around to be sure no one was within earshot.

"Daniel, about John Kile's visit to the schoolhouse yesterday—it's obvious you haven't said anything to anyone. I appreciate that."

His face sobered. "I don't know people to exchange gossip with. But I would not like to think that my children's teacher was being influenced by her English friend."

"He's not—" She stopped, trying to organize her thoughts. Naturally he'd assume John was there out of interest in her. "John Kile was Amish once."

He nodded, his gaze serious on her face. "I thought that when I saw him."

"How could you tell?" She had thought John typically English herself, with his fancy car and his blue jeans.

"Something about the way he looked at the school, maybe. As if he'd belonged there once."

"He attended school there for eight years." Sorrow swept over her, taking her by surprise. "I didn't let him go inside."

Had she been unkind? She'd thought only that she didn't want to be alone with him, not that he might have feelings about the place.

"He gave up that right when he left the church," Daniel said, his tone uncompromising. "Still, I'm sorry if his visit upset you."

It had. Rachel, not knowing that she had something huge to face, was helping Mamm put two rhubarb pies and a cake on the picnic table under the trees.

"He's Rachel's brother," she said softly, her heart aching for her friend. "Her twin. He came to me because he wants me to be—well, a go-between, I suppose. I must talk to her about whether the family is willing to see him."

"I see." His expression was veiled. "So he's just the brother of your friend."

Her chin came up at that. "Have you listened to gossip about me already, Daniel Glick? If so, you may as well hear it from me. John and I planned to marry once, but he chose to go English instead."

For a moment he didn't speak, and she had no idea what he was thinking. His face had tightened again. In disapproval? She wasn't sure of his emotion, but it was something dark.

"I see," he said at last. "No, I didn't know, but I'm sorry for your loss."

The sincerity of his tone was so intense that she couldn't doubt he meant it. His sympathy wiped away her irritation and made her ashamed that she'd spoken so abruptly.

"I'm sorry. I'm the one who should apologize." She took a deep breath, trying to ease the tightness in her throat. "It's just— People will talk about it again, once they know he's back."

"You could be careful, not give them anything new to talk about."

"Like meeting him at the schoolhouse?" Her temper, always so controlled, flared.

Daniel's strong face was impassive. "You are my children's teacher, an Amish schoolteacher, chosen for the position because of your faith and your character. What you do, who you see—that matters to all the children who are your responsibility."

Before she could say a word, he walked off toward the croquet game.

. . .

Leah stood at the end of the picnic table, setting out forks and napkins while she rehearsed all the things she should have said to Daniel. Unfortunately, he'd spoken nothing but the truth. It was too bad that he seemed to have the ability to bring out the emotions she usually kept under such careful control.

Rachel slipped an arm around her waist. "Why so deep in thought?"

Leah shook off the fear that there might have been a veiled threat in Daniel's final words. Time enough to worry about that later. Now—now she had to tell Rachel about Johnny.

"I must talk with you, Rachel." There was no easy way to break this news. She'd just have to come out with it. At least at the moment everyone else seemed occupied, either with the game or with their own talk. "I've seen Johnny."

Rachel's breath caught. "Our Johnny? Seen him? He's here in Pleasant Valley?"

"He came to the schoolhouse yesterday, wanting me to talk to you for him, to tell you why he's back."

Sudden hope blossomed on her friend's face. "He wants to come home? To repent and be one of us again?" Her voice lifted in joy.

It hurt Leah's heart to destroy that hope, but it was best to do it quickly, since it must be done. "No. I'm sorry, Rachel."

The hope faded, and Rachel's eyes filled with tears. She turned, hiding her face from the playing children. Leah gave her time, her arm encircling her friend's waist. She longed so deeply to help her, but some pains couldn't be soothed by even the most comforting words.

Finally Rachel managed a feeble smile. "Ach, I never really thought that would happen. Johnny always wanted the outside world too strongly."

"You couldn't stop hoping he'd come back to us," Leah said softly.

Rachel shook her head. "Why is he here, then? What does he want if not to rejoin the community?"

Leah picked her words carefully, feeling a flicker of anger toward John. He should be explaining this himself instead of putting it onto her.

"He's working with that doctor who's doing the research on genetic diseases that affect the children. He said he'd be here for six months, at least."

"Six months?" Rachel bit her lip. "It will be hard, having him near that long but not one of us."

"Did you have any idea of what he was doing?"

"No." The sidelong look seemed a little guilty. "Just that he'd gone to college for some kind of science."

"You never told me that." She'd thought that she and her closest friend shared everything.

Rachel's gaze slid away from Leah's, and she fiddled with the forks much as Leah had done, as if her hands needed to be busy. "You seemed like you'd forgotten him. I didn't want to bring it all up again and make you feel bad. Did I do wrong?"

"No. It's all right." But she hadn't forgotten. She'd just learned to hide her feelings.

"What does he want from us, then?" Rachel's eyes went dark with misery, hurting Leah's heart. "Why did he come to you?"

"He wants to see you and the rest of your family. He asked me to tell you. He's coming to the schoolhouse tomorrow to hear your answer."

Her friend's eyes widened. "But I can't tell him anything, not so soon. Not until I talk to Mamm and Daadi about it. And how will I do that?"

"I know it's hard." She thanked the Lord that she'd never had to face that particular burden with her parents. "But you should tell them right away, before they hear about him being here from someone else."

"But if no one knows but you—"

"Daniel Glick saw him at the school," she said quickly, before Rachel could imagine this secret would keep. "He hasn't said anything, but anyone could see John, could start talking about his coming back. You know how fast that news would spread."

"You're right. I can't be a coward about it. I'll talk to them tonight." She shook her head, worry darkening her eyes. "I don't know what to say. I don't want to hurt them."

Leah squeezed her in a quick hug. "They haven't forgotten about him. Maybe they'll be relieved to know what he's doing. Anyway, it must be done."

"Oh, I know that. It's just so hard. I want to protect them from hurt. You'd feel the same, wouldn't you?"

Leah glanced at her mother. Mamm sat in a lawn chair, watching the children play. She was smiling, but her face seemed thin and tired.

"Ja, of course I would. I do. It's strange. All these years we've relied on our parents, and now we need to care for them. It seems we're changing places, doesn't it?"

Rachel nodded in quick understanding. "How is your mamm?"

"She says she's doing fine, but fighting the cancer has taken a lot out of her. She and my father have decided to move to the grossdaadi haus."

Rachel's face expressed all that she might be reluctant to say. "So your brother and his family will be moving into the house. What about you and Anna?"

"That's what Anna wants to know." It was a relief to pour it out to someone who would understand and keep it to herself. "Levi and Barbara say that nothing will change, that we should keep our own rooms, but she's expecting again, and—"

"And it's only a matter of time until she wants those rooms for her family." Rachel shook her head. "Even if she didn't, you know how hard it will be to live in another woman's house." Now it was Rachel's turn to give a comforting hug. "What will you do?"

"Nothing for a bit. I haven't had time to think it through. I knew it would come sometime, but I didn't think it would be so soon."

Rachel nodded, eyes clouding. "I know. It's odd, isn't it? One day life seems settled and routine, and the next it's turned upside down, as if a storm came and tipped us all on our heads."

"Ja." That was surely how she'd felt lately. She took a breath. "Well, we can get through it. Somehow."

Rachel shot her a sidelong glance. "I saw you talking to Daniel. It looked as if you were finding a lot to say to each other."

"Don't matchmake," Leah warned. Was everyone in the community trying to team her up with Daniel?

"Well, don't you dismiss the idea too quickly." Her expression was serious. "I know it's early to be thinking this, but wouldn't it be better to be living in your own house with a family to love, rather than feel like a boarder in your sister-in-law's house?"

"I don't plan to marry." And even if she did, it wouldn't be to Daniel Glick. She valued her independence too much for that. "Never mind about Daniel. What shall I tell John?"

"Say I love him. Say he must give me more time. That's all I can tell him now."

John wouldn't like that, any more than she'd like telling him, but there was nothing she could do about it.

Daniel found his gaze straying to Leah Beiler, even while he talked with her father about the best place to buy a buggy horse. Teacher Leah was an interesting mixture of gentleness and spirit. He just hoped that spirit wasn't leading her toward trouble.

Did her father know about the return of his daughter's onetime sweetheart? The older man's face was placid as he puffed on his pipe, but he suspected Elias Beiler wasn't one to show his feelings easily.

"Your young ones settling down in school all right?" Elias nodded toward Matthew, who was helping Elizabeth knock a croquet ball through a wicket.

"They seem to be doing fine. Teacher Leah has made them feel right at home already."

A faint smile creased Elias's weathered face. "Our Leah is a gut teacher, she is. Not that I wouldn't rather see her married and with young ones of her own, but we must take what the Lord sends."

Daniel nodded. At the moment, Leah was in close conversation with Rachel, probably about the return of John Kile. Sooner, rather than later, it would be public knowledge, but despite his concerns, he was just as glad the spreading of it hadn't come from him.

"Will you be missing lots of kin back there in Lancaster County, Daniel?"

Elias only meant to express kindly interest, but even so, Daniel felt himself stiffen. Talking about his life there would lead inevitably to the reasons he'd left, and he wasn't ready to discuss that with strangers. Not yet, anyway.

"My parents hope to come for a visit later in the summer, once we're settled in. Maybe help with the harvest."

"Good to have extra hands around when the crops start to come in, especially for a man without a wife to help him."

Was that meant to be a question about his wife, or was it a hint as to whether he might be looking for a new helpmate now that he was settling in Pleasant Valley? That was how an Amish father's thoughts would go, for sure. Daniel managed a meaningless smile.

"It'll be wonderful gut to have them come for a visit. Now I'd best get Jonah. He's probably getting tired."

His younger son, who had just run across the lawn to throw himself at Teacher Leah, didn't look in the least tired, but it was a way to end a conversation that was cutting too near the bone.

He couldn't fool himself any more than he could anyone else. Most folks here had kin back in Lancaster County, and sooner or later someone would receive a letter with all the details about what had happened to his wife. To his children.

Time. That was what he wanted now, time for the children to settle down and feel at home. Then it would hurt less to have everyone know about them.

Leah smiled, bending over Jonah to say something that made him giggle, and a flicker of concern went through Daniel. Leah said she wasn't yearning for her fence-jumper fiancé, but maybe she was. He didn't want his children getting too close to a woman who could be tempted by the life outside their community.

He went quickly to them, then grabbed Jonah and tossed him in the air.

"Are you a bird then, Jonah Glick?"

"I think he's a barn swallow," Leah said, laughter filling her green eyes. Hair the color of corn silk was drawn back to the bun under her kapp, but a few tendrils had worked their way loose. They curled against the creamy skin of her cheeks.

And what was he doing noticing that about Teacher Leah? Despite his new community's obvious wish to marry him off, he was not looking for a bride. After what had happened with Ruth, he wasn't sure he'd ever take that chance again.

And if he did, it wouldn't be with a woman who seemed to be flirting with the English world in the shape of her former sweetheart.

He made Jonah swoop up and down in imitation of a barn swallow, and then set him down and gave him a tap on the bottom. "Go and tell your brother and sister it's almost time to go home," he said.

"So soon?" Leah looked honestly regretful. "Be sure you don't leave without taking the basket of leftovers that Mamm has for you. It will save you having to cook tomorrow."

"That's kind of her. I'm grateful for your hospitality." He looked into her face, detecting a hint of strain there. "I'm sorry if Jonah interrupted your conversation with your friend."

"It's all right. We had finished what we had to say." She gave him a straightforward, serious look. "I'm sure you can guess what we were talking about."

He nodded. "How does Kile's family feel about his coming back?"

"They don't know yet, other than Rachel." Her smooth brow furrowed. "She must tell her parents before they hear from someone else."

"That would be wise."

"Many Amish have children and grandchildren who have chosen not to join the church." She seemed to look inward, as if arguing with herself. "They still find ways to have some relationship with them."

She couldn't know why the very mention of that thought made him stiffen. And he wasn't going to tell her.

"We live separate from the world. Accommodating it can only lead to trouble."

His words came out harshly, but perhaps that was just as well. Teacher Leah may as well know now where he stood on that issue, because where his children were concerned, he would not take any risks at all.

CHAPTER FOUR

*I*t was perfectly normal for her to stop and see Rachel after school, Leah assured herself on Friday. So normal, in fact, that Betty turned her head toward the lane to the Brand farm even before Leah's hand tightened on the harness lines.

Her errand, however, wasn't so normal.

Surely Rachel would have talked to her parents about Johnny by now. Leah's stomach roiled at the memory of her conversation with John on Wednesday when he'd learned she had no answer for him. He'd hated being put off. And she hated being put in the middle of this tangle.

She slowed Betty to a walk as they approached the house. On either side of the lane, the Brand dairy herd munched contentedly on April-green grass, and she spotted Becky and her younger brother, five-year-old Joseph, heading for the barn.

Gut, she'd timed this visit right, then. She'd hoped to get here while Rachel's husband, Ezra, was still busy, and while the kinder were at their chores. That way she and Rachel could have a private talk.

She stopped at the back door and slid down, a prayer for guidance forming in her heart. She didn't know what to pray for in this situation, but certainly the Lord knew what was right for Rachel, for her parents, and even for Johnny.

She was fastening Betty to the hitching rail when Rachel appeared at the door, holding it open in welcome as always.

"Leah, wilkom. I hoped to see you." Her smile was warm, but those lines of strain around her eyes were not normal for easygoing Rachel.

Leah's heart sank. This situation was hurting her friend, she knew, and there was probably worse to come. No matter what Rachel's parents had decided, the way wouldn't be smooth.

"Komm, sit." Rachel led the way through the mudroom to the kitchen, warm and smelling of supper cooking already. "I have apple kuchen and coffee ready. You'll have some."

"Only if you join me." Leah sat at the well-scrubbed table, taking off her bonnet and cape, and smoothing her hair back under her kapp.

"Ja." Rachel glanced at the pot on the gas stove. "The chicken is stewing already, so I can sit for a bit."

Their conversation was natural enough, as if this were just any visit. But the cups clattered as Rachel took them from the tall pine cupboard, and the movement of her hands was stiff and clumsy.

Leah kept silent as Rachel grasped a pot holder and poured the coffee. She waited while Rachel put a slice of pastry, thick with apples, on a plate in front of her.

Only when Rachel stopped her nervous fidgeting and sat down did she think it was time to speak.

"I'm sorry. This is hard for you."

Rachel nodded, her hands clasping the thick white mug that held her coffee. "Not for me only. Ezra is upset, because Johnny was his dear friend. The children, because they sense that something is wrong even though we haven't told them. And Mamm and Daadi—"

She stopped, her voice choking with tears.

"You've told them, then." However little Rachel had wanted to break the news, she couldn't risk having her parents hear of John's return from someone else.

Rachel seemed to struggle for composure. "Ja. Ezra watched the little ones so I could go over alone to talk with them." She clenched her hands together, the knuckles white. "Leah, I have never seen them look like that. It was worse, I think, than when he went away the first time."

Probably, that first time, distressed as they'd been, they'd expected Johnny to come home eventually, like so many others did. But he hadn't, and the years had slipped away, each one making it less likely he'd return.

They wouldn't have forgotten him. How could they? Her own heart ached with the thought.

But maybe they'd been able to make peace with his leaving. Now, that peace was ripped beyond repair.

"Will they— Do they want to see him?"

"Of course they want to see him!" The words burst from Rachel's lips on a sob, and she raised tear-drenched eyes to Leah's. "But they won't. They can't."

Leah clasped Rachel's hand in hers, tears filling her eyes, too. "I know." Her throat was tight. "They feel they're doing the right thing by refusing."

"The only thing," Rachel said. "The meidung is the only thing that might make him return to the community, if that's possible."

Leah nodded in sympathy. The outside world probably thought of shunning as a punishment, but it wasn't that. It was the church's last, desperate effort to bring the stubborn rebel to his senses, and she had no doubt it hurt the family and the community more than it hurt the one who left.

She took a deep breath, knowing she had to press on with this while she could still say the words without breaking down. "If they were convinced that Johnny would never be Amish again, would they see him then?"

"I don't know." Rachel wiped tears away with her fingers. "If he came back to us penitent, ready to confess his sin and be restored to the body, it would be as if his leaving had never been. But if he's determined to live English . . ."

Her voice died out, as if she didn't have the strength to consider that possibility.

"There are those in the church who have accepted that in their children," Leah reminded her. "The Muellers and the Stoltzes both have sons who've left, but they've maintained ties with them and their families."

Everyone knew that accommodations could be made. Folks obeyed the letter of the meidung by not eating at the same table as the shunned person, not taking food from their hand, not riding in a car that person was driving. Otherwise, with goodwill on both sides, life could go on.

"I know they do. It's hard for them, but they've accepted that their children will never come back. I don't know if Daadi can ever accept that." She gave Leah a watery smile. "You know how he was about Johnny. His oldest son. His only son."

Unlike most Amish families, the Kiles only had two children. Something had gone wrong for Ella when the twins were born. Rachel and Johnny were all the more precious for that reason.

Rachel turned her mug, making rings on the scrubbed pine tabletop. "Daadi wouldn't admit to being proud of him, but they were so close, and Johnny so smart and hardworking. Daadi was glad to have a son to pass the farm to. After Johnny left, the heart just seemed to go out of him."

"He saw his life's work being discarded."

Leah thought fleetingly of Daniel and Matthew. There was another father determined to have a farm to pass on to his son. But Matthew—surely Daniel didn't fear that Matthew would leave the church.

"Leah, do you think—" Rachel hesitated. She was looking down at the cooling coffee in the mug, and Leah couldn't read her expression.

"Think what?" She patted Rachel's hand in encouragement.

"Do you think there's any chance Johnny could change his mind and come back to us? If there was, I would do anything to make it happen."

"I guess there's always a chance." She said the words slowly, not wanting to dash whatever hope Rachel might still cling to.

Rachel clasped Leah's hand in a tight grip. "You knew him as well as anyone. You must still be able to tell what he's thinking, no matter how much he's changed." Her voice compelled an answer. "Please, Leah. You must be honest with me."

She thought of the stranger Johnny had become, with his clean-shaven face, his modern clothes, his fancy car. But those were externals, easily changed.

What of the man himself? Rachel was right. Once, she'd have said she knew Johnny's heart as well as she knew her own.

The passion in his voice when he'd talked of his work at the clinic, the way his eyes looked for a future she couldn't imagine. Those were the things that told who John Kile was now.

"I don't think so." Her throat tightened at the pain she must be causing. "I can't be sure, but I don't think so."

The muscles of Rachel's neck worked. She slapped her hands down on the table and pushed herself back, her face twisting.

"He should never have come back, then!" she cried, her voice harsh.

"You know as well as I do, Leah. He should never have come back to Pleasant Valley at all."

Daniel stood looking across a field full of people on Saturday afternoon. The spring Mud Sale to benefit the local fire company was in full swing. True to its name, the sale took place when the ground, still wet from winter's snow followed by April showers, was rapidly turning into a sea of mud.

That didn't seem to deter any of the crowd. Amish and English alike, intent on finding a bargain, moved from used Amish buggies to lines strung with quilts to food stands offering everything from warm soft pretzels to cotton candy to funnel cakes.

He could only hope his children weren't talking Rachel Brand into buying them anything to eat. She had offered to have the younger ones walk around with her and her children, so that he could take a look at the tools that were spread out on several long trestle tables. And Matthew had gone off on his own with Jacob Esch and some other boys from his class.

Their acceptance was a sign that Matthew was settling down here, and he was relieved at that. He'd been worried about the boy, but not sure whether his worries were justified or not. Matthew had changed, and there was no way of ever getting back those lost years.

He glanced up from the harrow he was inspecting, his eye caught by someone coming from behind the small brooder coop next to the henhouse on the host farm. Even at this distance, even after meeting him only once, he had no trouble identifying the man. John Kile.

His eyebrows lifted. That was a surprise, for sure. Anyone could come to the Mud Sale. Plenty of Englischers were here, but Kile couldn't hope to pass unnoticed, not with the number of Amish in attendance. This was a public announcement of his return.

How would his family take that? They'd no doubt been through plenty of grief already. His stomach twisted. He knew that feeling only too well.

Kile moved quickly, almost like he was running away. Shoulders stiff and hands clenched, he headed for the nearest cluster of people gathered around a stand selling sausage sandwiches. He disappeared into the crowd.

Someone else came from behind the brooder coop. Black cape, black bonnet hiding her face. But as soon as she moved, Daniel knew it was Leah. Teacher Leah meeting with her old sweetheart in a not-so-secret place.

He stood, irresolute, for a moment. It was not his place to confront her. But if he had seen, others might have as well.

Even as he hesitated, she turned slightly and saw him. She stopped, her body stiff. Then she came toward him across the stubble of grass.

He waited. If she wanted to talk to him, he wouldn't avoid it, although he didn't think she'd want to hear anything he was likely to say.

Leah stopped a few feet from him. A couple of men who'd been looking at the tools moved off, leaving them alone.

"I suppose you saw." Her mouth was firm, but her face was pale with strain.

"Ja." He hesitated. She'd be angry if he told her what he thought, but—

"I met John Kile to give him his family's answer to seeing him."

For some reason, that gave him a sense of relief. She hadn't been with Kile on her own accord, then, but had been trying to do the right thing for her friend.

"I take it the answer was no."

She nodded. "How did you know?"

"He didn't look like someone who'd just had gut news when he went off." He searched her face, understanding the strain he saw there. "It was not easy for you."

"He was very hurt."

And she'd had to be the one to deliver that hurt. Given their history, it was probably more painful for her than for him.

"I'm sorry for him," he said gravely, praying that he honestly meant it. "And for you, having to be the one to tell him. But I understand why they decided that."

Her face was still troubled. "If he had come back sorry, they'd have forgiven him in a moment. The prodigal son, home where he belongs."

"That would only be right."

But he thought of his wife and his hands tightened, pressing against his legs. If Ruth had returned, wanting to be accepted into the church again, wanting to resume their marriage, he'd have forgiven her.

But would things ever have been the same between them? He didn't think so.

Still, the relationship between a man and his wife was different from that of a parent to a child.

"They're in so much pain." She turned to start walking back toward the crowd, seeming to assume they'd walk together.

"They love him and want him back. It's hard that the only way they have to push him to return is to stay separate from him." He fell into step with her.

The brim of her bonnet moved as she nodded. "I know that's what they're thinking, and they could be right. But what if you're dealing with a person who will never come back, no matter what?"

Leah couldn't know that she was causing him pain with every word. If she knew about his wife, she would never have spoken to him about this.

But this was what he'd wanted when he'd come here, wasn't it? The chance to start fresh, where everyone didn't look at him, at his children, with pity for what had happened to them?

They'd reached a wide muddy patch, and he touched her sleeve lightly to guide her around the edge of it. "It's not so bad over here where the cars are parked."

She nodded, moving with him. It had been a long time since he'd walked anywhere, even through a muddy field, with a woman. It felt odd, but somehow natural, too.

She glanced up at him, and it seemed the strain had eased from her face a little. "Do you have no answer to the problem, then, Daniel?"

"I don't." He managed a smile. "I know that surprises you, Teacher Leah."

"It does. But you'd best be careful of expressing too much wisdom, anyway. Someone might think you'd make a gut minister."

He shook his head. "Like most, I pray the lot never falls on me. My father is the bishop of our church district back in Lancaster County, and I know how heavy a burden it can be."

Her steps slowed, and she smiled. "Now I've learned something more about you."

"Is that gut?" He could get used to that smile, to the way it made her green eyes fill with light.

"It satisfies my regrettable curiosity, I'm afraid. Yours is the first new family in our church district in quite a few years. You've given us something to talk about besides who's courting whom and whether the price of milk will go up."

That sort of curiosity was the last thing he wanted, but it was inevitable. "Both of those things are more important than anything you might learn about me."

"People are always more interesting to me than cows," she said lightly.

He found himself wondering what she had been like at eighteen, before John Kile had left her behind. More like her pert sister than he'd have originally guessed, perhaps, before grief and disappointment had taken that liveliness away.

"Not more important to a dairy farmer," he said.

They rounded a row of cars. At the end of the next row, two motorcycles were parked.

Three Amish boys surrounded one of them, gawking at the boy who'd been brave enough, or foolish enough, to climb onto the motorcycle. Daniel stopped, taking in what he saw. The boy was Matthew.

For a moment Daniel froze, feeling as if he'd taken a pitchfork in the stomach. Then he surged forward, grabbed his son, and pulled him off the contraption.

"What are you doing?" It was all he could do to keep from shaking the boy. "Is this how you behave when I let you go with your friends? Is it?"

He was vaguely aware of Leah drawing the other boys away.

"Jacob and Thomas Esch and Gabriel Stoltzfus." It was very much her teacher voice. "You go back to your parents right now, before you find yourselves in trouble."

Murmurs of agreement, and the other boys ran off, leaving them alone. Daniel looked at his son, and Matthew stared back at him.

"Well? What do you have to say for yourself, Matthew?"

His son's face was white and set. "I didn't do anything so bad. It's just a motorcycle."

"It's not for us, as you well know."

Something flashed in Matthew's eyes, an expression he'd begun to dread. One that made his son look like a stranger.

"I rode on one once, with a friend of Mamm's." He spat the words out. "She didn't think it was wrong. I didn't either. It was fun."

The pitchfork in his belly twisted. He heard the quick intake of Leah's breath. He turned to her, knowing his anger was irrational but not able to stop it.

"Ja." He snapped off the word. "You heard. My children lived in the English world for two years. Now you really know something about me."

Holding Matthew by the arm, he charged off.

"*Don't* you bother to tell me you're not interested in Daniel Glick." Barbara paused at the kitchen door on her way out on Monday afternoon, clearly determined to have the last word on the subject. "I saw you together at the Mud Sale with my own eyes already."

She waved, chuckling a little at her comment, and scurried off the porch toward the waiting buggy.

Leah counted to ten, keeping a smile pinned on her face with an effort. By the time she reached eight, Barbara was in her buggy and heading down the lane.

Leah turned to her mother, frustration building to the boiling point. If she didn't say something to someone, she'd burst with it.

"When is this matchmaking going to stop? Can't I even speak to a man without the busybodies making plans for a wedding?"

Mamm continued moving a batch of snickerdoodles from the cooling rack to a plastic container, her face placid. "Ach, Leah, you take Barbara's teasing too much to heart. She doesn't mean anything by it. Anyway, you know how she is."

"I know too well how my sister-in-law is, but she's not the only one. I heard the whispers after church yesterday."

Leah picked up a dish towel and began drying the bowls and spoons left in the sink from Mamm's baking. The whole house had smelled of cinnamon and sugar when she'd come in from school, setting her mouth watering as if she were a scholar herself, running into the kitchen ravenous.

Her mother stopped what she was doing to look at Leah. "I heard whispers, too, but they were about Johnny Kile and how he's back in Pleasant Valley. Did you know about this already, Leah?"

"I've known for a few days." Her towel slowed on the mixing bowl. "I'm sorry I didn't tell you and Daadi, but Rachel asked me not to say anything until she'd had a chance to talk with her parents about it. She's worried about how they're taking it."

Her mother nodded, but her gaze was troubled. "They are grieved, I know. But does it bother you again, knowing he's here in the valley?"

"Not as much as having half the church trying to pair me up with Daniel Glick," she said tartly. At least she thought that was true. "Whatever feelings I had for Johnny Kile were boy-and-girl notions, over a long time ago and forgotten."

"It's gut, that." Her mother put the cookie container into a basket and added several jars of rhubarb sauce. "It makes no sense to be crying over the past. Let the troubles of the day be sufficient."

"I suppose so." Mamm had a thought from Scripture for every eventuality, though Leah had never found that one especially comforting.

Her mother tucked a cloth over the basket's contents. "There. You have time before supper to take this over to the Glick place, you do."

The cookie sheet Leah was holding clattered onto the counter. "Mamm, what was I just saying? You're as bad as Barbara is, trying to match me up with Daniel just because he's a widower."

"Nonsense." Her mother bridled, but her eyes didn't meet Leah's. "I'm trying to be neighborly, that's all. I don't suppose Daniel has time to be baking cookies for those young ones of his, running the farm all on his own the way he's doing."

"If you were just being neighborly, you could have asked Barbara to drop them off on her way home," Leah said firmly. "She'd have loved an excuse to call, and she'd probably be talking up my virtues to Daniel along with delivering the cookies."

"Barbara's not—"

"What? A maidal?" Bad enough that the rest of the valley thought that she and Daniel made a perfect match, without her mother getting into it.

"I'm just being neighborly," her mother repeated stubbornly. "But if I were trying to bring the two of you together, is that so bad?" She reached toward Leah, her eyes suddenly filling with tears. "Is it bad that I want to see my oldest daughter settled with a home and family of her own before I die?"

The words were like an arrow to Leah's heart, and her breath caught painfully. She clasped her mother's hands in hers.

"Mamm, what's wrong? Why are you talking that way? Did you get a bad report from the doctor? What did he say?"

"No, no, nothing like that." Her mother patted her cheek. "Don't fuss over me. I'm just thinking of the future."

"Why would you be thinking that way if nothing's wrong?" She should have insisted on going with her mother to that last doctor's visit. Then she'd know for certain what they faced.

"The doctor says I'm well. That the tiredness is to be expected." She sighed, putting her palm against her cheek as if to comfort herself. "I just never thought we'd be moving into the daadi haus so soon. I hoped and prayed that you and Anna would be married before that happened. Barbara's a gut woman, but—"

"Ja." They both knew how that sentence would finish. Barbara was a fine woman, but neither Leah nor Anna wanted to live with her. "Mamm, are you sure that's all? You promise?" She looked intently into her mother's lined face, trying to read the truth there.

"That's all," she said firmly. She cradled Leah's face in her hands. "You have so much love in your heart to give, daughter. I want a chance for you to give that love to a gut man and children, the Lord willing."

Leah felt the words like a physical pain. So Mamm thought she had love to give.

After the way she'd failed Johnny, she doubted it. He'd said she was a coward, and he'd been right. She didn't have what it took to love the way Mamm did.

But it would only upset her mother if she said that.

"Well." Her mother turned to the table, picking up the basket. "If you won't take this over to the Glicks, I guess I'll walk over myself with it."

Leah took the basket from her. "I'll do it." She was at least smart enough to know when she was beaten.

CHAPTER FIVE

Leah tapped at the back door of the Glick farmhouse, the basket heavy on her arm. If she'd been able to tell her mother why she really didn't want to see Daniel Glick today—

But no. She couldn't do that. The thing she'd learned at the Mud Sale was private. It had to be, until she could understand.

"Teacher Leah!" Elizabeth opened the door, drying her hands on her apron. "Please komm in."

The pleased surprise in her face gave way to a look of slight apprehension as Leah entered.

Leah knew that look. She'd encountered it enough times on the faces of her scholars when she turned up unexpectedly at their homes. Elizabeth was probably scouring her mind, trying to think of anything she might have done wrong that would have brought the teacher to see her father.

Leah hefted the basket, smiling at the child. "My mamm sent over jars of rhubarb sauce for you. And I think there are some fresh snickerdoodles in the basket, too. Do you like them?"

That was no doubt a safe question. She'd never met a child who didn't like the sweet cookies.

"Oh, ja. My grossmutter makes them sometimes for us." Elizabeth, seeming reassured, led the way into the kitchen. "That is kind of you and your mamm."

Leah set the basket down on the long wooden table. The Glick kitchen was very like their own, with its wooden cabinets, gas appliances, and plain wooden table. Very like an English kitchen, she supposed, except that everything ran on gas instead of electric.

She lifted out the jars of rhubarb, admiring their bright pink glow, and then took out the container of cookies. She'd carry the basket home and leave the containers here, knowing full well that with the way folks carted food around to each other, it wasn't worth trying to keep track of them.

"Maybe you and your brothers will have the snickerdoodles after supper."

Elizabeth nodded, eyeing the container as if judging how many cookies it might hold. "Please sit down, Teacher Leah. I was just washing up the dishes."

Her cheeks flushed a little as if she were, like any good hausfrau, embarrassed at being caught by a visitor with dishes in the sink.

"We'll finish them up together," Leah said, folding her sleeves back. "Do you like to wash or dry?"

"Wash," Elizabeth said, but her brows drew together. "You are a guest in our house. You shouldn't be doing the dishes."

"I like to dry the dishes," Leah said firmly, picking up a dish towel from the rack. "Sometimes I think the best talks I have with my sister are when we're doing the dishes together."

Giving in, Elizabeth stepped up on the small wooden stool that stood in front of the sink. "You are wonderful lucky to have a sister. I have only brothers." She glanced through the window over the sink, as if keeping an eye out for them.

"Brothers can be fun, too." Leah started drying the plates that were already stacked in the drainer. "I have three of them, you know. Mine taught me how to ride a bicycle and catch a softball."

"They're all right," Elizabeth said a little grudgingly. "But Matthew thinks he knows everything, just because he's two years older than I am."

"My big brother always thought that, too," Leah said. "We know they don't."

She watched the child's face, intent on her washing chores. Elizabeth inspected each dish carefully before relinquishing it, as if it had to be perfect. So careful about that she was, as she seemed to be about her schoolwork, her appearance, everything.

Had that trait somehow been caused by the time she'd spent in the outside world? Two years, Daniel had said. Two years was a long time in the life of an eight-year-old. How much had Elizabeth been affected by that? How long ago had that been?

And the little one—that explained why Jonah spoke such excellent English for his age. No wonder Daniel had looked disconcerted when she'd commented on it.

So many questions burning in her mind. They weren't caused by idle curiosity. As the children's teacher, she could help them more if she knew the facts.

But she didn't imagine she'd learn much more from Daniel than she already had. He wouldn't have told her as much as he did if not for Matthew blurting out that uncomfortable truth.

The silence had stretched on too long between her and Elizabeth, and she'd be having the child worrying if she didn't say something casual.

"I enjoy having you and your brothers in my class. What do you like best in school, Elizabeth?"

"Playing with Becky," she said promptly, and then looked up at Leah, her lips forming an O of dismay. "I mean—I like reading best."

"I like reading, too." Leah tried to hide a smile. "But it's all right to enjoy making friends, especially with Becky. Her mother and I were best friends when we were young. We still are, in fact."

"Becky has a brother, too," Elizabeth said, as if that sealed the contract between them.

"Perhaps you can go to her house after school one day," Leah suggested. "I'm sure her mother would like that."

"That would be nice." Elizabeth lifted the last dish to the rack. "But I have to take care of things at home." Her small face was set with determination.

Leah's heart twisted. Elizabeth seemed too determined to take over all the household chores. Every Amish child accepted that work was a part of life, but children needed time to play as well.

She'd speak to Rachel and make sure that Elizabeth was invited to her house one day. That would be gut for both the little girls.

There was a rattle at the back door, and Leah looked that way just as Daniel stepped into the house. His gaze met hers, and his face stilled, eyes growing wary.

That wasn't surprising, was it? She undoubtedly looked the same way, with memories of the last time they'd been together sharp in her mind.

"Teacher Leah!" Jonah squeezed around his father and ran toward her, excitement lighting his face. He was too young to think a visit from the teacher anything other than an unexpected treat.

She bent to give him a quick hug. When she looked up again, Daniel had managed to produce a polite smile that didn't reach his eyes. He had one hand on Matthew's shoulder. It looked as if without that, the boy would have run back out of the room.

"Wilkom to our home," Daniel said formally. He and Matthew came into the kitchen, and he looked an inquiry at Elizabeth.

"Teacher Leah brought us rhubarb sauce and snickerdoodles that her mamm made," she told him. "And we talked while we did the dishes."

His gaze swung back to Leah, and there was accusation in it. For an instant she could barely control her anger. How could he think that she would question a child under the guise of helping her?

"We talked about how much we like to read," she said, her voice firm. "And about her friend Becky."

He nodded, and she thought there might be an apology in his face.

"Elizabeth is our reader," he said, touching his daughter's hair lightly. "And Jonah likes to be read to, don't you?"

Jonah flashed that engaging grin. "I like animal stories best."

"This year you'll learn to read some of them for yourself," Leah told him, relieved that the conversation seemed to have moved into safe channels. "That's the best thing about first grade."

"We'll read a story together tonight after we have some of your mamm's cookies and some rhubarb sauce," Daniel said. "It was kind of her to think of us and kind of you to bring them over."

That sounded like an invitation to leave. She picked up the basket. "I'd best be on my way. I'll see you in school tomorrow."

Elizabeth looked suddenly stricken. "But I didn't serve you anything."

"I couldn't eat anything now," she said quickly. "My mamm will have supper ready when I get home."

Elizabeth's lips trembled. "But we should give you something."

She didn't know what to say. Elizabeth was so determined to be the perfect hostess that she was on the verge of tears.

"I'm sure Teacher Leah would like some of our fresh green onions to take home," Daniel said quickly, seeming to understand his small daughter. "We'll stop at the garden to pull some."

"That would be a treat," Leah said. "Ours are not ready yet."

Elizabeth's face cleared in an instant, though tears glistened on her lashes. "Be sure and tell your mamm they are from us."

"I will," she promised. She glanced from Elizabeth's tear-drenched eyes to Jonah's gap-toothed smile to the wary look on Matthew's face that was almost identical to his father's.

What happened to you out there in the English world? she asked silently. *Why were you there?*

Daniel led the way to the garden, very aware of Leah walking beside him. She hadn't bothered to put a bonnet on to walk across the field between the farmhouses, and the late afternoon sun lit her hair, turning it the warm yellow of the earliest jonquil.

The silence between them was pulling taut. The longer he waited to speak, the harder it would be.

As it was, Leah got in first. "I did not come to your home to question Elizabeth about anything."

He didn't pretend to misunderstand her. She had read him so easily. "I know. I'm sorry."

They'd reached the edge of the garden, and he stopped, staring at it absently. Too early for much to be ready to pick yet, but the lettuce he'd planted had begun to unfurl the smallest of green leaves above the soil, and the green onions were just about big enough to eat.

Leah waited. He had to say something more. He owed her that, at least.

"I wanted my children to get settled here." His voice was husky, and he had to stop and clear his throat. "What happened to us, to them—it's hard. Can't they get used to their new life before everyone knows?"

He glanced at Leah, and what he saw reassured him. Her green eyes glistened with tears.

"No one will hear about it from me," she said.

He could breathe again.

"But I could be a better teacher to them if I understood more."

He'd like to argue the point, but she was right. For some reason that annoyed him. It would be easier if he could tell himself that she was wrong.

"Look at it." The words burst out of him, and he grasped her arm to turn her, praying she saw what he did when he looked at the fertile fields stretching out all the way to the woods that covered the ridges. "I could not afford a farm like this back in Lancaster County. My father's farm goes to my oldest brother, which is only right. I came here to give my children a new start."

"I know." Warmth infused Leah's words. "I understand that need."

He took a breath. "My children were taken from me. They lived two years in the outside world. I got them back four months ago."

His throat closed. He could not say more. He prayed she could accept that.

He felt a light touch on his arm and looked down into Leah's face. A tear had escaped to trickle down her cheek.

"I am sorry for your troubles. I'll do whatever I can for the children."

The tight band that clutched his throat eased. He nodded. "Ser gut."

It was more than good, but that was all he could manage. He put his hand over hers in a mute gesture of appreciation.

Her skin was warm against his palm. That warmth seemed to travel through him, startling him so much that his breath hitched.

His gaze met Leah's. Her eyes had gone wide with a shock that matched his.

He leaned closer, drawn—

"Daadi, did you get the onions?" Elizabeth came running toward them, and her voice was a splash of cold water in his face.

He took a step back, not looking at Leah. "I'm getting them now." He stooped to pull up an onion, not bothering to see if it was the largest one.

He had to be grateful. His daughter had called out at just the right time to keep him from doing something too foolish to be imagined.

. . .

Leah opened the stable door, stepped inside, and raised the battery lantern she carried to drive away the darkness. She gasped, and the lantern nearly fell from her hand.

"What are you doing here?"

Johnny pushed himself away from the stall he'd been leaning against. "Waiting for you."

Behind him, Betty reached over the stall door to nudge him with her head. She leaned toward Leah, whickering softly.

Johnny nodded toward the mare. "Some things never change. I figured you'd come out to give a good-night treat to your horse." He brushed at the shoulder of his leather jacket, where the mare had touched him. "What's her name?"

"Betty." Carrying the lantern with her, she went to the horse, murmuring to her as she fed her the carrot she'd brought from the house. "I've had her for nearly eight years already. She can take me back and forth to the schoolhouse without my touching the lines."

"She's in a rut," Johnny said.

"Then so am I." Her anger flashed like lightning in a summer sky.

He shrugged. "You said it, I didn't."

Her head began to throb. She'd come out to the stable to escape tension, not to find it.

Johnny had one thing right. She was predictable in this habit of hers. She made a last trip to the stable every night. Tonight it had been a reasonable excuse to leave behind the endless discussions about Mamm and Daadi's move to the daadi haus.

It was happening in less than a week now. Anna should be finding a way to accept the inevitable instead of making everyone's life miserable. And speaking of making people's life a misery to them—

"Why are you here?"

It was probably best to stay angry with Johnny, if she could. When she let herself feel sorry for him or start remembering the past, then she was likely to give in and agree to do something she didn't want to do, just out of pity.

"We have to talk." He moved next to her, stroking Betty's silky neck.

"Not here." She sent an apprehensive glance toward the stable door. "Someone could come in. Someone might have seen you."

"No one saw me." Johnny's hand stilled on the horse's neck. "I was careful, just like I always was when we used to meet here. Remember?"

There it was—the plea to her memory. She remembered. It would be far better to say that she didn't, but it would be a lie. So better to say nothing.

Still, he knew. They'd used her habit of visiting her horse every night to steal some quiet time alone together. She'd rush in, a carrot or sugar cube for the mare in her hand, and find him waiting. His arm would encircle her waist, his lips brush her cheek.

They'd been innocent times, but she'd felt guilty, nonetheless, sitting on a straw bale, leaning against Johnny's shoulder, talking about the future. But it was a future they'd never had.

"You remember," he whispered, and he was close enough that she'd feel the touch of his breath if he moved another few inches.

"It doesn't matter."

She took a step back and was reminded of Daniel, stepping carefully away from her when his daughter called him. For a moment her mind clouded with confusion. Too much was happening, too soon.

"It doesn't matter," she said again, more firmly. "I've done everything I can for you, Johnny. I cannot change your parents' minds for them."

"I can't believe they refuse to see me." He turned away with a quick, restless movement. "I'm their only son. How can they treat me this way?"

She forced her heart to harden against him. "You are the one who left."

"Now I've come back. Even the prodigal son had a warmer welcome than this."

"The prodigal son admitted his wrong and was willing even to be a servant," she reminded him.

"Is that what you expect of me?" He threw his anger at her.

"I don't expect anything," she said. "But I can see what's in front of my face."

"And what is that?" The sudden sarcasm that hardened his voice made it easier to feel that this was not the Johnny she knew.

Gut. That would make it easier to say no to whatever it was that had brought him here tonight.

"You want to keep your English life and have the advantages of being Amish, too. You can't have it both ways. You should know that by now."

Some emotion crossed his face—regret, she thought.

"Maybe so." He shook his head. "But that's not what's important right now."

Her stomach clenched. They were getting to it, then. To whatever it was he wanted from her.

"What is important, if not your family's grief?" Could he dismiss that so easily?

"I accept that I can't change them, and I'm sorry. But that doesn't alter the reason why I came back to Pleasant Valley to begin with."

"Your work at the clinic." Somehow she'd known they'd get around to it eventually.

"I need cooperation from the families of affected children. They're not going to open their doors to me." He paused, his gaze intent. "But they might to you."

The breath went out of her. She took a step back. "No. I can't."

"Of course you could." He dismissed that with an impatient gesture. "It's not difficult—it's just a matter of interviewing the parents and writing down their answers."

She fought to control her irritation. Did he really think that she'd refused because she thought herself incapable of such a simple task?

"That's not the point. I'm too busy with my teaching and with the duties I have at home as well. I can't take on another job."

"This wouldn't be a real job. Just volunteer work. You could probably get it done in a few hours a day, plus the travel time, of course."

"I don't have a few extra hours in my days."

"You could wait until after school is out to start," he countered. "As long as I know that the data will be coming in, I can get to work."

He was as impatient as always, eager to bend everyone else to suit his needs, and that enthusiasm of his had always had a way of sweeping her along with it. Not this time.

"I can't," she said firmly. "There would be too many problems with my family and the church if I were to do such a thing."

Especially with Johnny involved. There would probably be fewer objections to the clinic than to her seeing so much of him.

He brushed that away with a sweep of his hands. "You're an adult. You can make up your own mind what to do."

Her eyebrows lifted. "Have you been away so long that you've forgotten what it means to be Amish? It is not just a matter of what I might want to do. You can't judge me by English standards."

"Fair enough." He had the grace to look a bit abashed at the reminder. "I won't judge you, Leah. If you feel you need to consult the bishop about it, that's fine."

"No, it's not fine. I'm not going to work with you on this, Johnny."

He'd have to make of that what he would. She wasn't going to put herself in a situation where every day might be spent reliving the past.

He took a quick step toward her, coming into the circle of light from the lantern. His face was set, his gaze steady.

"This isn't about you and me. This is about those children. You can dismiss me if you want. But can you dismiss them so easily?"

Her heart twisted, thinking of the children she knew who suffered from the genetic diseases. Not as many here, probably, as back in Lancaster County, but even one was too many.

There were two of the Miller children, over near the crossroads, spending hours of the day and night under the special blue lamps that helped the children affected with Crigler-Najjar syndrome. Without a liver transplant, they'd never be well.

And there were the babies gone in an instant, it seemed, from a form of sudden infant death syndrome, turning a family's happiest time into one of grief.

Others, some in their own church family, suffered from diseases that seemed to have no known remedy.

No, she couldn't dismiss the children. The fact that her own siblings and their young ones had escaped the inherited diseases didn't mean her heart didn't break each time she heard of a child's suffering.

She looked at Johnny. He must still know her too well, since he'd stood quietly, letting her think. Knowing where her thoughts had gone.

"How could anything I do help those children? I'm not a scientist."

"No, but gathering the information is nearly as important as applying the science." He took a quick step toward her, his face lighting with enthusiasm. "We have the tools to start unlocking the secrets of some of those diseases. But without the cooperation of the families, even those who seem free of the illnesses, we can't use the tools we have." He held out his hand to her. "Isn't that something you'd want to do, if you could?"

She was so tempted simply to agree—to be swayed by his enthusiasm and by the ache in her heart for any hurting child. But she needed to think this through, away from John's passion about it.

"I'll think about it." She lifted the lantern so that she could see his face more clearly, see him start to speak. "No, don't try to persuade me. Just let me think it over and come to a decision. Surely you can do that."

He nodded, reluctance in the movement. "All right. But at least come to the clinic and see for yourself the work we're doing on genetic diseases. There's no reason not to do that, is there?"

"I'll think about it," she said again.

His face fell, but he nodded, maybe seeing that further argument would push her away. "I guess that's the best you can do. I'll go now. Thank you for listening, at least."

He walked to the door, his stride quick and impatient. Slipping out, he turned away from the house so that the open door would shield him from the gaze of anyone looking out the windows.

He probably thought she was a coward for refusing to jump at the chance he offered her. She stroked Betty's neck, taking comfort in the solid warmth of the animal. But then, he already knew she was a coward, didn't he?

CHAPTER SIX

Leah sat at the small pine table in her bedroom, going over lesson plans. The gas lamp cast a yellow glow on the page, and she leaned back in the chair and rubbed her eyes. She'd fallen behind on schoolwork this week, and she didn't like to do that, especially with the end of the year barreling at her like a runaway wagon.

But it couldn't be helped. Mamm and Daadi were moving to the daadi haus tomorrow. Levi and Barbara were moving into the farmhouse at the same time. Her days had disappeared into a haze of trying to organize, pack, keep her mother from doing too much, and keep her sister from exploding.

She certainly hadn't had time to give more than a passing thought to Johnny's proposal. She could imagine how annoyed he'd be to know that, but he didn't have family to consider in his plans. That was sadder than he realized, to her way of thinking.

She hadn't exchanged more than a few words with Daniel, either. Her heart still ached for those children. Whatever had happened to send them away from the world they knew, it must have been traumatic.

When she tried to imagine it, she ran up against a blank wall of ignorance. If Daniel could only bring himself to confide in her about it—

She didn't think that was likely. He clearly wasn't ready to talk about his family's trials.

As for the surge of attraction that had flared so surprisingly between them—well, neither of them would want to discuss that.

She pulled the sheaf of lesson plans toward her again, but as she did so, she heard her mother calling her name up the stairs. She went quickly toward the hall. She'd expected Mamm to head straight to bed. Surely she hadn't thought of something else she wanted to do tonight.

Her mother grasped the newel post at the bottom of the stairs, sagging as if she needed its support. "Barbara is here. Will you come down and help her with these boxes?"

Leah nodded, starting down the steps. Barbara certainly had an abundance of energy. She hadn't thought to see her again before tomorrow morning, when the official moving would begin, and plenty of church members would be here then to help.

Barbara was in the kitchen, trying to maneuver an overfilled box onto the table.

"Let me take that." Leah slid the carton out of Barbara's grip. "We'll want the table clear in the morning to feed people."

"Ja, that's right." Barbara relinquished her hold. "It's kitchen things, though, so I thought best to put it in here."

"I'll stow it in the pantry. That's already cleaned out." She suited the action to the words, sliding the box out of sight into the pantry. "You look tired, Barbara. I'm sure that could have waited until tomorrow. Do you want coffee? Tea?"

Barbara slumped into a chair and fanned herself with her bonnet. Her face was flushed, her eyes bright with barely suppressed excitement. Surely she didn't anticipate the move that eagerly.

"Water would be gut," she said. "But I must tell you something."

Mamm, who had been hovering near the door, seemed to resign herself to the fact that this wasn't going to be a short visit. She took the seat across from Barbara, leaning back heavily in the chair.

Leah filled a glass with water, her movements stiff. Couldn't Barbara see that Mamm needed to go to bed?

"Can it wait until tomorrow?" she suggested. "I'm sure we're all ready for a good night's sleep."

"No, no, I must tell you, because he'll no doubt be here to help." She gulped down half the glass. "It's about your neighbor. Daniel Glick."

Leah froze. Barbara definitely had a nose for news. If something happened in the valley, she wanted to know it first. Was Daniel's secret out already?

"What about Daniel?" She kept her voice noncommittal. This might be nothing at all.

Barbara leaned forward, her eyes bright. "Miriam Miller, my neighbor, she had a letter today from her cousin back in Lancaster County. It seems that she knew all about Daniel and his family. They belonged to the same church district."

"I suppose she would know him, then." Mamm's voice was stern. "And you know that I don't hold with gossip, Barbara."

Looking a bit abashed, Barbara sat back in her chair. "Not gossip. Truth. That's all. Just the truth about him. And I thought you ought to know, being close neighbors and Leah so interested in the children, and all. I thought to myself, 'Leah can help those children better if she knows all about it.'"

"All about what?" Best just to get it out. Then it could be dealt with.

"His wife left him." Her voice lowered, as if she didn't want anyone else to hear. "A Muller, she was, Ruth Muller before they wed. Anyway, Miriam's cousin says that it was a grief to all of them when Ruth just up and went one day, fence-jumping to the English. And taking the kinder with her."

"No." Mamm winced, as if the very thought of it caused her pain.

"She did that. Took them away, and Daniel was nearly mad with the grief of it. Two years they were gone, with him not knowing what had become of them all that time."

"What a terrible thing," Mamm murmured. "That poor man. Those poor children."

"So young to have such a thing happen to them." Barbara's eyes filled with tears. She might enjoy being the first to know, but she had a soft heart and was easily moved by a child or an animal that was hurting.

"How did he get them back?" Mamm clasped her hands in her lap, as if sending up a swift prayer for Daniel's children.

"His wife died. Killed in a car crash, she was, and drinking besides. She'd left the children all alone to fend for themselves while she went out." Barbara shook her head. "A gut thing, as it turned out, that they were not in the car with her."

"God watched over them," Leah murmured, her throat choking with tears.

Small wonder that Daniel didn't want to talk about what had happened. To go for two years not knowing where his children were—it was unthinkable.

"You can see why I thought you should be told right away." Barbara thrust herself back from the table. "He'll be here tomorrow to help, I shouldn't wonder, and folks maybe will be already talking about it. Maybe our Leah should just drop a word in his ear, let him know that folks have heard."

"I'm not sure I should—" But if she didn't tell him, who would?

"You're the teacher." Barbara patted her hand. "You'll know how to say it to him, so he won't be upset."

"It's for the best," her mother added. "The news will get around, everyone will talk about it for a day or two, and then it will be forgotten and things will get back to normal for them."

She was looking at Leah for agreement, and Leah nodded. But she wasn't so sure her mother was right.

Or at least, that Daniel would think so.

"*Hold* on, Daniel."

Mahlon, Leah's brother, hoisted one end of the heavy wooden cabinet they were lugging from Levi's wagon to the house. Cradling the weight against his chest, Mahlon craned his neck to see into the kitchen, and then grinned and jerked his head to the side.

"We'd best wait a bit. Barbara's changing her mind about where she wants it."

They set the load down on the grass, and Mahlon leaned against it, pushing his straw hat back on his head. "Be glad when this movin' is done, so the women will stop buzzing around like bees."

"It's a lot of changes." Daniel propped his elbow on the cabinet. Around the corner of the farmhouse, another group of the brethren were carting furniture into the grossdaadi haus. "Two families moving in one day is enough to cause upsets."

Mahlon shrugged. "I don't see what all the fuss is about, but Mamm wants everything just so in the new place, and Barbara—" He raised his eyebrows expressively.

Daniel grinned. He liked young Mahlon, with his easygoing manner and his open, pleasant face. And it was a fine thing to feel accepted so readily by him.

Not that he wouldn't have come in any event to help his neighbors with their move. But it was the first work frolic he'd been involved in since he'd come to Pleasant Valley, and that made it a positive step toward belonging.

Some women of the church were setting up lunch tables under the trees, while others helped to unpack boxes and put things away in both houses. Men carted boxes and furniture from here to there. The children darted in and out among them, some of the older ones helping, others just getting in the way.

Matthew had been entrusted with the job of taking water to the workers, and he seemed to be taking the job seriously. Even now he came toward them, carrying a full bucket, stopping to offer Mahlon a drink first.

Such a simple thing, but it made Daniel's heart swell with pleasure. That was what he'd longed for during those years apart—just the simple tasks of Amish life, shared with his children.

Elizabeth also had a job to do. She and her friend Becky had been put in charge of some of the younger children, whom they led in a game a safe distance away from all the activity.

"A drink, Daad?" Matthew held out the dipper.

He wasn't thirsty, but he took it anyway just for the pleasure of sharing the moment with his son. "Do a gut job, now."

"I will." Matthew hurried off around the house, his face intent with responsibility.

"A fine boy, that," Mahlon said. "Not a schnickelfritz like Levi's boy."

"He gets into mischief already," he said, remembering the motorcycle. "I understand you might be setting up a family for yourself sometime soon," he said.

Mahlon flushed. "Ja, we will that." He glanced toward the kitchen, where the debate apparently still went on. "Just as well, I think, with Mamm and Daadi moving into the daadi haus. Barbara will want this place for her family, especially with another babe on the way."

"Your sisters will still be here though," Daniel pointed out.

Mahlon shrugged. "Anna's old enough to start thinking about a wedding instead of running around all the time. And Leah—well, Leah's a gut aunt."

It seemed the unspoken thought was that Barbara would be foolish to think of causing problems for Leah in the house. Still, the change couldn't make for an easy situation for Leah.

His gaze sought her out, and he realized that he'd known all along where she was, spreading a cloth over the picnic tables, even though he hadn't been consciously thinking about her.

Her situation was not easy in a lot of ways. She didn't fit in with the other unmarried girls, all younger than she, who were giggling and flirting as they went about their chores. And the young married women, who were more her age, were occupied with babies and growing families.

"She would be a gut mother herself, as well as an aunt."

The fact that he'd said the words aloud startled him. He didn't want people getting the wrong idea about him and Leah.

Mahlon looked startled as well. "Leah? She always says she's past getting married. Although I suppose—"

He stopped, apparently thinking that Daniel could be a prospective suitor. Mahlon flushed to the tips of his ears. "She's a fine person. I didn't mean—"

He stopped again, maybe because everything he tried to say seemed to lead in the wrong direction. He bent and grabbed the bottom of the cabinet.

"Let's get this inside. Maybe then Barbara will make up her mind. I'm ready for middaagesse."

It looked as if the servers were about ready for lunch, too. Women were carrying baskets to the tables, where Leah supervised setting them out.

He picked up his end of the oak cabinet. "We'd best do some carrying to earn our lunch."

Would he talk with Leah then? They hadn't spoken all week, but he felt as if that conversation in the garden had happened minutes ago.

They hoisted the cabinet into the kitchen. Faced with its size, Barbara seemed to realize there was only one proper place for it, and it was deposited there without further trouble.

"That will do it." She glanced at him. "It's kind of you to help, Daniel."

He gave the nod that was the only right response. Barbara seemed to look at him with more interest than he'd expected. True, he was new in the district, but this wasn't the first time they'd met. He'd expect her to have gotten over her curiosity by now.

Mahlon nudged him. "Let's get some food before the others hog it all. Komm."

He'd guess that Mahlon was still filling out his long frame, but he followed him outside to the picnic tables. Leah, seeing him coming, stepped a little away from the table to meet him.

"Your brother is ready to eat," he said.

"My brother is always ready to eat." She waved her hand at Mahlon as if she shooed away a fly. "Go on, fill your plate already."

Mahlon grinned and took a ladleful of potato salad that filled half his plate.

"He's still a growing boy," Daniel suggested. "I seem to remember feeling like that."

Leah didn't smile in return. Instead she looked at him with a kind of sweet gravity. "I must tell you something, Daniel."

For a moment he could only stare at her. Then certainty pooled inside him at her expression.

"Someone has found out about what happened to us."

She nodded. "I'm sorry. One of Barbara's neighbors had a letter from a cousin in Lancaster County."

He looked for his children—Matthew and Elizabeth going about their chores, Jonah playing happily with some of the younger ones. They were fine for the moment.

"I'd hoped for a little more time."

"I know," she said softly. "But it won't matter, you'll see. The brethren will care about you and yours all the more. It will be fine."

"I hope so." His throat tightened. He didn't mind for himself. Folks could talk about him all they wanted.

But the children—how did he protect them?

Leah waved good-bye to another buggy as the Miller family left. Almost everything had been moved into the farmhouse or transferred to the daadi haus. They'd have some sorting and storing ahead of them, but at least the worst of it was finished.

She glanced around the yard. Matthew was helping his father carry a box toward the daadi haus. Her heart winced at Daniel's expression. Withdrawn, stoic—it was the face of someone prepared to endure whatever was necessary.

And Matthew looked very like him at the moment. Did that mean Matthew realized people knew about that period in his life? It was hard to tell.

She picked up a tray of dishes from the picnic table and carried them toward the kitchen. She sympathized with Daniel's feelings, but really, he had to have known that everyone would find out soon.

As Mamm had said, the brethren would be sympathetic to his troubles, wanting to help.

But they would talk. My, how they would talk. She couldn't blame Daniel for wanting to avoid that as long as possible.

She entered the kitchen to find that Barbara was busily putting dishes in the cupboard, talking all the while to Mamm. As for her mother—

One look, and Leah crossed the room quickly to put her arm around her mother's waist. "Mamm, it's time you had a rest. Barbara and I will take care of whatever else needs to be done here."

Drawn to attention by Leah's words, Barbara climbed down from the stool she'd been standing on. "Leah is right. I should have said something. You go right along to the daadi haus and rest, and I'll bring you a cup of tea as soon as the water boils." She was already putting the kettle on the stove as she spoke.

Leah smiled at her sister-in-law. Barbara might be unaware of people's feelings sometimes, but she was kind at heart despite that.

She would try harder, Leah promised silently. She would remind herself of Barbara's fine points and ignore the rest.

For once her mother didn't argue, which must be a measure of how tired she was. She went slowly out the side door that led to the daadi haus.

Leah straightened her back. She couldn't stop yet, however attractive that sounded. "I'll bring the rest of the dishes from the picnic table."

She no sooner reached the yard than Anna came toward her, half running. She grabbed Leah's arm.

"You need to come right away." The words tumbled out in an urgent undertone. "It's Elizabeth. She's in the barn, crying, and I can't get her to stop."

Leah's heart twisted. "I'll get Daniel—"

"That's what I said, but she doesn't want him." Anna's eyes were dark with concern. "When I said I must call someone, she asked for you."

She should tell Daniel, but maybe it made sense to find out what was wrong first. She followed Anna, who was already hurrying toward the barn.

If the child had hurt herself—but surely if that was the case, she'd want her father. The fear that Daniel felt curled around her heart. Was this because people knew about Elizabeth's mother taking the children away? If so, Leah was out of her depth in dealing with it.

She caught up with Anna at the barn door. "What were you doing out here? Did you hear her?"

Anna shrugged, slid out of Leah's grasp, and sidled through the door. Leah followed. And stopped.

Elizabeth had apparently climbed into the hay mow. She curled there, hands over her face, her little body shaking with sobs. And a few feet away, looking embarrassed and uncomfortable, stood an English boy.

For a moment she could only stand there, amazed at Anna's effrontery. How could she have the boy here today, of all days, with half the church around? It was as if she wanted to get caught.

"I tried to comfort her, but she just keeps crying." He shoved his hands into the pockets of his jeans, hunching his shoulders.

"We'll take care of her," Leah said crisply. She climbed over the low barrier to the hay mow, sending Anna a glance that should have singed her. "Send him away at once," she said in Pennsylvania Dutch.

"I don't see why—" Anna began, looking mulish.

"Now," she snapped. "We'll talk about this later. There are more immediate things to deal with."

Sulky, Anna grabbed the boy's arm and shoved him toward the door, muttering something to him that Leah couldn't hear. Maybe that was just as well.

Leah sank down in the hay next to the crying child. "There, now, Elizabeth. Can you tell me what's wrong?"

She shook her head.

Leah pulled the child toward her, wrapping her arms around the small figure. "All right." She held her close. "It's going to be all right."

Some hurts went too deep for talk. She knew that for herself. Sometimes all you could do was hold someone.

Guide me now, dear Father. I don't know what to do for this suffering child. Please give me the right words to comfort her.

She held Elizabeth, rocking back and forth, crooning softly in a mix of lullabies and comforting words. She could only hope that the little girl understood enough to take comfort, at least from her presence, if not from her words.

After a while the sobs began to lessen in intensity, though the little body still shook with involuntary spasms. Elizabeth reached up to run her hand along her hair in a futile effort to right herself.

"There, now, it's all right." Leah continued in dialect instead of the English she'd have used with her in school. "Don't worry about how you look."

Elizabeth drew back a little, not meeting Leah's eyes. She sniffled, her hands twisting in her lap. "I'm sorry." She whispered the words.

"Don't be sorry." Maybe a calm, matter-of-fact approach was best. "Everyone needs to cry sometimes, and the hay mow is a good place for it. Usually it's nice and private, but today you had company, didn't you?"

"Anna came in with her friend." Elizabeth hiccoughed. "I wanted to hide, but I was crying too hard. I didn't want her to see me."

Leah stroked Elizabeth's hair, smoothing the tumbled strands. "Anna won't say anything to anyone. Besides, she's done her share of crying out here from time to time."

"She comes here to cry?" Elizabeth looked up at her, eyes round.

"She used to." Today she'd come with something different in mind, and that was still to be dealt with. "Or she'd climb up in the willow tree when she wanted to be by herself. Once she went too high and couldn't get down, and Levi had to bring the ladder to fetch her."

That brought the faint smile to the child's face Leah had been hoping for.

She used her handkerchief to wipe the last traces of tears from Elizabeth's cheeks. "Were you upset because people found out about when you . . ."

She hesitated. What was the right phrase? She wasn't sure.

"They were talking about my mamma." Elizabeth burst out with it before Leah could come up with the proper words. "I don't want them to."

Leah's throat tightened. "I'm sorry, Elizabeth. Sometimes people talk, but they're not really being mean. They're just not thinking about the fact that you might be missing her."

"I don't miss her." The child's hands clenched. "I don't. I don't want to talk about her ever again!"

The vehemence in the child's voice took Leah aback.

"It's all right. You don't have to."

Was this grief or anger? She wasn't sure, and not knowing the circumstances made it impossible for her to respond the right way. If Daniel had seen fit to open up a little more, maybe she'd be better able to deal with this.

Elizabeth was looking at her with a doubting expression, and all she could do was try to reassure her.

"Really. You don't have to talk about her at all if you don't want to."

Elizabeth stared at her for another moment. Then her face seemed to relax, and she sighed. "Ser gut," she murmured.

Was it good? She didn't think so, but she didn't have the right to interfere.

The barn door creaked open. Daniel loomed for a moment on the threshold, probably to let his eyes grow accustomed to the dim light. Then he strode toward them, scooped his daughter up in his arms, and turned away.

Leah scrambled out of the hay, shaking her skirt. "Daniel—"

He glanced at her, his face shuttered tight against her. "I'll take care of my daughter," he said, and walked out.

CHAPTER SEVEN

*L*eah tapped lightly on Anna's bedroom door. At a murmur from within, she opened it. Barbara and Levi were on the back porch, watching the children play as twilight drew in. This was probably the one chance she'd have to talk to Anna without anyone hearing.

She closed the door and leaned on it. Anna was rebraiding her hair, meaning that she intended to go out again. A small navy duffel bag lay on the bed, zipped closed.

If Leah looked, which she wouldn't, she'd probably find it contained English clothes. Many, if not most, Amish teens tried out modern clothing at one time or another during their rumspringa.

If only that was all Anna was doing. It was one thing to have English friends. It was another to be meeting a strange boy in the barn. She murmured a silent prayer for guidance.

"Well?" Anna, apparently tired of waiting, swung toward her. "Say what you've been waiting the whole day to say already."

Leah sank down on the bed. She wanted to have this conversation without blaming or scolding, but how could she?

"What were you thinking, Anna? Why did you invite that boy here today, of all days? With all that had to be done and with half the church here—well, it was foolhardy, at best."

"I didn't invite him today." The defiance in Anna's face faded, and she shifted her gaze away from her sister. "I'm not that dumb. He just showed up. And don't call him 'that boy.' His name is Jarrod Wells."

"All right." At least her little sister had more sense than she'd been fearing. "Why did Jarrod Wells come today, then, if you didn't ask him?"

Anna shrugged. "I don't know. He just wanted to talk, that's all."

"Talk?"

"Ja, talk," Anna flared. "I have a right to my own friends, don't I? You and the boys had your rumspringa, and I'm having mine. Don't tell me you didn't do things you wouldn't want Mammi and Daadi to know about."

"I suppose I did." But those things had been pretty tame, it seemed, by Anna's standards.

She suddenly felt the more than ten years' difference in their ages. Those years separated them as if they stood on opposite banks of a river.

She had been nearly twelve when Anna—the much longed-for baby sister after the boys—was born. Leah had been her second mother, so happy to take care of her and play with her. She'd thought they would always be as close as they had been then.

"Anna, please." She tried to put all those years of love into the words. "You must know I don't want to be the interfering older sister, out to ruin your fun."

"Then leave me alone. Trust me." Anna grasped the footboard of the bed, leaning forward with urgency in her voice, every line of her body proclaiming how passionate she was about this.

When Anna wanted, she wanted with her whole heart. Her emotions were always on the surface, ready to burst out in an instant. Maybe that was what frightened Leah so about her sister's choices.

She put her hand over Anna's. "I just want you to be safe."

"I'm careful."

"Is it careful to be meeting that . . . Jarrod in the barn? How many times has he met you there?"

Anna jerked her hand free. "All right, so I met him there a few times. Don't tell me you never smooched with Johnny in the stable when you were young, because I wouldn't believe it."

That hurt, but she wouldn't let it show in her face. "That was different."

"Different why?" Anna demanded. "Because Johnny was Amish? Because you were going to marry him? But Johnny's not Amish anymore, and you didn't get married."

The pain sharpened, all the worse because the hurtful words came from her precious little sister. She wrapped her fingers around the bed-post, trying to focus on the present.

"Are you in love with Jarrod?"

Please, she murmured silently. *Please.*

Anna shrugged. "I don't know. I might be."

"Anna, stop and think what you're saying. You can't fall in love with him. He's—"

"Englischer. Auslander." She threw up her hands in an extravagant gesture. "Listen to yourself, Leah. You talk as if a person can control who they fall in love with. Love isn't like that."

Leah's fingers tightened; her stomach twisted. She had to find the words that would turn her sister from her headstrong course.

"What is love like, then?"

Anna looked startled at the question. "Love is—well, it's over-whelming. It takes you over and makes you willing to do anything, anything for the person you love."

"What about the other people you love? The people who love you and want what's best for you? What about your duty to them?"

"You don't understand." Anna swung away from her. "Honestly, Leah, sometimes I think you don't have any feelings at all. You can't talk about duty when you're in love. If you were really in love, that wouldn't matter at all."

No feelings. That was what Johnny had said to her, too, long ago, when she'd sent him away. But if she had no feelings, what was this pain in her chest, so sharp it took an effort to breathe?

But she would breathe. And she would control her emotions, because that was what she did. It was for the best.

"Anna, I just want you to be careful. And I want Mamm not to have to worry about you. Is that so much to ask?"

Anna's lips tightened. She grabbed the bag and headed for the door.

But when she reached it, she stopped, hand on the latch. She didn't look back at Leah.

"I'll be careful, all right?" Her voice was impatient. "I promise I'll be careful."

She opened the door and was gone.

. . .

"Come in, come in." John Kile stood in the center hallway of the medical clinic a few days later, holding the door open for Leah. "Let me show you around our facility."

She stepped inside a little gingerly, not sure what awaited her. She'd hired a driver to bring her, because the clinic was too far to go with horse and buggy after school and still get home by dark. Her driver, Ben Morgan, would be waiting for her when she finished.

It wasn't that the idea of the clinic was foreign to her. She'd certainly spent a great deal of time in medical facilities last year when Mamm had been ill.

But this was different, both because Johnny was here and because of what he wanted from her.

The decision to come, even to look around, hadn't been easy. She'd struggled with it for over a week, praying endlessly, staring at the ceiling when she should have been sleeping.

Finally she'd realized why it was so hard. Because of Johnny. Because Johnny was the one who'd asked her.

If anyone else had approached her, her thoughts would have been for the children and how she could help them. Chastened, she'd made her decision.

"You can hang your bonnet there." Johnny nodded to a row of wooden pegs on the wall of the hallway. His blue eyes were alive with excitement, and he was as eager as a child with a new scooter.

She took her time removing her bonnet and straightening her head covering, trying to get accustomed to the place.

On the outside, the clinic had clearly been designed to make Amish visitors feel welcome. Although new, it was built in a style reminiscent of a sturdy Pennsylvania Dutch barn. A row of hitching posts lined one side of the parking lot under a row of shade trees.

"This is the clinic area." Obviously impatient, Johnny seized her elbow and steered her through the archway into a waiting room lined with chairs.

Leah had to pause and blink. In contrast to the mellow exterior, this room fairly shouted at her. The walls were covered with bright wallpaper in an abstract design, the plastic chairs bore brightly colored pads, and posters were plastered on the walls over the chairs.

"Great, isn't it?" Johnny gestured. "We even have a play area for the children."

The play corner was filled with bright plastic toys, some of them representing objects Leah couldn't identify, but she nodded and smiled.

He ushered her over to the counter that lined one end of the room. "I'd like to introduce our receptionist, the person who keeps us all on track. Leah, this is Julia Alcott. Julia, Leah Beiler."

Johnny gave Julia his most charming smile, and in that moment Leah realized that underneath his outward assurance, he was nervous. With all his education, did he still question his acceptance here?

Julia nodded, her eyes cool. She was probably in her midthirties, although Leah found it difficult to judge the ages of non-Amish women, and the beige suit she wore made her look more like one of the professionals than a receptionist.

Before Leah could decide what, if anything, to say, a door behind the counter opened. The man who loped through was tall and thin, with keen gray eyes behind his glasses and an eager, youthful smile. He came quickly through the break in the counter and extended his hand to her.

"Welcome, welcome. I'm Alex Brandenmyer. You must be the friend of John's who's going to help us. I'm pleased to meet you."

"Leah Beiler," Johnny said, and his voice had an undertone of increased nervousness.

It was little wonder. Leah shot a look at Johnny. She had said she'd consider this job, and the doctor acted as if her acceptance was an accomplished fact. Either Johnny was overly optimistic about persuading her to do this, or else he felt he knew her so well that there was no question of her cooperation.

With no help for it, Leah shook the man's hand, feeling awkward. "I'm not completely sure that I will be able to help you."

His eyebrows lifted at that, and he gave Johnny a questioning glance. "Well, we'll just have to convince you that we need you, won't we? Tell me, what do you think of our waiting room? We want it to be comfortable and welcoming for our Amish clients."

"It's . . . It's very nice." She found it anything but comfortable, but she couldn't say that.

"That isn't really what you think, is it?" He smiled, but his gaze was keen and assessing. "Tell me. I'd like to hear your opinion."

He was quick to size people up. A good quality in a doctor, she supposed, but she found it a bit uncomfortable when it was turned on her.

"Well, I . . ." She glanced at Johnny, hoping he could get her out of this awkward situation, but he was gazing attentively at his mentor. "It's very . . . busy. If your visitors are already nervous about being here, they might find it a little overwhelming."

"Good point. See, you've helped us already."

The doctor beamed, apparently pleased, but Julia looked annoyed. Had the woman picked out the colors and patterns? Leah hadn't meant to offend anyone, but he'd forced her to give her opinion.

"This is the clinic area, as you can see."

Dr. Brandenmyer seemed determined to take over the tour. She'd find it less intimidating to be shown around by Johnny, but he faded back in the presence of Dr. Brandenmyer.

"We see patients daily, but over here on the other side of the hallway is where the real work is done."

He moved quickly, towing her along as he crossed the hallway and opened the door. A completely different atmosphere permeated this side of the entry area. A hallway stretched the depth of the building, with rooms and cubicles off it to the left.

Dr. Brandenmyer gestured as he walked, giving her the impression that he liked to do more than one thing at a time. "Here we have an exam room with an area for drawing blood. Next we have the laboratory to analyze that blood." He nodded to a young man in a blue lab coat wearing goggles.

"The Amish provide a unique opportunity to study genetic diseases, you know." He paused. "Genetic diseases are those that are carried in the genes, passed on from parent to child."

He apparently assumed that she had no understanding of the problems at all.

"Like the Crigler-Najjar syndrome and the maple syrup urine disease," she suggested.

"Yes, exactly." He looked at her approvingly, as if she were a brighter pupil than he'd anticipated. "You see, most Pennsylvania Amish are descended from the same small group of ancestors. That means that genetic diseases can be more prevalent. If we're able to trace the family trees of those who are affected, we can come that much closer to identifying the causes."

"And finding a cure?" Her heart clenched at the thought of the families who would be touched by such a thing.

"We're a long way from that right now," he admitted. "But everything we learn moves us forward. Early testing and intervention can help many of the affected children live a much more normal life."

He stopped at the entrance to a room that seemed completely filled with computers. Johnny brushed past her and crossed to a woman who swung away from one of the screens as they came in.

"Leah, this is Stacie Corson." He rested his hand lightly on the back of her chair.

The slight, dark-haired young woman shot Johnny an intense glance before nodding at Leah.

"This is where Stacie and I analyze the data," he said, gazing around at the computers the way her father might look at a field overflowing with ripe corn. "But we need more information to work on."

"That's where you come in," Dr. Brandenmyer said. "You see, the information you bring us will be keyed into the computer." He moved to one of the machines, patting it lovingly. "This is the most advanced equipment on the market today." He bent over to tap something, so that a complex chart appeared on the screen. "You see, this is a sample of the—"

"It's not necessary to give Leah a crash course in computers." The woman who spoke had been sitting behind one of the machines in the corner of the room, and Leah hadn't noticed her until that moment.

But she was relieved at the interruption. Very relieved. Her head had begun to ache with the strain of trying to follow Dr. Brandenmyer's explanations. She'd been keeping up all right, she thought, until they'd reached the computer room, but here she was totally out of her depth.

"Lydia, I didn't see you back there. This is Leah Beiler, the young woman John told us about. Leah, this is Lydia Weaver."

"Leah is the teacher, I know," Lydia said, coming toward them.

Her smile was piercingly sweet, lighting her plain face with an inward beauty. She wore a simple dark dress with low-heeled shoes, her graying hair short and swept back from a face that was frankly middle-aged and didn't attempt to hide that fact.

"Goodness, look at the time," Dr. Brandenmyer exclaimed. "It's a good thing you stopped me, Lydia. I must go. I have a conference call with those researchers in Luzerne in a few minutes. John, you'd better come with me. Stacie can show Leah the charts and explain about the interviews."

In an instant they were both gone. Stacie didn't look especially happy at being left behind. She shoved her chair, and it rolled to the next desk so quickly that Leah had to step out of the way.

"It's very simple, really," she said, sounding doubtful that Leah could manage no matter how simple. "We'd expect you to visit families who have an instance of genetically linked illness and persuade them to cooperate. There's a family-tree form to fill out." She shoved a paper into Leah's hands. "And an interview form." She passed her another one. "We encourage all the members of the family to come in for DNA testing. You know what that is, don't you?"

Leah's hands tightened on the forms that had been thrust into her hands. This woman didn't like her, and she wasn't sure why. Because she was Amish? Plenty of Englischers were prejudiced against the Amish, but this would be a funny place to work if you felt that way.

Or did this have something to do with Johnny?

"I said do you know about DNA testing?"

"Yes."

Leah clipped off the word and put the papers down on the desk carefully because she wanted to throw them. If Johnny thought she'd be convinced to help them by making her the object of condescension and rudeness, he was mistaken.

"I'm sure there's time for all of these explanations once Leah has had a chance to think about this," Lydia interrupted smoothly. "I always have a cup of tea about this time." She touched Leah's arm lightly. "Please, come and join me."

Leah would rather leave, but she would not return rudeness for rudeness by saying so. "That is very kind of you."

With the sense that the woman had unexpectedly come to her rescue, Leah went with her.

Lydia led the way into yet another office, but this one was totally different. There was not a computer in sight. The room was simplicity itself, with off-white walls and matching fabric shades on the windows, drawn up to give a view across green pasture. In the distance, an old orchard spread along the hillside, its apple trees gnarled and bent, but still bearing blossoms.

There were blossoms inside, as well, with pots of African violets filling the windowsills. Though there was a desk in the far corner near crowded bookshelves, the focus of the room seemed to be two comfortable-looking padded rockers on an oval hooked rug.

"I like your office." At an inviting gesture from Lydia, Leah sank into one of the rockers. Its bentwood back fit her perfectly.

"My aim was to make it look as little like an office as possible."

Lydia turned on what seemed to be an electric kettle and put two mugs on a tray. Her movements were slow and smooth. Calming.

Leah leaned her head back, feeling the last of her stress drain away. "You succeeded. It's peaceful here." She hesitated. "You rescued me. That was kind of you."

Lydia opened a tin and began arranging cookies on a plate. "You looked as if you needed it. I'm afraid this place can be overwhelming."

"Ja." The word was heartfelt.

"I've noticed that scientists become so focused on their own subject that they're totally unaware of other people's reactions." The kettle was boiling already, and she poured hot water into the cups. "You can be staring at them with a totally blank expression, and they'll just keep talking."

That surprised Leah into a laugh. "I'm afraid blank is a wonderful gut description of how I felt when they started talking about the computers."

"I'm a little familiar with computers, but I confess, the complex programs John and Stacie work with are beyond me."

Lydia carried the tray to the small, round table that stood between the rockers and put a steaming mug down next to Leah.

Once Leah had taken the tea and an obviously homemade oatmeal cookie, Lydia served herself and sank back in the other rocker.

"That's better. I always want a break in the late afternoon."

"This is pleasant." Leah looked at the woman, curious. "You talk about the scientists as if they're different from you, but you work here, don't you?"

"Yes, but I'm a psychologist, not a genetics researcher. I help the families and the children cope with the difficulties of their situation."

"It is very hard," Leah agreed. "I know of several children who ought to be in my school, but their condition doesn't permit. I try to do what I can, taking them books and learning activities, but it's not enough."

Lydia nodded in understanding. "Whatever we do never seems enough, does it? Still, no matter what their condition, the children are a blessing. And those we lose—well, they're safe in the hands of Jesus."

Leah studied the woman, caught by the turn of phrase, the way she dressed, even the way she sat. "Lydia, are you . . ."

She stopped, realizing that the question she wanted to ask might be considered rude.

"Am I Plain?" Lydia finished the question for her, smiling. "I was raised Amish, yes." She shrugged. "But I wanted more education, more choices about the life I would have. So I chose not to join the church."

"Are you—" Questions flooded her mind. "Do you have a relationship with your family?"

"Oh, yes. It took some time, but we're close now. They live in Indiana, so I don't see them as often as I'd like, but we write often, and my nieces and nephews visit in the summer."

"That's gut."

At least, she supposed it was. So far, Johnny didn't have that chance, but perhaps it would come, given a little patience. Unfortunately, patience had never been one of his strong points.

"You're happy?"

Lydia considered the question. "Not entirely, I suppose. Sometimes I long to be an Amish woman again, sitting in my own kitchen with my children around me. But none of us gets everything we want, Amish or English. I am content. And I'm very satisfied to be part of the work we're doing here."

"I know that it is important work." Leah stared down at the dark brew in her cup, a little troubled. "But I'm not sure it is right for me."

For a long moment Lydia didn't speak. Then she nodded. "I understand. It would be difficult for you in any event, but having John here makes it worse."

She wanted to deny it, but Lydia saw too much. Or maybe Johnny had been talking about her. That thought was distasteful.

Lydia's chair rocked as she patted Leah's hand. "Think about it. Pray about it. See what God's answer is. That's all we can ask of you."

Leah managed a smile, grateful that Lydia, at least, didn't intend to pressure her. "All right. That I will do."

CHAPTER EIGHT

*H*e shouldn't be letting his mind stray to Teacher Leah when he was worshipping, Daniel reminded himself. He would not glance toward the other side of the aisle to where the women sat, even though he knew perfectly well that she was on the fifth bench back, sitting on the end of the row next to her mother.

His interest was only drawn in that direction because Elizabeth had asked to sit with Teacher Leah, he reasoned. Instead of staying with her father and the boys, she wanted to be on the women's side of the barn for the worship service, like a grown-up woman.

The Miller family's large barn had been cleaned and scrubbed until it shone, so that it would be ready to host the service today. The backless benches, which would have arrived by wagon sometime during the week, were arranged in rows so straight that someone might have measured the distance between each of them. When they'd entered, black copies of the Ausbund, the songbook, lay on each bench, ready for the singing.

With the number of families in the district and the every-other-Sunday schedule for worship, Daniel would estimate each family's turn probably came around only once a year. Twenty-six families was considered ideal for a district back home for that reason, but often the number went up or down a few. If it went up too many, or the homes were too far apart for everyone to make the drive easily by horse and buggy, the district would have to be split into two congregations.

He'd not be added into the schedule here in Pleasant Valley until next year, but when the time came, he'd have to use the barn, just as the Millers did. Some of the brethren had homes large enough to hold worship in, but that seemed to be more common back in Lancaster County, where houses were built with that in mind.

The three-hour service was drawing to a close, as one of their three ministers concluded his sermon. Jonah sagged against Daniel, and he put his arm around the boy. Little ones couldn't help but grow sleepy during the long service with its slow hymns. Jonah would liven up plenty when it came time to eat.

He felt his gaze stray toward Leah again, and he pulled it back. He hadn't seen her to speak to in more than a week. He'd best be honest with himself about it. The reason he felt so compelled to see her now was plain and simple—guilt.

He'd misjudged her when he'd found her with Elizabeth that day of the moving. He'd thought she'd overstepped her boundaries, prying into his grief by talking to his daughter instead of calling him and leaving it to him to deal with.

It had been a few days later when he'd brought up the subject with Elizabeth, hoping she was ready to talk about it, and learned that Elizabeth, upset at hearing folk talk, had asked for Leah. Not him. That bitter pill still choked in his throat when he thought of it.

Gracious Lord, guide me to deal with these children You've given me. I hoped everything would be fine once I had them back with me, but it's been hard. Each day I question whether I'm doing the right thing.

They are my responsibility, Lord, given by You into my care. Guide my words and my choices.

That couldn't be the extent of his prayer, and he knew it. He'd wronged Leah in his thoughts and in his attitude, and that must be confessed.

Forgive me, Dear Father, for my hasty thoughts and attitudes where Teacher Leah is concerned. I was wrong. Forgive me.

He stared down at his hand, clenched on the black fabric of the broadfall trousers of his best suit. That wasn't enough. His confession wouldn't be complete until he'd mended matters with Leah herself.

He stood with the others for the final prayer, lifting Jonah in his arms as Bishop Mose spoke the words. Maybe he'd be able to speak with Leah during the visiting that went on before the brethren sat down for lunch. He had to mend things with her.

"Komm." He grasped the boys' hands, and the community surged out of the barn into the sunshine.

Jonah tugged at his hand. "My friends from school are here, Daadi. Can I go and see them?"

"Ja, both of you can go. Just mind you komm schnell when the lunch is served."

Elizabeth, he noted, had already gone over to the picnic tables, probably offering to help. She was very much the little mammi already.

He glanced around. Women were intent on helping with the lunch, while men gathered to catch up on the week's events. He spotted Leah, carrying a large jar of what looked like lemonade from her buggy. This might be his best chance for a private talk, although he hadn't figured out the right words yet.

He walked toward her, hoping it didn't look to the others as if he were seeking her out.

"May I carry that for you?" He reached for the jar as he spoke.

Leah looked up at him, green eyes wide and unguarded for an instant. Then her gaze slipped away from his. "I can manage."

She wasn't going to make this easy, but that was only fair.

"I know that you can carry it, but helping gives me an opportunity to speak with you."

Again that startled look, but she surrendered the jar without further argument. They moved together toward the tables.

"Is there a problem with the children?"

That would always be her first concern, of course. She only thought of him, if she thought of him at all, as the father of his children.

"The children are well. I am not. I must apologize to you."

"You mean about what happened with Elizabeth last Saturday." She stopped under the shade of an overhanging willow tree, and he stopped with her.

"I was rude to you when you were trying to help. That wasn't fair."

"It's all right." Her quick forgiveness shamed him. "You were concerned about your daughter. You felt you should have been told about her immediately. That's natural."

"She told me she asked your sister to find you. And not to tell me."

He tried to keep the hurt out of his voice but probably didn't succeed very well.

Leah's eyes darkened with concern. "Anna didn't know what else to do. Elizabeth was so upset that she felt it best to do as she wanted."

"Elizabeth asked for you. Not me." The words came out flatly. He hadn't intended to say that, but Leah's obvious caring made it easier than he'd expected to bring up the thing that still pained him.

Leah looked up at him, her gaze filled with sympathy. The leaves of the willow, moving in the breeze, dappled her face.

"I understand that bothers you, Daniel, but I'm sure Elizabeth was trying to protect you. She knew you would be worried if you realized how upset she'd become. She didn't want to hurt you."

"I hope that's all it was." His throat tightened, and the worries he had for his children rushed in upon him. "Those years we were apart— I don't know what they've done to my relationship with my children."

He was sorry he'd spoken the instant the words were out of his mouth. It sounded as if he was inviting Leah to help him, and he didn't want that. He was the father. He had to figure this out for himself.

"You love them," she said quietly. "That's the most important thing."

"Ja." He grappled for steadier ground. "We will be all right. We just need time."

"Time to adjust." She seemed to agree, but her eyes were troubled. "Elizabeth and Matthew struggle more than Jonah, because they're older. Elizabeth is trying so hard to be perfect that it concerns me."

He took a step back. "She's a helpful and conscientious child. That's a gut thing."

"Sometimes it's too much of a gut thing." She softened the words with a smile.

Still, they annoyed him. He had not asked for advice. Leah, however well-intentioned, was not a parent.

"You are kind to be concerned about my children. But I think you have enough worries of your own about your sister."

Her chin came up at that. "Elizabeth told you about Anna's friend."

"Ja, she did." He paused, struggling to be fair. "She said that he was kind to her. But he was English."

"Anna did not invite him to meet her in the barn, if that's what you're thinking." She paused, probably trying to get her irritation under control. "But you're right. We do each have our own problems to deal with."

Taking the jar of lemonade, she walked quickly over to the picnic tables, her back very straight.

Leah reached the picnic table and set down the lemonade. As was traditional, the host family had prepared a cold lunch. There were trays of bologna and Swiss cheese already on the table, and Naomi Miller came out the back door of the farmhouse, carrying baskets of whole wheat and white bread.

"Naomi, I don't know how you found the time to bake two kinds of bread."

Naomi Miller was busier than most young mothers, since two of her three preschool-aged children were among those in the valley suffering from the Crigler-Najjar illness.

"Ach, what I would do without my mother-in-law, I don't know," Naomi said, putting the tray on the table. "Her baking is wonderful gut, it is." Her eyes twinkled. "And your Mahlon will soon be as fortunate as I am, I think."

"Shh," Leah whispered, smiling. "Mahlon thinks no one has figured it out yet. As if no one notices him and Esther looking at each other all the time."

"Or the amount of celery my husband's daad has planted this year." She turned to go back to the house, probably for more food.

Leah caught her arm. "Since you and I are almost family, let me help bring things out."

"That is kind of you, Leah." One of her young ones rushed up to grasp her skirt just then, and she nodded. "Everything is on the kitchen table."

Leah went quickly into the house. She would have offered to help in any event, but she was just as happy to be safely away from the group for a moment. That exchange with Daniel had shaken her more than she wanted to admit.

He knew about Anna and the Englischer. Well, that in itself was not so bad. As Anna herself had said, it was her rumspringa. Such goings-on were tolerated, if not welcomed, by the community. Parents turned their eyes away and prayed for the best.

The danger lay in what Anna made of the situation. *I might be in love,* she'd said. It was tempting to believe that her younger sister wasn't old enough to know what love was, but she'd been Anna's age when she'd fallen in love with Johnny.

And look how that had turned out. She certainly couldn't hold herself up as any sort of example.

Sometimes I think you don't have any feelings at all.

Anna's words echoed relentlessly in her heart. The very fact that she couldn't forget them told her that she feared they were true. Certainly Johnny would have agreed with that, once at least.

And now? Well, now he simply didn't care.

Forcing herself to move, she picked up a tray and began filling it with the dishes on the table. Naomi, and perhaps her mother-in-law, had gone all out. There were sweet pickles and dill pickles, red beets, even peanut butter and strawberry jelly for the children. Additional plates were filled with sweets: pumpkin, chocolate chip, and sugar cookies.

She gripped the tray, but for a moment didn't move. Whether others would accept Anna's flirtation or not, Daniel was the worst person to trust with it.

She could understand why he felt as he did. With just the little she knew about his wife's jumping the fence to the outside world and taking the children with her, the reason for his feelings was clear. She could sympathize with his pain.

But she wished he didn't know about Anna.

She started out the door with the filled tray and nearly bumped into Elizabeth, coming in.

The child looked up at her, small face intent. "Naomi said that I could help carry things out."

"That's kind of you, Elizabeth, but wouldn't you rather play with the other scholars? I can take everything out."

"But I said I would help." Elizabeth's lower lip trembled. "I must do as I said."

"Ser gut," Leah said quickly. "You can take the plates of cookies that are on the table."

Elizabeth nodded and hurried to the table. Leah watched as she picked up the first plate carefully, holding it with both hands.

Dear Father, help me to understand this child. There is something not right about her frantic need to be good. Help me to see.

And if she did see, would Daniel listen to her? The way things were going, she doubted it.

She shoved through the screen door, holding it open against her hip while Elizabeth came out. They carried their burdens to the picnic tables, where people already clustered, plates at the ready.

Naomi seized the tray, putting its contents quickly on the table, the bishop lifted his voice in prayer, and the fellowship meal began.

In spite of her concerns about Daniel and his children and her worries about Anna, Leah began to relax. This time—this bonding with her community—was surely one of the great strengths of Amish life. Sharing worship and a common meal, they did what the earliest followers of Jesus did, and it built the ties between them more surely with every bite, every joke, every shared story.

By the time folks were settling into groups with their coffee and cookies, the peace of the day had calmed Leah. She sat down next to Naomi, who had her five-year-old son on her lap. Leah reached over to stroke light brown hair out of the boy's eyes.

"Eli, will you be coming to school in the fall?"

Eli burrowed his face in his mother's shoulder.

"Ach, now, answer Teacher Leah," Naomi chided.

The boy stole a glance at her face. "Ja, Teacher Leah," he whispered.

She smiled. "I will be glad to have you in my class, I will."

"You will be teaching in the fall, then?" Naomi asked.

Leah blinked. "Ja, of course I will, for sure. Why not?"

Naomi's gaze slid away from hers. "No reason. I just thought—folks were saying—maybe you'd be doing somethin' else in the fall."

For a moment her mind spun. And then it settled on the right answer. Daniel. Folks were saying she would wed Daniel.

She managed to smile. Managed to force her tone to be light. "I see the matchmakers are busy as always. I hate to disappoint them, but I have no plans to do anything but continue to teach."

Naomi's gaze met hers, and for a moment it seemed the young mother could see into her heart. "Sometimes it surprises us what God has for us."

A thin wail sounded from the second-floor window of the house. "It sounds as if young Jacob is awake." Leah was relieved at the interruption.

Naomi moved, starting to put Eli down, but Leah stopped her with a hand on her arm.

"Let me get him, please? I haven't seen him in weeks, it seems."

Naomi hesitated a moment, and then she nodded. "His clothes are hanging on the rack by the crib."

"I'll take care of him." She hurried toward the house. Escaping again? She'd hate to think that.

The wail grew louder as she mounted the enclosed staircase. Little Jacob was growing impatient. "I'm coming, Jacob."

The bedroom at the top of the stairs was typical of a small child's room in most Amish houses, with one dramatic exception. Over Jacob's crib hung a metal rack filled with blue lights, sending an eerie blue glow through the room. Run by a generator, the lights were the only thing that kept Jacob and his sister, who was two years older, alive.

Crossing to the crib, she switched off the lights and lifted them out of the way. Jacob, clad only in his diaper, reached chubby arms to her, and she picked him up, holding him close.

Jacob looked like any other fourteen-month-old, except for the golden color of his skin and the yellow whites of his eyes, caused by the jaundice that built up in his little body. Without spending twelve hours a day under the lights, Jacob would die.

Bouncing him a little, she carried him to the changing pad on top of the wooden dresser. "There we go, little man. We'll get you all dressed and take you down to your mammi."

Jacob stared at her intently for a moment and then gave her a grin. She tickled him, and he chortled, clapping his hands.

Her heart turned over, and she knew that she had one answer, at least, to the difficulties that surrounded her. She might not know what to do about Daniel and his children, or about Anna, but if it meant helping Jacob and those like him, she would ask Bishop Mose for permission to volunteer at the clinic.

"*I'm* wonderful glad to have a chance to talk to you." Rachel sat down beside Leah in the back row of schoolroom desks. "We've been too busy to visit lately, we have."

At the front of the room, the teacher's helper who came in to assist Leah several days a week was beginning to rehearse the scholars for their end-of-year program.

"Of course," she murmured, her mind only partially on Rachel. "I can't believe school will be out so soon. The years go faster all the time."

"That's because we're older all the time," Rachel said. She nodded toward Leah's seventeen-year-old helper. "How is Mary Yoder shaping up? Will you make a teacher of her?"

"I will if she keeps at it and doesn't let herself stray off after a job in town, as so many girls want to do."

Rachel's gaze sought out her own Becky, whispering with the other eight- and nine-year-olds as they practiced their parts. "That's a worry, for sure."

Already Rachel feared the world would lure her child away. *Be ye separate. In the world, not of the world.*

Those were the teachings they lived by, ingrained from birth, but still, the world called too loudly for some.

Like Rachel's twin. Leah glanced at her friend's face. Was she remembering Johnny?

"I hear that you are going to volunteer at the clinic where Johnny is." Rachel said the words softly, her face averted.

Leah hesitated, not sure of Rachel's reaction. When they were girls, they'd told each other everything, but now— Well, life was like that, wasn't it? They couldn't stay girls forever, and they wouldn't want to.

"I am. Once school is out, I'll start calling on folks, getting information about those who have the inherited illnesses."

Rachel looked at her then, her gaze troubled. "Are you sure that's wise?"

How could I be sure? No, she wouldn't say that. It would be giving in to her own doubts and fears.

"I've talked with Bishop Mose about it. He's approved." She stopped, not willing to repeat to Rachel the gist of Bishop Mose's concerns about her being near Johnny again.

"Have you seen him? Johnny, I mean?" Rachel lowered her voice, though none of the children could hear their conversation.

"Ja." She hesitated. "Are you upset with me for doing this?"

"No, no." Rachel put her hand over Leah's. "Not upset. Just worried."

"Don't be," she said, her tone firm. "There's nothing between John and me now, and that's as it should be."

"That's gut, much as I hate to say it." She paused, and her eyes grew wistful. "How is he?"

Leah's heart twisted. "He seems successful. Driven to succeed in his work, I'd say."

"But something about him worries you," Rachel said. "Don't deny it. I know you too well."

Leah spread her hands, palms up. "I'm not sure. The others seem to respect him, but he still is nervous, as if he's not quite sure of himself among them."

"Because he was Amish?"

"I don't know." She struggled with feelings she didn't fully understand. "Sometimes I catch flashes of the old Johnny, and I understand him. But then he becomes someone so different."

Rachel nodded. "If I could see for myself—"

"You could, if you wanted." Leah's hand closed over hers.

Rachel shook her head. "Not now. Maybe later." She focused on Leah's face, her blue eyes piercing. "Just tell me one thing for sure. Are you going to help there because of Johnny?"

In that, at least, she knew her own heart. "No. I'm going because of the children. Little Jacob and Naomi Grace Miller, and all the rest. And those yet to be born."

Her heart clutched. Mahlon was marrying into the Miller family. She wouldn't want him to give up his Esther, but she feared for the children they would have.

"Gut." Rachel patted her hand. "That's gut."

Mary came halfway down the aisle toward them and stopped, obviously not wanting to interrupt. Leah smiled at her.

"What is it, Mary?"

"The middle-grade scholars are ready to practice for us."

"Ser gut. We'll come a little closer." She rose and moved toward the front of the classroom, Rachel following her.

This end-of-year program was one she'd written her first year of teaching—so long ago she hoped no one would remember it. Although if any of her scholars from that year came to the program, which they probably would, they might still be able to recite the poetry by heart.

She settled herself to listen attentively, smiling and nodding encouragingly at each child as he or she spoke. Mary, who was prompting as needed, looked a bit worried. She'd have to assure her that mistakes were normal at this stage. Experience had taught Leah that just when you thought the program would be a complete disaster, it all came together.

Elizabeth stepped forward, her hands linked on her apron, her gaze on the ceiling, as if she looked for inspiration there. "I am but a little scholar," she began. "Still I've learned to—" She stopped, her hands tightening as she sought for the elusive words.

"—listen well," Mary whispered loudly.

Elizabeth didn't seem to hear. Her eyes grew panic-stricken.

"It's all right," Leah began.

But it was too late. Elizabeth burst into tears and ran from the room.

CHAPTER NINE

*M*atthew!" Daniel, on his knees in the vegetable garden, pushed himself to his feet, scanning the area between garden and barn for his son. "Matthew, wo bist du? Where are you?"

No answer. He glanced at the tomato plants, ready to be put into the ground now that the threat of frost was past. He'd hoped he and Matthew could get the job done quickly once the children got home from school.

He could have done it himself, but he'd wanted to share it with his son. He longed to have the pleasure of working beside him, planting something that would help to feed the family.

But Matthew, while never openly rebellious, had found many ways of avoiding chores lately. He'd been sent to the barn on a simple enough errand to bring back an extra trowel. He'd had time enough to do that a dozen times by now.

Daniel looked again at the two dozen tomato plants he'd decided would be enough for them. They'd begin to wilt in another few minutes. Blowing out an irritated breath, he headed for the barn.

Matthew seemed to get more distracted every day. Before Ruth left, Daniel had thought that he and Matthew were as close as a father and son could possibly be. He'd never expected that could change.

Now, he wasn't so sure. He didn't know his oldest son any longer, and that cut him to the heart.

The barn door stood open a few feet, where Matthew had gone in. Daniel gave it an impatient shove and stepped inside.

At the sound, Matthew popped up from the hay mow, eyes round with surprise. He made a quick movement with his hand, as if shoving something out of sight.

Daniel crossed to him, his jaw tightening.

"I'm sorry, Daadi. I—I guess I forgot to bring the trowel." He scrambled out of the hay mow. "I'll get it right now."

Daniel brushed past him, heading for the spot where the boy had been sitting.

"Daadi, let's go plant the tomatoes." Matthew's voice held an edge of nerves, a sure sign that he was trying to hide something.

Leaning on the low wall of the hay mow, Daniel bent over, probing into the hay with his hand. In an instant his fingers met something hard and rectangular.

He pulled it out and stood staring, hardly believing his eyes. It was some sort of game, with blinking lights and figures moving on a tiny screen.

He swung around, holding it up in front of his son. "What is this thing?"

Matthew stared back, sullen and defiant. "It's called an electronic game."

"Where did you get it?" His head started to throb. He had no desire to interrogate his son, but the boy wasn't being open with him.

Matthew didn't answer. He just stared, and Daniel couldn't tell what was going on behind that blank expression.

"Matthew?"

Matthew's jaw clenched, too. Daniel felt as if he looked into a mirror. Then Matthew's gaze slid away. He focused on the wide planks of the barn floor.

"It's mine." He muttered the words.

"Yours? How can it be yours?" How could an Amish child come by something like this?

"Mammi gave it to me." The words burst out of him. "It's mine."

Daniel froze. He tried to swallow, but his throat seemed paralyzed.

Help me. Show me what to say. If I say the wrong thing, I could drive a wedge between us we might never get rid of.

He took a long, slow breath. "I thought I had seen everything you brought from your mamm's house. I have not seen this."

Matthew's face seemed to ease a fraction at his father's calm tone. "I hid it."

"Why did you do that?" He'd tried hard to be gentle and understanding in the aftermath of Ruth's death. Had he failed so badly?

"It is English, so I knew you wouldn't want me to have it."

He didn't. That was his first instinctive reaction. And then he realized that he was asking himself what Leah would advise. Leah, with her quick intelligence and her knowledge of children, would know what to do.

But Leah wasn't here. And his children were not her concern.

"Matthew—"

"Mamm would let me have it," Matthew blurted out. "She would."

For just an instant he saw Ruth's face, lit with love when she looked at their son for the first time. His heart twisted. If only they could wipe out all the pain since that moment.

But there was no going back. He could only move ahead, trying to do what God willed.

He looked at the game—so small it nestled in the palm of his hand. Its light blinked at him.

He took a deep breath, praying he was making the right choice, and held it out to his son.

"I can keep it?" Matthew stared at him, disbelief in his eyes.

"You can keep it because your mammi gave it to you. But I don't want Elizabeth or Jonah to see it. Do you understand?"

"Ja. They won't. I'll keep it where they won't see it."

"And it's not to interfere with chores."

"It won't, Daadi. I promise." Matthew scampered to the hay loft and quickly rehid his device. "I'll get the trowel right away."

Matthew would come with him and plant tomatoes. But would he be thinking of planting and growing? Or would his mind be on that remnant of his English world?

"Don't walk in the living room," Barbara said the minute Leah came in the back door from school. "The floor is still wet." She stood at the kitchen sink, wringing out a cloth, her sleeves pushed back.

Leah nodded. The quilt frolic Barbara was hosting would be tomorrow, which meant that the house must be spotless. Leah pushed aside her plan to go over the materials from the clinic this afternoon.

"Mamm will enjoy the quilting, for sure." She hung her bonnet on the peg in the back hall. Her mother's quilts were works of art, with love in every stitch. "What are you working on tomorrow?"

"That tumbling blocks quilt. It'll go to one of the wedding couples in November." Her eyes twinkled. "Maybe Esther and Mahlon, if they get around to announcing in time."

Leah smiled back at her sister-in-law. "I think they will, if Mahlon has anything to say about it."

"Before you know it, it will be time to start a baby quilt," Barbara said. She hung the cleaning rags on the wooden rack to dry.

"I guess so." She thought again of Naomi's children under their blue lights. Would Esther and Mahlon have healthy babies? "I'll put my school things upstairs and come down to help you."

Barbara nodded. "Ser gut. Oh, and if you have any nice tea towels in your dower chest, maybe we could use them tomorrow. I tried to look, but the chest is locked, it is."

Leah's hands tightened on the case that held her school materials, and she forced the grip to ease before she spoke. Barbara had been in her room, trying to open her dower chest.

Rachel's words about living in another woman's house surfaced in her mind. Rachel had been right, but how many choices did she have?

"Leah?" Barbara questioned.

"I'm not sure what I have. Is there something wrong with yours?"

"Ach, they're worn through with using. Would be nice to have something pretty out when the sisters are here tomorrow."

Given the number of times Leah had told her family that she didn't intend to wed, Barbara's request was only natural. She didn't like it, but surely a few dish towels weren't worth starting a family argument over.

"I'll look and see what I have," she said, and made her escape to her room.

Once upstairs, with the bedroom door closed behind her, she massaged her temples. Barbara meant well, she reminded herself. And this was her house now.

Still, some rebellious part of her wanted to lock the door, something she'd never done before in her life.

She put her school materials on the table under the window and turned to look at the dower chest that stood against the wall opposite her bed. Daadi had made it for her sixteenth birthday, and even though she'd known that would be her gift, she'd been overwhelmed by it.

She bent, stroking the warm grain of the wood. Daad had saved the pieces from the walnut tree near the spring after it came down in a storm. She and her brothers had played under that tree from her earliest memories, and touching it was like touching a piece of her life.

The key was in the top drawer of her dresser. She took it out, sat down on the rag rug, unlocked the chest, and lifted the lid.

She had put a clean sheet over the contents to protect them. Touching the fabric, she remembered the day she'd done that. It had been nearly a month after Johnny left the valley.

To her shame, it had taken her that long to face that he wasn't coming back. The life they'd planned together would never be. She had to stop looking for him to return, put on a calm face, and never let anyone know how much it hurt.

She grasped the sheet and pulled it off in one quick movement. All this time, and still she didn't want to face it.

There was a light knock at the door, and then it opened a few inches. She stiffened. If it was Barbara, come to press her about the dish towels, she might not be able to hang on to her temper.

"Leah? May I come in?" It was her mother.

"Of course." She started to get up, but her mother had already entered, waving her back to her place.

"Sit, sit." Mamm sank into the rocking chair. "Go on with what you were doing."

Leah's fingers clenched on the edge of the chest. "Barbara wanted to borrow some tea towels for tomorrow. I was just going to look for them."

"I know." Mamm's voice was soft. "You don't have to do that. I'll settle it with Barbara."

She shook her head. "No, it means nothing. It's time I sorted these things out." She lifted out the quilt that lay on top.

Mamma reached out to touch it. "That is the log cabin quilt that you and your grossmutter made together."

"She did most of it." Leah unfolded it, and the colorful geometric pattern spread between her and her mother. "I'll never be the quilter she was. Or that you are as well. Look at those tiny stitches."

"She loved making it with you, for sure. It's something to treasure."

Leah stared at the quilt. Once, she'd expected that it would cover her marriage bed. Now . . . Well, how foolish was it to keep it hidden away instead of using it?

"I should have it out, where I can see it every day and remember her."

"Ja, that would be gut." Mamm's tone was careful.

Leah managed a smile. "I'm all right about it, Mamm. Really I am. I should have gotten these things out and made use of them a long time ago."

"They were put away for your wedding. They come with memories."

They were tangible reminders of the life she'd expected to have with Johnny. She'd been so happy with each thing she'd added, thinking about how she would use it in their new home. She lifted out a stack of tea towels.

"Life doesn't always happen the way we think it will. It's foolish to live in the past."

Mamm's face was troubled. "Does it still grieve you, thinking about Johnny? His coming back to the valley makes it harder, ain't so?"

Did it? She wasn't sure how to find an honest answer to that question. She looked into her mother's worn face, trying to find the right words.

"It's made me think about those times, for sure. I'm sorry for the way it ended."

"Do you still love him?"

Did she? "I love the boy he was. I can't stop doing that. But the man he is now—I don't even know him. So how could I love him?"

Mamm leaned forward to touch her cheek lightly. "The heart has reasons of its own. I just don't want you to be hurting any more because of him already."

"I know, Mamm." She covered her mother's hand with hers, taking comfort from the gentle touch. "I'm not."

"And I don't want you to give up thoughts of marriage because of what happened with him." Mamm sounded as stern as she ever could. "That wasn't your doing, it was his."

Leah pushed down the doubts that assailed her at that. "I know you want me to be happy, Mammi. But I don't think marriage is for me. I am happy with my teaching."

"You spill out so much love on other people's children. Don't you want to have your own to love?"

There was an odd little pain in her heart at that. "I'm contented," she said firmly, remembering Lydia saying those words. "As much as most, married or single, I think." She scrambled to her feet. "Now, let's get these dish towels down to Barbara before she comes up looking for them."

Six thirty in the morning that Saturday, and already the buggies were pulling in at the Stoltzfus farm. Leah watched the line of buggies ahead of her in the lane, letting Betty take her time. Aaron Stoltzfus's barn had been destroyed by fire in a spring thunderstorm, and this was the day appointed for the barn raising.

In a few moments she was pulling into a grassy area, one of a veritable fleet of buggies parked in a neat row. No sooner had she stopped than several boys ran up to tend to the horses—their first job of the day. She greeted them before turning to her mother.

"Here we are, Mamm." She considered asking her mother not to overdo, but that would be futile. And really, Mamm looked bright-eyed and excited about the prospect of spending the whole day with the church family, doing a gut work.

Mamm was already sliding from the buggy, not waiting for help. "Hand me one of the baskets down, and I'll take it."

Obediently, Leah lifted the smallest of the baskets and gave it to her. "I'll bring the rest," she said firmly. "One of the boys will help me."

Mamm trotted off toward the kitchen, and Leah unloaded the rest of the food and joined the chattering crowd of women and children moving along the lane. Daad, Levi, and Mahlon had come even earlier than they had, eager to get a start on the day's work. Barbara would be along later, in their family buggy, wanting to let the little ones have their sleep.

Crews had come already to clear away the rubble, prepare the site, and lay the foundation. Today, with the entire church involved, the barn would be built.

Englischers sometimes wondered at the Amish reluctance to buy insurance on their property, probably seeing it as foolhardy. To the Plain People, that would be like trusting in the insurance instead of in God.

And if lightning did happen to strike, well, that was God's will, and the whole community would join in rebuilding. Perhaps that was part of His plan, too, teaching them to rely on one another, building community at the same time that they raised the barn.

She followed the crowd into the kitchen, joining the group that would produce enough food to satisfy more than a hundred hungry folks come noon. The necessary chores, familiar to everyone, were quickly parceled out, just as they were outside among the men.

Leah found herself paired with Rachel and Naomi to slice bread and make sandwiches. The three of them were soon deep in conversation as they sliced and spread and piled meat and cheese high.

By ten, the food was ready as ready could be, and Leah's head had started to ache with the constant chatter and clatter of pans.

"I'm going to help take drinks out to the men." She spread a linen tea towel over a tray of sandwiches. "Want to come?"

"I'd best check on my young ones." Rachel wiped her hands on a towel.

"Ja, me also," Naomi said. For a moment her eyes clouded, and Leah suspected she was mentally counting the hours until she'd have to get the children home and under the lights again. "Gut to see you both. We don't get to visit often enough." She gave them a quick hug and scurried off.

Rachel stood motionless for a moment, watching her. "I wonder sometimes," she said softly, for only Leah to hear. "I wonder if I would cope with such grace as Naomi does."

"You would," Leah murmured. "You do."

Rachel looked startled for a moment, and then she nodded. "Ja. But having a brother go English is not as bad as if the grief were for my husband or my child. I think of her often."

Leah nodded. She knew that Rachel really meant she prayed for Naomi, just as she did.

When Leah emerged from the house carrying a pitcher and paper cups, she had to blink at the scene that met her gaze. The ribs of the new barn rose toward the sky, the uprights pale and new-looking. They swarmed with men, busy as so many worker bees.

In their black pants, colored shirts, and straw hats, they might have looked alike to someone else, but she picked out individual people easily. There was Daad, consulting with Ammon Esh, who had overseen every barn raising in the valley since before she could remember.

Mahlon was up in the rafters, where he loved to be. Her breath caught as he walked along a beam as easily as strolling down the road. He'd always had a head for heights. He was the one called on when the kitten got too far up the tree or a kite was stuck in the branches.

Levi, hammer in hand, pounded away steadily and methodically, as he did everything.

Her brother Joseph wasn't hard to find, since he was running the gas-powered winch that carried materials up to the top. Joseph's talent with machinery was put to good use today.

Daniel worked not far from him, frowning a little as he framed in a door. She looked for Matthew and found him with the crew of young boys who were fetching and carrying for the men. They learned as they watched, handed nails, and held boards. In a few years they'd be taking their places in the work crew.

Was Elizabeth here today? She hadn't seen her yet. The child worried her, especially after the incident at the rehearsal. She'd smoothed it over with Elizabeth, encouraging her to try again. Still, it worried her. Maybe she should have talked with Daniel about it, but she didn't want to make too much of it.

She waved at Naomi, who had joined the cluster of younger children, and carried her pitcher and paper cups toward the barn. She'd start with Joseph, since she hadn't seen him in more than a week.

"Leah." His face lit when he saw her. "I wondered when you were going to remember your thirsty brother."

She gave him a quick hug. "Thirsty, indeed," she teased. "Looks to me as if you have it easy here in the shade with your machine."

He grinned. "Daad always says, use your head and you won't have to use your feet. Have you seen Myra yet?"

"Not to talk to so far, but I'll catch up with her soon."

There was a movement beside her, and she turned to find Matthew, staring at Joseph's contraption with fascination.

"Matthew." She touched his shoulder. "Joseph, this is our new neighbor, Matthew Glick. Matthew, my brother Joseph."

Joseph nodded to the boy with his usual friendly smile. Matthew seemed almost too engrossed in the machinery to pay proper heed to the introductions.

"Did you make that?" he asked.

"I did. Are you interested in machinery?" Without waiting for the obvious answer, Joseph began describing how the winch worked, how he'd built it, and why it was an improvement over the last one.

Knowing that once Joseph had started on his precious machinery he'd go on for ages, Leah left his cup of water for him and started working her way along the perimeter of the barn.

In a few minutes she'd come to Daniel. "Water, Daniel?"

He put down his tools and took the cup she held out. He drained it quickly, the strong muscles of his neck working.

"Gut." He handed her back the cup and wiped his forehead with the back of his arm, resettling his hat. "Though it might feel better to pour it over my head."

"I can give you another for that," she offered.

He shook his head, smiling, but then he seemed to sober as he glanced toward his son. "Is that another of your brothers?"

"Joseph. He's between me and Mahlon in age. He has the farm machinery shop."

Daniel's face tightened with a concern she didn't understand. "I hope Matthew isn't being a pest."

"Not at all. Joseph loves to find someone as interested in machinery as he is."

"Matthew is that." For some reason, that seemed to deepen his frown. Was he imagining his son deserting the farm to run a shop, like Joseph?

"A farmer has to know how to take care of his equipment as well as his animals," she said.

"Ja." He picked up his hammer and turned back to the door frame.

Well, that was that. Her conversations with Daniel always seemed to end in frustration, if not outright annoyance. And yet she couldn't help being drawn to him, which made no sense at all.

By the time she returned from the barn, tables were being set up under the trees. She joined her sister-in-law Myra in covering them with tablecloths.

"I saw you talking with Daniel Glick," Myra said as the tablecloth billowed between them. "Nice to have a new neighbor who is so helpful. And single and good-looking, too."

Leah pulled her end of the cloth down sharply. Apparently the matchmaking had reached further than she'd thought.

"He's very nice," she said flatly. "And how are you? It's hard to believe, it is, that you and Joseph have been wed six months already. It seems yesterday that you were getting back from your wedding trip."

"It seems that way to me, too," Myra said, a flush coming up in her fair skin. "Being married is wonderful gut, Leah."

The implication that she should try it wasn't lost on Leah. She'd expected shy, sweet Myra, who always seemed a bit in awe of her school-teacher sister-in-law, to refrain from joining the matchmaking.

"When you find the right person it is," Leah said firmly. "You and Joseph are so gut together that it makes work light."

"We are that." The flush deepened, but at least she was distracted from marrying off Leah. "I'm not telling anyone else yet, but I wanted to tell you. I think, I pray, I might be pregnant."

Leah went quickly to put her arms around Myra. "That would make us all so happy."

"Don't tell," Myra cautioned. "I want to wait until I'm sure. But keeping it in today just seemed too hard—I had to tell someone or I'd burst."

"I won't say anything," Leah assured her. She hugged her again.

Surely that wasn't a tinge of envy she felt, was it? That would be wrong, and foolish besides.

"I just—" Myra hesitated, then seemed to gather up her courage to go on. "You are always so kind, Leah. You make me feel welcome in the family. I wish for you the happiness I feel, and Daniel seems so right for you. Especially since—"

She stopped, but Leah thought she could fill in the rest of that sentence. Especially since Johnny Kile had come back to the valley, making everyone fear that he might lure her away.

"I'm happy as I am," she said, turning away. "Now I think it's time to start getting the food ready to come out."

But she couldn't ignore the feeling, as she walked toward the kitchen, that gazes followed her, then turned to Daniel as folks wondered and speculated and wanted to make something happen that wouldn't be.

She loved her community—loved the closeness, the mutual support, the love of God and each other that made them strong—but at moments like this, she almost wished they didn't care so much.

CHAPTER TEN

D"*a Herr sei mit du*. God be with you." Verena Stoltzfus stood in the kitchen doorway, waving good-bye to another buggy-load of folks headed for home. She turned back to Leah, who was up to her elbows in hot, soapy water at the sink.

"Leah, it's kind of you to stay, but are you sure you don't want to go along home already?"

"I'm fine, Verena. Barbara and Mamm took the children home, so I'm free to stay as long as you need help." She waved a soapy hand.

Verena heaved what might have been a sigh of relief. "I'll go and bring the rest of the crockery in from the table, then."

The screen door banged behind her, and the farmhouse kitchen filled with quiet after the hustle and bustle of the afternoon. The day was winding down, though she could still hear the occasional shout of a child from the kickball game in the backyard.

She looked out the window over the sink. A fine new barn stood where there'd once been nothing but charred timbers. It was complete down to the coat of red paint that was probably still wet in places. Even as she watched, the oldest Stoltzfus boy led the cows in for the evening milking.

Many of the women had left, ready to get their children settled for the night. Some of the men lingered, though, a cluster of them standing looking at their handiwork, or maybe rehashing the building of it, others sitting on the grass, gossiping.

She concentrated on washing the large platter with its design of hearts and birds. By her count, five people had commented to her today on what a fine man Daniel Glick was. Three others, bolder, had come right out and said she'd be a gut mother to his kinder.

It had been a long afternoon.

The door swung open with a rattle of dishes on a tray. She glanced over, prepared to see Verena. She didn't. It was Daniel.

He stopped, probably startled by the glare she sent his way, and then he crossed the room and set the tray carefully on the table.

"Verena sent me in for a basket of leftovers she'd fixed for the family."

She felt sure that wasn't Verena's only reason. She nodded toward the basket, waiting on the dry sink. "It's there."

Daniel made no move to pick it up. Instead, he walked over to stand next to her. "Have I done something to offend you, Teacher Leah?"

It wasn't fair to take her frustrations out on Daniel. "No. But I see that they're still at it."

His eyebrows lifted. "At what?"

"Matchmaking." She snapped out the word. "Don't tell me you haven't noticed."

He braced his hands on the counter next to her, his expression more amused than offended. "No, I can't say I have."

"Didn't you wonder why Verena sent you into the kitchen for the basket, instead of carrying it out to you, which would be much more natural?" She blew out an exasperated breath. "She wants to get us alone together, and she decided this would do it."

There was definitely a twinkle in his blue eyes now. "So we are. It's not such a bad thing, is it, to talk with me for a moment?"

She set the platter down carefully. "I seem to remember that our conversations often end up in disagreement."

"That's one way to get to know someone."

He was close to her, so close that the sleeve of his blue work shirt brushed her arm. He smelled of soap and good, honest work, and his hands were strong where they pressed against the counter.

She drew her hands from the soapy water and dried them, using the movement to put a few more inches between them. "It's gut to know our neighbors," she said. "It's the idea that other people are trying to push us together that bothers me."

He turned so that he was facing her more fully, the deep blue of his gaze searching her face. "I can see that it does, but why? It amuses them, but it doesn't affect us."

"I don't like folks talking about me, wondering if I'm thinking of . . ." She stopped, not liking where that sentence was going.

His brow furrowed a little. "Perhaps their thoughts are running that way because John Kile has come back to the valley, not because of me."

She wanted to deny it, but that would be foolish when they both knew it to be true. "No one needs to worry about that. What was between John and me was over a long time ago. It's just a memory."

"Memories can be powerful things." He said that as if he spoke from personal experience, and she wondered again about his wife.

"I am not affected by having John here."

"Yet you're volunteering at the clinic where he's working."

"I see him sometimes. But only in a working way, not even as friends." She hesitated, wondering why she was saying this to Daniel, of all people, a virtual stranger.

Maybe that was why. He didn't speak, and the moment stretched out.

Finally she let out her breath, trying to ease the tension that gripped her shoulders. "I don't even know him any longer. I have no intention of marrying, and if I did, it wouldn't be to him."

Daniel's gaze searched her face again, seeming to penetrate to her very soul, and she read nothing but kindness there. "This determination of yours not to wed—is it caused by John Kile's leaving?"

"Not by his leaving. By what it told me about myself."

She wanted the words back, but it was too late. They hung there in the air between them—the thing she hated to admit, even to herself.

She couldn't look at his face, so she focused on his hands instead, tightening on the edge of the counter. It was a long moment until he spoke.

"Leah." He touched her hand, a featherlight touch that was gone in an instant but that brought her startled gaze to his face. "I haven't known you for very long. But I can't imagine that whatever happened between you could possibly cause anyone to think ill of you. Or would cause you to think ill of yourself."

Her throat tightened at his perception, and it was a moment before she could speak. Maybe that was just as well. It was past time to get the conversation off her personal business.

"You are very kind, Daniel. Denke." She cleared her throat, trying to get control of her voice, which had gone suddenly soft. "Enough about my maidal state. You and your children are at least half the reason for this spate of matchmaking, you know."

He nodded, as if recognizing the barrier she'd chosen to put up. "True enough. A widower with young children is assumed to be in need of a wife."

There was something behind the light words, but she wasn't sure what it was. "You don't feel that way?"

He didn't move, and at first she thought he would ignore the question. But then he spoke.

"For a long time, I thought that I wouldn't marry again. Now— well, maybe the brethren are right that my children need a mother."

He frowned, and shutters seemed to close over the blue eyes that had been so warm and caring a moment ago.

"But if I wed again, there's one thing I'm sure of. The marriage will be based on common sense and shared needs. Not on love."

Daniel leaned against the smooth warmth of the cow's side, hands moving automatically in the milking rhythm. He'd been doing this since he was younger than Matthew, and sometimes he thought he could do it in his sleep. But he always found it comforting.

He glanced over toward his son, milking at the next stanchion. He couldn't see the boy's face—only his legs, spread out on the milking stool, and the movement of his hands.

"Gut job," he said. He glanced at the barn cats, lined up at each animal in anticipation. He aimed a squirt at the nearest cat, and she caught it deftly. "Give the cats a drink now already."

"I always miss," Matthew said, but then he aimed and squirted. The cat, surprised, took some of the milk on its face, but it quickly cleaned it off with a long pink tongue.

"Your aim is getting better." Daniel glanced down at the milk foaming into the bucket. "Next year we can add to our herd. Elizabeth will be big enough to help then."

"We'll need a bigger tank, ja," Matthew said.

It was satisfying, talking about the future of the farm with his son. It was something he'd once thought was robbed of him forever.

"We've been working on our program for the end-of-school picnic. Will you be there, Daadi?"

His heart seemed to clench that his boy had to even ask the question. "Certain sure," he said quickly. "I wouldn't miss it for anything."

That was one of the remnants of their time apart—that hesitation Matthew had to take it for granted that his father would be there. Daniel couldn't wonder at that, though every day he prayed it would soon be a thing of the past.

A year ago, he hadn't known what his children had done at the end of the school year. He hadn't known where they were or what they were feeling. Were they well? Did they cry for him? Had they forgotten him? The questions had haunted him for so long. But no more.

"What are you doing for the program?"

Matthew, his bucket full, carried it carefully to the cooler. "It's a surprise." He grinned as he passed, the expression so like the boy he'd been before Ruth took them away that it nearly brought tears to Daniel's eyes. "It's going to be outside, so folks can sit at the picnic tables, and Teacher Leah's brother came today to help."

"Ja? Levi came?" This natural conversation was so much better than the long weeks when every word from Matthew was strained and stilted.

"Joseph. The one that has the farm machine shop." His bucket empty, he came back. He paused, his eyes lighting up. "He helped us make a platform, and we used pulleys to put up real curtains that pull apart. He let me help with that, too, and showed me how the pulleys work."

Daniel swallowed his concerns about Matthew's fascination with all things mechanical. Nothing wrong with that, but he feared that interest would lead him past the things that were approved for Amish life and further, into things of the outside world.

He had taken too long to respond, and Matthew would be thinking that he disapproved. "It's gut of him to show you that. Useful, it will be, when we start bringing the hay in." He nodded toward the large pulleys, high above them, that would help with that work.

"Ja." Matthew studied them. "Maybe—"

But the door slid open then, and Jonah ran in, distracting Matthew from whatever idea he had.

"I finished my chores, Daadi. Can I help with the milking? I'm big enough."

Matthew suppressed a laugh.

"Well, let's see." Daniel took Jonah's small hands in his. "Maybe these hands are big enough to get some milk out. What do you think, Matthew?"

"Enough for the cat, maybe," Matthew said, beginning to clean up.

"I can fill a bucket," Jonah declared. "I can."

"Ah, but Daisy doesn't have a bucket left in her, I'm afraid. Here, you can help me get the last bit."

Guiding the boy's hands as they finished, he felt a sense of satisfaction move through him again. This was what he'd been missing. What the children had missed, too. Now that they were together again, everything would be well.

The contentment stayed with him as they started back toward the house. Sunlight slanted across the fields, and the boys romped ahead, playing tag. It had been right, moving to the valley. The children were happier. He had a gut farm. Next year they'd add to their dairy herd, and they'd make a fine living here.

But for now, he'd do well to think about what he was going to fix for supper. He'd never been much of a cook, but a man without a wife had to learn.

That reminded him of the conversation with Leah on Saturday at the barn raising. Strange, that they'd been so open with each other, but maybe it was good, too. They'd be easier with each other now.

"Daadi, Teacher Leah is coming!" Jonah cried, and set off at a run.

He looked toward the Beiler farm, shielding his eyes against the setting sun with his hand. Sure enough, Leah Beiler came toward them across the field, a basket on her arm.

He went quickly to the outside pump, folding back his sleeves. By the time she drew near, he'd done a quick washup.

"Teacher Leah. This is a nice surprise."

"It's even nicer than you know," she said, smiling. She lifted the towel that covered the basket's contents. "Mamm was making chicken potpie today for the family, and she made extra for you."

"It smells wonderful gut," he said, speaking no more than the truth. "It's kind of her to think of us." He lifted an eyebrow and said softly, "Matchmaking?"

"Probably." Leah's smile lit her eyes. "I've decided to ignore it."

"That's gut." It was better between them, now that they had this matchmaking business out in the open already. "I—"

A crash and a cry from the house cut off his words.

"Elizabeth!" He spun and ran toward the kitchen, vaguely aware of Leah following him, of the quick murmur of prayer from her. Elizabeth—

His heart twisted, and he bolted through the mudroom and into the kitchen.

"Was ist letz? What happened?"

Elizabeth had stumbled back against the table, her face white. She held her right hand outstretched, gripping the wrist with her left hand. Then he saw the skillet, tipped from the stove, sausage spilling onto the floor.

"She's burned." He lifted her in his arms, his mind racing. "The doctor—"

"Here." Leah brushed past him, shoving the basket onto the countertop and turning on the water full force in the sink. She grabbed a bowl and shoved it under the spigot. "Bring her here. We want to get the hand cooled off as quick as we can."

Leah had such an air of calm command that it didn't occur to him to argue. He carried his sobbing child to the sink, and Leah grasped the reddened hand and thrust it into the water.

"There, now, there." She held it firmly, in spite of Elizabeth's instinctive withdrawal. "Just leave it there, Elizabeth. The water will make it feel better. I promise it will."

"Maybe some butter," he said, with distant memories of his mother's remedies.

"That just seals in the heat. We need to get the heat out, and then it will stop hurting so."

Sure enough, Elizabeth's sobs lessened, and she leaned her head against his shoulder. The two boys pressed close, their eyes round, and Jonah's lower lip trembled.

Leah glanced at them. "Elizabeth is going to be fine," she said, still in that calm manner that he realized was her teacher attitude. "Matthew, do you think you can bring me some ice from the refrigerator?"

"Ja, Teacher Leah." Matthew hurried across the kitchen.

Jonah tugged at her skirt. "I want to help Elizabeth, too."

"Fine. You can get me some dish towels. Do you know where they are?"

Jonah nodded, scurrying to pull out the drawer that held dish towels, spilling several on the floor in his haste.

"Should I hitch up the buggy?" Daniel asked in a quiet undertone.

Leah turned the small hand, still in the water, studying it carefully. "I don't think so. I don't see any signs of blistering. Let's just keep cooling it down."

Matthew returned with the ice cubes, and she directed him to drop them into the bowl, giving him a quick smile of approval. Elizabeth whimpered a little, the sound tearing at Daniel's heart. Leah turned to her, patting her cheek.

"You're tired of leaning over to keep your hand in the water, I know," she said. "But it's making you better. I see you were cooking sausage."

"I was making supper for Daadi and the boys," she said. Her voice trembled. "But it's all spoiled."

"Elizabeth, I told you I would fix supper after the milking." He didn't want to scold her, but she shouldn't have attempted to manage that on her own.

"Well, the dog will have a fine meal instead. He'll be wanting to come inside," Leah said. "Luckily my mamm made a lot of extra chicken potpie today, so your daadi and the boys won't go hungry. Do you like chicken potpie?"

"Mmm-hmm." Elizabeth nodded.

"Maybe you can come over one day when she's making it and help her," Leah said. "Now, let's get you a little more comfortable."

She eased the hand out of the water. Elizabeth caught her breath when the air hit the burn, but Leah was there instantly with a cold compress, wrapping it gently.

"You can sit on Daadi's lap at the table." Leah deftly transferred the bowl of ice water and the extra towel to the table. "I'll clean up the sausage."

"You sit," Daniel said, urging her toward the chair. "I'll do better cleaning up, I think."

She didn't dispute it but sat down, taking Elizabeth on her lap, guarding her hand from any contact. His daughter leaned against her trustingly.

He turned away, bending to pick up the pan and sausages, glad to hide his face for a moment. His fear had subsided, but its remnants lingered, tight in his stomach, stinging his eyes. He hadn't been here, and Elizabeth had been hurt.

He dumped the pan and its contents into the sink. Matthew began picking out the sausage, putting it into the pail of scraps for the dog.

Daniel glanced toward the table. Elizabeth, calm now, leaned against Leah's shoulder, her gaze intent on Leah's face as Leah told her a story. Jonah leaned against her knee to listen as well.

His heart clenched. He'd admitted his children needed a mother. He was looking at the woman who would be perfect—for them and for him, if not for that dangerous link she kept to the outside world.

It had been natural enough to stay for supper with Daniel and the children, Leah told herself as she dried the last dish. She glanced out the window. The boys were practicing baseball in the backyard while Elizabeth watched from the porch, seeming to enjoy her invalid status at the moment.

Natural enough to stay, she repeated to herself, but now it was time to go home, before she gave folks even more to talk about than they had already. She was hanging the towel on the rack when Daniel came in the back door.

"Leah, you did not need to wash the dishes. I said that I would do them later."

He bent to stow the pail he carried under the sink. His hair was thick, growing vigorously from the whorl on the top of his head, and the brown had lightened where the sun hit it.

"It made no trouble," she said. She'd best be going home, if she was noticing things like that about her neighbor. "I'm just happy that Elizabeth is all right."

He straightened. "You don't think I need to have a doctor look at it?"

"Well, I'm not a doctor, for sure. But my brothers managed to hurt themselves on a regular basis, and Anna wasn't far behind, so I've seen my share of burns. I think it will be fine, as long as you keep it clean and put the burn ointment on it often."

"That much I can do." His voice roughened. "Even if I did let her get hurt."

Her heart twisted, but she kept her voice firm, even tart. "That's nonsense, Daniel, and you know it. Children hurt themselves."

"Not like that." His face tightened with pain. "You told me that she was trying too hard to be perfect, and I didn't listen to you. And this is the result."

"I certainly wasn't imagining anything like this. I just thought that it worried her too much when she didn't do things perfectly."

"She shouldn't have tried to fix supper." He glared at the gas stove, as if it were to blame. "I should have come in from the barn more quickly or taken her out with me and the boys."

"It's natural to blame yourself when a child in your care is injured." She knew that well enough as a teacher. "But you couldn't have predicted that would happen. As for her attempts to be perfect—" She hesitated, but it had to be said. "Have you thought that maybe she is trying to take her mother's place?"

He stared at her, eyes wide and appalled. "No." He tried to push the thought away with his hands. "No. I never wanted, never expected—" He stopped, seeming to catch his breath. "I've never wanted Elizabeth to do more than the chores that would be normal for a child her age."

"I'm sure that's true. I didn't mean that it was coming from you. But often a girl models herself on her mother, and she may be sensing the lack—"

She stopped, because he was shaking his head. Because he disagreed with her? Or because he feared what she said was true?

"Have you talked to her much about her mother?" she asked gently.

Anger flared in his eyes at that. "No. Do you think I wanted to remind them of that time when we were apart? I want them to forget that. To forget that they ever lived in the English world."

"They can't forget their mother." Didn't he see how wrong that would be?

His face twisted. "How do I separate it? How do I divide what I feel about what Ruth did—" He stopped. Shook his head. "You don't understand. She took my children away. For two years I didn't see them. I didn't know where they were. I didn't even know if they were alive or dead."

His voice broke. Hurting for him, she put her hand on his arm, feeling the muscles so tight it seemed they'd never release.

"I'm sorry. That's the worst thing I can imagine."

To be without your children was dreadful enough. Not to even know if they were alive—the utter desolation of it swept her soul.

"Ja." He took a strangled breath. "I didn't go to the law. That's not the Amish way. But now I wonder if I did right. Ruth—" He shook his head. "When she said she'd marry me, I was the luckiest man in the world, I thought. She was so bright, so lively, so happy that she made everyone else smile, just to be near her. Half the Amish boys in the county wanted to marry her, but she picked me."

Did he even realize he was telling her this? Or was he just talking out of a soul-deep need to say it out loud to someone? It didn't matter. If all she could do was listen, she'd listen.

"Something went wrong," she said softly.

"Ja." His voice was rough. "When the babies were born, she seemed so happy, but afterward—she couldn't settle down to being a wife and mother. She always wanted more. Not more things, you understand. Just—" He shrugged, as if he couldn't find the words for it. "She was restless, always. As if looking for something and not knowing what it was."

He stopped. Blaming himself for that, the way he'd blamed himself for Elizabeth's accident?

"She started working at a quilt shop that her cousin ran. Lots of English shopped there, some of them taking lessons in quilting. She started wanting to be like them—to wear pretty clothes, have everyone looking at her the way they did when she was a girl." He spread his hands. "I tried to understand, tried to pay more attention to her, tried to make her happy. What did she want?" He sounded baffled.

She hurt for him, sympathized with him. But somewhere in her heart, she had sympathy for Ruth as well. She'd known what it was like to long for more.

Not pretty clothes, like Ruth. But more learning, more knowledge, more experiences than she could ever have in Pleasant Valley.

"I don't know," she said softly. "Maybe she didn't know, either."

"She took my children." The pain in his voice was as fresh as if it had happened yesterday. "Two years, and every minute of it I was asking God to keep them safe and bring them back to me."

"He answered your prayer."

"Ja. But Ruth—" His lips twisted. "The state police troopers came to tell me. How she'd been out with a man. Drinking, both of them, and she was driving. She ran the car into a tree. The police went to the place where she'd been living—a couple of rooms, it was. They found the children there alone. Nothing to eat, no one to watch them."

She made a small sound of pain and distress.

He looked at her. "Ja. I forgive her, because God commands it. I try to forget, and that's what I want my children to do. That's what they must do." He sounded desperate.

He had trusted her with this, and she had to do the best for him she could. That meant she had to say something he wouldn't want to hear.

"I understand why you feel you can't talk to the children about it," she said carefully. "But I think Elizabeth needs to talk to someone. Some adult who can help her sort it all out, help her find out why she's trying so hard to be grown-up before her time." She hesitated. "There is a woman at the clinic, a psychologist. I think she could help Elizabeth—"

"No." It came swift and hard. "I will not turn to the English to help my daughter. She cannot help a child adjust to being Amish."

It was on the tip of her tongue to say that Lydia had once been Amish, but that would hardly recommend her to Daniel under the circumstances.

"Elizabeth needs help," she said. "Perhaps maybe more than you can give her. There's no shame in seeking out a specialist when you need one."

His hands shot out to grasp hers in a firm, warm grip. She couldn't turn away from the intensity in his eyes. "We are an Amish community. You are the teacher, with more knowledge and experience than most. You are our specialist. You can help her."

All her instincts told her to refuse. Told her that deeper involvement with Daniel and his family could only lead to difficulty later.

But her heart was thudding to the beat of the pulse she felt in his hands, and his need struck at her core. She couldn't say no. She was afraid to say yes.

She took a breath. "All right," she said, feeling as if she took a step from which there was no going back. "I'll try."

CHAPTER ELEVEN

*S*he was being confronted with one thing after another that she didn't feel capable of handling. Leah gripped the set of interview papers in her hands as her taxi driver, Ben Morgan, the elderly Englischer who enjoyed driving the Amish for a small fee, stopped in front of the clinic.

It was the last week of school, and she should be dealing with a hundred last-minute details for the picnic and program. But Johnny had recommended she do a trial interview and bring the forms in to discuss with him before she started working on the project in earnest once school was out, so here she was.

Thanking Ben, who had brought a book and announced his plan to park in the shade and wait for her, she headed for the door, her mind going faster than the car had.

She was avoiding thinking about the most serious problem facing her, she knew. Elizabeth Glick. How had she let Daniel persuade her to attempt to counsel Elizabeth? A wave of panic went through her. She wasn't equipped to do that. What if she tried and made things worse?

Father, was I becoming too confident, too prideful in my own abilities? Have You sent me these things to show me that it is You, and You only, who is capable? Guide me, Lord, and show me the path You would have me follow. Amen.

Taking a deep breath, she opened the door to the clinic.

Two Amish families waited in the reception area, and she stopped to greet them. It gave her a breathing space before she realized that she was stalling, putting off the moment when she'd see Johnny again.

With a final smile for the children, she removed her bonnet, hanging it on a peg in the hallway, and entered the door to the research side of the building. A young man with long hair tied back at the nape of his neck glanced at her, dark eyes curious, before turning back to something he was doing with vials of blood.

He didn't challenge her, so she walked down the hallway. Perhaps she should have asked Johnny exactly where she was to meet him. The place still felt alien to her, with its whirring noises and the equipment whose function she couldn't even guess.

The young woman she'd met on her first visit—Stacie, her name was—walked swiftly out of the computer room and came to a dead stop when she saw Leah. "Oh. It's you."

"Yes." There seemed no other answer to that question. Who else would she be? "I am supposed to meet John Kile this afternoon. Can you tell me where he is?"

"He's not here. He asked me to go over the interview form with you and make sure you know how to do it properly."

Her tone said that she doubted that was even possible, and her demeanor was so unwelcoming that Leah wanted to flee.

"I can come again when John is here—" she began, but Stacie cut her off with a decisive shake of her head.

"Dr. Brandenmyer has him assigned to a much more important project." Stacie held out her hand. "Let me see them. I'll have to take time from my work to catch your mistakes, I suppose."

Leah had been treated more rudely than that at other times, she supposed. Most Amish had. But she wasn't sure it had ever bothered her quite so much. When a tourist stuck a camera in your face, it was rude, but it was also not aimed at you, specifically. Any Amish person would do.

Stacie's attitude was personal, and she had no idea how to handle it.

Submit. The word echoed in her mind. That was the Christian response, the Amish response.

She nodded, not speaking, and followed Stacie to a desk. Stacie flung herself into the chair behind the desk, fanning the interview sheets out in front of her. Leah perched on the edge of the chair opposite her, folded her hands in her lap, and waited.

Frowning, Stacie stuck a pencil into her mass of dark hair and stared at the papers. Leah forced down her resentment that the woman obviously expected to find something wrong. Of course there would be something. That was why she was here—to be corrected, so that she would do it right in the future.

Still, she'd rather have met with John. Only because he'd have done this in a friendly manner, she assured herself. Not because she wanted to see him again.

But it was better this way. The Ordnung—the rules by which the congregation lived, discussed and prayerfully accepted by the people— would find her meeting with an English woman on a matter of business perfectly acceptable. Meeting with a person who was under the bann was considerably trickier.

That could be done, of course. She knew families who lived that way, setting a separate table for those under the meidung, so that they didn't actually break bread together. Would the Kile family come to that, eventually? She couldn't guess.

Stacie came to the end of the form and tapped it with her pencil. "Not bad," she said, her tone grudging. "Going back several generations is helpful, but only if it's accurate. How can you be sure some of these are facts, not just family stories?"

Family stories *were* facts, but it was hardly worth arguing the point.

"The information came from the genealogical records in the family Bible," she said. "Amish families usually keep very complete records. However, if you don't wish me to provide that—"

Stacie shook her head quickly. "No, don't stop. It's great as long as you make accurate notes. I don't suppose you could get a photocopy of the Bible page and bring it in, so we wouldn't have to rely on your accuracy."

Leah tried counting to ten. Supposedly that helped one control an unruly temper. "I don't believe the families would like to have the Bibles taken out of the house to be copied."

"This will have to do, then." Stacie shuffled the papers together and put a paper clip on them. "If you could type instead of print them, it'd be easier to read, but I guess you Amish don't use newfangled inventions like typewriters, do you?"

Leah wanted to ask the woman why, if she looked down on the Amish so much, she was involved in research here. She didn't. She kept her voice colorless. "We do use typewriters in business, but I don't have access to one, and I'm sure I can print them more quickly."

"And Leah always had the neatest printing in the whole class," said a voice behind her.

"Johnny." She couldn't stem her pleasure at the sight of his warm smile as he came in, dropping a case of some sort on the nearest desk. It was a joy to see any friendly face after Stacie's open antagonism. "I thought you weren't here today."

"Just got back." He moved toward her with such enthusiasm she thought for a moment that he intended to hug her, but then he seemed to recall himself and touched her shoulder lightly instead.

"You brought back all the information?" Stacie interrupted.

"The files are on my computer," Johnny said, turning his attention to her, and then embarked upon a discussion that was so technical that, to Leah, they might as well have been speaking in Russian.

Today he wore what she supposed was a business shirt, with a collar that buttoned down and a tie. How long, she wondered, had it taken him to learn how to tie one of those? How long to feel comfortable with a belt instead of suspenders?

Johnny swung back to her so quickly that perhaps he'd felt her looking at him. "If you're finished, let's go have a cup of coffee or a sandwich. We have a lot of catching up to do."

He smiled at her, and she was transported into the past, becoming again the young girl whose pulse had fluttered when he'd held out his hand to her at a danze with just that smile.

And that was why it was so dangerous. She wasn't that girl now, and Johnny wasn't that boy.

"I don't think—"

His mood changed, lightning fast as always. "You're not going to let some ridiculous rules stand in the way of talking to an old friend, are you?"

He should know her well enough to know that he was making her uncomfortable.

"I can't."

"Leah promised to have tea with me today." Lydia Weaver emerged from behind one of the shoulder-high partitions in the room. She smiled at Leah. "If you're ready, I have the water hot."

"That is kind of you," Leah said quickly. She walked away from Johnny without looking back.

You have rescued me again," Leah said as soon as the door of Lydia's office closed behind them. "But it is not necessary to give me tea."

"It is a pleasure to give you tea," Lydia replied, nodding toward the rocking chair Leah had taken the last time and busying herself with the tea things. "And I don't think you needed rescuing. It was obvious from your face that you would say no to John's invitation, not because of the Ordnung but because that was what your conscience told you to do."

Leah sat, the rocker giving instant comfort. "I don't want to be unkind to him, but as much as I like seeing him again, I'm not sure it's wise to spend time alone with him."

"John Kile is a gifted researcher, but he doesn't understand people well, including himself. He wants two contradictory things at the same time." Lydia set the cup of tea on the table next to Leah.

Leah appreciated the gesture. Lydia was, without making an issue of it, allowing Leah not to have to take the cup from her hand, which was the letter of the law in most communities in regard to eating and drinking with those under the meidung.

Johnny, on the other hand, had been only too ready to make an issue of it.

Lydia sat down opposite her, holding her own cup. She seemed very willing to let the silence stretch out comfortably between them.

Leah sipped the hot, fragrant brew. Her thoughts drifted to the past, measuring the Johnny she knew against Lydia's words.

"You're right," she said finally. "When he was a child, if he had to choose between a jumble cookie and a snickerdoodle, he'd end up with none if he couldn't have both."

Sharing a laugh with Lydia dissipated the last of her tension, but it still left a question in Leah's mind.

"Tell me, if you will. Is Stacie like that with everyone or just with me?"

"Especially with you." Lydia smiled. "Although, like many researchers, she is impatient of anything that gets in the way of her work, including good manners."

"But why? She doesn't even know me."

Lydia's pale eyebrows quirked. "I think you know the answer to that, don't you? She's interested in John."

"Well, but—" Leah paused, trying to assimilate that. She would want for John to find someone to love, wouldn't she? "I'm not a threat to a relationship she might have with Johnny."

"Aren't you?"

"You mean she knows that we once planned to marry, and she's jealous? But I can't compare to her."

"You're his first love," Lydia said. "She's afraid that knowing you again will make him realize that you are what he wants."

She wanted to deny it, to say it couldn't be. In a way, this was the opposite of her experience. Those who loved her were pushing her toward Daniel because they feared she would be lured to the English world by her first love. Meanwhile, the person who loved John feared that Leah would draw him back to the Amish world.

She shook her head finally. "He would never return. She doesn't have to worry about that. But if she cares about him, why is she so derisive of the life that he came from? She has so many misconceptions about the Amish that it's hard to understand why she's here."

Lydia shrugged. "As for that, I think the research is all that matters to her. The Amish are only of interest because their custom of marrying within the church provides such a classic genetic workshop."

"You could clear up some of her false ideas," Leah suggested.

"I could." Lydia looked down at her cup. "Not doing so is one of the accommodations I make to get along in the English world."

Leah didn't know how to respond to that. It seemed that jumping the fence was not so simple as shedding one life and picking up another.

They were quiet again for a few minutes. Leah let her gaze drift over the wall of books behind Lydia's desk. How much pleasure must it be to have a room like this, with more books than you could have time to read?

"May I . . ." She hesitated. Daniel would not allow her to bring

Elizabeth to see Lydia. But there was no reason why she couldn't use the woman as a resource if Lydia were willing. "May I ask you—consult you—about something?"

"Of course."

"I've been asked to help a family." She chose her words carefully. "The three children were taken away from their Amish home by their mother. They lived in the English world for two years before she died in an accident, and then they came back to their father."

There, that was a neat, anonymous recounting of the facts. Lydia wasn't from the community, so she was unlikely to know about Daniel and his family.

"They're having problems adjusting?" Lydia looked interested. Probably something like this didn't come her way very often.

"The middle child, the only girl, is eight, one of my scholars. She is so determined to be perfect at everything she does that she becomes overly upset when she can't." She censored herself, not feeling she should trust Lydia with the story of Elizabeth's injury. "She wants to take on duties that a woman would do, instead of a child's chores."

"Does the father push her to do that?"

"No. Just the opposite, in fact. He's very concerned about her." She hesitated. Her opinions weren't facts, but perhaps it would help Lydia to know them. "I wondered if she's trying to emulate her mother, but her father doesn't agree. He has difficulty talking with them about their time in the outside world."

Lydia nodded slowly, as if she sifted the facts through her mind. "Would he allow me to see his daughter?"

"I suggested that already. He refused. He feels that I am the one to help her." She opened her hand, as if exposing her inadequacy. "I know how ill equipped I am to do any such thing. But if I don't help, there will be no one."

"I don't think I can counsel at secondhand," Lydia said.

Leah's heart sank. She hadn't realized until that moment how much she'd hoped for from Lydia.

"But what do your own instincts tell you the child needs?"

"To talk to an adult who cares about her," Leah said promptly.

"Probably not her father, since he finds it so hard. Someone who will listen and reassure her."

Lydia smiled. "You're a good teacher, I'm sure. Your instincts are sound." She stood, going to the bookshelves. "I may not be able to counsel her, but I can lend you some materials that might give you guidance."

"That would be so appreciated." Leah stood, accepting the books as Lydia pulled them from the shelves and handed them to her.

Lydia's hand rested for a moment on the stack of books. "Just—be careful. What you are doing is risky, both for the child and for you."

"For me?"

Lydia studied her face intently. "It is difficult enough in a counseling situation to stay detached from the client's problems. In your case, I think that will be nearly impossible. You'll risk caring too much."

Lydia's words gripped her heart. She'd failed Johnny when it came to caring enough. She couldn't fail a child who depended on her.

"I can only do my best and trust God with it," she said.

"Da Herr sei mit du," Lydia said softly, like a benediction. "The Lord be with you."

Leah pressed her hand. She'd reached the door when Lydia spoke again.

"One thing you should be aware of. In the situation you describe, chances are good the little girl isn't the only one affected. The whole family may need help in working through their feelings about the mother." She paused. "Especially the father."

Daniel. Daniel might need help. But he wouldn't allow her anywhere near his feelings about his dead wife, would he?

The makeshift curtains, probably sheets from someone's bed, pulled together for the final time, and the audience, gathered on benches under the trees in the schoolyard, burst into applause. Daniel clapped as heartily as the rest.

Every parent was nervous when his or her child performed, of course, but he might have been more jittery than most. This was his children's first end-of-school program in Pleasant Valley, and it was more than a marking of the end of classes for him. It was another sign of their belonging here.

The scholars marched out, beaming broadly now that the difficult part was over, and the audience clapped again, the clapping growing deafening when Teacher Leah appeared. The community must realize how fortunate they were to have such a dedicated, skillful teacher.

Lest he be caught staring at Teacher Leah, he sought out his own young ones. He'd held his breath while Elizabeth said her part, fearful of what might happen if she faltered. She'd held her friend Becky's hand and been letter-perfect.

The curtains, operated with care by Matthew and another boy, had opened and closed on cue, something that clearly mattered to Matthew far more than the piece he'd gotten through.

As for Jonah—well, Jonah forgot his poem before he reached the end and turned to the assistant teacher to be prompted with such an engaging grin that everyone had chuckled.

Women started uncovering the dishes that marched down the centers of the rows of tables, while the men moved benches and tried to stay out of their way. A buzz of conversation and laughter filled the air.

On an afternoon like this, with the sun shining, the church family around him, and all going well, he wondered why he'd told Leah all that he had. More, why he'd asked for her help.

They were going to be all right. Surely that incident with Elizabeth had been a onetime thing. He'd talked to her, getting her to promise that she'd never again try anything so foolish.

Still, he had to admit that it might be gut for Elizabeth to spend time with a woman she admired as she did Teacher Leah. He disliked Leah's continued association with her former sweetheart, but he couldn't doubt that she had the interest of the children at heart.

Elias Beiler, Leah's father, came over to him, a broad smile on his face. "They've done well, those young ones of our Leah's, haven't they?"

"They have indeed. I was just thinking that the community is fortunate in our teacher."

Since Leah's father was looking at her, it seemed natural that Daniel look as well. The excitement of the day had brought a flush to Leah's cheeks, and her green eyes sparkled with pleasure.

"I understand we're to have your little Elizabeth around a bit this summer," Elias said.

Daniel nodded. "I hope she won't be in the way of things your wife is doing."

Leah and her mother had hatched a plan whereby they would teach Elizabeth quilting over the summer. He didn't doubt that the teaching would branch into some cooking and baking and other things that girls her age were normally learning from their own mothers.

"Not a bit of it," Elias said quickly. "My Mattie loves showing young ones how to do things, and your Elizabeth is a sweet, quiet child, not like those schnickelfritzes of our Levi."

Since the two young boys in question were wrestling in the grass at the moment, the comment seemed apt, but Elias looked at them with an indulgent eye.

"Elizabeth will enjoy it, I know. My mamm and daad hope to come for a long visit, but with my sister about to give birth, they won't get away for another month or two, at least."

"Well, they'll be most welcome any time."

Another man wandered over with a comment about the corn crop, and the conversation turned more general. Daniel listened attentively, figuring that Elias, like his own father, had no doubt forgotten more about farming than he'd learn in a lifetime.

His gaze wandered over the crowd while they talked. Elizabeth and Becky were helping Rachel, Becky's mamm, spread things on the table for lunch. It looked as if they'd all be called to the food shortly. Bishop Mose Yoder, white-bearded and saintly, stood at the head of one of the tables, surveying the food he'd be called upon to bless.

Fortunate, Daniel thought again. The Lord had blessed the families that settled in Pleasant Valley. He had been right to bring the children here. With no reminders of Ruth, it was easier to forget.

Jonah raced by, and Daniel reached out to collar his youngest. "We'll be eating soon. You'd best wash your hands. Where is your brother?"

"I dunno, Daadi." Released, Jonah ran off in the general direction of the outside pump.

Scanning the hosts of children, Daniel failed to come up with Matthew. But Leah moved toward him, her smile a little tentative. Perhaps she worried that her knowing so much about his past would make the situation uncomfortable between them.

"A grand program, Teacher Leah."

Her smile eased. "The scholars did well, I thought."

"Speaking of scholars, do you know where Matthew is? We're about ready to eat."

She glanced around. "He and Thomas were taking the curtains down. They're probably packing up in the schoolroom."

With a nod, he retreated toward the schoolhouse. The trouble with talking to Leah was that he always wanted to prolong the conversation. But when he did, it seemed they got into things he'd rather not discuss. Or into a disagreement.

The door stood open. He stepped inside. Sure enough, the two boys were there, but they didn't seem to be putting things away. Ropes, pulleys, and curtains lay on the floor between them, and they faced each other like two roosters squaring off over who was to rule the henhouse.

"I tell you I did." Matthew's voice was shrill. "I flew on an airplane and I rode on a motorcycle, and lots of other stuff, too."

"I don't believe it." The other boy's jaw came out. "You're making it all up, Matthew Glick. When did you do all those things, tell me that?"

"When I was English." Matthew practically shouted the words. "When I was English."

It was like an axe handle to the belly. Daniel grabbed the door, just to keep standing upright as the wave of fury hit him.

Ruth. This was Ruth's fault. His children would never really be his again because of her betrayal.

He knew, in that moment, that he'd been lying to himself. Lying to Leah, too, for that matter. Because he hadn't forgiven Ruth. She was six months dead, and he hadn't forgiven her at all.

Chapter Twelve

*L*eah closed the kitchen door behind her, shutting out the sound of her two nephews squabbling over a toy train, and crossed the covered walkway that led to the daadi haus. Mamm had seemed unusually quiet at supper, and since Daadi had gone out, she'd best check on her.

She tapped gently as she opened the door. "Mamm?"

How many times over the years had she come this way to see Grossmutter? She'd invariably found her grandmother in the rocking chair by the window, fingers busy with a quilt for someone's new baby or a hooked rug to cover a bedroom floor on cold mornings.

Now it was Mamm who looked up with a smile from that same rocker. Instead of a quilt patch, her lap was covered with the massive family Bible.

"Leah. Am I needed for something?" She started to close the Bible.

"Nothing at all." Leah went quickly to pull a chair over next to her. "I thought you might like a little visit is all. But if you're busy reading—"

"Not reading," Mamm said, patting the Bible, which Leah saw was opened to the family tree that covered several pages in the front of the book. "Just remembering. Come sit with me if you have time."

Leah sat, guilt crowding in on her. She was busy, but she could have found the time to sit quietly with Mamm more often.

She leaned on the arm of her mother's chair to scan the fine, faded printing on the genealogy chart. Since her work with the clinic, she'd never look at a family tree in the same way again.

"What are you remembering, Mamm?" She looked more closely, realizing it was the Lapp family Bible—her mother's family. "I didn't realize you had this one. I thought Uncle Jacob and Aunt Emma kept it." The Bible, like the farm, usually went to the oldest son of the family.

"Ja, they do, but Em wanted me to fill in names and dates for Levi and Barbara's children." Mamm's finger traced a line. "Look, there is me and all my brothers and sisters. Twelve of us, there were. Such a noise when we sat down to supper that you couldn't hear yourself think."

"I can imagine." She squinted to read the faded ink in the failing light. "Was that Uncle Mose who came after Jacob?"

"Elizabeth," Mamm corrected, her fingers seeming to caress the page. "Elizabeth came next, you remember. Only eight when she died."

Again her newly acquired information surfaced. "Was she ill, Mamm? What did she die of?"

"She fell." Tears glistened in her mother's eyes. "Such a daring girl she was. Like our Anna. Always had to try and climb the highest or run the fastest."

"I'm sorry. You were close."

"Only thirteen months apart." Mamm wiped away a tear that had spilled onto her cheek. "Ach, it's foolish to cry. She has been safe in God's hands these many years, but still, sometimes in my mind I see her scrambling up that tree."

Leah clasped the hand that had always been so strong, so comforting. Frailer now, but still, the comfort was there. "I wish I could have known her."

Her mother seemed to look into the past. "I wonder, sometimes. What would she have been like as a woman? How many babies would she have had?" She smiled a little. "Brothers are fine, in their way, but sisters are closer, I think. Ain't so?"

"I guess so." Were she and Anna close? Once she'd thought so, but that had changed in recent years. It was as if the gap between their ages had suddenly started to matter more, instead of less.

"Uncle Jofie, now, he and his twin sister were close as could be, but maybe that came of bein' twins. You remember him, don't you?"

Since Uncle Jofie, for whom her brother Joseph was named, had died before she was born, she didn't. "I remember you talking about him."

"You remember him," Mamm repeated. "Hair the color of ripe horse-chestnuts he had. You remember."

"Uncle Jofie died before I was born." She forced her voice to gentleness, trying to deny the panic that rose in her. Did Mamm really not realize—

"Ach, how foolish." Her mother shook her head. "Of course you don't remember Jofie. How silly I am. Seems like my memory gets mixed up sometimes, ever since I had that chemo."

"That must be it," Leah said soothingly. "Mammi, you're— If something is wrong, you'd tell me, wouldn't you?"

Her mother's gaze focused on her face. "Now I've scared you, making you think I'm getting sick again, when I'm fine. Just a touch forgetful now and again, is all."

Reassured, Leah smiled at her. "You seemed—well, a little tired and a bit confused."

"I'm fine." Her mother's voice seemed to gain strength on the words. "But you know, having the cancer showed me how true it is that our time is in His hands. God could call us at any moment."

"You beat the cancer." Leah infused confidence into the words. "You're going to be with us for many more years."

"If God wills." Her mother stroked the page. "There's comfort here, Leah, in looking at those I loved who are gone ahead of me. Here or in Heaven, I know I am surrounded by the family's love."

"I hadn't thought of it that way," Leah admitted.

She touched the page, running her fingers along the generations. Her family. Spread out through time and space, those were her kin.

The names of the women drifted through her mind like dandelion puffs carried on the breeze. They were women who had held their faith strong, who had passed it on to their children and their children's children. Women who mourned for those who died young and those who left, who rejoiced and welcomed those who came back.

Love welled in Leah's heart. She was connected to all of them.

She ran her finger down the page until she found her name. She was connected to all of them, but nothing led from her name. It sat there alone.

"We were more fortunate than some," her mother said. "Not many of our family jumped the fence to the outside world."

It almost sounded as if there were a question in that.

"That's right, Mammi. Not many from our family."

Her mother looked at her, and Leah had the feeling that she saw right into her heart.

"You are worrying about Anna. About what she's getting up to in her rumspringa."

"N-no." How had her mother guessed that? "I mean, not exactly. Our Anna is a smart girl."

"Smart, ja. But maybe not so much common sense as you had at her age."

"She'll be fine." *Please, God.*

"Everyone feels the pull of the world at one time or another," her mother said gently. "For Anna now it is pretty clothes and parties. For others—" Her mother hesitated. "For others it might be something different."

Something different. For an instant Leah was back in Lydia's office again. She knew what she'd really wanted, looking at all those books. She'd thought what a pleasure it would be to have Lydia's life, to be an educated woman with a serious job to do.

Mamm was right. The world tempted different people in different ways.

"Remember this, Leah." Mamm clasped her hand firmly, leaning toward her. "No matter what my children do, I will never stop loving them. Never."

A chill went down Leah's back. Were Mamm's words for Anna? Or for her?

Leah walked into the clinic for her reporting session with Stacie, a determined smile pinned to her face. She would not allow the woman to irritate her this time. As for Lydia's idea of what was behind it—well, she wasn't going to think about that at all.

But when she reached the desk, it wasn't Stacie who waited for her. It was John.

He rose, giving her that sweet smile that made him look like the boy he'd been once. If Lydia was right about Stacie's feelings, it would be that smile that had snared her heart.

"I'm looking for Stacie." She gestured with the sheaf of papers in her hand. "I have my latest interviews."

"Great." John took them from her. "But as you can see, Stacie is occupied." He waved a hand down the long row of computers. Stacie sat at the far end, frowning at the screen in front of her. At his movement, she transferred the frown to them.

"I can wait—" Leah began.

He shook his head, sitting down and riffling through the papers. "Not necessary. I've switched places with her for today. I'll go through the reports with you." That smile again. "Though if I know you, Teacher Leah, everything will be perfect."

Teacher Leah. Had he ever called her that before?

She could continue to argue, but he was looking at her in a faintly challenging manner, and the lift of his eyebrow seemed to dare her.

She sat down, and he turned to the forms.

Well, fine. She realized that her hands were clenched in her lap, and she smoothed the fingers out. This was business, and she would handle it that way. Meeting with Johnny would not be a difficulty either for the Ordnung or for her conscience.

She turned slightly, not wanting to stare at him while he read her carefully written reports. But doing so brought her around so that Stacie was in her line of sight. The woman's head came up again, and she stared at Leah.

Taking a deep breath, she ordered herself not to fidget. She was not a nervous scholar, turning in sloppy homework. She was a conscientious volunteer, and the interviews had been conducted to the best of her ability. If John found something to criticize, she would learn from that and do better the next time.

The desk was a pale gray metal, and when John moved slightly, his knee bumped it, making a small thumping sound. Behind him, a coffeemaker burbled on a countertop.

Two long-haired young men passed them, arguing loudly about something to do with the computers, she thought. The terms were so unfamiliar that she couldn't be sure.

John glanced up, frowning in annoyance, as they seemed to settle in front of the coffeemaker to continue their conversation.

He gathered up the papers.

"I can't hear myself think in here." He beckoned to Leah. "We'll move this to the conference room." He turned and walked away, leaving Leah to follow.

Conscious of the men's gazes on her, Leah went after him down the hall, around a corner, and through a glass-paneled door. A rectangular table with chairs around it filled most of the room.

John jerked out a chair and slumped into it, spreading the papers out with an intentness that made her uneasy. Was something wrong with her work?

She slid into the chair that stood at right angles to his and waited. At least here she was away from Stacie's gaze. She was used to the stares of the curious when she was out among the English, but she wasn't used to having someone look at her with such open dislike.

On the other hand, here she was alone with Johnny. Business, she reminded herself. He seemed perfectly able to keep this on a business-like basis, and she could, too.

Finally he pressed his hands against the sheets. "Who told you to do a family tree?" He shot the question at her.

"Well, I . . . I think Stacie said something about how seeing the family Bibles would be useful, but I told her I didn't believe people would be willing to lend them out. I thought perhaps a transcription of the tree would work, but if not—"

"If not?" That smile lit his face again, this time tinged with something like triumph. "Leah, this is fantastic. It's exactly what we need."

A footstep sounded in the hallway outside, and Dr. Brandenmyer poked his head in the doorway. "Do I hear the noise of a scientific triumph in here?"

Johnny waved the paper. "Leah has brought us a complete family tree for the Miller family, going all the way back to the early 1700s. It gives us exactly when the genetic illnesses began showing up."

"I copied it just as it was worded in the original." Her hands twisted in her lap again, and she forced them to be still. "I hope—"

"Excellent, excellent." Dr. Brandenmyer studied the sheets and then beamed at her. "We've never had such a detailed source before, not even from the families seeking treatment here. You've done a superb job, Ms. Beiler. Superb."

She could feel the heat rushing to her face. It wasn't the Amish way to lavish praise, and to accept it was prideful. She lowered her gaze.

"The Miller family has a very complete family tree in their Bible, and because we are nearly related, they were willing to let me copy it. I can't hope to obtain such results every time."

"If you bring in something half as good, we'll be pleased." Dr. Brandenmyer reached out, as if he intended to pat her shoulder, and then drew his hand back. "Excellent," he said again. "Well, I'll leave you to it. Get those results into the computer as soon as possible, John. Well done."

"I will, sir." Johnny straightened in his chair, looking almost as if he would like to salute, as the older man walked away with that long, loping stride.

Once he was gone, Johnny turned to her, his expression exultant. "I knew I was right to bring you in on this, Leah. You have access the rest of us couldn't possibly get."

Her hands gripped each other. "Don't count on that much information every time. Please. I can't promise to do that with every family."

"It's fine," he said quickly. Maybe he thought he was putting too much pressure on her. "I don't mean to make you uncomfortable, Leah."

"Praise is what makes me uncomfortable, as you well know." She felt a trace of annoyance with him. She couldn't expect the English to understand, but Johnny certainly should.

"Oh, yes." His mouth tightened. "I remember. Accepting a compliment would be prideful. Lacking in proper Amish humility."

She would not apologize for her beliefs. "The instruction to have a humble and contrite heart is not only for the Amish."

He lifted his hands in a gesture of surrender. "I'm sorry. I guess I still have trouble with that one. What's so bad about accepting that people think you did a good job?"

For a moment she couldn't speak. John did sound like an Englischer now. He'd been raised on the same Scriptures she had.

Blessed are the meek. Do not think yourself better than anyone else, but humble yourselves in obedience to God.

Apparently he had forgotten.

"I don't want to argue with you about it." She started to rise. "If that's all—"

"Leah, don't. Please don't leave. I didn't mean to offend you." He rubbed the back of his neck with his palm, as if trying to wipe away tension.

"Is it hard?" She asked the question abruptly, thinking about his obvious eagerness to please Dr. Brandenmyer. "Feeling you belong in this world now?"

A muscle jerked at the corner of his mouth. "Sometimes not at all. Sometimes every minute of the day."

"I'm sorry." She was. Not trying to convince him he'd been wrong in his choice. Just sorry it was hard for him.

He shrugged. "It was worth it."

Did he really feel that? Apparently so.

He stared down at the chart of the Miller family. Finally he cleared his throat.

"I remember Naomi. So she married Nathan Miller. Everybody thought they'd make a match of it."

"Ja." Everyone had thought that. Just as they'd thought she and Johnny would.

He smiled suddenly. "Remember when Nathan and I took our daads' buggies out on that dirt road behind the Esch farm and tried to have a harness race?"

"I remember that Naomi and I told you not to. And that you both ate your meals standing up for a few days."

"Don't give me that." His eyes laughed at her. "I distinctly remember Naomi jumping up and down waving her bonnet, and you yelling at me to go."

She couldn't prevent the chuckle that escaped her. "We did not."

But she remembered that day so clearly—the dust hanging in the air like fog, the buggy wheels flashing, the boys standing up in the buggies like chariot racers.

Johnny laughed, a delighted chuckle that was so familiar it plucked her heartstrings. "You're a liar, Leah Beiler." He closed his hand over hers. "You were just as ready to get into that mischief as I was, but you got off easier." His fingers tightened, and his gaze was warm on her face. "Admit it."

For an instant they were Leah and Johnny again—young and in love. A flush mounted her face.

They weren't, and she couldn't let herself think that way.

She pulled her hand away. "We did plenty of foolish things when we were young. It was a long time ago."

"Afraid, Leah?" His voice mocked her. "Afraid holding hands for a minute with a fence-jumper will ruin your reputation as the perfect Amish schoolteacher?"

She clasped her hands in her lap and took refuge for the tumult of feelings in anger. "At least I can accept who I am."

Anger, quick as summer lightning, sparked in his face. "What's that supposed to mean?"

"It means that if you were as confident you made the right choice as you claim you are, you'd correct your friend Stacie's misconceptions about what it means to be Amish."

His chair scraped as he stood, planting his hands on the table. "And are you so convinced you've made the right choice? Maybe that's what you tell yourself, Leah, but don't expect me to buy it. I know you—I know how much you've always wanted to learn and know and experience the world you can only dream about."

Would his words hurt so much if they weren't true? "I know my place," she said, fighting to keep her voice even. "I have my family, my faith, the children I teach. That is what matters to me."

"Is it? You give kids an eighth-grade education that doesn't prepare them for the real world and think you're doing a good job. Well, you're not."

She looked at him steadily. Johnny said he knew her. Maybe he did and maybe he didn't, but she knew him. That moment when he'd admitted his struggle had shown her too much, and she could sense the pain beneath his words.

"I'm not preparing them for the English world," she reminded him. "I'm preparing them to be Amish men and women. But I don't think you're talking about my scholars, anyway. I think you're talking about yourself."

Her hands were shaking, and she had to concentrate in order to pick up the folder with the unused forms.

"I think I'd best meet with Stacie in the future," she said, and walked quickly from the office.

A car approached the buggy from behind, going fast, if the sound it made was any indication. Hands firm on the lines, Leah kept Betty moving at a steady pace. She darted a glance to the side of the road—hardly any berm and then a drop-off to a deep ditch.

A horn blared. Leah's nerves tightened but Betty, bless her, merely flicked an ear. And then the car whizzed past the buggy, so close that she could have reached out and touched it, cutting in again sharply in front of the horse.

The horn blared again, a harsh, derisive sound. Leah stared after it as her pulse steadied. Bright red it was, filled with teenagers, it looked like, and one—

Her fingers tensed on the lines. That sheet of pale blond hair flying in the wind as the girl turned to look back at her looked familiar. Too familiar.

Anna. But it couldn't be, could it? Anna was supposed to be working at the bakery this afternoon. She couldn't be riding around out on the Hedgeville Road in the farthest reaches of the district. The only reason Leah had come so far up the valley was to do an interview with another family.

It had been a branch of the Stoltzfus family, this one with four affected children. The mother had been willing to talk, but unfortunately hadn't known much about the ramifications of her husband's family.

The grossmutter knew it all, she'd said, but she was on a visit to a married daughter over near Mifflinburg. Teacher Leah was welcome to come back another time and talk with her.

Leah glanced down at the black case that sat beside her feet. That would mean another long buggy ride, eating up time that could have accommodated visits to two or three closer families. She would not have anything near as satisfying to report this week as her triumph with the Miller genealogy.

She backed away from that word, frowning. *Triumph.* What a decidedly un-Amish concept that was. If God led her to learn anything that helped the children, His was the glory, not hers.

There was more traffic on the road as she approached Hedgeville, and she had to concentrate on that, putting aside for a moment thoughts of the work. And especially worries about the girl in the red car who could not possibly have been Anna.

Hedgeville sported a small area of strip development on its outskirts—an auto parts store, a donut shop, a fast-food place. She frowned. A red car, surely the same one, was parked at the fast-food restaurant.

Without giving herself a chance to think too much, she turned Betty into the parking lot. It was hot, and she had a long way home yet. A cold drink would taste good.

As was usual in Pleasant Valley, the restaurant provided a hitching rail at the back of the parking lot, under the shade of the trees that lined it, for their horse-and-buggy customers. She drew up to the rail and Betty halted. Before she could get down, someone was there, beside the buggy, blocking her way.

Anna. But not the Anna she knew. This Anna had a wave of straight, silky hair falling nearly to the waist of her tight jeans. Her gray T-shirt bore the logo of a local college. Only the sneakers on her feet were familiar.

"You recognized me."

"Barely." A flicker of anger went through Leah. "You might have told your friend not to blare the horn at a buggy horse."

Anna dismissed that with a flick of her fingers. "Betty's too stolid to let that bother her."

"Every buggy horse in the valley is not so well-trained as Betty. Driving like that could cause an accident."

"The way the English see it, roads are for cars. It's the horses and buggies that cause the accidents."

"And is that what you believe, Anna?" Leah studied her sister's face, trying to find some indication of the Anna she knew.

Anna shrugged, her gaze evading Leah's. "No. I mean, I guess I can see their point. It wasn't my doing. I was just a passenger."

"And why were you a passenger at all? You're supposed to be at work this afternoon, aren't you?"

Another shrug. "We weren't busy this afternoon. Mrs. Schatz said I could go home early. My friends offered me a ride."

So she could racket around the county with a boy who drove too fast, wearing English clothes, pretending she was one of them. "This isn't the way home."

"We stopped for something to eat." The flippant tone grated on Leah's nerves. "There's nothing wrong with that. What are you doing out this way, anyway?"

"I had a family to interview." Worry for her little sister replaced the annoyance she felt. "Why don't you get your things and come along with me now?"

"I'm not ready to leave yet. Don't worry about me. I'll be back in time for supper."

"Not worrying is easier said than done." She wanted to reach out, to touch that silky hair she'd brushed and braided so often for her little sister, but she was afraid Anna would pull away. What had happened to them, that there was such distance between them now?

She moved, intending to get down. Anna's hand shot out to grab the buggy, blocking her way.

"You're not coming in, are you?"

She froze. "I thought I'd get something cold to drink. Are you ashamed of me, Anna?"

Anna's face turned sulky. "Well, you're ashamed of me, dressed this way, aren't you?"

"Not ashamed. Never ashamed." Now she did reach out and touch her sister's hair lightly. "Just worried that you are flirting too much with the English world. I love you, Anna. I don't want you to be hurt."

"I can take care of myself."

"I know you think that, but—"

"I can." Now Anna did jerk away from her. "And you're a fine one to talk about that to me when you're doing the same thing."

Leah's heart seemed to turn cold in her chest. "What are you talking about?"

"You. Johnny Kile." Anna took a step back, throwing the words at her. "All that work you're doing at the clinic." She shot an angry glance toward the black case. "Everyone knows you're only doing it to get close to Johnny Kile again. So maybe you'd better save your lectures for yourself."

CHAPTER THIRTEEN

*L*et's pick out the colors you want to use for your doll quilt," Leah said, spreading out the contents of her mother's scrap basket on the table in the living room at the daadi haus.

Elizabeth looked at them doubtfully and shrugged. "I don't know. Whatever you think is best."

Elizabeth's impassive little face didn't give Leah any clues to her feelings. Did she want to learn how to quilt, or was she going along only because her daadi wanted her to?

Leah moved scraps of colors around, hoping for an inspiration. She had suggested teaching the child to quilt, thinking that it would lead to conversations while they worked together. Most Amish girls of eight were already fairly accomplished with a needle, but then, most had a mammi or grossmutter to guide them.

She glanced at Elizabeth's solemn little face. Did she feel that something was missing in her life, without a mother to teach her the skills of Amish life?

Or was she longing to go back to the English world her mother had taken her to? If that was the case, it would devastate Daniel, who was trying so hard to restore his relationship with his children after their time apart.

"These might be pretty together." She moved a dark blue piece next to a coral rose.

"That's a nice color." One small finger touched the rose fabric. "Do you have a dress made of that?"

"No, that piece is left from a dress my sister Anna made."

Leah kept her voice calm, but her mind winced away from thoughts of her sister. She and Anna had been painfully polite to each other in public since the incident at the fast-food restaurant. In private, they had been silent, living in the same house without speaking.

The hurt would go away in time. They'd be normal to each other again. Just not right now.

"This is a doll quilt that I made when I was about your age."

Leah unfolded the small, faded one-patch quilt. With its simple arrangement of seven squares across and seven squares down, it would be the simplest design to start with.

"I remember I thought the yellow and the green would look fine together, but once it was done, I wasn't so sure." She'd sat in this room with Grossmutter, trying so hard to make her stitches as smooth and tiny as her grandmother's had been.

"I think it's pretty."

That was the first positive thing Elizabeth had said, and it pleased Leah, even if the child was just being polite.

"Your quilt will be really pretty, too, I know. And I'll make one along with you. I think I'd like this light blue piece for one of my colors." She took a good-sized piece of fabric, hoping that would encourage Elizabeth to do the same.

Elizabeth looked at her, forehead wrinkling in a frown. "Do you have a doll bed?"

"Well, not anymore. I gave it to my little sister when she started playing with dolls. But I'll make a quilt anyway, and I can put it away to give when I need a gift for someone."

Elizabeth picked at the piece of rose fabric. "I don't have a doll bed, either." Her mouth seemed to tighten on the words, and Leah had a sense of some emotion quickly suppressed.

"You have a doll, don't you?" She couldn't imagine any Amish girl without at least one of the faceless cloth dolls that were so much a part of childhood.

Elizabeth nodded. "But she has to sleep on my bed, because she doesn't have one of her own."

Again Leah sensed that tension. She longed to find out what the significance was of a doll bed, but if she probed, Elizabeth would retreat, and they'd be left in silence again.

Best to let it go for the moment. Perhaps Daniel would be able to shed some light.

"I'm sure your doll will like to have her own quilt, even if she's sleeping on your bed." She was going to have to move things along, or she had the sense that Elizabeth would sit looking at the fabric pieces until it was time for Daniel to come for her. "Let's decide what colors we want." She pointed to her old doll quilt. "How many colors would we need to make a quilt like this?"

Elizabeth studied the design, obviously counting to herself. "Seven." Her fingers lingered on the rose fabric. "May I use this one? And the light green?"

"Ser gut." Leah's heart warmed at the show of interest. "Choose five more, now, and then we can start cutting them out."

Nodding, Elizabeth began moving fabric pieces around, face intent as she considered each one.

Somehow Leah had attracted the child's attention. That was the first hurdle, and she'd have to be content with that for today.

She watched Elizabeth's face, longing to do more. The trauma of what had happened to Elizabeth had made her put up barriers against showing what she truly felt. Leah, of all people, knew about that. She had guarded her own feelings just as carefully after Johnny left.

The thought hit her, taking her breath away for a moment. She hoped to help Elizabeth surmount her fears, but how could she do that when she hadn't succeeded with her own?

And if she did, through God's grace, manage to help Elizabeth, who would help her?

Matthew and Jonah darted ahead of Daniel as he headed across the field to the Beiler farm to collect Elizabeth. Matthew seemed more settled in recent days, for which Daniel was truly thankful.

As for Jonah—he had to smile as his youngest grabbed Matthew's hat and took off, Matthew in hot pursuit. Nothing ever seemed to dampen Jonah's spirits. He had the gift of taking things as they came, unlike the other two.

Still, even Elizabeth had been better lately, making him wonder if this business of having Leah work with her was necessary. Maybe all his daughter needed was time to adjust to her life here.

"Daadi!" Matthew, having retrieved his hat, came racing back to him. "Mahlon and Joseph are working on something at the barn. Can we go see?"

"Go, but mind you stay out of their way."

Matthew ran off again, Jonah chugging along behind him like a little shadow. The Beiler brothers would make time for them, he knew, and maybe that was the answer with Elizabeth as well. Whether or not she really needed the counseling, as Leah thought, it would be good for her to be around a family like the Beilers.

When he reached the back porch, Leah and Elizabeth were just coming out. As usual, Elizabeth's face didn't give anything away.

"How was the quilting?" He hated that his voice sounded too hearty, as if he still couldn't be at ease with his own child.

"It went very well," Leah said, resting her hand lightly on Elizabeth's shoulder. "Elizabeth has a natural talent for needlework, I think."

Elizabeth darted a glance at her, as if checking to be sure Leah really meant it. Apparently she was satisfied with whatever she saw on Teacher Leah's face, because a smile played on her lips.

"I'm making a one-patch quilt for my doll," she announced. "Can I go tell Matthew about it?"

Leah nodded slightly over the child's head. She wanted to talk with him privately, then. Apprehension tightened his stomach.

"Your brothers are out at the barn. Go and find them, but don't get in the way."

"There's no need to worry about that." Leah sat down on the porch swing as Elizabeth crossed toward the barn. "Mahlon and Joseph are working on some project, but they always have time for company."

He sat down next to her. "What's wrong?" He said the words bluntly, not willing to wait for her to lead up to whatever troubled her.

"Nothing." She reached out toward him, a tentative little gesture. "I'm sorry if I gave you that impression."

"There is something, Teacher Leah, or you would not be so cautious. Just tell me."

She looked troubled. "Daniel, it's important that Elizabeth not feel I'm reporting to you on what happens between us."

Irritation flickered. "I'm her father. I have a right to know what concerns her."

"Please understand." Leah's voice went soft with caring. "I won't keep anything important from you, but Elizabeth must know that she can trust me, or she won't open up at all. You can see that, can't you?"

He pushed past his annoyance, past his instinctive response that he was the only one responsible for his daughter's happiness. If Leah could help Elizabeth, he must swallow his pride and let her.

"Ja," he said. "I see. I'll be careful."

"Ser gut." She glanced toward the barn, as if checking to be sure that Elizabeth was well out of earshot. "When we were planning the doll quilts we're making, Elizabeth said that she doesn't have a doll cradle. It seemed to upset her a little, so I wanted to ask if it means something I should be aware of."

For a moment he looked at her blankly. The doll cradle—

"I made one for her," he said slowly. "For her third birthday, that was. It was one of the things Ruth took with her when she went away." He could feel the tension tightening inside him like a spring.

"Do you know what happened to it?" Leah's voice was carefully neutral.

"When I went to pick them up, I stopped at the place where they'd been living." He had to force himself to remember that, hating the fact that his children had lived in a place with dirty dishes in the sink and clothes strewn on the floor. "I wanted to pack up their things, but the cradle wasn't there." His voice roughened. "There was nothing left to remind them that they'd been Amish. Ruth must have gotten rid of all of it."

"I'm sorry." Leah's green eyes went dark with sympathy.

His hands had curled into fists on his knees. He forced them to relax, one finger at a time.

The anger is still here, Father. How am I ever to be rid of it? Please, take it away.

Leah put her hand over his, her touch startling him. "It's so hard, I know. But they were things. Things don't make us Amish." She paused, as if groping for words. "It is Gelassenheit that defines who we are. If they've forgotten, your children will learn it again, now that they're safe with you."

Gelassenheit. It meant humility, but it was so much more, encompassing all that was simple and humble and good about their way of life.

He took a deep breath. "I pray you are right," he said. "Certainly I can make a new doll cradle for Elizabeth."

"Her birthday is later in the summer, isn't it?" Leah drew her hand away, flushing a little. "We'll try to finish the quilt by then, too, so that she can have both the cradle and the quilt together. And my mamm has already started making a doll for her."

"That is kind of her. And you."

"It's a pleasure for both of us. We're glad to have Elizabeth in our lives."

The warmth in Leah's voice touched the sore place in his heart, soothing it. He glanced at her, liking the delicate line of her profile, the warmth and caring that flowed from her so effortlessly.

His family kept telling him that he should marry again, that his children needed a mother and he needed a wife. If he intended to do that, wasn't Teacher Leah the logical person to ask?

She had been kind to them from the moment they'd arrived, had gone out of her way to help his children. And he was attracted to her— he couldn't deny that.

But balanced against that was her work at the clinic, bringing her again and again into contact with her onetime intended. He knew, better than most, the trouble that could come from flirtation with the outside world.

And even if he did decide to risk it, the truth was that despite her kindness, despite the attraction that he thought was mutual, he had no idea how Leah would react if he courted her.

. . .

Leah got up, setting the porch swing moving slightly. She was getting too close to Daniel, and that was a problem. She neither wanted nor was ready for any further changes in her life. She was dealing with enough already.

"Shall we go out to the barn and see what they're up to?"

Daniel nodded, standing and falling into step with her. The silence between them bothered her, filled as it was with the things unsaid.

"It's hard to tell what Joseph and Mahlon might be doing," she said to fill the gap. "When the two of them get together, they turn back into young ones again, ready for all kinds of foolishness."

"They've always been close?"

She nodded. "They're near each other in age and sandwiched between the girls, so maybe that accounts for it."

"My brother Caleb and I were like that." His smile flickered, reminiscent. "Mamm declared we gave her more gray hairs than the rest of the family put together."

"She probably enjoyed it, even if she didn't want you to know."

He glanced toward the barn, as if looking for his own young ones. "Maybe so. I'd like to see Matthew and Jonah be closer."

"When they've grown a bit, the age difference between them won't mean as much," she suggested.

He nodded, frowning a little. In this, as in everything connected with his children, Daniel wanted so much to have everything be right. He was a good man, trying hard to be both mother and father to his family.

She admired that, as she should, but that didn't mean she ought to be drawn any deeper into a relationship that might not be what either of them wanted for their lives.

Daniel slid the barn door back. Joseph and Mahlon were bent over a piece of machinery, and Matthew knelt next to them, obviously intrigued. Elizabeth and Jonah were in the hay mow, engrossed in some game of their own that seemed to involve Elizabeth putting strands of hay into her little brother's hair.

"Don't tell me you're still trying to get that corn binder working. Last year it broke down so often that Daadi said it was simpler to do it by hand."

Joseph, a streak of grease on his forehead, grinned at her. "That's why we're working on it early this year. Come time to harvest the corn, we'll have this running like a top."

"That's what you said last year," she reminded him.

"This year we have Matthew helping us," Mahlon said, reaching out to tousle the boy's hair. "He's a natural with machines already."

"That he is," Joseph said. "I could use a bright boy like this as an apprentice in a few years."

A slight movement drew Leah's gaze to Daniel. His hands pressed tightly against the sides of his trousers, and his mouth was a firm, straight line.

"We'd best be getting along home now." He softened the words with a smile, but she thought it took an effort.

Matthew scowled. "But I want to see the corn binder work. Please, Daadi, can't I stay until they get it working?"

"No." The word was sharp and uncompromising, sounding loud in the quiet barn.

Mahlon and Joseph exchanged glances, and then Mahlon gave Matthew a friendly cuff on the shoulder. "Knowin' my brother, that could be a long wait. You come again another time, all right?"

Matthew's lower lip came out, but he bobbed his head and got to his feet. Elizabeth and Jonah slid over the low wall of the hay mow, and in a moment the Glick family had gone.

Leah stood still, fingers clenched. *It's not your place to interfere. You're not going to get any more involved, remember?*

But it was no good. She crossed the barn floor quickly and hurried after them.

The children were already running ahead. Since Daniel seemed to have no intention of stopping when he saw her coming, she fell into step with him.

"What is it?" A plain, frank question seemed to be the only thing that worked with Daniel. "Why did you pull the children away like that?"

"It's time we were getting to the chores." But his gaze evaded hers.

"Do you object to using the corn binder? It's been approved by the bishop long since, and most farmers in the valley use them. As long as they're pulled by horses—"

"It's not the corn binder," he snapped.

"Then what?"

He stopped, swinging to face her. "I don't like Matthew's interest in things mechanical, that's all. He won't be looking for any apprenticeship, either, because he's got a gut farm waiting for him."

"Joseph didn't mean anything but to encourage the boy."

"I don't want him encouraged."

She struggled to understand. "Surely it's right for a farmer to understand the machinery he uses. Levi always says he'd be lost if he didn't have Joseph to keep things running."

Daniel's jaw tightened. "If it was only farm machinery—" He stopped, as if thinking that he didn't need to explain himself to her.

But she thought she understood. "You're afraid Matthew's interest in how things work draws him closer to the English world."

He wore the expression of a man goaded too far. "I know. I know it will. I've seen it already. 'When I was English,' that's what my son said to me. 'When I was English.'"

Her heart twisted. She reached toward him. "Daniel—"

He shook his head, clearly fighting to regain his composure. "I'm grateful for your help with Elizabeth, Teacher Leah. But this I have to take care of on my own."

CHAPTER FOURTEEN

*L*eah, it's been too long since you stopped to visit me like this."
Rachel chided Leah gently as she poured glasses of lemonade and
arranged cookies on a plate. "You've been even busier since school let
out, it seems like."

Leah felt a combination of pleasure that she'd stopped at Rachel's
place on her rounds today and guilt that she hadn't done it sooner. This
was just like the situation with Mamm. She shouldn't let her new
responsibilities affect her old relationships.

It was gut to be in Rachel's kitchen again, able to talk with her about
anything. The two older children were outside, but little Mary played
with blocks in the corner.

"I'm sorry I haven't come before this." She took a sip of the lemonade, tart on her tongue, and accepted a crisp, cinnamon-topped snickerdoodle. "It does seem that I have a lot to do lately."

"I've heard." Rachel's lips twitched, as if she tried without success
to hold back a smile. "It seems like you've been spending a lot of time
with Daniel Glick and his young ones this summer."

So that was the way the talk was going. She might have known her
actions wouldn't have gone unnoticed in a community as tightly knit as
theirs was.

"Rachel . . ." she began, then realized that she was gripping the edge
of Rachel's pine kitchen table so tightly her fingers hurt. She relaxed her
grip and deliberately took another sip of the lemonade.

"I have been seeing a lot of Elizabeth Glick lately." She hesitated. Daniel had talked about his wife in confidence, and she couldn't repeat his
words, even though it would probably silence the gossip about the two

of them. "She wants to learn to quilt, and since she doesn't have a mother or other female relative here to help her, I've been trying. And Mamm is working with her, too." She smiled, thinking of her mother with the solemn little girl. "Mamm's enjoying it as much as Elizabeth, for sure."

"That poor little girl." Rachel's quick sympathy overflowed. "I should have been thinking of that, too. I'll have her over to do some things with my Becky this summer. The two of them are sweet together."

"That would be wonderful gut. Anything we can do to fill the gaps in those children's lives, we should do."

"And in Daniel's life, too." Rachel's smile said that she might have been distracted for a moment, but she wasn't giving up on her matchmaking. "He's a gut man, for sure. I bet he appreciates what you're doing for his child."

Clearly Rachel wouldn't be diverted from her conviction that Leah and Daniel were meant to be together. Leah bit back her frustration. Denying it would only subject her to more teasing. Maybe it was best to ignore the topic entirely.

"I'd like to do more, but I've been traveling from one end of the church district to the other several days a week, interviewing families with sick children."

"For the clinic. I know." Rachel's blue eyes seemed to darken with concern. She pressed her lips together, as if to keep back words she wanted to speak.

Leah hesitated for a moment. She leaned across the table to put her hand over Rachel's. "Go on. Say whatever it is that's put those worry lines between your brows. We've been too close for too long to hold back now, that's certain sure."

Rachel clasped Leah's hand warmly. "I just— I don't know what to say. I want to warn you about gettin' too close with Johnny again, while a little piece of me hopes that loving you might be the thing that will bring him home."

Leah's throat tightened with pity. "Rachel, I'm sorry. But I'm afraid there's nothing that will bring John back to the church. I hoped you'd accepted that."

Rachel sighed, shaking her head a little and blinking back tears.

"It's not so easy. Hope keeps slipping back in. And when you started working at the clinic, well, I thought maybe Johnny was the reason."

"He's the one who asked me. But I didn't agree because of him. I'm doing this for the children. If anything I do keeps a child from suffering, that's worth it."

Rachel wiped away tears with her fingers, much as she'd done when they were girls. "God gave you a heart for children, that's for sure, Leah Beiler. I just wish you had some of your own to love."

Little Mary chose that moment to knock her block tower down, sending blocks skidding across the floor and surprising Leah into a chuckle. "There's one of your little blessings in action."

"Ach, Mary, don't do that. Someone might trip on them."

But Mary had lost interest in building, it appeared. She trotted across to Leah and dumped a handful of blocks into her lap.

"How kind of you, Mary. Can I play with these?" Any interruption that got them safely off the subject of her childlessness was a good one.

Mary stared at her with round blue eyes, her fine blond hair curling loose from her braids. Then, suddenly, she smiled, dimple showing, and held out her arms to Leah.

"Up," she demanded.

"There now, little girl, you're a sweet child." Leah picked her up, holding her close.

Mary looked so like Johnny that it shocked her that she'd never noticed it before. Not surprising, since Mary's mamm and the uncle she might never know were twins.

If Leah and Johnny had had a babe, this was what he or she might have looked like. She brushed a kiss against the soft cheek, a peculiar ache spreading in her chest. She'd have said she'd accepted never having children of her own, but in this moment, she wasn't so sure.

"She looks like Johnny, doesn't she?" Rachel seemed to understand Leah's thoughts. Her voice was soft, and her eyes glistened with tears.

"Ja." Her own voice was thick all of a sudden. She shouldn't ask the question that pressed against her lips—she shouldn't, but she had to.

"Rachel, if I could arrange it, would you see him? It hurts so much to think of the two of you apart."

Something that might have been hope dawned in Rachel's eyes. "Do you think— Should I? I wouldn't want the folks to know, but oh, how I'd love to see him again."

"You could talk to him." At least, she could if Johnny put his pride aside and agreed. "Surely there's someplace the two of you could meet and talk. Maybe that would even ease the way for your parents to accept seeing him eventually."

"I don't know about that." Rachel clasped her hands, hope and doubt warring in her expression. "But I would do it, if you can set it up. Will you talk to Johnny about it, Leah? Will you?"

Doing so would mean involving herself more deeply with Johnny, something she'd been determined not to do. But how could she refuse the longing of her dear friend's heart?

"I'll try." She held little Mary close, somehow drawing strength from her. "I'll do my best."

Leah gathered her clinic materials together, breathing a silent sigh of relief. She'd met with Stacie to turn in her reports, and this time the woman had been almost—well, not friendly, but at least not antagonistic.

As she stood, Stacie looked up from the desk. "Good work," she said curtly.

Leah nodded in acknowledgment. As she started to turn away, Stacie slapped her hand down on the desk.

"What's wrong with you people? Can't you even say thank you for a compliment?"

Leah blinked. "I didn't mean to offend. It's just not our way."

"Why not?" Stacie shoved herself to her feet, both palms on the desk. "A little simple politeness can't be against your rules, can it?"

"It's not that." Although the woman's tone was irritated, she did seem to want to understand, and that was surely a step in the right direction. "The Amish way is that of humility. For me to say thank you would imply that I agreed I had done a good job."

Stacie shook her head. "I don't get it. What's wrong with that? I always figure if I don't think well of myself, nobody else will."

This was like the conversation she'd had with John, which had turned so quickly into a quarrel. Their part of the English world didn't seem to think very highly of humility.

"We believe that God calls us to not think more highly of ourselves than others. To put others first." Trying to explain something that was so fundamental to her beliefs in a way this educated, intense woman would understand seemed impossible.

Stacie shrugged. "You wouldn't get very far in the academic world with an attitude like that."

"I suppose not."

Johnny seemed to have been able to leave that attitude of mind and heart behind. Had it been easy for him to erase the habit of a lifetime?

"Well, I'll see you next week, I guess." Stacie gathered up the forms, tapping them together. "Have a good one."

Nodding again, Leah headed back through the maze of offices. Had Johnny told Stacie that Leah had requested to report to her rather than to him? That might account for the change in her attitude.

But now she had to seek him out for a private talk in order to set up a meeting with Rachel. This could only complicate matters with him, but that couldn't be helped. A little embarrassment on her part was a small price to pay for Rachel's happiness.

She'd just begun to wonder how she'd find Johnny when he came around the corner. His step checked at the sight of her. He nodded stiffly and began to turn away.

"John." This was going to be difficult, given how they'd parted. "May I speak with you?"

His eyebrows lifted. "That's the last thing I expected from you. Had a change of heart, have you?"

She was probably flushing. "This isn't about the clinic. It's about your family."

For a moment she thought he'd walk away. Then he gave a curt nod and gestured toward the door at the end of the corridor.

"Come out on the back porch. We won't be interrupted there."

She followed him, trying to arrange what she needed to say. She'd expect Johnny to be eager to see his twin sister, but did she really know him well enough any longer to say?

The back porch stretched the length of the building, and it seemed to be a repository for things no one had a use for at the moment. Cartons were piled against the wall, and beyond them metal folding chairs leaned against each other.

To her right, someone had attempted to arrange a small sitting area, with a glass-topped table and a couple of benches. John brushed off the seats with the palm of his hand, and they sat down.

She folded her hands and banished the intrusive memory of sitting on the back porch swing with Daniel. How to begin?

"They're all right, aren't they?" The concern in his voice disarmed her. "The family."

"As far as I know."

"Did my parents change their minds? Do they want to see me?" He shot the question at her.

"I'm afraid not. But—"

He planted his hands on his knees as if to rise. "Then there's nothing to talk about."

"There is." She put out a hand to stop him. "Please, Johnny. Just listen to me for a few minutes."

His fingers clenched. Then he nodded, not looking at her.

She took a breath. "It's not that they don't want to see you. You must know that."

"What difference does it make?" He looked at her, and she saw the flash of pain in his eyes. "They won't. That's the bottom line. They're so tied up by the rules of the church that they won't see their own son."

"You're the one who left with hardly a word of explanation." And with no hint of farewell for her. "Can't you see how many people were hurt by that? If you wanted to really come back, we—they—would hold out their arms to you."

"Are you talking about my parents, Leah?" His voice went soft. "Or about you?"

For a moment she couldn't speak. She looked into his face and saw again the boy she'd loved—the boy whose leaving had broken her heart.

She tried to rally her defenses. "This isn't about me."

"Still determined to hide your emotions under that perfect Amish exterior? Can't we talk honestly about it at least once?" He reached out impetuously to clasp her hand. "Maybe then we can be friends again."

She forced herself to take a deep breath. "The blame is not on one side or the other, I know that. We hurt each other."

His fingers tightened. "I left you. I promised to marry you, and then I left."

The words seemed to wrench open a hole in her heart. Could she, this once, accept the truth about herself?

"And I promised to love you forever." Tears stung her eyes. "But I couldn't go with you. I was afraid."

There. That was the truth, as plainly as she knew how to speak it. She felt as if a brisk wind blew through the hole in her heart, chasing away the last shreds of guilt and bitterness.

"I'm sorry." His voice broke a little on the words, and all the pride seemed wiped out of him in the truth of the moment. "Maybe we were both too young."

"Ja. We were. I blamed you for a long time." She looked at him steadily. "I blamed myself even longer."

It was an astonishing relief to say the words out loud to him after all this time.

"I wish—" he began.

"Don't," she said quickly. "I know you don't regret leaving, no matter how hard it's been."

"No. But I regret hurting people to do it."

She let the silence stretch between them for a moment. For the first time since his return, she felt comfortable with him.

"Can we be friends again, Johnny?"

He squeezed her hand. "Friends."

She nodded. "Then, as your friend, I'm here for Rachel. She wants to see you."

His eyes widened, as if he couldn't believe what he heard. "She does? Really?"

"Really." She smiled, relieved. There could be no doubt about Johnny's reaction to that.

"I'll go right now. I can leave for the day and drive over there—"

"Wait." She grasped his arm to stop him. "Not right away. She'll meet you someplace. She asked me to arrange it."

She felt him stiffen, saw the softness leave his face. "You mean I'm not welcome at my own sister's home. She wants to see me someplace where no one will know, as if I'm a criminal."

He was pulling away, and somehow she had to make him see what he was doing.

"Don't, Johnny. Don't deny the very thing you want out of some foolish, worldly pride. Rachel loves you. She wants to see you again. That's the only important thing, isn't it?"

For a moment it hung in the balance, and she held her breath. Then, a little shamefaced, he nodded.

"You're right." He squeezed her hand tightly, and the bond between them ran so strong that it frightened her. "You set it up. I'll be there."

"Those are nice, small stitches, Elizabeth. Your quilt is coming along already."

Elizabeth nodded, not looking up from the patch she was working on. Her brows were furrowed in concentration as she wielded the needle.

Leah suppressed a sigh. She sat in her grossmutter's chair, but she didn't seem to have her gift for drawing out confidences. Elizabeth's quilt might be progressing, but their relationship wasn't.

Should she be pushing more? She studied the little girl's face, but it gave nothing away, and she feared probing might only make Elizabeth retreat further into her shell.

Perhaps she should discuss it with Lydia again. Her books had been helpful, but talking it out would be even better.

Better yet would be having Lydia counsel the child, but she had no hope that Daniel would agree to that.

She frowned down at her own quilt patch. Her life seemed more like a crazy quilt lately than this neat geometric design. Trying to balance Elizabeth's troubles, her apprehension over bringing Rachel and Johnny together, her tangled feelings for him, her growing closeness with Daniel . . . Maybe they all made some sort of pattern in God's sight, but she couldn't see it.

Guide me, Father, she prayed as she set one tiny stitch after another. *I don't see my path clearly just now, and I need to know where You want me.*

Someone knocked at the front door of the daadi haus. Murmuring a silent *Amen,* she went to answer it.

"Leah, you're just the person I hoped to see." Paula Schatz, the Mennonite woman who owned the bakery where Anna worked, peered past her. "Is your mother here?"

"I'm sorry, but she had to go out—"

"No, no, that's good."

Paula thrust a paper bag with the bakery logo on it into Leah's hands as she came in. With her graying hair pulled back into a bun under her prayer cap and her comfortable girth enveloped in a modest dress, she might have appeared Amish to an outsider.

It was true enough that the Amish and the Mennonites were cousins in belief, so to speak, though sometimes their differences could be bitter. But she knew Paula nearly as well as she did her own church family.

Paula chuckled. "Listen to me. I'm so distracted that I made it sound as if I didn't want to see your dear mamm. Give her that from me—it's some of my pumpernickel bread."

"She and Daadi will love it, for sure. But if you didn't come to see Mamm—"

Paula clasped her arm. "I thought I'd bring this problem to you, Leah. You'd be the one to handle it, and I didn't want to put another burden on your mamm when she's still recovering."

A problem with Anna, then. Leah's heart sank. She'd just begun to feel as if things were getting back to normal between her and Anna.

Paula caught sight of Elizabeth and blinked. "I'm sorry if I interrupted."

"This is my neighbor Elizabeth Glick. We're making quilts together."

Elizabeth gave a polite nod, seeming to retreat a bit further into herself in the presence of the stranger.

"I'm glad to meet you, Elizabeth." Paula shot a glance at Leah. "Can we talk in private?"

There was nothing to be gained by putting it off, whatever it was. Leah nodded, gesturing toward the kitchen.

"Just keep on with your stitching, Elizabeth. I need to talk with Mrs. Schatz for a few minutes." She went into the kitchen with a silent prayer.

"I'll make a long story short," Paula said, bracing her hands against the back of a kitchen chair. "Seeing as how you have a guest."

Her brown eyes twinkled with curiosity, and Leah knew she was aching to ask about her relationship with the Glick family. Paula, like everyone else in Pleasant Valley, took a deep interest in her neighbors.

"Is there a problem with Anna?" Leah came out with the question before Paula could get sidetracked.

"Now, Leah, you know how much I care about the girls I hire to work in the bakery." Paula's round face, seeming to be made for smiling, grew serious. "They're like my own kin, they are, and I feel responsible for them."

"Ja, I know." That was why Mamm and Daad had felt safe about Anna working there.

"And I don't want to be telling tales on any of my girls, no, I don't." Paula shoved her wire-rimmed glasses up her nose. "But I'm that worried about Anna that I had to talk to someone. 'Teacher Leah's the one,' I said to myself. 'If anyone can get through to Anna, it'll be Leah.'"

Paula couldn't guess how wrong she was about that. Leah seemed to have no influence at all over her baby sister these days.

"What has she done?" She braced herself for the answer.

"Coming late. Leaving early. Not showing up at all sometimes. I tell you, Leah, I'm at my wit's end with her." She hesitated. "It's not my business, but I've seen the boy who waits for her when she leaves— Englischer, he is, with a fancy red car."

Even though Paula herself drove a car, it was a sedate black sedan, with even the bumpers painted black.

Leah let out a breath she didn't realize she'd been holding. She couldn't even say she was surprised. "Have you spoken to her about it?"

"I've tried to talk sense to her, but it's done me no good at all. I might as well save my breath to cool my porridge. No, you're the one to handle this."

"I'll try." Though she doubted that Anna would listen to her, either. "Thank you for coming to me, rather than Mamm. You're a gut friend, for sure."

Paula patted her hand. "I do my best by those girls, but if ever I saw someone going near the edge, it's Anna. Well, well, we do our best, but sometimes young people have to make their own mistakes."

She headed toward the front door, apparently satisfied that she'd said what was necessary. Leah trailed behind her, impelled by hospitality when she'd rather curl up and weep.

"I'm grateful to you. I'll do my best."

"I know you will." Paula gave her a quick hug. "You're a good, responsible girl, you are. Anna could stand to be a little more like you."

Leah managed a smile. "I don't think she'd like hearing that."

Paula shook her head, chuckling a little as she went out. "No, I don't suppose so. Mind, now, if she doesn't straighten out soon, I'll have to let her go. I wouldn't want to put that burden on your mamm, either. It would worry her."

"It would." Leah's heart sank at the thought of Mamm's reaction to that. She and Paula were old friends, and that would hurt her. Still, what else could Paula do? She had a business to run.

Leah stood watching as Paula drove off, her mind searching for a way to reach Anna. Here was another errant patch for her imaginary crazy quilt, and it threatened to be the most difficult to deal with.

But in the meantime, she was neglecting Elizabeth. She went to look over the child's work before sitting down again.

"Ser gut," she said, picking up her own work. "I'm sorry about the interruption."

Elizabeth fixed her with an apprehensive gaze. "Is something wrong with your mamm?"

Odd, that out of all she must have overheard, that was what she'd fix on. "Not exactly. Mrs. Schatz didn't want to worry her just now, that's all."

"Because she's sick?"

Obviously Elizabeth wasn't going to be content with evasions. Maybe she was relating this to losing her own mother.

"Mamm was very sick last year," Leah said carefully, wanting to be honest without frightening the child. "She's doing much better now, but we still try to keep her from being worried and upset, or from doing too much."

"Is she going to die?" Elizabeth's lips trembled.

Leah's heart clenched. "Everyone will die sometime, but I think my mamm will be with us for a long time."

"My mamm died."

Was this the breakthrough she'd been looking for, coming at her from an unexpected source? She breathed a quick, silent prayer for guidance.

"I know she did. I'm sorry. You must miss her an awful lot."

Elizabeth clenched the quilt patch tightly in her hands. Her face worked. "I was angry at my mamm." Her mouth twisted. "And then she died."

Calm, be calm. Don't overreact. "You got mad at her before she died. We all get mad at the people we love sometimes."

Elizabeth was shaking her head, her face contorted. Leah longed to put her arms around the child, to comfort her and tell her she didn't have to talk about it. But talking about it might be the very thing that would help her heal.

"It's all right, Elizabeth," she said softly. "You can tell me anything you want. I won't tell anyone."

"I prayed to go home again." She seemed to force the words out. "All the time after Mamm took us away, I prayed to go home. But I didn't mean for her to die. I didn't!" Elizabeth burst into tears.

Now Leah did have to hold her. She scooped the child into her arms and settled in the rocking chair, holding her close.

"Hush, hush, now. It's all right. Really, it's all right." She smoothed her hair and stroked her back. "Elizabeth, your prayers didn't bring about your mamm's accident."

"But I prayed to go home." A choked sob punctuated the words. "And after Mammi died, Daadi came to take us home."

Leah rocked back and forth, patting her, trying to find the right words to comfort her. The poor child, carrying a burden like this for months and not telling anyone.

"I know it seems that way," Leah said carefully. "But your mamm was in an accident because she drove a car when she'd been drinking. God didn't make her do that. She decided to do that on her own."

Leah couldn't guess what had led Ruth to the choices she'd made. She could only do her best to deal with the results.

"Her accident was a terrible thing, but you weren't to blame. It's all right to be thankful that you were able to come home."

She felt some of the tension ease out of Elizabeth's body. She seemed to relax against Leah's shoulder, much as she'd done the night she'd burned her hand.

But this was a much deeper, more painful hurt. A professional would know how to deal with it so much better than she did.

Please, Lord. Help this dear child to understand. Take away her burden.

"It wasn't your fault," Leah said again, her words soft. "You weren't to blame."

Elizabeth sighed, hiccoughing a little. "I didn't want her to die. I just wanted to go home again."

"I know. I know. It's all right. God has brought you home, where you belong." She took a deep breath, praying she was saying the right thing. "Maybe you should tell your daadi what you told me. I know he'd want to help you feel better about it."

She shook her head. "I can't. I don't want to say it again."

"Would it be okay with you if I told him?"

At least Elizabeth didn't refuse that entirely. "I . . . I don't know. What if it makes him think I wanted Mammi to die?"

"I promise you he wouldn't think that." She smoothed Elizabeth's hair. "But I won't say anything to him unless you tell me to. All right?"

Elizabeth looked at her for a long moment, as if weighing her trustworthiness. Finally she nodded. "All right," she said.

CHAPTER FIFTEEN

Leah was up before the sun the following day. She may as well be—she'd spent a mostly sleepless night with her mind bouncing between the revelation of Elizabeth's feelings about her mother and the visit from Paula Schatz, with her concerns for Anna.

She'd prayed, caught herself worrying, and prayed again.

Why can't I be confident in Your answers to my prayers, Father? I feel so torn. For years I felt so sure that I knew the right thing to do, and now everything seems to be a challenge.

Maybe that was the point. Maybe God was reminding her that only through relying on Him would she find the right path.

I can rely on You for myself, I think. It's so much more difficult to relinquish control when it's a child I love.

Daniel had to know the anguish of guilt that had Elizabeth tied up in knots, but how could she break the child's confidence? If she did, that could destroy any hope of a further relationship between them.

And if she didn't—she didn't want to think about his reaction if she kept this from him.

She couldn't discuss this with anyone else, but she could talk to Lydia. If God had brought Lydia into her life for a reason, this might be it.

And as for Anna—

Sometime in the long night, she had come to a decision. She couldn't deal with this situation on her own any longer. Trying to protect Mammi's feelings was a good thing, but not at the cost of Anna's future.

She would talk to Daad about it. She went softly down the stairs, feeling her familiar way in the predawn darkness. Perhaps Mamm would never need to know how worrying Anna's behavior had been. And if she did, Daadi would know the best way to bring it up.

She went quietly out the back door and across the lawn toward the stable, the dew-wet grass dampening her sneakers. The eastern sky brightened already, and the world seemed hushed, as if it held its breath, waiting for the sun's appearance.

Daadi would be in the stable, feeding the horses, talking to them as he always did. She could have a few quiet moments alone with him before the rest of the house was up and busy.

The stable door stood open, letting out a shaft of yellow light from Daad's lantern. She went in, pausing a moment on the threshold, appreciating the fact that all was just as she'd imagined it.

Daad leaned on Betty's stall door, pouring oats into her feed bucket, talking to her in that same gentle tone that he'd always used with his children as well. He looked up at her step, smiling in welcome.

"You're up early, daughter."

"Not so early as you."

Her father never changed, it seemed to her. His beard might be more white than brown these days, but he still moved with the same quick, wiry strength he always had. His hazel eyes watched her with love and maybe a little question.

She leaned against the stall door next to him, patting Betty's neck. The mare, nose deep in her oats, flickered her ears in greeting.

"Greedy girl," she said, stroking her.

In the next stall Dick, one of the big Percherons, pawed and snorted impatiently. Daad chuckled.

"We'd best get the rest of them fed, if we don't want to hear about it." He handed her a feed pail. "While we're doing it, you can tell me what has you so worried already."

"You noticed that." She took the pail, going to fill it at the barrel that held the oats.

"Ja, I noticed." Daadi poured oats into Dick's feeding pail, glancing at her with a faint trace of a frown between his brows. "Is it Johnny's coming back that has you upset?"

She blinked in surprise. Other people might be talking, but—

"You know me better than that, don't you, Daad?"

"I know you're a levelheaded, responsible girl. But I also know that once you loved him with all your heart."

"That was a long time ago. I don't have feelings for him now." *Do I?* She hoped that was true.

"Are you sure you're not gettin' involved with him again, seeing him as you do?"

"No, Daad." Unless she considered setting up a meeting between Johnny and Rachel getting involved.

He looked at her searchingly for a moment, as if he sensed that she was hiding something. "Ser gut," he said at last. "So what is it then that has you worried?"

"Anna." It was a relief to say it. "I know she has to have her rum-springa, just as the rest of us did, but I'm concerned about what she's doing."

He nodded, leaning his elbow on the top of the last stall. The sound of contented munching filled the stable.

"I know. She's been running with English friends, maybe even a boy, hasn't she?"

She studied his weatherworn face. "Daadi, if you know, why haven't you talked to her about it?"

He smiled a little. "Five times we've gone through this, your mamm and me. Five times we've worried and prayed."

"The rest of us didn't go so close to the line, did we?"

"Well, you were the one we didn't think we needed to worry about, settled as you were on Johnny so early. But when he left, it seemed we should have been more careful with you."

"No one could have predicted that." Not even her, apparently.

"And you don't know what foolishness your brothers got up to." His eyes twinkled a little. "Them I understood a little better than you girls. Your mamm knows you and Anna best."

Maybe that was part of the problem. With Mamm's illness, perhaps they hadn't concentrated on Anna enough.

"I haven't wanted to upset Mamm. But I think you should talk to Anna."

He folded his hands, almost as if in prayer. "We've always believed rumspringa to be a useful time. We give our young people a taste of what life is like on the other side, and then they can make a decision of commitment without regrets."

She didn't have regrets, at least not about that. But still, sometimes she wondered. What would her life have been if she'd gone with Johnny? Could she have thrived, as he apparently had, without family and church?

"You're still worried." He patted her shoulder. "Try to have trust that Anna will sow her wild oats and then come out the other side, just as the rest of you did."

She wished she had his faith. "It's not just the English friends," she said. "Paula Schatz stopped by yesterday to talk to me. She didn't want to upset Mamm, but she says Anna has been coming late, leaving early, sometimes not showing up at all. You know Paula. She wouldn't come to us without cause."

Her father straightened. "That's so?" At her nod, he frowned. "This will not do. It is not right for Anna to be taking her wages without putting in an honest day's work. I'll talk to her."

Leah gave a rueful smile. "I feel as if I've shifted my worries to your shoulders."

He patted her hand. "That is where they belong. I'm glad you care about your sister, but you shouldn't carry the burden for her. It's enough for you to deal with your own concerns." His fingers tightened on hers. "I'm always here for you, Leah."

She nodded, her throat tightening. "I know you are, Daadi."

He was still worrying about her, she could see that. But she couldn't reassure him that everything was all right with her. She didn't know that herself.

"*What* if he doesn't come? Or what if we're late?" Rachel twisted her hands in her lap, peering out the window of Ben Morgan's car. Leah had arranged for Ben to drive them to this meeting with Johnny.

"Calm down already." Leah patted her hand, trying to ignore the fact that her own stomach was tied in knots. "I've never seen you so ferhoodled."

"I haven't seen my own twin in ten years." Rachel transferred her grip to Leah's hand. "Is it any wonder? What if he doesn't come?"

"Johnny wouldn't let you down that way." She glanced toward the driver, but Ben could be trusted to keep quiet about this trip. That was why she'd asked him to bring them.

"I hope not. But ten years with hardly a word . . . I know I'm being foolish, but I can't decide whether I want to hug him or box his ears for him."

"Maybe both," Leah suggested.

Ben slowed the car, peering out at the houses they passed, obviously looking for the number she'd given him. They must be nearly at Lydia's now.

Setting up this meeting had been so difficult that she'd felt at times as if she were negotiating a peace treaty. Rachel didn't want to go anyplace where she might be seen by someone who'd relay the news to her parents, and Johnny had shown signs of getting prideful again about the whole thing.

Finally Lydia had stepped into the breach, offering her home in Mifflinburg, and the time was set.

Leah and Rachel had come early, giving themselves plenty of time to do the fabric shopping that was the stated reason for their trip.

Leah hadn't expected to enjoy the shopping part of the day, but as it turned out, Rachel had found fabric for new dresses for Becky and shirts for the boys, while Leah had bought the lining and backing material for her and Elizabeth's quilts. They'd taken their time, weighing the merits of one bolt against another, but even so, they were arriving at Lydia's place a little early.

"Here we are, ladies." Ben pulled into the driveway of a small white cottage, his gaze meeting Leah's in the rearview mirror with a look of encouragement. "You can leave your bundles in the car. I'll just sit and read the paper."

He slid his seat back a bit and unfurled the newspaper from the seat beside him.

"Ser gut." She opened her door, but Rachel was already out ahead of her.

The yard was tiny but beautifully kept, and several varieties of roses bloomed in a bed across the front of the house. They followed a flagstone path that led to the front door. If it were not for the electric lines running to the house from the street, this might be an Amish home.

"All right?" Leah glanced at Rachel when they reached the stoop.

Rachel nodded, her face pale but determined.

Almost before she could knock, Lydia opened the door. "Welcome to my home. Please, come in. This must be your friend Rachel."

Rachel gave a quick nod, looking around with a certain amount of apprehension in her blue eyes. "It's kind of you to have us."

"My pleasure." Lydia led the way into a small living room, gesturing to the sofa. "John called a while ago to double-check the address, so I imagine he'll be along soon." She glanced at Leah. "Perhaps when he comes, you'll join me in the kitchen for a cup of tea."

Leah nodded.

"Maybe you should stay—" Rachel began.

Leah grasped her hands firmly. "You'll be fine. John is still your brother."

"But he's different now. A fence-jumper. Englischer." She glanced at Lydia.

Lydia smiled. "Like me, yes. There's no need for you to feel uncomfortable about it. My situation and John's are similar."

Similar, but not entirely alike. Lydia had already gone over the difficult bridge to establishing a relationship with her family. John had yet to do that, but Leah hoped and prayed that today would be a first step.

A car pulled into the driveway—she could hear the tires crunch on the gravel. Her fingers pressed taut against the skirt of her dress, and her stomach seemed to turn over.

"He's here," Rachel whispered, her eyes wide and apprehensive.

Please, Lord. Leah's throat was so tight that she couldn't have said the words aloud. *Please let this go well. I long so much for Rachel and Johnny to be brother and sister again.*

The knock came at the door, and they could hear the soft murmur of Lydia's voice as she opened it. Rachel gasped, and her hand squeezed Leah's convulsively.

There was the sound of a familiar step, and Johnny appeared in the archway. He stood, hesitant, looking at his sister.

With a strangled sob, Rachel catapulted herself across the room and into his arms. In a moment the two of them were hugging and laughing and crying all at the same time. Leah exchanged a glance with Lydia and followed her into the kitchen.

On the verge of tears herself, Leah sat in the kitchen chair Lydia pulled out for her. She pressed her fingers against her eyes.

Lydia, not speaking, turned the gas on under a teakettle and began rattling cups and saucers, obviously giving her time to calm herself.

By the time Lydia brought the cups to the table, Leah was able to smile at her. "That's kind of you."

"I always think a hot cup of tea does wonders for emotional upset." She poured the brew from a squat brown teapot and then sat down across from Leah.

"I don't think they'll be ready for refreshments for a time." Leah glanced toward the door to the living room.

"I didn't mean them," Lydia said. "I meant you. This surely is emotional for you as well."

"I suppose it is." She held the cup between her hands. "Seeing them together—well, it feels so right. They were always very close, and for a long time, I couldn't get used to seeing Rachel without knowing Johnny was around somewhere."

Lydia nodded, staring down into the contents of her cup. She and her siblings had come to a relationship, she'd said. It must have been a difficult road.

"Everyone's actions affect so many other people," Leah went on. "Rachel just hasn't seemed heart-whole without him. Maybe she'll be better now."

"I hope she's not counting on his coming back." Lydia traced the rim of her cup with her finger. "It would be a nice dream, but it won't happen."

"You think he's too happy where he is?"

"Happy?" Lydia seemed to look at the word. "I'm not sure that describes it. When you fence-jump, you never entirely leave the past behind. How could you?"

"So you never really fit into the English world." That was what Johnny had hinted.

Lydia intrigued her, and she'd like to understand the woman better. Lydia apparently loved her work and was probably very good at it, but she didn't seem entirely to match with the life she'd chosen.

"Something like that." Lydia smiled, her gaze meeting Leah's. "I've told you that sometimes I wonder if I'd be better off right now if I were still Amish, and I can never really leave that yearning behind. But that's not the choice I made."

"You could change." Leah ventured the words tentatively.

Lydia shook her head. "Some can't go back because they invest too much in the English world, like John. Others, like me, might long to return, but there's something they can't give up. For me, it's my work."

Leah nodded. She might not entirely understand what made someone leave, but she could understand why a woman like Lydia couldn't go back.

She hesitated, wondering if it would be intruding to ask the question in her mind. "Do you think, twenty or thirty years from now, you'll have regrets?"

"I'll be alone here in my little house then, you mean. With no family and community to look after me."

Leah thought about Mamm, surrounded by people who loved and cared for her. That was the old age an Amish woman expected to have. They didn't worry about being left alone.

"I didn't mean to offend you," she said.

"I'm not offended." Lydia's smile had a tinge of sadness. "It's an honest concern. Yes, I think about that. But I've made my choice."

Leah nodded. Each time she met Lydia, the woman gave her something new to think about.

"You know, Leah, if you ever left, it would be for reasons like mine. For the work, not for love."

Her breath caught in her throat. She couldn't answer. Couldn't even think about it, because she was afraid Lydia had verbalized something that might possibly be true.

. . .

This welcome should go a long way toward convincing his mother that he and the children were fitting in here in Pleasant Valley. Daniel smiled, relaxing a little as he saw that Mamm had settled into a folding chair in the shade of the big maple in the Beilers' backyard.

His mother had arrived on yesterday's bus from Lancaster County, fresh from helping at the birth of his sister's new babe, and already the Beiler family had planned a picnic to welcome her.

"I hope your mamm wasn't too tired from her trip."

Leah paused next to him, a basketful of rolls in her arm that must be intended for the serving table that was filling up with more food as each family arrived once evening chores were done.

"If she was, seeing her grandchildren has more than made up for it." He nodded toward his mother. "It seems like she and your mamm are finding plenty of things to say to each other."

"Ja." The faintest shadow crossed Leah's green eyes at the thought.

Perhaps she still worried about the persistence of the matchmakers who were determined to yoke them together. That didn't seem as annoying to him as it once had.

"It is gut for her to see that we're fitting in and happy here. She can't help but worry."

"That comes with being a parent." Leah smiled, the shadow vanishing. "My mamm certainly hasn't stopped yet, no matter how old we are."

He nodded, looking down at Leah. She'd be that kind of mother, too, he felt sure. You could see that in the care she had for every one of her students.

"When my children were gone—" He paused, his throat tight at the memory. "I don't know how I'd have gotten through it without my family."

"They must have been overjoyed when the children came home at last." She hesitated. "I wonder if—" She stopped, perhaps not wanting to voice the thought.

But he knew what it must be. "They didn't really understand why I wanted to move afterward. They hated seeing me take the children away from Lancaster County, but once they knew I felt it was the right thing, they supported my decision."

"It's hard to let go, for them and for you." Her understanding was as quick as ever. "But I suppose sometimes it's needed. You had to get away from the reminders."

"Getting the children away was the important thing. The older ones, especially. They couldn't seem to settle down after they came home. I felt as if they were always looking for Ruth. They're better here."

Elizabeth raced up to them at that moment, tugging on Leah's skirt. "Did you see that my grossmutter is here for a visit, Teacher Leah?"

"I know." Leah smiled at her. "That makes you both happy, doesn't it?"

The tenderness in Leah's face when she looked at his daughter touched Daniel's heart. Elizabeth darted off again, giving him the opportunity to say something that was on his mind.

"She was happier even before my mamm arrived. She told me—about her feelings over Ruth's dying that way. About feeling guilty over it."

It was difficult even to say the words, but if he'd learned one thing from this, it was that speaking was better than keeping silent. "She said you wanted her to tell me."

Her face filled with the concern she felt for his child. "I did my best to reassure her, but I knew she needed to hear it from you as well. I hope you're not upset that I didn't tell you about it right away."

Maybe he had been, just for a moment, but then he'd realized that Leah had done exactly what she'd said she would. "I can't be, when it's turned out so well. My little Elizabeth acts as if a weight has been lifted from her shoulders."

"That's wonderful gut. I'm so glad." Her free hand moved, as if she'd reach out to him, but then it stilled.

Maybe she was too aware of the people who watched them. No one came near to interrupt them, though. They were being given a chance to be together, even in a crowd.

There was one thing more he had to say—had to admit—to Leah.

"I should have seen long before this that something was eating at her. You tried to tell me, but I thought I knew better."

"Maybe there are times when things are easier seen by an outsider instead of a parent. It won't help Elizabeth for you to be blaming yourself, you know."

"I know. But you're wrong about one thing, Teacher Leah."

She looked up at him, her gaze puzzled. "I am?"

"Ja." He touched her hand lightly, and even that small contact seemed to send awareness of her flowing through his body. "You're not an outsider."

Her eyes darkened as they met his. Was she as aware of the attraction as he was? His grasp tightened, and her fingers pressed his in response. The noise and activity around them receded, and all he could see was Leah.

He took an abrupt step back, dropping her hand as if it were a hot coal. He'd told himself he should think of remarrying, giving his children a mother. And physical attraction was important, wonderful important, in a woman he might think of courting.

But not if it overpowered his common sense. He'd already made a mistake that had nearly cost him his children. He couldn't make another.

That would sound foolish if he tried to explain it to anyone—the idea that he didn't trust feeling too much for a woman he might want to wed. But he couldn't let his head be ruled by his heart, not in something as important as this was to his family's happiness.

CHAPTER SIXTEEN

*L*eah shuffled through her reports for the week, double-checking to be sure she had everything. She'd be meeting with Stacie in a few minutes, and she didn't want to give the woman any reason to criticize her work. Their relationship was difficult enough already, although it had seemed a little better the last time.

She heard a step and glanced up, tensing a little. But it wasn't Stacie— it was Dr. Brandenmyer, coming down the hallway with his long stride.

He paused when he saw her. "Ms. Beiler, how nice to run into you. Are you here to see John today?"

Her fingers tightened on the sheaf of papers as she shook her head. Why would he think that? Did he know about that private conversation between them the last time she was here?

"I'll be meeting with Stacie in a few minutes to go over my interview reports."

She expected him to hurry off, but instead he sat down next to her, his long white coat flapping around his legs. He peered at her over the top of his glasses, his eyes keen.

"How do you feel about the work, now that you've been at it for a while? Is it satisfying?"

She considered. "I like talking with the families, and I suppose I'm satisfied when I draw something out that I didn't expect. But—" She hesitated.

"Go on." He nodded encouragingly.

She smoothed the papers in her hands, staring down at them. "I just wonder sometimes. Is this really going to help the children?"

"You have one particular family in mind?" His voice was warm and interested, giving her the courage to continue.

"I suppose I do, although naturally I'm concerned for all the affected families. But Naomi Miller—hers was one of the first interviews I did. Two of her three children have Crigler-Najjar disease." She forced herself to be honest. "She is a friend. And my brother is marrying her husband's sister, so naturally, that is a personal interest."

"Nothing wrong with that," he said quickly. He reached out, as if he'd pat her hand, and then seemed to reconsider. "Many of us have personal reasons for becoming involved in a particular line of research. My younger sister was a Down's syndrome child, and she died when she was eight."

"I'm sorry for your loss." Her heart filled with sympathy. So that was what drove him—not just science, but love for a small sister.

He nodded. "I don't tell that to many people." He looked a little surprised at himself. "But even though research doesn't bring about instant results, every small step forward brings us nearer the goal of healthy children." He waved his hands, and she saw the light of passion in his eyes. "There are so many things that can make a difference. Genetic counseling, early testing, even organ transplants . . . Those solutions are here already, and there are more to come."

She nodded, moved by his obvious dedication.

"Your brother and his fiancée should come in for genetic counseling, if they're willing. It may not make a difference in their choices, but at least they'll know what the risks are."

That was a positive step, as the doctor said.

"I'll talk with them about it. Perhaps I can persuade them."

"You do that. I imagine if anyone can, it's you."

She blinked. "Why would you think that?"

"Because you are the teacher. You're a person who affects many lives. If you urge your people to have genetic counseling or to have their babies tested immediately after birth, they'll listen to you."

"I'm not so sure of that."

"I am." He touched the forms she held. "Look at the progress you've made already. You're reaching families who would never talk to us.

That's important." He did pat her hand then. "I'm not saying that to make you feel prideful, as you Amish would say. I'm telling you that because you are doing good, important work that could touch lives in ways you can't imagine right now."

"I hope what you say is true." Perhaps, as the Scripture said, she was planting a seed, even if she wouldn't be there to see the harvest.

"It's what keeps me going." He stood, giving her a smile that made him look younger than his years.

The door behind him swung open, and John came in quickly, checking at the sight of them. "I didn't mean to interrupt . . ."

"You're not, you're not." Dr. Brandenmyer glanced at his watch. "I must be off. I have patients." He hurried off toward the exam rooms of the clinic.

John looked at Leah with a quizzical expression. "It's not often Dr. Brandenmyer slows down for a private conversation."

"He was asking how I like the work." Actually, the doctor had given her a new image of herself and what she might do, and she wanted to consider that privately. "How are you?"

"Great." He smiled, looking more relaxed and open than she'd seen since he'd returned. "I can't tell you how much it meant to see Rachel again." He shook his head. "Hard to believe she's a wife and mother. I wish I could meet my nieces and nephew."

"Maybe that will come, in time."

"Maybe. Anyway, I owe you, Leah. Not just for making the arrangements, either. For helping me not to let pride interfere."

She smiled in return. "I seem to recall you often needed someone to do that."

"Good thing I had people who cared enough about me to do it."

She suddenly realized that she was at ease with him. With who he was now, not just thinking about who he used to be. That was another step forward, wasn't it?

"*That's* all you managed to get this week?" Stacie's voice was sharp.

Maybe she had honestly expected more interviews from Leah. Or perhaps her current ill will had been caused by having seen Leah in conversation with Johnny.

"I had other responsibilities this week." She had no intention of betraying to Stacie that some of those responsibilities had involved Johnny. "And now that I'm going to the farther-off homes, I can't do as many in a day."

"If you took a car, you could do more."

Stacie seemed to have forgotten that she was a volunteer. "I'm afraid I can't afford to hire a car each time I make a visit."

Stacie looked momentarily abashed. "No, I guess not."

She frowned down at the forms for a moment, but Leah had the feeling she wasn't really concentrating on them. Her lips were pressed tightly together, as if she were holding something back.

She flipped a page over and slapped her hand down on it. "Maybe if you weren't spending so much time with John, you'd be able to accomplish more."

For a moment Leah stared at her. How open could she be with Stacie? She didn't know anything about Stacie's background or family, and she couldn't imagine how she'd lived her life.

But the emotion she felt now was surely common enough to both Amish and English.

"I'm afraid you have a mistaken idea about the two of us." Leah kept her voice quiet, not wanting to be seen as confronting the woman. "There is nothing between John Kile and me but an old friendship."

Stacie's eyes narrowed. "Is that why he went off someplace to meet you the other day?"

So Stacie had somehow gotten hold of that, but she obviously didn't know that the meeting had been between John and his sister, not between John and Leah. It was easily explained, but if John hadn't chosen to confide in her, Leah could hardly do it for him.

"That was not . . ." She hesitated, not sure what to say. "That was not personal. I'm still close with his family, you know."

Stacie sniffed. "Tell that to someone who might believe it. The only reason you're here is John."

Funny, she was getting the same response from the English at the clinic as she had from some of her own people. But she didn't feel like laughing.

"John is the person who asked me to volunteer, that's true," she said carefully. "But I've continued with it because it's important work, not because he's here."

Stacie slapped her hands down on the desk in the gesture that seemed to be habitual with her. "Maybe you really believe that, or maybe you don't. But I've seen the way John looks at you." Her face twisted a little, and she was suddenly vulnerable. "He has feelings for you."

"No. No, he doesn't." All she could think was to deny it. It wasn't true. It couldn't be, because if it was, her life would be complicated beyond belief.

Stacie ran her fingers through her hair, shaking her head. "Okay, maybe you really haven't seen it. But trust me, he's completely different when he talks to you than he is with anyone else."

Relief washed through Leah. "But that is because we are old friends. The bond between us goes deep. And I am Amish."

Stacie shrugged. "So what? He gave all that up years ago."

It seemed impossible to make Stacie understand, but she had to try. "He left the church, but a person can't stop being Amish so easily. If you met someone who'd grown up in . . . in Africa, for example, you wouldn't expect that person to be able to turn off how he was raised in the flick of a switch, would you?"

"I guess not." The admission was grudging. "But John didn't grow up in another country."

"His life is closer to that than to anything else you might imagine. He didn't learn English until he went to school, for instance. All the things you take for granted"—she waved her hand toward their surroundings—"the computers, the television, the cell phones, the constant information about the outside world. Try to imagine growing up without ever being exposed to that."

"I can't." Stacie's gaze met hers, and for the first time, there seemed to be no antagonism in it. "I guess that means I can't ever really understand him."

"You care about him." Leah said the words softly. "That's all that's important."

Stacie shook her head a little sadly. "I used to think that. But he doesn't seem to see me that way. And nothing you've said changes the fact that he has feelings for you. Not for me."

"No." Denying it might not convince Stacie, but maybe it would reassure her. Because if Johnny really did have feelings for her—

A flicker of panic went through Leah. She couldn't deal with that. Not again.

Daniel smoothed the sheet over Elizabeth's shoulders. Her face was relaxed in sleep, clearly visible in the light of the full moon pouring through her bedroom window.

She stirred a little, as if she felt his touch, and then slipped deeper into slumber. Heart full, he turned and walked softly across the hall to check on his sons.

Jonah slept on his side, one hand under his pillow. But Matthew knelt by the window, a piece of paper in front of him on the sill.

"Was ist letz?" Daniel whispered, tiptoeing to the window. "What's the matter? Why are you still awake?"

Matthew moved his hand over the paper. "The moon is so bright, I couldn't go to sleep."

Daniel knelt beside the boy, resting his hand on Matthew's shoulder. "What are you writing?"

He could feel tension in his son. "It's a drawing."

"A drawing of what?"

Matthew hesitated. Finally he pushed the paper over to Daniel. "For when we bring the hay in next time. To use with the generator, is all. Not electric."

For a moment Daniel struggled to keep from crumpling the paper. Would the boy's interest in mechanics never leave? He took a deep breath, trying to come up with the right thing to say.

Matthew must have sensed his negative reaction. He pulled back. "It's not electric, Da."

He wanted to shut down the idea. But even as his hand tightened on the paper, he seemed to hear Leah's voice in his head, telling him to listen, to talk, to explain instead of order.

He smoothed the paper out, studying the detailed drawing, and his admiration for his son grew. How many ten-year-olds could come up with something like this?

"I see." He tried to sound neutral. "What made you think about this? Because you like machines?" *Things that pull you toward the English world?*

Matthew eyed him warily. "It's hard to run the farm mostly by yourself, with only me. Jonah's too little to do much. I thought this would help us do more."

For a moment Daniel couldn't speak. His throat was too tight.

He ruffled his boy's hair, feeling the fine strands under his fingers. "That's smart thinking, Matthew."

The tension left the boy's face. "You think so, Daadi? It's not against the Ordnung. Even the Beilers use one, Mahlon says."

"I know." He hesitated. Leah would say this was a moment he should use to teach his son. "You understand why some things are against the Ordnung, don't you? Because they might take us away from our family and our church, or connect us too much to the outside world. The rules aren't meant to punish us, but only to keep us from being worldly. You understand?"

Matthew studied on it for a moment. "It's hard, isn't it, to figure out why some things are okay and some aren't?"

Daniel nodded. "That's why the whole church will talk and talk about a new thing, trying to figure out what God's will is for us, until Bishop Mose helps us come to an understanding."

Matthew nodded slowly, and Daniel had the sense that he was pondering something deeper.

"Daadi—" He stared down at his hands, clasping the windowsill. "Is that why you didn't try to get us back?"

Daniel's heart stopped, as if it had turned to a chunk of lead in his chest. "Is that—" He had to stop and clear his throat. "Is that what you think? That I didn't try to find you?"

He hadn't talked about it when they'd come home, thinking that it would be like probing an open wound. Better to try to forget, he'd told himself. But Matthew, at least, hadn't forgotten.

"Did you?" Matthew glanced at him then.

"I looked," he said, his voice hoarse. "You know that we don't go to the law to settle disputes among ourselves, but that doesn't mean I didn't look. I thought, if I could find you, maybe I could talk to your mamm about coming home."

Should he have done more? Could he have? The questions haunted him.

"Matthew, didn't you know I loved you and would look for you?"

Matthew's gaze met his then, his eyes wide in the moonlight. "I thought so. But Joe—he was one of Mammi's friends—he said you'd have forgotten about us, and when you didn't come—"

Daniel grabbed his son, pulling him tightly against him. "I love you." He muttered the words against the boy's silky-fine hair. "Don't ever think that I could forget you. I never stopped thinking about you for a single moment when you were gone."

Matthew's arms wrapped around him. "I missed you, Da."

"I missed you, too." He kissed his son's forehead. "But now you're here, and we're together." He cupped Matthew's face in his hands, looking at him seriously. "Always. I promise."

Matthew nodded, a smile trembling on his lips. "Always."

Daniel blinked away tears. "Ser gut," he said softly. "Now I think you should be in bed."

Matthew stood and then paused, turning toward the window. "Daadi, that sounds like a buggy on our lane."

The boy's ears, quicker than his, had caught it first, but now he could hear the clop of hooves and the creak of a buggy. Who would be coming at this time of night?

"To bed with you. I'll take care of it." He started toward the door, mind churning. People didn't come calling this late on a summer night. Was something wrong?

CHAPTER SEVENTEEN

A sound woke Leah from the fringes of sleep. She shifted in the bed, puzzled. What had that been? Not one of the usual noises, or it wouldn't have wakened her.

Moonlight still poured through the window, so it wasn't very late. It felt as if she'd just gotten to sleep, in fact. Perhaps it was Anna, coming home. Had Daad talked to her yet? What had he said? More importantly, would it do any good?

She shoved her heavy braid back over her shoulder and settled her head on the pillow again. If it was Anna, Leah wouldn't get any thanks for showing concern.

The sound came again, but this time, awake, she could identify it. Gravel. Someone had thrown a handful of gravel at her window.

She slid from the bed and ran barefoot to the window, her heart thudding. She wasn't a seventeen-year-old, expecting a sweetheart to wake her for a late-night talk. Something was wrong.

She shoved up the window and leaned out. Below her, silhouetted clearly in the moonlight, stood the horse and buggy Anna had taken when she'd left tonight. Anna was a huddled, dark figure on the seat.

A man stood looking up at her window, his face a pale oval in the moonlight. It was Daniel.

If he spoke, she couldn't hear him for the rush of blood thudding in her ears. "What's happened? What's the matter?" She whispered the words, praying no one else would hear.

Daniel seemed to glance at the other windows of the sleeping house, then at the figure on the seat. Anna didn't move. He looked up at her again and gestured for her to come down.

She waved to signify that she understood. Ducking back inside, she grabbed a shawl from its hook and threw it around her. No time to worry about her hair, tumbling in a braid to her waist, or her bare feet and nightgown. Something had happened to Anna.

She fled silently down the stairs, her mind a jumble of prayers. *Please, Father, please, Father, help her. Help us.*

No sound broke the stillness of the house as she hurried through the kitchen to the back door. Levi and Barbara were sound sleepers, and their windows faced the other way. And Mamm and Daadi were staying at Joseph and Myra's tonight to get an early start going to market tomorrow, so the daadi haus was empty.

She swung the door open carefully, mindful of its creak, and hurried across the porch and down the steps to where Daniel waited.

"What are you doing here? What's happened to Anna?" She threw the questions toward him in a hoarse whisper as she hurried past him to the buggy. "Anna—" She reached for her sister.

Anna, slumped against the seat, didn't stir. She turned to Daniel, furious that he just stood there. "She's hurt or sick—"

"She's drunk," he said, his voice low and flat. "Asleep by now, and you won't be able to wake her anytime soon."

Not content with his explanation, she climbed the buggy step to get close to her sister. "Anna," she said again, pulling at her arm.

Anna moved her head a little, seeming to attempt to rouse herself, and then sank back against the seat again, letting out a small snore. With it came the stench of alcohol.

Leah stared at her for a long moment. Then she stepped down again, turning to Daniel. She could only pray that in the dim light, he wouldn't be able to tell how embarrassed she was.

The horse shifted a little, probably wondering why he was standing here instead of being turned into his comfortable stall. The crickets, their noise interrupted for a few moments by the goings-on, began their ceaseless chirping again.

She took a breath. "How is it you're bringing her home?" Daniel would hardly have been wherever it was Anna had been drinking.

"I heard her buggy coming down my lane." He stepped closer, whispering. "She near enough put it in the ditch before I got to her."

Tears stung Leah's eyes—for her sister and the trouble she was in, for herself and her inability to protect Anna. "Denke," she murmured. "It is kind of you—"

"That can wait." He clasped her wrist, holding it loosely in one strong hand. "We're got to get her settled before the whole house is awake. Can we get her to her room?"

Why he was helping, when he so clearly disapproved of Anna, she couldn't imagine, but she was grateful. She'd never be able to manage on her own.

"No." Her mind raced. "The daadi haus. My parents are away for the night. If we can get her in there, she'll be all right for the moment." She turned, starting to climb into the buggy. "I'll get her—"

Daniel clasped Leah by the waist and lifted her down. "She's too heavy for you." He climbed up in one long stride, leaned over, and slid his arms around Anna, pulling her to the edge of the seat and then lifting her down.

She lolled in his arms like a rag doll, her unbound hair falling to cover her face.

Anna, what were you doing? Where is this going to end?

"This way." She led the way quickly across the grass toward the daadi haus, safely away from the vicinity of Levi and Barbara's bedroom. She was thankful, in a numb sort of way, for his help. She could never have carried Anna's dead weight on her own.

They went quickly up the stairs, with a little less need to be silent here. Leah pushed open the door to the small extra bedroom, thanking God that the moonlight was still so bright. She hadn't had to put on the gas lamps and risk waking anyone.

Daniel carried Anna's inert figure to the bed and put her down. She wore English clothes, of course. Blue jeans and sneakers, with a knit shirt so short it showed a strip of bare skin.

Leah pulled a coverlet over Anna. She'd have to get her changed, but that could wait until she'd gotten rid of Daniel. He'd seen enough of her family's troubles for one night.

She straightened, well aware that it was impossible to look dignified in her bare feet and nightgown, with her baby sister lying there drunk.

"You've been most kind, Daniel. I'm grateful. I can take care of everything now."

And if he'd just go away home, she could stop wondering what he must think of them.

Not that it was all that unusual for Amish boys to have a drink too much during their rumspringa, but folks were much less likely to turn a blind, indulgent eye when it was a girl.

If Daniel was aware of her embarrassment, he gave no sign. "I'll take care of the horse and the buggy for you. You'll have your hands full enough here."

Was there no end to the things for which she would owe him gratitude?

"It's gut of you," she said, clasping her hands together to still their trembling. "I don't want to keep you away from the children any longer—"

"My mamm is there, remember?" He turned away, giving her the ghost of a smile. "I'll tend to things outside, and then I'll come back to the daadi haus porch. Come down if you can, just to let me know everything is all right."

She managed to nod, managed to smile. But she didn't think "all right" was going to describe anything about her life very soon.

Anna didn't wake as Leah pulled off her clothes, finding the task harder than she'd expected as she fumbled with the unaccustomed fastenings. Finally she got the jeans off and pulled one of Mamm's nightgowns over Anna's head.

How they were going to explain Anna being in the daadi haus, she didn't know, but that was a problem for later. Now she had to see Daniel again and send him off home.

She bundled the English clothes into a pillowcase and stuffed it into the bottom of the chest of drawers. Then she hurried back down the stairs as quickly and quietly as possible.

She peered through the glass of the door to the back porch. A tall form emerged from the darker shadows of the lilac bush.

She opened the door and beckoned to him. "Come into the kitchen," she whispered. They'd been wonderful lucky already, and she didn't want to risk rousing the house when they were so near done.

She was aware of him behind her, a tall, silent shape that sprang to life when she turned up the gas light in the kitchen, thankful that the windows faced away from the main house.

She took her time turning toward him, not eager to hear his disapproval of Anna and her behavior. But when she looked up at him, she didn't see anything but concern in his expression.

"I don't know how to tell you how much this means," she began, but Daniel shook his head.

"It makes no trouble," he said, his voice low, as if the silence around them impelled him to be quiet even if no one could hear. "I cleaned up the buggy as best I could without drawing any attention to the stable."

"There was no damage?"

"None that I could see. I don't think anyone will notice that anything happened." He fell silent, but he looked at her steadily, as if waiting.

Waiting to hear what she would do. He was willing to let her handle it, it seemed, but he probably doubted her ability.

Well, fair enough. She doubted it, too.

"I talked to my daad about Anna." She pulled the shawl tighter around her, needing its warmth. "I hated to burden him, but I couldn't take the responsibility on myself any longer."

"You did the right thing, Leah." His response was quick and comforting.

Her fingers tightened on the soft fabric of the shawl. "Did I? I hoped it would make a difference—that Anna would change once Daad talked to her. And then she goes and does something ferhoodled like this."

Tears welled in her eyes, and she fought to blink them back.

Daniel took a step closer, his hand going out to encircle hers. His grip warmed and comforted her. "As much as you love your sister, you can't take the responsibility of trying to be her mamm."

She resisted the impulse to lean on his strength. "There are so many years between us—by the time another girl baby came along, I was old enough to be the little mother to her. I guess I still feel that way."

"That's only natural. And with your mamm's sickness, you've tried your best to spare her from worry."

"Right now I don't feel as if I've done a very gut job."

His fingers smoothed the skin on the back of her hand, as if he gentled one of the children with his touch. "You've done your best. Anna is old enough now to bear the consequences of her actions herself."

Leah looked up, very aware of how close he was. "Yet you were ready to help me cover for her."

"I was." He looked a little surprised at his own actions. "There seemed no need to let your brother and sister-in-law in on it. Besides, I owe you."

"Owe me? If you're talking about Elizabeth, I just encouraged her to talk."

He shook his head. "Elizabeth, but not only her. There's Matthew, too."

"What about Matthew?" Much as she'd like to help Matthew adjust to his new life, she couldn't see that she'd done much there.

"Things came to a bit of a head with the boy." He looked down at their clasped hands, but he seemed to be seeing something else. "I felt— well, I almost reacted the wrong way, but I thought about what you would do and say. That you'd say it was better to listen, no matter how hard it was to hear what my son had to say."

"And you did?" She had trouble concentrating on his words, too aware of the way his fingers traced circles on the back of her hand.

"Ja." His brows drew together. "It wasn't easy to hear, for sure. Matthew— I guess he thought I didn't care for the children enough to fight to get them back."

Her heart clenched with pain for him. "He must know you love them. Deep inside, I'm sure all three of them have no doubt about that." Now it was her turn to want to comfort him.

His fingers tightened on hers. "I hope so. If I should lose them again—"

That was the fear in his heart, she realized. Deep down, what terrified him was the thought that once his children were old enough to choose, they'd leave.

She clasped his hand in both of hers, hoping he could feel her caring. "It will be all right. They're doing better all the time, really they are."

"Because of you."

Their fingers entangled, and Leah's breath hitched at the sudden passion in his voice. "I haven't done much."

"You've understood. And you've made me see how much they need a mother."

Her heart was thudding so loudly that she could hear it, beating in her ears. A step would close the distance between them. A word of encouragement, and Daniel would propose. She could almost hear the words, and panic flooded her.

She couldn't. She couldn't let him take such an irrevocable step, not when she wasn't ready to give him an answer.

She took a cautious breath and then a deliberate step back. "The children are very dear to me." She loosed her hands, and he let her go instantly. "But it is late now, and I should check on Anna."

"It is late. I must go." But his gaze held hers for a long moment, and the unspoken question seemed to sizzle in the air between them.

He hesitated a moment longer. Then he nodded and went quickly out.

Leah glanced across the crowded kitchen at Rachel's house. The group of women had been there since five this morning, making sandwiches for a hoagie sale to help with medical costs for Naomi Miller's children.

The volume of chatter continued unabated, as it had since before sunrise. White kapps fluttered like so many birds in flight around the long tables that had been set up in the farmhouse kitchen. In all that time, Anna had managed never to look at her.

It had been that way for the entire uncomfortable week. Daad had been upset to hear what Leah had had to say, Anna had avoided speaking to her, and she had been haunted by the memory of what had nearly happened between her and Daniel.

Mamm handed her a hoagie. She rolled it in wax paper and secured it with tape, then added it to the waiting cooler. She stole a glance at her mother's face. It was as serene as ever, her eyes intent upon her task.

At least Mamm didn't know about any of it, so there was nothing to worry her. Daadi had decided that the situation with Anna was best handled by him. And she certainly hadn't confided her thoughts about Daniel to anyone.

"Anna has been very quiet today."

That jerked Leah's gaze back to her mother. Was there a concern hidden in that comment? Or was it her own sense of guilt at keeping something from Mamm that made her feel so?

"Is she?" She wrapped the next hoagie. "She's been busy, I guess." She managed a smile. "And she's not at her best in the morning, is she?"

Mamm shook her head, smiling a little. "Remember how hard it was to get her out of bed when she was little? That must be it."

"I'm sure it is." *I wish it was.*

Mamm sighed a little. "I'd like it fine if she'd just settle down to one sweetheart." She lowered her voice under the chatter of women around them. "Do you think she likes Jonas Stoltzfus?"

"I'm afraid she finds Jonas a little—well, too settled and serious for her." Actually, Anna had said that Jonas was as dull as dishwater, which didn't say much for Mamm's matchmaking hopes.

"Settled and serious are good things in a husband. Anna's trouble is that she doesn't think about what her life will be like a few years down the road, when she has a home and children to care for."

"Maybe in a year or two she'll start looking at it that way."

"Maybe so, but it's time already for her to think of something besides running with her friends." Mamm used a table knife to stuff the sandwich filling into the roll a little more emphatically than was necessary. "A girl her age should be thinking of marriage."

It looked as if Mamm had been worrying about Anna despite all their efforts to shield her. "She might be waiting to fall in love first."

Anna's words echoed in Leah's mind. Anna already thought she might be in love with that English boy.

"Falling in love is wonderful gut, but it's not everything." Mamm's expression grew reminiscent. "Your father and I didn't really understand what love was until we'd been married a few years and gone through some trials together."

"You and Daadi are special. Anna—well, Anna doesn't think of marriage that way."

"And what about you, Leah?" Her mother's gaze probed, seeming to peel away the layers of her protection. "A gut marriage can be made without starting out as boy-and-girl sweethearts."

She could feel her cheeks growing warm. How much did Mamm know, or guess, about Daniel and her? "I . . . I don't . . ."

"It's all right." Mamm pressed her hand. "I don't mean to embarrass you, daughter. But think about it. Listen for God's guidance."

"I will." That she could promise, and it seemed to content her mother. She turned back to the sandwiches with a satisfied look.

How could her mother know what had nearly happened between her and Daniel that night? She couldn't, that was all. But Mamm seemed to have an extra sense where her daughters were concerned.

It was fairly obvious what her mother thought she should do. She herself wasn't so sure.

She'd gone over and over every word, every gesture. Sometimes she'd almost convince herself that she was imagining things, but then she'd remember the warmth of Daniel's gaze, the strength of his hands, and she'd be convinced again that she'd been right.

Daniel Glick would propose to her if she gave him the slightest encouragement. And she didn't have the faintest idea what she should do.

She'd decided, after Johnny left, that marriage wasn't for her, and she'd been content with that decision all these years. She hadn't been able to love Johnny enough to have the courage to leave or the strength to convince him to stay. How could she think she could love Daniel enough to be a mother to his children and a wife to him?

"Here is Daniel, come for his order," Mamm said. "You fix it for him, Leah. I'm ready for some coffee." She flitted away.

Mamm wasn't exactly being subtle. Leah could only hope Daniel would attribute her flushed cheeks to the warmth of the kitchen.

Daniel stepped aside to let the Klopp boys hurry past him with the boxes of orders for the men who worked at Bishop Mose's harness shop. Nodding and smiling to those he passed, he came straight to her table.

"Rachel said you'd fill my order." His smile grew warmer when he looked at her.

"Ja, I have it here." She pulled his slip from the pile and began to stack hoagies in a paper bag, trying to find something light to say to him. "You're surely not going to eat all these yourself."

He shook his head, leaning against the table so that he was close to her. "Some of the brothers have come to help with the first cutting of hay today. Mamm wanted to cook for them, but she has enough to do with the children. And they'll enjoy the sandwiches fine."

Since he didn't have a wife to make the lunch. Was that a reminder of his need? He was watching her with such warmth in the deep blue of his eyes that she lost count of how many sandwiches she'd put in the bag and had to start again.

"They'll like these," she said, rallying. "And the money goes to a good cause."

He nodded. "It's a joy to help."

"Ja." It was, wasn't it? That was woven deeply into their way of life, the joy and satisfaction that came from helping your brothers and sisters whenever they had need. And knowing that, in turn, if you needed, they would be there.

It was part of what she loved about being Amish, part of what made them belong to each other.

Maybe, if she were Daniel's wife, she'd lose this disturbing sense she had of never quite fitting. But was it fair to him to marry for a selfish reason?

She glanced at Daniel, and their gazes met. Tangled.

She took a strangled breath. The attraction was there, certain sure, even in the midst of a crowd. That was important to a marriage.

But love?

Daniel had given her the impression, through everything he said about his wife, that if he offered his hand, that didn't mean he was offering his heart.

Still, maybe that was for the best. Maybe, as Mamm had hinted, it was possible to build a good marriage anyway.

CHAPTER EIGHTEEN

Leah had gone to her room after supper, saying she had to work on her reports. That was true, but a stronger reason was to get away from the tension she seemed to feel everywhere she went lately.

The door opened before she had so much as looked at the first page. Anna stepped into the room, closing the door behind her.

The wave of gladness that swept through Leah was startling in its strength. Anna was ready to talk at last, and for a moment she dared hope that the old, easy relationship between them could be restored.

Anna took an impetuous step toward her. "How can you possibly be friendly with that man?"

It looked as if her hope had been a little premature. She tried to swallow her disappointment. "Come, sit down. If you're talking about John Kile, I've told you already—"

"Not John." Anna dismissed him with a wave of her hand. "Daniel Glick. I saw how you two were talking this morning."

"Daniel." She readjusted her thinking. "Why would you care if I'm friends with Daniel? I should think you'd be happy about it. Everyone else is busy trying to match us up."

"He fits right in with all the rest of the interfering busybodies." Anna's hands clenched against her skirt.

"If you're embarrassed because Daniel saw you . . ." She hesitated, not wanting to say the word. ". . . saw you the other night, you shouldn't blame him."

"I'm not embarrassed." But Anna's cheeks flushed slightly.

Leah longed to grasp the clenching hands in hers, wanted to smooth away the hurt and shame that her little sister surely was feeling. But

Anna wouldn't accept comfort from her now, and maybe she needed plain talking more than she needed comfort.

"I would say you owe Daniel your thanks. He found you, he helped you, and more than that, he kept silent about it."

"And now he can look down on me. I hate that he's involved."

When she was six, Anna would have sat in the corner for talking that way. Leah felt her exasperation rising. It was a pity that wouldn't work now.

"You were the one who involved him," she said flatly. "You got drunk, you drove into the wrong lane, you nearly ended up in the ditch. You should be on your knees thanking the Lord that it was Daniel who found you and not someone who'd be quick to spread the news all over the valley."

At last Anna's gaze evaded hers. Her cheeks flushed. "Maybe," she muttered. "But I still don't see why you're so close with him."

"I've helped with the children, as any neighbor would when there are motherless children."

Anna stared at her, eyes widening. "You're not thinking— Leah, you can't be thinking about marrying him just because his children need a mother!"

Now it was her turn to glance away. "He hasn't asked me," she said, knowing she was equivocating.

"How could you think of it? To marry a man you don't love— sometimes I think you don't even know what love is."

The control Leah had been exercising suddenly slipped away from her. She clenched her hands to keep from grabbing her sister and shaking her.

"And I suppose you know all about love at eighteen."

"More than you," Anna snapped back. "I said it before, and it's true. You don't have any feelings at all."

Leah did grab her then, startling herself as much as she did Anna. Grasping her sister's arms, she held her fast.

"How would you know what feelings I have? You don't spare a thought for anyone's feelings but your own. I know what it is to love and to lose and to spend your days trying to hide the pain. I don't need a child like you trying to give me lessons in what it is to love."

Anna stared at her for a moment, eyes wide in a white face. Then she jerked free and ran out of the room.

She might not feel at ease at the clinic, Leah decided, but at the moment, being here was better than being at home. She settled on a bench in the hallway, planning to go through her list of potential interviewees until her driver returned for her.

But her hands lay idle on the sheet. The days since that dreadful scene with Anna had been so strained that even Barbara, occupied as she was with her pregnancy, the house, and the children, had noticed it. Unfortunately her well-meant attempts to interfere had only made things worse.

Forgive me, Father. I sinned. I expressed anger with my sister instead of trying harder to help her. Now she won't even speak to me, and I fear I've driven her away. Please, forgive me and show me how to help Anna.

"Leah? Is something wrong?"

It was a measure of her distraction that she hadn't even heard Johnny approach. She shook her head, but the lump in her throat kept her from speech.

"I can see—" He stopped when a woman came out of the waiting room, leading a small boy by the hand. He waited until they'd left, then held out his hand to Leah. "We can't talk here. Come out to the back porch."

There wasn't anything Johnny could do. There wasn't anything anyone could do, but Leah couldn't resist the concern in his face. Avoiding his hand, she rose and walked down the hallway with him.

A couple of rocking chairs had been added to the back porch furniture. She sat down, pleating her skirt with her fingers.

"So tell me." Johnny sat down opposite, reaching out to still the nervous movement of her hand. "It must be something bad for you to look that way."

"It's Anna." It was a relief just to say the words. "I'm worried about Anna."

"What has Anna been up to that causes you this much distress?"

His voice, warm and gentle, was the voice of her friend, of the person she'd known and cared about her whole life. "Running around too much with her friends? Trying to land you with her chores?"

That coaxed a reluctant smile from her, but almost immediately it trembled from her lips. "If only it were that." She shook her head. "I know I can't expect her to have so tame a rumspringa as I did . . ."

He patted her hand. "No, I'm sure not." There was amusement in the tone.

She pulled her hand away, straightening. "Don't laugh. It's not funny." She looked at him, her eyes welling with tears. "Johnny, she came home so drunk that she was within inches of wrecking the buggy. Only the grace of God kept her from injury."

She was relieved to see that her words wiped the amusement from his face.

"I'm sorry, Leah. She wasn't hurt, though?"

"No. Oh, I suppose my brothers probably did as bad, but this is my baby sister."

"You've tried to talk to her?"

She felt the flood of sympathy, and it warmed her. "Tried and tried again. Daad has talked to her, too, with no results either. I'm afraid she's—"

She stopped, unable to put her fear into words.

"What?" His voice was gently insistent. "What do you think is going to happen to her?"

Her breath caught in her throat, and she had to force the words out. "I think she might leave."

He didn't immediately respond, giving her time to think that maybe Johnny wasn't the best person to talk to about this. After all, that was just what he'd done.

"I'm sorry," he said at last. "I know how scared that must make you."

"It does." The tightness in her throat eased just a little. "I don't begrudge her running-around time. I even understand it. And she's the baby, so maybe she's had her own way a little too much. But this—"

She stopped, shook her head. "I'm sorry. This is probably hard for you to talk about. I shouldn't burden you with it."

"You're not." He smiled slightly. "We're friends. Old friends, no matter what else happened. You can say anything to me, and I promise it won't go any further. You don't have to worry about that."

"I don't." She managed to return the smile. "I know I can trust you." Johnny wouldn't talk. And he wouldn't condemn, either.

"You've been keeping this to yourself. That only increases the worry." He shook his head. "Leah, you're always trying to take care of everyone. Look, what's the worst thing that could happen?"

"I could lose her." She looked at him steadily. *The way Rachel lost you. The way I lost you.* She wouldn't say it, but he must know she was thinking it.

"If she left . . ." He paused. "Maybe I'm not completely impartial, Leah. But would it be such a terrible thing? You could still have a relationship with her. Maybe that's what she needs to do."

"No!" She rejected that with every fiber of her being. "Anna is too young. She's rebellious, and she doesn't really understand what it would be like. Or what she'd be giving up."

He leaned back in the rocker, his gaze intent on her face. "Maybe so. But sometimes, for some people, it's the right thing to do."

"No. Not Anna." She had to cling to that, because the alternative was too frightening.

"Maybe you're right. Maybe Anna is too young, or thinking about it for the wrong reasons. But you're not too young, Leah. Is it possible you're so worried about Anna because you're thinking about it, too?"

She jerked back as if he'd hit her. "No. I'm not."

He brushed that aside with his hand. "Well, maybe you should be."

She started to rise. She didn't want to hear this, and all the comfort she'd felt from Johnny was gone in an instant.

He grabbed her hand. "Wait. Just let me say this one thing. Can't you do that?"

She sat, perched on the edge of the chair, ready to flee. "Go on."

"You're a good teacher, Leah." He leaned toward her, hands braced on his knees. "I know that. But think how much more you could do if you were able to develop your teaching gifts to the fullest. You could get a degree, you could learn all the latest methods, you could—"

She stood, shaking her head. "No. Don't. You have no right to say that to me, John."

"Why not?" He stood, too, and passion filled his voice. "I'm the person you said you loved once. Doesn't that give me a right to be concerned about you?"

Still shaking her head, she hurried to the door. "That was a lifetime ago."

"It's still true." His voice roughened. "Leah, let yourself think about it. Don't you fear that you aren't preparing your scholars for the world they have to live in? Haven't you thought that maybe the right place for you isn't here?"

She couldn't listen. She hurried through the hallway, out the front door, and down the steps to the parking lot where her driver was waiting.

But she couldn't outrun his words. They echoed in her heart, and she knew what she was afraid of. She was afraid they were true.

He'd been on the verge of proposing marriage to Leah. Daniel frowned down at the road disappearing under the wheels of his buggy. The night that he'd taken Anna home, those quiet moments in the kitchen together . . .

Leah had been the one to draw back. He could only be grateful for that. He'd known, in the clear light of day, that he'd almost acted on impulse, something he'd vowed never to do.

He should have been able to think the situation through and come to a sensible conclusion. That was the only way to approach marrying again. Practical. Logical. Make a decision on what would be best for himself and his children.

Unfortunately, every time he tried to do that, the memory of Leah's caring face, her vulnerable eyes, got in the way.

There was the lane leading to the schoolhouse, and sure enough, Leah's buggy stood at the hitching post. He'd stopped by the Beiler farm, and Barbara had been delighted to tell him that Leah had gone to the school to do some work on her teaching materials. Barbara had obviously hoped there was a romantic reason for his visit.

Romantic wasn't the word he'd have picked, he guessed. He had to talk to Leah, had to make a decision, one way or the other.

And then, of course, she'd have her say. He smiled ruefully as he stopped at the hitching post and climbed down. Maybe he was kidding himself even to think that her answer would be yes.

He went quickly to the open door and hesitated on the threshold. Without the children, the schoolroom was a little forlorn, as if it waited for their return.

Chiding himself for his fanciful thoughts, he stepped inside. Leah stood at her desk, a stack of books in front of her, watching him.

"Daniel. What brings you here?" She brushed a strand of hair back from her face and came around the desk toward him.

"I wanted to ask how things are going with Anna." He went toward her and rested his hand on the corner of the desk. "Each time I've seen you since then, there have been so many other people around that I didn't want to bring it up."

"I'm grateful for your silence. I told Anna she should be, too. There are others who'd have been hard put to hold their tongues if they'd found her that night."

"Judging by the cold shoulder she's given me each time I've seen her, I don't guess she feels very grateful about it."

"No. But she should." Leah's eyes darkened with worry, making her look vulnerable. "I don't understand her anymore. I never thought I would say that."

"Is she not sorry for what she did, then?" He'd think the embarrassment alone would be enough to bring the child to her senses.

"If she is, she's doing a fine job of hiding it." She smoothed the errant strand of hair back again. "All she seems to think about is going out with her friends."

"English friends." He filled in the word.

"I suppose so. She doesn't confide in me." A spasm of pain crossed her face as she said the words.

It made him want to put his arms around her, comfort her, tell her everything would be all right. But he couldn't. Because he didn't have the right, and because he couldn't be sure it would. He barely knew Anna, but he feared for her.

Leah sighed, shaking her head. "I'm sorry. I shouldn't have poured all that out to you. It's not your burden. It's ours."

True enough. But if he did ask her to marry him, Anna would become his problem, too. And there was something—something he felt driven to say, even if it made Leah angry.

"I'm sorry for your troubles. I wish I could be of more help."

She managed a smile, but the life seemed to have gone out of it. "You've already helped more than you know."

"If I have, I'm glad of it," he said. He hesitated. "There's something that's been on my mind since that night. And I don't know what to do except just to say it."

Her eyes grew wary. "I don't think—"

He shook his head, knowing he had to blurt the words out before he could change his mind. "Are you sure your work at the clinic isn't setting the wrong example for Anna?"

Leah's eyes widened with shock and pain, and the look cut him to the heart. But it had to be said, didn't it?

"I don't want to hurt you. But isn't it possible that she sees you spending time with the English, working with them, and thinks it's all right?"

"That's completely different!" Leah had recovered, and now it was anger that flashed in her green eyes. "I volunteer at the clinic because I want to help the children, and for no other reason."

"You didn't go there until John Kile came back." It couldn't be jealousy he felt when he said the fence-jumper's name.

"I didn't know that there was anything I could do until John told me about it." She threw the words back at him.

"You're there often, working with those people." He pushed doggedly on, even knowing he was antagonizing her with every word. "Maybe you've started enjoying it."

"And maybe you're talking about Ruth, not me." She looked shocked that the words had come out of her mouth.

No more shocked than he felt. For a moment he could only gape at her.

But he owed her an honest answer. "I guess what happened between me and Ruth affects how I look at it. But can you be sure I'm not right?"

She hesitated, her hands straining against each other. She took a deep breath. "I'd like to say that it's not your concern."

"That wouldn't be true, would it?" He took her tense hands in his. "We both know we've been moving toward something, Leah, even if no words have been spoken."

She stared down at their clasped hands for a moment. "You're saying that my work at the clinic is a barrier between us."

"I guess I am." He didn't want to draw a line between them, but what else could he say? No one could go through what he'd been through and come out unchanged.

She drew her hands away slowly. Her shoulders straightened. "I don't think I can be the woman you want, Daniel."

Her words, her voice, her expression all told him that that was an end to it.

CHAPTER NINETEEN

When she saw the headlights coming down the dark lane to the farmhouse, Leah knew deep in her soul that something bad had happened to Anna. Maybe it was that instinct, stronger than words, which had kept her awake this night.

Pulling her shawl tight around her, she pressed her face to the living room window. The lights belonged to a police car. She could make it out now, see the dome on its roof and the reflective letters on the side.

Her heart thundering in her ears, she ran toward the door that led out to the daadi haus, but before she could reach it, Daad was already there, pulling suspenders over his shoulders. His face was bleak.

"Anna," he said.

"She's not home." Leah's voice broke, and she clutched his arm. "She's not here. It must be—"

"Ja." His face tightened until the skin seemed stretched over the bones. "You should go and stay with your mamm."

Before Leah could move, her mother came in, clad like Leah in a nightgown and holding a shawl tightly around her, as if it would protect her from whatever was coming toward them.

"No need," she said. "I'm here."

Daadi patted her shoulder. "Go back, now. Let Leah stay with you until we know what is wrong."

She shook her head, her graying braids swinging. "I must hear it, Elias. She is my baby."

Footsteps echoed on the porch, heavy and authoritative. The knock on the door hammered against Leah's heart.

Mamm clung to Daad now, so Leah went to open it. The tall state trooper was young—young enough to look embarrassed at the sight of her in her nightgown.

"Is this the home of Anna Beiler?"

She stepped back, opening the door wide and gesturing for him to enter. "Yes." She struggled to catch her breath. "I am Leah Beiler, her sister. Our parents, Elias and Martha Beiler." She clutched her hands together, framing a wordless prayer. "Anna—how bad is it?"

He frowned, looking as if he were trying to remember whatever he'd learned about how to break bad news. "There's been an accident out on the Fisherdale Road—a car and a buggy. Anna—"

He stopped as Levi thudded down the stairs, followed by Barbara, voluminous in her nightgown. Mahlon came last, stumbling and rubbing his eyes.

"Was ist letz?" Levi said, face white. "What's the matter?"

"It's Anna." Leah was astonished that the words came out so calmly. "An accident."

"How bad?" Mahlon clutched the railing, looking young and scared. She turned back to the officer.

"Anna Beiler was injured," he said stiffly. "And three other people were hurt, too. They've all been taken to the county hospital. I have instructions to drive you people there."

"How bad is she hurt?" she said again. *Please, Lord, please don't take our Anna away.*

His official mask slipped a little, and she saw the conscientious young man beneath it. "I don't know, ma'am. Honestly. They didn't tell me that. Just to break the news and drive you." He glanced at her nightgown and then away. "I'll wait while you folks dress and take you in."

"Ja. We all go," Levi began, but Daadi shook his head at the words.

"No, no. Leah will go with us, to talk to the doctors. She'll understand better how to deal with them. Mahlon, you must hurry to tell Joseph, so they don't hear from someone else. And Levi, you fetch Bishop Mose and ask him to come to the hospital."

Mahlon looked as if he'd argue for a moment, but then he nodded. He ran upstairs.

"I'll dress and then help Mamm—" Leah began.

"I'll do that," Barbara said quickly. She gave her a gentle push. "You just get ready."

Nodding, Leah ran for the stairs, her mind spinning more rapidly than she could believe. She tried to grab on to something reassuring.

Injured. Anna was injured. It might not be serious—maybe nothing more than a broken bone.

And the others who were hurt—three, the policeman had said. What other families were getting a visit like this one right now?

Praying, the words tumbling over one another in her haste, Leah pulled her clothes on, fumbling with the straight pins that secured her dress.

Hurry, hurry. The words echoed to the thud of her heart. *Hurry.*

In moments she was racing back down the stairs again. Mahlon and Levi had already hustled out the back toward the stable. Better, as Daad said, to send them off to tell folks—better that than have them all tripping over each other at the hospital, waiting, not knowing . . .

Barbara came in with Mamm, and together they walked her out to the waiting police car. Barbara urged Mamm into the middle of the backseat, so that she'd have Daad on one side and Leah on the other.

Leah shot her a look of thanks. Barbara had her faults, maybe, as they all did, but she was steady and calm in a crisis.

The doors slammed, and the car pulled out. Mamm's hand closed tightly over Leah's. She wrapped it warmly in hers, wanting to say something encouraging, unable to think of anything.

All she could think of was Anna—of all that bright, eager life tumbled into a ditch someplace in the wreckage of her buggy.

Leah glanced toward the front of the police car. The dim lights on the dashboard showed her the young policeman's profile, his hands on the wheel.

"Do you know anything else about the accident? Were you there?"

"No, ma'am, I wasn't. All they told me was what I've told you." They reached the road, and the vehicle seemed to spring forward. "We'll be at the hospital in a few minutes, ma'am. The investigating officers will be there. They'll be able to answer your questions."

The car passed the turnoff to the Glick farm, and she could see that the house was dark and still. Daniel would be a tower of strength at a time like this. But Daniel wasn't there. Wouldn't be there.

Her father reached over to wrap his hands around theirs. "We must pray."

Nodding, Leah closed her eyes, letting the sound of her father's voice roll over her as he led them in prayer for Anna.

"*The* doctors are still running tests." The emergency room nurse gave them a look of such sympathy that Leah's courage failed her. She wouldn't look that way unless it was serious.

Please, Father. Give me Your strength, for I have none of my own.

The Lord must have heard her, since she didn't crumple to the tile floor, although her hands gripped the counter's edge so hard that it cut into her fingers.

"Can we see her?"

The woman consulted her computer. "It looks as if she's just been taken to a patient room. You can go up, and the doctor will tell you what they know so far."

Leah forced herself to ignore the stares of the English who sat in the waiting room. The nurse checked the room number and then pointed out the direction to the elevator. Putting her arm around her mother's waist, Leah led the way.

When they reached the proper floor, she had to urge Mamm forward out of the elevator. How long was Mamm going to be able to hold up? Her face was gray and drawn, and the hand that gripped Leah's strained.

She glanced at her father. Daad, always so strong and controlled, looked almost frail in this setting.

My parents are old. The thought shocked her. *They have grown old, and I didn't notice.*

Leah checked the room numbers and led the way down the hall. As they neared the room, a doctor strode out and then stopped at the sight of them.

"We are Anna Beiler's family." Leah spoke, because her parents seemed unable to do so. "Can you tell us how she is?"

He shot a glance over his shoulder into the room and then turned back to them. "We're still waiting for the results of some of the cranial tests we've run—an EEG, CAT scan . . ." He paused, looking at her doubtfully. "Do you understand what I mean?"

It wasn't the first time she'd encountered the assumption that the Amish were ignorant, and it probably wouldn't be the last.

"Yes, doctor. My sister has a head injury, and you are trying to determine the extent of the damage."

He nodded, looking relieved. "She's unconscious but stable right now. We're hoping surgery won't be necessary, but a lot depends on the results we see and on how she does during the next few hours."

He stepped to one side, clearing the doorway for them.

"You can go in and sit with her. Don't touch any of the equipment."

She bent her head in obedience and ushered Mamm and Daadi into the room.

Anna lay in the high metal bed, as still as if she lay in her coffin. Her head was bandaged, her face scraped and bruised. Machinery hummed and buzzed, and what seemed like dozens of tubes snaked around her. A nurse in blue scrubs appeared to be checking a monitor.

Leah felt her mother sag and grasped her waist, supporting her. "It's all right, Mammi. Look, we'll pull a chair over so you can sit right next to Anna."

The nurse gave a sympathetic smile and pushed a green plastic chair across the floor. "That's right, honey," she said. "Sit down right here. Don't try to wake her, but you can talk quietly to her. It might comfort her to hear your voice."

Mamm, given something positive to do, straightened and walked to the chair. Leaning forward, hand on the bed as if she wanted to touch Anna but didn't dare, she began to talk softly in the dialect that Anna would know, even if the nurse wouldn't understand.

Daad moved to the other side of the bed and clasped his hands, eyes closing, lips moving in prayer.

The nurse gave Leah an assessing look. "You'll make sure no one touches or bumps the equipment?"

She nodded.

"I'll have a couple more chairs brought in for you."

"Is there anything else we can do?"

The nurse shook her head. "Just wait, I'm afraid." She glanced at Leah's father. "And pray." She went out, leaving the door open.

The chairs arrived, and Leah persuaded Daadi to sit. Minutes ticked by. Anna didn't move.

Leah's heart seemed almost too full to pray, and she struggled to find the words.

Gracious Lord, extend Your hand to my little sister. Guide the doctors, and give her Your healing.

Her hands clasped tightly together, and she began to murmur the words of the Twenty-third Psalm, reaching for the comfort of the familiar, beautiful words.

Someone would come. Sometime, someone would come to tell them if Anna would live. If Anna would be whole again.

Finally a footstep sounded in the hall outside the door. She glanced up to see a uniformed figure peering in—the township police chief, face somber. He caught her eye and gestured.

With a murmured explanation, she went out to him, faintly relieved to see a face that was at least familiar. The People knew and respected Chief Walker—he was said to be both fair and kind.

"Teacher Leah, I'm sorry for the trouble that's come on you folks." He pushed his hat back on his head, his lean, weathered face worried. "How is your sister doing?"

"We don't know anything yet. The doctors are waiting for some test results."

He nodded. "Well, that's something. The other three young folks got off with minor injuries—a broken wrist, some cracked ribs."

She was ashamed to realize she hadn't given them much thought. "I'm glad of that."

"The folks in the buggy got off light, too. Lucky to escape with bumps and bruises."

For an instant his words didn't seem to register. She frowned, shaking her head a little. "I'm sorry, but what you do mean? Was someone in the buggy with Anna?"

His face changed, and he looked at her with what must be pity. She seemed to freeze. Something bad was coming. She knew it as surely as she'd known there was trouble when she saw the lights.

He cleared his throat. "I'm sorry. I thought you knew. Anna wasn't in the buggy. Anna was driving the car."

An abyss seemed to open before her. She reached behind her for the stability of the wall, pressing her hand against it as she tried to make sense of this.

"That . . . That can't be. I'm sorry, but someone has gotten it wrong. Anna left home in her buggy."

He shook his head, sorrow carving deeper lines in his face. "I'm sorrier than I can say for this, but Anna wasn't driving a buggy. I don't know where she left it. She was behind the wheel of the car when it sideswiped the buggy."

Leah grasped for sanity in a world gone askew. "But she doesn't know how. She doesn't have a license. Who would let her drive a car?"

"We both know she's not the first Amish teen to drive a car. It belonged to one of the other kids, so I suppose he let her drive it. I haven't gotten the whole story from the other teenagers yet, but you can be sure I'll keep after them until I have the truth."

He was trying to reassure her, she supposed, but she still grappled to get her mind around it all. "The buggy—who was the family?"

"Aaron Esch, his wife and two children. They live over toward Fisherdale. Not in your district, I guess, but I reckon you'd know them."

She nodded numbly. Before their district had gotten so large that it had to be split into two, the Esch family had been part of their church. Aaron was first cousin to Jonah Esch, whose children were her scholars.

"They were all right, you said?" She grasped for something hopeful in this dreadful situation.

He nodded. "Seems like Anna swerved, trying to avoid them, and lost control. The driver's side hit a tree. She had the worst of it."

"Ja." She glanced toward the room.

"I'm awful sorry," he said again. He shifted from one foot to the other. "I sure don't want to add to your troubles, but . . . well, maybe you should think about hiring a lawyer for Anna."

A wave of dizziness swept over her, and she fought it off. She had to hang on. The family depended on her.

She had to clear her throat before she could speak. "You know that it is not our way to go to the law."

"This time the law's going to come to you, I'm afraid. It seems like Anna's been doing a lot that's not your way. Now, you know I'm not one to come down hard on Amish youngsters who are just having fun during their rumspringa. But this time folks got hurt."

Pain had a stranglehold on her throat. She forced out the words. "What will happen to Anna?"

He shrugged. "Not really up to me. I just investigate it. The district attorney will have to decide whether he wants to prosecute."

Prosecute. The word had a terrifying sound.

The chief patted her hand. "You take my advice and talk to your folks about getting a lawyer for Anna. That's the best thing they can do right now." He settled his hat firmly on his head and walked off toward the elevator.

Leah sagged against the wall. She had to have a moment to gather herself before she could go back into the room. Had to think, had to decide.

But she knew that no matter how long she thought, she wouldn't come up with any satisfying way to tell her parents.

CHAPTER TWENTY

Daniel stepped off the elevator at the hospital. It wasn't hard to figure out where to go—a waiting room was spilling folks out into the hallway, as most of the church district seemed to be here to give support to the Beiler family.

That was the strength of being Amish. The People were always there for one another. Not saints, just ordinary folks with their share of faults, but when one was hurting, all were there to lend a hand.

He halted in the doorway, returning muted greetings and nods as his gaze searched the room for Leah. There she was, making her way from one person to another, probably expressing her parents' appreciation for their kindness.

Bishop Mose Yoder clapped him on the shoulder, a smile lighting his gentle face. "Have you heard the good news? Anna has been waking up, even talking to her mamm and daad. Praise God, it looks as if she will be well."

"That is good news." Daniel murmured a silent prayer. Both of them knew that even if Anna recovered physically, she'd have other troubles that needed praying for.

His gaze followed Leah's progress through the room. He'd had his final answer from her, but that didn't keep him from wanting to help her, as a friend and a neighbor, if nothing more.

She turned toward him, and he sucked in a sharp breath. Suffering had drawn her skin taut. Her eyes were dark and shadowed with it, and she looked as if she couldn't manage another word.

He slid through the crowd and took her arm. "Komm," he murmured, and led her out of the room, not caring what anyone thought of that.

The hallway wasn't much better, with people moving back and forth, soles squeaking on the tile floor. He steered her down the hall and around the corner. There was a small, empty room with benches, a sort of chapel, he supposed. He steered her inside and led her to a seat.

She sank down with a sigh and then looked at him with a question in her eyes. "Did you need to talk with me, Daniel?"

"Not as much as you needed to sit down and be quiet for a bit."

That startled the ghost of a smile from her. "They are being kind, but you're right. It is tiring to keep saying the same things over and over."

"I won't make you say them again to me, but I understand from Bishop Mose that Anna is waking up. That's wonderful gut news."

Her eyes lightened. "It is. She knows us, that's the important thing. The doctors say it looks as if she won't have to have surgery." She brushed away a tear that had spilled onto her cheek. "I know it's foolish of me, but I can't help wondering what people are saying about what she did."

He leaned toward her to take her hands in his. "It doesn't matter," he said firmly. "Whatever Anna did, once she confesses she will be forgiven and loved."

She nodded, her gaze downcast, as if she looked at their hands. "I know. Just as I know that everyone is helping. Mahlon told me that you'd been over to do the milking. Matthew, too."

"It's gut for the boy. It helps him to remember what it means to be Amish."

If it made her feel better to talk about that, he would oblige, but he couldn't help but see that thinking of Anna's confession before the church distressed her.

"The horse and buggy are back safe, too," he went on. "One of the Esch boys showed up with them this morning."

"Ser gut," she murmured, but he thought her mind was elsewhere.

"If you want to be by yourself—" he began.

Her fingers tightened on his. "No." The word came out quickly, and then she bit her lip. "I'm sorry. I shouldn't impose on you."

"You are not imposing." He cradled her hands in his, wishing he knew some way to ease the burden she carried. "You can say anything you want to me, Leah. It will go no further."

"I know." She looked at him then, her eyes dark with misery. "The police chief talked to me last night. He said that Anna may have to face charges in a court." Tears spilled over again. "I don't know what to do." Her voice dropped to a ragged whisper. "I don't know how to help her."

Her pain pummeled his heart. He moved to the bench next to her. Tentatively, he put his arm around her, intent only on giving comfort.

She turned into his shoulder, her tears wetting his shirt. Her whole body shook with the sobs.

He stroked her back, murmuring softly to her as he would to one of the children. "It will be all right."

That was the best thing to say right now. The only thing. He just prayed that it was true.

Leah frowned down at the quilt patch she was piecing as she sat in Anna's hospital room. She'd have to take those erratic stitches back out again. It was surely true that they reflected her state of mind.

She glanced at her sister. Anna napped, face turned away from her. In the three days that had passed since the accident, things had settled into a more normal routine. She, Mamm, and Daad had taken turns being here at the hospital, but it had been a battle to convince Mamm that she didn't have to be with Anna twenty-four hours a day.

The plain truth was that every time Leah heard a step in the hallway, she feared it might be the police. The prospect of her sister being charged hung over her, and she still didn't feel they'd gotten from Anna a complete story of what had happened. If the worst came, somehow they must try to protect Mamm.

Leah couldn't think about that trouble without remembering weeping in Daniel's arms. He'd comforted her without question when that was what she'd needed. She'd never realized before how much it meant to have someone to lean on.

She stared down at the quilt patch. Her life still resembled a crazy quilt rather than this neat arrangement of geometric shapes.

Was her volunteer work at the clinic really so important that she couldn't give it up for the sake of marriage to a good man? For the sake of those children she already loved?

Maybe the truth was that she was afraid. Afraid she'd fail at loving, as she had with Johnny.

Not that Daniel was offering love. Everything else—a stable life, children, a home, support, and security. But not love.

Anna moved slightly in the bed. Her eyes flickered open, then shut again at the sight of Leah.

Leah touched Anna's hand, shaking off her own perplexities. This time, perhaps, she could get the full story from her sister. Anna couldn't keep escaping into sleep. She had to face the situation.

"How do you feel?"

"Tired. I need to sleep some more." Anna kept her eyes closed. She'd done that as a child, refusing to face doing something she didn't want to do.

"You've slept enough," Leah said briskly, pushing the button to elevate the head of the bed. "The nurses say you should be getting up more now. You need to get your strength back."

"I don't want to." Her eyes snapped open, and she frowned at Leah. "Where's Mamm?"

"Home, getting some rest, I hope."

Anna had grace enough to look a little embarrassed at the reminder. "Is she all right?"

"As all right as she can be under the circumstances." They both knew that Mamm was troubled by more than Anna's being hurt.

Anna's fingers pleated the edge of the sheet. "What about—what about the other people in the accident? How are they?"

It was the first time Anna had seemed willing to have a real conversation about what had happened. That was a good sign, surely.

"The Esch family is fine, they say. Just some bumps and bruises. Daad is making arrangements to have their buggy fixed."

Anna smoothed out the pleats. "And the others?"

"Your English friends were not badly hurt. They've all gone home from the hospital."

"Have any of them come to see me?"

"No." Better the plain truth than soft evasions. None of the English teens who'd been with her that night had come to see her.

"They—they want to. I know that."

Leah couldn't say the words that trembled on her lips about the kind of friends who had led Anna into such trouble and then left her there. That would only make her sister more defensive.

"Maybe so," she said, her tone neutral. "Everyone from the church has been here, though, at one time or another. And brought food to the house, and took over the chores for Daad and Levi so they could be here."

Anna nodded, head down.

Leah felt exasperation mixed with the love she had for her sister. "Anna, why did you do it? Did the others talk you into driving that car?"

"Nobody talked me into it." She stared at Leah, her face set. "I wanted to. It's not so bad. I'll bet the boys drove cars lots of times."

"If they did, at least they never had an accident. That buggy—" Her throat tightened. "Anna, don't you see how dangerous it was? If you'd hit the buggy full on, that family would be having a funeral right now. You of all people should know what to watch out for."

Anna's lips trembled, and her eyes filled with tears. "I didn't mean to drive too fast. The car just went so easy when I touched the pedal. All of a sudden I saw the reflector on the buggy, coming up so fast. I swerved to avoid it, Leah. I did."

In that instant she was Leah's baby sister again. Leah bent over the bed, putting her arms around Anna in a fierce hug. "I know. I know you're sorry for what you did."

For an instant Anna clung to her. Then she stiffened and pulled away.

"Well—I'm sorry they got hurt. But I bet lots of people have accidents when they're learning to drive."

In other words, she wasn't sorry about driving the car. Leah grasped the bed railing. "You're not lots of people, Anna. You're Amish. We don't drive cars."

Anna didn't respond. She averted her face, staring out the window.

The closeness Leah had felt with her sister disappeared as quickly as leaves blown by the wind. With her face set and averted, in her print hospital gown, Anna looked like a stranger.

Leah should talk to her. Should try to impress on her how wrong she'd been, how much trouble she might be in.

She looked at the sister she no longer seemed to know. Would anything she said reach her? Or was it too late?

With Anna taking refuge in sleep again, Leah headed for the elevator. Maybe a cup of hot coffee and a few minutes out of the hospital room would ease some of the tension.

She rounded the corner and came to a stop. John Kile stepped off the elevator. He carried a tissue-wrapped bunch of flowers in one hand.

"I know." He smiled with a touch of regret. "You're going to say that it's not a good idea for me to visit Anna."

"No. I was just going to say that I'm surprised to see you here. But it is kind of you." Her throat choked with tears. What was wrong with her that she allowed simple gestures of kindness to affect her so? "I'm sorry—" The rest of the words wouldn't come out, not without tears, in any event.

John grasped her elbow and piloted her through the nearest door. It was the same meditation room where Daniel had brought her for refuge. John took her to the nearest bench. The same bench.

He sat down next to her, laying the flowers aside and taking both her hands in his. "Don't take it so hard. Please, Leah. I know Anna is your baby sister, but she's not your responsibility."

For a moment she just took comfort from the gentleness of his touch and the caring that was obvious in his voice. Then the words penetrated, and she shook her head.

"That's what makes her my responsibility, no matter how old she is." Her voice might be wavering a little, but she was sure. She looked at Johnny, the tears wet on her cheeks. "Don't you know that?"

He blinked. "I didn't mean— Well, of course you love her and want to take care of her. But Anna's eighteen now. You have to let her make her own choices."

Part of what he said was right. But part of it was wrong. Anna was and would always be her baby sister, and she could never stop trying to protect her and take care of her. That was what siblings did.

If she said that to him, it would be the same as telling him that he'd let his sister down, and she couldn't do that, not when he and Rachel were just beginning to restore their relationship.

He seemed to take her silence for agreement. "You'll see. She'll come out of this a stronger, better person."

Anna needed to come out of it a humbled, repentant person, but Johnny had gone far from that Amish viewpoint, it seemed.

He stroked her hands gently. "Leah, I didn't really come here because of Anna. You must know that. I came because of you."

"Because you're my friend."

"Because I have feelings for you." His grip tightened, and he leaned toward her, face intent. "Maybe the timing's bad, but I can't hold this back any longer. I still care about you. I knew that the minute I saw you again. We were always meant to be together. You know that, don't you?"

She could only stare at him, her mind spinning hopelessly out of control.

"You feel the same way, I know you do." He sounded exactly like the young, impetuous Johnny of ten years ago. "I was going to give it more time, but I can't. Dr. Brandenmyer has offered me a two-year contract, and I have to give him an answer. I know you wouldn't want to stay here, but we can go away together. We can get married, you can go to school, we can travel—we can do all the things you've always just dreamed about."

The spinning stopped. Certainty pooled in her heart and mind. Somehow, in these past difficult days, she'd come to know where she belonged. She knew the place to which God had called her.

Maybe Johnny understood before she even spoke, because the eagerness faded from his eyes.

"I'm sorry," she said gently. "I'm sorry."

Anger flashed in his face. "You're still afraid."

How could she explain it so that he would understand? It was so clear to her now.

"I'm not afraid. I'm just sure."

"Is there someone else? Is that why?" He drew his hands away.

Sorrow was a weight on her heart. There might have been, but Daniel had made that impossible.

"No. At least, not the way you mean." Words weren't enough for this, but they were all she had. "You told me that I wasn't doing enough for the children I teach, but you're wrong. I'm not teaching them just by the subjects they learn. I'm teaching them by my life and my actions."

"You can't live your life for other people's kids. You deserve more."

"There is nothing more than this." She shook her head. "I am being a part of the community where no single piece is more important than any other. What anyone does affects everyone, especially the children."

He sat with his face averted, like Anna had.

"Johnny, I'm not blaming you for the choice you made." She wanted to comfort him, as she would one of the children. "I just know that if I left, ripples would spread out from that action, affecting so many lives. You were right, in a way. I suppose at some level I was thinking about what the English world would be like, the way a child wonders what it would be like to be a bird. But I couldn't leave. I would be lost if I did."

"I'd take care of you." But there was no confidence in his words.

"I know you'd try." She took a breath, feeling the peace that settled into her. "I'm sorry I've never been able to give you what you want. Ten years ago I refused to go with you out of fear. But now—now the answer is the same, but the reason is different. I can't go, because I know where I belong. It's here."

CHAPTER TWENTY-ONE

*L*eah would never have imagined that she'd be dreading seeing her baby sister. But as she walked down the hospital corridor the next day, she realized that *dread* was exactly the right word for what she felt.

She'd spent the night praying for Anna and praying for guidance. Her newfound peace about who she was and what God intended for her life didn't seem to extend to her relationship with the sister she loved.

Why, Father? Why can't I reach her? Why can't I show her what is right?

To that, there didn't seem to be an answer.

Leah pushed the door to Anna's room open. She froze, fingers gripping the edge of the door. The room was empty, the bed stripped, the cards and flowers Anna had received gone.

She forced herself to cross the room to the small closet. The dress, cape, shoes, and kapp she'd brought yesterday in anticipation of Anna coming home soon were still here. Only Anna was gone.

The door swished behind her, and she whirled. The smile died on her face when she saw it was one of the nurses, a plump, comfortable, middle-aged woman in blue print scrubs.

"My sister." She nearly stammered the words. "Where is she?"

The woman's gaze slid away from hers. "She's gone. She checked herself out of the hospital first thing this morning."

"Gone!" Leah's mind spun dizzyingly. "How can she be gone? Where did she go? We were told that we might be able to take her home tomorrow."

"The doctor wanted her to stay another day, but she was very insistent." Faint sympathy crossed the woman's face. "Your sister is eighteen. Legally she's an adult, and she could check herself out."

Leah gripped the bottom rail of the bed. "But where did she go?"

"I'm sorry. I'm afraid I can't give out any information without the patient's permission." The nurse looked as if the sorrow was genuine—surely that was pity in her face.

Leah took a breath, trying to calm herself, trying to frame the words that would convince the woman to tell her where Anna was. "Please—she's my baby sister. You have to tell me where she is."

She shook her head, lips pressed together as if she wanted to speak but couldn't.

Please, Lord . . .

"She was still so weak. How could you just let her walk away?" Leah tried to keep her voice steady, but it wobbled despite her best efforts.

The nurse glanced behind her at the closed door and then turned back to Leah.

"We wouldn't let her walk, of course. I took her out myself in a wheelchair, and her young man brought his car right up to the sidewalk and helped her in. They drove away together."

The woman looked at her meaningfully. Leah's hands clenched. The English boy. Of course. For a moment her mind was blank, and then it came to her, as clearly as if she heard Anna speaking.

Jarrod, Anna had said. *His name is Jarrod Wells.*

"Thank you." Her eyes filled with tears as she pressed the woman's hand.

The nurse gave her a quick hug. "Don't thank me," she said. "I didn't tell you a thing."

"*This* is it." Ben Morgan, who'd come at once when Leah called from the hospital, pulled to a stop in front of a large, elegant home set back from the street in a suburban neighborhood. He patted Leah's shoulder as she started to slide from the car. "I'll wait for you. Good luck."

She nodded. Murmuring a silent prayer for guidance, she started up the walk.

She felt—small, she supposed. Out of place. Surely every one of these fancy homes looked in disdain at the sight of a Plain woman disrupting the modern style of their neighborhood.

She rang the doorbell, half expecting Anna or the boy to come. But when the door opened, she found herself facing a woman who must surely be the boy's mother, even though her carefully styled blonde hair and flawless makeup made her look too young to be the parent of a boy that age.

"I am here to see my sister." There seemed little point in beating about the bush. They both knew why she had come.

The woman stiffened. "I don't think she wants to see you. She's made a choice of her own free will. Why don't you people just leave her alone?"

She made it sound as if they were persecuting Anna.

"Anna is my baby sister. I will not go away without seeing her." She stepped boldly into the hallway, the woman stepping back as she did.

She flushed. "You can't—"

"It's all right. I'll talk to her." The voice was Anna's. But the young woman who stood in the archway wasn't Anna—not the Anna she knew.

Blue jeans, sneakers, a bright knit top that clung to her body and a dangling necklace that hung between her breasts. Makeup drew attention to her delicate features, and—Leah's breath caught—her hair. Anna's hair was cut to her chin in a shining bob that swung when she moved her head.

"All right," the woman—Mrs. Wells, she supposed—said doubtfully. "If you're sure. Go in the sunroom. You'll be private there."

"Thanks." Anna gestured to Leah. "This way."

Wordlessly, Leah followed this new Anna down the hallway. The sunroom had tile floors and glass all around, with plants blooming so profusely that it looked like a greenhouse.

Anna swung to face her, not offering her a seat. "I'm not going back, so there's no point to your saying anything." She flicked her hair with her fingers. "Cut my hair first thing. You like it?"

"I liked it the way it was." Leah took a step toward this girl who was and yet wasn't her beloved sister. "Anna, don't do this. Come home with me. It's not too late. Everyone will welcome you—"

"Everyone will be glad to see the last of me, you mean."

"You know that's not true. We only want you to come home."

"And be exactly like everyone else." Something that might have been hurt flickered in her blue eyes. "I can't. I don't want to. Jarrod's mother says I can stay with them until I figure out what I want to do."

It seemed incredible that the boy's mother would encourage this. Surely she must think that her son was too young to form a lasting attachment.

"I know you think you love him, but this is only going to bring unhappiness. You're both so young—"

"You wouldn't say that if I were talking about marrying Eli Stoltzfus or Martin Brand." She shrugged. "Anyway, it's not like that. They're just helping me because they think I have a right to make my own decisions."

"I will not argue that. But what about the police? The chief said—"

"That's taken care of. Mrs. Wells got a lawyer for me. I just plead guilty to driving without a license, and I'll be put on probation for a few months. See? My friends are taking care of me."

"It's gut of them to help you." Anna was getting off easy, Leah felt. Because of the Wells family involvement? She didn't know.

"It is." Anna's face was stony.

Leah reached out a tentative hand toward her sister. "But we love you. How can you decide to leave us this way? Don't you love us anymore?"

For a moment she thought Anna wouldn't answer. Then her lips trembled a little, and her eyes filled with tears.

"I love you." She blinked rapidly. "That's what makes it so hard. But this is right for me. Really." She flung out her hands. "Don't you see? I have to find out what the world is like. I have to see for myself. I can't just settle down and get married and never know anything else. Can't you understand that? Sometimes I feel as if I'm going to explode if I don't get away from here."

"I know things have been upset, with Mamm's health and Mamm and Daadi moving into the daadi haus—"

"It's not that." She shook her head decisively, her hair flaring out and then fluttering against her cheek. "I admit that's pushed me along, but this has been coming for a long time." She smiled a little sadly. "You just didn't notice. Leah, please, try to understand. Try to forgive me for hurting Mamm and Daad. I'm sorry. But I have to go and see what the world is like. I have to."

Leah didn't want to understand. She wanted to take Anna's hand, the way she had when Anna was little, and lead her back home. But she couldn't.

Leah was meant to stay, she knew that now. But it seemed that Anna was equally convinced that it was her time to go.

"I will miss you. More than you know."

Relief flooded Anna's face. "You understand."

"No, not entirely. But I accept that you feel you have to go." She opened her arms to Anna, her heart full of love and pain. "Da Herr sei mit du. The Lord be with you."

Anna threw her arms around Leah in a fierce hug. "I love you, Leah." Her voice cracked with emotion. "Thank you."

Leah stroked the silky hair. "Just don't disappear, the way Johnny did. Don't forget us."

"I won't." Anna pressed her cheek against Leah's.

Pain ricocheted through her, and she remembered the first time she'd held her baby sister, her heart overflowing with love.

Please, Father. Please. Bring our Anna back to us one day.

She was almost home already, and she still hadn't figured out what she was going to say to her parents. Leah reached across to touch Ben's sleeve, knowing he was unlikely to hear her with his favorite country music blaring from the radio.

"Just drop me here. I'd like to walk the rest of the way."

His eyebrows lifted. "You sure of that?"

"I have some thinking to do."

He pulled up at the edge of Daniel's pasture. "I'm sorry about this business with Anna. Hope everything works out all right."

"I do, too." Her throat thickened, and she couldn't say more. But Ben was a good friend to the Amish, and he'd understand.

She slid out, raising her hand in a wave as he drove away.

Walking along the road, even in the heat of the summer sun, was better than being cooped up in an automobile. She took her bonnet off and let it dangle from her fingers.

Tiger lilies had begun to open along the side of the road, their orange blossoms unfurling, and Daniel's cows surveyed her from the other side of the fence. It was beautiful, and peaceful, and Anna was rejecting it. Rejecting the life she'd always lived in favor of the unknown.

Mamm and Daadi wouldn't take her word for Anna's decision, of course. They'd insist on trying to talk to her themselves, sure that they could make her see sense.

But Anna wouldn't change her mind. She was set on this course. One day, if God chose, she might realize that here was where she belonged.

Leah's vision blurred with unshed tears, and she closed her eyes for a moment. When she opened them, she saw Daniel, working on the fence at the corner where his lane met the county road.

Maybe that was why she'd had that urge to get out of the car, if she were truthful with herself. She'd hoped to see Daniel. Hoped to borrow a little of his strength for the ordeal ahead of her.

He saw her coming and straightened from his work, watching as she approached. "Was ist letz?" he asked as soon as she was close enough. "What's the matter?"

She stopped, finding it harder than she'd expected to answer the question.

He touched her hand gently, drawing her closer. "Anna? She's not coming home, is she?"

So he'd guessed. The tears spilled over before Leah could stop them. "She's gone to her English friends."

"She might change her mind once she's thought about it a bit." He brushed away the tears on her cheek, and his fingers were warm against her skin. "Maybe it's not too late."

"I don't think so."

Anna wouldn't come home. She wouldn't kneel before the congregation, confess her sin, and receive their forgiveness and love. Leah fought back tears so she could speak.

"Maybe for now, that's the right thing. It seems she'll never be happy unless she's seen some of the world. Maybe, once she's seen it, she'll realize her place is here."

He took her hands in his. "Is that what you believe?"

"It's what I hope and pray."

"Then I will hope and pray that also." His fingers tightened on hers. "Has she left it to you to tell your parents?"

She nodded. "I wish I could find the words to break it to them gently."

"They will not be surprised."

She looked up at him, startled at the comment, and realized he was probably right. She longed to protect them, but they wouldn't be surprised. They knew Anna.

"What makes you so wise?"

He smiled, shaking his head. "I'm not so wise. But I care." The smile faded, and his blue eyes grew very serious. "This is not the time or the place, but I cannot wait any longer to ask this. Leah, will you be my wife?"

Her breath caught in her throat, and the waving meadow grass blurred. She looked at him—at the strong column of his neck, the firmness of his jaw, the kindness in his eyes.

Looking at him, she seemed to see the life that would be hers if she said yes. The children, the laughter, the sharing. It was all there within her grasp. But she couldn't take it.

"I'm sorry." The words came out in a whisper, and she took a deep breath and lifted her chin. She wouldn't be a coward about this. "I thought I could do without love, but I've learned something about myself in the past few months. I can't marry without it. You can't offer me your heart, Daniel. So I'll have to settle for being your friend."

"Leah." His voice was husky, and his fingers tightened on hers when she tried to pull free. "Knowing you has turned all that I thought I knew upside down. I've been so foolish, comparing you with Ruth and thinking that if you were around the English, you'd want to be one. I see now that the gut work you do at the clinic has only made you stronger."

He let go of her hands then, but only so that he could cup her face between his palms. "I love you, Teacher Leah. With all my heart. I believe that God led me to this place because we are meant to be together, and I will never try to change the strong, faithful woman you are, if only you will be my wife."

Her heart was so full that she could not speak, but he must have read the answer in her eyes, because he bent his head and kissed her. After the first surprised moment she put her arms around him, secure in his warm embrace.

He lifted his head after a long moment.

A smile trembled on her lips. "Are we really standing at the end of your lane, kissing in broad daylight? The People will think for sure we are ferhoodled."

He drew her closer, his lips brushing her cheek tenderly. "There is no one to see but the cows, and they don't mind. You haven't answered me, you know."

"I thought I had." For a moment she pushed away all thought of the troubles yet to be faced. "I love you, Daniel, with all my heart. Ja, I will marry you."

Here was the answer she'd been seeking, even without really knowing it. In all she'd done, God had been preparing her for this role—Daniel's wife, the mother of his children, the woman who could fill a role at the Englischer clinic without compromising being Amish.

She lifted her face for Daniel's kiss. God had chosen this role for her from the beginning. He was just waiting for her to be ready to step into it.

Rachel's Garden

*This story is dedicated to my husband, Brian,
with all my heart. Without your unflagging support and
belief in me, it would never have happened.*

CHAPTER ONE

A flicker of movement from the lane beyond the kitchen window of the old farmhouse caught Rachel Brand's eye as she leaned against the sink, washing up the bowl she'd used to make a batch of snickerdoodles. A buggy—ja, it must be Leah Glick, already bringing home Rachel's two older kinder from the birthday party for their teacher.

Quickly she set the bowl down and splashed cold water on her eyes. It wouldn't do to let her young ones suspect that their mamm had been crying while she baked. Smoothing her hair back under her kapp and arranging a smile on her lips, she went to the back door.

But the visitor was not Leah. It was a man, alone, driving the buggy.

Shock shattered her curiosity when she recognized the strong face under the brim of the black Amish hat. Gideon Zook. Her fingers clenched, wrinkling the fabric of her dark apron. What did he want from her?

She stood motionless for a moment, her left hand tight on the door frame. Then she grabbed the black wool shawl that hung by the door, threw it around her shoulders, and stepped outside.

The cold air sent a shiver through her. It was mid-March already, but winter had not released its grip on Pleasant Valley, Pennsylvania. The snowdrops she had planted last fall quivered against the back step, their white cups a mute testimony that spring would come eventually. Everything else was as brown and barren as her heart felt these days.

A fierce longing for spring swept through her as she crossed the still-hard ground. If she could be in the midst of growing things, planting and nurturing her beloved garden—ach, there she might find the peace she longed for.

Everything was too quiet on the farm now. Even the barn was empty, the dairy cows already moved to the far field, taken care of by her young brother-in-law William in the early morning hours.

The Belgian draft horses Ezra had been so pleased to be able to buy were spending the winter at the farm of his oldest brother, Isaac. Only Dolly, six-year-old Joseph's pet goat, bleated forlornly from her pen, protesting his absence.

Gideon had tethered his horse to the hitching post. Removing something from his buggy, he began pacing across the lawn, as if he measured something.

Then he saw her. He stopped, waiting. His hat was pushed back, and he lifted his face slightly, as if in appreciation of the watery sunshine. But Gideon's broad shoulders were stiff under his black jacket, his eyes wary, and his mouth set above his beard.

Reluctance slowed her steps. Perhaps Gideon felt that same reluctance. Aside from the formal words of condolence he'd spoken to her once he was well enough to be out again after the accident, she and Gideon had managed to avoid talking to each other for months. That was no easy thing in a tight-knit Amish community.

She forced a smile. "Gideon, wilkom. I didn't expect to be seeing you today."

What are you doing here? That was what she really wanted to say.

"Rachel." He inclined his head slightly, studying her face as if trying to read her feelings.

His own face gave little away—all strong planes and straight lines, like the wood he worked with in his carpentry business. Lines of tension radiated from his brown eyes, making him look older than the thirty-two she knew him to be. His work-hardened hands tightened on the objects he grasped—small wooden stakes, sharpened to points.

He cleared his throat, as if not sure what to say to her now that they were face-to-face. "How are you? And the young ones?"

"I'm well." Except that her heart twisted with pain at the sight of him, at the reminder he brought of all she had lost. "The kinder also. Mary is napping, and Leah Glick took Joseph and Becky to a birthday luncheon the scholars are having for Mary Yoder."

"Gut, gut."

He moved a step closer to her, and she realized that his left leg was still stiff—a daily reminder for him, probably, of the accident.

For an instant the scene she'd imagined so many times flashed yet again through her mind, stealing her breath away. She seemed to see Ezra, high in the rafters of a barn, Gideon below him, the old timbers creaking, then breaking, Ezra falling as the barn collapsed like a house of cards . . .

She gasped a strangled breath, like a fish struggling on the bank of the pond. Revulsion wrung her stomach, and she slammed the door shut on her imagination.

She could not let herself think about that, not now. It was not Gideon's fault that she couldn't see him without imagining the accident that had taken Ezra away from them. She had to talk to him sensibly, had to find out what had brought him here. And how she could get him to go away again.

She clutched the shawl tighter around her. "Is there something I can do for you, Gideon?"

"I am here to measure for the greenhouse."

She could only stare at him, her mind fumbling to process his words. The greenhouse—the greenhouse Ezra had promised her as a birthday present. That had to be what Gideon meant.

"How do you know about the greenhouse?"

The words came out unexpectedly harsh. Ezra was gone, and plans for the greenhouse had slipped away, too, swamped in the struggle just to get through the days.

He blinked, apparently surprised. "You didn't know? Ezra and I went together to buy the materials for your greenhouse. He asked me to build it for you. Now I'm here to start on the work."

The revulsion that swept through her was so strong she could barely prevent it from showing on her face.

Perhaps he knew anyway. The fine lines around his eyes deepened. "Is there a problem with that?"

"No—I mean, I didn't realize that he had asked you. Ezra never said so."

"Perhaps he thought there was no need. I always helped him with carpentry projects."

True enough. It wasn't that Ezra couldn't build things with his own hands, but he was far more interested in the crops and the animals. Since his childhood friend Gideon was a carpenter, specializing in building the windmills that had begun to dot the valley, Ezra had depended on him.

But that was before. Now . . .

Now the thought of having Gideon around for days while he built the greenhouse that was to have been a gift of love from her husband—

No, she couldn't handle that. She couldn't. It was, no doubt about it, a failure on her part, one that she should be taking to the Lord in prayer.

"Rachel?" She had been silent too long, and Gideon studied her face with concern. "Was ist letz? What's the matter?"

"Nothing," she said quickly. "Nothing at all. It's just that I hadn't thought about the greenhouse in months." Her voice thickened—she couldn't help that.

Gideon heard it, of course. A spasm of something that might have been pain crossed his face.

"It gave Ezra great pleasure to think about giving it to you." His deep voice seemed choked.

She blinked, focusing her gaze on the barn beyond him, willing herself to be calm. Think. What could she say that would not hurt Gideon, but would get him to go away?

"I haven't—I haven't decided what to do about the greenhouse." As she hadn't decided so many things in the past few months, lost as she'd been in grief. "Will you give me a little time to think?"

"Of course."

But his voice had cooled, as if he knew something of what she was feeling. His gaze was intent on her face, probing for the truth, and all she could think was that she wanted him to leave so that she didn't have to talk about the bittersweet nature of Ezra's last gift to her.

The creak of an approaching buggy broke the awkward silence between them. She glanced toward the lane.

"Here is Leah, back with the children." She probably sounded too relieved as she turned back to him. "Perhaps we could talk about this some other day."

His expression still grave, Gideon nodded. "Ja, another time, then." He turned away, but then glanced back over his shoulder. "I promised Ezra, ain't so? I have to keep that promise."

He walked toward his waiting buggy, back stiff.

Leah shook her head, cradling between her hands the mug of tea Rachel had given her. "I don't understand. Why are you so ferhoodled at the idea of Gideon putting up the greenhouse for you? He'd do a good job, that's certain sure."

"Ja, he would." She couldn't argue with that. Everyone knew how skilled a carpenter Gideon was. "I just . . . it makes me feel . . . makes me remember . . ." Her voice trailed off.

Leah reached across the scrubbed pine kitchen table to cover Rachel's hand with her own. "It's hard, I know. I'm sorry."

"Ach, I'm being foolish." She shook her head, determined not to slide into burdening Leah with her sorrow and her worries. She'd done that enough lately. She freed her hand and stood. "I think I'd best take a look out at those children. I haven't heard any noise from them in a while."

Three-year-old Mary, building a house with her favorite blocks in the corner of the kitchen, chose that moment to knock it over, chortling when the blocks crashed to the floor. Leah laughed, and Rachel shook her head.

"Plenty of noise in here, though. Mary, pick those up, please. It'll be time to help with supper soon."

"I set the table," Mary announced, and began to pick up the blocks, putting them in her wagon.

Rachel leaned against the sink to peer out the window over the plants that crowded the sill. Her daughter Becky and Leah's stepdaughter, Elizabeth, seemed to be in a deep conversation, side by side on the wide swing that hung from the willow tree. Her first-grader Joseph and Leah's Jonah, who was a year older, were romping with Dolly, the nanny goat.

"All seems well at the moment." She sat down again, pushing the plate of snickerdoodles toward Leah.

"That's usually when they're the most ready to get into mischief," Leah said. She took another cookie, sighing a little. "I shouldn't eat this, but it tastes like more. Since the morning sickness finally went away, I've been eating everything in sight."

Rachel studied Leah's glowing face. "Being pregnant agrees with you, for sure. I've never seen you look better."

Leah shook her head, smiling a little, and patted her rounded belly. "I look like a hippo."

"I'll bet Daniel doesn't think so."

Leah's cheeks grew pink, but instead of answering, she shoved the plate of cookies back toward Rachel. "You have another. You need all the energy you can get."

Leah undoubtedly thought she had grown too thin in the past months, just as her mamm did, but Leah was too kind to say so outright.

It was strange, how much their situations had changed. A year ago Leah had been the devoted teacher at the Amish school, single and content to remain so, while Rachel had been completely occupied as a wife and mother, helping Ezra to run the farm, far too busy to think about anything else.

Now they'd switched places, it seemed. Leah was happily married to Daniel Glick, instant mother to his three children, and glowing with the joy of her pregnancy.

As for her—Ezra was gone, and she struggled to raise their children without him, caught in a web of indecision about the future.

Leah must have guessed at her thoughts, because her green eyes darkened with concern as she leaned toward Rachel. "Are you all right? Are you getting enough help? Daniel would be glad to come over, or we could send Matthew to do chores."

"That's gut of you, but we are managing to get everything done. There's not so much this time of the year. William comes every day to deal with the milking, and he's so willing to do anything he can. I think it helps him with his grief, knowing that he's doing what Ezra would have wanted."

She didn't need to explain further. They both knew how Ezra's shy younger brother had loved him.

"He's probably glad to get out from under Isaac's thumb a couple of times a day," Leah said, her tone tart.

Rachel had to hesitate for a moment to think of something positive to say about Ezra's oldest brother. "Isaac means well, I'm sure. He just believes he's the head of the family now, and so everyone should heed what he says."

"I'm convinced William's stuttering wouldn't be nearly so bad if Isaac listened and encouraged him instead of snapping orders at him." Leah spoke like the teacher she had been for so many years.

"I try to do as you suggested, listening to him and making him feel comfortable, and I do think he speaks more when he's here with us."

"That's good. I'm glad it's helping. I used to get so frustrated when he was one of my scholars and I'd see his sisters speaking for him, instead of helping him try." For a moment she studied Rachel's face, as if she hadn't been distracted from her concern by the talk of William. "Still, you will let us pitch in, any way we can."

"I will." Rachel could feel her forehead wrinkling into the frown that came too often these days, and she tried to smooth it out. "The real problem is that I can't seem to make up my mind about anything. I was spoiled."

"Spoiled?" Leah's eyebrows lifted. "That's silly."

"I was. My life went so smoothly. You know that. I loved Ezra and he loved me, we were able to buy the farm from my aunt and uncle, the children came along easy and healthy—everything went the way I wanted it to. Until the day Ezra and Gideon went off to look at that barn." Her hands clenched so tightly that her knuckles were white.

Leah put her hand gently over Rachel's. "Is that why you don't want Gideon to build the greenhouse? Because you blame him for Ezra's accident?"

Rachel shook her head, tears choking her throat. "I don't know. Forgive, that's what God commands. Besides, it was an accident, no one's fault. Everyone knows that. But when I see him—"

She broke off. She couldn't explain to Leah. She couldn't even explain to herself.

"Forgiveness is only right, but our Father must know it is hard. But Ezra and Gideon were as close friends as you and I are," Leah said, her voice gentle. "You know he wouldn't want you to hold Gideon at fault."

That hit home, and her heart clenched in her chest. Ezra had loved Gideon like a brother. But how could she look at Gideon and not feel the pain of Ezra's loss?

She took a deep breath, forcing her hands to relax. "I know," she murmured.

Leah patted her again, seeming reassured. "Just think how much you'd enjoy having a greenhouse." She nodded toward the windowsills, crowded with the plants Rachel had started from seed. "By the looks of those windows, your plants will be pushing you out of the kitchen soon."

She managed a smile. "True enough. But I'll be selling them at the Mud Sale next Saturday, so that will clear off my windowsills."

Leah had a point, though. With a greenhouse, she'd be able to produce many more plants for sale.

"Ach, I'd best be getting along home." Leah seemed satisfied that she'd made her point. "I'll see you at the sale, if not before."

She rose, but stopped partway up, her breath catching as she clutched her belly.

Rachel was beside her in an instant, fear shooting through her. "Leah, was ist letz? Are you all right?"

"Ja." Leah laughed a little as she straightened. "Just a muscle spasm, I think. All the books say to expect them."

"You and your books," Rachel teased, reassured by the laugh. "I think you have a book about everything, ain't so?"

"You can never have enough books," Leah said. "Anyway, I have you to ask for advice when it comes to being pregnant."

Rachel put her arm around Leah as they walked toward the door. "That's right. That's the only subject on which I'm the expert, instead of you."

Over the years she'd turned to Teacher Leah and her books whenever she'd had a question, and Leah had usually found the answer. For the first time in their relationship, she was the knowledgeable one, and it was gut, knowing she could help Leah.

They hadn't yet reached the door when it burst open. Becky and Elizabeth surged inside. Elizabeth looked to be on the verge of tears, but Becky wore the rebellious pout that Rachel had seen on her face too often lately. Her heart sank. What now?

"Mammi, my shoes are all wet," Elizabeth wailed.

Exchanging an understanding look with Rachel, Leah went to her. "Well, that's not so bad. Sit up here on the chair, and let's see how wet they are."

Rachel focused on her daughter, knowing perfectly well that if anyone had instigated mischief, it would have been Becky. "Becky, how did this happen?"

Becky's lower lip came out, her gaze sliding away from Rachel's.

"I'm waiting, Rebecca."

The pout deepened, and Becky shrugged her shoulders. "I wanted to see if the ice is melting on the pond. That's all. Elizabeth didn't have to follow me."

Unfortunately they all knew that where Becky led, Elizabeth would follow.

"You know you are not allowed on the ice without a grown-up there. Go find some dry stockings for Elizabeth to wear home. You will go to bed early tonight so that you'll have time to think about being disobedient."

"But, Mammi—"

The pout melted into the threat of tears, and Rachel had to force herself to remain unmoved. "Now, Rebecca."

Becky scurried out of the room. Leah, having soothed away Elizabeth's tears, was scolding her gently for being so foolish. "Run along with Becky and get something dry to wear home."

She gave her stepdaughter a little shove. Her face brightening, Elizabeth hurried after Becky toward the stairs.

"I'm sorry—" Rachel began.

"Don't be silly," Leah said quickly. "It's not your fault. I'm sure we did much worse when we were their age."

Had they? Those days seemed very far away just now.

"I don't think either of us was quite so gut at leading others into trouble as Becky is. And it seems to be getting worse, not better."

"She's had a lot to handle since last year." Leah's voice was soft. "I'm sure that's all it is."

She nodded, because she didn't want Leah to have another cause to worry about her.

But the truth was that she was no longer so sure that she was the gut mother she'd always thought she was. What if it had really been Ezra's influence that ensured the children's obedience and happiness? What if she couldn't do it on her own?

Loneliness swept over her—loneliness mixed with longing for something she'd never have again.

"Don't you have any snapdragons?" The English woman leaned across the stand at the Mud Sale on Saturday afternoon, peering at Rachel's remaining plants and seeming to dismiss them at a glance.

Only the success of the sales she'd made already gave Rachel the confidence to speak up.

"It's too early to plant snapdragons here. You won't want to set those out until the danger of frost is past. What about some of these nice pansies?"

The woman eyed the cheerful faces of the pansies. "I suppose they'll do. Do you have two dozen of them?"

Taken slightly aback by the sudden agreement, Rachel did a quick count. "Ja, I can just manage that."

Exultant, she began putting the plants into the boxes she'd brought for the purpose. This sale cleaned her out, and it was only two o'clock.

Leah had been right. If she'd had the greenhouse already, she could have made two or three times the money today.

She couldn't go back. She accepted the money and thanked the woman. But she could go forward.

She glanced down the row of booths that had been built for the sale in the field adjoining the township fire house. True to its name, the Mud Sale had turned the field into a sea of mud, with furrows filling with moisture where pickup trucks and buggies had made their way.

Mud Sales were a rite of spring in Pleasant Valley, and probably folks—Amish and English alike—enjoyed them so much because their appearance meant winter was over. People who hadn't seen much of their neighbors for months were visiting even more than they were buying, it seemed, at the couple of dozen booths that had been set up.

A few booths down, she could see her daadi, buying bags of popcorn for his grandchildren. She could only hope the kinder hadn't been eating junk food since he'd taken them off her hands an hour ago.

"Rachel, are your plants all gone so soon?" Her mother, who was sharing the booth with Rachel, looked as pleased as if she had just sold all her jams and jellies. "That is wonderful gut, that is."

"Ja. It makes me feel . . ." She paused, searching for the word. "Hopeful, I guess." Her mood seemed to have flipped around in the week since she'd talked to Gideon.

She studied her mother's kindly, lined face, knowing every wrinkle had been honestly earned. Mamm's hair might be snowy white now and her vision starting to fail, but the sweetness in her face would always make her beautiful.

"Mamm, is that the way of grieving? To be weak and doubting one day and then confident and hopeful the next?"

Her mother's faded blue eyes seemed to be looking at something in the distance. "Ja, you have it right. That's the way of it." She patted Rachel's arm. "It will get better. You'll see."

Rachel clasped her mother's hand in hers. "I'm sorry. I've made you think of Johnny, haven't I?"

A kind of longing crossed Mamm's face. "I never stop thinking of him, Rachel. Just as I never stop praying that one day I'll see him again."

"If Daadi would change his mind—"

Her mother shook her head. "Don't, Rachel. It's not your daadi's fault. He's only trying to do what's right. You know that."

No matter how much it hurt. Rachel finished the thought for her.

Daad held hard to the letter and spirit of the Ordnung, the rules by which the Amish lived. Some might choose to bend the rules, but not Amos Kile.

A customer approached Mamm's side of the stand, and she moved away quickly, as if relieved to be distracted from thoughts of her only son, gone nearly eleven years now.

It had been hard for Rachel, too—terribly hard—to lose her twin when Johnny deserted his family to go English. Still, even a twin brother wasn't so close as a husband, and Johnny hadn't died.

She'd even seen Johnny a number of times in the past year, thanks to Leah's intervention. Leah understood too well herself the grief of having a beloved sibling go English, since her younger sister, Anna, had jumped the fence.

Rachel leaned against the counter, watching her mother wait on the customer. She should have thought twice before she'd asked her mother that question. With no other children but her and Johnny, the loss of him weighed heavily on her parents.

Daadi hadn't seemed able to reconcile himself to the truth—Johnny was never going to come back to the church. So he clung to the bann, refusing to see Johnny, even though it hurt him and Mammi more than it did Johnny, busy and happy with his work at the medical research clinic.

Her parents were growing older, more frail it seemed, with each passing month. Daad wanted so badly to help her with the farm since Ezra's passing, but his health just wasn't good enough. She knew it was a constant worry to him.

Mamm, having sold three jars of her raspberry jam, came back to her, studying Rachel closely. "You've been fratched about something. I can see it in your face. Is it too much for you, trying to keep the farm going?"

She shook her head, suspecting she knew the direction of her mother's thoughts. "I'm doing all right. William helps a lot."

"Still—" Mamm put her hand on Rachel's arm. "Won't you think about your daadi's idea? Sell the farm and move home with us. We'd love to have you and the kinder living with us. You know that."

"I know, Mamm," she said gently. "I just can't bring myself to do that. The farm was Ezra's dream. It's what he had to leave to his children. How can I let him down?"

Mamm's eyes clouded with concern. "You can't run a dairy farm alone. Who knows how long Ezra's brothers can continue to do so much? If you sold, you'd maybe get enough to start a small business of some kind. Wouldn't that be better?"

It was tempting, so tempting. To be back under her parents' roof, having them share the responsibility for the kinder. Being able to lean on them when things got difficult. But—

"I can't, Mamm. I just can't make up my mind to that. Not yet, anyway."

But she had to, didn't she? She had to stop drifting along and make some definite decisions about their future, hers and the children's.

Isaac and William, Ezra's brothers, came up to the stand just then, relieving her of the need to keep talking about it, even if she couldn't dismiss it from her thoughts.

"How are your sales today, Rachel? Gut, I hope." Isaac, bluff and hearty, his beard almost completely gray now, stopped in front of her counter.

"They're all gone." She swept her hand along the empty countertop.

"Gut, gut," he said, and William nodded in agreement, giving her a shy smile.

The nearly twenty years between the oldest of Ezra's siblings and the youngest accented the many other differences between them. Isaac was stout and graying, with an assured manner that seemed to have grown since the death of their father had left him the head, as he thought, of the family.

William, just turned eighteen, hung back, shy as always. He had huge brown eyes that reminded Rachel of a frightened deer and blond hair so light it was nearly white. He seemed always on the verge of growing right out of his clothes.

"Are you having a pleasant day at the sale?" The guilt she felt over her uncharitable thoughts toward Isaac made her voice warm with interest.

"Ja. For sure. Made a couple of deals and have a line on someone who has a fine colt for sale." He gave William a hearty slap on the shoulder. "Maybe I'll let William train this one."

Not sure what William felt about that, she could only smile. But for the most part, William did what Isaac said without questioning, as far as she could tell.

"By the way, Rachel, I found a buyer for those greenhouse supplies you've got in the barn," he went on. "You won't want it now. I'll come by and pick those materials up on Tuesday."

For a moment Rachel could only gape at him. Slowly, the temper she rarely felt began to rise. Not only did Isaac assume he knew what she should do—he thought he had the right to make decisions for her.

Forcing down the anger, she managed a smile. "That is kind of you to go to so much trouble. But I don't wish to sell."

He blinked. "Not sell?" His voice rose in surprise. "But what will you do with all that lumber and glass?"

"Build a greenhouse." The words came out almost before she thought what she'd say. She'd been having such difficulty in making decisions, and suddenly she'd made one on the spur of the moment. Yet Isaac had pushed her into this one.

Annoyance flared in Isaac's face, quickly masked by an air of concern. "Ach, Rachel, don't be so foolish. The money will be of much more use to you than a greenhouse."

"Ezra gave it to me for my birthday. I don't want to sell his gift. I want to use it the way he intended."

"Ezra would want you to do the sensible thing." Clearly the sensible thing, according to Isaac, was to listen to him.

The smile was so tight it felt her face would split with it. She shook her head. "I appreciate the trouble you've taken, but I've made up my mind."

Temper flared in his eyes, and his fist clenched on the counter. "How do you expect to get a greenhouse built? I don't have time to do it for you. And you certainly can't do it yourself."

"I w-w-want t-t-t—"

William didn't get any further before Isaac turned on him. "Forget that idea. I need you at the farm. You'll have no time to indulge this whim of Rachel's."

Her teeth gritted at the way Isaac disregarded William's wishes. Just because it took the boy a long time to say something didn't mean he couldn't have an opinion.

But that was how most of the family treated him, finishing his thoughts for him instead of having enough patience to hear him out.

"If that is indeed what William intended to say, it is very kind of him." She smiled at him, and he blushed to the tips of his ears.

"William is not available." Isaac ground out the words.

William's jaw clenched as if, for once in his life, he might go against Isaac's wishes. But she couldn't let the boy get into trouble on her account.

"I can't take him away from his work—he does so much for me already. I'll manage."

"How do you plan to do that?" Isaac's face darkened to a deep red, and he looked dangerously close to an explosion.

It seemed she didn't even consider the words before they were out of her mouth.

"Gideon Zook is going to build the greenhouse for me."

She caught a glimpse of movement from the corner of her eye. Gideon was standing there, watching them, close enough to hear every word.

Chapter Two

Gideon winced inwardly as the expression on Rachel's face hit him. She'd just announced that he was going to build the greenhouse for her. But as soon as she'd seen him, she'd regretted her hasty words.

He hadn't been listening intentionally. He'd just noticed that her stand didn't seem to be busy at the moment, and he'd thought this might be a good opportunity to see if she'd made up her mind about the building.

Well, now he knew. She had, and if he wasn't mistaken, she'd been driven to that by Isaac's attempts to boss her around.

Ezra had always said his eldest brother was a little too fond of giving people orders. Even when they were boys together, he remembered Isaac trying to rule the roost. But Ezra had been a peaceable person. He'd listened politely to what Isaac advised, and then he'd gone his own way.

The surprise was Rachel. Who would have thought that someone who seemed as soft and gentle as Rachel would display such a stubborn streak when she was pushed?

Isaac, apparently following the direction of Rachel's gaze, turned and saw him. His face darkened a little.

"Gideon." He jerked his head in greeting. "Is this true, what Rachel is telling us?"

"Ja."

Sometimes the less said the better, and Isaac, though a good enough man in his way, had an uncertain temper to go with his bossy ways.

Isaac hesitated, and his expression said he was trying to adjust his attitude. "That's kind of you." It sounded as if he had to push the words out. "Still, Rachel's family is well able to help her."

It didn't seem the moment to point out that he'd just refused to do that very thing. "It makes no trouble. I promised Ezra that I would build the greenhouse if he got the materials." He kept his voice even with an effort, Ezra's face filling his mind, head thrown back, laughing as he'd done so easily. "I want to fulfill that promise."

Isaac's jaw hardened at the words, his eyes narrowing. He'd probably be surprised to know that Rachel had reacted much the same way.

And neither of them would ever know that his determination to do this thing went far beyond a matter of wanting to fulfill a promise to a dead friend.

A fresh spasm of pain went through him. He would do this because Ezra had been closer than a brother, and because he owed it to him. Ezra was dead, and he was alive. The pain deepened.

"Ja, well . . ." Isaac's words trailed off. "We can talk about it more later, when Rachel has thought this whole thing through."

When Rachel had come to her senses, Isaac clearly meant. His piece said, Isaac nodded to Rachel's mother, then turned and walked away. William, with a slightly apologetic smile directed toward Rachel, followed him.

Gideon watched the brothers walk down the now-muddy stretch between the rows of booths. He hesitated for a moment. The expression on Rachel's face wasn't very encouraging.

Still, since she'd committed herself openly to the project, he'd best nail it down before she had any more regrets than she already did. He approached the stand and leaned against the waist-high wooden counter.

"It looks as if you had a fine sale day, Rachel." He gestured to the flats that had been filled with blooming plants when he'd passed by her stand earlier. He'd not only taken note of them—he'd directed several people to her stand for flowers.

"Ja." She glanced at the counter, as if surprised to find it empty. "It's the first Mud Sale of the year, so everyone's eager to get something blooming, they are."

"We've had a wonderful fine turnout today, with the sun finally shining. The fire company will have a nice profit when all's said and done."

Mud Sale season would run for a few more weeks, probably, but their township volunteer fire company liked to be the first, especially this year, with the fund drive for a new fire engine. He'd been a fire company volunteer for years, and even though he and the other Amish couldn't drive the fire truck, they knew well how important it was to have up-to-date equipment.

"Ser gut." Rachel seemed to relax a little with the conversation safely off her own affairs.

He couldn't leave it at that, or she'd be backing out again. "You'll be able to grow a lot more plants for sale once you have your greenhouse up and running."

"I guess so." Her gaze evaded his, and she began stacking the flats, as if she wanted to keep her hands busy. "About the greenhouse. I—well, I spoke hastily. You don't have to feel obligated to do the building."

He studied her downcast face for a moment. Rachel had always been a pretty girl back when they were in school together, with those big blue eyes and the light brown hair that curled rebelliously out of her braids. She had become thinner since Ezra's passing, and dealing with loss had given a new maturity to her face.

Why did she dislike the idea of his helping her so much?

He brushed bits of potting soil off the counter's surface, trying to find a way to bring her to acceptance. It was strange, in a way, that he knew so little of how Rachel's mind worked, when Ezra had been his lifelong friend. Somehow his relationship with Rachel had always been a tenuous thing. Ezra had been the focal point, and with Ezra gone, he wasn't sure how to talk to her.

But he had to try.

"You know, it's more than a year ago now since Ezra showed me the sketch you made of the greenhouse you'd been dreaming about. He said he'd had to sneak it out when you weren't looking, trying to keep it secret until he was sure we could do it. I used that sketch to work up the plan and figure the materials."

She looked at him then, her face suddenly soft. "Really? Ezra started planning it that long ago?"

He nodded, glad that he'd been able to bring some pleasure to her. He remembered that day so clearly, hearing the love in Ezra's voice when he talked about his wife. "He knew we wouldn't get around to building it for a bit, but he was wonderful happy to find a gift you'd like."

"He knew how much I love growing things." Her fingers toyed with a leaf that lay on the counter.

"Ja." Memory blossomed in his mind. "He told me once that you had such a green thumb that you could put a stick in the ground and it would grow a flower."

Her eyes were wet suddenly. Maybe his were, too, as Ezra's words brought him back in the minds of the two who'd loved him.

He had to clear his throat before he could speak. "There's something I've been wanting to say to you. I had a lot of time to think about this while I was laid up."

After the accident. He sensed her withdrawal. Was she shying away because she didn't want to think about Ezra's death? Or was it because she blamed him?

If she did, that seemed only fitting, since he blamed himself.

She started to turn away, as if to end the conversation, and he touched her sleeve to halt her. She froze instantly.

"I need to get this said once, and then I'll never mention it again." His voice thickened, and he fought to control it. He'd be fortunate to get the words out once, with the pain and guilt riding him constantly. "I couldn't make any sense out of the fact that the Lord let me live when Ezra died."

His throat tightened at the thought of the other, older pain that was so similar, hovering over him, darkening his life. With Ezra's death the darkness might never leave, and then how would he keep going? He pushed the thought back and concentrated on saying what he had to.

"It seems to me the only reason I survived was so I could help Ezra's family." Surely she could hear the truth of it in his voice. "And that's what I plan to do, God willing."

It had been raining nearly every day since the sale, and the well-trodden paths where the cows approached the barn were a sea of mud. Rachel peered out the kitchen window, streaked with the latest shower. William was working in the barn. She must catch him and give him a cup of coffee when he finished.

She hadn't seen Gideon since the day of the sale. He'd probably been kept away by the rain. At least that would stop him from doing anything more about the greenhouse.

Just as well. She hadn't figured out yet how to deal with him. Most of the time, she didn't even want to try. That moment when they'd seemed to share their grief—that had unsettled her, shifting her perception of him, she supposed.

He grieved for his friend. Somehow she had too easily forgotten that. She'd been so absorbed in her feelings that she hadn't made room in her heart to remember that he suffered, too.

The barn door moved, and William came out. Thankful to be distracted from the difficult thoughts, she hurried to the back door and waved at him.

"Komm out of the wet and have something hot already," she called.

He hesitated a moment, then nodded and started across the expanse of wet grass that seemed to be greening more and more by the day, maybe even the hour.

By the time William had removed his boots and reached the kitchen, she had a mug of coffee poured for him and had set a plate of cinnamon rolls within reach.

"Sit down. What are you working on so hard out there?"

William sat and took a gulp of the steaming coffee, then grabbed the largest of the cinnamon rolls.

She smiled. At eighteen, William was still growing.

"B-b-broken b-b-board," he said briefly. He always found the shortest way of answering any question, having learned the hard way that most people didn't like waiting around for an answer.

"That's kind of you," she said. "I didn't even realize anything was broken. I guess I haven't been out there in several days." She spoke casually, busying herself with the coffeepot. Given a little time and acceptance, William's stammer improved remarkably. "You've been taking care of things so well that I haven't had to."

He nodded, taking a huge bite of the roll and speaking around it. "Okay n-n-now."

He was relaxing already, she could see. Filling her own mug, she sat down opposite him. If only there was a way to make it easier for him to communicate. He suffered so, locked out of the easy talk that should flow between him and his friends.

"I w-w-anted to d-do the greenhouse for you." He blurted the words out, his hand tightening on his mug.

"I know you did, William." She hurried to assure him. "It's all right. I understand that your work for Isaac has to come first."

"Not just that. We should d-d-do it, not Gid." He frowned, his mouth setting in a firm line.

William took his responsibilities seriously—too seriously, maybe. He was still a boy who should be enjoying his rumspringa, his running-around time, instead of trying to take care of her.

"I know what you feel," she said carefully, not wanting to make it seem that she was angry with Gideon. "I didn't want Gideon to do it either, at first. But he was Ezra's good friend. It's only natural that he wants to keep his promise."

A red flush ran up William's face to the roots of his straw-colored hair. He clutched the edge of the table. "It's not r-r-right. That he lived when Ezra d-d-died."

The words caught her on the raw, and it was a moment before she could respond. "Du muscht schtobbe. You must stop thinking that. If we want God to forgive us, we must forgive others."

She patted his hand, taut on the table's edge. It was big and raw-boned, the wrist protruding a little from his shirt—the hand of a boy still growing into a man.

William shouldn't be angry that Gideon survived when Ezra died. That was wrong. And yet, didn't she sometimes feel that herself, despite all her prayers to forgive?

She wasn't alone in feeling it. Gideon himself felt it, judging by his words to her.

"I sh-should help you."

"You do." She was comforting him as she'd comfort one of the children. "You help every day, me and the children."

"I'm g-g-glad to." He flushed a little, his gaze almost too intense for comfort.

Maybe it was time to change the subject. "Speaking of the kinder, is Joseph still out in the barn?"

Becky would rather stay in and read when it was raining, but Joseph had hurried out as soon as he spotted William coming.

He nodded, his face breaking into a grin. "W-w-wants me to make a b-bed for the goat."

She shook her head, smiling in return. "He treats that goat better than he does his little sister. What Ezra would think about that, I don't know. He never believed in making a pet out of a farm animal." Her smile faded. "Still, Joseph seems to get comfort out of it. I don't have the heart to discourage him."

They were silent for a moment, and she knew they were both thinking of what Joseph had lost.

"I'll d-do it."

"You're a gut onkel," she said, her voice filling with affection for him. "I don't know how we'd get along without you."

William flushed again. "I been thinking about th-that. You n-n-need someone to take c-c-care of you." He seemed to be growing nervous, the stammer increasing.

"The family already does that."

"N-not enough." He leaned toward her, his face suddenly filled with intensity. "R-Rachel, will you marry me?" He said the words as formally as if in worship.

For a moment she thought she'd misunderstood him, but a look at his face told her he was serious. The boy actually felt so strongly about taking care of them that he'd propose marriage to a woman old enough to be . . . well, not his mother, but certainly his big sister.

She didn't know what to say. Whatever it was, she couldn't let him think she was laughing at him. He was so young, so vulnerable already because of his stammer.

Please, Lord, give me the right words to do this without hurting him.

"William, that's so kind of you." She infused the words with caring for the little brother Ezra had loved. "I know you want to help us, but that's not the way."

His lips trembled, and he pressed them together for a moment. "You're s-s-saying no."

It was kinder, surely, to make this clear. "I'm saying no. You're my bruder, William. That's how I've always seen you, and you're very dear to me."

He was only doing this for Ezra's sake, she was sure. But still, he would be hurt by the rejection.

"D-dumb idea." Tears welled in his eyes, and he knuckled them away like a child would.

"Not dumb. Just very kind." She smiled at him. "I'm too old for you, William, and that's the truth. I can't take you away from the sweet girl God has planned for you."

"N-nobody w-w-would have m-m-me." He turned away, face sulky, his ears red with embarrassment.

"Someone will love you for the gut person you are. I promise." She patted his hand. She felt about a hundred and two in comparison to him, and in a moment she'd start to laugh hysterically. "Why don't you go on out and give Joseph a hand before he tears down Dolly's pen?"

He jerked a nod, shoved himself to his feet, and rushed out the back door, letting it slam behind him.

She could laugh now, but somehow the impulse had left. Poor William, thinking he could make up for Ezra's death that way. Thinking that marriage to him would solve her problems.

Bless him, dear Lord. He has such a gut heart. Surely You have a girl in mind who will love him for that and will set him free to love her, too.

Rachel drove her buggy down the road that led to Daniel and Leah's farm a few days later. Brownie, her mare, could probably take her there and back home again without any guidance, they'd made the trip so often.

Letting the lines lie slack in her hands, Rachel glanced down at the boxful of baby things at her feet. She'd had a gut clearing out and packed up things that Leah might need for her little one. Smiling and sometimes tearing up a bit while she did it, for sure. It seemed incredible that lively Mary had ever been small enough to fit in those clothes.

She tilted her face up so that the sun's warm rays reached beneath the brim of the black bonnet she wore for traveling. Her daffodils grew so fast now that it seemed she could almost see them moving, and even the green spikes of the tulips stood taller each day. Spring was nearly here, and with its coming her spirits lifted.

At worship yesterday it had felt as if everyone seated on the backless benches in the Millers' barn had shared her feelings. Except, possibly, for William.

Her fingers tightened on the lines, and Brownie glanced back over her shoulder, as if to ask what was wrong. Brownie couldn't offer her any advice about the boy, but Leah could. And that was another reason for coming here today.

Brownie turned in at the lane, and in a few minutes the mare stopped at the back porch, lowering her head immediately to snatch a mouthful of grass. Leah, not even bothering with a shawl, came to the door, smiling.

"Wilkom, komm in. I'm wonderful-glad to see you today."

Rachel slid down and pulled the box of baby clothes out. "You'll be even happier when you see what I've brought. Mary's outgrown things for the boppli."

"Ach, how kind of you. It'll be another six weeks before I'm needing them, if the doctor is right." She held the door to let Rachel into the spotless kitchen. "And where is Mary? You didn't bring her with you?"

"Her grossmutter wanted to spend time with her this morning." She set the box on the table and gave Leah a hug. "That was gut, because I wanted to spend some time with you. And it's never too soon to get the swaddling clothes ready. Your little boppli might surprise you by coming early."

Leah patted her belly, laughing. "Not a bad idea. I can barely get close enough to the stove to cook now. Sit. I have coffee ready, and I think the young ones have left some of the apple kuchen my mamm brought yesterday."

"Sounds gut."

Rachel settled down, nearly as comfortable in the Glick kitchen as she was in her own. Leah hadn't moved far when she married, only to the farm next to the one where she'd grown up, where her parents still lived.

While Leah busied herself at the stove, Rachel began sorting the baby things she'd brought, laying them in rows on the pine tabletop. She unfolded a gown so tiny it seemed hardly likely it would fit a baby doll, let alone Mary. Her fingertips smoothed the fine stitches her mamm had sewn into the soft fabric—smoothed and clung, reluctant to let go. Reluctant to think that Mary would be the last boppli she'd have.

Leah brought the coffee and apple kuchen, leaning over to touch a baby shawl, letting it run through her fingers. "Your mamm made this, didn't she? Maybe you'd rather keep it for—" She stopped, biting her lip. "I'm sorry. I shouldn't have said that."

"It's all right, Leah. Really. I'm not upset at that."

Leah eyed her, still looking a little flushed at her mistake. "If not at that, then at something. Are you still concerned about Gideon Zook and the greenhouse?"

"No. Well, maybe a little," she said, trying to be honest. "But I'm as sure as I can be that going ahead with it is the only choice. He's coming over later this afternoon to go over the plans with me."

"No regrets at standing up to Isaac?"

She shook her head. "I surprised myself, I did. But Ezra never let Isaac make decisions for him. And if I once start, I don't know where it would stop."

"You might be like William, afraid to do anything unless Isaac approves," Leah suggested.

"William can be surprising, too." She blew out a frustrated breath. "You wouldn't believe what he said to me the other day."

Leah's hands paused on the tiny nightgown she was folding. "Tell me."

"He offered to marry me, that's what." She could feel the color come up in her cheeks at the thought of it. "Oh, it was kindly meant, I know. He thinks that with Ezra gone, I need someone to take care of me. And since he loved Ezra, I suppose he feels it's his duty. I turned him down as gently as possible, hoping he would understand."

"Did he?"

"I thought so. But then at the Millers' yesterday for church, he wouldn't even look at me—just scuttled off every time he saw me heading his way." She shook her head, still upset when she thought of it. "It has me downright ferhoodled, trying to see how to deal with William, and Isaac, and my folks pressing me to sell the farm and move back home with them. To say nothing of Gideon, all set on helping us whether we want it or not."

Leah leaned across the table to clasp her hand. "It sounds as if you have too many people thinking they know what's best for you."

"That's it exactly." She could count on Leah to understand. "Ezra always said you couldn't hurt Isaac's feelings with a two-by-four, but William is a different story. He's so self-conscious about his stuttering, anyway. Ach, I must have handled it badly, for him to be that eager to avoid me yesterday."

"I don't know what you could do other than make it clear to him." Leah's tone was practical. "You certain sure don't want William walking around imagining that you're going to marry him. You're old enough to be his—"

"Don't you dare say I'm old enough to be his mamm." She smiled, realizing she felt better about it already. "Big sister, maybe."

"Maybe. But I think you've missed something about him. Don't you know that William is stuck on you?"

She stared at Leah as her words penetrated. "William? Me? That's silly. He only did it because of Ezra, because he thought Ezra would want him to. He doesn't—"

"He does." Leah shook her head, lips quirking a little. "Do you really not know that?"

"No, and I don't believe it." But the words didn't come out sounding as convinced as she expected.

"That's because you don't see his expression when he watches you, times you're not looking at him."

She still shook her head. But if Leah was right—

"Leah, what am I going to do?" She nearly wailed the words. This was the last thing she'd expected to have to cope with. "It's impossible."

"Why is it impossible? William is at the age of looking around for someone to love, and he sees how lovable you are."

Her stomach twisted in protest, and she pressed one hand against her middle. "I'm not. I mean—of course Ezra loved me, but I've never thought of anyone else . . ." Her voice trailed off.

"If you haven't thought of it, you should. It'll soon be a year since Ezra passed, and folks are already thinking to match you up with someone. I bet more than one man has been looking your way, and you haven't even noticed."

"I don't believe it. You're making that up. No one is thinking about that at all."

Leah shook her head, green eyes dancing. "Ach, Rachel, you are ferhoodled for sure. Don't you remember how set you were on matching me up with Daniel when he came to the valley? Well, now it's your turn to feel like the target."

She stared at Leah, sure that the consternation she felt was written on her face.

Chuckling a little, Leah started to get up. "If you could see your face right now—" She broke off with a gasp, clutching the chair, and doubled over.

"Leah!" Rachel was there in an instant, putting her arms around her friend, her heart beating a wild rhythm of love and fear as she helped her sit down again. "Are you all right? Is this happening often?"

Leah gasped a little, leaning back in the chair, her face taut with pain. "Not—not too often. That was the worst one yet. But all the books say—"

"I don't care what the books say." Now it was her turn to be the practical one. "If you have a pain bad enough to make you turn white and double up with it, you need to talk to the doctor. Where's Daniel?"

"In the barn, I think. I'm sure I'm all right. It's just a muscle spasm."

"Maybe so. I hope so. But Daniel had best take you to the doctor now, and I'm going to tell him so."

Without waiting for an argument, she hurried across the kitchen and out the back door, her heart pounding in time with her feet.

Please, Lord, please. Let it be nothing at all. Let Leah and her babe be safe. Please.

CHAPTER THREE

*A*nyway, the doctor says that Leah and the boppli are both all right, but she has to start taking it easy, getting off her feet more every day if she doesn't want to be stuck on complete bed rest."

Rachel's brother, Johnny, looking out of place sitting at Rachel's kitchen table in his buttoned-down shirt and khaki pants, stirred his coffee with an absent frown. "If I know Leah, she won't like that. She always has to be up and doing."

"This time she'll do as she's told. Daniel and I made a pact to see to that."

She had gone to the doctor's office with Leah and Daniel, knowing that her mother wouldn't mind staying with Mary, and feeling that her friend needed her support. Daniel had been as happy at her presence as Leah. There were times when only another woman would do.

"I'm glad she's going to be all right." Johnny's voice had a strained note, and he bent his head over the tax forms she'd asked him to look at for her, as if to avoid the subject.

When Johnny had come back to Pleasant Valley a year ago to work at the medical research clinic, he'd tried to renew his friendship with Leah, the girl he'd promised to wed before he'd run off to turn English. He'd ended up imagining himself to be in love with her again, but Leah had chosen to marry Daniel.

Johnny seemed to have adjusted to that, but Rachel wasn't sure how much it bothered him. Once she'd have said that she knew her twin's every feeling, but that had been a long time ago. Now she was just happy to have a relationship with him, knowing they could never go back to what they'd been.

When Leah had first helped bring them together, they'd met once in a while on neutral territory, usually at the home of a friend who understood. Ezra, seeing how important it was to her, had encouraged her to talk the whole situation over with their bishop, Mose Yoder.

Bishop Mose, who saw those kinds of situations more and more as the years went on, had been helpful. As long as she kept to the letter of the bann, not eating at the same table with Johnny, not taking food from his hand, not riding in a car he was driving, the bishop saw no problem.

The outside world probably thought their rules silly. But the rules, the Ordnung, agreed to by every baptized member, spelled out how they remained Amish. How they lived in the world but not of the world.

Rachel's gaze lingered with affection on the dark gold of Johnny's hair as he bent over the papers. It was such a joy to be in the same room with him after all those years apart. And how much Mammi must long to see him, touch him.

For just an instant she toyed with the idea of setting up an "accidental" meeting. But that would be foolish, causing more harm, putting her mother in a position of choosing between husband and son. As long as Daadi held to his determination not to see Johnny, she could do nothing.

Johnny finally pushed the forms back and tapped the yellow pad on which he'd been figuring. He looked up at her, shaking his head a little. "Almost anyone would probably do this better than I can, Rach. I do my own taxes, sure, but a dairy farm is a different matter." A smile flickered across his face. "Would you believe that some people think the Amish don't pay taxes, just because they rely on themselves instead of the government?"

"I hope you straighten people out if they say that to you. 'Render unto Caesar . . .'" She didn't finish the Scripture, because Johnny would know it as well as she did.

He shrugged slightly, as if to evade answering the implied question. She didn't press him. Maybe not correcting people's misconceptions was one of the compromises he made to live English.

"Even if you can just give me a rough figure," she said, "that will help me to plan."

"I might be missing something important. Why don't you have Daad do it?"

"He would, for sure. But I'm trying not to depend on Daad and Mammi too much. If he knew, he'd insist on paying the taxes for me. As it is, he and Mamm are pushing me to sell the farm and move back in with them."

Johnny turned to face her more fully, his face grave. "Nobody knows better than I do how stiff-necked Daad can be, but maybe he's right about that. How long can you keep on trying to run a dairy farm with people volunteering to help you?"

If Johnny was telling her to take Daad's advice, the tax news must be bad. She clasped her hands together. "How much do I owe?"

"I could be wrong. Probably am. Why don't I take these to a regular tax preparer for you?"

He was being kind, but his kindness just seemed to make things worse.

She took a breath, steeling herself for the worst. "I'll need to do that, I guess. But first I want to have at least an idea of what I'm getting into. I won't hold you to it, Johnny, but tell me what you think."

His blue eyes, so like hers, darkened with concern. "Okay. It looks to me as if you're going to owe around ten thousand, give or take a thousand."

She leaned back against the counter. "That much."

"I'm sorry." He pressed his fingers to his forehead, massaging, as if his head ached over giving her such bad news. "Look, I could be wrong. I might be missing some big deductions. Maybe it's not as bad as that."

"Maybe it's worse." She forced herself to be practical. It wouldn't do to let Johnny see how upset she was. "Don't worry. I do have money in the bank. Probably enough to make the payment."

"And then what will you have to live on?"

"We'll manage."

They could manage on very little, living as they did. Johnny, with his English standards, had probably forgotten that.

Still, she would find it difficult, just keeping up with the normal expenses of the farm. If she could find some additional source of income . . .

Or maybe everyone else was right. Maybe she was making things harder by clinging to the farm, not just for herself but for everyone who helped her.

"I don't make much money as a research assistant, but I can get by on a couple hundred less a month. Let me give you that much."

Her heart was touched. But it was impossible; surely he saw that.

"I can't. Thank you for offering. It is so kind."

He moved back, his face tightening. "You mean you won't accept it because I'm under the bann."

"I love you for offering to help me, but I need to do this on my own."

"Don't try to sugarcoat your answer for me, Rachel." His tone hardened. "I'm not one of your children. You're willing to see me, but you won't take money from me no matter how much you need it."

Johnny was getting that mulish look that meant he had his back up, and she knew only too well how that would end. As dearly as she loved him, she wasn't blind to his faults.

She took a breath, trying to be patient. "You know I love you. But keeping my covenant with the church is important. Don't ask me to do something that would cause problems for me with the other people I love."

He shrugged, reaching for his jacket. "Some things never change, do they? I'd better get out of here before I say something I'll regret."

It seemed to her that he already had, but she wouldn't make things worse by telling him so.

"Denke for helping with the taxes. Komm again soon."

He gave her a quick peck on the cheek. "I'll see," he muttered. "We're pretty busy at the clinic just now."

Rachel watched him leave, trying not to feel upset. Johnny's attitude would be understandable if he really was English, but after eighteen years of being Amish, he ought to know better.

The truth was that he and Daadi were too much alike—both too stubborn and too proud to see beyond their own opinions.

Rachel dug her hand spade deep into the moist earth, loosening the roots of the weed that was already taller than the thyme uncurling its leaves delicately in the herb garden. This end of the bed was shady and moist, and the mint loved it here. She was eager to see how the variety of lemon thyme she'd planted last year had survived the winter.

"Weed, Mammi."

She grabbed Mary's hand just before her daughter could uproot the tiny plant. "Not that one, Mary. See, look for ones like this."

She showed her the weed she'd just removed, and Mary nodded solemnly, intent on doing it right. If taking pleasure in digging in the dirt was any sign, little Mary would turn into the gardener of the family.

The air was still chilly, but the sun felt warm on Rachel's back. Already the rhythmic movements and the scent of fresh-turned earth relaxed her. She might be tired and aching after her first hours in the garden, but it would be a happy tired. She glanced at Mary, smiling at her daughter's intent face as she worked away with her own little spade.

Rachel's heart warmed with the sun. This was what she'd longed for throughout the long, lonely winter. This was where healing would come for her.

I know You love gardens, Lord. I feel as close to You here as I do when we're in worship. That's not wrong, is it?

The bucket of weeds was nearly full when Mary sat back on her heels. "Look, Mammi. Onkel Isaac."

She followed the direction her daughter pointed, and her peace fled. Sure enough, it was Isaac, walking across the field that separated their farm from his.

It was unkind to feel that his coming tore up her peace as surely as she had torn the weeds from her garden.

Forgive me, Father. Help me to be patient with him and to remember his good heart.

Even as she prayed, she couldn't help hoping that Isaac would conclude his business quickly. Gideon was supposed to stop by with the final plans for the greenhouse, and life with Isaac would go more smoothly if he were not reminded of that.

Besides, she found the whole business stressful enough, without having Isaac there looking on while she tried to arrive at some conclusion with Gideon.

She rose as Isaac approached, brushing the earth from her hands and shaking out her apron. "Wilkom, Isaac."

"Onkel Isaac." Mary, seldom shy, threw herself at his knees.

He caught the child, lifting her skyward, and tossed her in the air. His stern face softened into a smile at her giggles.

Warmth flooded Rachel's heart at the sight. Isaac, having only sons, had always had a soft spot for her two girls. Whenever she became exasperated at his bossiness, she should remind herself of how kind he was to her children.

"There, now, little Mary, that's enough flying for today." He set her on her feet and patted her head gently.

"I'm afraid she'll never think it's enough." Rachel steered her daughter back to her spade before she could demand more. "You know she loves it when you play with her."

"Ja." Isaac's face was soft as he watched her daughter. "She's a gut child." He turned to her. "And how is Leah Glick? We heard she's been ailing."

"Doing much better." The relief she felt sounded in her voice. "I went over this morning to help a bit with the kinder and make sure she's resting."

"Gut, gut," he said, a bit absently. He gazed past her, toward the barn, as if his mind were elsewhere.

"Did you want to talk with me?" she nudged, mindful that Gideon could show up at any minute.

"Just wanted to check on you and the little ones."

"That's kind of you. We're doing all right, thanks to everyone's help."

He nodded. "I didn't want to bring this up until after you'd had some time to get used to the way things are now, but have you been giving thought to the future?"

The way things are now. He meant her life without Ezra, but he was making an effort to be considerate.

"I think about it all the time. Making decisions, that's the difficult part."

"Ja. Ezra always took gut care of you. It's hard, a woman on her own."

Tension crept back along her nerves. Surely Isaac wasn't suggesting that she remarry, was he?

"I've been considering the situation. You know, Caleb's nearly nineteen now."

Caleb, Isaac's oldest, was actually a month older than his Onkel William, a thing that wasn't so surprising when families were large and spread out in age.

"He hasn't given you much worry during his rumspringa, has he?" Some youngsters did, especially the boys, taking their freedom to extremes, but Caleb had always seemed too serious and responsible for that.

"No, no, he's too wise for that. Thing is, he's ready to take a wife."

A suggestion that she consider marriage to Caleb, coming after William's proposal, would drive her to hysteria. "Is he?" Her voice sounded strangled.

"Ja, ja. He and Ellen Stoltzfus have decided between them, and we're agreeable, though we're not telling anyone but family yet, of course."

She could breathe again. Really, she was being ridiculous, having such thoughts. "I'm happy for them."

"Ja, so are we, but having five boys to get settled isn't an easy thing, you know. In the normal way of things, Caleb would take over my farm, but I'm nowhere near ready to move to the grossdaadi haus."

He chuckled, to show that was a joke. Naturally Isaac wouldn't want to give up the reins yet.

"I'm sure Caleb is willing to wait until you're ready." That seemed the proper answer, although she had no idea why Isaac would be talking to her about it.

"Well, and that's just what we don't want him to do. A young couple like that, just starting out, it's a gut thing to have their own place. Helps them to be steady-like, knowing what they're working toward."

"I see." She was beginning to, actually. "Are you talking about my farm?"

He looked a little nettled, as if he didn't care to be rushed toward the point he wanted to make, but then his face smoothed out into a determined smile.

"Don't hurry into answering me. I just want you to think about this. Seems it would be the best solution all around. Ezra's farm would go to his kin, as I'm sure he'd want, and we'd pay you a fair market price. Set it up any way you want, with monthly payments or a lump sum."

Ezra's farm, he'd said. Of course that was the way he'd see it, conveniently forgetting that the farm had come to them from her aunt and uncle. Childless themselves, they'd made it easy for their favorite niece and her husband to buy their place.

That didn't really matter, did it? The point was that if she was going to have to sell, it would be better to sell to family, as Isaac said.

The familiar indecision settled on her. "I'm not sure . . ."

"What aren't you sure about?" His voice sharpened. "You can't run a dairy farm on your own. You must be sure of that much. It was hard enough for Ezra, with the children not old enough to help yet."

Ezra had worked too hard, tried to do too much, but he'd loved it. No matter how tired he was, he always had a smile and a dream for the future. That was what he'd been working for—to have the right life for their family.

"You have to think about the children's future," Isaac said, gesturing toward Mary, who'd begun arranging pebbles around the edge of the bed. "Suppose you try to hang on to the farm and you fail. You could get into trouble with the taxes and end up losing everything Ezra worked so hard for. Better to make the decision now, while it's yours to make."

He made it all sound so sensible. It was sensible, she supposed. It just seemed wrong, somehow. This wasn't the way Ezra's dream was supposed to end.

"I . . . I'll think about it." Her voice sounded weak and indecisive, even to herself, and she hated that. Had she really been so dependent on Ezra that she couldn't make up her own mind?

"Gut, gut." Isaac rocked back on his heels, smiling. "You think on it. Pray on it. I know you'll decide right."

It was easy for Isaac to say. He wasn't the one who'd have to live with the results.

. . .

Gideon's hands tightened on the lines as his buggy rolled down the lane to the Brand farm. That was Isaac Brand he'd spotted, heading back across the fields to his adjoining farm.

Judging by what he'd seen of Rachel's relationship with her brother-in-law, he probably wouldn't find her in a tranquil temper after a visit from Isaac. That didn't bode well for the success of his mission today.

He'd have to be persistent, that was all. He'd been trying for well over a week to get Rachel's final approval on the plans for the greenhouse. He'd figured that once she'd committed herself to letting him build it, that would be the end of the discussion, and he could get on with it.

But each time he'd tried to pin her down, Rachel had found yet another reason to avoid giving him the final go-ahead. At first he'd thought she just couldn't figure out what she wanted. Now he was beginning to wonder if she still thought she'd find a way to get out of it entirely.

He didn't have all summer to get this job finished, not without having it affect the other projects he'd committed to. After the months of recuperation that he'd begun to think would never end, his shattered leg was finally healing. He might not be ready to climb on any scaffolding yet, but a small job like the greenhouse was the perfect place to start.

His hands tightened in the frustration that was becoming too familiar a companion. Orders for the windmills that were his specialty were stacking up. If he didn't start filling them soon, he risked losing the business to someone else.

Folks had been willing to wait for him so far, some because they were Amish and so were brethren, others because they wanted the skill he provided.

But they wouldn't wait forever. The doctors kept saying he had to be patient, that he'd regain much of his mobility in time. Unfortunately, patience was not something he'd ever had in great supply. Maybe that was why God had sent him this particular trial—so that he could practice developing it.

Truth was, he'd almost welcomed the pain of his injuries. The guilt he carried every day demanded some penalty. "Survivor guilt," the doctor had called it. Having a name didn't help him cope with it.

He stopped at the hitching rail, making an effort not to favor his left leg as he climbed down. Acting as if he were whole must be a step to getting there, he'd think.

Rachel had obviously seen him coming. She stood waiting for him by the herb garden near the back porch, with little Mary digging in the bed next to her. Motionless, she looked oddly forlorn in the slanting rays of the early spring sunshine.

Maybe she saw that he was watching her, because she squared her shoulders and smiled. He thought it took an effort. Her hands weren't gathered into fists, so apparently her encounter with Isaac hadn't made her angry, but it had had some sort of effect on her.

"I hope I'm not coming too late, Rachel. Mary, how are you?" He smiled down at the little girl. So like her mother, she was, her blue eyes fixed on him in an unwavering stare.

"No, it's fine. We're finished here." Rachel glanced at her daughter. "Mary, what are you doing?"

Mary had come over to him. She tugged on his pants leg, and then she linked her fingers together in a rocking motion.

"It's all right." He grinned at the child. "She remembers that I made her a cradle from my handkerchief once. That's been over a year ago. Think of her still remembering that."

Mary tugged at his pants leg again.

"Persistent, aren't you?" Chuckling a little, he pulled out his handkerchief. He folded it into a triangle and then did the double roll and twist that transformed a handkerchief into a cradle with a baby in it, if you had the imagination of a child. He rocked it once between his fingers and then handed it to Mary.

She laughed and swung it back and forth. "Schloofe, boppli. Schloofe."

Rachel was staring at him, and he couldn't read her expression. "You're very talented," she said.

He shrugged. "I have nieces and nephews who sometimes need distracting."

"When did you do this for Mary?" Her voice seemed to have cooled.

He didn't care much for the disapproval he sensed in her. She'd never really liked the time Ezra had spent with him, it seemed. Had it been jealousy of their close friendship? Or resentment that he took Ezra away from family sometimes? She certainly couldn't imagine he was leading Ezra into mischief. During their rumspringa, it had been Ezra who always came up with that.

"When she went with Ezra and me to an auction, I think." He held up the plans he'd tucked under his arm. "Are you ready to take a look at these?"

She blinked at the abrupt change of subject. He could see her scrambling to come up with an answer.

"I . . . I was thinking that maybe it doesn't make so much sense to start the greenhouse right now. I mean, the frost danger will be over in another month, and I probably wouldn't get much use from it for a while. If you have other projects to do first—"

He kept a rein on his temper. Rachel had been a pliant girl, and she'd always seemed eager to do as Ezra wanted. Now it seemed she didn't want to be told what to do, and he wouldn't fall into the same mistake that Isaac made in dealing with her.

"Now is the perfect time to get on with the greenhouse. My leg's not up to the high work on windmills yet, but I can certainly handle a greenhouse."

He wasn't going to tell her the rest of it—his sense that if only he could start doing something for her and her kinder, he'd ease the weight of responsibility that he felt each time he thought of Ezra.

Her face had tightened with the reminder of his injury, but she gave a jerky nod. "Makes sense, I guess. It's getting chilly. Komm inside. We can work there."

Success, of a sort, he supposed. He followed her into the haus, and Mary trailed after them, crooning a soft lullaby to her imaginary infant.

Obeying Rachel's gesture, he spread the plan out on the table, smoothing it down, while she poured coffee from the ever-present pot on the stove. She carried two mugs to the table, handing one to him, and stood for a moment staring down at the simple plan.

"You're right," she said. "I've hesitated about this long enough. If this is a gut time for you, let's go ahead already."

"Fine." He kept it matter-of-fact and leaned over, tracing the shape with his finger. "Here's the area we talked about adding along the side. It'll make the greenhouse a bit bigger than the original plan, but it'll give you more light, especially early in the spring."

She bent over the plan next to him, studying it. "I didn't think about it being bigger—will we need more materials, then?"

He heard a trace of anxiety in her voice, making him wonder if the cost was an issue. "I don't think so."

And if they did, he'd take care of that himself. She need never know.

"That's gut." Her fingertips glided over the outline almost lovingly. "I was just thinking that—" She hesitated, as if reluctant to voice the thought.

"What?"

"Well, it could be a little extra income for me, ain't so? Growing the plants and selling them. If I had more, I could maybe go to all the spring Mud Sales, even the farmer's market, ferleicht."

"No 'perhaps' about it. You could do that."

Now it was his turn to hesitate. Had Ezra not left her provided for? He'd always assumed this was a prosperous farm, but Rachel sounded as if finances were a worry.

He had been Ezra's closest friend. He had the responsibility to ask. "Is the money a problem? I thought the dairy herd brought in a gut income."

Rachel sighed, a little catch of breath that brushed his heart. With her eyes fixed on the plan she wasn't looking at him, and his gaze traced the clear line of her profile. She stood very close, and the air around them was so still it seemed even the room held its breath.

"I never had to worry about it when Ezra was taking care of things." She stopped, shaking her head. "But with Isaac and William doing all the work for the dairy herd, it's only fair that they share the money from the milk."

His own breath seemed to be strangling him. Fair? Well, they deserved something for their work, but—

"How big a share?"

She didn't have to answer, but he hoped she would.

"We go halves." She glanced at him then, troubled. "That's only right."

"Does Isaac also pay half the expenses—the feed, the taxes?" Because it would be Isaac who expected the payment. He felt sure that young William was doing this because he had a gut heart and because he'd loved Ezra.

"Well, no. I mean, it's not his farm."

No, it wasn't. And if anyone accused Isaac of taking advantage of his widowed sister-in-law, all he'd have to say was that she'd pay as much or more if she had to hire the work done.

And saying anything to Isaac would only cause trouble in the family and dissension in the church. It was better, much better, to keep his opinions of Isaac's doings to himself and find some other way to help Rachel.

"I think your plans for the greenhouse are very sound. You might go a little further, if you wanted."

"Further?"

"Fresh flowers for the farmer's market, say. My brother Aaron and his wife go twice a week in the growing season. I'm sure he'd be willing to take them for you. And if you potted up some of the perennials you grow, that would be another thing to sell."

His enthusiasm for the idea built as he talked. A fine gardener like Rachel had plenty to offer that folks, especially the English, would pay for.

"Those herbs of yours, too," he added. "You might even go into growing some ornamental shrubs and raspberry or blackberry bushes and such-like for sale."

Rachel's eyes had widened, as if she could see all the possibilities. For a moment her face lit with enthusiasm, but then the light went out like a snuffed candle.

"There would be expenses. And besides, I don't know anything about running a business."

"I can help you with that."

He saw in an instant that he should have stopped at offering the ideas. Those she might take. Actual assistance, at least from him—that she didn't want. She was only accepting it with the greenhouse because she couldn't find a way out.

She pulled away from the table. "That's kind of you, Gideon. But I can't let you do anything else for me."

"Can't?" If he didn't do some plain speaking, this would always stand between them. "Or won't, because you don't forgive me for Isaac's death?" There. It was out, though his heart hurt with it.

Her face blanched. "It was an accident. You're not to blame. And even if you were, I would forgive."

It was the Amish way. They both knew that. Forgive as you would be forgiven. God didn't offer His forgiveness on any easier terms, no matter how much His children might want it.

"Forgiveness is more than words." He paused, but maybe it was best to say the rest of it. "The truth is that you didn't like my friendship with Ezra long before the accident. Every time he went off with me, I could see it in your face."

"No."

He ignored the denial, because they both knew what he said was true. "You resented our friendship. I never really understood why. And now you resent it that I'm still alive." The face of his dead wife flickered through his mind. Ja, he was still alive, for a reason only God understood.

He took a harsh breath. "I loved him, too, Rachel. I mourn for him. And I am going to do everything I can to help you and his children, so I hope you can find a way to live with that."

CHAPTER FOUR

Folks in the outside world probably had people they went to when they had a problem. Doctors and other advisors, Rachel shouldn't wonder. When the Leit, the Amish of Pleasant Valley, needed someone to talk to, they went to Bishop Mose. So that was where she was headed today.

The weather had turned gray and chill again, as the end of March often did, and the wind had whipped at the brim of her bonnet as Brownie clip-clopped along the narrow blacktop road to town. If March was going to go out like a lamb, it had best start warming up. But she was here now, and Mose's workshop would be warm.

She swung down from the buggy seat and fastened the lines to the hitching rail. She reached back under the buggy seat for the piece of harness with the loose buckle. That needed mending anyway, so it gave her a good reason for coming to Mose Yoder's harness shop, just in case her courage failed her and she couldn't bring up the thing she wanted to talk with him about.

Bishop Mose, like all ministers and bishops among the Amish, worked at his trade as the apostle Paul had, accepting their Christian duties in addition.

There were two steps up to the little wooden porch, hollowed with the passage of many feet over the years. The glass-paneled door bore a hand-lettered sign. *Horse People Only, No Tourists*, it read. Beneath those directions Mose had added, in firm black-marker letters, *No Picture-Taking*.

She smiled a little. Once, the signs wouldn't have been necessary, but in recent years tourists had discovered the Amish of Pleasant Valley. Bishop Mose did business with the English horse-owners in the area, some even coming from as far away as Mifflinburg to get good handcrafted tack. But he could do without the tourists.

She opened the door, the bell jangling, and stepped inside. Bishop Mose stood behind the cash register, busy with a customer, but he gave her a quick, welcoming smile. Since the customer was English and not anyone she knew, she moved to the side counter, keeping her gaze politely averted from the business they were transacting.

The rich scents of leather and oil transported her back through the years. She'd been coming to Mose's harness shop since her father brought her and Johnny when they were little more than Mary's age. The shop fascinated her—the harness and tack hanging from pegs and lining shelves up to the ceiling; the mysterious, to her child's mind, machinery that Mose used on the leather; and most especially Bishop Mose Yoder himself.

She slid a sideways glance as he bent over the counter, listening courteously to some story the Englischer was telling. As always, Mose wore a heavy apron over his black trousers and blue shirt to protect them from his work.

Had he really not aged since she was a child? Somehow she'd always thought him old, with his long beard and hair a snowy white and his face a patchwork of tiny wrinkles, much like a piece of his own leather.

Running her fingers along a fine Western saddle with elaborate leatherwork, she tried to figure out how old Mose must be. Close to eighty, surely, wasn't he? An Amish bishop was a bishop for life, just as the ministers were, chosen by lot through God's guidance. Had Mose started out looking like a patriarch of the Old Testament, or had the look grown on him as he ministered to his flock?

The customer finally headed for the door, apparently satisfied with the new bridle he had slung over his shoulder. He gave her a polite nod as he passed.

The door closed behind him, and Mose turned to her.

"Rachel. It's fine to see you today. How are you? And the kinder?"

"We're all well." Now that she faced his keen gaze, she was doubly grateful she'd brought the harness. She handed it across the counter to him. "I hoped you might have time to fix the buckle on this for me."

"Ach, I always have time for you, ain't so?" He took the harness, running it through his hands as if he saw with them, as well as with his eyes. "I mind when I made this for Ezra. Five years ago, it must have been, at least."

"About that."

She glanced past him, toward the alcove behind the counter where the big sewing machines sat, all connected to a massive belt that ran through a hole in the floor to a generator in the cellar. Sometimes Mose had several men helping him there, when he was especially busy, but today all was quiet.

She was alone with him in the shop. She wouldn't find a better opportunity to ask for his advice, if she could just get the words out.

Mose adjusted his glasses and began picking out the loose stitches that held the buckle, staying at the counter probably because he guessed that she wanted to talk.

She felt tongue-tied. How could she just come out with her mixed-up feelings about Gideon?

"Have you seen anything of John lately?" Mose gave her a keen glance, as if to assess whether her English brother was the source of her worry.

"A few nights ago." She remembered too well Johnny's annoyance at her for keeping to the Ordnung. "He is doing well, I think. I just wish—"

She paused, but Mose probably knew the rest of that thought.

"Your daad still refuses to see him?"

She nodded. "I don't bring it up much, because it upsets Mamm. Even though Daadi knows other Amish parents find a way to have a relationship with their children who have jumped the fence, he won't consider it."

"Ach, your daad always was one to do everything the hard way. No doubt he still hopes being cut off from his family will push Johnny into coming back to the church."

"It won't." Once she might have hoped that, too, but she'd seen enough of her brother in recent months to know the truth. He was committed to the English world and to the work that seemed so important. He would never come back.

"No. I never thought he would return." Mose's face showed regret and acceptance. "Some just aren't a fit for the life, even when they're born to it."

She'd never thought of it that way, exactly, but Bishop Mose was right. "From the time we were little, Johnny was always restless, always wanting more. Impatient."

He nodded. "I think—"

The bell over the door rang. Mose glanced that way, and his face stiffened. "No tourists," he said.

She darted a quick look. A man and woman, both with cameras hanging from their necks, had just come in. Surely they couldn't have missed the sign on the door.

"We just want to look around." The woman lifted her camera. "Just take a few pictures."

"No pictures. No tourists." Mose's tone was polite but firm. "That's what the sign says. I ask you please to leave."

Rachel stole another glance. The man's face had reddened. "Listen, if you people want to have any tourist trade in this town, you'd better be a little nicer when folks come in here."

"My harness shop is a business. Not a tourist attraction." Mose's face was as stony as Moses's must have been when he'd broken the stone tablets.

"Come on, Hal." It sounded as if the woman was tugging her husband toward the door, but Rachel didn't turn around again to see, wary of the camera the woman still held up. The brim of her bonnet cut them off very nicely. "There's a cute quilt shop down the street. I'm crazy about Amish quilts."

The door slammed, and footsteps thudded on the wooden steps. Rachel glanced around, just as the woman raised her camera to the glass and snapped a picture. Then, smiling in satisfaction, she went off down the street.

Mose grunted. "It spites me when they do that. Some folks don't have the sense the Lord gave a chipmunk. Can't they read?"

The flash of the camera had unsettled her, but she tried to shake it off. "They think they're the exception to the rule. If they try that on Ruth Stoltzfus at the quilt shop, she'll chase them out with a broom."

Mose chuckled, his good humor quickly restored. "I'd like to see that, I would."

"So would I." She smiled, picturing plump, irascible Ruth's reaction.

"Now, then." Mose returned to the buckle, but his wise old eyes surveyed her over the rims of his glasses. "I think you did not come all the way to town today just to have this buckle replaced or to talk about the ways of tourists. Or even of your brother."

"No, I guess not." How to say this? "I . . . I'm concerned about something." She took a breath and plunged in. "It's Gideon Zook. You've maybe heard that he insists on building the greenhouse that Ezra promised me for my birthday?"

He nodded. Of course he'd have heard. The Amish might not have telephones in their homes, but they had a very efficient grapevine that passed on all the news.

"I know Gideon is not to blame for the accident." She said the words she'd been repeating to herself, staring down at Bishop Mose's weathered hands, darkened by the stain he used on the leather. "It was an accident, just that."

"But?" His voice was gentle.

"But when I see him, I feel resentment. It's as if I blame him for being alive when Ezra is gone." She clasped her hands together. "That's wrong. I know it. I have prayed to be able to forgive, to stop thinking this way, but God hasn't taken the feelings away."

"We forgive, as God forgives us," Mose said. "But God is God. We are not so gut at it as He is."

"I must forgive." She could hear the desperation in her voice. "I can't go on feeling this every time I see him."

"Rachel, child, when we suffer a great loss, as you have, we start by saying the words. That is gut, but we still have to go through all the grieving." His voice had thickened, as if he thought of his own losses—a son gone in an accident when a car hit his buggy, his wife dying of a stroke a few years after that.

Other people lost those they loved. Other people found a way to forgive and go on with their lives. Why not her?

"Gideon says that I never liked his friendship with Ezra." The words burst out of her. She'd been denying them for days, and that had made her no gut at all.

"Is he right?" Mose's voice didn't condemn. It just asked the question.

"I don't know." Her fingers twisted together, as if they fought it out. "I hope not. But maybe—well, since Gideon didn't have a wife, I guess it seemed like he was freer than Ezra. When the two of them went off together, even if it was just to an auction, it was like they were still having their rumspringa."

The words that came out of her mouth surprised her. Had she really felt that? She stared at Mose, longing to hear him say she was wrong. He didn't speak. He waited.

"Gideon was right, then." She said the words softly, almost to herself. "I did feel that."

"Rachel, Rachel," he said. "That's natural enough already. For sure a young frau wants to have her husband to herself. When there's a boppli, she wants him home with her."

Guilt was a rock in her chest. "Ezra worked so hard. I shouldn't have questioned it if he wanted to go off to do something with Gideon."

"Ach, child," he chided gently. "Don't start fretting about that, now. It's foolish. You were a gut wife to Ezra, and he loved you. Don't worry that you weren't perfect. We're not meant to be perfect this side of Heaven."

"But what do I do?" Her throat was tight. "I have to make it right. I shouldn't feel this way."

"The Lord calls us to obedience, not feelings."

"I don't understand."

His face hinted at a smile. "You try so hard, Rachel. Too hard, maybe. Just think about what you would do if you truly had forgiven. Then go and do that. Du Herr will take care of the feelings in His own gut time. Ja?"

She nodded slowly. *Think what you would do if you had truly forgiven, and then do it.* That was simple enough in one way.

And in another, given Gideon's determination to be involved in her life, it was not simple at all.

. . .

"*What* are you doing?"

Gideon looked up at the question to find Ezra's young son staring at him, his expression open and curious.

He set aside the trowel he'd been using to smooth the wet cement for the floor of the greenhouse. Squatting, he propped his elbows on his knees to pay attention to the boy. "This will be your mammi's new greenhouse. Today I am making the floor."

Joseph nodded. "Daadi gave the greenhouse to her for her birthday. I remember."

"You have a wonderful-gut memory, then. Do you think she'll like it?"

"It's a nice floor," the boy said, maybe wondering if that was all.

Gideon smiled. Young Joseph was a lot like Ezra had been at that age in looks, but not in character. Somehow he didn't think Joseph was as daring as Ezra, who'd found far too many ways to get into mischief, usually dragging Gideon along with him.

"The floor is just the beginning. I still have to put up the walls and all the glass. And maybe build some tables for your mamm to put her plants on. It will take me a few days to finish it."

"I could help you. I helped Daadi a lot." Joseph's eyes clouded a little, as if the memory grieved him.

Gideon hesitated, not because he wouldn't be happy to have Joseph around, no matter how little help he was, but because he wasn't sure how Rachel would feel about that.

"You'd best go and ask your Mammi first. She might have some other chores for you to do."

Joseph considered that for a moment. Then he nodded and scampered off toward the kitchen door.

Maybe Rachel would have no objection. She had seemed welcoming enough when he'd turned up today. She'd even brought him out coffee and offered to make lunch for him. But that might be nothing more than a temporary truce.

He didn't know whether to apologize for what he'd said about her attitude toward his friendship with Ezra or let it be. Not that he'd changed his mind. But just because something was true didn't mean a person had to say it.

In a way, he could understand why she'd felt as she did. Young married couples usually had best friends who were in the same situation. If Naomi had lived, they'd have been friends as couples, sharing each other's lives as the children came along.

But Naomi hadn't lived. The baby hadn't. Even after all these years, letting himself think of that was looking into a bottomless pit.

Ezra had talked to him, just once, about remarrying. "Naomi wouldn't expect you to live your life alone, Gid." Ezra's normally merry face had been solemn as he leaned against the wagon they'd been fixing. "Everyone thinks it's time you were looking around for a wife."

He expected it from everyone else. Not from Ezra. He thought Ezra understood. The wrench he held clanged against the wheel rim.

"I can't." His voice rasped, and he forced the words past suddenly numb lips. "I let Naomi and the babe die." He saw the argument forming on Ezra's face. He didn't want to hear it. "Don't, Ezra. No matter what anyone thinks, I'll not be marrying again. I won't take responsibility for another life. I can't."

The back door banged, forcing him back to the present. Joseph raced across the lawn, his face alight with eagerness. "Mammi says yes, but I shouldn't be a nuisance, and I have to give water to my goat first, and keep her penned up so she doesn't get in the way."

It sounded as if he quoted Rachel. "Fine, do that."

The boy spun toward the barn, then paused, darting a measuring look toward Gideon. "Do you want to see my goat?"

Something in Joseph's expression said that this was a rare treat, so he got up from his knees. "I'd like that."

He followed the boy across the backyard toward the barn. The light breeze ruffled the boy's hair as he raced ahead.

Joseph ran the last few steps to a pen attached to the barn. A small Nubian nanny stood at the door, bawling for the boy as if he were her kid. Joseph opened the pen door and slipped inside, fending off the goat's attempt to get out.

"You must stay in now. Later I'll take you for a walk."

The little Nubian wore a collar, as if she were a dog instead of a goat. Her coat was glossy from much brushing. She was a beloved pet, obviously.

Joseph kept his arm around her neck and smiled proudly. "This is Dolly. She's beautiful, ain't so?"

"Ja, she is." Ezra's son might look like him, but he had Rachel's smile. Not that he'd seen much smiling from her lately, but he remembered the look.

"She's going to have a kid. Maybe two. Onkel William says that it might be twins. I'd like it if she had twins. Don't you think that would be nice?"

Gideon nodded. If his boppli had lived, he'd be a bit older than Joseph. They would have been friends. His heart twisted in his chest.

Joseph patted the little nanny's side. "I don't see how she's going to know what to do when the babies come, with no other goats around to show her."

"I'm sure it's in her nature."

"Maybe." Joseph didn't look reassured by the glib answer.

"I tell you what. I'll ask my brother Aaron about it, if you want. He raises goats, so he'll know. Then I can tell you what he says the next time I come."

"Would you?" Joseph's smile blossomed.

"Ja. Now, what do you say we get some work done?"

"I'm ready."

With a final pat for the goat, Joseph hurried out, fastening the pen door carefully. Then he darted across the yard toward the construction.

Gideon followed more slowly. He was a fine boy, this son of Ezra's. Rachel was doing a gut job with him, and it couldn't be easy for her, bringing up a boy without a man in the house.

He spotted her then—coming out on the back porch to shake out a rag rug. She paused, glancing from Joseph to him.

Taking that as an indication she wanted to say something, he detoured by the porch.

"Don't let him be a pest, now," she said.

"He's not. He was just showing me his goat, and now we're going to get down to work."

"That goat." She shook her head. "Ezra wouldn't approve of Joseph treating her as if she were a pet, but it's hatt."

Hard, ja, it was hard for Joseph. For all of them. "Ezra would have been happy the boy found comfort. You must stop worrying about it, because that I'm certain sure of."

There it was, then—that smile that softened her cheeks and warmed her eyes. Just like Joseph's.

But Rachel's smile was having a funny effect on him, and he wasn't sure he liked that. Or at least, not sure that he should.

"*Stretch* your hand out, now."

Rachel watched as Gideon helped little Mary press her palm into the still-damp cement floor for the new greenhouse. Mary giggled a bit, but her tiny handprint took its place next to those of Joseph and Becky, marking the spot that would be the entrance.

Joseph leaned over Gideon's shoulder, looking at them. "My hand is bigger than Mary's," he observed.

"But mine is the biggest," Becky said quickly.

"It's not a contest to see whose is biggest." Gideon lifted Mary back away from the floor. "We put your handprints there so that years from now, when you're all grown, you'll look at them and see how small you were the day we started the greenhouse."

Rachel had a lump in her throat already, and that comment just made it worse. Panic gripped her for an instant. Where would they be, years from now? What if Isaac was right? If she couldn't keep the farm, someone else might be looking at the handprints, wondering at them.

The moment Gideon released her, Mary made an instinctive move to wipe her sticky hand on her dress. Rachel grabbed her just in time to avert disaster.

"Ach, no, Mary. Becky, please take Mary and wash her hands at the pump—real gut, now. Joseph, you go, too."

She kept her face turned away from Gideon, hoping he wouldn't see that she was upset. Or at least, that if he did see, he'd respect her privacy and not question it.

"Rachel?" He rose to his feet, brushing off the knees of his broadfall trousers. "Was ist letz? What's wrong?"

"Nothing." Despite her efforts, her voice didn't sound quite natural.

"Something, I think, or you would not have tears in your eyes." He stood, waiting, as solid and immovable as one of the sturdy maples that had been here since before there was a farm on this spot.

"I hope . . ." She had to stop. Start again. "I hope the children are still living here when they are grown."

"Why wouldn't they be?" His tone sharpened.

"If I have to sell the farm, it won't be the same." Even if she sold to family, and she and the children came back often, they wouldn't really belong here.

"You're not going to sell the farm." He reached out, as if to grasp her arm, but stopped, his hand falling back to his side. "You can't just give up."

"Give up?" Anger spurted through her, surprising her. "Do you think it's easy, trying to run the farm on my own?"

"No, I don't think that. But you have Ezra's brothers helping you with the dairy herd."

"There's more to it than that."

He didn't understand the constant worry. He couldn't. He was responsible for no one but himself. How long could she hold on? Even if she did start making money from her plants, would it be enough?

"Rachel, the farm was Ezra's dream." He did take her wrist then, holding it lightly in the circle of his fingers as if to keep her from walking away until he had the answers he wanted. "He wouldn't want you to give that up already."

"You make the same arguments as Isaac does. But to a different end."

He frowned. "What are you talking about? What arguments?"

She didn't want to tell him, but she seemed pinned to the spot by the intensity of his frowning gaze.

"Isaac wants me to sell the farm to him, for his oldest boy. He says that way it would go to Ezra's kin and still be in the family." Her fingers clenched. "He says that's what Ezra would want. You say Ezra would want me to keep the farm. The truth is that neither of you really knows what he would want."

"Maybe that's so." Gideon spoke slowly, his gaze intent on her face. "Maybe it's wrong to try to judge what Ezra would want. I don't know what Isaac is going on, but I'm saying it because I heard Ezra talk about his dreams for this place. About how it would be his legacy to his children, how one day Joseph would be running it, and you'd be adding on a grossdaadi haus for the two of you."

She seemed to hear Ezra's laughing voice, talking about the two of them growing old together in the grossdaadi haus he'd build. Her throat choked with tears.

"Do you think I don't know that?" She fought to speak around the tightness. "A wife knows her husband's hopes better than a friend, no matter how close he is. I lived the struggle to get established here. Even with the help my aunt and uncle gave us in buying the place, it wasn't easy."

His lips parted as if he'd speak, but she swept on, determined to have her say.

"This was our dream, but we never imagined that I'd be running it alone. I can't do it. If I didn't have Isaac and William's help, I'd be done. What if Isaac were no longer willing to help with the herd? What would I do then?"

"Isaac surely has not threatened to do that." His fingers tightened on her wrist.

"No. He seems willing to wait for my answer." She straightened, pulling her hand away, and he let her go instantly. "And it will be my answer, no one else's. I am the one with the kinder to raise, and I must decide what is best for them."

It sounded lonely. It *was* lonely, but it was also true.

For a long moment, Gideon stood looking at her. Finally he nodded. "I'm sorry if I spoke out of turn. You're right—the young ones must come first."

He turned, picking up the tarp that lay folded on the grass. He began to spread it over the cement.

She picked up an edge and helped him cover the new floor. The tarp slid over the small handprints, hiding them from her sight.

He fastened the corners with stones and then straightened, looking at her for the space of a heartbeat, his face very grave.

"I hope you will not have to leave, Rachel. But if you do, I'll make sure that every part of the greenhouse can easily move with you, except for the floor."

The tension that had been holding her up went out of her like a balloon deflating, and she felt flat and tired. "That's kind of you, Gideon. I don't know what the future will hold. Maybe that's for the best."

"Maybe so." His mouth closed firmly on the words, as if he wanted to say something else but was afraid to upset her.

She couldn't help smiling. She'd grown to know Gideon better in the past few days than she had in all the years before.

"You may as well go on. There is something more you want to say, so just say it."

He didn't quite smile in response, but his mouth seemed to gentle, somehow. "Just this. Ezra heard a lot of advice from Isaac all his life. He listened, but he always made his own decisions, whatever Isaac said." He paused, surveying her gravely. "I hope that you will do the same."

Chapter Five

*B*ecky!" Rachel called her daughter's name for the third or fourth
time, still with no answer.

She could guess where Becky was. William had brought Ben and
Bess, the Belgian draft horses, back from Isaac's this morning, intending to do the plowing. Becky, as fascinated as her father had been by the
massive, gentle creatures, had raced for the barn the moment she got
home. She was probably still there.

Grabbing her shawl, Rachel wrapped it around her as she hurried
off the porch. Fickle April had turned cold after a few days that tempted
with a promise of warmth.

Still, the ground was soft underfoot. William would be able to plow
tomorrow. Perhaps she ought to have him add a strip or two to the
kitchen garden, so that she could grow extra vegetables for market. And
maybe some small shrubs, as Gideon had suggested.

She glanced toward the greenhouse. The uprights were in place now,
so that she could visualize the completed project. It would be near as big
as her kitchen, which made sense since she'd rather garden than cook.

Gideon hadn't come today—off to bid on another job. Just as well.
She'd felt awkward with him since the day he'd helped put the handprints in the greenhouse.

Annoyance flickered through her. Gideon didn't understand how
dependent she was on Isaac's goodwill. Without William here to handle
the draft horses and do the plowing, she didn't see how she'd manage.

She'd try if she had to, but she shuddered at the thought. Ezra had
teased her, but she'd always been in awe of the massive beasts, gentle as
they were.

All Gideon could think about was what he imagined Ezra would want. Well, that was what she wanted, too, wasn't it? Why did it annoy her so much when Gideon voiced it?

I'm not making sense, even to myself, Father. Please help me to know what Your will is for our future, because I do not see the path clearly just now.

She reached the barn door, which stood ajar, and shoved it wider so that she could enter. She stepped inside and stopped, shock freezing her to the spot.

Becky—Becky was in the stall with Ben. The giant draft horse stood, perhaps dozing, facing away from the front. Becky looked like a doll next to him as she tugged at a hind leg the girth of a young tree.

Terror stifled the cry that rose to Rachel's lips. She mustn't do anything that would startle the animal. He was a gentle creature, but his sheer size made him a danger. The step of one of those dinner-plate-sized feet could break a bone, and the horse probably didn't even realize Becky was there.

She took a cautious step. "Becky." She fought to keep her voice soft when she wanted to scream. "Komm schnell."

Becky's face swiveled toward her. Her lower lip pouted, as if she were about to argue. A thud resounded from the loft overhead, reverberating through the barn.

Ben threw his head up, massive body shifting. Before she could breathe, Becky had disappeared, caught between the horse and the wall.

"Becky!" Rachel flung herself toward the stall, heart pounding in her ears, terror speeding her feet.

Becky, Becky, Dear Father, protect her . . .

She heard pounding boots above her, and then William dropped straight down from the hayloft. He vaulted into the stall, shoving at the horse's hindquarters. In an instant he lifted Becky over the stall door and into Rachel's arms.

"Are you all right?" She knelt, holding her, running her hands quickly along Becky's limbs.

"I'm fine, Mammi." Becky's voice trembled a bit, and her face was white. "Ben didn't hurt me. He wouldn't."

"N-n-no." William climbed out of the stall more slowly than he had gone in, and the horse stamped a giant foot as if to emphasize the word. "He w-w-wouldn't hurt you on purpose. He d-d-didn't know you w-were there."

"Are you sure you're okay?" Rachel smoothed Becky's fine hair back into its braid.

Becky pulled away, her lower lip coming out. "Don't fuss."

Fear slid easily into anger, fueled by the guilt she always felt when one of the children was in danger.

"That is no way to speak to your mother. What were you doing in that stall? You know better than to go in there."

Becky's gaze slid away from hers, a sure sign she knew she was in the wrong. "Daadi always checked the horses' hooves to be sure they hadn't picked up a stone. He showed me how to do it. I did it just like he did."

The picture filled her mind—Ezra bending over the horse's leg, knowing just where to pinch so that Ben would lift his hoof for checking, explaining it all in his confident voice to his small daughter.

She had to swallow before she could speak. "I'm sure Daadi didn't mean for you to do so now. When you are bigger, you will, when a grown-up is there to watch."

Becky's face turned sullen. "I'm big enough."

"No, you are not!" She was on the verge of losing patience with the child, and that was surely a failure on her part.

"B-Ben would squash you like a bug and n-n-not know he did," William said.

"But Daadi said—"

"Enough." Her voice was sharper than she intended. "Onkel William knows well how to take care of the animals. He will do it."

"Ja, I will, for sure." William tugged on Becky's kapp string. "D-don't worry."

"Tell Onkel William denke for taking care of you."

"Denke," Becky whispered.

"Ja, it's okay."

"Go to the haus." Rachel gave her a little shove toward the door. "I'll be right in."

She gave Becky a moment to get out of earshot before she turned to William, because she knew that her voice was going to betray her.

"Denke, William." She clutched both his hands in hers. "If you hadn't been here—" Tears overwhelmed her.

"Ach, it was n-nothing." He flushed to his ears. "I sh-sh-should have been w-watching her better."

"That is not your job. It's mine." She brushed away the tears impatiently with the back of her hand. She was embarrassing William, and that wasn't fair to him. "I'm so grateful to you. I don't know what we would do without you."

His flush deepened, and his blue eyes seemed to darken with emotion. "I w-would do anything for you and the ch-ch-children. Anything."

Leah's idea that William had feelings for her forced its way into her head. Here she stood alone in the barn with him, their hands clasped.

Carefully she drew her hands away. "We're very grateful. Now I must go and find some suitable punishment to keep Becky from being so foolish another time."

It was on the tip of her tongue to tell him to come in for coffee when he'd finished, but Leah's words had made her wary of doing so. That was foolish, wasn't it?

Still, she turned and walked quickly back toward the house. It *was* silly, she was sure of it. She'd let Leah's comments change the way she reacted with William.

William had been upset, maybe a little emotional, too, just as she had been. But that was because he loved Becky. It couldn't possibly be anything else.

"They'll be opening the doors soon." Aaron Zook, Gideon's brother, gave Rachel a reassuring smile. "Are you ready?"

"Ach, she's been ready this past hour." Lovina, Aaron's wife, turned from arranging the loaves of bread she'd placed in a large basket on the counter of their stall at the farmer's market in Petersburg. "This is Rachel's first Saturday at market, so she hasn't been running around being a blabbermaul to the neighbors like me." Lovina chuckled, her round form jiggling.

"It is so kind of both of you to share your stall."

Gideon had arranged it, of course—Rachel had no doubt of that, even though it was Lovina who had come to see her a few days earlier with the suggestion.

Her plants—pansies and a variety of potted mints, basil, rosemary, and dill—were ready on the end of the counter they had given her. She had hung bunches of dried herbs from the overhead rack. There weren't many of those, because when she'd dried them last fall she hadn't been thinking of bringing them to market. This year she would do more, if this effort proved successful.

Lovina had been right. She had never even visited the market before, let alone been part of it. The rectangular brick building in the center of town was crowded with vendors of all sorts, some Amish, some English, all of them calling to each other in cheerful, familiar tones.

Lovina and Aaron participated with the ease of long practice. Had being out among the English ever seemed as strange and scary to them as it did to her?

Aaron, four or five years older than Gideon, shared a strong family resemblance with him, although Aaron's beard held a few traces of silver. Perhaps, if Gideon had not had so much sorrow in his life, he'd also share Aaron's jovial good humor and ready laugh.

Aaron had chosen a mate who matched him. Lovina had a round, merry face, snapping brown eyes, and a laugh that came often. She was spreading comfortably into middle age and ruled her large family with cheerfulness unimpaired by the mischief their four boys and three girls seemed to get up to, judging by the stories she'd told on the drive to town. Since they'd started out at five this morning, there had been plenty of time for talk.

"Here they come," Aaron said.

Rachel's gaze shot to the doors, and her breath caught in her throat. People poured through the openings, spreading out into streams that flowed down each of the aisles in the long building. The noise bounced from the high ceiling, and she feared she'd drown in the hubbub.

Lovina pressed her hand in a quick squeeze. "Don't fret. You'll soon get used to it."

She doubted that, but she managed to return Lovina's smile. Then those leading the stream of people reached them, and Lovina turned with a smile to her customers.

Folks headed toward the baked goods and Aaron's cheeses first, giving her a chance to watch the two of them in action. When customers approached her end of the counter, she knew what to do.

After she'd waited on a few people, her tension began to slip away. This wasn't that different from the Mud Sale, except that she'd known most of the people there.

Finally, the initial rush slacked off. "There now," Aaron said, grinning, "that wasn't so bad, was it?"

She shook her head. "I guess not. Is it over?"

"Ach, no." Lovina brushed up the crumbs that had fallen on the countertop. "This is just the lull. There's always those who think they have to be here right when we open. Then it settles down. It'll get real busy again around noon, probably. Meantime, I'll go and get us all some coffee. You'll mind my baked goods, ja?"

"Sure thing." Coffee would taste good about now. And Aaron was there to be sure she didn't make any mistakes while Lovina was gone.

No sooner had Lovina left than a woman appeared at Rachel's end of the counter, looking at the potted herbs with a faintly disdainful air. She carried a large basket that already held several bunches of dried flowers.

"May I help you?" Rachel asked, echoing the way she'd heard Lovina do it.

"Is this price correct?" The woman flicked at the small tag Rachel had attached to the dill.

Rachel took a second look. "Ja, that's right." Lovina had helped her price things, and Lovina knew what was right to charge.

"It's too high. I'm certainly not going to pay that." The woman glared as if Rachel had offered her an insult.

Taken aback, Rachel could only gape. "I'm sorry—"

Someone elbowed her lightly to the side. She glanced up and blinked. Not Aaron, as she supposed, but Gideon. Where had he come from?

She couldn't ask, since he was already dealing with the customer. He consulted the price tag gravely.

"That's the price for one," he said, as if they were his plants, not hers. "If you wanted a half dozen, we'd be glad to bring it down to six plants for five dollars."

Rachel opened her mouth to speak, and then shut it again as the woman scrutinized the plants.

"Hmm . . . don't know that I want that many. How about three for two-fifty?"

"You won't find finer herbs anywhere you look," Gideon said, his tone persuasive. "Our Rachel grows nothing but the best. Take six, and you can make it a mixed batch—say two each of three varieties. That's the best we can do."

For a moment she thought the woman would turn and walk away. Then, meek as a lamb, she picked out six of the potted herbs and handed over the money.

When the woman had moved on to another stall, Gideon shot a look at her, as if to assess her reaction. What he saw on her face must have reassured him, because his mouth relaxed into a smile.

"D'you mind my butting in on your business?"

"Not when you can sell the customer six plants instead of one. But how did you know how to deal with that woman? And what are you doing here?"

She thought, too late, that the question was rude, but Gideon didn't seem to mind. He rested one elbow on the counter.

"I usually stop by on Aaron and Lovina's market days unless I have a job. I spell them so they can take a break. But I guess you're taking over that job today."

"Lovina went for coffee."

Aaron was busy with a customer at the other end of the counter, but otherwise all seemed quiet enough for the moment. She could ask the question that bothered her.

"But you didn't explain—how did you know what to say to that woman?" She had stood there like a dummy, not knowing how to respond to what had seemed an insult.

He shrugged, seeming at ease in this situation. "Experience, that's all. When someone starts out by saying your price is too high, that usually means they want to haggle. It makes them feel gut to bargain over something they're going to buy anyway." He grinned. "No one ever outsmarted a Dutchman when it comes to a bargain."

True enough. She'd seen her daad and Ezra haggle over price. But she'd never been the seller, out among the English this way. "I don't think I can do it."

"It just takes a little practice. And a little nerve."

"Maybe I don't have that." She concentrated on the remaining plants, pushing them around to show them to their best advantage. "I never worked outside. Not like girls who work at the shops or restaurants until they marry."

If she had, maybe she'd have been better prepared for the life she had now.

"Why was that?" Gideon leaned his elbows on the counter as if he had all the time in the world to listen.

"My folks didn't want me to take a job." She said it slowly, seeing the situation more clearly now, looking back. "Daad said there was enough to do at home, and that I'd be better off learning what Mamm could teach me. But I suppose it was really because of Johnny."

"They held you closer because they'd lost him." Gideon's voice was a low rumble under the background noises of the crowd.

"That, I guess. And maybe also they didn't want me to be out among the English so much. Afraid I'd do what Johnny did. Not that I would have." She glanced at him, seeing the understanding in his face. "I mean, Ezra and I knew we'd marry from the time we went to a singing when we were sixteen. I didn't need to prepare for any other life."

He nodded, the lines of his face seeming to deepen, as if he looked at the naive youngsters they'd been and found it sad. "We don't know what tomorrow will bring." He echoed what she'd said to him. "That's just as well."

She didn't want to talk about the spouses they'd lost. "Anyway, I didn't want my folks to worry. They'd had enough of that with Johnny."

"How is he? Ezra said you were seeing him again."

She studied Gideon for a second, but she didn't find any condemnation in his face. "Since he came back to the valley I see him now and again. He's busy with his new life. Happy, I guess, in his work. It wonders me though . . ."

She let that trail off, but he picked up on it.

"What? If he'll come back?"

"No, I'm sure he won't." The familiar worry sounded in her voice. "I just wish Daad could accept that. Make it easier for Mamm to see Johnny again. Like I said, he's happy with his work. But for all he's changed, I don't think he really fits in the English world, either."

"You want to make it better for all of them." Gideon sounded almost surprised.

"Ach, for sure I do. But Johnny and Daad are cut from the same cloth—both too stubborn for their own gut."

"Families are like that. Drive you crazy sometimes, but you can't do without them." He glanced toward his brother as he spoke, and affection was written in his face and voice.

"Aaron and Lovina have been so kind to include me." She hesitated, but she might as well say it. "I know this was your doing, Gideon, and I appreciate it."

"All I did was to mention it to them. Then Lovina took over." He smiled. "That's what she does best. And here she comes now with the coffee, and none for me."

Lovina bustled up to the counter, shoving a steaming cup at Rachel. "If I'd known you'd be here, I'd have brought some for you. You go get your own, and bring back some crullers from Ida Mae's stand already. We could use a little something before the next rush."

Holding up his hands in surrender, Gideon pushed open the half-door that was built into the counter. "See, what did I tell you? Lovina's the boss, and it's just as well to do what she says to begin with. It saves arguing."

He moved off, and Lovina took his place behind the counter, clucking a little. "That Gid—he's a caution. He has a gut heart, he does." She slanted a glance at Rachel. "It's time he should be forgetting the past and having a family of his own."

A warning tingle slid down Rachel's spine. Was that aimed at her? Leah said folks were already talking about when and who she'd marry.

She couldn't very well say anything to Lovina, but if that was her idea, this was one time when she wouldn't get her way. Gideon had no intention of marrying again, according to what Ezra, who would have known, had told her.

And she—well, she wasn't ready to marry again, either. She didn't know if she ever would be.

But if she were, it certainly wouldn't be to a man who would be forever tied in her mind to Ezra's death.

Two English women in the booth opposite them stared avidly at the four figures in Amish dress when they stopped at their favorite restaurant for supper after market. They didn't bother Gideon, and Aaron and Lovina were used to it. Stopping here for supper was a tradition, and if the tourists wanted to stare, they were welcome to it.

He glanced at Rachel, sitting next to him on the padded bench, hands in her lap, eyes downcast. She wasn't so used to being the target of curious gazes. He wanted to wipe the strain from her face, but he didn't know how.

Rachel had had little experience with the English world. Now her situation forced her to deal with it.

It wasn't easy to live in the world, but not of it. Some found it simpler, but Rachel wasn't one of those.

He wasn't, either, but he'd had to adjust to it once he'd started his business. Now—well, he'd just as soon be dealing with Amish customers, because he understood them. But the English were gut customers, too, and becoming friends as well, some of them.

He let Lovina's stream of chatter about the success of market flow past him. It was a balancing act, to be Amish in twenty-first-century America. Rachel would face plenty of challenges, trying to hang on to the farm without Ezra.

She'd been right to flare up at him about that. He'd been thinking only of Ezra's dreams, instead of what was best for Rachel and the children without him.

Still, how could he dismiss Ezra's plans for his family? From the time they were boys, Ezra had talked about the dairy farm he'd have one day, even knowing that his daad's place would go to Isaac. Gideon had lent a hand with the milking now and then, and Ezra liked to lean his head against the cow's warm side and talk about running his farm. Wouldn't he expect Gid to help Rachel stay?

"Gid, did you hear me?" Lovina's voice sounded as if she might have asked the same thing several times.

"He tunes you out," Aaron teased, sopping up the last of his beef gravy with his bread. "He's so used to your gabble that he doesn't listen."

"Sorry, Lovina." He brought his thoughts back to the bright restaurant, the clatter of dishes, and the buzz of English conversation. "My mind was wandering."

"Your mind and Rachel's, too, I'd say," Lovina said. "Rachel, what deep thoughts are going through your head to make you stare so intently at your plate?"

Rachel's cheeks grew pink. "Just that this is nice, is all. Do you always stop here for supper on a market day?"

"Just about," Lovina said. "I'm certain sure I don't want to go home and start cooking." She chuckled. "It's a little treat we give ourselves without the kinder along. Much as we love them, we like some time apart."

"It's a nice place, anyway." Aaron glanced around the brightly lit dining room, with its painted versions of Pennsylvania Dutch art on the walls. "Gut food. Not so gut as Lovina's, but okay."

"Nice big servings, you mean," Gideon said. He smiled at Rachel, hoping to put her at ease. "Aaron wants to feel like he's got his money's worth when he eats out."

"Nothing wrong with that," Aaron said. "We worked hard, up since before dawn. We need a gut meal."

"And to take time to enjoy our profit," Lovina added.

"Speaking of that, here is your share, Rachel." Aaron pulled an envelope from his pocket, double-checked it, and shoved it across the checked tablecloth to Rachel.

Rachel opened the envelope, riffling through the bills, and her gaze widened. "But—this is too much. My plants didn't bring in this much, I'm sure of it."

She tried to push the money to Aaron, but he shoved it back. "It's a mite extra," he said. "It's only what's fair. You helped Lovina with her sales, so you deserve a cut."

"But it's your booth." Rachel paled a little. "I can't take money for helping when you are letting me use your booth."

Aaron shot Gideon a look, as if to ask for help in handling such a stubborn woman. "Your plants and dried flowers drew more people to the stand, and then they bought from us, too. So we benefit from having you there."

"Besides," Lovina cut in, her tone firmly practical, "we need the extra help. Having you there lets me do some other things besides standing in the booth all day already. We'd have to pay anyone else who helped out."

"You wouldn't have to pay Gideon," Rachel said, giving a sidelong glance at him.

"Oh, Gideon." Lovina's tone dismissed him. "He's a help, sure enough, when he's there, but lots of times he's not. We need to have someone we can rely on, like you."

She patted Rachel's hand and pushed the envelope into her lap. "Let's hear no more about it. We'd be grateful if you come along as often as you can, even if you don't have much to sell. We can use the help and the company."

Rachel didn't look entirely convinced, but she gave in, curling her fingers around the envelope of cash.

"I've been thinking on that," she said. "I can pot up more herbs, and there'll be perennials ready to go soon." Her eyes lit with enthusiasm.

Gideon liked seeing her that way, with the tiredness and grief erased for the moment. "You should find lots of buyers for your perennials," he said.

"When the greenhouse is ready, I can start petunias, marigolds, cosmos, and such from seed, without waiting until after the last frost." Her smile flickered. "I won't have to crowd my windowsills with pots."

"Gut idea." Lovina glanced toward the dessert buffet. "And that double chocolate cake looks gut, too." She slid out of the booth, nudging Gideon. "You heard what Rachel said. You work a bit faster on that greenhouse, so Rachel can get her seedlings started. What's taking you so long?"

"The job takes as long as it takes," he said mildly. "I don't tell you how to bake bread, so don't you be telling me how to build a greenhouse."

Lovina laughed. "You're just spinning it out so you can spend more time with Rachel. You can't fool me."

She walked off, still chuckling, before Gideon could think up a suitable retort.

But he'd have to come up with something. He couldn't have Lovina imagining there was going to be something between him and Rachel when there wasn't.

He glanced at Aaron, hoping to read some evidence of support in his brother's face, but Aaron's gaze evaded his.

"Guess I'll go take a look at those desserts myself," Aaron said, pushing himself out of his chair.

So they were both thinking that. He'd have to do some straight talking to the two of them. It'd be embarrassing all around, but most of all for Rachel, if they started in on matchmaking that was bound to fail.

Aaron and Lovina knew, better than anyone, why he'd avoided involvement with any woman since Naomi's death. To be the only one left when his wife and baby died had made him shutter his heart for so long that he didn't think it could open again. And if he had begun to change, Ezra's death had ended it. He couldn't take responsibility for the life of someone he loved. What if he let them down, too?

Rachel moved slightly, clasping her hands in her lap, the fingers twining together. He met her gaze, to find her regarding him with worry darkening the vivid blue of her eyes.

The color came up in her cheeks a bit. "Was ist letz, Gideon?"

He shoved away the unwelcome thoughts. Better to keep them safely buried, he knew.

"Nothing's wrong." He tried to smile.

"Maybe you're thinking that I should not have taken that extra money that Aaron insisted on giving me. I didn't want to, but it seemed so hard to keep on refusing—"

"Ach, no." This was what came of letting the dark memories out. "Aaron was right. You were a great help."

"But really, I didn't do much." Her face was still clouded, faintly troubled.

He wanted to put his hand over hers, to stop her fingers from straining together that way. But it would be too familiar a gesture and embarrassing besides, here in a public place. He contented himself with leaning a little closer as he searched for the words that would convince her to accept what they offered.

"You did plenty. Aaron worries that Lovina does too much, pushes herself too hard with the children and the house and the farm, besides all the baking she does to get ready for market day. If she'll accept help from you, Aaron is only too glad. Please don't back out now."

He did touch her hand then, very lightly. The warmth of her skin made him want to linger, which was all the more reason to snatch his fingers away quickly.

There was a bit of a stir as the English women who'd been watching them slid out of their booth, dropping shopping bags in the process and exclaiming as they picked up their belongings. It distracted Rachel, which was just as well, and her face relaxed in a small smile.

The women had themselves together at last and started toward the door. A high-pitched voice came floating back over the shoulder of one as she stole a last look at them.

"Aren't they just the cutest couple you ever saw? They're like those Amish dolls we were looking at in that shop this afternoon."

Color flew into Rachel's cheeks again. Gideon spared an uncharitable thought for the tourists while he tried to think of some way to ease the situation for her.

"Like those Amish dolls," he mimicked. "How would they like it if we were buying dolls dressed like them?"

She managed a smile, but it didn't reach her eyes. He could see her distress, and he couldn't do anything about it.

Except leave her alone. The thought occurred to him, and his negative reaction to that startled him.

He couldn't leave her alone. This wasn't just about fulfilling his promise to Ezra any longer. It was all tangled up with Rachel's valiant efforts to do her best for the children and with his instinctive need to help her, regardless of the cost.

CHAPTER SIX

The final slow hymn had been sung, and Bishop Mose stood to pray. His gentle face radiated love as he blessed the people. Rachel's heart warmed with it. Tired as she had been after the long day at market yesterday, worship had rejuvenated her.

Talk rustled through the Stoltzfus farmhouse as the service ended. "Mammi, can we go outside?" Becky tugged on her arm.

"Ja, but walk out nicely with your grossmutter." She knew her mamm found it a joy to greet her friends with her grandchildren by her side. "I must speak with Leah."

Mamm, hearing her words, nodded and took Joseph's hand. "We will save a place at the table."

Daadi stood, cradling a sleeping Mary against his shoulder. "You go, and give our best to Leah. Maybe this one will sleep a little longer."

Rachel made her way between the rows of backless benches, heading for the spot where Leah sat with Elizabeth snuggled close to her side. She liked seeing the bond Leah had formed with her stepdaughter.

She didn't like the fact that Leah had come to worship today. Nearly four hours on a backless bench wasn't her idea of the rest the doctor had ordered.

She moved along the row, exchanging greetings with those on the women's side of the worship area. The Stoltzfus place was ideal for worship, built so that the living room and dining room opened into each other, giving plenty of space for the service.

House worship was held every other Sunday, rotating among the members. Depending on whose turn it was, they might be in a house one time, in someone's basement the next, and in a barn the following one. When she and Ezra had hosted worship, they'd spent a week cleaning out the barn beforehand.

She had to see if there was anything she could do to help Leah. And then she'd tell Leah of her plans for the greenhouse. The ideas had been bubbling since she got home, tired but satisfied, from market yesterday. It would be gut to hear Leah's words of encouragement.

Some of the men had already begun removing the benches, carrying them outside for the lunch that would follow worship. She skirted past them, smiling and nodding, and fetched up beside Leah, bending over to enfold her in a warm embrace.

"What are you doing here? I'm sure the doctor wouldn't approve of this."

Leah rose, leaning a bit heavily on Rachel's arm. "I asked and he said it was all right." She winced, rubbing the small of her back. "Of course, he probably doesn't know how long our service is."

"Ja, that's for certain sure." Leah's mother, who'd been seated on the other side of her, ran a soothing hand along her daughter's back. "You go along with Rachel and have a nice visit. Elizabeth and I will see if we can help with the food, won't we, Elizabeth?"

"Oh, ja." Elizabeth's eyes filled with love when she gazed at her adopted grandmother. "We'll help."

"Wish I had a daughter so eager to help," Rachel said once Leah's mother and daughter had left. "My Becky is probably getting into mischief already, if Mamm has let her go off."

"I'd be pleased if Elizabeth felt secure enough to seek out some mischief." Leah's smile lit her face. "Sounds like we're always wishing for something we don't have."

"I guess so." Her arm around Leah's expanding waist to support her, Rachel led the way toward the door. "Let's find a real chair for you to sit in, and I'll get you a cool drink. It feels like summer in here already."

"It does at that."

They worked their way toward the door that stood open to the sunshine. Folks still stood in small knots, talking. Judging by the grave faces, Rachel knew the topic of conversation.

"Bad news about Eli Fisher," she said. "Everyone's upset to think he'll not be with us much longer."

Leah nodded. "He's a gut man and a gut minister. It sounds as if the Lord has need of him in Heaven."

"And that means we'll be praying on who will be the next minister."

"It's a weighty decision, to think of the name you wish to whisper to the bishop." Leah grasped the porch banister to help her descend the two steps. "At least we know that the final decision will be made by the Lord."

The Biblical tradition of choosing the new minister by lot from among those recommended by the people of the congregation meant that everyone accepted the decision with gratitude for God's guidance. Still, Rachel had to confess that she had not been overjoyed when Ezra's name had been put forward the last time there had been an opening.

Had the lot fallen on him, their lives would have changed in ways she couldn't even imagine. A minister had to continue with the work he already had, tend his own family, and still find time to minister to his flock and preach on Sunday.

The lot hadn't fallen on him, but their lives had changed anyway. *It was God's will*, she murmured to herself, hoping that one day she'd think those words and really mean them.

Betty Stoltzfus saw them coming toward the picnic tables. "Wait, wait." She hurried to drag a padded rocking chair from the porch to the end of one of the long tables. "Sit down and be comfortable." She patted the chair.

Rachel helped Leah to sit, concerned about how cautiously Leah lowered herself. "Are you having pain?"

"Not much. I'm all right, Rachel. Don't fuss so."

Rachel and Betty exchanged glances over Leah's head—the look of women who'd already had children and knew how uncomfortable the final month could be.

"You sit, too, Rachel, and keep Leah company. I have some lemonade ready to come out." Betty bustled away toward the kitchen.

Leah glanced at Rachel, looking a little embarrassed. "I'm sorry I snapped. Daniel said coming to worship would be too much, and he was right, but I'm trying to keep things as normal as possible. Anyway, there was something I wanted to speak to you about, and I knew I'd have a chance here."

"I would come to you, anytime." Rachel was assailed by guilt. "I'm sorry I didn't get over this week." She'd been busy, but that was no excuse to ignore Leah.

"I was fine." Leah patted her arm. "Mamm has been coming by every day, and folks have brought food. With the children in school, there's not enough for me to do."

"Get plenty of rest and enjoy it," Rachel said promptly. She didn't have to think twice about that. "Once the baby comes, you'll be only too busy. But what did you want to talk to me about?"

Something about babies, she'd guess. It was hard for Leah to think of anything else right now.

"It's Anna." Leah's voice dropped on the word, as if she didn't want anyone to hear the name of her young sister, who'd run off to the English world nearly a year earlier. "I've heard from her."

The smile slid from Rachel's face. "Oh, Leah."

Rachel clutched her friend's hand, not sure whether to be happy or not. She knew how much suffering accompanied the loss of a beloved sibling. And as the elder, Leah had felt guilty, too, as if she somehow could have prevented it. "How is she? Is she all right?"

Leah nodded, tears sparkling. "She seems to be, though whether things are as rosy as she pretends, I don't know."

"Where is she? Did she tell you?"

"She didn't say, but the envelope was postmarked a town in Illinois." Leah sighed a little. "I don't know why she feels she has to hide. She knows we accepted her decision."

"Maybe she's not so sure of it herself."

Leah swallowed, probably because of the tears that clogged her throat. "She's not with that boy anymore. I never thought that would last. But she has a job and a room to live in. She says she's gotten her GED, and she's even planning to take some college courses in the fall." She sighed. "It seems wrong to be hoping that she'd find things difficult out there."

Out there among the English. Rachel knew what Leah was feeling, because she'd been there herself—almost longing for Johnny to fail, if that was what it took to bring him back to them.

"I'm sorry," she said softly.

"I know." Leah squeezed her hand. "It's funny. It almost seems as if Anna and I have traded places. Imagine our Anna actually wanting more learning."

"Maybe she's grown up some since she's been away."

"That was what I always wished for. I just never thought it would come this way." Leah sighed. "Anyway, I wanted you to know about it, because you understand."

"Ja, I do. I know what it is to feel helpless to make things better. But at least you've heard from her. You know she's well and taking care of herself. That's better than wondering. Imagining."

"My imagination is too gut, that's for sure. But I trust that God is watching over her, and now I can picture her life."

Rachel's throat tightened, remembering all the times she'd struggled to picture what Johnny was doing, how he was, during those years when they hadn't been in touch.

Leah must have known what she was thinking, because she touched her hand lightly. "Enough worry about things we can't affect. Tell me how it went for you at market yesterday."

"Ach, better than I ever imagined." She couldn't stop the smile that bloomed on her face. "Leah, I made more money in a day than I've ever made before in my life. It felt so gut to be earning for my children."

"That's wonderful-gut news. I'm happy for you."

Rachel glanced toward where the children played, but instead of their running forms, she was seeing rows of flowers and shrubs, blooming in her garden.

"If I can just get seedlings started in the greenhouse, I'll have plenty of plants to take to market every week. And I was thinking that I would put in more perennials and even some small shrubs and trees. I could have a regular nursery business if I work at it."

She turned to Leah. But instead of the enthusiasm she expected, there was a look of caution on Leah's face.

"Are you sure that's a gut idea? I mean, won't it be a lot of work?"

"For sure, it will be work. But if I can make enough to provide for the young ones without selling the farm, that will be worth any amount of labor."

"It will take so much of your time. And then there's the bookkeeping you'd have to do if you actually started a business. And the taxes, and . . ."

"You think I can't do it." A chill settled around Rachel's heart. Leah was her best friend, the person who knew her better than anyone, and Leah thought she wasn't capable of this project.

"It's not that," Leah said, but her voice betrayed the truth. "I just feel you ought to think on it more. Talk to your parents."

"I know what they think without talking to them. They think I should sell the farm and move in with them."

Leah leaned forward, putting her hand over Rachel's. "I don't want to discourage you. I just think you have to be careful, that's all. You understand, don't you?"

"Ja. I understand." She tried to keep the flatness she felt out of her voice. She'd thought she'd known what to expect from her friend. It seemed she was mistaken.

"Rachel . . ."

"Ach, there's Becky, halfway up the apple tree." She didn't know when she'd been so glad to see her daughter getting into mischief. "I'd best go and see to her." She hurried off before she could let Leah see how disappointed she was.

Becky is all right, ja?"

Mary Yoder, their schoolteacher, watched as Becky scurried off to her grossdaadi once Rachel had gotten her down from the tree. She'd approached while Rachel was still looking up at her errant daughter. Maybe it was the presence of her teacher that had cut short Becky's complaints.

"She's fine, though I sometimes wonder why." Rachel made an effort not to let her frustration show in her voice as she smiled at the young woman. "She's far too daring, that's what she is. Takes after her daadi in that."

Mary nodded, but she didn't smile in return, and that set off all Rachel's maternal alarms.

"Mary? Is there some problem with Becky in school?"

"She's a fine scholar," Mary said, almost too quickly. "I've just been thinking—well, perhaps I could come by the house sometime this week to talk. Would that be all right?"

Rachel opened her mouth to ask the questions that flooded her mind and then shut it again. Obviously Mary didn't want to talk about school issues at the after-church meal.

She took a breath and tried to erase the worry from her face. "I'll be happy to have a chance to talk. Stop by any afternoon, whenever it suits you."

Teacher Mary moved off toward the picnic table, leaving Rachel with more questions than answers. It wasn't unusual for the teacher to come calling, but it hadn't happened before with Becky.

Am I making mistakes with the children, Father? I want so much to do that right. Please, guide me and grant me patience and humility.

"And how was your day at market, Rachel? You didn't find it too tiring?"

Isaac had come up behind her, and she was uneasily aware that he might have overheard her conversation with Mary. Still, what difference did it make if he had? Isaac was family.

"It was a long day, but very gut." The enthusiasm she'd felt when she talked about market with Leah had disappeared, and she tried to regain it. "Everything I took with me sold, so I'm thankful for that."

"Gut, gut." But Isaac didn't sound convinced, and his gaze avoided hers.

Her heart sank. Isaac no doubt intended to say something she didn't want to hear—probably more about selling him the farm. She'd hoped he'd respect her request for time to consider.

"About this business of going to market. Do you really think that's appropriate, with you widowed not even a year already?"

For a moment she couldn't answer. *Widowed not even a year.* The words sank into her heart. Soon it would be a year since the morning

Ezra had driven off in Gideon's buggy. Would things be better once that terrible landmark passed? She didn't know.

But Isaac was still waiting for an answer.

She cleared her throat, so that she could reply gently, quietly, as was the Amish way. "I don't think anyone could complain about my behavior in trying to support my children as best I can."

"Not that, for sure, but in such a public place, among all them English."

"I was well-chaperoned by Aaron and Lovina, if that's what you're thinking." She reminded herself that Isaac meant well.

"They're gut folks, but they're not family. You should be relying on family just now."

"Isaac, I do. You should know how much I rely on you and the rest of the family." Was he thinking that it was a slight to him that she turned to others? "The children and I couldn't get along without your help, that's certain sure. You know how much we appreciate all that you do, don't you?"

"Ach, there's no need for thanks." He patted her hand. "Now, I won't talk business on the Sabbath, but I want to be sure you're thinking about my offer."

There it was, just the subject she didn't want to discuss. "You're right, Isaac. We shouldn't talk business on the Sabbath."

He looked a little disconcerted at having his words turned back to him that way. "I see your mamm and daad coming to collect you for the meal, so I won't say more. Just . . . don't let this business with your little greenhouse affect your decision."

Sure enough, her mother and father approached, Mary awake but clinging to her grossdaadi's hand. If Rachel asked them, they'd no doubt agree with Isaac and take the opportunity to urge her to move back home with them.

No one, it seemed, thought her plan at all reasonable. Well, except maybe Gideon, and Gideon was convinced, no matter what he said to the contrary, that she should do what Ezra would want.

Guide me, Lord. Her heart whispered the prayer as Mary rushed to grab her skirt. *I need to know what is right to do.*

. . .

It had been two days since that Sabbath meal, but Rachel still struggled with the opinions that had buffeted her. Most of all, she hadn't been able to reconcile herself to Leah's negative reaction.

Was Leah's approval really that important to her? Apparently so.

She'd been trying not to think about it, but this quiet moment at the end of the day, cleaning up the kitchen as she glanced through the window over the sink at the slow settling of dusk on the farm, seemed to let the concern slip back in.

She'd turned that conversation every which way in her mind. She'd told herself that Leah had just been tired, or was feeling overly cautious because of her pregnancy.

But the end result was the same. Leah didn't support her plan. She didn't think Rachel was capable of doing it.

Rachel hung the dishcloth on the drying rack and then grasped the edge of the sink with both hands, bowing her head in the stillness. She could hear the children's voices, coming softly from upstairs as Becky helped Mary get ready for bed. Otherwise, the farmhouse was quiet with the end-of-day serenity.

Dear Father, I confess that I have been annoyed with Sister Leah over her lack of support for my plans. Please, Lord, if she is right about this, help me to see that clearly. And if she is wrong, if this is the right step for me and the children, please help me to rid myself of these feelings.

She seemed to be praying the same prayer over and over these days, first for her feelings toward Gideon, now for those she harbored toward Leah. The advice Bishop Mose had given her was harder to follow than she'd thought it would be.

The soft voices from upstairs were suddenly no longer so quiet. She straightened, appalled to hear Becky practically shouting at her little sister. Hurrying toward the stairs, she tried to quell the frustration that rose in her.

Ezra used to joke that this was the time of day when even gut children turned into little monsters. How she missed his steady hand with them!

She reached the door of the bedroom Becky and Mary shared to find Mary sitting on her bed in her white nightgown, tears running down her cheeks. Becky stood in the center of the hooked rug between the beds, her hands clenched and her face red.

Joseph, who'd probably been drawn by the noise, slipped past Rachel and out of the room, obviously having no desire to get into this, whatever it was.

"Hush, Mary, hush." First things first. Rachel sat down on the bed and drew the little one into her arms. "Quietly, now. It's all right. Mammi is here."

Mary clung to her, burying her face in Rachel's shoulder, her sobs lessening already. Rachel stroked her, murmuring softly, until they calmed into little hiccupping sounds.

"Now, then." She kept her voice low as she focused on Becky. "Tell me what has Mary so upset. And you also, I think."

For a moment Becky didn't speak. Her fists were clenched tightly against her apron, and strong emotion twisted her lips.

"She doesn't remember!" The words exploded from her. "Mary says she doesn't remember what Daadi looks like!"

That brought a fresh outburst of tears from Mary. Rachel held her close, murmuring to her, patting her back. Poor Mary, who probably didn't even understand what was happening, only that Becky was angry with her.

And poor Becky, too. Rachel understood what Becky felt, because her own heart was sore at just hearing the words.

Could Mary have forgotten Ezra so soon? If so, it was her fault. She should have talked about him more, made sure his image was fresh in the children's minds. Without photographs, words and memories were all they had.

"Hush, little girl." As Mary's sobs lessened again, she tilted the small face up so that she could see it. It was blotched red with tears, and just the look of it wrenched her heart. "It's all right. You remember Daadi. You remember how he used to lift you high in the air, so high that you touched the ceiling, and you loved it. You'd say, 'Again, again!' to him."

Mary nodded, wiping the tears away with the back of her hand.

She must tell the child more, say the words that would bring Ezra clearly back into her memories. But panic swept through her like a cold wind. Ezra's image, his dear face, the sound of his laugh, the look in his eyes—they were fading, all fading.

Rachel was terrified at the thought of losing him, but even more terrified at letting the children know how she felt.

Please, help me, dear Father.

"His beard tickled you and made you laugh." Somehow the words came, as if the Lord had heard. "And his eyes were so blue—just as blue as yours are. He was strong, so strong he could lift all three of you children up at the same time. Remember? Remember how he'd make a Mary sandwich, with you in the middle?"

"I remember." Mary smiled at that, the tears banished. "I remember Daadi."

"Of course you do." She put Mary down on the bed, pulling her quilt up and tucking it around her. "You remember, and if you start to forget, we'll all help you remember."

She glanced at Becky. "Come and kiss your baby sister, and tell her how sorry you are that you made her cry."

Becky, looking on the verge of tears herself, crawled up on the bed and wrapped her arms around Mary, kissing her cheek. "I'm sorry," she whispered. "I love you."

Mary clutched her in a throttling embrace. "I love you, Becky."

"Now is time for sleep." Rachel kissed Mary, holding her close for a moment. "Good night, my little one."

Mary snuggled down under the quilt, turning her face to the side as she always did for sleep. Rachel slid off the bed and put one hand on Becky's shoulder to shepherd her out of the room. She pulled the door to, leaving it a few inches ajar as she always did, so that she could hear if one of them cried in the night.

"Komm," she said to Becky. "Sit down here on the steps and let's talk."

She sat on the top step, trying to push away the weariness and the tears that would come too easily if she let them. Becky sat down next to her, her face downcast, the nape of her neck so exposed and vulnerable-looking that Rachel's heart twisted again.

"Mary is still a boppli in some ways, ja?" She put her arm around Becky. "She was only two when Daadi went to Heaven. She doesn't have as many memories as you do of Daadi, because she didn't get to be with him as long."

Becky nodded. "I'm sorry, Mammi," she whispered.

"It's forgiven and forgotten." She hugged her close. "We will keep Daadi alive in Mary's heart by our love for him and by our stories about him. Ja?"

"Ja, we will." Becky tilted her head up so that Rachel could see her face. The tears still lingered in her eyes, but she was smiling.

Rachel pressed a kiss to her forehead. If only she could always solve her children's problems with a little talk and a lot of love.

"Why don't you read for a bit before bedtime," she suggested. "I'd best see to Joseph."

Becky, nodding, went down the steps. Her book would be tucked under the cushion of the small rocking chair that her grossdaadi had made for her, and she'd lose herself in the story for a while.

The door to Joseph's room stood open, but he was not there. Rachel glanced quickly into her bedroom and the spare room before hurrying down the stairs, hand running along the wood rubbed smooth by generations.

She glanced into the living room, where Becky had lit one of the lamps. "Have you seen your brother?"

"No, Mammi." Becky slid off the chair, her finger marking her place in the book. "Do you want me to look for him?"

"I'll do it." She walked through the dining room, peeked into the pantry. Empty.

The kitchen had grown dark since she'd been upstairs. She lit the ceiling lamp that hung over the table, its yellow glow banishing the shadows. "Joseph?"

No answer, but the back door stood open. Hurrying, a nameless fear clutching her, she rushed onto the porch.

All was still quiet. But the barn door, which should have been closed, was open, a yawning dark rectangle. Before she could gather breath to call again, a massive dark shape erupted from the barn.

CHAPTER SEVEN

*R*achel's heart nearly failed her until she heard Joseph's panicked voice.

"Mammi! Wo bist du?"

"Here! I'm here, Joseph!" She jumped down the steps and ran toward the sound of his voice. "Are you all right?"

Joseph barreled into her, and she clutched him, torn between thanks and fear.

"Was ist letz? What's the matter?"

"The draft horses—one of them got out." He sounded close to tears. "I'm sorry, Mammi. I'm sorry. I didn't mean to do it."

"We'll talk about it later." Her eyes were adjusting to the light now, and she could see his face—a pale, anxious oval. She grasped his hand. "You must stay up here on the porch, you understand? Don't come off the porch."

She waited for his nod, and then she patted his shoulder. "It will be all right. Just let me get the lantern, and then I'll put the horse back in the stall."

He nodded again, which she hoped meant she sounded more confident than she felt. She reached inside the door for the battery lantern that hung there on a hook. Lighting it, she managed a smile that seemed to chase the worry from Joseph's face.

"Stay here," she repeated, and stepped off the porch.

Luckily the horse didn't seem to have any immediate plan to run off—Ben, she saw now, the more skittish of the two. He'd dropped his head and was cropping the grass next to the lilac bush. If he went a little farther, he'd be munching on her tulips.

Well, he wouldn't have the chance. She went forward, repressing the butterflies that danced in her stomach. Stupid, to be so nervous of the animal. If only it were Brownie, her buggy mare—Brownie would come right to her when called. The big geldings were another story.

"There now, Ben." She spoke as soothingly as if she were talking to one of the children. "This isn't where you belong. What are you doing out here at night?"

And why on earth had Joseph let him out? That seemed to be what he had been saying, but it made no sense.

"Let's get you back in the barn where you belong." She was almost to the animal. She reached out gingerly for his halter.

Ben flung up his head and danced away from her, his eyes rolling so nervously that she could see the whites even in the glow of the lantern.

The lantern—that must be what had frightened him. She set it on the grass. She didn't really need the light it provided. The western sky was still streaked with purple, and night hadn't quite claimed the farm yet.

She had to quiet her own nerves before she could proceed. She tried to picture Ezra in this situation. He would probably walk right up to the gelding and grasp the halter, wouldn't he? Then that was what she should do.

Except that Ezra seemed very far away, and she did not feel very brave. *Please, Father.*

Ben had settled back to his eating. She moved closer, reached out, and patted his shoulder. His skin rippled as if she were a pesky fly, but he didn't move. More confident, she reached for the halter. She almost had him—

The door banged, the sound like a shot in the still night. Ben shied away from her. He wheeled, his huge hooves coming dangerously close to her legs, and ran straight for the road.

She spared one quick glance toward the house as she ran after him. Becky had come onto the porch, probably looking for them. Her mouth was a round O of surprise.

"Stay there!" Rachel ordered, sprinting after the animal. "Stay there."

They would obey, wouldn't they? The last thing she needed was to have them to worry about, in addition to the horse. If Ben got out onto the road—

She didn't want to think of that. Too often animals were hit, and a car or pickup coming fast along the narrow road wouldn't have a chance of stopping in time.

That pair of Belgian draft horses were one of the farm's biggest assets. She couldn't afford to lose Ben.

She pressed her hand against the stitch in her side and ran on down the lane. How far would he go? Surely, after he got over his initial fright, he'd stop to eat the lush grass along the side of the lane, wouldn't he?

But Ezra always said that horses were not the most sensible creatures, as apt to take fright at a blowing paper as at an oncoming freight truck.

Rachel rounded the slight bend in the lane. She could see the road now. Could see, too, the pair of headlights that pierced the darkness. A car was coming. If the horse ran out onto the road, what was the chance the driver would be able to stop?

She forced herself on, too breathless to cry out, not that it would have helped her anyway. *Please, God, please, God.* The words kept time with her running feet.

A dark shape loomed ahead of her on the lane. Then, coming closer, it separated itself, and she could see. The gelding, not free any longer, plodded toward her, his halter in the hand of a man who also led a horse pulling a buggy. Something about the size and shape of the lanky figure identified him.

"William! You caught him."

"Ja."

William was close enough now that she could see his grin. All the tension went out of her in a whoosh of relief.

"G-gut thing I was on my way home chust n-n-now."

"A very gut thing." Thankfulness swept over her. "I was afraid he'd run onto the road and be hit." The car swept past the lane, accentuating her words.

"He's s-safe now." William fell into step with her. "Don't you worry."

"Denke, William. I don't know what I'd do without you." She seemed to be saying that too often lately.

"I'll p-put him in the barn."

Nodding, she took the buggy horse from him, leading it to the hitching rail as William led the gelding on toward the barn.

She tied his horse to the rail, thankful that William hadn't repeated what he'd said the last time she'd had cause to be grateful to him. Maybe he realized that his words then had made her uncomfortable.

She crossed to the porch, almost too tired to put one foot in front of the other. When she sank down on the step, Joseph and Becky threw their arms around her.

"There, now, it's all right." Somehow she found the strength to comfort them. "Uncle William is putting foolish Ben back in the stall where he belongs. There's no need for tears."

Although she had to admit, she felt like shedding a few herself.

"I'm sorry, Mammi. I shouldn't have slammed the door." Becky hugged her, arms tight around her neck.

"It's no matter." Rachel turned to her son. "Joseph, how did this happen? How did Ben get out?"

Joseph sniffled a little. "I went to check Dolly, because she was bawling. She must have tipped her water bowl over, 'cause it was empty, and I filled it before supper, I really did."

"I'm sure you did." Joseph would no more neglect his precious goat than miss his own supper. "Why did you go in the barn?"

"I heard something moving inside. I could tell it was one of the draft horses, 'cause it was so loud. It sounded like he was out of his stall, so I thought I'd better check." He hung his head. "I should have come to tell you."

"Ja, you should." She ruffled his hair. "You will next time. So Ben was out of his stall?"

He nodded. "When I opened the door, he ran right out the barn door. I couldn't stop him. I'm sorry, Mammi."

"I know you are." She drew him closer, a chill running through her. If he hadn't gotten out of the way of the animal—

She suppressed that line of thought, looking up as William approached.

He stopped at the foot of the steps. "Everything else is all r-right."

"Ser gut. But how did he get out of the stall?"

William glanced at Joseph. "J-Joseph d-d-didn't let him out?"

"No!" Joseph looked up at his uncle. "Honest, Onkel William, I didn't. He was already out when I opened the barn door."

William shrugged. "Don't know. He was in and s-settled when I l-left."

It was troublesome, to say the least. Rachel couldn't doubt William's word. He wasn't careless. But Joseph's story had the ring of truth, too.

"No harm was done, thanks to you." She smiled at William, giving the children another hug. "Now I must get my little schnickelfritzes to bed. Say good night to Onkel William."

She kept a calm smile pinned to her face while the children bade William good night. It wouldn't do to let them know she was worried.

But how had the horse gotten out? She'd give a gut deal to know the answer to that.

Gideon stood back, hands on his hips, to survey the panel of glass he'd just set into place. He was close to putting the finishing touches to the greenhouse.

Rachel must surely be itching to move her plants in as soon as he pronounced it done. The chilly weather of the past couple of days had reminded everyone that the valleys of central Pennsylvania couldn't count on frost-free nights until about the middle of May, at least.

Some folks put their plants in early, if they felt reckless, but then ended up having to cover them or lose them.

Truth to tell, he'd be sorry when the day came that he'd be finished. He wouldn't have a reason then to come to Rachel's as often, and he'd have to think of some other way to help Ezra's family.

Rachel would continue going to market, surely. Aaron and Lovina would do their best to see to that. The problem might be to keep Lovina from being too enthusiastic in her pushing.

Joseph came running across the yard toward him, and Gideon's face relaxed into a smile. One of the best things about being here every day was getting to know Ezra's small son. He'd come to count on the boy rushing to help him the moment he got home from school. Nothing compared with working together to build a bond between them.

"You put the first glass in!" Joseph skidded to a halt. "Can I help? Can I?"

"Sure thing. I'm planning on you holding the panels for me while I put the putty in already."

"I *told* Mammi you'd need me to help you."

Gideon paused in lifting the next pane. "You're not skipping other chores to do this, are you? That wouldn't be right, with your mammi counting on you and all."

Joseph shook his head, his fine blond hair bouncing on his rounded forehead. "I have some watering to do, but Mammi said I can do it later."

"Gut." He lifted the pane of glass into place, letting the boy steady it while he tapped in the metal glazing points that would hold the pane even without Joseph's small hands on the glass.

This was how children learned to do the things they'd eventually need to do as adults. He hadn't given that much thought before he'd begun coming here. Joseph, with his father gone, would absorb what it meant to be an Amish man from his grandfather, his uncles, and maybe even a little from him, if the gut Lord willed.

"Did Mammi tell you about the horse getting out last night?" Joseph frowned at the pane, his palms flat against it.

"No, she didn't." He glanced toward the house. He hadn't seen much of Rachel today, as a matter of fact.

Joseph stared fixedly at the pane. "I didn't mean to let it happen."

"I'm sure you didn't." He smoothed the putty into place, his voice calm.

"I was checking on Dolly. I could hear that one of the horses was out of his stall. You know how their hooves go clump-clump on the boards?"

He nodded. The sound was different, more hollow when it wasn't muffled by the straw in the stall.

"I thought I could get him back in by myself." Joseph's voice trembled a little.

"You wanted to help Mammi." He certainly understood that feeling. He wanted to help Rachel, too. "Which horse was it?"

"Ben. He's the big draft horse. He ran right out when I opened the door."

"That must have been scary." And dangerous, but he figured Rachel had already pointed that out to the boy.

"Ja." His eyes met Gideon's then, and Gideon saw how troubled the boy was. "I wanted to help, but Mammi said to stay on the porch with Becky. And then Ben ran toward the road, and Mammi ran after him."

Joseph didn't need to say how frightening that had been. It was written on his face.

"You did what your mother said?"

He nodded.

"Well, then, you did the right thing."

"I wanted to help," he repeated, his voice shaking. "But Mammi couldn't get him either. Gut thing that Uncle William came by then. He brought him back."

"That was fortunate." William was a kindhearted lad, obviously willing to do anything he could for Rachel. Or maybe more accurately, anything that Isaac would let him do. "And you did the right thing by listening."

Joseph nodded again, but his forehead was still knotted with worry. Gideon thought he knew why. Joseph was trying hard to fill his father's shoes. That was natural enough, but those shoes were much too big for any six-year-old boy.

All three of the children had to be affected by the loss of their father. Mary seemed the least bothered, young as she was.

As for Becky—well, at the moment Becky had been dispatched to take the clothes down from the clothesline. Instead, the basket lay forgotten on the grass while Becky shinnied up the clothes pole.

He had to smile. Ezra had been like that as a boy—always willing to try anything, and like as not, leading Gideon into trouble, too. Ezra would know how to deal with that tendency in his daughter, having been that way himself. Gideon wasn't sure that Rachel did.

But here came Rachel now, crossing the lawn toward Becky, the breeze sending the strings of her prayer covering streaming out behind her. She said something to Becky—he couldn't hear what—and Becky slid down the pole and picked up the basket.

Rachel glanced his way, hesitated a moment, and then came toward him, pressing the skirt of her dress down with one hand when it flapped in the wind.

"You are making wonderful-gut progress," she said. "The windows going in already!"

"Thanks to my fine helper." He smiled at Joseph.

"I don't want to take him away when he's working, but Dolly is bawling, and no one will do for the silly creature but Joseph."

"She's not silly," Joseph said loyally. "She's going to have her babies soon, and that makes her nervous, ain't so?" He appealed to Gideon.

"That could be. Why don't you take a break from this and see to her? I can manage until you do that."

"I'll come right back," Joseph said, and sprinted across the yard toward the goat's pen.

"How long do you think it will take to finish the work?" Rachel was obviously counting the moments until she could put her plants in her new greenhouse.

"I should finish up in a day or two, if all goes well." He picked up the next pane. "I hear you had some trouble here last night."

"Joseph told you?" Her smooth brow furrowed with concern. "He shouldn't have opened the barn door, of course. But how did Ben get out of the stall? That's what worries me. I'm sure William wouldn't make such a mistake."

Without seeming to think about it, she moved around so that she could take Joseph's place holding the pane. Now it was her palms that pressed against the glass instead of the child's.

"William's the careful sort, I'd say." It was odd. And dangerous to the animal even if he hadn't gotten out of the barn.

"That's what makes it so puzzling." She shook her head, her face troubled. "Joseph shouldn't have been out there alone that late anyway. If it hadn't been for—" She stopped.

"Hadn't been for what?" Gideon prompted.

A small sigh passed her lips. "Becky was upset with Mary. And Joseph hates any rumpus, so he went outside to get away from it. For him, that was just a short step to going to check on Dolly."

She tried to smile, but he could see that she was bothered by more than just the boy being outside that late.

"What was going on between Becky and Mary? They always look as if they get along pretty well."

"They do. But apparently Mary didn't remember something about her daadi that Becky thought she should, and Becky got upset. She just doesn't understand that it's natural Mary isn't going to remember much about Ezra."

"That's too bad." He hated the thought that Ezra's youngest wouldn't have memories to keep him alive in her thoughts.

"Ja. Sometimes I almost wish we could have photographs, so we'd have an image of him. But I know the Scripture says not to make graven images." She shook her head. "And I suppose maybe if we had one, we'd make too much of the picture, instead of using our hearts to remember him."

Gideon's heart ached, just listening to her. If he could make the grief better—but he knew from his own loss that that was something no one else could do for you.

"Seeing so much of the children has made me think about Ezra a lot," he said. "They're each like him, but in different ways."

Now Rachel's smile chased the sorrow from her face. "That is what I think, too. Mary has his smile, but Joseph looks the most like him. And Becky—well, Becky has his manner, sometimes."

"His daring, too. She's like Ezra was as a boy." He glanced toward the clothesline, but Becky was doing her chore now without looking for mischief.

"Always getting into trouble. I know." Rachel seemed to look back through the years, but they were happy memories, he could tell.

"We did a lot together when we were boys," he said. "If you wanted it, I could talk to the children about him."

He sensed her immediate withdrawal. If she hadn't been holding the glass, she'd have moved away from him.

"I—I'll think about it."

But her voice was strained, and he could already tell what her answer would be. It seemed they hadn't moved as far as he'd been hoping they had.

. . .

Rachel washed the dishes, lingering over the job as she gazed out the window over the sink. As Gideon had said yesterday, the greenhouse was nearly done. Her last gift from Ezra would soon be a reality.

Gideon had done a wonderful-gut job. Everyone knew that he was a fine carpenter, none better. He worked steadily now, his movements deft and calm.

He'd gotten stronger over the course of building the greenhouse. She could see that now as she studied him. His leg wasn't so stiff as it had been that first day he'd come, and he moved more easily and more surely.

He turned from the greenhouse, glancing toward the window where she stood watching. Heat flew into her cheeks. What must he think of her staring at him?

Looking down at the pot she held, she scrubbed so vigorously that she was in danger of rubbing through the metal. She hadn't been admiring him. Of course she hadn't. He couldn't think that. She just liked watching anyone who did a gut job of something, like Mamma with her jams and jellies. Ja, that was all.

Once the pot was dry, she bent to put it in its proper place and walked across the kitchen to hang the towel on the wooden drying rack. She glanced out the side window. From here, she could see the schoolhouse, nestled in its little hollow. The scholars were coming out the door now, so Becky and Joseph would soon come running across the field.

And if Mary Yoder intended to come today, she'd soon be here, as well. Rachel's fingers tightened on the drying rack. She hadn't told the children that she expected a visit from their teacher. And she hadn't attempted to find out from them why Mary Yoder was concerned about them.

No, not them. Becky. Rachel had been able to read that much in Mary Yoder's face.

Well, she would find out when Teacher Mary came. And then she'd deal with it, whatever it was.

As Rachel turned away from the window, movement caught her eye. She swung back, leaning over to peer down the lane. Something came, all right, but it wasn't a buggy. It was a car.

Johnny? She tidied her hair automatically. She wasn't expecting him, but it was typical of her brother's impatience that he would come rather than sending a note through the mail.

But when she stepped out onto the back porch, she could see immediately that it wasn't John. She recognized the Englischer, though—Thomas Carver, it was. Mr. Carver owned the dairy that bought the milk from them.

Had he come with a problem? Her nerves tightened with dismay. William did everything just the way Ezra always had, so surely it wasn't that. But the man had never come to the farm before, not in all the years since Ezra had signed on with him.

She smoothed her apron down and stepped off the porch as Mr. Carver got out of the car. Middle-aged and balding, he wore the blue jeans and plaid flannel shirt over a white T-shirt that was the common dress among the English farmers in the valley.

"Mrs. Brand. Nice to see you." He approached, starting to extend his hand and then seeming to think the better of it.

"Mr. Carver." She nodded politely. "It's kind of you to call."

Her hands pressed against her sides, hidden by the folds of her skirt, as she waited for him to go on. It wouldn't be polite to ask what he was doing here when he'd never come before.

"Yes, well, I had a little business I wanted to talk over with you." He glanced toward Gideon. "Mind if we go inside and have a chat about it?"

He moved toward the step. She held her ground. He may be a perfectly nice man, but she'd feel more comfortable talking with him here, rather than in the house.

"It's a pleasant day. Perhaps we could talk here."

His face seemed to tighten. "Yeah, sure. I guess maybe you people wouldn't think it right for a widow to be alone in the house with a man who isn't Amish."

Since there was no reasonable answer she could give to that, she didn't try, but just waited.

"Guess this is fine." He leaned forward to rest his hand on the porch railing, bringing him uncomfortably close to her. "No need for you to be worried about the milk. Young William is doing fine with that. I got no complaints."

"This is gut." So what did he want, in that case?

"Still, it has to be rough for you, running a place this size without a husband."

He was trying to be kind, she supposed. "We are doing all right. The family has been taking care of things."

"Sure, I know how you Amish stick together. One for all and all for one, huh? Though I guess you wouldn't say it that way."

Again, there seemed no proper response, so she just inclined her head in a nod.

"Yes, well, anyway, I figured things might be getting a little difficult for you by now, without your man. Thought I'd stop by with a business proposition for you."

He was talking in circles. Maybe she could move him on toward a conclusion.

"And what is this business proposition?"

"Right to the point." He chuckled. "I like that in a woman. Well, see, it's this way. I hear tell you don't want to sell the farm, but you're having a tough time making a go of it."

Her stomach lurched. How could this Englischer know that about her? How could he know anything about her?

"Maybe there's a way you don't have to sell, but you can still make a decent living off the place. And you wouldn't even have to give up the house or that little greenhouse you've got going there."

"And what is that way?"

A year ago she wouldn't have been capable of having a business discussion with anyone, let alone an Englischer. But then, a year ago she wouldn't have had to. Maybe her introduction to bargaining at the market helped.

"I'd be interested in buying the dairy herd from you." He must have seen that she was about to say no, because he held up his hand to stop her. "Now, just hear me out. What I propose is buying the herd and just leasing the barn and the pastures from you."

"I don't think—" she began.

"See, that way you don't have to let the farm go." He rolled on as if he hadn't heard her. "You have a nice steady income coming in, and you get to stay in your house." He cocked an eyebrow at her. "Pretty good deal, don't you think?"

She took a breath, trying to steady herself. Coming out of the blue as it did, the idea had her brain spinning.

"I appreciate your offer, Mr. Carver. But I don't think that's the right thing for me to do."

"Now, you haven't considered it yet." He moved uncomfortably closer. "You have to stop and think a bit."

She tried to step back, but she was against the steps, and there was nowhere to go. "I'm sorry—"

"This is the perfect answer for you. Don't you want to be able to take care of your kids and keep them in this house? Trust me, you're not going to do any better than this. I wouldn't cheat you."

He was right in her face, and she felt his insistence pushing at her. "I don't—"

"Rachel, was ist letz?" The quiet question, coming in dialect, seemed to go right to the heart of her tension, soothing away her nerves.

Thomas Carver turned to stare at Gideon, and she took advantage of the opportunity to put some space between them.

"I'm fine." She answered in English, so that Carver would understand. "My business with Mr. Carver is finished."

Carver's smile was a mere twitch of the lips. "Not finished, Mrs. Brand. You think about what I said. I'll be in touch."

Gideon stood beside her while Carver got into his car. The man turned in the narrow lane, spraying gravel and clipping one of her rose bushes, and drove off toward the main road.

"What's wrong?" Gideon repeated his question as soon as the man pulled away. "You didn't look fine. Was it bad news about the dairy's deal with you?"

"No, nothing like that." She managed a smile. "He wanted . . ."

Did she really want to discuss that with Gideon? Maybe not. After all, Gideon had his own ideas of what she should do with the farm.

"Well, it was nothing important." She phrased her words carefully, intent on not telling a falsehood. "He wanted to talk to me about my arrangements for the dairy herd. If they'd be continuing the way they are."

Gideon's mouth firmed. He knew she wasn't telling him all of it, she supposed, but it would have to do.

She stared past him—toward the fine barn that had been in her family for generations, toward the pastures lush with spring growth. Sell? Lease? It seemed much the same to her. It meant someone else would be tending the farm that Ezra had loved.

She was being offered too many chances to do something she didn't want to do at all.

CHAPTER EIGHT

*R*achel had been standing in the backyard for several minutes, watching him put the finishing touches to the greenhouse while Mary trotted around, busy with her little bucket and shovel. But Gideon could see that Rachel's mind was far away.

Probably she was still caught up in that conversation she'd had with Thomas Carver, the Englischer. He didn't for a minute think that she'd told him everything about it.

Why should she? He frowned at the latch he was screwing into place. He didn't have the right to expect that. Her business with the dairy was just that, hers. And Isaac's and William's, he supposed, in a certain sense.

Still, in that moment when he'd seen her pull back as if she were intimidated by the man—well, his instinctive reaction was nothing to be proud of. For himself, he'd long since learned to turn the other cheek, as the Lord taught. For Rachel—he couldn't deny the bone-deep need he'd felt to protect her, not that she'd wanted or would welcome his protection.

Rachel had made that clear time and again. He was the one who didn't seem to be getting it.

"Becky and Joseph are coming." He nodded toward the two scholars as they raced across the lane on their way home from school, detouring to drop their books on the back porch.

"Ja." Rachel's solemn look disappeared into a smile when she saw the children. She seemed to dismiss whatever had been troubling her, or, most likely, put it away to think about later. "Mary, look." She turned the little girl with a light touch on the shoulder. "Here they are."

Mary's short legs churned as she hurried to meet her brother and sister.

Gideon dropped his screwdriver back into his toolbox. "Maybe you'd like for the young ones to help set up your greenhouse."

Rachel's breath caught. "Now?"

He nodded. "It is finished at last."

"Wonderful gut." She clasped her hands together, her face lighting up with pleasure at the thought. "Children, come see. The greenhouse is ready."

All three of them swarmed over the greenhouse, opening and closing the door. The girls darted inside and out again as if it were a toy house just for them.

After a quick inspection, Joseph came to stand next to him, surveying the greenhouse much as he did. He could sense the pleasure the boy felt at having been a part of the building.

He rested his hand on Joseph's shoulder. "Gut job we did here, ja?"

"Ja." Joseph leaned against him for a moment. A hand seemed to reach out and grasp Gideon's heart, squeezing it.

Before he could come to terms with the feeling, Joseph had darted off to his mother. "Can we bring the plants out and set them up on the tables? Can we?"

"Let's do that." Rachel's gaze met Gideon's, and hers brimmed with happiness. "Komm, everyone help."

They all seemed to figure he'd help, too, so he followed Rachel into the house. Pots of seedlings that she had started perched on every sunny windowsill.

"I didn't know you had so many. You have been busy."

She pulled trays from the cabinet under the sink and began putting the tiny pots on it. "Ach, I love to do it. My mamm used to say that I was never so happy as when I had my hands in the dirt. I'm sure Daad was sorry it was his daughter with the green thumb instead of his son."

A shadow dimmed her face on the words, and he knew she was thinking about her brother.

"How is Johnny?" He wouldn't let her feel that she had to be wary of discussing John with him. "Have you seen him lately?"

"Not for a while. He came over one night to help me with the tax forms."

That seemed to make the shadows deepen in her face, unfortunately. He took another tray and began to fill it with the contents of the windowsill above the sink. "He's well?"

"Ja." She sighed. The children's voices echoed from the living room as they apparently divided up the plants to carry out. "He was unhappy with me because I wouldn't take money from him. I wish he'd understand about that."

Gideon nodded. "Not so easy to balance between him and your daad, I guess."

"They're both too stubborn." Her mouth set.

"That trait didn't pass you by, either, I think."

Her gaze met his, startled. "I'm not stubborn." A faint color came up in her cheeks, and she focused on the plants. "Well, only about some things."

Some things that included him, he suspected.

"These are ready," he said, as the children marched through the kitchen, each carrying a share of the plants. Mary had one grasped in each chubby fist, and she frowned as if daring them to fall. "I'll hold the door."

Coming along behind Rachel and her children as they crossed the lawn to the greenhouse, he felt a sense of—what was it? Belonging?

Not that, maybe, but as if for this moment, anyway, he could share in their happiness. He'd fulfilled his promise to Ezra, and he'd made things a little better for Rachel and the young ones. That should be enough for him.

Just ahead of him, Mary reached the very entrance to the greenhouse before she stumbled, the plants waving wildly as she tried to save them. Balancing his tray with one hand, Gideon scooped her up with the other, setting her on her feet before she lost her cargo.

Mary tilted her face up toward his, leaning against him confidingly. "Denke, Gideon," she whispered.

The small warm body in his grasp seemed to set something echoing through him, as if the door of his heart, long since closed, creaked ajar. First Joseph and now Mary, making him feel again.

No. He could not let that happen. He would help them, would try to do what he could for Ezra's sake, but he could not let himself care. His faith would never survive another loss, and the only way to prevent the pain was not to risk his heart again.

He set his mind to helping them arrange the plants on the plank tables he'd built for the greenhouse. The children, enthusiastic at first, lost interest quickly, and Rachel sent them off to the kitchen, putting Becky in charge of getting them a snack.

It soon became clear that Rachel had her own definite opinions as to what should go where. Her face wore a serene expression as her hands busied themselves with her plants. She'd forgotten he was there. He had no gut reason to stay longer, so he began gathering up his tools.

"Ach, let me help you get your things together." Rachel shook her head. "Forgive me. I'm so eager to work on my plants that I haven't even told you how much I appreciate your kindness."

"Not necessary." He opened the lid of his toolbox. "Seeing your pleasure in the greenhouse is thanks enough."

"My last gift from Ezra." Her voice had grown soft. "It would have been treasured, whatever it was, but especially so since the greenhouse will help me support the children."

"You'll be going back to market again?"

"Ja. And this time with many more plants to sell, thanks to your help."

He shook his head. "I told you—"

She put her hand on his arm, the touch of it startling him into silence.

"I know. You did it because you promised Ezra. But I can still appreciate your actions, can't I?" Color flooded her cheeks. "Especially after the way I behaved that first day you brought it up. I'm still embarrassed to think about that."

"That's of no matter," he said carefully, wary of trying to press too far into her confidence. "Then, you couldn't see me without being reminded of Ezra's passing. It was only natural for you to blame me."

"I didn't. I don't. I know the accident wasn't your fault." She lifted her face to his, and she was so near he could almost feel her breath on his skin as she spoke. "You must accept that, too, Gideon. It would not be right to blame yourself for something that was in the hands of God."

She was too close, and he was far too aware of her. But he couldn't bring himself to move away.

Maybe she felt that, too. Her breath seemed to quicken, her eyes to widen.

And then suddenly she was looking down at the toolbox, as if searching for something to distract her. Or him.

"Is this a design for one of the windmills you'll be building this summer?" She touched the sketch he had tucked into the lid of the toolbox.

"Not exactly." He forced himself to focus on the paper, instead of on the curve of her cheek. He spread it flat. "I was playing around with an idea for a model windmill—something that folks might want to buy to put in their garden. It was just a thought I had when I was laid up. Don't suppose it amounts to much."

"Don't say that. I think it's a wonderful-gut idea. Think of all the ornaments the English like to put on their lawns and in their flower beds. I bet you could sell those easy. When are you going to make one?"

He folded the sketch and tucked it back into the box. "I'll tell you what. I'll make some when I get time, if you'll sell them along with your plants. That would be a gut deal."

He was only joking, of course. But he'd like it fine if he could make it come true.

Rachel tucked another marigold seedling into its own peat pot. The seedlings should be a nice size by the time frost danger was past. She stood back a little from the trestle table, admiring the lineup of plants. Ser gut. She'd have plenty to sell when the time came.

Picking up a water bottle, she began spraying the seedlings with a fine mist. Only a day had passed since the greenhouse was completed, and already it felt as familiar to her as her own bedroom.

Not only that—it had given her courage, it seemed. She'd asked William to help prepare an addition to the garden for some more ambitious plantings. Lavender would be simple to grow, and folks liked that. She'd put in a variety of small shrubs, maybe even some dogwood trees if she could afford them. She could get young plants cheap and bring them along until they were ready for sale.

Thanks to Ezra's gift, she had hope for the future. She and the children didn't need much, after all—just enough added income to make up for the portion of the milk money that went to Isaac. She wouldn't have to sell, and the children would have the security that went with a gut farm.

Thanks to Gideon, as well. She couldn't forget that. If he hadn't made her dream about the greenhouse again, with his insistence on fulfilling his promise to Ezra, she might never have pursued it.

Gideon had become close to them in the past few weeks—closer than she'd have imagined possible. Her hands stilled on the sprayer.

Forgive me, Father, for my attitude toward Gideon. I'm trying to do better. Please help me.

A shadow fell across the tray of seedlings in front of her. She looked up, startled, to find Isaac standing there, staring in through the glass at her.

Her stomach tightened even as she smiled at him. In her enthusiasm, she had forgotten that Isaac had his own idea of what should happen to the farm.

She put the sprayer back on its shelf and took a last look around the greenhouse, soaking in its peace. Then she opened the door and stepped outside.

Isaac's expression didn't give anything away as he surveyed the completed greenhouse, but that very lack of expression told her he wasn't pleased.

"See Gideon got it finished at last." He tapped on the framing around the door.

"Ja, just yesterday. It turned out nice, I think. I'm very grateful to him."

He peered through the glass at her tables, his forehead creasing in a frown. "You got a mighty big lot of plants in there. More than you can use yourself, I'd guess."

"They're to sell," she said, schooling her voice to patience. "I'll take them to the farmer's market, alongside Aaron and Lovina's things."

He grunted a response that might have meant anything and turned away from the greenhouse. He seemed to transfer his gaze to her newly plowed garden. "William told me you're talking about putting in a bunch of new things this year, bushes and whatnot."

This was what bothered him, she could see. She should have realized that he'd disapprove of those plans. The greenhouse he could rationalize moving to a new location, but if she started something bigger, like an actual nursery garden, he'd know she was determined to stay put.

"I'm hoping to grow enough to make a little income from it. For the children, you know."

"Is this your idea? Or did Gideon Zook come up with it?"

She blinked at the hardness of his tone. "Mine. Well, I did talk to Gideon about it, maybe."

"It seems to me you'd want to talk to family about this idea first, instead of an outsider."

"Gideon isn't an outsider."

"Not English, no, but he's not a member of your family, either. Just because he was Ezra's friend doesn't give him the right to interfere."

"He's not—" She stopped herself. The only way to deal with Isaac in this mood was to be patient with him. And he was right, in a sense. It would have been proper to discuss it with Isaac ahead of time. "I'm sorry I didn't talk with you about it first. I'm sure you'd have had some gut advice for me about what to plant."

"There's no reason for you to be planting anything. I told you that. Caleb will be glad to take over the farm, and then you won't have to worry about such things."

So this wasn't about her failure to talk to the family about her plans. It was about *his* plans—his plans to wipe out Ezra's dreams as if they'd never existed.

She actually felt a flicker of anger. She'd deferred to her father and to Ezra when it was needful. They'd had the right to be concerned with what she did, and they'd always wanted the best for her.

But Isaac—it seemed that Isaac wanted what was best for him and for Caleb.

She took a deep breath, quenching the anger before it could grow into a flame. Impossible to come to an actual breach with Isaac. He was family, he was one of the brethren, and she counted on his help.

But it was equally impossible just to cave in to him.

Please, Father. Give me the right words.

"I know you feel it's for the best that Caleb takes over the farm," she said carefully. "But I'm not sure that's what Ezra would want me to do. Isn't it my duty to carry out what I believe are his wishes in the matter?"

For a long moment Isaac just stared at her, as if he were measuring the extent of her stubbornness. Then he shrugged.

"Maybe you're right, but maybe not. I guess we can't say for certain, since Ezra is not here to speak for himself. But I do know he wouldn't want you to start in on something risky without thinking it through."

"What is risky about putting in a few more plants and shrubs? I'm able to take care of them, and the older children are big enough to help me."

"It would be risky if you invested money in them and didn't have enough water to keep them going over the summer."

She blinked. It took a moment to understand his meaning, and then her hands tightened into fists that pressed against her skirt. "Why would I not have enough water?" If he was going to threaten her, he'd better come right out with it.

"When your well has run low in the past, our spring has always had plenty of water to share." He hesitated, and she thought he was wondering just how far he wanted to go. Then his face tightened. "Could be that this summer we'll need all that we have."

"I see." She stared at him steadily, and his gaze shifted away from hers.

"Think about it." He turned away, his movements jerky. "I'm sure you'll see that my plan is best for everyone."

He walked away, leaving her fighting down unaccustomed anger.

I'm sorry, Lord. I must not be angry with a brother. But what am I to do?

"*Ach,* they're having a gut game, they are." Lovina Zook leaned back in the lawn chair she had dragged over to the edge of the field at the Zook farm.

"They are that." Rachel relaxed in the seat next to her.

Lovina and Aaron had invited her to come to supper and bring the children. She'd thought perhaps Lovina wanted to talk about plans for market, but so far Lovina seemed more concerned with making sure everyone had enough to eat. Their four boys and three girls made for a hungry, cheerful group around the supper table, especially with her three added.

And Gideon, of course.

His presence was only natural, since he lived here and had his shop in an old barn on his brother's farm. He and Aaron had organized an after-supper ball game.

At the moment Gideon was pitching, sending an easy ball toward Becky. Aaron seemed to be coaching her on how to hold the bat.

"I hear tell when the English play ball, there's lots of yelling and cheering, even loud teasing." Lovina smiled fondly at her brood. "Sounds funny, ain't so?"

"Maybe they'd think we're funny," Rachel suggested. "Playing a game so quiet-like." The more she saw of the outside world, the more she realized how strange Amish ways would be to them.

"There's no need to make a lot of ruckus to have a gut time. I'd say Aaron and Gideon enjoy it as much as the children."

"Ja. It's nice to see how well your family works and plays together. You and Aaron must be doing a fine job, with raising seven of them."

The bat cracked, and they both leaned forward to watch Becky race for first base, apron fluttering, a huge grin on her face.

"A big hit for such a little girl." Lovina glanced at Rachel, her usually merry face turning serious for once. "I'd guess that being around other families makes you miss Ezra more sometimes, ja?"

"I guess it does." Rachel hadn't thought about it that way, but Lovina had a point. "I don't begrudge others their happiness, you understand. But Ezra was such a gut father. And husband. I miss that feeling that there's someone who's always there to help and support me."

She'd felt that keenly when she'd heard what Teacher Mary had to say about Becky. The young teacher's eyes had been filled with concern when she talked about how daring Becky had become—challenging even the older boys to climb higher or run faster at recess. Teacher Mary had been forced to discipline her more than once.

Ezra would have known what to do. Rachel didn't.

Lovina nodded. "I plain don't know how I'd deal with my seven if I didn't have Aaron," she said, an echo of Rachel's thoughts.

Somehow it was easier to talk about it with Lovina, who wasn't family. Rachel's mamm would listen, but she wanted so much to help that it almost hurt to talk to her.

"It's hardest when the children worry me." *Like Becky.* "I think about how it felt to be able to share it all with him."

"Ja." Lovina reached over and patted her knee. "But you're still a young woman, Rachel. Losing Ezra doesn't mean that you can't ever have that kind of partnership with a man again."

Rachel realized she must be healing, since that comment didn't pain her as much as the implication usually did. "I don't know. I guess I can't imagine loving anyone else the way I loved Ezra."

"Well, of course not." Lovina's tone was one of brisk common sense. "I mean, it stands to reason you're not going to love someone the same way when you're thirty as you did when you were sixteen."

"No, but—" It was certain sure that her love for Ezra had changed and deepened over time.

"I figure it's like loving your children." Lovina's gaze followed her oldest girl, chasing a fly ball. "They're all different, so you love them in different ways, but you don't love one more than another."

Rachel wasn't sure that applied to loving a man, but she did understand what Lovina meant about the children. "It is a challenge, knowing what each of them needs. My three are all so different."

Her gaze sought them. Mary, safely out in right field, was picking dandelions with Lovina's youngest. Becky danced off third base, daring Gideon to try to pick her off. And Joseph was at bat, his small face intent and serious.

"Imagine what it's like with seven." Lovina chuckled. "Course, we've had Gid around a lot of the time. He's a gut onkel, he is, in spite of having lost his own wife and the boppli. It helps having him here, but I'd sacrifice that gladly to see him married again."

Rachel wasn't sure what to say to that. Was it a hint?

"It's been a long time since the accident. I'm sure he's had plenty of chances to marry, if he wanted to."

Lovina shrugged ample shoulders, as if in agreement. "Has he maybe talked to you about it?"

"No."

That probably came out too sharp, but she couldn't seem to help it. Her mind had suddenly filled with an image of Ezra talking about Gideon. Explaining why it had been important for him to go off and do something with his friend on one particular day.

Rachel's cheeks flushed, just thinking about it. Had she been petty, nagging, wanting him to stay home with her?

It's the anniversary of losing his wife and boppli, Rachel. In her mind's eye, Ezra frowned at her in disappointment at her attitude. *I couldn't leave him alone today. He'll never talk about it, but he needs a friend right now.*

She'd been embarrassed, of course. Apologetic. But she'd still probably harbored a little resentment.

Maybe it's time he started looking for someone else.

At the memory of her words she cringed. She hadn't understood, then, the power that grief could wield.

I don't think he can. Ezra's eyes had gone dark with pain for his friend. *I don't think he ever will.*

"Aaron says I'm too eager to manage everyone else's business." Lovina's cheerful voice interrupted Rachel's thoughts. "And maybe he's right, but I don't like to see anyone alone. It's not what the gut Lord intends for us, to my way of thinking."

Joseph hit the ball at that moment, saving Rachel the difficulty of answering. The boy just stood looking at it in astonishment until Gideon called to him to run. Then he scrambled toward first base.

The hit was an easy fly ball that Aaron unaccountably failed to catch. That gave Becky the chance to score. Laughing, Aaron declared it was time for a snack, and the game was over.

The players flooded toward the picnic table, where Lovina had put out a pitcher of lemonade and a platter of cookies. Joseph ran to Rachel, his face lit up.

"Mammi, did you see? I hit the ball."

"I saw." She gave him a quick hug. "Go and have your lemonade and cookies now. It'll soon be time for us to head home."

"Not yet," he said, dancing with impatience. "Gideon promised to show me Aaron's goats first."

She'd like to get started before the sun set, but there was still time. And she couldn't deprive him of something that was so obviously important to him. "Go along then, but don't pester Gideon, all right?"

Joseph nodded and ran off.

"Ach, don't let that fret you." Lovina grasped the chair arms and shoved herself up. "Gideon is always talking about that *bu* of yours. He's very fond of Joseph and happy to show him the goats. I'm surprised Aaron's not going along, too. He's so pleased with those creatures that he loves the chance to show them off. Komm, let's have some cookies and lemonade, too."

Rachel followed Lovina toward the picnic table, wrestling with the thought. Gideon was fond of Joseph, always talking about him, according to Lovina. Well, that was a gut thing, she supposed. A child couldn't have too much love, and Joseph needed a man to look up to.

She just wasn't sure that Gideon was the man for the job.

Becky was full of herself over having scored the winning run, and Rachel sat on the picnic bench, listening to it twice over. Mary crawled up on the bench next to her, settling down with a cookie in each hand. In only a moment she was leaning against Rachel's shoulder.

Rachel patted her. "We'd best think about getting along home."

"Not yet, Mammi," Becky protested.

"Soon," she said, getting off the bench. "You finish your treats, and I'll go and see if Joseph is finished looking at the goats. Then we must be leaving."

She crossed toward the fenced area next to the barn. Aaron's herd of goats was larger than she'd expected. He must be having good luck with the goat cheese he sold at the market.

Gideon and Joseph leaned on the fence watching them, their backs toward her. The goats clustered close to them. Gideon had probably let her son hand-feed them, or they wouldn't be so eager to be petted.

She drew closer, her sneakers making little sound on the grass. Gideon and Joseph seemed so intent on whatever they were saying to each other that she hated to interrupt them.

". . . Becky says it's silly to have a goat for a pet. She says goats are farm animals, not pets." Joseph's voice reached Rachel clearly. "I guess Aaron's goats aren't pets, are they?"

"I guess not, but Aaron is a farmer." Gideon sounded as if he were torn between saying what was true and reassuring her son.

"I'm going to be a farmer, too, when I'm bigger." Joseph's profile tilted toward Gideon. "But Dolly—" He stopped.

Gideon put his hand on Joseph's shoulder. "Dolly is special to you, isn't she?"

"My daadi gave her to me, for my very own."

Rachel's heart twisted. Why hadn't she seen that? The greenhouse was important because it was Ezra's gift to her, and Joseph loved that goat for the same reason.

"Well, then, if you're asking me what I think, I'd say that Becky is wrong."

"Wrong?" Joseph's eyes widened, as if that thought hadn't occurred to him.

"Not about other things, mind. But about this."

The boy reached between the rails to scratch the muzzle of a persistent little goat. "But you said Aaron doesn't think his goats are pets, either."

Joseph, like the little goat, was persistent. She should intercede, but somehow she wanted to hear how Gideon would answer that.

He hesitated for a moment. "You know, I remember another boy who had a pet most people would think was silly. He was just about your age at the time, too."

"Who?"

"Your daadi."

"He did?" Joseph breathed the words. "What was it?"

Rachel's breath caught. Gideon had said he'd wait for her permission before talking to her children about Ezra as a boy. Now, it appeared he was about to do exactly that.

"A duckling."

"A duckling?" Joseph blinked. "But that's silly."

"Maybe so, but that's what it was." Gideon seemed to be looking back through time, and his face softened into a smile that made him look younger. "The little thing hatched out when its mammi wasn't there. I guess it thought your daadi was a gut substitute. It used to follow him around, quacking."

"Did folks laugh at him?" There was a world of feeling in Joseph's words.

"They did. But he never let that bother him, not one little bit. He figured they could think what they wanted to, but that little duck depended on him, and he wouldn't let it down."

Joseph seemed to mull that over for a moment, and then he gave a decided nod. "My daadi was right." He stood a little straighter. "I want to be just like him."

Tears choked Rachel's throat and blurred her vision. Gideon had just given her son a gift that she'd been unable, or unwilling, to give. She stifled a sob.

CHAPTER NINE

A soft sound behind him had Gideon turning. Rachel stood there. She'd obviously been listening, and her blue eyes were bright with tears.

Regret pierced him. He shouldn't have spoken to Joseph about his father. That was Rachel's responsibility, and the one time he'd brought it up, she'd evaded the subject. She hadn't wanted this, and now he'd done it anyway.

Still, even though it was wrong to talk to the boy without his mother's permission, the idea itself wasn't wrong. He'd be sorry to face Rachel's anger about this, and sorrier still that he'd caused her more pain.

But he felt as sure of this as he'd been of anything in his life. All three children needed to have stories of their father to remember, but Joseph needed it most of all, because those stories would help him grow into a man like Ezra.

Rachel came toward them, not looking at him, all her attention on her son. "Here you are, Joseph. Have you seen all of Aaron's goats already?"

"Ja, Mammi." Joseph hurried to her, his face lit with excitement. "Aaron has a fine herd, but he doesn't have any Nubians like Dolly. He said I could come another time with Gideon and learn how he makes the cheese, if you say it's all right."

If Rachel objected, she wasn't letting it show on her face. Her smile for the boy was gentle. "We'll talk about it," she said. "But now I need you to run back to the table. Tell your sisters I'll be there in a moment."

She waited while the boy hustled across the yard, her face turned away from Gideon so that he saw only the curve of her cheek. He stiffened, preparing himself to bear the brunt of her anger, preparing to tell her—

The child out of earshot, Rachel turned toward him. A single tear glistened on her cheek, and the sight of it wiped away everything he'd thought he'd say to her.

"Don't, Rachel." He longed to smooth the tear away, but he didn't dare. "I'm sorry. Don't mind so much."

She dashed the tear away herself with an impatient gesture. "No, I'm the one to be sorry. I didn't understand." She took a step toward the fence, grasping the rail with her hands and looking at the goats without, he thought, really seeing them.

He studied what he could see of her averted face. The line of her profile was as sweet and innocent as that of one of the children. She wasn't angry, it seemed, but he couldn't be sure just what she was feeling.

"I'm sorry," he said again, figuring that, at least, was safe. "I should not have spoken with Joseph about his father before asking you if it was all right."

She shook her head, still not looking at him. "I'm glad you didn't wait." She swallowed, the muscles of her neck working as if it took an effort. "Joseph came to you with a problem. I might wish he'd come to me instead, but maybe this was for the best. You gave him an answer that will help him much more than whatever I would have said."

"If you truly feel that, then I'm glad, too."

Rachel's eyes glistened with the tears she didn't want to shed. "You're a gut man, Gideon Zook. My children and I are fortunate to have you as a friend."

She was setting the boundary for him, and it was one he should be happy to accept.

He nodded. "Denke, Rachel. It is my pleasure."

For a moment they stood there, hands close on the fence rail, looking at each other. If Lovina was watching, she probably thought her matchmaking efforts were bearing fruit. She couldn't know how far from that they were.

He cleared his throat. "Are you ready to go to market again on Saturday?"

"Ja." She frowned slightly, but then seemed to chase the expression away. "My parents are so happy to have the children for the day that it makes it easy for me to go."

"Lovina will be pleased to have your company." He would, as well. He knew without even thinking about it that he'd show up, because it would mean a little extra time with her. And he'd keep talking about it at the moment for the very same reason. "You have many plants ready to take?"

"Ja. I think I will take some of the marigold and snapdragon seedlings, even though it's early for them. Some folks might want to risk putting them in."

He forced himself to concentrate on her plans for the flowers instead of on the play of expressions that crossed her face. "Did William get the soil ready for the other things you want to put in your garden?"

"He did." She stopped, but her troubled frown told him there was more to it. "He must have mentioned it to Isaac, because Isaac came to see me about it. Not that I would try to keep a secret from him, in any case."

Judging by the look on her face, he thought she might be wishing that she could.

"What does Isaac have to do with your plans for planting?" He tried to keep his voice neutral, even though the question itself probably announced how he felt about Isaac's actions in regard to his brother's widow and children.

"Isaac is family, after all." She sounded as if she were making excuses for him, which must mean that Isaac had not approved of her plans. "And he's still hoping that I will decide to sell the farm to Caleb. He probably thinks that the more I become involved in the nursery business, the less chance there is that I'll sell." She shrugged. "And that's true, of course."

"As Ezra's brother, he should be happy that you're doing what Ezra would want."

"He doesn't see it that way. And I suppose he's right when he says that we none of us really know what Ezra would advise."

He bit back the impulse to say that he knew. That wasn't helpful to

Rachel right now, with her brother-in-law being difficult. And this was about Rachel's needs, not about his own feelings.

"I know you want to keep peace in the family," he said carefully, not sure how far he could go. "But I would hate to see you give up things that are important to you and the children because they might upset Isaac."

"No, but—" Her hands twisted together, as if they were fighting with each other. "I depend on him, you see."

"I know William does all the work with the dairy herd, but you're paying for that, ain't so?"

"It's more than just that." Her forehead furrowed. "Ezra was always going to work on the well. Maybe even put in a new one or pipe water from the spring. But there was always so much else to spend the money on, and . . ."

"I'd forgotten. Ezra piped water down from Isaac's place in dry weather." Now he frowned, too. "Isaac wouldn't deny you the water just because he wants you to sell the farm to his boy."

Her mouth tightened. "Maybe, if it came down to it, he wouldn't. But he hinted at it pretty strongly."

That was so wrong that Gideon wasn't sure what to say. Not just wrong as a family member, but contrary to everything the church taught about supporting each other.

Words sprang to his lips, but he held them back. Better to be slow to speak and be sure that what he said made things better, not worse. "Maybe it would be gut to take this to Bishop Mose . . ."

"No." Something that might have been panic whitened her face. "Not that. I won't be the one to make a breach in the family known to the whole church."

"Bishop Mose could talk to Isaac. Make him see how wrong that would be. Other people don't need to know about it."

She shook her head. They both knew that if a dispute among the brethren could not be resolved by a private talk with the bishop, he would take it to the church.

"I won't do that," she repeated. "I'll have to find another way. Maybe it will be a wet summer."

"Maybe," he agreed, mind busy with possible answers to the problem. "But maybe you need to think about something else."

"Like what?" Her face flushed with exasperation. "I can't afford to have another well dug."

"No. But it could be that a windmill would give you the power to pump enough water from your existing well."

For an instant, hope dawned in her face, but it faded just as quickly as it had come. "I can't afford a windmill, either."

"I'd be glad to build one—"

She cut him off with a quick gesture. "Building windmills is your livelihood. The greenhouse was one thing, a promise you made to Ezra. But a windmill is totally different. I couldn't let you do that unless I could pay for it, same as anyone else would."

Maybe she didn't need to know what he would charge anyone else. "The cost wouldn't be near as much as having a well drilled."

"By the time I pay the taxes, I'll have barely enough to keep us going until the next payment from the dairy comes in." She shook her head. "No, Gideon. I know what you're going to say, but there's no point in discussing it. Unless I can pay for having a windmill put up, it's out of the question."

He nodded in seeming agreement. But he wasn't done with the subject, not yet. Let her think about it for a time. Let her mull over how gut it would feel not to be dependent on Isaac's generosity.

Obviously she didn't want to depend on his generosity either. She wouldn't let him build the windmill unless she could pay for it. So he'd have to find some way to make sure she could do just that.

Mammi, please can we have some? Please?" Becky tugged on Rachel's arm, pointing to the popcorn stand at the firemen's carnival.

The mingled aromas of popcorn, cotton candy, sausage sandwiches, pizza, and who-knew-what other treats were beginning to be overwhelming. "Becky, we have popcorn at home. Why—"

"Ach, let the little ones have popcorn if they want." Her father was already reaching for his wallet. "The carnival is a special event, ain't so?"

Rachel shook her head, smiling in surrender. "It'll be even more special if they end up with tummy aches from all the junk food they're eating."

But Daadi had already stepped up to the stand, Becky and Joseph on either side of him, ready to supervise the purchase. Mary clung to Rachel's hand, and already she drooped a little from all the excitement. Rachel exchanged looks with her mother.

"Let him do it," her mother said. "They won't suffer from having a few extra treats, and it gives your daadi pleasure to do things for his grandchildren."

"You do so much for us already." Rachel pressed her mother's hand. "You know how grateful I am."

Her mother dismissed it with a quick shake of her head. "It's nothing." She touched Mary's hair gently. "We'll be able to do more once you move back home with us. Daad and I were just talking about it last night. He's thinking he'll add on another room to give everyone a bit more space with growing children in the house."

"Mamm—" The sinking feeling in her stomach had nothing to do with eating junk food. "You know I don't want to give up the farm."

"Chust think about it already. Think about how much easier it will be on everyone."

There didn't seem to be any doubt in her mother's mind that sooner or later Rachel would be moving in. That made it all the more difficult to bring up the subject she'd been circling around since her parents had picked them up for this outing.

Should she ask them for the money to build the windmill? And if she did, what would they say?

She'd had a successful day at market on Saturday, even better than the first time, building her confidence that she could actually do it. But whether her parents would agree—whether they'd even consider it when they were so firm in their notion that she and the children move in with them—well, that was another thing entirely.

The popcorn bought, they started moving along the row of stands, the children's gazes darting from one unfamiliar sight to another. Rachel let Becky and Joseph go ahead with their grossdaadi while she and her mother lagged behind, suiting their steps to Mary's.

Mary's small bag of popcorn tipped, spilling onto the sawdust pathway. Rachel grabbed it before it could all go.

Her mother's eyes twinkled. "I know what you are thinking chust now, my Rachel."

"You do?" Whatever Mamm imagined, it certainly wouldn't be that her daughter's mind was caught up in the subject of windmills. That even her dreams had been filled lately with their paddles spinning against a clear blue sky.

"You are thinking that your daadi didn't spoil you and Johnny the way he wants to spoil your young ones."

It took an effort to conceal her surprise at her mother's bringing up Johnny's name. "That's certain sure. Though Johnny did a pretty gut job of wheedling."

"Ach, that was his way. That boy could charm the birds out of the trees when he wanted to." Mamm glanced down at Mary, who was staring openmouthed at a clown on stilts. "We know that you see him, Rachel." Her voice grew soft on the words. "Even if your daad will never willingly mention it."

She'd been reluctant to bring it up, telling herself she didn't want to cause more pain. Maybe she'd just been a coward. "Does that upset you, my seeing him?"

"No, no. Don't think that. I'm glad that he has you. I chust wish . . ."

She let that trail off, but Rachel could figure out the rest of it. Mamm would never go against what Daad said, but she longed to see Johnny for herself.

Rachel squeezed her mother's hand. "I know. I wish it, too."

"Look, Mammi. It's Elizabeth." Becky darted away from her grandfather to greet her friend, while the rest of them followed a little more slowly.

"Daniel, it's gut to see all of you." Rachel smiled at Daniel Glick and the three young ones. "Leah is home resting, I hope?"

"Ja." Daniel grinned. "And complaining all the time about it, too. I had to promise to bring her a caramel apple when we return."

"That was always her favorite treat, even when we were your size."

She tapped the brim of young Jonah's straw hat, and the seven-year-old gave her a gap-toothed grin.

"We appreciated the food you brought on Thursday," Daniel said. "That was kind of you. Cheered Leah up, it did."

Rachel nodded, hoping he was right. She saw Leah just as often as ever, of course, maybe more often, as she tried to help at this difficult time. On the surface, things were the same between them, but the truth was that she'd felt a constraint since the day she'd told Leah her plans and come away shaken by her lack of support.

"Can Elizabeth walk around with us, Mammi?" Becky held hands with her friend.

Rachel glanced at Daniel, but he shook his head. "Not this time. We're going to pick out desserts for everyone and then be on our way home."

"Ja, we'll be going soon as well. I have one almost asleep on her feet already." She patted Mary's shoulder as she smiled at Elizabeth. "Maybe you can come to spend the afternoon sometime soon, ja? We'd like that."

Becky and Elizabeth brightened immediately, the hint of a pout vanishing from Becky's face. "Soon, Mammi?" She obviously wanted to nail it down.

"As soon as Elizabeth's daadi and mammi say it's a gut day." She glanced at Daniel. "Just let me know. Anytime. And give our love to Leah."

He nodded. "We will." He raised his hand in farewell and shepherded his children away.

"Leah is doing all right?" Mamm asked as they moved on.

"The midwife is happy with her progress, she says. But Leah frets at having to be off her feet so much, wanting to tend to the family herself."

"Well, she'd best listen. It's no easy thing to have a first boppli at her age."

"She's just as old as I am," Rachel protested.

"But you've already had three. That makes it easier. If you were to marry again . . ." Her mother darted a look at her, as if waiting for a reaction.

Rachel did her best to keep her face from expressing anything at all. If she were to marry again. Everyone seemed to have ideas about that. Everyone but her.

"Rachel?" Her mother's voice was questioning.

"We'll have to wait and see what the future holds," she said. Mary stumbled, and Rachel bent and lifted her into her arms. "And right now, I think the future must hold bedtime for this little girl."

"Ja, you're right about that. I'll tell your daadi that we're ready to go."

Mamm moved forward briskly to intercept Daad and the children, who'd gotten a few yards ahead of them while they'd talked. Rachel stood where she was, Mary heavy in her arms, and suddenly found her breath catching in her throat.

Johnny. Johnny came toward them, walking with an English woman, carrying a paper plate of funnel cakes in his hand. His head was bent toward the woman as she talked, and he didn't see them until he was almost upon them.

He stopped. Daad stopped. For a moment Daad's face softened, as if he would reach out, would say something.

And then Daad turned sharply away, muttering, "Komm," over his shoulder. Mamm sent Johnny one pleading, loving glance before clutching Joseph and Becky by the hands and following.

Rachel reached her brother in a few steps. "I'm sorry," she said softly.

"Don't be." Johnny's face hardened until he no longer resembled the brother she loved. "I didn't expect anything else." Taking his friend by the arm, he walked off.

Rachel made her way toward the buggy, her heart as heavy as the child asleep in her arms. Was there no possibility of peace between them?

She already knew the answer to that, didn't she? As long as Daadi believed there was a chance to bring Johnny back to the fold by his attitude, he'd continue, no matter how much it hurt.

Maybe that was the answer when it came to asking Daadi to fund the building of the windmill. She'd be asking him to pay for something that allowed her to continue on a path he didn't approve. Whether he said yes or no, it would create tension between them.

And tension was something they already had in abundance. There had to be another way. She'd just have to find it.

Gideon settled on the polished bench in the hallway of the medical clinic, his hat on his knees. The English woman behind the reception desk had given him an odd look when he asked for John Kile, as if that was an unusual request.

Well, it most likely was, at least coming from an Amishman. Every Amish person in Pleasant Valley knew that John was under the bann, even those who weren't members of his former church district. They wouldn't willingly seek him out. But Gideon had to.

He'd been turning Rachel's problem over and over in his mind for the past few days, methodically considering all the possibilities for a solution. Ezra had often chided him for his slowness in coming to a conclusion about things, but he wasn't inclined to change now, and the situation between Rachel and Isaac was too delicate for any rash solutions.

Rachel certainly knew that Bishop Mose would intercede if she took the problem to him. Isaac would not be acting in accordance with Scripture or the Ordnung if he went so far as to cut off Rachel's water, and Gideon doubted that any member of the church would support his action.

But the decision wasn't up to him; it was up to Rachel, and he understood why she'd long for just about any solution that would avoid such an open breach in the family. To take her late husband's brother to the judgment of the community—such a thing could not be undertaken lightly.

Indeed, he wondered how serious Isaac's threat was. Would he actually follow through with it, knowing it could bring the condemnation of the community? Or did he hope to bend Rachel to his will without the need to carry it out?

Gideon frowned down at the brim of his hat, considering, and then quickly changed the frown to a smile when he realized he was being watched by an Amish mother and child from the waiting room. The little boy, probably not more than four or five, had the golden skin and yellowed eyes that marked children who suffered from Crigler-Najjar syndrome.

Gideon didn't know this family, which told him they weren't from the valley, but Dr. Brandenmyer's work with the genetic diseases that afflicted the Amish was widely known. This family might have come from as far away as Ohio or Indiana to seek out his help.

The door beside him opened, and John Kile came through with a quick, businesslike stride. He glanced around, and his face registered surprise when he saw who waited for him.

"Gideon?"

Gideon rose. "John. You look well."

Actually he was nearly unrecognizable. The Amish boy Gideon had once known seemed present only in the shape of his features. His hair was a bit darker now, and cut so short that it appeared even darker. He wore a pale blue shirt with a pair of tan pants, topped by the sort of loose coat doctors wore. If Gideon had passed him in a crowd of English, he wouldn't have known him.

"Gideon Zook." John said the name slowly, his eyes narrowing a bit. "When the receptionist told me an Amishman was waiting to see me, I found it hard to believe."

Would Johnny have thought—or hoped—that it would be his father? Everyone knew how strict Amos Kile was when it came to holding to the bann. And Gideon knew how much that situation was hurting Rachel and her mother.

"I'm sorry to interrupt your work. I'd like a few minutes of your time, if you can spare it."

John's jaw tightened. "Aren't you afraid someone will see you talking to me?"

Natural, maybe, for John to be less than friendly. It couldn't be easy for him to be back in the valley and have folks avoid him. Still, leaving had been his choice. As had coming back.

"I wouldn't be here if I were worried about that. We need to talk about Rachel."

John just stared at him for a moment, and Gideon couldn't begin to guess his thoughts. Then he held open the door he'd come through. "Come on back. We'll find someplace private to talk."

Nodding, Gideon followed him.

This side of the building was entirely different from the ordinary medical clinic that occupied the opposite side. He glanced into the rooms they passed as they walked along a hallway that seemed to run the depth of the building. Medical labs and computer rooms lined the hall—the tools of Dr. Brandenmyer's trade, he supposed. And John's now, as well.

They passed a door marked Conference Room and came to an outside door, which John pushed wide. "Come out on the porch. Nobody will bother us back here."

The porch was furnished with a small table and a couple of chairs, and some cartons were stacked at one end, as if a delivery hadn't been put away yet. A driveway curved around the building, and beyond it pasture stretched all the way to the distant line of trees. A hitching post had been conveniently placed under the shade provided by a couple of maples.

It was a pleasant spot; some would probably say a funny spot for a medical research laboratory. Dr. Brandenmyer had been smart enough to know that he'd have to go to the Amish if he wanted to study their diseases.

John leaned against the porch railing, as if he didn't expect to prolong this visit. "What brings you to visit me today? Nothing medical, I'm guessing, or Rachel would have come herself instead of sending you."

"No."

Gideon would know how to talk to the boy he'd grown up with, but John Kile was English now. There was pride in him, Gideon would guess—pride in his education and his position. That might make it more difficult to gain his agreement.

John raised an eyebrow. "Well?"

No choice but to plunge into it and trust to the gut Lord that he was doing the right thing.

"You maybe know that I've been helping Rachel out some."

John nodded, his face softening at the mention of his twin. "She told me you were building that greenhouse she wanted so much. That was good of you."

He shrugged that off. "She's been working with her plants a lot—taking things to sell at market, at my brother Aaron's stand."

"She always did have a green thumb, didn't she?"

John smiled, and all of a sudden that made him look like the boy he'd been. The antagonism Gideon had felt at first disappeared once John mentioned Rachel. Those two had always been as close as two halves of a heart.

"Ja, she did. She still does." He took a breath. He was skirting the issue, and that wasn't helping either of them. He'd best get to the point. "But she needs help."

John seemed to stiffen, his hands pressing hard against the railing, his face shuttered. "What business is that of yours? Did Rachel send you here, or is this your idea?"

Looked like he'd said something wrong, but there was nothing for it but to push ahead now. "Rachel didn't send me." He felt a twinge at the thought. No, Rachel hadn't asked him to do anything for her.

"Then what are you doing here?" John's tone made it a demand.

"I guess I'm interfering." He shrugged. "Somebody has to. And Ezra was my friend. I feel like I owe it to him to do what I can."

"You two always did hang together, didn't you?" John seemed to take a cautious glance at the past they'd shared. "All right. So tell me what it is that's so serious you have to butt in to it."

Gideon's tension eased a hair. Johnny would listen, anyway. That was progress.

"Rachel maybe told you that she's thinking of expanding what she's doing with her plantings, maybe even turn it into a regular nursery. She could make enough money from it that she wouldn't have to sell the farm."

"I knew money was tight. And that she doesn't want to let go of the farm. I guess that's as good a solution as any. So where does the problem come in? Does she need financing to get started?"

Gideon hesitated. Isaac's role in this wasn't his story to tell.

"The water supply from the well isn't always reliable. Putting in a windmill would solve it, and I'd be glad to do it. But she won't let me unless she can pay." He shrugged. "Your sister can be a stubborn woman at times."

John's jaw clenched. "I've already offered her money. And been turned down. You can guess why." His very tone was a challenge.

"That's so," Gideon said slowly, his gaze on John's face. "But it seems to me that a smart, educated man like you could figure out a way around that, if you really set your mind to it."

For an instant anger flared in that set face, and Gideon thought he'd failed. Then slowly, maybe reluctantly, John nodded. "You have an idea how we could accomplish that?"

Relief moved through him. This was going to work. "Not exactly. But I know who will help us, because I've already asked him. Bishop Mose."

CHAPTER TEN

*I*just can't believe this is happening so quickly already." Rachel stared from her kitchen window at the windmill that had risen almost overnight, it seemed, in the field beside the barn.

"The children aren't getting in the way of Gideon and the workers, are they?" Leah grasped the kitchen table, as if she was about to heave herself to her feet. "Maybe I should check on mine."

Rachel got to her in two quick steps and nudged her gently back into her chair. "You'll do no such thing," she chided. "It's a wonder to me Daniel let you come over here today. If you overdo, he'll never let me hear the end of it."

"But the children . . ."

"Are playing in the barn, well out of the way. Did you think Gideon would let them climb the windmill tower?"

Leah chuckled, subsiding. "I guess you're right." She smoothed her hand down over her bulging belly. "Seems like the closer this little one comes to being born, the more I fuss and fidget. Please tell me that's natural and not just me."

"Definitely not just you." Rachel sat down opposite her and stirred her own cooling tea. "I remember driving Ezra and the oldest two crazy with my fussing the month before Mary was born."

Funny, now that she thought about it, that she could talk about Ezra so naturally now. It felt gut—bittersweet, maybe, but gut.

Leah stroked her belly. She wore that looking-inward expression that pregnant women seemed to get, as if communicating with the babe inside them was far more important than anything that happened outside.

"The midwife says I've probably three weeks to go, but I keep feeling as if this little one won't wait so long." Her lips curved in a soft smile. "How much I want to hold him. Or her."

Rachel had to blink back tears. She remembered that feeling, too. "That will come soon enough. But hopefully not before the quilting bee at your house."

Leah nodded. "If everyone comes, there will be enough to finish two baby quilts that afternoon. People are being so kind—it's almost overwhelming."

"You were our schoolteacher for nearly ten years," Rachel reminded her. "Lots of folks have reason to be grateful to you. They want to share your happiness."

Despite her pleasure in having Leah here for a visit again, she couldn't prevent herself from taking another quick glance at the windmill, rising raw and new against the sky. That was Gideon on the top level now, working steadily and without hurry, as he always did.

And how she could recognize him at this distance in a group similarly garbed, she didn't want to think about.

"Enough about the baby," Leah said, putting her cup down on the table. "I want to hear all about the windmill. How did this come about? I didn't even know you were thinking about building one."

"It's not so surprising, really. You know we often had trouble with our water supply in the summer."

Leah nodded, not saying the obvious—that Ezra and Rachel had always been able to count on pumping their water over from Isaac's. But she was probably thinking it, wondering about it.

"Anyway, I needed to do something." She hurried on past the difficult patch. "Gideon suggested that the windmill would let me be . . . would increase the amount I could pump. Ezra had talked about that several times, but it seemed like there was always something else to spend the money on."

"Now Gideon is doing it for you."

If there was a double meaning in the words, Rachel decided to ignore it. "Not for free. I couldn't let him do that. And the truth was that I didn't see how I'd ever pay for it."

"Your parents . . ."

Rachel shook her head. "I didn't feel right about asking them. They're so eager for me and the children to move back in with them. They see this as just another thing holding me here. No, this help came from Bishop Mose."

"Bishop Mose gave you the money?" Leah leaned forward, face alive with interest.

"Not gave. It's a loan, and I'll pay him back." Rachel hesitated, the longing to talk this over with Leah strong. "I'm not even sure how Bishop Mose knew about it to begin with. It wasn't as if I was going around talking about it."

"Gideon must have told him." Leah glanced toward the window in her turn.

"I suppose so. Of course I told Bishop Mose no, but—have you ever tried to tell him no about something?"

Leah's lips twitched. "I can't say I have."

"For every argument I had, he had an answer. First he was rational. It was a gut investment and it would increase the value of the farm, so that even if I sell sometime, I'll get more."

"He's probably right about that. But if I know you, you didn't give in that easily."

"Well, no." Rachel fiddled with her teaspoon, balancing it on her fingers. "But he questioned my pridefulness, saying that's all that was keeping me from accepting help from one of the brothers when I needed it."

The spoon dropped from Rachel's finger, landing on the wooden table with a tiny *clink*.

"If the bishop tells you that you're falling into sin, you sit up and take notice. Thing was, I could see how he had it right. I *was* being prideful, thinking that I was the only one who could take care of my children, and not trusting others to help me."

Leah leaned across the table and put her hand over Rachel's, her grip warm and firm. "I'm glad."

"Are you?" Rachel flushed. "I mean—I know you don't think I can succeed at this nursery business, and that's mostly why I need the windmill—"

"Not think you can succeed?" Leah interrupted her, her fingers tightening on Rachel's. "Rachel, where did you get an idea like that?"

"That Sunday, after worship, when I told you about my idea. You . . . Well, you discouraged me. As if you didn't think I had it in me to make a success of it."

"Ach, Rachel, that isn't what I meant at all." Leah's face crinkled with such distress that Rachel had to believe her. "I was just worried about you, that's all. I was afraid you'd work yourself to death, not accepting any help and thinking you had to do it all on your own. That's what I was thinking. Goodness, I know you'll do anything you set your mind to."

Rachel flushed, this time with pleasure. "I thought—well, never mind. I'm just glad you feel that way."

Leah's eyes were bright with unshed tears. "I've felt, lately, as if there was something between us. I didn't like the feeling. Are we all right now?"

Rachel nodded, her own throat thick. There had been something between them, thanks to her own misunderstanding.

"Ser gut," Rachel murmured.

Before she could say another word, a ruckus erupted outside. Men's voices, shouting—something had happened.

She and Leah exchanged one quick, frightened look, and then she was rushing to the door, with Leah following more slowly.

She burst out onto the back porch and took the steps in a jump. Men were running toward the barn, Gideon in the lead. Rachel's heart thudded against her ribs.

Something was wrong—something bad.

Please, Lord, please, Lord. She didn't know what to pray, only that prayer was needed.

Elizabeth raced to them and clutched Rachel's apron with both hands, her face tearstained and frightened.

"Elizabeth, what is it? Tell me!" She grasped the child's shoulders.

"Becky." The word came out on a sob. "Becky climbed up into the barn rafters. She can't get down. She's going to fall."

Becky . . . please, God, protect Becky.

"Go to your mamm," she ordered, and she set off running toward the barn, fear clawing at her heart, breath coming in terrified gasps.

Please, Father. Please.

Gideon's leg throbbed as he reached the barn seconds ahead of the other men. He thrust the door wide and plunged in, blinking, trying to adjust his vision to the gloom after the bright sunshine outside.

He spotted the two boys standing in the middle of the barn floor, their heads tilted back, faces pale, shocked ovals as they stared upward. He followed the direction of their gazes, and his heart seemed to stop.

Becky. High in the rafters, thirty or forty feet up, Becky teetered on a beam, hands outstretched to clutch nothing but air.

For a second he couldn't move—couldn't do anything but utter a wordless prayer. Then the others rushed in, and his mind started working. Be calm, be rational, think only of what must be done, and not of what was at stake.

"Get a rope," he ordered. "And a tarp, a canvas, anything you can use to stretch out in case—"

He didn't finish. He didn't need to. They understood. In case she fell.

Murmurs of agreement. He grasped the ladder that led up to the loft level. "I'm going up."

"No, I will."

He hadn't seen William come in, but he was often around the farm. His round, beardless face was pale, and his voice had shaken on the words.

Gideon didn't stop his scramble up the ladder, but he threw the words over his shoulder. "I'm more used to working at heights. Stay with Rachel."

Not waiting to see if the lad agreed, he scaled the ladder to the loft and then paused to assess the situation. A rough ladder nailed to the wall led upward into the angled timbers that braced the roof. Becky must have gone that way, but how she'd gotten that far out on the cross-beam, he couldn't imagine.

"Gid, here." Aaron, who'd been helping with the windmill, tossed a coil of rope up to him.

Gideon caught it and slipped it over his head, then thrust his arm through the middle so that it crossed his body.

"What else?" Aaron said the words softly, as if afraid of disturbing Becky on her precarious perch.

Gideon measured the angle at which he'd have to bring the child down if he reached her. *When* he reached her. "Stay here on the loft. I might need to lower her down to you."

He wouldn't consider any other conclusion to this. He couldn't.

Aaron nodded, seeming to understand all that he didn't say. "Da Herr sei mit du," he murmured.

The words seemed to follow Gideon as he started up the ladder. *The Lord be with you.*

Gideon's gaze was fixed on Becky. He could see her better now that he was higher. Her face was as white as her kapp, her arms stretched out in an effort to balance herself.

Below, he heard the rush of running feet. Rachel. It had to be. She'd look up; she'd see her child in danger. Pray God she didn't cry out. The slightest thing could disturb Becky's delicate balancing act.

Straining his ears, his body tense, he heard a faint gasp—that was all. Rachel would see, would understand. She'd be strong, no matter how afraid she was.

And he—he couldn't look down, couldn't let himself be distracted by the pain he knew she was suffering. All his attention had to be on Becky.

He reached the top of the ladder. Not close enough to reach her yet, but at least he could probably talk to her without causing her to move.

"I'm coming to get you, Becky." He kept his tone low and easy. "Got yourself in a bit of a pickle, I'm afraid."

She didn't speak, but her head moved in the faintest of nods.

A diagonal beam crossed beneath her. That must be how she'd gotten up there, but he couldn't imagine it. Still, if she had done it, then he could.

He eyed the beam she stood on. If he could loop the rope over it, that would help to stabilize him as he worked his way up the diagonal toward her. But he'd never do it from here. He'd have to edge his way up closer first.

Meanwhile, Becky was visibly tiring, and that increased the danger. He risked a glance down. If she fell from where she was now, she'd miss the loft edge where Aaron stood. The other men were already positioned below with a canvas stretched between them, their eyes and their prayers fixed on the child.

"Becky, can you sit down on the beam instead of standing, do you think?"

Frowning, she bent her knees slightly. Her arms waved, and someone below them gasped.

Then she caught her balance again, shaking her head slightly.

"That's all right." He edged upward along the beam. "You're fine just where you are. That beam is nice and wide. I'd guess you could stand there all day if you had to."

She seemed to straighten a little, as if she were trying to prove him right.

He edged a foot closer and grasped the beam with one hand while he lifted the rope free with the other. He would not let himself imagine the day Ezra had been above him in another barn. He would not think about Rachel, far below, watching in terror. He would only concentrate on the child.

"Becky, I'm going to throw my rope up around your beam. I don't want you to move or reach for it, okay? I'm just going to use it to help me balance."

Seeing that she understood, he loosened the loop, measuring the distance to the beam with his gaze. He knotted the end of the rope to give it a little more weight, swinging it several times to get the feel of it. Then he swung it upward.

It missed, falling back toward him. The momentum of his swing threw his body off balance. He lurched, stumbling on the beam, clawing at thin air, nothing beneath him but the canvas, which wouldn't hold his weight. He was going to fall—

His left hand brushed the beam, caught, held, and his body slammed into it, his legs dangling.

Hug the beam, don't look down, don't think about the pain, he thought, as his bad leg took all the weight when he dragged himself back onto the beam . . .

Gripping it, he looked up, shaking off the red haze that clouded his vision. Bless the child, she still held her position, though every muscle must be trembling with the effort it took.

"Missed, but I'll get it this time." He forced his voice to be calm. "Hold on, Becky. Only a few more minutes now."

Slowly, painfully, he inched back up along the beam. It was harder this time, his strength waning. He readied the rope again. Breathed a prayer. Threw it. This time it swung around the beam, the knotted end dropping almost into his hands.

Gripping the ends, he wrapped them around his left arm, leaving his right free to grab Becky. With the stability the rope gave him, he moved up the beam.

Then he was as close as he could get, and he still wasn't quite close enough.

"Becky, I need you to help me, okay? I need you to bend just a little, so that you can reach for my hand."

"I can't." Her lips barely moved. "I'll fall."

Be honest with her. "Maybe," he conceded. "But if you do, I'll catch you." *Please, Lord. Please.* "It's the only way to get you back down to your mammi. All right?"

She pressed her lips together firmly. Then she gave a slight nod.

"Wait until I give you the word." He strained toward her, stretching until his muscles screamed. Sweat poured into his eyes, and he blinked it away. "Okay, Becky. Now."

She wavered. Her small body bent slightly—her hand neared his, still a painful few inches away, but he couldn't quite reach. *Please, God—*

Then, as her body tumbled from the beam, he got a glimpse of her white, terrified face, heard a cry from below, grabbed, held, and pulled her tight against him.

He couldn't move. He could only balance there, clinging to the rope, holding her close against him, feeling the frightened beating of her heart, so quick, so light, like a little bird in his arms.

Thank you, Lord.

He could breathe again, move again. He edged back down the beam, aware of the sounds below him, the others scrambling up the ladder to the loft.

Finally he reached the relative safety of the crossbeam. Becky's arms were tight around his neck, her tears wet on his shirt.

"Almost there," he said. "You have to be brave a little longer, all right?"

She nodded, and he felt the movement against his shoulder.

He edged his way to the rough ladder nailed to the barn wall, his strength nearly gone. Would his leg hold them both to get down the rest of the way?

But he didn't have to find out. There was Aaron, already halfway up the ladder, reaching toward him.

"Becky, I'm going to hand you down to my brother Aaron. But you have to let go of my neck. Can you do that? Just hang on to my arm instead. We won't let you fall."

For an instant longer she clung to him, her cheek pressed against his. Then she let go. Grasping her firmly with his arm across her chest, he lowered her into Aaron's waiting arms.

Aaron carried her quickly down. He could hear the murmurs of those below, the muffled sobs that must come from Rachel.

He should climb down, but he couldn't seem to move. He could only lean against the rough, warm wood, his heart hurting as if the Lord had taken a chisel to it and wrenched it open.

By the time supper was over, it seemed to Rachel that everyone in the community had heard about Becky's mishap, and half of them had stopped by to marvel and praise God over her rescue. Much as she appreciated their prayers and concern, she'd begun to wish that they would leave the subject alone for a while, for Becky's sake if not for hers.

Her parents had come, too, and stayed to eat supper, with Mamm taking over the kitchen the moment she walked in the door. Although Daad had yet to say anything to her about it, Rachel suspected that his somber expression meant he found this incident just one more reason why she and the children should move home.

"Ach, Becky, you don't have to dry the dishes." Mamm patted Becky's cheek. "You deserve a reward for being such a brave girl."

"Don't say that." The words spurted out of Rachel's mouth before she could stop them. "Don't give Becky the idea that she's done something brave. She was naughty. She did something she knew was wrong, and she caused a lot of trouble."

Becky's eyes widened at her tone, and her lower lip trembled.

"Rachel, Rachel," her mother chided. "You should be praising God that she is safe."

Taking a deep breath helped, just a little. "I'm sorry, Mamm." She pulled her daughter close against her. "I am praising God you are safe, Rebecca. We owe our thanks to the quick work of Gideon and the others who helped." She tilted her daughter's face up gently. "But that doesn't change the fact that you did wrong, does it?"

"No, Mammi." Becky's lips quivered, and she pressed them together for a second. "I'm sorry."

"Ser gut. Now I think you will help finish up the dishes, won't you?"

Becky nodded and turned back to her work.

Rachel glanced at her mother. Mamm's lips were pressed together much as Becky's had been. Obviously Rachel hadn't heard the end of this, but at least maybe her mother would wait until the children were in bed to discuss it.

By then, she'd have to find some measure of calm to deal with her parents' concerns, and she wasn't sure where that was going to come from.

"I'm going out to check the animals before it gets any darker." She dried her hands quickly on a dish towel. "I'll be back in a few minutes."

She escaped out the back door before her father could offer to do it for her.

Dusk had drawn in while they were in the kitchen, and the lilac hedge cast a long shadow on the lawn. There was still enough light to see, though, once her vision adjusted, so she didn't go back inside for a flashlight.

She walked quickly past the greenhouse. Then, knowing she was out of sight if her mother watched from the kitchen window, she stopped, putting her hands over her face.

I'm sorry, Father. I'm sorry. I was wrong to speak that way to my mother. But that is what it would be like if we moved in with them. With the best intentions in the world, my parents would begin to take over with the children. As dearly as I love Mamm and Daadi, these children were given by You for me to raise.

She blotted the tears that spilled over onto her cheeks. Even here, she shouldn't let herself cry, because the signs would be there on her face when she went back inside.

She glanced at the darkening sky. The children were the most important thing in her life. Was she doing right by them? She'd tried to continue handling them as she had when Ezra was alive. Maybe that wasn't enough. What if Becky's foolish act today was a sign that her parents were right?

Shadows deepened by the moment. She'd best get this finished before she couldn't see at all. She started for the barn, and then stopped again.

A buggy stood next to the barn, and a horse was still in the paddock. Gideon's buggy. Gideon's horse. Had he ridden home with his brother, or was he still here?

Her steps quickened. She slid the barn door back and grasped the torch that always hung just inside, switching it on.

The barn's interior sprang to life in the flashlight's beam, and her stomach clenched with the memory of what had happened here earlier. But Becky was safe, thanks to Gideon. She couldn't let the memory control her actions.

She took a step. "Is someone here? Gideon?"

A rustle answered her, and she swung the beam in the direction of the sound. Gideon sat slumped on a bale of straw, his bad leg stretched out. He lifted a hand to shield his face from the light, but not before she saw that it was wracked with pain.

Lowering the light, she hurried to him. "Gideon, was ist letz? Are you hurt?"

He shook his head, but she knelt next to him anyway, touching his bad leg gently.

"Your leg is paining you, ain't so?"

"It will heal." His voice was choked, alarming her still more.

"Daad is in the house. I'll get him to come and help . . ."

"No." He grasped her hand to keep her from moving. "I'm all right. I'll go now."

Bracing his hand on the stall behind him, he attempted to lever himself to his feet. A spasm of pain crossed his face, and his leg seemed to buckle under his weight.

"No, no." Sliding her arm around him and dragging his arm across her shoulder, she helped him sit back down. "I'm so sorry. Becky's foolishness has ended up with your leg getting hurt."

He leaned back, seeming spent, but he shook his head. "The leg will be better in a few days." He closed his eyes. "My heart will take longer."

She saw, then, and wondered why she hadn't realized it sooner. "This is about Ezra. When you saw Becky—it was just like Ezra."

His hand clenched spasmodically on hers. "I can't talk about it. Not to you, of all people."

She took a breath, reaching inside for calm. *Please, Father. I didn't see that he was hurting so much. Please, give me the words to help him.*

"You're wrong." She saw it now, if only she could make him understand. "It is hard to talk about. Hard to hear about. But maybe we two are the only ones who can really understand. Really help each other. Because we both loved him."

He shook his head again, but she sensed the need inside him to get it out.

"I know," she said softly. "When I saw Becky on that beam, I saw Ezra, too."

"I should have stopped him." His voice was harsh with pain. "I should have kept him from going up. If I hadn't been so slow, if I'd moved more quickly, maybe I could have stopped him."

"Gideon—"

"I shut it away. Tried not to think about it. But it didn't work. And seeing Becky today just tore it open."

His head moved again, and he was like an animal in pain seeking relief. Her own heart seemed clutched in a vise that tightened with every word. Somehow she had to ignore that so that she could ease his grief.

"You're not thinking straight. How could you have stopped him? You know what Ezra was like."

Even as she said the words, she realized that she was seeing Ezra more clearly than she had since the day he died. For the first time, she thought of that day without seeing him falling. Instead she saw him laughing, climbing higher just as Becky had, probably chiding Gideon for taking his time.

"He was daring, too daring sometimes. You know that better than anyone else." The hand that clutched hers feverishly seemed to relax just a little. He was listening to her, and for his sake she had to get this all said, just this once. "I know he teased you about being slow, but that was just his way."

"If I had—"

"No." She snapped out the word. "Don't you think I've been down that road a thousand times myself? If I had done something differently, maybe he wouldn't have gone. If I hadn't told him to hurry home, maybe he'd have been more careful."

"It wasn't your fault." He leaned toward her, and she knew her words had jolted him out of his absorption with his own imagined guilt. "Nothing you did caused Ezra to fall."

"No. And nothing you did caused it either." She gripped his arm with both hands, wanting to force him to understand. "Gideon, think about it. Ezra asked you to go and check out that barn for soundness because he knew that you would do it thoroughly, the way you do everything. He knew you would be careful and methodical—that's why he valued your opinion, isn't it?"

He nodded slowly, almost reluctantly.

"Ezra was a gut man, and I loved him with all my heart. But he wasn't perfect." She saw him with such precision now, as if he stood in front of her, with no need for a photograph to prompt her memory. "He was always daring, and Becky is too much like him in that. He was quick and impatient, and that day—" Her throat tightened, but she had to say the rest of it. "That day he should have been more cautious. But he wasn't, because that was who he was."

Something that had been tied up in knots inside her seemed to ease, and she could think of him without pain. "It was an accident, that's all. We both know that, don't we?"

His gaze fixed on hers, and her heart seemed to lurch. Then he nodded. "Ja. I guess we do."

CHAPTER ELEVEN

*R*achel misted the snapdragon seedlings, pausing to touch the creamy edge of a blossom that had begun to show already. These plants would be a beautiful addition to someone's garden.

Maybe hers. If she was going to sell plants from her home eventually, she'd have to have an overflowing flower garden herself. That would be what buyers expected.

William had painted a neat sign for the end of the driveway last year, advertising the strawberries she'd had for sale. Maybe he'd do another one for her plants.

She turned, movement drawing her eye, and her breath seemed to catch in her throat. Gideon was back to work on the windmill. Even as she watched, he pulled his wagon up close to the site, which probably meant he had supplies in it.

Or maybe that his leg was still bothering him and he didn't want to walk. If so, he shouldn't be here at all, although he wouldn't welcome her saying so.

They hadn't talked in several days—not since Saturday evening, when she'd found him in the barn. She'd seen him at worship on Sunday, moving cautiously, his brother or one of his nephews always close to lend him an arm. He hadn't come near her after the service, and she'd tried to respect his obvious wish to avoid talking with her.

He was embarrassed, she supposed, over having revealed so much of his inner feelings to her. He wasn't a man who did that easily in any event, and especially not when it came to something bound to be so painful to both of them.

She put down the mister and tried to focus on thinning out a tray

of marigolds. Without her willing it, her gaze kept straying back to
Gideon. He was starting up the structure now, making her hold her
breath until she saw that he was wearing a safety harness.

Mostly the Amish didn't do that, and she'd seen enough of Gideon
at work to know that it was unusual for him. Was he doing it because
his leg was still paining him?

What happened on Saturday had been painful both physically and
emotionally. And yet, for her at least, that encounter had been healing,
too. She could see Ezra more clearly now, as if the fog of grief and guilt
was lifting. She could only hope that was true for Gideon as well.

She finished the tray of seedlings before she let herself look again. And
jumped to find someone staring in through the glass at her. William.

Smiling, she went to the door. "William. I didn't see you. Will you
come in and look at my greenhouse?"

He took a step forward and then paused. "I—I—maybe I shouldn't.
I mean, b-b-bother you."

"It's not a bother. I want to show you what I've been doing with the
flowers."

She held the door wide in invitation, but still William hesitated,
standing a few steps away and surveying the building as if it were a
skittish colt about to buck.

"William? Do you disapprove of the greenhouse so much that you
won't even come in?"

"No, no. F-f-for sure it's not that." Clutching his straw hat in his hands,
he stepped inside, ducking his head to avoid the hanging pots of plants.

She stepped back, giving him as much space as she could in the confines of the greenhouse that was really made for one. "I thought maybe
you agreed with Isaac—that I should forget this foolishness and sell the
farm to Caleb."

He didn't respond, and she immediately regretted putting him on
the spot. Hadn't she just been telling herself that she couldn't contribute
to a family quarrel?

"I'm sorry, William. I shouldn't have said that to you."

He shook his head. "N-n-no, it's okay. I'm g-glad for you, that
you have the greenhouse Ezra w-wanted to give you." His big hands

tightened on the hat's brim. "J-j-just sorry G-Gideon was the one to build it for you."

She paused, not sure what to say to that but knowing she had to say something. "William, you're not blaming Gideon for Ezra's death, are you?"

"You d-d-did."

Her throat tightened, making it difficult to speak. "I didn't blame him. Not that. I just couldn't seem to forgive him for living through the accident when Ezra didn't."

"Now you d-d-don't f-f-feel that way." He said it almost accusingly.

"I think I see things more clearly now." She tried to marshal her thoughts. If only she could help William take the step that she seemed to be taking, it would be a comfort to him, she was sure. "You remember how Ezra was—always a little more daring than everyone else, always needing to go first, even to take chances."

"You th-th-think it was his fault." He threw the words at her.

"No, not at all. I mean that we both know what he was like. It was part of what we both loved about him, wasn't it?"

William jerked a nod.

She was talking out of hard-won insight, and her assurance grew as she formed the words. "It was in Ezra's nature to go first, just as it was in Gideon's nature to move more slowly, to check things out methodically, just as Ezra wanted him to." She found herself smiling. "Maybe that was why they were such gut friends. They each had something the other one needed."

William was frowning, but he seemed to be listening, even understanding.

"For a long time, when I thought about that last day, I could only see Ezra falling." Her throat tightened, but she forced herself to go on. "Now I can see him the way I know he would have been—climbing higher, enjoying it, maybe laughing at Gideon for taking his time. I can see how his eyes would sparkle when he did something daring." She touched William's hand. "It's better to see him that way. It is. Don't blame anyone else. All right?"

He jerked a reluctant nod. "Ja." He hesitated. "But I still wish I— w-w-we were the ones helping you."

She patted his hand, relieved at his acceptance. "Isaac wouldn't want you to be helping me with something he doesn't approve of. He hasn't said anything to me yet about the windmill, but I can guess what his opinion is."

"He says you are w-w-willful. I don't think that."

"Gut. I'm glad you understand." She wouldn't let herself dwell on what Isaac thought. "I just have to take care of the children the best I can. I wish everyone could see that."

"I—I do." He gripped her hand suddenly, his fingers tight on hers. "I'm on your s-s-side. Always."

"Denke, William." But she didn't feel comfortable with the intense expression on his face. Better to change the subject, if she could. "In that case, come with me and see the new windmill. Once it's finished, this farm will have plenty of its own water. Bishop Mose says that will make the farm more valuable, so that's gut, isn't it?"

She moved around him as she spoke, gently loosening the grip of his hand. She stepped outside, feeling as if she were stepping out of a situation that was getting increasingly uncomfortable.

William followed, ducking his head to get through the door. Funny. She always saw him as Ezra's little brother, but he was growing into a man now, and no one in the family seemed to notice.

She led the way toward the windmill. "The children have been fascinated to see it go up so fast. Isn't it amazing?"

"I d-d-don't know m-much about those things." William sounded sulky, but he followed her.

Gideon spotted them coming and began to descend more quickly than he had gone up. In contrast, William's pace seemed to slow when he saw Gideon.

"What do you think?" She turned toward William, but he was already stepping back.

"Ser g-gut. I—I have to g-g-go." And he strode off before Gideon could reach them.

Gideon unbuckled his safety harness, watching as William Brand strode off toward the barn. What ailed the boy? He'd always been a bit shy because of his stammer, but he seemed more distant than ever since Ezra's death.

But Rachel was standing there, giving him a tentative smile, and he tried to return it, tried to think of something ordinary and commonplace to say that wouldn't remind either of them of what had happened Saturday night.

"Have I scared young William off?"

Rachel glanced after the boy, a wrinkle forming between her brows. "William's not so young."

"I suppose not." What was there about William to bring that worried look to her face? "I guess I always think of him as Ezra's baby brother."

"His family treats him like a child." She bit off the words. "They don't see him as he really is."

"How do you see him, Rachel?"

And what troubled her about him? He couldn't ask that, but he found that he was losing the constraint he'd expected to feel with her. After what happened Saturday, after showing her all his weaknesses, he'd thought he wouldn't be able to talk comfortably with her.

Now, he just wanted to wipe away that anxious expression on her face.

She met his gaze, concern still filling her blue eyes. "I'm not sure. I just know that he's turning into a man now, and no one seems to recognize that. They continue to treat him like a child, just because he doesn't speak normally."

Rachel's concern seemed to be catching. He looked in the direction William had gone, but he'd disappeared into the barn.

"That's not a gut thing, to be holding someone back from growing. Ezra cared a great deal for him." Even when they were boys, Ezra had been remarkably patient with his little brother, quick to protect him if anyone should think of teasing.

"He was a buffer between Isaac and William, I think," Rachel said. "I'm just beginning to see that. I'd like to help William, but I don't know what I can do."

She probably had enough to worry about with her own situation, but he figured Rachel could no more keep from being concerned about other people than the sun could keep from rising.

"Just listen to him." The words were out before he realized how close they came to the very subject he wanted most to avoid. But it was true. That was what Rachel did so well. "That will help him more than any advice, I'd guess."

She nodded, but now she switched the concerned look to him. "About Saturday—"

"You were kind to listen to me, especially when I—when it—"

He was beginning to sound like William, and he understood how frustrating that must be. He couldn't take back what he'd told her on Saturday, and maybe that was a gut thing. But he didn't want it to stand as a barrier between them, either.

"I'm glad you told me." Her voice went soft on the words, but there were no tears.

"It hurt you. I shouldn't—"

She grasped his hand, silencing him. "Maybe it did hurt to talk about when Ezra died. It hurt you, too. But since we talked, it's been better."

She paused, shaking her head, as if frustrated in her turn at the inability of words to show what she was feeling.

"You don't need to say anything more—"

"I want to." She took a breath, seeming to calm herself. "Since we talked, I can see Ezra more clearly now. I'd been so busy blaming you and blaming myself for the fact that he was gone that I risked losing him twice over. I don't know why, but talking to you about it helped me to see him clearly again. That's what I was just saying to William. Ezra wasn't perfect." She stopped, as if surprised she'd said that.

"No, he wasn't perfect." Gideon actually managed to smile a little. "If he were here, he'd be the first one to laugh at that, for sure."

"He would, wouldn't he?" Her face lit with a smile in return, and she seemed to have forgotten that she was holding his hand.

"Ezra was always one for a joke, and he laughed at himself more easily than anyone." He seemed to hear Ezra's hearty laugh.

Rachel was right, he realized. Just saying the words gave him such a vivid picture of Ezra in his mind, and there was no sorrow with it. No sorrow—just joy in remembering Ezra as he had been.

"Ja, he did." The smile clung to Rachel's lips a moment longer.

Then she seemed to notice that she was still holding on to him. She let go of his hand.

"Are we friends?" There wasn't a hint of embarrassment in her words or her expression, and he was glad of it.

"Friends," he agreed.

"Ser gut." She gave a quick little nod.

He glanced over her shoulder. "It looks as if your little scholars are home from school already."

"Ach, where has the time gone? I forget it when I get working in the greenhouse, that's for sure." She turned away. "I'll send Becky out with a cold drink for you."

She walked briskly across the lawn toward the children, the light breeze tossing her kapp strings and apron, and held out her arms to them.

He turned back to his toolbox, his heart lightened. Rachel had made things all right between them, and he was glad.

He was still organizing the tools he needed when Becky came trotting across the yard toward him, a thermos swinging from her hand. She stopped a few feet from him and held it out.

"Mammi sent this for you."

"Denke, Becky." He took it, tilting it up for a long drink of lemonade. "That tastes gut."

She nodded. "I'll have some with the brownies my grossmutter made for my snack."

"That was nice of her." He put the thermos down and began buckling on the safety harness. "She must know you like them."

"Ja." Her gaze was fixed on the leather straps. "You didn't wear a harness before."

"No, I didn't." He paused, and the memory of Rachel's words made it easier to say what was in his mind. "I thought maybe you got the wrong idea about it when I didn't wear a harness."

Her blue eyes went round with surprise. "You're wearing the harness now because of me?" Her voice went up in a little squeak.

"Ja." He fastened the buckle and adjusted the straps. "Working up high can be dangerous, like climbing up high for no gut reason."

Her gaze slid away from his, and she kicked at a clod of mud. "Mammi says I should thank you for helping me on Saturday."

He studied what he could see of her averted face, but couldn't make out what she was thinking. "You don't have to thank me if you don't feel it. It's better to be honest with people, I think."

"Elizabeth told on me."

He hesitated, thinking this conversation should be between Becky and her mamm. But she had said it to him, and he owed her an honest answer or he'd be running counter to what he'd just said.

"Elizabeth is your friend, ja?"

She nodded, her lower lip coming out. It made her look like Ezra as a little boy. His bottom lip would come out like that when he was told he couldn't do something. His grossmutter had teased him, saying that a bird would come and perch on his lip if he weren't careful. Funny, how fresh that memory was after all this time.

"A friend has a duty to see that you're safe." His heart twisted. He hadn't kept Ezra safe, had he? "She thought you were going to fall, so I think she did the right thing in getting help. Wouldn't you have gone for help if it had been Elizabeth up on that beam?"

"Elizabeth wouldn't climb up high. She's scared of that."

The words shot back at him, almost defiantly.

"It's sensible to be scared of some things." *Father, give me the right words to say to this child.* "I was scared when I climbed up after you."

"You were?" Now her gaze met his. Now she was listening.

"Ja, sure. It's gut to be scared, so long as it makes you careful. If I hadn't been careful, I might not have made it all the way up to you. Then what would you have done?"

"I . . . Maybe I could have got down by myself."

He looked at her, not speaking. She needed to face the truth of this one herself.

"I guess I couldn't have." She pressed her lips together, as if she wanted to say more but wouldn't let herself.

"No. You couldn't." What would Ezra have said to her in this situation? Gideon didn't know. He could only offer what he felt in his heart was the right answer. "It can be gut to dare enough to try new things. But it's foolish to risk your life doing it."

She didn't look convinced. Probably Ezra wouldn't have been at her age, either.

"Your daadi was my friend from the time we were younger than you." He hadn't spoken of Ezra to her before, and maybe it was a mistake now, but he had to try. "I wonder what he would say if he'd been the one to climb up in the barn to get you."

Becky stared at him for a long moment. Tears sparkled, beginning to spill over onto her cheeks. Then, without speaking, she turned and ran back to the house.

He'd hurt her, maybe. But it was worthwhile, wasn't it, if it kept her from taking foolish chances? He wasn't sure, and not knowing made him feel like he'd failed.

Rachel glanced into the living room once the stew she'd decided on for supper was well under way. All three children were there, instead of outside as they usually were at this time of day. She'd called them in when she realized that dark clouds were massing over the hills to the west. Rain was coming, and they were better off inside.

Joseph and Mary stacked blocks into a tower, which Mary was certain sure to knock down sometime soon. Becky sat in the rocking chair with a book, her gaze pinned to the page.

Was she actually reading? Or was she thinking about whatever it was that had brought her into the house earlier, trying not to cry?

Becky had been talking to Gideon. She'd come into the house upset. And that was all Rachel knew. Becky had shaken her head to questions, saying nothing was wrong.

But something was. And it was something Becky didn't want to tell her. Rachel's heart clutched. Her daughter was keeping secrets from her already. What had happened to the little one who'd leaned on her so confidingly? She'd changed in so many ways in the past year.

Rachel walked back to the kitchen, pausing automatically to check the heat under the stew. Maybe she should have asked Gideon what was wrong, but that seemed like interfering. She pressed her hands on the edge of the stove, staring at the pot without really seeing it. If something had happened that she should know about, Gideon would tell her, wouldn't he?

A few fat raindrops patted against the windowpane, and she went to lean on the sink to peer out. Gideon, ignoring the rain, was stowing his tools with steady movements.

At least he was off the windmill tower. She was developing a dislike for seeing anyone working up high, no matter what the circumstances. She'd have to conquer that feeling before the next barn raising.

If she talked to Gideon—

"Mammi, Mammi." Joseph rushed into the kitchen. "I didn't feed Dolly yet. I have to go back outside."

He was headed for the door when she grabbed him by the suspenders that crossed his back.

"It's starting to rain outside. Dolly can wait until later."

"But she's hungry. And she's going to have her babies soon, so she needs to eat."

"It won't hurt her any to wait a bit."

"Daadi always said the animals have to come first, 'cause they depend on us. And I won't melt in the rain. Remember how he used to say that?"

She heard Ezra's voice for a brief second. "I remember." She managed to smile at him. "But you go back and watch Mary for me. I'll take care of Dolly."

"Dolly's my job, Mammi." He pressed his lips together, for a moment his expression very like his father's.

"Well, you're my job, ain't so?" She ruffled his hair. "And I don't want you getting wet. I'll do it. Now scoot." She turned him toward the living room and gave him a little shove.

Fortunately the rain wasn't heavy yet. She swung her shawl around her as she went out the back door and started toward the barn. Sure enough, Dolly was bawling in her pen, used to having Joseph show up promptly with her dinner.

"Hush, now, you spoiled creature. I'll get your feed for you." She picked up the grain bucket and headed for the shed where the chicken and goat feed was stored, hunching her shoulders as the rain began pelting down.

Lifting the latch, she stepped inside. Then stopped and stared, dismay building. The lid to the large metal can where she stored the goat's mixture lay on the floor, and even as she watched, a mouse scurried out of sight.

Worse, water dripped from the roof, directly into the barrel. She blinked back frustrated tears. If the grain spoiled—

A sudden gust of wind tore the door from her hand, slamming it back against the shed wall and driving cold rain into her face.

"R-Rachel! What are you d-d-doing?" William was behind her, reaching out to grasp the edge of the door and pull it so that it shielded her from the worst of the wind. "Go in. I'll t-t-take care of the g-g-goat."

"The feed." She grasped the edge of the barrel and tried to drag it out from under the drip, which was rapidly becoming a steady stream.

William, seeing what was wrong, ducked his head and stepped into the shed. In an instant, he had wrestled the container out from under the leak.

Rachel put her hand on the surface of the grain. It felt as if only a small amount of the top layer was wet, thank the gut Lord.

"H-h-here." William picked up the bucket and began scooping out the damp grain. "It's not t-t-too bad."

"Be sure to get it all." Seeing how quick he was, she stepped back out of his way. "I'd rather throw away some that might be all right rather than risk mold spoiling the whole barrel."

"Ja." He focused on the grain. "Gut thing you c-c-came when you did to find it."

"The lid was off." She stared at it, as if the circle of metal could answer the questions that buzzed in her mind. "I can't believe that Joseph would be so careless."

William didn't answer, but he shrugged, as if to say anything was possible.

The door swung wider, and Gideon peered in, water dripping from the brim of his hat. "Was ist letz? What's wrong?"

She gestured mutely toward the barrel. "When I came to feed the goat, I found the lid off. And it was right under that leak in the roof." She frowned up at it. "I don't understand. How could it get so bad so fast? It was fine and dry in here during that heavy rain we had last week."

Gideon reached up, exploring the roof with his fingers. "I'll have a look and . . ."

"I—I—I'll fix it." William slammed the lid back on the can. His voice was determined, almost angry.

For a moment the two men stared at each other, and animosity seemed to sizzle in the close confines of the shed. Finally Gideon shrugged.

"Gut. I'll help you do a quick patch so Rachel doesn't get any more water in here today."

"Denke," she said quickly, before William could reply. "You're both very kind."

"Why don't you go inside? The children will be worried when you don't come back."

Gideon's tone was persuasive. It was clear he and William wouldn't be content until she'd gotten out of their way. And he was right, as well. She didn't want Becky or Joseph to come looking for her.

"I'll feed the goat on my way in." She grabbed a dry pail and scooped up the grain mixture, putting the lid back firmly.

As she edged past Gideon on her way out the door, she sent a worried glance toward the shed roof. Surely that was odd for such a bad leak to develop so quickly. She glanced at Gideon, to find that he was staring at the roof, too, a frown deepening on his face.

Drawing her shawl tightly around her, she hurried to Dolly's pen and dumped the feed in. The goat's complaints ceased abruptly, and Rachel ran for the house, wishing she could outrun her worries as easily.

"Mammi?" Joseph was waiting on the porch. "Was ist letz?"

She shepherded him inside the kitchen and shook out her wet shawl, draping it over the drying rack beside the stove. Then she turned to look at him.

"Joseph, are you sure you put the lid on the grain barrel the last time you fed Dolly?"

His mouth formed an O. "I did. Really. I wouldn't forget that. Honest."

She didn't think he would, either, but the fact was that the lid had been off. "The lid was lying on the floor beside the barrel. Are you sure you didn't do it in a hurry and forget?"

"No, Mammi. Anyway, I don't ever put the lid on the floor. I put it on top of the chicken feed when I get Dolly's meal out."

True enough. She'd seen him do that numerous times. "Maybe a raccoon got in and took it off. They can get into all kinds of things. I'll have Onkel William check for any hole where they might get in." She patted his cheek, wanting to chase the worry from his small face. "We won't worry about it. All right?"

He nodded.

"You go and watch Mary for me while I finish supper."

"Ja, Mammi." He ran toward the living room, his worry disappearing.

Getting out a bowl, she began mixing up dumplings for the stew. She did it at the counter where she could look out the window, staring through the rain at the men moving around the shed.

By the time the dumplings were ready, Gideon was approaching the back door. Setting the bowl aside, she went to meet him.

"Come in." She gestured. "You must be drenched. Do you want some coffee?"

He shook his head. "I'm too wet to come into your clean kitchen, and I'd best get along home anyway. I just thought I should tell you what we found."

She stared at him, dread pooling in her stomach. "What is it?"

"That hole in the roof." His voice went hard. "It didn't get there naturally. Someone took a pry bar and pulled the boards loose. It was done deliberately."

Chapter Twelve

*T*he sky was clear and cloudless. The only sign Gideon could spot of yesterday's rainstorm was the refreshed green of the pasture grass and the plants in Rachel's garden. The storm had been swept away, but the worry it left behind lingered like a stain on the crystal-clear sunshine of the day.

He studied the shed from his perch on the windmill. Seen from above, the shed roof was plainly visible. If he'd been up here when someone had taken a pry bar to the tar paper, he'd know who'd done it.

There was no doubt in his mind that the action had been deliberate. Someone, or more than one person, had set out to cause harm to Rachel's property.

Teenagers, intent on vandalism? That sort of thing was known to happen. English kids, even Amish ones sometimes, didn't always use common sense when they were out for mischief.

Still, he couldn't imagine any Amish teenager, knowing Rachel, who would pick a struggling widow to play a trick on. As for the Englischers—well, he didn't understand them well enough to say, maybe, but it seemed to him they'd do something more obvious than this. Splashing paint around, knocking over an outhouse—those were more the kinds of tricks you heard of from them.

One thing kept pushing its way back into his thoughts, as annoying as a protruding nail. That story Joseph had told him about the draft horse getting out of his stall one night—did that connect with the damage to the shed roof? Or was he imagining a pattern where none existed?

The screen door slammed, and Rachel came out of the house carrying a load of laundry she must intend to hang on the clothesline. She reached the line, paused for a moment, and then seemed to make up her mind about something. She dropped the basket in the grass and started toward the windmill.

He came down from the tower nearly as fast as she crossed the yard, reaching the ground seconds behind her.

She hesitated again, looking at him, the breeze blowing strands of fine blond hair across her face. He could read the doubt in her eyes. Whatever brought her here, she hadn't made up her mind to it.

"I shouldn't have brought you down from your work."

He shrugged, loosening the harness. "It makes no matter. I wanted to talk to you anyway. I see William got the shed roof finished, ain't so?"

"Ja. He worked on it this morning, soon as he finished with the herd. He made a gut job of it."

She said that as if she were trying to convince herself.

"I'm sure he would." He waited, knowing that something more had set that wrinkle between her eyebrows.

"I told William what you said." Her hands gripped each other so tightly that the knuckles were white. "That you believe it was done deliberately."

He wanted to hold those straining hands in his, but he couldn't. Instead he leaned against the windmill upright, taking the pressure off his leg.

"What did he have to say about that?"

"At first he said it must be just an accident. But finally he agreed that you were right. That someone had damaged the roof on purpose."

"Anyone who saw it would say the same."

Odd, that William would even try to deny it. Wouldn't he want Rachel to know the truth?

"He struggled with admitting it so much." Her hands pulled against each other, as if she fought to say the words. "It made me think . . . made me wonder, anyway . . ." Her lips pressed together, trying to keep the words in. Then she shook her head. "Maybe William suspects Isaac of doing it."

"Isaac." He said the name slowly, turning the thought over in his mind.

"I shouldn't think that!" The words burst out of her. "It's wicked, even to think that about Ezra's brother."

"Not wicked, no." Finally Gideon couldn't resist the impulse to touch those anguished hands, stilling them as he'd gentle a frightened animal. "Of course you don't want to think that of Isaac. Or of anyone you know."

"Am I imagining things?" She threw the words at him, demanding an answer.

He had to be honest with her. But . . .

"Tell me something first. Joseph told me about the night the draft horse got out. Did you ever figure out how that happened?"

Three vertical lines formed between her brows as she considered the meaning behind the question. "No. No, I didn't see how it could happen. Any more than I can see how the shed roof got damaged with the grain barrel left open right under it. You think the same person did both things?"

"I wouldn't go that far." His native caution asserted itself. "But it's two odd things happening without any reason we can see. They didn't happen by themselves. Somebody had to do them."

She nodded slowly. "Isaac—would he do something like that to show me that I can't manage the farm on my own? I don't want to believe that of him. I don't."

"You asked what I think." He gazed down at her hands, still held loosely in his. "I'd say that Isaac always wants things to go his way. If he sets his mind on something, he figures other people will fall in line."

"Ja. That is Isaac."

"It's hard to picture him doing something like this. But if he convinced himself it was for your own gut, he might be able to justify it in his mind."

She let out a long breath. "That's what I fear, too. I don't want to, but I do."

"There's someone else you haven't considered, though." He hated to add to her worries, but it needed to be said. "What about Caleb?"

"Caleb." She repeated the name, and he could almost hear her mind working. "I can't believe Caleb would want the farm badly enough to do something like that."

He shrugged. "I'd say that about both of them. Still, neither incident was really costly or dangerous."

"Not dangerous!" Sudden fury blazed in her eyes. "If someone let the horse out, they risked Joseph's life. How can you say that's not dangerous?"

He didn't want her anger turned on him. "Maybe whoever it was didn't think about Joseph being the one to open the door."

"Maybe so, but it was. If something happened to one of the children—" Her voice choked.

His fingers tightened on hers, and the need to take care of her was so strong that it nearly overwhelmed him. "Rachel, I don't want you to have to carry this burden by yourself. I wish—"

Now he had to stop. What did he wish? Where exactly were these feelings leading him?

"I know." Her chin firmed, as if she were determined not to show weakness. "You're a gut friend, Gideon."

A gut friend. Ezra's friend. That was how she saw him. That was who he was.

"Ja. Well, if there is anything I can do—anything—you must ask me, all right?"

She nodded. Seeming to become aware that he still held her hands, she drew them free.

She would be embarrassed, would walk away from him. He cast around for anything to regain a safe footing between them. "I've been thinking about Becky. How is she doing after her mishap?"

"I wish I knew." Rachel pressed her lips together, her worry seeming to deepen. "I'm afraid—" She pleated her apron between her fingers, then smoothed it down again. "Do you think she might have done that because she was trying to be like Ezra?"

The question hit him like a blow to the stomach, taking his breath away for an instant. "I . . . I don't know. She is like him in temperament, I'd say. Did you ask her?"

"No. But I wondered—William was talking to the children one day about how daring Ezra was as a boy. He didn't mean anything by it— just remembering. He always looked up to Ezra so much, you know."

"Ja. And the children did, too. But would Becky go that far?"

Rachel chewed on her lower lip. "She won't talk about it. And she won't tell me why she came in the house almost crying after talking to you, either."

That took him by surprise. After everything else that had happened yesterday he'd almost forgotten that troubling exchange with Rachel's daughter.

"I'm sorry. I didn't realize she was that upset."

That wasn't true, and he knew it as soon as he said the words. He'd known that the child was close to tears over his words. He'd just hoped that what he'd said was sufficient to keep her from trying something so dangerous again.

Rachel was waiting, and he knew he had to tell her.

"Becky said you had told her she had to thank me for coming to her rescue. It was pretty clear that she didn't want to. She claimed she could have gotten down by herself."

Rachel made a small sound of distress.

"I couldn't let it go at that." He could only hope she'd understand. "I had to help her realize how dangerous it had been. So I asked her what her father would have thought if he'd been the one to climb up after her."

Rachel sucked in a sharp breath. "You—that was hurtful. You shouldn't have taken it upon yourself."

"Maybe not." He had to be fair. "But she came to me, Rachel. I had to answer her, and I said the one thing I thought might keep her from doing something so dangerous again."

Rachel's lips pressed firmly together, but tears sparkled on her lashes, as Becky's had. Then, like her daughter, she turned and hurried away.

Rachel strode across the lawn, not sure where she was going, only that it had to be away from Gideon, at least for a while. How could he have said that to Becky? He didn't have the right. No wonder the poor child had been on the verge of tears.

Dolly bawled plaintively at the sight of her, so she changed course and walked toward the pen, glad of the distraction. Joseph had been as nervous as a first-time expectant father as the time neared for Dolly's twins to arrive, insisting that his mother had to check on the goat often while he was at school.

Rachel knelt in the grass beside the pen, reaching through the wire to scratch Dolly's muzzle. "Was ist letz? You just want some company, don't you?"

That reminded her of Leah, who no doubt wanted some company even more than the little goat did. It seemed Rachel was failing there, too.

"I wish I knew what to do," she murmured as the goat nuzzled her hand.

She wanted to hang on to her anger against Gideon, but she couldn't, not after he'd risked his life to save Becky. And if what he'd said kept Becky off any more high beams, maybe it was worth it.

She leaned her forehead against the pen's upright. Daadi had used Becky's misdeed as an argument to again urge her to sell the farm and move home. It had been hard to maintain her position that she could handle the farm and the children by herself when Becky had just risked her life that way.

"You're lucky, Dolly." She patted the little Nubian's side, feeling the life that moved within. "Your babies will be content with milk and loving. They won't worry you and make you doubt yourself."

Dolly just gazed at her, seeming happy to hear her voice no matter what she said.

Once, her babies had been like that. No longer. Now every day they seemed to give her fresh reason to wonder if she knew what she was doing.

She stood slowly, her hand resting on the pen. She should get the clothes hung. She turned, but a sound from the barn brought her up short. A sound—like a footstep—in the barn she knew to be empty at this time of day.

She paused for a moment, staring at the barn door. She could go and call Gideon. She glanced his way. He was up on the windmill again, hard at work.

Calling him down was foolish. She was just scaring herself with this talk of someone causing accidents.

Besides, hadn't she been trying to reassure herself that she could manage things herself? Well, here was a chance to prove it.

The barn door stood slightly ajar. She went to it quickly, before she could change her mind, grasped the handle and shoved it open, letting sunlight pour inside. Not a creature moved. Dust motes swam in the shaft of light.

But she'd heard something. Or someone. She took a step forward. "Who's here?"

For a moment her voice echoed in the stillness. Then someone moved, coming from the shadows into the light. She blinked in surprise. Thomas Carver. The dairy owner. What was he doing here?

"Mr. Carver." She found her voice. "I'm surprised to see you. Were you looking for me?"

"Yes, well, not exactly." He gave an unconvincing smile. "Truth is, Mrs. Brand, I wanted to have a look around before I talked to you about my offer again. Sorry. I guess I should have asked permission before coming into your barn."

There was nothing she could say to that but yes, and he knew it, so she said nothing.

He came toward her, still smiling. "Well, anyway, I hope you've had a chance to think about my offer. Seemed to me that maybe you'd have come up with some questions about it."

If he'd come for that reason, he should have come to the house. "I really don't have any questions."

"You sure? Anything at all, I'd be happy to explain it to you. That's only fair. You can ask anyone you like to go over the paperwork for the lease."

"I'm not ready to go into it just now, Mr. Carver. I thank you for your interest, but I haven't decided yet what I'm going to do."

"You shouldn't wait too long, you know." He moved closer, almost uncomfortably so. "The offer won't stay on the table indefinitely. I'm ready to invest now, but if your place isn't available, there are some others in the valley I could make an offer on. I just thought of you first, because I knew how hard it must be for you, trying to stay on here with your husband gone and all."

She took a step back. "I will just have to risk your finding another property that suits you, I'm afraid."

"Now, you ought to think this through." Again he moved closer to her. "I know how you Amish like to deal with each other, but you won't get a better offer than mine."

He was so near that the scent of him filled her nostrils. She stepped back again, tension like ants crawling on her skin.

"Rachel?" A tall shadow bisected the shaft of sunlight. Gideon stood in the barn doorway. "Is there a problem?"

"Everything is all right." Now. She hoped her relief didn't show in her voice. "Gideon, you remember Mr. Carver."

"It is gut to see you," Gideon said politely, although he didn't sound happy.

"Zook." Mr. Carver gave a short nod. "I have some business with Mrs. Brand, so if you'll excuse us—"

"We are finished, I think." She moved quickly to the doorway, and Gideon stood aside while she passed through and out into the sunshine. "I appreciate your coming, Mr. Carver."

The man had no choice but to follow her out of the barn. He stood for a moment in the doorway, hands on his hips, and then stepped outside.

Gideon moved out behind him and stood quietly, his gaze not leaving the other man.

"I can bring those papers over sometime this week, Mrs. Brand. Just give them a look-see."

"I will let you know if I want to talk about it any further." She turned to Gideon. "Mr. Carver is interested in buying or leasing some of the land and the dairy herd."

The Englischer nodded. "Just stopped by to have a look around today. See if Mrs. Brand had any questions."

"I did not see your car, Mr. Carver."

Gideon made the observation quietly, but as he said it, Rachel real-

ized how odd it was. Carver didn't seem the type of man to go anywhere on foot.

"Yeah, well, I wanted to have a walk along some of the boundary lines.
Just checking things out. I left my car down the road." He gave Gideon a
speculative look. "I see you're here to build a windmill for Mrs. Brand."

"He is also here as a friend." Rachel said the words firmly. Perhaps it
was best that the man see that she was not without people to advise her.

"Well, you consider my offer, now. Remember, it won't stay on the
table forever. You'd better decide pretty soon if you don't want to be
left stranded."

"Thank you, Mr. Carver." She kept her tone polite. She didn't want
to encourage the man to haunt the farm pestering her for an answer, but
she didn't want to discourage him entirely, either. "I will think about
what you have said."

"Good." He nodded to her, ignoring Gideon. "I'll hope to hear
from you soon, then."

He walked off down the lane. Gideon made no effort to go back to
his work, but stood watching until Carver disappeared around the bend
in the lane. They heard the sound of an engine, and a moment later a
pickup truck pulled out onto the road and sped away.

Rachel turned to Gideon. "Why did you come to the barn? Didn't
you think I could handle Mr. Carver on my own?"

That came out more sharply than it should have. She had a feeling
she was snapping at him just because she'd been so relieved to see him
there.

Gideon leaned against the barn door, probably to ease his leg after
climbing and standing so much. Because of her. "I did not know that
Mr. Carver was here, Rachel."

"Of course not." She took a breath, consciously trying to relax her
tense shoulders, unclench her hands. "I'm sorry. That wasn't kind of me."

"No need to be sorry. I wasn't trying to pry into your business." He
gestured toward the windmill tower. "From up there, I couldn't help
but see you staring at the barn. You stiffened as if—well, as if something
wasn't right. When you went in and didn't come back out right away, I
thought I should check."

That was natural. She should be grateful, instead of feeling that Gideon, like everyone else in her life, was trying too hard to manage things for her.

"Denke. I appreciate your kindness." She frowned. "It was odd, I think. Carver not letting me know he was here."

"He's made you an offer, you said?"

She nodded. She'd avoided telling Gideon about it once before, and the same reason held now. Gideon was so intent on doing what Ezra would want. She already knew what he'd say about the possibility of her making such a drastic change.

Still, their relationship had changed since that day. Gideon was already too involved in what went on here to keep him in the dark about this.

"This offer he talked about—he wants to buy the dairy herd outright, and then rent the barn and the pastures from me. That way, I could keep the house and as much land as I need for my own use, and the rest would be bringing in money for me and the children without the worry of the animals."

"And you are thinking about doing this?"

Something about his even tone raised her hackles. "I know what you will say, Gideon. You want everything to stay just as it was when Ezra was here, but—"

"No, Rachel, that is not what I would say."

"It's not?" Her voice lifted with surprise. "But I thought—"

"Maybe once I would have said that." He seemed to be looking inward. "All I could think was that I had to make amends to Ezra. I couldn't seem to see any further than that. Now—well, now maybe I am seeing him a little more clearly."

He was quoting her own words back to her, she realized. Maybe that meant he was moving out from under the suffocating cloud of guilt that had burdened him. If so, she was glad.

"Ezra would never have imagined a situation in which you'd be going on without him." His voice was flat. "We both know that."

He was right. She did know that. "Ezra never let himself worry over what might happen. That's not a bad thing."

"I didn't mean that it was. I'm just saying that trying to think that he would want this or that is fruitless. All we can really be sure of is that he would want what is best for you and the children."

"Ja." She felt lighter, as if something had lifted from her, too. "You think that I should take Carver up on his offer?"

"I would not go that far." Gideon was cautious, as always. "Maybe just that you might consider it. If you're going to go ahead with the nursery business, you need to keep enough land for that. This might be better than taking Isaac's offer and selling out entirely."

"The People would not look on it favorably, if I did business with an Englischer instead of one of us." Carver had been right about that, if nothing else.

"Then one of our people should make you the same offer, before they judge your actions."

"Isaac would never understand. Or forgive."

The word dropped between them. *Forgive.* They both struggled with that, didn't they? Forgiving each other, forgiving themselves.

Forgiveness was never easy. Maybe that was why it was so important.

"I don't know the answer to that, Rachel. It may be that Isaac will not forgive any choice but the one he wants."

"Ja." That was certain sure, but wasn't doing what was right for her family more important?

"One thing that I think about Carver's offer—" Gideon paused, his gaze focused on the lane where the man had disappeared. "He is yet another person who might want you to decide that the farm is too much for you. And who might do something to force you to that decision."

CHAPTER THIRTEEN

*M*ary put one block too many on top of the huge tower William had been constructing with the children, and it collapsed with a satisfying clatter. Mary giggled, not a bit sorry, while William groaned nearly as loudly as Joseph did.

William grabbed Mary, tickling her. "Schnickelfritz," he exclaimed. "You did that on purpose, ain't so?"

She just giggled all the more, clutching him around the neck.

Joseph's lower lip came out. "Mammi, Mary did that on purpose. Onkel William said so."

William exchanged glances with Rachel as he set Mary back on her feet, and he seemed to sober with an effort.

"I was teasing, that's all. Komm, let's pick up the blocks."

Rachel suppressed a smile. William went from playing as if he were one of the young ones to being the serious adult, but she suspected he didn't do it easily. Playing with them was more to his taste than enforcing any rules, much as he might try.

"It is time to clear up anyway," she said. "Becky and I will finish up the supper dishes while you do that."

"Not so soon, please, Mammi," Joseph protested. "I want to play with Onkel William some more."

"Not now," William said. "Now you must do as your mamm says. And I must get home to bed myself, so I can be back here early to tend the cows."

Amazing, that William could talk to the children without stammering at all, but could barely get out a sentence among adults. When he finally fell in love, would he find that with his special girl there would be no stammering either?

Rachel paused in the doorway long enough to be sure there'd be no more grumbling from Joseph. Then she and Becky headed back to the kitchen sink.

"Onkel William likes to play games," Becky observed as she picked up the dish towel.

"I was just thinking that myself." Rachel plunged her hands into the warm, soapy water. "Ach, he is not so very older than you, ain't so?"

Becky nodded, wiping a plate with careful circles of the towel. "He is not very much like Onkel Isaac."

"No, I guess not." Was there disapproval of either of her uncles in that? Rachel hoped not. "Brothers and sisters are sometimes alike and sometimes very different from each other."

"Onkel William is more like Daadi, I think." Becky set the plate on the counter and took a cup from the rack. "Daadi liked to play with us, too."

The towel might as well be tightening around her throat. "Ja, he did."

William came in from the living room, silencing whatever else Becky might have said about her father. Would she ever know? Did she want to?

She wiped her hands on a dish towel as she turned to William. "Denke, William, for playing with the little ones. You are a gut onkel."

He colored, ducking his head. "S-s-supper was a fine meal. You were kind to invite me."

She'd probably said too often how much they owed him, so she just patted his sleeve. "We'll see you tomorrow."

"Ja." For a moment he hesitated, as if he'd say more. Then, perhaps thinking better of it, he went out, the door banging behind him.

The house was quiet when he'd gone, with only the soft voices of Joseph and Mary from the other room to make a sound. Rachel turned back to the dishes.

Or maybe it just seemed quiet because she was the only adult in the house now. Once, she'd have been looking forward to Ezra coming back in from the evening round he'd always made to check on the animals. She'd have been thinking of the things she wanted to tell him after the little ones were in bed—the small details of her life that interested no one but him.

And now interested no one at all.

She washed a plate with conscious care. The gloomy thoughts could gather too quickly in the evening if she weren't careful. She would not let them take control.

"My mamm and I used to do the dishes together always. Course, I was the only girl. Soon we'll have Mary to help, too."

Becky's nose crinkled. "She'd break things, Mammi."

"Well, and you did when you started, too. Breaking things is part of learning to do them right."

Becky made a small sound that indicated doubt. "Did you know that English people have a machine that washes and dries the dishes? That would save a lot of time."

"I guess so. But if we'd had a machine to wash the dishes, my mamm and I would have missed out on a lot of talking with each other. And I'd surely miss talking to you. So I'd rather do things our way."

Becky considered that for a moment. "I guess maybe I do, too."

"Gut," she said softly.

"I brought a new book home from school," Becky said, with the air of one veering away from an emotional moment. "Teacher Mary said that since I liked the Little House books so much, I might like this one."

"Maybe we can read together for a bit after the younger ones are in bed. Would you like that?"

Becky nodded.

It was tempting, so tempting, to be content with the fact that things seemed easy between them again. To believe that everything was all right.

But it wasn't. Becky had done a dangerous thing in climbing up in the barn, and Rachel still didn't really know why she'd done it. She'd hoped Becky would bring it up herself, given a little time, but she hadn't.

As Becky's mother, she must push it, no matter how easy it would be to let it slide. That had been Ezra's way with the children, not hers.

Her hand stilled on the casserole dish she was washing. That thought had been almost critical of him. She hadn't meant it that way, had she?

She set the casserole dish in the drainer and took Becky's hand when she would have reached for it.

"Just let that drain. I'll put it away later. Now I want to talk to you."

Becky's small face tightened. Natural enough, wasn't it? Every child knew that the talk probably wasn't going to be a happy one.

"I have to understand, Becky. Why did you climb up in the barn?"

Becky shrugged, turning her face away. "I just did."

"That's not an answer." She took Becky's chin in her hand, turning her face gently. "Tell me."

Something that might have been rebellion flared in Becky's eyes. She shook her head, pressing her lips together in denial.

Rachel would not show the pain that squeezed her heart. "Komm." She drew Becky to the rocker. Sitting down, she pulled her daughter onto her lap.

Becky came, limp as a faceless doll and betraying just about as much emotion.

Please, Father. Show me. Give me the words. There was more than a little desperation in the prayer. How had she and her daughter gotten so far apart?

She set the rocking chair moving almost automatically, closing her arms around the unresisting, unresponsive child.

"I am your mamm, and you are my dear daughter." Through a shimmer of tears, she stared at the part in Becky's hair. It was almost, but not quite, straight—a sign that she had done it herself.

Pain tightened its grip on Rachel's heart. How had they slipped away, those days when her child depended upon her for everything? Not that she wanted to keep Becky a boppli forever—no, not that. But somehow, in the past year, preoccupied with grief and the struggle just to keep going, she hadn't even noticed the steps of her daughter's growth.

She pressed a kiss to the crooked part. "It has been too long since I've rocked you like this."

"I'm too big for rocking." But she didn't pull away.

"I hope you will never be too big for Mammi to love you." She smoothed her hand down Becky's back, feeling the sharp little angles of her shoulder blades. "Or to worry about you. Did you climb up because you remember Daadi doing that?"

Becky made a convulsive movement, and Rachel hugged her close.

"Daadi was a gut climber," Rachel suggested. "Were you trying to do what he would have done?"

For a moment Becky was still in her arms. Then her small face turned into the curve between Rachel's shoulder and neck, snuggling into place, gentle as an infant at the end of a feeding.

"I don't know," she whispered. "Maybe. We were playing in the barn, and Elizabeth said how high it was, and the next thing I knew, I was saying I could climb up."

Rachel's breath seemed stuck. Whatever she said now could mean the difference between learning and rebellion.

"I expect you had a picture in your mind of Daadi climbing up in the barn." She fought to keep her voice calm. "I do, too. Daadi liked to do things that were a little daring. But—"

"He wouldn't want me to do it." Becky muttered the words against her collarbone, so that she seemed to feel them as well as hear them. "If he'd had to climb up and get me, would he have been angry with me?"

Becky was echoing the question Gideon had asked her. So he had made her think. That was more than Rachel had been able to do, it seemed.

"Not angry, no. He'd have been afraid for you, first of all. And then—well, I think he might have been a little bit disappointed that you'd do something—"

"Foolish," Becky finished for her.

"Yes." She wouldn't gloss it over by calling it anything else. "But he would hug you very tight and love you just the same. You know that, don't you?"

Becky nodded, her face rubbing against Rachel's dress. "I guess so." Her voice was very soft. "Mammi—do you ever think you're forgetting Daadi?"

The question pierced her heart. Forget? Did her children think she was forgetting him when she talked so much, thought so much, about the things she did now that she'd never done with him?

Was she? How often in the past few days had she thought about him, not wondering what he'd think of her struggles with Isaac or her worries about the children, but just thought of him, pictured his dear face, imagined the feel of his arms around her?

". . . talking to Gideon."

Preoccupied with her own self-doubt, she'd missed the beginning of what Becky said, and the words were like a blow to her heart. Was Becky thinking that her mother was turning to Gideon in the way she'd once turned to her daadi?

"He remembers when Daadi was a little boy," Becky added. "I like to hear about that."

Rachel could breathe again. Becky was talking about herself, not her mamm.

"It's nice to hear other people's stories about Daadi," Rachel said. "We can see him through their eyes then, can't we?"

Becky nodded. She leaned against Rachel's shoulder, as relaxed as the babe Rachel had imagined moments ago. She snuggled her face closer to Rachel's.

"I'm glad we talked, Mammi," she murmured.

"I'm glad, too." A barrier that had been separating her from Becky dissolved as simply as a patch of snow in the spring sunshine.

Thank You, Father.

But another worry had sprung up in its place. Would she have jumped to that conclusion about Gideon if the thought hadn't been in her mind to begin with? Was she talking to him too much? Confiding in him too much?

If she was, what did that say about her feelings for him?

"I said, are you going to hold this board straight or not?" Aaron's exasperated tone penetrated Gideon's thoughts.

"I am." He leveled the top stall board by a fraction of an inch. "It's fine. There's nothing wrong with my eye."

"Not when you're paying attention, there's not." Aaron's tone was that of every older brother who'd ever lived, Gideon suspected. And the truth was that he had been woolgathering.

"Mahlon and Esther Beiler will be back from their wedding trip tomorrow, I hear. We didn't get this work frolic scheduled any too soon."

Aaron drove a nail home with a single swift stroke. "I hear tell they were going to stay out in Illinois a bit longer, but decided to come back early. The Beilers will have been missing Mahlon, him being the youngest boy."

"Ja." Not that any son wouldn't be missed, having been away for months on an extended visit to kinfolk out in the Midwest.

But Leah's parents had lost her little sister, Anna, their youngest, to the English world a year ago. No doubt they were still grieving that. They'd be glad to have the newlywed couple to fuss over.

And the community was made stronger when they gathered for a work frolic, getting the couple's new home ready for them. Rachel was here somewhere, he had no doubt—maybe working with some of the other women in the house.

"Rachel Brand will be here today, ain't so?" Aaron's words, echoing his thoughts, made Gideon blink.

"Guess so." Gideon turned the question over in his mind. Aaron wasn't one to say something for the sake of hearing his own voice. If he asked about Rachel, there was a reason.

Aaron was frowning down at his toolbox, face turned away.

Gideon planted his hands on the stall bar, giving it a shake to be sure it was secure. "Why the interest in Rachel?"

Aaron shrugged. "No reason. I was just thinking—well, you're spending a lot of time over there. Lovina will have it that you're courting her. Are you?"

"No." He bit off the word. "I'm being a friend. If a man can't help out a neighbor without folks thinking he's courting—"

Aaron raised his hand to stop him. He clamped his mouth shut. Not because of Aaron, but because of what he might give away if he responded too strongly.

"I wouldn't think anything about it. But the thing is—well, Isaac Brand's been to see me about Rachel. And you."

Gideon wouldn't have been more surprised if Aaron had swung a two-by-four at him. "Isaac?" He forced back the angry words that sprang to his lips. "What has Isaac to say about my doings? Or Rachel's, for that matter?"

Aaron shrugged heavy shoulders. "Nothing to yours, I'd say. As for Rachel—well, as her brother-in-law, I guess he feels he has a duty to be concerned about what she's doing."

There were a lot of things Gideon would like to say to that, but only one that really made a difference. "Why did he come to you?"

"I had a little trouble figuring that out myself." His eyes crinkled. "Talked around and around about how worried he was about Rachel and those children and how he wanted what was best for everyone. But when he finally got to the point, it seemed he doesn't like our taking Rachel to market. 'Encouraging her to be willful' was what he said."

Gideon could only stare at him. "What is willful about earning money to support her children?"

The twinkle in Aaron's eyes brightened. "I expect Isaac thinks anyone's being willful who doesn't do exactly what he says."

Gideon found the twinkle reassuring. "And what did you tell him?"

"That I appreciated his concern, but that decision was up to Rachel."

Gideon blew out a breath. "That's what I'd expect from you. So why did you look so worried when you asked about me and Rachel? Just because Lovina's not happy unless she's matching folks up in pairs—"

"It's not that." Aaron leaned his elbow on the railing, turning toward him. The pose was casual, but his expression wasn't. "Rachel Brand is a fine woman, and nothing would make me happier than to see you settled with a wife and children."

Gideon started to speak, but Aaron was clearly not finished, so he held his tongue.

"We'd be happy if you and Rachel made a match of it, that's certain sure. But if you were doing it out of a debt to Ezra, that wouldn't be right for either of you."

He couldn't be angry with his brother, not when Aaron was looking at him with such caring in his eyes. But he also couldn't tell Aaron what he felt, when he didn't know himself.

"Don't worry," he said finally. "I promise you, that wouldn't be the reason if ever I did ask Rachel Brand to be my wife."

He shoved himself away from the stall and headed for the door.

"We're not finished in here. Where are you going?"

"To find Rachel. To tell her what Isaac is trying to do."

Aaron moved quickly. He put an arm the size and strength of a young tree trunk across the doorway. "Just hold on a minute. You go find Rachel looking like a thundercloud, do you think people aren't going to notice?"

"Let them notice."

"And then there will be more folks thinking the same way Lovina is." Aaron clapped him on the shoulder. "Komm, simmer down a bit first. You can talk to her more natural-like over lunch."

Gideon itched to push his way past his brother—to find Rachel and tell her exactly what Aaron had told him.

But maybe Aaron had a point. If people were already talking about them, speculating about them—well, did he really want to stoke that fire any hotter?

And then there was the fact that this would hurt Rachel. She was so sensitive to Isaac's feelings, even if he didn't seem to return the favor.

Gideon's jaw clenched. Probably the real reason that he wanted to put his fist through the board they'd just put up was that this was going to make Rachel's decisions even more difficult, and there wasn't a thing he could do about that.

It was wrong to be angry with a brother. Rachel kept reminding herself of that as she worked her way toward Isaac. It was against the teaching of the Bible, and against the beliefs of the church.

She should not tell herself that Isaac had been wrong to try to control her actions by intervening with Aaron that way. One sin did not excuse another.

She would talk to him calmly. She would make it clear to him that she had no intention of giving up the market with the Zooks. That she needed the income it provided to support her children.

Around her, the work frolic was coming to an end. Some buggies had already moved off down the lane, mostly women who were headed home to fix supper for their families. Small groups of people still clustered here and there—the women chatting as they packed up boxes of cleaning supplies or food left over from the lunch; the men catching up on the latest news now that the work was finished.

Isaac was at the center of one such group. He leaned back against the split-rail fence, elbows resting on it as he talked, looking relaxed and expansive, the center of attention.

Rachel halted a few feet from the group. What she had to say wasn't for everyone else to know. If she waited until later—

Isaac caught her gaze, just for a second. Then he turned back to his conversation.

He was keeping her waiting deliberately. A fresh spark of anger ignited and had to be extinguished. She'd been fighting that battle since Gideon spoke to her.

Gideon had been reluctant to tell her, she suspected, but he'd been right to do so. If Isaac was going to people behind her back, she needed to know that. As for what she was going to do about it—

The men's conversation ended on a rumble of laughter, and Isaac turned toward her. "Do you need something, Rachel?"

His tone seemed to imply that of course she did and that it was natural for her to come to him with her needs. Fortunately no one could see how tense her hands were under the concealment of her apron.

When she didn't speak right away, he raised heavy brows. Then his gaze shifted to someone behind her, and his features rearranged themselves into a smile.

"Isaac. Daughter." Her father came to a stop next to her, surveying Isaac with an expression she didn't understand. "You wouldn't be talking business, would you?"

Isaac straightened, as if reminding himself that his casual pose was disrespectful to the older man. "Not on my account. Rachel's the one who wants to see me."

The men's gazes swiveled toward her, pinning her to the spot. Was it going to be easier or more difficult to bring this up in front of her father? She wasn't sure. She simply knew that she couldn't keep silent. Isaac had gone too far.

"Perhaps we could talk more privately," she suggested.

Isaac stared at her for a moment, then shrugged and moved a few feet off to the side. It was hardly out of earshot of the other men, but they drifted off, leaving her alone with her father and her brother-in-law.

She took a breath, willing herself to calm. "I understand you had a conversation with Aaron Zook about me. About the fact that I've been going to market with him and Lovina."

"I might have done. Hard to remember everybody I've talked to." But his gaze slid away from hers, denying the casual tone of his words.

"According to Aaron, you want him to stop taking me to the market."

"I suppose Gideon told you that." Isaac's voice snapped the words, and she could sense her father turn to look at her.

"Does it matter how I learned of it? Aaron would have no reason to make up a story about it."

"No, he would not." The low rumble of Daad's voice startled her. "Is this true, Isaac?"

Isaac's jaw clenched until he looked as stubborn as the mules he used to pull his plow. "It seems to me that Rachel would be better off staying home with her children than leaving them to spend the day at the market, talking to outsiders, taking advice from folks who aren't even her kin."

She was ready to defend herself, but before she could speak, her father beat her to it.

"Are you saying that Rachel's children are being neglected because they spend her market days with their grossmutter and me?"

"Now, now, I didn't mean that." Isaac backpedaled away from the implication she was sure he'd intended. "But a young widow has to be careful about the appearance she creates."

Words pressed at her lips, demanding to be let out. "A young widow who is earning money to support her three young children is surely creating the right impression, don't you think?"

"You wouldn't have to earn money at all if you'd just listen to me." Goaded, Isaac's temper, always a little uncertain, slid from his control, his face flushing and his hands closing. "You're just being stubborn, clinging to the farm instead of taking my offer for it, as Ezra surely would want."

There it was again—that idea that he, and he alone, knew what Ezra would have wanted. Rachel had to clamp her lips shut to keep from flaring out at him. They were dangerously close to an open breach, and she would shrink back from that, whether Isaac did or not.

"We none of us know what Ezra would want." Her father said the words that she was thinking. "The farm belongs to Rachel and her children now, and it's for Rachel to decide about selling."

Given how her father felt about the subject, that statement astonished her. If Isaac had gone about this in a different way, he'd have probably been able to get Daad lined up firmly on his side. Maybe she was fortunate that Isaac didn't have a lot of tact.

Isaac glared. "You can't think that Rachel can make a go of the dairy farm herself. It's nonsense. And who is she going to sell to, if not to me? That Englischer who's been hanging around?"

Daad swung to stare at her, and she could feel the warmth mounting her cheeks. Isaac had done that deliberately, but how had he even known about the man?

"Rachel?" Her father was looking at her with doubt and questioning in his eyes.

"I suppose you're talking about Mr. Carver from the dairy. He has been to see me twice."

"About dairy business?" Daad looked a little reassured at that. After all, most of the Amish dairy farms in the valley did business with Carver.

"In a way." She wasn't ready to talk about this yet, but she was being pushed irrevocably toward a decision she wasn't sure she wanted to make.

Isaac snorted. "He wants to buy the farm, ain't so? Everyone knows he's trying to expand. I'd never believe that my own brother's wife would think of selling his farm to an Englischer instead of to his own family."

"It's not like that at all." She pressed her fists hard against her skirt, trying to hang on to the calm that was rapidly deserting her. "He's not trying to buy the farm."

"Then what does he want?"

Daad's question demanded an answer. She was going to have to come out with the man's offer and why it mattered to her. She'd have to find out if the dream that had been drifting through her mind more and more lately would stand the light of day.

She fixed her gaze on her father's face, praying he'd understand. "He offered to buy the dairy herd. He'd lease the barn and the pastures, paying me rent for them. That way, I could keep the farm for the children's future, and I'd still have the house and enough land for my needs."

That was hurt in his face now—hurt that she was considering this without talking to him first and embarrassment that he was hearing about it in public.

"You might as well break up the farm completely as do that." Isaac had found his voice, and it exploded with fury. "The idea that you'd deal with him—and what do you need land for, anyway?"

There was the question. She had to answer it. Ready or not, as the children called when they played at hide-and-seek in the twilight.

"I need it for the flowers and shrubs I'm growing. I'm going to start a nursery business of my own."

Silence greeted her words. She looked at her father, praying she'd see support, or at least understanding, in his face.

He stared at her. Everyone within earshot stared at her. And no one spoke.

She had never felt so alone in her life.

CHAPTER FOURTEEN

Rachel could almost tally the opinions of her community by counting up the number of people who'd come to call the next day. It was an off-Sunday, when they didn't meet for worship, so it was given over to visiting family and friends.

Her parents had been notable by their absence today. Even the children had noticed it, wondering aloud where Grossmutter and Grossdaadi were. She hadn't had an answer.

She gave the counter a last wipe, knowing she was making work simply to avoid the moment when she'd have to sit down alone in the silent living room.

Enough. She stalked through to the room, sat down in her favorite rocking chair, and picked up the basket of mending that sat near at hand on the table.

Moments later the dress of Becky's that she was shortening for Mary lay in her lap, the needle stuck through the hem, while her mind was caught in the now-familiar groove of worrying about her relationship with her parents.

Leah had sent Daniel over with the children for a short visit, a mute gesture of support. Aaron and Lovina had stopped by, Lovina's merry chatter filling up the silent corners of the old house. But Mamm and Daadi hadn't come, their absence clearly proclaiming their disapproval for all to see.

Johnny had been strong enough, or willful enough, to pursue his dream without their consent or support. She didn't think she was. How could she keep insisting that her way was right, if those who loved her best thought it wrong?

A tear dropped on the light blue cotton of the child's dress, and she blotted it away.

Lights crossed the front windows, and tires crunched on the gravel lane. She put the mending basket on the floor, her movement jerky. What if it was Carver, come to press her for a decision again?

She crossed to the window and peered out. Relief swept through her, gentling every frazzled nerve. It was Johnny.

By the time he reached the porch, she had the door open.

"I didn't expect you tonight." She hugged him, pressing her cheek against his clean-shaven one, aware as she always was of the sense of oddness about that. "How gut it is to see you."

"Good to see you, too." He gave her an extra squeeze, his gaze sweeping the room. "It's okay?"

She nodded. "No one else is here." She turned away, busying herself with taking his jacket and hanging it on the back of a chair. "It's been quiet today."

"I heard."

She swung toward him, staring into the blue eyes that were so like her own. "Heard what?"

"That you announced at the work frolic that you were starting your business. That the folks weren't exactly supportive."

"But . . ." Her mouth was probably gaping. "How did you find out about that?"

He shrugged, the movement fluid under the fine knit of the shirt he wore—blue, to match his eyes. "I have my sources."

"I don't understand what you mean." Who among the Plain People in the valley had a relationship with Johnny, other than herself? "Did Leah tell you?"

His gaze slid away from hers. "Never mind that." He set the bag he carried on the round table where the children had played a board game earlier. "I know you're disappointed about Daad, but you can't let it get you down."

"That's not so easy." Her hands gripped each other. "I'm not like you. I can't go against them."

"You won't have to." He clasped her tense hands in his, and his strong grip warmed her. "Daad will come around. You'll see. Give Mamm a chance to work on him."

"He didn't come around for you." Her fingers tightened on his. How much Mamm would give to be here right now, touching him, even just looking at him.

"Think a minute." Johnny's tone was brisk, as if he'd willed all emotion away. "The two things aren't the same at all. What you want to do isn't against the Ordnung. It isn't anything that dozens of other Amish right here in Pleasant Valley aren't doing. Starting a business, especially one that you can run right out of your home, is perfectly acceptable."

"Those other dozens aren't young widows whose family thinks she ought to do something else." But even as she said the words, she felt heartened by Johnny's support.

"Daad will come around," he repeated. "You know he wants what's best for you and the children, and once he sees this is it, he'll be there for you."

"Maybe." She wanted to believe that. "And will Isaac come around, too?"

"You worry too much about what people think." He pulled out a chair and sat down at the table, unzipping the bag he'd carried in. "Who cares what Isaac thinks? I want you to take a look at this instead." He slid a folder onto the table.

She cared, although it seemed her brother had moved so far from the Amish way of thinking that he wouldn't understand that. She cared about the opinions of every member of her church family, and especially about those of Ezra's brother.

Still, did that caring mean she should give up something she felt was right for her?

She pressed her fingers against her temple, wishing that would still the argument that raged in her mind.

Please, Father. Please guide me, because I don't know what to do. I want to follow Your will, but I must understand what it is.

"Okay, here it is." Johnny spread out a sheaf of papers. "Tell me what you think of this."

She looked. Blinked. And looked again. It seemed to be—it was—an advertisement, like one that might appear in the newspaper.

Rachel's Garden, it read. *Perennials, annuals, shrubs—40 Black Creek Road. No Sunday sales.*

She touched the page with her fingertips, marveling that seeing the simple words in black and white should make her dream seem so close to reality.

"It's beautiful." She blinked back the tears that filled her eyes. "But I can't—it's not appropriate—"

"Sure it is." Johnny flipped open another folder. "You think I didn't do my homework on this? Look, here are the ads put in by other Amish businesspeople. If they can do it, why can't you?"

She leaned over his shoulder to look. That was true enough. No one objected, so far as she knew. Even Bishop Mose's harness shop had an advertisement.

"Most people put small box ads in the local shopping paper. And in the booklets put out by the tourist association. You can put this up on the bulletin boards in stores, too." He swung around to face her, his gaze intent. "I'm not urging you to do anything that would cause problems with the church. I wouldn't do that."

The concern in his voice touched her. Johnny, who had seemed so impatient with her need to follow the rules, was now going out of his way to do so for her.

She touched his shoulder lightly. "You've done all this for me?"

Johnny put his hand over hers. "You've done more than that for me." His fingers tightened. "Just seeing me—making me a part of your life again—"

He stopped, his voice choking, and ducked his head. The light from the lantern above the table reflected from the gold of his hair, cut short over his ears.

"Johnny—" A mix of love and loss wrapped tightly around her throat. "I didn't see that it mattered so much to you. I thought you were happy in your new life."

His shoulders shrugged, the movement jerky under her hand. "Happy? I don't know if *happy* is the right word. I'm satisfied, I guess."

His fingers tightened on hers so hard she nearly gasped. "I wouldn't give it up, Rachel. Understand that. I couldn't. I'll never come back. But it still feels as if a part of me is missing. It still hurts."

She wrapped her arms around him, pressing her cheek against his hair. He was her brother, her twin, the other half of herself, she'd always thought. "I wish I could make it better."

"I know." For just a moment he leaned into her. Then he straightened. "I made my choice, and I don't regret it. But I can't forget about you, or stop trying to help you. When Gid told me about it . . ."

He stopped, his voice trailing off.

"Gideon? You were talking to Gideon Zook?"

"Yeah, well, I ran into him." He rustled the papers into order, needlessly, it seemed. "Just happened to see him, and we got to talking. Anyway, I should have heard about it from you, shouldn't I? Why didn't you let me know what was going on?"

"I . . . I wasn't sure how you'd feel about it. The last time I saw you—"

He grimaced, as if that memory was still sore. "Guess that wasn't one of the good times, was it? Well, it doesn't change anything between us. You're still my sister. I still love you."

"Ser gut." She smiled, touching his face lightly. "I love you, too."

But even as she sat down next to him and listened to his ideas for her business, she wondered if starting it was really possible.

And she wondered even more how and why her brother had been talking to Gideon Zook.

"Why did you talk to my brother about me?"

Gideon's gaze jerked to the doorway of his shop, the metal piece he'd been working on clattering to the table.

Rachel stood there, her slender shape dwarfed by the giant doors of what had been one of the earliest barns built in the valley.

"Rachel?"

He walked toward her, his mind trying to process her words. Had she found out about his arrangement with Johnny? How could she have?

"I'm sorry—I'm just surprised to see you." Playing for time, he gestured her in. "You've never been in my shop before, have you? Komm. Welcome."

She stalked into the barn with quick, determined strides, very unlike the way she usually moved. Waves of irritation, if not outright anger, swept toward him, and she shook her head, either to say that she hadn't been there before or to shake off his question.

"I need to talk to you. You didn't come today."

"I have to finish the blades for the windmill before I go any further." He motioned toward the worktable behind him. "Would you like to see?"

She gave the work area a cursory glance. "I want to know about you and Johnny."

Maybe it was a gut thing to have the reputation of taking things slow and steady. At least he didn't have to rush an answer to that. He leaned against the worktable. "What about Johnny?"

She made a short, chopping gesture with her right hand. "Johnny said that you'd told him about—about what happened at the work frolic. About Daad . . ."

Her voice faded. The annoyance in her face faded, too, as if a lamp had been extinguished. Pain took its place, so strong that it punched him in the heart.

He longed to protect her. Comfort her. He couldn't, but he also couldn't resist touching her shoulder.

"I'm sorry," he said softly.

She leaned against him. It startled him, the feel of her head against his shoulder. He held her, not letting himself think of the past or the future, just cherishing the moment.

It was over too soon. She straightened, pulling away, giving a shaky laugh.

"I'm sorry. I didn't mean to be so foolish. I just . . . I just need to know what's happening."

"I see." He did. But if he told her everything, how would she react? "I saw Johnny, ja."

She swung toward him. "But why? I mean—you know he's under the bann. Why did you talk to him—tell him?"

"Ja, I know, but it seemed to me he had a right to know." Memory painted an image in his mind, and he smiled. "I remember how you two were as children. Like two peas in a pod, you were, and just as close, ain't so?"

Her lips curved, almost reluctantly, her face softening so that for an instant she was that child he remembered. "Ja. We were that."

"Well, so, I thought you could use some family support. He's family, for all he looks and sounds like an Englischer."

"He is family." She looked stronger, just saying the words. Taking a deep breath, she seemed to shed some of the tension that had been driving her. "But your talking to him without telling me—that I didn't like."

"I'm sorry." If she didn't like his speaking to Johnny, he could just imagine how she'd feel about his plotting with Johnny behind her back.

"But I guess you did it for the best." She reached toward him in a movement that seemed impulsive. "Denke, Gideon."

He clasped her hand gently in his, nodding.

For a moment they stood there, hands clasped. And then she moved away.

Now it was his turn to take a deep breath. He needed it. But apparently the storm was over.

She was looking around the shop, seeming to see it for the first time since she'd walked in the door. "You said you had to work in the shop today?"

"Ja." Relief at the change of subject washed through him. He swung his hand toward the work table. "Once I finish the blades, I'll be back up on the tower again."

She moved between the table and the workbench, glancing around at the workbenches, the generator for his power tools, the wooden partitions against the back wall that held lumber. The corner nearest him was fitted up as his office, with his always-cluttered desk and his filing cabinets.

He perched on the corner of the desk, watching her. What did she see when she looked around? He always saw the work that had saved his life when he hadn't wanted to go on.

"It's a gut big space for your work."

"Believe me, Aaron hated to give up this old barn, even though he has a fine new one. Lovina says he'd have filled it up with more goats if she hadn't jumped in and convinced him I needed it for my shop."

"Lovina is a determined woman."

"Ja, she is." Interfering, some might say, but he appreciated her. She'd known what he needed. He patted the gray metal file cabinets. "If not for her, I'd probably keep my records in a shoe box."

Rachel stared at the cabinets for a moment, her expression unreadable. "Tell me something. If I looked at those records, would I find that you charged me the same amount for the windmill that you charged other people?"

The swing back into dangerous territory took him off guard. He cleared his throat. If he were the kind of man who could think quickly on his feet, he might come up with an answer for her. Instead he could only sit there, feeling like a dumb animal.

Rachel's eyebrows lifted in a mute repeat of the question. He couldn't evade an answer.

"No. You wouldn't."

She made a pushing away motion with her hands and started to turn. And he knew that he couldn't let her reject this.

He slid from the desk and caught her arm, turning her back to face him, trying to ignore the fact that he could feel the warmth of her skin through the fabric of her sleeve.

"Stop, Rachel. Think this through. If I had been building the windmill for Ezra, like I offered to do several times, would I have expected to charge him the same as I'd charge a stranger?"

She kept her gaze stubbornly averted from his. "We're not talking about Ezra."

He stifled the urge to give her a gentle shake. "Answer the question. Would I?"

"No." She glared at him. "But that's different."

"How is it different?" He would not repeat all the things he'd already said. If she didn't understand the reason behind his need to help her by now, she probably never would.

"It . . . it just is." For a moment confusion clouded the clear blue of her eyes. "You're trying to put me in the wrong. That I don't like. It *is* different, and you know it. Ezra was able to help you out with things, just as you helped him. I can't."

Anger flicked him. "Are you saying that my friendship with him was some kind of business arrangement? That we'd do for each other only because we'd get paid back?"

That got through to her. "No. Of course I'm not saying that. It's just that . . ." Her voice trailed off. For once, it seemed, Rachel could think of no argument to make.

"Bear one another's burdens," he quoted softly. "If Ezra had come away from the accident injured, I would have done his work gladly. Since he didn't come away at all, how much more must I want to help? Would you deprive me of that?"

"You are right. I know that." But still, her gaze was troubled. "But building the windmills is your business. You're probably losing someone else's business while you're building mine, ain't so?"

"Ach, I'm sure I'm losing a wonderful heap of business." Relief that she seemed to be accepting his words brought a smile to his face.

"Well, you might be."

"Listen to me, Rachel Brand. I would do it anyway. You know that. But it's a gut thing that I can work on your windmill at my own pace." He slapped his bad leg. "This still isn't as strong as it should be. Anyone else might expect me to be going full speed. You don't seem to mind if I take a day off now and again."

"No." She returned the smile. "No, I don't mind."

"Are we all right now about this?"

"Maybe I overreacted a little bit." She shook her head. "I don't know. I just don't like the feeling that other people are making plans for me behind my back. Talking about my business, like you and Johnny did."

"I explained about that." Would she never let it go? "I just ran into him at—"

His mind went blank. Where might Johnny have said they'd run into each other, when they'd actually met at the home of one of her brother's friends?

Suspicion tightened Rachel's lips. "Were you lying to me about meeting my brother then, Gideon Zook? Because if you were, you'd best tell me the truth of it right now."

"I . . . Maybe you should ask Johnny that." That was a feeble answer, and he knew it. How had he managed to get himself into such a pickle, anyway? Because Rachel was one stubborn woman, that was how.

"I will ask my brother." The anger that flared in her eyes didn't bode well for John. "Right now I'm asking you, and I'm expecting a truthful answer."

"All right. The truth of it is that I have seen Johnny. Several times over the past month. Sometimes at the clinic, sometimes at the home of a friend of his."

Was it only his imagination that she'd paled? He didn't think so, and he blamed himself for it.

"Why?" Her breath seemed to catch on the word. "Why, Gideon? Why have you been meeting with my brother behind my back? Why didn't you come right out and tell me, whatever it is?"

"Because you're too stubborn, that's why." It was a relief to feel a bit of anger at her. "You didn't want to let me help you, even when you needed it. You wouldn't accept help from your brother, either."

She was definitely paler. "You know the reason for that, just as well as I do. Johnny is under the bann."

"I know." His voice gentled. This wasn't easy for her, and probably Johnny, with that stubborn streak that matched hers, hadn't made it any easier. "But Johnny's not coming back, no matter what. And he had to find a way to help you. There has to be a way to help those we love."

Her lips trembled, and she pressed them together. "What did you do, the two of you?"

"Johnny wanted to help. I wanted to help. Bishop Mose wanted to help. So I was the go-between for Johnny and Bishop Mose."

She looked horrified. "You don't mean—that money that Bishop Mose insisted on lending me for the windmill—he never took it from Johnny. He wouldn't."

"No, no, he wouldn't." That had been a tricky negotiation, and he had no intention of telling her just how tricky, trying to satisfy Johnny's pride and Bishop Mose's need to stay on the right side of the Ordnung. "Bishop Mose wanted to put up all the money himself. But Johnny—"

Rachel gave the slightest nod. Well, she had to know how stubborn and prideful her twin could be.

"The end of it was that the clinic threw some extra work Bishop Mose's way." He put up a hand to block her protest. "I don't know anything about the arrangement between Johnny and the folks at the clinic, and I'm not planning to ask. If the bishop is satisfied, I am. And so should you be, if you have any sense."

She opened her mouth and then shut it again. "You've left me without anything to say."

"That's a relief." He tried a smile. "You shouldn't be angry with kindness, Rachel. Be angry with us for not telling you, if you want, but don't be angry because people love you and want to help you."

"All right." Her giving-in was hardly more than a whisper. "I won't be."

"I'm here." Rachel maneuvered the folded-up quilting frame through the back door at Leah and Daniel's farmhouse. "Leah? I've brought the quilting frame."

Leah came through from the living room, skirting carefully around the kitchen table. "I'll help you with that."

"No, you will not." She pulled the frame away from Leah's hands. "Tell me where to put this. And then tell me how you're feeling. Are there any signs that this babe plans to arrive before tomorrow's quilting?"

"I wish there were." Leah crinkled her nose, half-laughing, half-serious. "Well, not really, I suppose. Everyone is looking forward to the quilting, and I wouldn't want to disappoint them."

"We'd all understand how that feels, having been through those last weeks of being pregnant ourselves." Rachel followed her into the living room and set the frame where she indicated.

Leah grasped one side, helping her to snap the legs into place. "This is such a nice frame. I love how it folds up. If I actually did as much quilting as my mamm, I'd want one like it."

"It is nice." Rachel ran her hand along the side pole nearest her. "Ezra put it together from a kit, he did." He'd been so pleased with how it turned out that she seemed to see his smile each time she used it. "I shortened the poles to sixty inches for the crib quilt."

"Ser gut. Using two frames will be faster and easier, I think." Leah lowered herself into a rocking chair. At nine months' pregnant, she was ready to sit every chance she got.

Several feet away, another frame occupied one corner of the room. "I see you have your mamm's frame up already, ja?"

Leah nodded, rocking a little. "Daniel and Daadi set it up last night. They're willing enough to help get things ready for the quilting, but they're both planning to make themselves scarce while the work is going on."

"Gut. We don't want them listening in on our conversation. They might blush." Rachel brushed her hands together, not that there had been any dust on the quilt frame. "I'll just go and bring in the food I brought for tomorrow."

"I'll help—"

"You'll sit still." Rachel bent to press her cheek against Leah's. "You're supposed to be staying off your feet, remember?"

Leah's lips curled upward. "How can I forget, the way everyone keeps reminding me? Anyway, the midwife says it's not so crucial, now that I'm about full-term."

"Rest anyway. I'll put things in the kitchen, and then we can set up the quilts and get ready for tomorrow."

"Gut. We'll have a chance to talk while we do that."

The wistful note in Leah's voice registered, and guilt trickled through Rachel. She hadn't spent near enough time with Leah this past week. And even now, when she was here, her mind skittered off like a waterbug to all the other things she had to do.

"As much talk as you have energy for." She gave Leah a quick hug. "I'll be right back."

Two more trips to the buggy, and she'd brought in everything she'd prepared for the quilting—the pieced tops for the baby quilts, several loaves of banana nut bread, a huge tin of jumble cookies that her mamm had made, and a couple jars of strawberry preserves.

Plenty more food would arrive tomorrow. Every woman who came would bring something, so there'd be lots left for Leah's family to enjoy, for sure.

She carried the quilt tops, wrapped in clean sheets to protect them, into the living room and laid them on the table, then got out the backing pieces and her pincushion.

"You have to let me help with this, at least." Leah levered herself out of the chair with her arms, sighing a little. "I feel as if I need a crane to get me up and down these days."

"Give it a little time, and you'll be feeling as if you need one to pry your eyes open." Rachel spread the backing piece for one quilt carefully over the frame, stretching it firm, and then began to pin.

Leah took a handful of pins and started on the opposite side. "We've done a lot of things together over the years, but I never thought we'd be doing this for a babe of mine."

Heart full, Rachel touched Leah's hand. "It's wonderful gut to share the excitement of the boppli coming along."

"You never expected it to happen either." Teasing filled Leah's voice. "Admit it, now. You thought I was destined to be a maidal forever."

"That's not true." Although it had seemed, at times, as if Leah had been almost too content with her single life. "I'm the one who pushed you toward Daniel, remember?"

"You and the rest of the church." Leah ran her hand down over her belly in a caressing movement. "I don't regret it now, but there were certainly times when I wished everyone would mind their own business instead of mine."

"I know just what you mean." The words had brought Rachel's concerns about Gideon and Johnny back to the fore, not that they were ever far from her mind. "There's something—"

She hesitated. But if she couldn't talk to Leah about this or anything else, then the world had turned upside-down already.

"Something that's worrying you?" Leah caught her mood instantly. "Tell me."

"I'm maybe being foolish about it."

She unfolded the batting piece and spread it over the backing. Was she? She just couldn't decide. She'd told Gideon she wouldn't argue with him about it, but it seemed she couldn't stop arguing with herself.

"You'll feel the better for talking, then." Leah slid a pin through the batting. "Out with it."

Rachel nodded, concentrating on lining the batting edge up perfectly. "You know about Bishop Mose lending me the money to pay Gideon for the new windmill, already. Well, for one thing, I got Gideon to admit that he's not charging me full price for it."

"I wouldn't expect anything else." Leah's voice was firm. "Rachel Brand, if that's what's bothering you, you're foolish indeed. Gideon was Ezra's closest friend. Naturally he wouldn't expect the same amount from you as he would someone he doesn't even know."

"That's what he said."

"Well, he's right."

"But he told me something else—" She sent Leah a troubled look. "You must agree not to say anything of this to anyone."

The laughter faded from Leah's face. "Of course."

"Somehow Gideon got together with Johnny. I don't know how, exactly. And they hatched a . . . a plot, that's what it was. And Bishop Mose went in on it." She still found that hard to believe. "Gideon says that Johnny's clinic is throwing extra work to the harness shop. It's all a way of letting Johnny help out, even though they won't admit that."

"What did Gideon say when you told him that?"

"That he didn't know what the arrangements were, and that if Bishop Mose was satisfied, then I should be, as well."

Leah was quiet for a moment, as if absorbing it all. "Gideon gave you gut advice. I think you should take it."

"But—"

Leah shook her head, lines crinkling around her green eyes. "Rachel, no buts about it. Bishop Mose would not do anything wrong. And besides, we both know that's not what you're fussed about anyway."

"What do you mean?"

"I mean that you're annoyed at all of them for going behind your back and trying to help you. That you're so bent on providing for the children yourself that you think no one else can do anything."

"If it was you—"

"If it was me, I'd maybe make the same mistake. But I hope I could count on a gut friend who'd point it out to me."

Rachel was still for a moment, absorbing Leah's words. Was she being prideful, holding back from accepting the love and help others wanted to share?

"You should accept all the support you're offered," Leah said. "All of it."

Something—some note in Leah's familiar voice—sounded an alarm in her. She knew Leah so well. She knew when something was being left unsaid.

"What, Leah?" She reached across the frame to catch Leah's hand and hold it tightly. "You're thinking of something beyond this. I can tell."

Leah's lips pressed together tightly, as if she'd hold the words back. "I wasn't sure whether I'd tell you this or not. It's just gossip, when it comes right down to it, and maybe nothing behind it at all except someone's imagination embroidering what was said."

A cold compress seemed to press against the back of Rachel's neck, dripping its chill down her spine. "I'd still rather hear it, whatever it is."

"Daniel heard it when he went to the farrier's to have the horses reshod this morning. Some of the men were talking. You know how they linger there and gossip, even though they insist that it's only women who do that."

Rachel could picture the scene well enough, the men leaning against wagons, watching the shoeing, exchanging all the news of the day. She'd never expected that she'd be the subject of their talk.

"Just tell me, Leah."

"It maybe means nothing at all." Reluctance dragged at Leah's words. "But they were saying that Isaac is furious about the idea that you might be leasing the farm to an Englischer, instead of selling it to him for Caleb."

Rachel's tension eased. If that was all it was— "I already knew Isaac was angry about that, but I haven't made a decision yet. I'm thinking on what Mr. Carver said, that's all."

"The talk is that Isaac isn't willing to wait for your decision." Leah took a breath, seeming to push the words out. "They're saying that he's going to the bishop and the ministers with a complaint about your conduct."

CHAPTER FIFTEEN

Rachel worried at it all the way back to her parents' place to pick up Mary. Leah had continued to reassure her, repeating that it was rumor, nothing more. And even if Isaac had said that in a fit of temper, he might easily have changed his mind once he'd calmed down. And even if he did complain about her . . .

Rachel's mind refused to go there. Leah could say that she should present her own argument to the elders. That they would understand if she explained it to them.

Leah was braver than she was, for sure. Leah, with her years of teaching behind her, had a self-possession and ability to express herself that Rachel would never achieve, no matter how she tried.

If it came to an open conflict, Rachel knew perfectly well what would happen. She'd give in, restoring peace and harmony to the church.

The English world wouldn't understand that. It seemed to be built on competition, and even Johnny had been influenced by that, talking about doing better than a colleague to compete for a position.

Things were not like that among the Leit, the Amish people. Cooperation was valued, not competition. She would give up what she wanted rather than cause a rift in the family that was the church.

She turned into the lane and slowed the horse to a walk as they approached the house. Daadi was at the edge of the garden, in conversation with Jacob Esh, the son of his second cousin. Jacob, just a year out of school, was working the farm with Daad, learning as he earned a bit of money. At the moment he was plowing the garden, and he looked as if Daad was giving him a bit more advice than he thought he needed.

Fortunately for Jacob, Daadi saw her. He waved and headed across the lawn toward her.

He reached her as she mounted the porch steps.

"You're putting the garden in already, I see."

"Ja." He sent a glance toward Jacob, toiling across the length of the garden. "Jacob thought we should wait another week for the soil to dry more, but I'm ready to get peas and spinach in the ground."

"How is Jacob shaping up?" She'd be happy to keep the conversation on someone other than herself for as long as possible.

Daadi gave a snort, but his eyes held a twinkle. "Like most young folks. Thinks he knows more than his elders. He's a gut boy, though, and does what I ask, I will say that."

"He'll learn a lot from you." She studied her father's face as she spoke. She'd have said that he never seemed to age, but something— worry or tension, maybe—was exaggerating the lines around his eyes.

"Ja, well, he'll turn into a gut farmer, I have no doubt. Maybe he'll be taking this place over one day." He gazed across the field toward the orchard, shielding his eyes with his hand.

Her breath caught. That was the first time her father had spoken of the future he envisioned for the farm, now that Johnny was gone.

She didn't know what to say to that, so maybe it was best to say nothing. "I'd best get Mary ready to go home."

Before she could reach for the door, Daad stopped her with a quick gesture. "She's still napping, I think, judging by the quiet. Walk down to the pond with me, ja? Komm."

He turned, not waiting for an answer, and she fell into step with him.

He didn't speak as they walked side by side across the lawn. When she was young, she'd trailed him everywhere around the farm. Most of the time he'd been silent, but that hadn't bothered her. It had been a comfortable, accepting kind of silence, and she'd learned much even from the things he didn't say.

She waved at Jacob as they passed the garden. Both hands gripping the plow, he couldn't wave back, but he gave her a nod and a smile.

The day was warming, even though the grass dampened her shoes as they started through the grove of trees to the pond. She and Johnny had come this way together more times than she could count, on their way to catch tadpoles in the pond, most likely, or to grasp at fireflies in the dusk.

A pang of longing pierced her heart. If she had those days back again, she would cherish her moments with him, knowing that the time would come when they'd be few and far between.

Daadi stopped at the bench he'd built on the edge of the pond, so Mamm could enjoy sitting there in the evenings. He sat down, patting the space next to him.

Rachel sat, too, bracing herself. A private conversation with Daad would undoubtedly be on the subject of her stubbornness.

"Never heard the spring peepers as loud as they are this year." He leaned his elbows on his knees, gazing out over the still water of the pond. "You should bring the kinder down here in the evening sometime soon."

"I will," she said. She leaned back, staring as he did at the pond.

Maybe she was wrong. Maybe he hadn't brought her here to lecture her. The still surface of the pond reflected the drooping willow tree, already dressed in its pale green, and the puffy white clouds that drifted across the sky.

In the marshy area around the pond, the tan heads of cinnamon ferns lifted above the vibrant green of the unfurling fans of skunk cabbage. It was quiet, and peaceful, and as familiar to her as her own body.

Daadi spoke without turning to look at her. "Have you any new answer for me about moving back here with your children, Daughter?"

Well, she had known that was what was in his mind, hadn't she?

"No, Daadi." Best to come right out with it. "You know how I feel about that. I appreciate that you want us, but . . ."

"Don't say that." He turned toward her, his face tight with a tension she hadn't recognized. "Think about it, child. Don't tell me that you appreciate it. You need help, and we're your parents. You're a parent yourself, now. If one of your children needs, don't you have to go to the rescue?"

"Ja, I do." She took a breath, despairing of ever making him understand. With Daad against her plans and Isaac threatening to complain to the elders, was there any hope for her?

"Well, then," Daad said.

"Please, try to understand." She put her hand on his, willing him to listen to her. "Of course I would run to the rescue, but my children are hardly more than babes."

"The love doesn't change, no matter how old the child becomes. Your mamm and I want nothing so much as to help you raise those children. We don't want to see you wearing yourself down to nothing trying to run the farm and take care of them."

"I'm not. You know that I'm not doing any of the work with the dairy herd now."

"And what will you do if Isaac withdraws his help? He could do that, and then where would you be? I heard . . ." He let that trail off, but she knew what he'd intended to say.

"You've heard that he's talking of complaining to the elders about me." Surprising that she was able to say the words so calmly.

"Ja, I've heard that." He gave a heavy sigh. "It's a bad thing, having conflict in the family."

Anger flared up like a candle in the dark. "And isn't it a bad thing for Isaac to try to force his brother's widow to sell out to him?"

"Isaac is as headstrong as he ever was. Maybe worse, since his father died."

"Then you understand." Hope blossomed for a moment.

"I know that he's difficult to deal with." Her father shook his head. "But to think of selling to an Englischer rather than your husband's kin . . ."

"But that's the point. I wouldn't have to sell if I accepted Carver's offer." Everyone seemed to have a different version of what the man had offered. "He wants to buy the herd, yes, but he would only lease the barn and the land."

"Is it so important to you, to hold on to the farm in the hopes that the children will want to farm it? What if they don't?"

He hadn't let bitterness into his voice on the words, or sorrow, but she knew he must feel both. She never talked to him about Johnny. Maybe she should.

"Daadi, you know what I'm feeling. You've kept the farm, hoping that Johnny would come back, even though . . ." She stopped, not wanting to finish that.

"Even though you know he never will." Her father finished it for her.

"Ja," she said softly. "That is what I believe."

Daadi closed his eyes briefly, as if he could shut out the pain. "I don't want to see you work yourself to death to hold on to the farm for the children," he said again. "I believe you'd be better off to sell, to Isaac or the Englischer, I don't care which, and move back home with us."

Nothing changed. No matter how hard she tried to explain, everyone around her stayed firm in his own belief that he knew what was best for her. The weight of all that disapproval was almost too much to bear.

Her father's fingers tightened on hers. "But I have already lost one child. I will not drive another away."

It took a moment for his words to penetrate. She looked at him, her heart lifting.

"Whatever you decide, Rachel, your mamm and I will support you. If you must go before the elders, we will stand with you."

"Denke, Daadi." Her throat choked with tears.

He put his arm around her and drew her close. She buried her face in his shoulder, feeling the fabric of his shirt against her cheek, inhaling the familiar scent that had always meant safety and comfort.

Daadi might not believe in her dreams, but he would stand with her anyway. Maybe that would be enough.

Gideon tightened a last bolt and glanced at the sky. He'd stayed longer than he'd intended at Rachel's today. Before the accident, he'd have been able to finish this part of the job in a few hours. Looked as if he wasn't up to his normal speed yet.

It will come. *Please, God, let my strength return so that I can do my work.*

He started to climb down, his bad leg protesting from the effort. Halfway down, he paused to give it a rest.

Movement from the ground caught his eye. Joseph, it was, over at the goat's pen as usual. That boy was certainly devoted to his pet.

Even as Gideon thought that, Joseph took a quick step backward, away from the pen, arms pressing rigid against his sides. He whirled, racing toward the house.

"Mammi! Mammi, komm! Schnell!"

Something was wrong, or he'd not be crying for his mother that way. Gideon made quick work of the rest of the trip and unhooked the harness. By the time Rachel and Joseph had rushed to the pen, he'd reached it, too.

Joseph grabbed his hand. "Something's wrong with Dolly. Look at her."

"Let us see," Rachel said, exchanging a glance with him. She moved Joseph away from the pen door and opened it. She paused, hand on the door. "Gideon?" There was a question in her voice. "You know more about goats than either of us does."

He pried the boy's fingers from his hand and knelt beside her at the pen door. "I couldn't live on Aaron's farm without picking up a bit. Let's have a look."

The little Nubian lay on her side near the pen opening, panting. He expected her to rise when he reached for her, but she just looked at him with what almost seemed like confidence in her eyes.

"There, now." He stroked his hand down her side. "What's going on here?"

The answer came as soon as the words were out of his mouth. A shudder rippled through her under the pressure of his palm—an unmistakable contraction.

He kept his hand there until the contraction eased off. He patted the little goat. "Well, Joseph, I think Dolly is about to become a mammi. That's what you've been waiting for, isn't it?"

The boy nodded, eyes wide. "The twins are coming. Ain't so, Gideon?"

"They are for sure."

Rachel rested her hand on Joseph's shoulder. "You have the box stall all ready for her. Let's move her into the barn now."

Joseph started to reach for the goat. He stopped, seeming not to know how to move her, and gave Gideon a pleading look.

"Won't she walk if you lead her?" Rachel said, holding the pen door wide.

Joseph took hold of the thin collar the goat wore, that looked, for all the world, like a pet dog's. "Komm, Dolly. Komm."

The goat struggled, legs waving, seeming unable to get to her feet.

"Suppose I carry her," Gideon said quickly. He didn't like the look of that, but no sense in alarming the boy if it wasn't necessary.

Joseph nodded, his breath coming out in a whoosh of relief. He stepped back so that Gideon could reach into the pen.

He slid his hands under the goat, moving gently so as not to frighten her, and lifted her out. His leg grumbled a bit as he rose, cradling the goat against his body.

"Lead the way, Joseph."

The boy rushed to the barn door, knocking his straw hat off in his hurry to slide it open. He scooped up the hat and raced to open the door to one of the box stalls.

The stall had been cleaned, he'd guess, to the last inch, and a fresh bed of straw covered the wooden planks. Gideon knelt, depositing the goat on the straw that Joseph fluffed up. The boy promptly sat down next to her.

"Joseph, she can probably do this part without you. Komm. Supper is ready."

Joseph's face crumpled at his mamm's words. "I can't leave her. She needs me." He reached toward Gideon, tugging on his pant leg. "You'll stay, won't you, Gideon?"

"I'm sure Gideon has much to do—" Rachel began, but he interrupted her.

"It's fine. I'm glad to stay." He sat down on the floor next to Joseph and leaned back against the side of the stall.

Rachel's face lit with gratitude. A man would do a lot for a smile like that, not that he wouldn't have stayed anyway, since Joseph seemed to need him.

"Well, if you won't come in for supper, I'll bring something out for the two of you." Her gaze met his. "Denke, Gideon," she said.

When she'd left, the barn seemed steeped in stillness. The big draft horses, who were the only other occupants, watched them curiously for a few minutes and then turned back to their feed buckets.

Joseph stroked Dolly's head. "What do we do now, Gideon?"

"Now we wait." He settled himself as comfortably as he could. "First births can take a while, and there's nothing to do for Dolly but let nature take its course."

An hour later, he'd begun to wonder if nature was going to be enough. He lit a lantern to chase away the gathering shadows so that he could get a better look at Dolly.

The little goat seemed to be struggling, and this wasn't progressing nearly as fast as the other births he'd seen working with Aaron's herd.

Rachel came in again while he was trying to urge Dolly to her feet. She studied his face, seeming to look past the facade he kept up for the boy.

She took Joseph by the shoulders. "I want you to go into the house now."

"But Mammi, Dolly needs me." His hand lingered on the little goat's head.

She hesitated a moment, and then knelt beside him. "You may come back out again. But I want you to say good night to Mary. Then go to the shed and get some of the empty feed bags that are on the shelf. We might need them when the kids come."

Joseph's small face lit with the prospect of something helpful to do. "I'll do it, Mammi. Schnell." He scrambled to his feet and raced for the door.

Rachel swung toward him as soon as Joseph was gone. "Something is wrong."

"I'm not sure." He gave up the effort and let the little doe rest on her side again. "I thought standing might help things along, but she doesn't seem to have the strength for it."

"Is there anything we can do?"

He spread his hands, hating feeling helpless. "Once she starts pushing, we may be able to help. I've done that often enough with Aaron's herd. Until then—I don't think there's anything."

"If we were to lose her, Joseph would take it so hard." Her lips twisted, as if she fought not to cry. "I can't bear for him to lose something else he loves."

"It's not come to that." Gideon reached out his hand and she took it, fingers twining tightly. "Goats are like people, I guess. Sometimes the first babe is a long time in coming." His thoughts flickered to his wife, his babe, and he yanked them away.

"Yes, of course." She took a breath, straightening. "I shouldn't be so foolish. But—do you think I'm right in letting him stay out here?"

She'd never asked his advice on anything to do with her children before. He'd best have the right answer.

"What would he do if you sent him inside?"

"Wait. Worry. Fret." She gave a slight shrug. "You're right. That would be worse than letting him feel he's helping."

"That's how you'd feel, ain't so?"

She nodded, bending to stroke the little doe's side. "Be strong, Dolly," she murmured.

"Here I am." Joseph burst in, burdened with a flashlight and an armload of feed bags. "Did anything happen?"

"Not yet." Rachel brushed his hair from his eyes. "It'll be a little while yet. You do as Gideon says. I'll be back out after I get Mary to bed."

Joseph nodded solemnly and came to sit next to Gideon. Once Rachel had gone, the barn seemed too quiet, too lonely. Was he right in encouraging the boy to stay? Joseph had certainly seen animals give birth before. He wouldn't be frightened by what was normal.

"Gideon?" Joseph rested his head against Gideon's sleeve. "Dolly isn't going to die, is she?"

"I hope not."

"But it shouldn't take this long, should it?"

"It does seem like a long time." He wouldn't lie to the boy. "But things may start to happen very fast. Kidding goes that way sometimes."

Joseph's face moved against his sleeve. "I love her," he whispered. "I loved Daadi lots, lots more, but I love her, too. I don't want her to die like Daadi did."

"I know." Gideon put his arm around the boy. He was skinny, like Ezra had been at that age, with sharp little bones that seemed fragile under Gideon's touch. A wave of protectiveness swept through him, so strong it scared him.

What was he doing, feeling this powerful a caring for another man's son? He'd set out to help Ezra's wife and children, thinking only of the debt he owed to Ezra.

He'd never imagined they'd become so dear to him. Too dear. How would he live with himself if he failed them, too?

Rachel paused before she reached the barn on her return, lifting her face toward the sky. Pinpoints of light clustered thick as clover in the meadow. The nearly full moon seemed fat with promise. Was it true, then, the old idea that the full moon brought on birth?

Please, Father. I don't know what Your will is for this little creature, but I ask Your guidance for helping Joseph to deal with whatever happens tonight. Thank You, that You've provided Gideon to aid us.

A few more steps brought her to the door. Again she hesitated, this time caught by what she could see inside. The glow of the lantern echoed the glow of the moon, illuminating the stall. Gideon sat, his back against the rough boards, and Joseph leaned against him, his head snuggled into Gideon's broad chest. The man's arm curved protectively around his shoulders.

Her throat constricted. Gideon was doing what Ezra would have in this situation. Did he even realize how wonderful gut he was with the children?

Gideon's attention seemed to sharpen on something out of her line of vision—no doubt Dolly. He moved, Joseph moving with him. As if it had been a signal, she scurried inside.

"Was ist letz? What's the matter?"

"Time to help her push." Gideon squatted next to the goat. "Will you?"

She nodded, kneeling in the straw next to him. "Show me what to do."

"I want to do something." Joseph's voice wobbled a little. "Let me."

"You will hold her head. Your mammi will put her hands here." He took her hands in his and positioned them against the goat's warm, smooth side. "When you feel her push, only then, you press along with her. I'll try to ease the kid out."

She nodded, breathing a silent, wordless prayer.

Gideon gave Joseph an encouraging smile. "We'll do our best for her. The rest is in the Lord's hands."

Even as he spoke, the goat's muscles contracted under her hands. Rachel sucked in a breath as if she were in labor as well and began to push.

"That's it, gut. The kid is in the right position. It won't be long now." Gideon had rolled up his sleeves, and he leaned over the animal. "Talk to her, Joseph. Tell her to push."

"Push, Dolly, push." Some of the fear eased from Joseph's face as he concentrated on the goat. "You can do it. I know you can."

"Come on, Dolly. Come on." Rachel pressed with her palms, feeling the progress of the contraction. "It's working."

"Ja." Gideon's glance at Dolly held concern. "Ease off, now. Wait for the next one."

Did he fear the little goat didn't have the strength in her to finish the job?

Rachel longed to ask, but didn't want Joseph to hear the answer. Before she could think of how to phrase it, the next contraction hit, and she was too busy to say anything.

"It's coming," Gideon exclaimed, and in a moment the tiny kid, front hooves first, came sliding out onto the feed bag, squirming and messy.

"She did it." Joseph hugged Dolly's head. "You did it, Dolly."

Gideon lifted the baby away a foot or so. "Ja, but I think she has one more to push out. You come and dry this one off, Joseph, while your mammi and I help her."

The worry in his voice was plain, but fortunately Joseph was too enraptured by the brand-new kid to hear it. He dried the baby off, crooning to it.

Dolly stiffened under her hands, and in what seemed little more than a moment, the second kid arrived. The doe lay back, eyes closing, side heaving with strain.

"Do you think—" Rachel began, studying Gideon's expression.

Grasping her arm, he turned her toward Joseph and the kids. "You help him with the babies. I'll tend to Dolly."

Gideon looked so grave that she feared Joseph could hardly fail to pick up on it, but he didn't seem to. So Rachel helped him dry the kids, marveling with him at them. It wasn't hard to keep his attention fixed on the babies instead of the mother.

"We should name them." Joseph stifled a yawn. "What do you think, Mammi?"

"I think you've been up far too long. Say good night to them, now, and get into bed." She stilled his protest with a gentle touch. "They need to rest, too, and so does Dolly. Go now. I'll come and check on you when I come in."

He hugged her and sidled over to Gideon. "Denke, Gideon." He hesitated a moment, then flung his arms around Gideon's neck in a throttling hug. "Denke."

Gideon patted him. "Sleep well."

Rachel handed him a flashlight. Standing in the barn doorway, she watched the light bob across the lawn, staying there until Joseph was safely into the house. Then she turned back to Gideon.

"Is she going to make it?"

"I don't know." He moved one of the kids to Dolly's head, but she closed her eyes and ignored it. "She's letting them nurse all right, but she should be cleaning them off and taking a bit of notice of them by now."

Rachel knelt next to Dolly's head. "Poor little thing. She's exhausted. Isn't there anything we can do?"

"Just wait. Pray."

"That I've been doing already."

Gideon moved fresh straw around mother and babies. He was limping, she realized as he straightened.

"You've been here all day. You should go home and get some rest yourself already."

"I'll stay." He sat down, leaning against the wall again. "You might need me."

"You've already done so much. I don't know how to thank you."

"You don't, that's all. Joseph is a fine bu, and you should be happy with him. He did a wonderful-gut job tonight."

"As did you. You would have been a gut father."

The moment the words were out of her mouth, she remembered, and she wished them back. But it was too late. "I'm sorry. I—"

He touched her arm. "It's all right. I hope I would have."

There seemed nothing to say to that. She just hoped he could sense her sympathy.

He drew his knees up, wrapping his arms around them. "When I think about that night, it's most often the boppli that I think of. He should have had his chance at life."

Her breath seemed strangled in her throat. Ezra had said that Gideon never spoke of it, not even to him.

"He lives in Heaven," she whispered.

"Ja." He stared at the goats, quiet now, but she didn't think he was seeing them. "It was raining that night. So hard that I could barely see to keep the buggy on the road." His hands tightened to fists against his legs. "We should have stayed at home and waited for the midwife, but Naomi wouldn't hear of it. She was so sure something was wrong, so sure that I had to take her to the hospital. If I'd insisted, maybe—"

He stopped, his voice choking.

Rachel's throat was tight with unshed tears. She knew the rest of the story. The truck, speeding in the driving rain, hitting the buggy, smashing it to pieces. Naomi and the baby dead, Gideon so badly injured that most had thought he'd never recover.

She put her hand tentatively on his shoulder. "Don't, Gideon. It wasn't your fault. You only did what Naomi wanted."

He turned, grabbing her hand in a fierce grip. "I knew it was a bad idea. I should have followed my instincts."

"Anyone in that situation would have done the same."

"Would they?" His eyes were dark with pain. "I don't know that. I just know that they died, and I survived."

And then Ezra had died, and he had survived again. The pain in Gideon's soul went so deep—what could Rachel possibly say that would be a balm for that?

Straw rustled. Gideon seemed to choke back a sob as he let her go and turned to the goats. One of the babies was nuzzling at Dolly's head, pushing her muzzle with an almost angry persistence.

"Ach, let her be." She reached toward the kid, but Gideon intercepted her, grasping her hand.

"Wait."

She held her breath, watching. Waiting. The kid bumped Dolly's muzzle again. The little doe opened her eyes. Wearily, slowly, she moved her head. Looked at her baby. And began to lick him.

"They're bonding," she breathed.

"Ja." Gideon moved the other kid up close, and Dolly licked her, too, seeming to gain strength even as they watched. "I think they're going to be all right."

He looked at Rachel then, and she realized that she wasn't the only one blinking back tears. Gideon's hand clasped hers again, warm and gentle. Emotion flooded through her.

She cared for him, more than she'd dreamed possible. He meant so much to her.

But the wound he'd revealed to her tonight—perhaps that would never heal. And if it didn't, how would he ever be able to care again?

CHAPTER SIXTEEN

*Y*ou look half-asleep today," her mother scolded gently the moment she walked in Rachel's kitchen door the next day. "Were the kinder up sick last night and you all by yourself here?"

Rachel hugged her. "No, nothing like that. Joseph's goat kidded, and we feared for a time she might not make it. But it ended well, with twin kids to show for a long night."

"You never should have let Joseph know that pet of his was in danger. The poor boy must have been worried out of his mind."

Mamm hung her bonnet on the peg and set a container of what looked like whoopie pies on the table.

"I don't think he realized how bad she was," Rachel assured her.

Mamm's eyebrows lifted in a question. "You said 'we.' I thought you meant you and Joseph."

"Gideon Zook was here." She tucked her packet of pins and her grossmutter's silver thimble into her bag for the quilting. "Thank the Lord he was. He knew just what to do."

The questioning look lingered in her mother's eyes. "He's a gut man, he is."

"Ja." Rachel was afraid to say anything more, afraid of betraying feelings that she didn't want to examine too closely in herself. "It's kind of you to watch the little ones while Becky and I go to the quilting."

Her mother seemed to accept the change in subject. "Ach, you know it's a pleasure."

"You'll probably be chasing them away from the goats all day."

"Well, and I want to see these little twins, too, so that will be chust fine. Is that where they are now?"

"Joseph and Mary are. Becky is supposed to be getting ready, but it's taking her a long while." She went to the hallway and peered up the stairwell, but there was no sign of her daughter. "Becky, come along now. It's time we were leaving."

No response, but she heard a drawer close in the girls' bedroom. Exasperated, she started up the stairs. "Becky, do you hear me?"

She reached the bedroom door to find Becky sitting on the bed, one shoe in her hand, the other on the floor. She had obviously been changing, but she'd come to a standstill.

"Becky, komm. I can't be late."

Becky didn't look up. "Maybe I should stay home today. I could help Grossmammi with the little ones."

That was so out of character for Becky, who always wanted to be on the go, that Rachel could only stand and stare at her for a moment. What was going through the child's mind?

"I'm sure your grossmutter can manage without you. I thought you'd been looking forward to going. Maybe you can put some stitches in the quilt for Leah's new baby."

Becky stared down at the log cabin design that covered her bed, picking at it with her fingers. "I don't want to go, Mammi. Can't I stay home?"

"You can't—"

She caught herself, stopped, and went to sit down on the bed next to her daughter. Something was wrong, and she wouldn't find out what by giving orders. She schooled herself to patience and tried not to think about being late.

"Komm, tell me what is going on. You always like to go to Daniel and Leah's."

Becky hunched her shoulders, not looking at her. "I just don't feel like it today."

"Is it because you might be expected to sew? You don't have to, you know. I just thought you might want to."

Becky didn't respond, but her lower lip jutted out.

Rachel caught her daughter's chin and turned her face so that she could see the expression. Pouting, definitely pouting. Becky's stubborn streak was making itself known.

"Rebecca, I want an answer now."

The pout became more pronounced. "I don't want to play with Elizabeth."

Rachel blinked. "Not play with Elizabeth? Why ever not? Did the two of you have a spat?"

Becky shook her head, the mulish look intensifying.

"What then?"

For an instant Becky clung to her silence, pressing her lips together. Then she shrugged. "I don't want to be her friend. She told on me."

Rachel's mind produced nothing but a blank slate. Then she realized what the child was talking about. So much had happened since Becky's misadventure in the barn that it had slid to the back of her mind.

"Let me get this straight. You're angry with Elizabeth because she ran for help when you were stuck up in the barn."

Becky flushed, as if she knew how ferhoodled that sounded but wouldn't admit it. "Ja. She told. Friends shouldn't tell on you."

"Becky, you needed help. You couldn't get down by yourself. If Elizabeth hadn't gone for help when she did, you might have fallen."

Rachel stared at her recalcitrant child with dismay. This had been preying on Becky's mind, and she hadn't known it.

Father, I should have known. Forgive me, and please give me wisdom now. I must have answers for my children, and I can't seem to find them on my own.

She put her arm around Becky. Her daughter stiffened, not giving in to the embrace.

"Sometimes it is right to tell. Sometimes that is what a true friend does." She sucked in a breath, praying that wisdom came with it. "What if Elizabeth had done what you wanted, and you'd fallen? She would have had to live with that for the rest of her life."

Becky did react to that—a tiny, almost undetectable wince.

"You are holding on to a grudge. You are not forgiving her, even though you know in your heart that she did the right thing."

The rigid little figure shook suddenly. "I can't help it! I know I shouldn't feel this way, Mammi. I don't want to. Why do I?"

Rachel hugged her, longing to make it better even while she knew there wasn't an easy solution. Every problem with raising children seemed to come back, in the end, to the teaching of faith.

"Forgiving can be hard. Maybe the hardest thing of all. That's why it's so important, and why we have to keep learning that lesson over and over again. Jesus forgives us, and He expects us to forgive others."

"I want to." Becky turned her face against Rachel's sleeve, wetting it with her tears, her voice muffled. "How can I?"

Rachel stroked her hair, knowing that she had the answer but hating to reveal so much of her own failure. But maybe that was part of the lesson God had to teach her.

"You know, for a long time after your daadi died, I had trouble forgiving." Her throat tightened, not wanting to let the words out. But she had to speak them. "I knew it wasn't Gideon's fault that he lived when Daadi died, but I was angry, and I blamed him for it."

Becky didn't speak, but Rachel knew she was listening with all her heart.

"It was wrong, that not forgiving, and it hurt me even more than it hurt Gideon. I had to find a way to forgive and let go of the hurt."

"How, Mammi? How did you do it?" Becky tilted her face back, looking up into Rachel's eyes, her whole body seeming to yearn for an answer.

"I talked to Bishop Mose. And you know what he told me? He said that I had to act as if I'd forgiven, no matter what I was feeling. He said I should think of what I would do if I had forgiven, and do that. He said the feelings would follow. And he was right."

Becky's forehead knotted as she struggled to understand.

Rachel stroked the wrinkles gently with her finger. She had to concentrate on teaching forgiveness now, and leave the difficult lesson of when it was right to tell on a friend for another day.

"What would you do if you really had forgiven Elizabeth for telling on you?"

"I would go to the quilting and play with her." That answer was obvious.

"Then that is what you must do."

Becky hesitated for a long moment. Then she gave a nod, slid off the bed, and fished for her shoe.

Have I said the right things, Father? More important, have I shown her forgiveness by my actions?

Forgiving others wasn't easy. Gideon's painful confession, never absent from her thoughts, demanded her attention. Gideon had to master an even more difficult task. He had to learn to forgive himself.

The living room at Leah's seemed about to burst from the sheer volume of conversation as the women gathered around the quilting frames. Leah's mamm was there, of course, and one of her aunts. Two of her sisters-in-law, also—Barbara, plump and cheerful, had her six-month-old on a blanket at her feet, while Myra divided her attention between the quilting frame and the boppli who slept in a cradle near her chair.

Leah had placed herself and Rachel at the second quilting frame with her other sister-in-law, Esther, newly returned from her wedding trip, and one of their running-around friends from school, Naomi Miller.

Was Leah thinking about the person who wasn't there as she handed round spools of white thread? Rachel knew how much Leah grieved over her baby sister, Anna, lost to the English world. How happy it would make her if Anna walked in the door right now, to take her proper place around the quilting frame. But it wouldn't happen, not today.

Rachel thought of Johnny. Maybe never.

She was not nearly as accomplished a quilter as some of the others were, so maybe she'd best focus on her work.

Esther glanced toward the other frame. "They are going to have theirs done long before we do, that's sure."

"The fastest quilters are all on one quilt." Leah sent a teasing look at her mamm's frame. "Maybe we should make them send one over to us."

"Or tie one of Barbara's hands behind her back," Naomi said.

"Ach, I have one hand occupied with the boppli as it is." Barbara chuckled, her good nature unimpaired by the teasing. "Wait until you all have babes to deal with."

Since both she and Naomi had children, that comment was obviously aimed at Leah and Esther. Leah ignored it, her hand swooping smoothly over the surface of the quilt, while Esther's rosy cheeks grew even pinker. Had Esther come back from her wedding trip pregnant? If so, she didn't seem inclined to announce it with her mother-in-law sitting at the other frame.

The chatter proceeded as quickly, as the tiny, almost invisible stitches traced their pattern across the quilt. No one would admit it, but each one wanted her stitches to be as perfect as possible. Not a matter of pride, Rachel hoped. Probably the others felt, as she did, that this baby quilt was a precious gift for the child Leah had never expected to have.

Rachel caught Leah's gaze across the frame, the delicate pattern stretched between them. Leah smiled, her eyes glowing with a kind of inward light, and Rachel's heart lifted. It wouldn't be long until Leah held that babe in her arms instead of beneath her heart.

By the time Rachel rose to follow Leah into the kitchen to set out the midmorning snack, the other group, for all their talking, had predictably made more progress than they had.

"They're showing us up," she murmured to Leah as they reached the kitchen.

"Let them." Leah glanced back fondly at the women around the frame. "It will give Barbara something wonderful gut to brag about."

Anything that kept Barbara focused on her own business instead of everyone else's was just fine. They both knew that, though they'd try not to say it. Leah exhibited endless patience with her tactless sister-in-law—far more than Rachel would be able to manage, she feared.

Leah lifted the coffeepot from the stove. "I'm so glad to see Becky and Elizabeth playing happily together again."

Rachel's fingers tightened, crumbling a piece of cinnamon-walnut streusel cake. "Leah, I am so sorry. I didn't even realize that Becky was holding a foolish grudge until today. I should have known. I should have seen."

"How could you if she didn't want you to?" Leah was calmly reassuring. "Now, don't start blaming yourself for that. Think of all the things we kept from our mamms when we were their age."

"I suppose so, but still." She couldn't dismiss her sense of guilt that easily. "Sometimes I think that Ezra was much better with the children than I am. I don't remember having these kinds of problems when he was with us."

Leah set the coffeepot on a hot pad and snitched a corner of the coffee cake Rachel had broken, popping it in her mouth. "Of course not. They were smaller then, and their problems were smaller. The bigger they get, the bigger the problems. My mamm always says that, and I'm beginning to think she's right about a lot of things."

"Maybe when we're as old as our mothers, we'll be as wise."

"You're already a wise mother." Leah patted her hand. "Never think that you're not. You're just not perfect yet, is all."

"That's certain sure." Rachel smiled, feeling some of the burden slip away just from sharing it. It was always that way with her and Leah. She hoped their girls would be as fortunate in their friendship. "Will I tell the others to come in now?"

At Leah's nod, Rachel went to the doorway to announce that the food was ready. The quilters flowed into the kitchen on a current of talk and laughter.

Rachel found herself next to Naomi as she took a slice of rhubarb coffee cake.

"How are the children doing?" she asked in an undertone. Two of Naomi's three children had the Crigler-Najjar syndrome that affected too many of the Amish, and it was always possible that Naomi didn't want to talk about it today.

"Doing well, denke." Naomi's smile blossomed. "We are wonderful lucky to have the clinic where your brother works. They are saving lives, I know, and one day perhaps they will find a cure."

Rachel's heart warmed to hear Johnny spoken of so naturally. Before she could respond to Naomi, Barbara said her name.

"Rachel, I hear you and Isaac are on the outs these days." Barbara's smile was as cheerful as if she were talking about the weather. "He can be a stubborn one, can't he?"

Several women sent sidelong glances toward Barbara and then looked studiously at their plates.

Rachel shrugged, hoping Barbara would take the hint.

"Your raspberry cake is delicious, Barbara," Naomi interrupted forcefully. "You must let us have the recipe."

"Ja," Leah's mother said. "It's wonderful gut."

Barbara flushed with pleasure. "I will. But I was talking to Rachel about Isaac."

"I don't think Rachel wants to talk about that." Leah's mamm tried to rein in her daughter-in-law, and Rachel shot her a look of gratitude.

"Ach, I'm just saying what everyone is thinking," Barbara insisted. "Naturally Isaac feels he has a right to interfere as head of the family. But if Rachel were to marry again, then it would be none of his business."

She stopped, finally, smiling as if pleased that she'd come up with the solution to all of Rachel's difficulties.

Several people tried to say something, anything, to cover the moment. If she'd been dipped into a pot of boiling apple butter, Rachel couldn't have felt hotter.

The spatula Leah was holding clattered to the table, startling every-one to silence. "That's enough." Leah's voice snapped in the tone she had used in the schoolroom on the rare occasions when her students had gotten out of line. "Barbara, whether it is Isaac's business or not, it is certainly not yours!"

Silence. Stillness. No one moved, no one spoke. Impossible to tell what they were thinking. Shocked, most probably. For Leah, calm, patient Leah, to lose her temper—Rachel could not have been more surprised if the table had cracked under the weight of all those dishes.

Barbara laughed. An unconvincing sound, but at least she made the effort. "Ach, I'm sorry. I'm talking out of turn again, I guess. Levi's always telling me to think before I speak, but I can't get in the way of doing it."

"Just keep trying," Naomi said, surprising them and reducing the tension in the kitchen by a few degrees. "Maybe it'll take."

To give Barbara credit, tactless as she was, she took the rebukes gracefully. "Forgive me, Rachel." She looked as if she wanted to say more but firmly closed her mouth on the temptation.

"Of course," Rachel murmured, grateful that the others had begun chatting, maybe a little desperately, on whatever popped into their heads.

The moment was over. She could forget it, couldn't she?

Perhaps not. Because if Barbara was saying it, that meant other people were thinking it, and she couldn't doubt that the person most of
them had in mind for her future husband was Gideon. And aside from
her own confused feelings, one thing was clear. Gideon would never
risk loving again.

If he could have gotten out of it, Gideon would not be helping to set
up for a singing at the Miller barn. He'd have been taking refuge from
his scrambled thoughts by working, as hard and fast as his body would
let him.

But getting out of it wasn't an option. He'd agreed to help chaperone
the singing, and that's what he would do. Aaron had come along, osten-
sibly to help, although he was more likely to enjoy a nice long chat with
Nathan Miller instead of looking after a barn full of young people.

"Watch out." He swung his end of a plank out of the way of several
running kinder who were as excited by the singing as their older brothers and sisters were.

Aaron grunted, taking a firmer grip on the long board as he headed
for the barn. "Time those young ones were in bed."

"Too excited."

Gideon paused just inside the barn doors. The barn had been
scrubbed as clean for the singing as it would be for worship. But instead
of the backless benches they'd have for worship, Nathan and a couple
of boys were creating long tables with planks set on sawhorses in the
middle of the barn floor. More sawhorses waited along one side, where
they'd need tables for the food.

"Come on, let's get this done with," Aaron grumbled.

"Anyone would think you'd never gone to a singing. Never kept
your eyes peeled for that special girl you were hoping to see. Hoping
she was looking for you, too."

His brother grinned, hefting one end of the plank onto a sawhorse.
"You're sounding like a youngster yourself tonight. Ja, I remember my
rumspringa. But I wouldn't go back and live those days over again for

anything. Too much time spent worrying about what the girls were thinking, that's certain sure."

"You didn't have to worry. Lovina was set on you from the first grade, as I recall."

"Maybe. But she led me a merry dance along the way, I'll tell you that."

Nathan finished the table he was working on and came over to them. "Denke." He rapped the board with his knuckles. "We can use more tables, if everyone comes we're expecting."

"More planks in the wagon," Aaron said. He nudged Gideon's shoulder. "Komm, Gid. Let's get the work done."

"I'll send the boys to do that." Nathan beckoned to the teenage boys who were helping him. "Here, you two. Go and fetch the rest of the planks from Aaron's wagon. Schnell."

Jostling each other, the two of them set off at a run.

"Better for you to do the setup," Nathan said. "They're so ferhoodled over the singing that any tables they knocked together would probably collapse halfway through. Glad you came, both of you."

"Gideon's a favorite of the younger crowd when it comes to chaperones. They must figure he's more likely to let them get away with things than us old folks with families."

Aaron didn't mean anything by his careless words. Gideon knew that. Still, they stung with the reminder. He didn't think he gave any outward sign, but his brother's face changed.

"Gid, I didn't mean—"

"It's okay. Let's get on with the work."

"Right." Aaron slid a long bench into place alongside the table Nathan had completed. "So, how is young Joseph's doe? Did she kid yet?"

Gut thing he was bent over to pick up one of the hay bales that Nathan was setting around the edges of the singing area. By the time he straightened, he made sure his expression didn't give anything away.

"Ja, she came through it fine. Twins, she had."

Fortunately a wave of boys came in just then, all of them helping to carry the planks. Pressed into service by their friends, no doubt. The barn was suddenly noisy enough and busy enough that Aaron wouldn't be asking Gideon any more questions.

Not that he'd been keeping it from Aaron. The trouble was that talking about the kidding brought that night back too vividly. Made him too aware of everything he'd thought and felt and said.

He'd told Rachel things he'd never confessed to a living soul. Was it the circumstances that had loosened his tongue? Or was it Rachel herself, with her caring eyes and her stubborn chin?

It didn't matter. He tossed a bale into place with unnecessary vigor. What he felt for her didn't count next to what had happened to him. He'd twice survived when he'd gladly have died in place of others. Even if he could forgive himself, he wouldn't risk living through that again.

And yet . . .

The yearning was there, deep in his heart. He had to find some way to deal with that.

The level of noise in the barn had steadily risen. Abruptly, it lowered—not ceasing, but changing in quality. Gideon glanced toward the door. The girls were coming in. Demurely, for the most part, in pairs or in giggling groups, they filed into the barn, stealing glances at this boy or that.

For a few minutes neither boys nor girls made a move. Then they began to drift toward the tables, the girls' dresses like flowers in the lantern light. The boys moved, too, in an awkward surge, as if in silent argument over who would go first. The girls took their places along one side of the table; the boys filed in opposite them.

A moment of silence, and then the high, clear notes of a familiar hymn soared toward the rafters. The boys, a little slower, joined in, and the sound grew richer, fuller.

Gideon realized he was holding his breath, and he let it out. Foolish, he supposed, to be so touched by the moment. They would spend the next couple of hours singing, with a lot of covert flirting thrown in. Then it would be time for the food, which was already appearing on the tables against the wall—eating, talking, maybe some discreet smooching in dark corners.

Some of them, the older ones, would pair off, with the boy driving the girl home if he was lucky enough to have a courting buggy. And in the fall, it might be that marriages would be announced.

Some of these very young folks, Gideon had no doubt, were engaging in riskier rumspringa behavior. Their parents, indeed their whole community, would turn their eyes aside and pray, trusting that God would bring them back to the fold in time. And mostly, it worked.

He stretched, tired. Aaron had already disappeared. Nathan, too, most likely. Duty said he should stay, but he could at least get something to drink and pull up a hay bale, while he was at it.

Cold jugs of cider, homemade root beer, and lemonade had already been placed on the table, along with trays of cookies. The rest of the food, tons of it, would be brought out from the kitchen before too long. He poured a glass of cider, snagged a couple of snickerdoodles, and headed for the nearest hay bale.

He rounded the end of the table and nearly collided with the woman carrying a tray full of moon pies. "Rachel." He steadied her quickly, dropping the cookies as he did. "I didn't know you were coming tonight."

She looked equally surprised to see him. "Naomi talked me into it." The tray wobbled a little, and he helped her set it down. "I must be clumsy tonight. I've knocked your snickerdoodles to the floor. Let me get you more."

"Leave it. I really just wanted a drink anyway." He lifted the cup and drained it quickly, the cider tart and cold on his tongue.

"You were helping to set up, I guess."

He nodded, reminding himself that he needed to deal with these foolish fancies he had where Rachel was concerned. If he had any brains, he'd make an excuse and walk off.

But Rachel's eyes glowed in the lantern light, and her head was tilted back to look at him, as if she really was glad she'd walked into him tonight.

She nodded toward the singers. "Remember when we were the ones sitting at those tables?" Her eyes went soft with the remembering. "We'd pretend we were concentrating on the songs, when instead all we could think of was each other."

His throat tightened. He did not want to remember, but he couldn't hurt her by saying so.

"You and Ezra were paired off right from the start, I remember." He hesitated. "Does that bother you, to think of how you were then?"

She tilted her head to the side, considering. Several other women came through the door with trays, and he guided her a step or two back, where they were out of the way of traffic. Out of the light, too, it seemed, but he could still make out her features.

"A few months ago it would have," she said. "But now—well, now it seems I can think of those happy times with joy, not pain." She put one hand on his arm as if eager to make him understand. "I've made my peace with Ezra's dying, maybe. Seems as if that's opened my heart to remember and cherish."

"I'm glad." He muttered the words. Did she really feel that? Or was she trying to fool herself into thinking that was true?

"Gideon." She said his name softly, her fingers insistent on his arm, so that it seemed he could feel her touch to his very bones. "Don't you see? You can't fight the pain. You have to walk through it and reach for the other side."

She was looking up at him, her tilted face very close to his, her eyes pleading. She wanted, so much, to heal his pain. And he wanted . . .

Without letting himself think, he lowered his face to hers and claimed her lips. He felt the sudden intake of her breath, inhaled the scent of her skin. Only their lips and their hands touched, but he was on fire with longing to hold her, protect her, love her—

The word jolted him back a step. He stared at her. Then, before he could say or do anything to make it worse, he spun and walked out the open door into the dark.

CHAPTER SEVENTEEN

Worship had ended, and folks were gathering to talk over the week's events, as always. How many of them were talking about her?

Rachel shepherded the children toward the picnic tables that were set up under the trees at Aaron and Lovina's farm. Prideful, that's what it was, to imagine that she was the topic of people's conversations. They had more important things on their minds than her little problems, didn't they?

"Rachel, over here," Mamm called, and she veered thankfully in her direction.

What if the rumors were true, and Isaac had talked to Bishop Mose and the ministers about her? That didn't necessarily mean they'd agree with him. At least that was what Daad said, and the strength of his support warmed her like the sun on her back.

"Can we go and play until the meal is ready, Mammi?" Becky tugged at her apron. "I want to see Elizabeth."

"Go, then, but mind you come straight back when it's time to eat." At least Becky's relationship with Elizabeth was mended, and that was certainly something to be thankful for. "Mary and I will be with Gross-mutter."

Mary went running to her grandmother, and Rachel followed quickly.

"I'll just go and see if Lovina needs any help in the kitchen, if you don't mind watching the little ones."

"Ja, go." Mamm scooped Mary up onto her lap, tickling her. "We'll be fine, ain't so, Mary?"

Before she could let herself glance at Gideon, who stood talking with his brother, she hurried toward the kitchen. Surely she had enough things worrying her to make it easy to avoid thinking about those moments at the singing with Gideon. Not so.

The kitchen swirled with activity as women grabbed filled trays and carried them outside, and fortunately the busyness made it possible to join the parade without getting caught up in conversation with Lovina. Lovina's quick curiosity might easily lead her to detect that something was different, just through an unwary word or expression.

No one must know what had happened between her and Gideon. Rachel could only pray no one had seen. Probably the young folks had been far too wrapped up in each other to notice anything about their elders. And surely, if anyone had seen, she'd have intercepted some knowing glances by this time.

She put the tray down, narrowly avoiding a collision with two running children. When she looked up, Gideon was standing a few feet away.

Her heart thudded against her ribs. He was going to speak to her, and she'd have to reply without reliving that moment when his lips had touched hers.

He gave her a curt, unsmiling nod, and walked away, joining a group of men who seemed to be discussing Aaron's goats, to judge from their gestures.

Carefully she straightened the tray she'd set on the table, as if the success of the meal depended on its alignment. Gideon's actions had made it only too clear that he regretted that kiss, regretted it so much, in fact, that he couldn't even come and greet her properly.

While as for her—she pressed her fingers hard against the wooden tabletop. For her it had been an awakening. It had brought to life feelings she'd never thought to have again. And now what was she to do with them?

"Daughter?" Her father touched her arm, and she hadn't even seen him approaching. "Bishop Mose is coming to speak with us."

A taut cord twisted inside her. Never would she expect to dread a conversation with the man she loved so dearly. At least Daadi stood at her elbow, waiting with her.

"Amos, Rachel," he greeted them. "A fine day. Everyone is grateful once we can have our meal outside, ain't so?"

Rachel opened her lips to reply, but her father spoke first.

"It might be that you should come to the house to talk to our Rachel." He stood very stiffly, his lean face seeming drawn against the bones.

Bishop Mose, on the other hand, looked as relaxed as if there was nothing on his mind but the weather. "Come now, Amos. A call from the bishop is just what I'm trying to avoid. If Rachel and Isaac have a bit of a disagreement, seems to me it's best to settle it quietly among ourselves, rather than dealing with it in church."

To stand in front of the congregation with Isaac, to confess that she was at odds with a brother—anything was better than that.

"If Isaac Brand thinks—" Daad began, but she put her hand on his arm to quiet him.

"I agree with Bishop Mose. Much better to settle things quiet-like if we can." *If.*

"That's gut, that is." Bishop Mose chuckled a little. "No need for everyone to know what we're talking about, is there? Now, you just tell me what you have to say. Isaac seems to have a whole list of complaints, but the only one I can see that affects the brotherhood is the idea that you'd sell to an Englischer, instead of one of us."

She took a deep breath, trying to compose her mind. "I'm not wanting to sell at all. That's the thing that has Isaac upset. He feels I can't run the farm. He wants me to sell it to him for Caleb."

For an instant she thought of telling Bishop Mose about the accidents—accidents that could be aimed at convincing her she couldn't manage the farm. But that would come dangerously close to accusing a brother. She couldn't. It would be a failure of faith to do so.

A small frown puckered the bishop's white eyebrows. "Where does the Englischer come in, then?"

"Thomas Carver, the dairy owner, offered to buy the herd. He wants only to lease the barn and pastures, not buy." How many times had she explained this now? "He's pushing me for an answer."

"And do you have one for him?"

"No." She met Bishop Mose's gaze. "It's not what I want. You know that. But I have to think what will be best for the children."

Relief filled his eyes behind the wire-rimmed glasses. "Gut, gut. If you haven't committed to Mr. Carver, let me see what I can do. I'll talk to Isaac, try to get him to think, see if there's not some other solution. See that it's a bad thing, straining the bonds of family over a farm. All right?"

"Ja." Her lips trembled, and she pressed them together.

He patted her hand. "Don't worry so much. As for your nursery business—well, seems like I've invested in that already, ain't so?" His eyes twinkled. "No one can object when your family is supporting you." He glanced toward her father.

For an instant Daad didn't say anything. Then he took a step closer to Rachel. "Ja. We do."

"Well, then." Bishop Mose studied her face, his callused hand resting on hers. "See if you can make peace with Isaac, child. It's not gut for brothers and sisters to disagree."

"I'll try." She would, because she agreed with everything the bishop had said.

But knowing Isaac, she feared there might be no compromise he'd be willing to consider. Then what? Did she give up her dream to keep the peace?

Gideon came back to work on the windmill the next day as calmly as if nothing at all had happened between them. Rachel was hanging laundry on the line when his buggy pulled in. He slid down, and if he hesitated when he saw that she was outside, he didn't let it show.

He started toward her, and Joseph came running from the barn, throwing himself against Gideon's legs. He used to do that with Ezra, and the memory squeezed her heart.

"And what are you doing home from school today? Did Teacher Mary kick you out for misbehaving?" Gideon took off Joseph's hat, ruffled his hair, and clapped the hat back on his head again.

Joseph giggled. "Teacher Mary wouldn't do that. She had a meeting today with teachers from all the other schools in the district, so we're staying home to help Mammi."

"Most of the helping so far has involved those goats." At least the goats made for a safe topic of conversation, and they were eased past the difficult spot.

"The kids are growing like weeds. They want to eat all the time." Joseph babbled on about the goats, giving her a moment to catch her breath.

It didn't seem to do her much good. She was still staring at Gideon, loving the way he gave Joseph all his attention, and then handing out equal shares to Becky and little Mary, when they came running over.

Gideon's quiet stability had always been a counterpoint to Ezra's livelier nature. Maybe he'd been a bit eclipsed by him. Now she seemed to notice his gentle strength more every day.

Not that it mattered. Gideon had made it clear that he regretted kissing her. He'd pulled away, and he'd clearly never talk about it.

Unless she did. The very thought embarrassed her. If she couldn't think about it without feeling her cheeks grow hot, she'd certainly never do it.

"Go on now." She made shooing motions at her children. "Gideon has work to do, and so do you."

"You'll visit Dolly and the kids before you go home, won't you?" Joseph had to get in one last question.

"They're beautiful," Becky added.

"Ja, I will." Gideon slung his tool belt around his waist and fastened it. "Before I go."

They ran off, satisfied. Rachel turned back to her sheets, picking one up by the corners and shaking it before starting to peg it to the line. Gideon headed for the windmill, his shoulders maybe a little stiffer than normal.

The sheet seemed to be wrinkling in her hands, and she shook it out again. She couldn't. Her cheeks burned again. But she was going to.

Quickly, before she could change her mind, she dropped the sheet back into the basket and strode across the grass to the base of the windmill.

Gideon snapped the harness into place before he looked at her. "Is there something wrong, Rachel?"

"No. Ja." She stopped, took a breath, tried again. "We should talk about what happened between us at the singing."

His fingers gripped the harness for an instant, and then he went on with his preparation to go up the windmill tower, avoiding her eyes. "Best to forget it."

"I don't want to forget it." A sharp little edge of anger caught at her.

"It shouldn't have happened." His tone roughened. "That's all."

"No, that's not all."

He didn't respond, just went on preparing to climb the tower. No doubt thinking that he'd be safe from her harping if he did that.

"Gideon, listen to me." Her fingers tingled with the desire to grab his arm and shake him. "It's one thing if you regret—" She had to stop, swallow. "—if you regret kissing me because you don't care about me."

He jerked as if he'd been hit, and somehow that gave her courage. If what she said could have an effect on him, it was worth saying.

"But it's another thing if it's because of Ezra. We're both free, and—"

He swung to face her, and the bleakness in his eyes stole her breath. "I'm not free, Rachel. I'm not."

He turned away just as quickly, scaling the windmill tower as if a pack of wolves snarled at his heels.

She watched him, her nails biting into her hands. He was not free. He was right about that.

Gideon was imprisoned by his grief and guilt as surely as those early martyrs had been imprisoned by godless governments. It hurt her heart, as much for him as for herself. Unless God worked a miracle in Gideon's soul, he would never be free.

Walk away. Get back to work. Don't let anyone see you watching him with tears in your eyes.

But even when she'd returned to her wet clothes, she couldn't keep her rebellious gaze from going back to him.

He'd reached the platform at the top of the windmill now. He stood there as easily as if he stood on the ground, silhouetted against the sky.

A violent crack sounded. Almost faster than she could comprehend, the platform crumbled beneath his feet, his body plummeting toward the ground.

She was frozen, caught as if ice encased her feet, unable to help, to cry out . . .

The harness caught him, stopping the mad plunge, slamming his body against the windmill frame. He dangled there, limp and very still.

Had she screamed? Her throat hurt as if she had, and she was running across the damp grass, heart pounding so loud in her ears that she couldn't hear, couldn't think . . .

She reached the windmill tower and clung to it, looking up, shielding her eyes to try to see him against the sun. He wasn't moving. She couldn't see his face.

"Gideon! Are you hurt? Can you hear me?"

Nothing. She grabbed the first crossbar. Gideon climbed up so easily, it seemed, but could she do it?

Becky barreled into her, her breath catching on sobs. Joseph came behind her, tears streaming down his face, and then Mary, not understanding what was happening but crying anyway.

Rachel's fists clenched. She had to get control of herself, for Gideon's sake, for the children's, too. This was not the time to fall apart.

"Stop the crying, now." Her voice was so sharp that the children were startled into silence.

"We must work together now to help Gideon." Calmly, calmly, don't frighten them any more. "Becky, you're the fastest. Run to Onkel Isaac's and get help. Schnell!"

Becky nodded and took off across the lawn, her feet flying.

"What must I do to help Gideon, Mammi?" Joseph stood tall, awaiting her orders.

"You will help me put the ladder up." Pray God they were strong enough to raise it. "Mary, you must go back five steps and sit on the ground."

Mary sniffled a little, but she did as she was told. Joseph rushed to help her with the ladder. Fortunately the men had left it lying on the ground next to the windmill tower.

Together they grabbed it. Heavy, it was so heavy. How would they ever get it up?

Please, God, please, God, give us Your strength.

Joseph strained, his small face pale. Rachel's arms screamed with pain as she struggled to raise the ladder. They forced it against the first crossbar.

"Stop a second. Rest." She tilted her head back. Was it her imagination, or had Gideon moved? "We're coming, Gideon. Hang on!"

"I'm ready, Mammi." Joseph took his position, hands braced against the side of the ladder. "We'll get it this time."

Please, God.

She grabbed, pulled, muscles crying. The ladder lifted, swung, and slammed into place against the tower.

"Gut." She shook it, making sure it was stable, and started up.

"Let me come, Mammi," Joseph cried.

"Stay where you are. You must be ready, in case I need you to run for anything."

Knowing he would obey, she climbed, pressing down the queasiness that cramped her stomach. Gideon needed her.

A few more rungs brought her within arm's reach of him. "Gideon." She reached out, grabbed his arm, and was relieved to feel it warm against her hand. "Answer me."

Slowly, very slowly, he turned his head. "What . . ."

"Hush, now. You're going to be all right. Just stay still."

He blinked, shaking his head and wincing with pain. A huge lump rose on his forehead, and he moved his hand, as if to touch it. His whole body swung at the movement, and awareness and alarm dawned in his eyes.

"Easy." How long could the harness hold his weight? *Please, please, don't let it give way.* "The platform broke, but the harness is holding you."

He moved, as if to assess the situation, and something above them creaked ominously. She didn't dare take her eyes off him long enough to see what it was.

"Can you grab hold of the frame with your right hand?"

He tried to move it and a spasm of pain went through him. "Don't think so."

"It's all right."

She drew him a little closer, so that his left hand could touch the ladder. He fumbled for a moment and then gripped it. She could reach him better now, and she anchored her arm around his waist.

He tried to pull free. "Don't want to take you with me."

If he fell, he meant. But he wouldn't. He wouldn't.

"Be still." She spoke as if he were one of the children. "Just be still. Everything will be all right."

Let my words be true, Father. Protect us.

And even as she prayed, she recognized the truth. She didn't just care about Gideon. She loved him with all her heart.

"Mammi, they're coming!" Joseph's shout was triumphant. "They're almost here!"

If everyone would stop poking and prodding him, he'd feel a lot better. Gideon tried to evade the light that the paramedic kept shining in his eyes, but the man held his face as if he were a child.

"I am fine." His voice sounded husky and uncertain, even to himself. "Just bumps and bruises is all," he added, putting more force to the words.

"Let the man examine you."

Rachel stood next to the porch steps where he sat. A stranger might think her perfectly possessed, but her eyes bore lines of strain around them, and her hands were knotted under the protective cover of her apron.

"Ja, that's right." Isaac, who'd come racing across the fields, his wagon hastily loaded with a ladder and extra timbers, planted his hand against the porch railing. "You didn't look but half-alive when we got you down."

Fortunately the paramedic didn't understand Pennsylvania Dutch, so he didn't know Isaac's opinion of his condition.

"Did you lose consciousness at all?" The man tucked the penlight into the pocket of his jacket.

"I don't think—" he began.

"He was out for several minutes." Rachel cut him off. "As long as it took Joseph and me to get the ladder up. He was starting to come round when I reached him."

"How you and the boy managed to put that heavy ladder up, I'll never understand."

Isaac actually sounded admiring. Apparently he'd forgotten his quarrel with Rachel in the excitement. Too bad he wouldn't stay that way—it would save Rachel some heartache.

"God gave us strength," she murmured softly.

By the time the paramedic was finished, a sizable crowd had gathered around—Isaac, William, and Isaac's two oldest boys had been the first to rush to help, of course. Someone must have sent for Aaron, because he was even now checking out the wreckage of the platform. Lovina had come with him, and she'd gathered up the children and swept them into the house for cookies and milk.

Every other minute, it seemed someone else turned up, demonstrating the amazing power of the Amish grapevine. Much as Gideon appreciated the love they showed, he'd just as soon be left alone. But he didn't figure that would happen anytime soon.

"Bruises, you're going to have plenty of those." The paramedic finished writing something on a clipboard. "Suppose you let us take you in to the hospital to have that head looked at. Just in case it's a concussion."

He shook his head and instantly regretted it. "No need. I'm fine. Nothing is broken." He flexed his right hand, wrapped in an elastic bandage. It was swollen already, and he wouldn't be doing any carpentry work for a while. "I'd rather go home."

"If they think you should go . . ." Rachel's voice died away. She'd be thinking that she didn't have the right to insist.

"We'll keep a gut watch on him tonight." Aaron joined the group. "If anything seems not right, we'll get someone to drive us in to the hospital."

The man nodded and thrust the clipboard at him. "Sign here."

Gideon scribbled his name, barely listening to the rest of the instructions. Instead he watched his brother's face, but Aaron wasn't giving anything away.

When the paramedics began gathering up their equipment, folks moved back to give them room. Aaron leaned in next to him.

"You know that platform . . ."

"I know." He kept his voice low. "Knew the instant I put my weight on it, but don't say anything."

"Don't say anything about what?" Rachel demanded.

"Ach, it's nothing." Aaron tried to turn her concern away.

"It's the platform, isn't it?" she demanded, her voice ringing out above the sound of the departing van. "That's why you were up there looking at it for so long. Someone did this."

Isaac put his hand on her arm. "Rachel, you're imagining things. No one would do a thing like that."

She shook the hand away. "Wouldn't they? And I suppose no one would let the draft horse out at night, or damage the roof of the grain shed. No one would do any of those things."

"Rachel, don't—" Gideon saw where she was headed and tried to stop her.

"Except someone who wanted to convince me to sell the farm."

Isaac's mouth sagged. He took a step away from her. "You . . . think about what you're saying. I couldn't—"

"He didn't!" The voice was so shrill that for a moment he didn't recognize it. Then William pushed his way to the front of the group, his face white, his eyes tormented. "It was my f-f-fault. I did it, n-n-no one else."

"William—" Rachel whirled toward the boy. "No! What are you saying?"

"I'm s-s-sorry, I'm so sorry." Tears welled over in his eyes, so that he looked more Joseph's age than nearly a man grown.

Isaac caught him by the shoulder. "You don't know what you're saying. You couldn't do such a thing."

"I did." He scrubbed his face with his knuckles, as if trying to force back the tears.

"Why, William?" Rachel's lips trembled. "Why would you hurt me that way?"

"N-n-not—" He stopped, shook his head in frustration. "Not hurt you." He seemed to force the words out. "I w-wanted you to n-n-need me. Depend on m-m-me. Not Gid."

Shocked, grieved faces looked from William to Gideon. When one hurt, they all hurt.

"I d-d-didn't mean you to get hurt so bad. I'm s-s-sorry. I'll do anything t-to make amends."

Gideon couldn't seem to speak. Rachel was the one who needed help and comforting right now. She was stiff, rigid, looking as if she'd shatter to pieces if anyone touched her.

Isaac reached toward her, but then drew his hand back. Maybe he saw in her what Gideon did. "I'm sorry, Rachel. I don't know what to say. I hope you and Gideon can forgive this."

Bishop Mose cleared his throat. "This will have to go before the church, William. You understand that, don't you?"

William bobbed his head. He would kneel before the church, confess his fault, and bear the punishment they agreed upon. Then it would be over.

But not for Rachel. Gideon needed to do something—something that would help to heal this breach, something that would take away the pain Rachel felt at this betrayal by the boy she loved.

"William." The boy swung toward him at the sound of his voice, but he kept his gaze on the ground. "You say you want to make amends, ain't so?"

He nodded, managing to lift his gaze to Gideon's feet, it seemed.

"Ser gut." He gestured with his bandaged hand. "I'm going to need a right hand if Rachel's windmill is to be finished. What do you say?"

Now the boy looked at him, hope dawning in his face. "Y-y-you'll let me help?"

"Ja." He deliberately stared at Isaac. Seemed as if Isaac, in his stubborn determination to get his own way, had contributed to all this mess. "If Isaac agrees."

"I agree," Isaac said. "That is only what's right."

Murmurs of agreement came from the others. The frozen chill began to leave Rachel's face.

"Ser gut," she murmured.

CHAPTER EIGHTEEN

Rachel patted Brownie as she slipped the harness into place on the mare. Brownie, with the ease of long practice, stepped back between the buggy shafts and waited patiently. If the mare had hands instead of hooves, she'd do it all herself, no doubt.

Rachel let her gaze slide cautiously to the windmill tower. In the days since Gideon's accident, she had struggled to accept the truth, and in some ways, it still felt impossible.

How could William, the little brother Ezra had loved and nurtured, the boy she'd treated as her brother, too, have done such a thing? Try as she might, she couldn't even picture him doing something to hurt her or the children.

I wanted you to need me, he'd cried. Her cheeks burned at the implication. That foolish proposal, which she turned away so lightly—he'd actually meant it. The poor boy thought himself in love with her.

She hadn't seen him or spoken to him since then. But today he was working on the windmill, attempting to be Gideon's right hand. It would be easy, so easy, to climb into the buggy and drive off to Leah's with no more than a wave. Easy, but not right. She should speak to him. Somehow, she had to find a way to deal with him.

And with Gideon. Could she talk to him without letting the love she felt show in her face? Or did he already guess?

She patted Brownie again. Then she turned and walked toward the tower.

Both men stood at the base. Gideon seemed to be demonstrating something to William. She'd face both of them at once.

But as she approached, William turned and hurried off toward the barn, ducking his head. Obviously she wasn't the only one dreading this meeting.

"I hoped to get things back to . . ." She let that die out. Gideon must know as well as she did that her relationship with William would change. "I wanted to express my forgiveness."

"You'll have to give him time. He's too embarrassed to talk to you right now, I'd say." Gideon put down the bolt and screw he was holding in his left hand. His right still wore the elastic bandage.

"Your hand—how is it?" She fought to keep too much emotion from coloring the words, but she couldn't look at him without seeing him dangling from the tower, dark and motionless against the sky.

"Better. I maybe could do this myself in another day, but it will do the boy gut to make amends."

He was the kind of man who would think that, even of someone who'd done him harm. How had it taken her so long to see what a gut man Gideon was?

"Ja, I think it will." Her voice had gone husky in spite of herself. "He seems able to face you, and it was you he harmed the most, not me."

"William doesn't love me," he said.

The words, gently spoken as they were, stabbed her to the heart.

"William has been hurting all this time. I talked to him every day, and yet I didn't understand that. How could I have been so blind? I should have seen, should have talked to him about it."

"I doubt you could talk him out of loving you, Rachel." Gideon paused, seeming to weigh something in his mind. "You should know something that William confessed to me." He stared down at his bandaged hand. "William saw us, the night of the singing. He saw us kiss. That's why he damaged the windmill platform."

She couldn't speak, but she could feel the tide of embarrassment sweep through her.

Maybe misinterpreting her silence, Gideon hurried into speech again. "Understand, Rachel, he's miserable about it. Seeing me get hurt was enough to bring him to his senses."

She cleared her throat. "Gut." It was all she could manage.

"It will be better once he confesses at the next worship. Better for him, better for all of us."

The act of public confession was difficult, doubly so for William, with his stammer, to have to kneel and confess his fault before the church. If Bishop Mose thought the bann was justified for a time, all who were present would have to agree.

Ich bin einig, I am agreed, each one would say, with varying degrees of pain and sympathy.

And then, when it was over, William's sin would be as if it had never been.

"I should confess, too." The words burst out on a wave of pain. "I didn't see."

"That is foolish, Rachel. Yours is not the sin. You couldn't have known."

But she still felt it.

Gideon cleared his throat, maybe feeling that they'd waded into water that was too deep. "Are you better now? No one has seen you for the past few days, I hear."

"Ja." She forced a smile. "I must be all right. The advertisements are already in the paper about the nursery opening on Saturday, and there is much to do."

He nodded toward the buggy. "You're going to pick something up for the opening, then?"

"Not now. I'm on my way to Leah's. The family is going to a farm sale over near Fostertown, and I told Daniel I'd stay with her. And I must be off, or she'll be wondering where I am."

She turned away, but he stopped her with a hand on her arm. His touch seemed to heat her skin right through the fabric of her sleeve. He snatched his hand away. Did he feel it, too?

"One thing—I'll be finished up here in another day's work, probably, depending on the weather." He shot a glance at the clouds that were massing along the western horizon. "I start a new job next week, putting in windmills for Elias Bender."

She turned her face away on the words, hoping he couldn't see her expression. Well, what had she expected? He would finish the job for her and move on.

Her smile seemed to stretch her face. "We will not see so much of you then."

"No."

And that was it. They would be friends, and she must be content with that. Gideon didn't want anything more.

"*Are* you sure another batch of pretzels is really necessary?" Rachel paused before adding the butter to the pan of scalded milk. "Haven't we already made enough?"

They had been baking all afternoon, it seemed, and still Leah wasn't satisfied.

"We may as well do another while we're making them." Leah sprinkled coarse salt over a tray of pretzels and slid it into the oven, glancing at the clock to note the time. "I want to have a nice treat for Daniel and the children when they get home. And you must take some for your family, too."

"We'll have enough for most of Pleasant Valley, it seems to me." Rachel set the pan aside to cool a bit before adding the yeast. "Not that I don't enjoy making pretzels with you, but I think you're overdoing it already."

Leah touched the batch of pretzels that was cooling on a rack. "I have to be doing something. I've been cooped up too long. Every time I move, someone tells me to rest. The children are as bad as Daniel is."

"They love you," Rachel reminded her. "That's not a bad thing, having people who want to take care of you."

"I know." Leah's mouth curved in the smile that Rachel had come to think of as her "mother" look. "I just feel so restless today." She grabbed a cloth and began to wipe the table with quick, hard strokes.

"You know what I think, Leah Glick? I think this baby is going to arrive soon. I remember the day before Mary was born. Ezra found me in the cellar, rearranging all the canned food alphabetically."

That brought on the laughter she'd hoped for. Leah sank into a kitchen chair, chuckling. "Ach, I can just see you doing it. Well, if it is a sign, I'm glad of it. I'm ready to meet him or her." She patted her belly.

"At the risk of getting hit with a pretzel, I'm going to suggest you sit awhile. Have something to drink. Eat a pretzel."

"I am thirsty."

"I'll get it—" she began, but Leah had already gotten up again.

She poured a glass of tea from the pitcher on the counter and added a sprig of mint from the bowl on the windowsill. Rachel watched her, torn between amusement and frustration.

"Now will you sit down?"

"I will." Leah made her way back to the chair and took a sip. "I think we've talked about everything imaginable this afternoon except about the situation with William. Would you rather not?"

"It's all right." Rachel dried her hands slowly, staring out the window absently. The rain that had begun shortly after she arrived continued without pause. Her plants could use it. "It's just all so sad. Poor William. I should have seen he was getting too attached to me."

"I wondered how long it would take for you to start feeling that it was your fault," Leah said. "You are not responsible for William's emotional needs."

"I suppose not, but I wish I could help him. He's too embarrassed even to talk with me about it now."

"Isaac is embarrassed, too, according to what Daniel has heard. Has he come to talk with you?"

"No. I wouldn't expect him to."

"Maybe not." Leah considered that, frowning a little. "Still, I hear he's dropped his complaint to the bishop."

"He has? Are you sure? No one has said anything to me."

"Maybe no one wanted to bring it up, but I'm sure as can be. Daniel heard it direct from Bishop Mose."

"Well, that is a relief." Rachel sank down in the chair opposite Leah. "I haven't slept easy since I heard about it."

Leah patted her hand. "Now you can. Unless you've found something else to worry about."

"William, of course." She sighed. "I wish I could help him find a girl to love, but he wouldn't welcome my help."

"Much as we all like to matchmake, some things are better left to the Lord. William is still smarting from his jealousy of Gideon."

"Gideon is being so kind to him. I just wish he could be as forgiving to himself as he is to other people."

She bit her lip. She shouldn't have said that. It was Gideon's private business.

"You love him, don't you?" Leah's voice was gentle, filled with the love she shared so freely.

There was no use trying to pretend. Leah knew her too well.

"Ja, I do. But it's no use."

"Don't say that." Leah gripped her fingers. "You don't know that. Maybe Gideon thinks it's too soon after Ezra to say anything to you."

Rachel shook her head, her eyes filling with the tears she was determined not to shed. "It's not that. It's something deeper in himself that keeps him from loving again. All he wants from me is friendship. That's all he'll let himself want."

"Rachel—"

"No, don't." She managed a watery smile. "I know you want to encourage me, but this time it's no use. I know that now, and the best thing I can do is get over these feelings. So you see I really do know how William feels."

"I'm sorry." Only two words, but they bore a world of caring and sympathy.

"It will be all right." She glanced at the clock. "I'd best check on those pretzels."

"I'll do it," Leah said, predictably.

"Sit. I have it." Rachel pulled the tray out with a hot pad, glad of something to do that would change the subject. She set the tray on the waiting rack. "They're just perfect."

"Gut." Leah started to get up, one hand on the back of her chair. "I think—"

The chair rocked. Heartbeat rushing, Rachel reached toward her friend, but she was too late. Her hand grasped empty air, and Leah fell heavily to the floor.

"Leah!" Rachel rushed to kneel beside her. "Are you all right? Does it hurt anywhere?"

Leah shook her head, grimacing a little. "Only my pride is hurt, that's all. You'd think I could at least get up from a chair. I told you I was going to need a crane pretty soon."

"Take it easy." Rachel got one arm around her. "Slowly. Don't rush. I'll help you."

"I'm all—" Leah bit off the words with a gasp. She clutched her belly, eyes wide and frightened as she looked at Rachel. "The pain—Rachel—"

"It's going to be fine." She could only hope her words sounded more confident than she felt. "Is it a labor pain?"

Instead of answering, Leah grabbed Rachel's hand and put it on her belly. She felt the contraction, hard against her palm.

She forced a smile. "I guess so. I told you this baby would be coming soon."

"But—it shouldn't start this hard, should it?"

The contraction eased, and Rachel glanced automatically at the clock. Keep her calm, that's what she had to do. Time the pains, and hope that nothing bad had happened when she fell. And pray that Daniel would come home soon.

"Everyone's different." She hoped she sounded reassuring. "Haven't you had any contractions at all today?"

"No."

"Now, stop thinking about all those descriptions in your books of how childbirth is supposed to happen. Remember, the baby didn't read any of them."

That brought a smile to Leah's face. "I guess not. Maybe I should try to get up, and we can start timing the contractions."

"I already have." Rachel slid her arm around Leah again. Hopefully she had enough time to get Leah comfortably situated before another contraction came. "Let's get you up and—"

She felt the contraction almost as soon as Leah did. Leah's face contorted as she struggled to remember her breathing exercises. "It's too fast," she gasped. "Rachel, why is it so fast?"

"You'll be fine," she soothed, stroking Leah's cheek. "You'll be fine, don't worry."

All very well to say don't worry, when her heart twisted with anxiety. Why was it this fast? In all the tales women told about their babies' births, she'd never heard of someone starting in labor with contractions so hard and so close together.

The contraction eased at last. Leah lay back, panting.

"Do you want to try to make it to a chair or the bed?"

Leah shook her head. "I'm afraid. Something is wrong."

"We don't know that." Rachel scrambled to her feet and grabbed a cushion from the rocker, returning to ease it under Leah's head. "But we need to tell someone what's happening. I'll help you through the next one, and then I'll run across the field to your parents' house . . ."

Leah was shaking her head. "No one's there. They all went to the sale, too." She grabbed Rachel's hand in an anguished grip. "What are we going to do?"

"We're going to be calm." Although she felt anything but calm inside. "Where is the nearest phone shanty? I'll have to go and call for help."

"My midwife's number is on the counter."

"Ja, I'll take it, but I think this babe is coming so fast that we can't wait for a midwife. Paramedics can get here quicker."

"I don't—" Another contraction cut off whatever Leah was going to say, and she clung to Rachel and breathed.

Murmuring nonsense, anything soothing that came into her mind, Rachel held her, stroking her while she watched the clock.

Leah lay back again, white and exhausted, and shook her head. "The phone is clear at the far side of my father's back pasture. It will take too long—Rachel, don't leave me. What if the baby came while you were gone?"

"I know, I know. But we need help—"

"Daniel will come soon. I know he will. The rain probably slowed him down. He'll go for help."

"Yes, yes." Anything to calm the panic in Leah's face.

Father, guide me, please, guide me. If I make the wrong decision, I could put Leah and the baby in danger. Hold them in Your hands, Father. Keep them safe.

"Pray for my baby," Leah whispered.

"I am."

"Out loud, so I can hear."

Rachel nodded. She stroked Leah's belly gently. "Our Father, we come to You now. We reach out for Your hand. We're afraid, and we need to feel Your presence. Be with us now, and protect Leah and her baby. Keep them safe and well."

And show me what to do, she added silently. *Please, Father, show me what to do.*

"You're going to be fine—" she began, and then stopped.

"A buggy!" Leah started up and then sank back. "Daniel—run and tell him."

Rachel scrambled to her feet and raced for the door. She plunged outside, to be hit by a shower of water as the wind blew the rain toward the porch.

"Rachel!" A man slid down from the buggy. But it wasn't Daniel. It was Gideon.

"*Your* mamm was worried. Asked me to check—" He stopped, registering the expression on Rachel's face. "What is it?"

Rachel grabbed his arm and tugged him to the door. "Leah's in labor."

He drew back instinctively. But that was foolish. He had to do what he could. "I'll go for help."

"Ja, you must. Her folks aren't home, so best to go to the nearest phone and call the paramedics." Still she pulled him into the kitchen. "First help me with Leah."

"Better I should go—"

Leah lay on the floor of the kitchen, her face contorting with pain. But he didn't see her—he saw Naomi, lying in the road . . .

Rachel rushed to Leah, grasping her hand. In another moment Leah sank back on a pillow, her face easing.

"Gideon is here. He'll call 911, but first he can help me get you onto the bed, so you'll be more comfortable." She glanced back at him, looking surprised, maybe at the fact that he'd backed himself flat against the door. "Komm."

That was a command, not a request. Forcing himself to focus, he strode to them and squatted down. "Show me what to do."

"We'll wait until after the next contraction. Then just slide your arms under her and lift her." She jerked a nod toward what he thought was a storage room next to the kitchen. "That's all ready for the delivery and the first day or two, so Leah won't have to go up the stairs."

Leah inhaled, eyes widening, and all Rachel's attention went back to her. "Here it comes."

He would have retreated, but Leah had grabbed his hand, squeezing it, and all he could do was hold on and send up wordless, incoherent prayers.

When the contraction finally eased, he felt as if he'd been put through a wringer.

"Now," Rachel said.

He slid his arms around Leah, half-afraid to touch her, and cradled her against him as he rose.

"In here." Rachel pushed the door open, moving swiftly to turn down the covers on the single bed that took up much of the small room. "This will be much better. You'll see."

She continued to talk, soothing Leah, he supposed, until she was settled on the bed. Leah sank back against the piled pillows, sighing.

"That's better."

"Ja." Rachel stroked her forehead. "You rest while I get a lamp. We'll need more light, since your boppli decided to come on such a gray day."

She caught Gideon's elbow and guided him back into the kitchen. He had the sense that she barely knew it was him. Anybody would do in this situation.

"I'll go right away."

She didn't let go of him. "Be sure they understand that it's an emergency." She'd lowered her voice with an anxious glance at the door.

"She fell, and the labor came on sudden and hard. Pains are only two minutes apart already. They must come at once."

Something's wrong, Gideon. Naomi's panicked voice sounded in his head. *Something's wrong. I'm going to lose the baby—I just know it. You have to get me to the hospital.*

"I'll make sure they understand." He clasped her hand in a quick, firm grip, but he couldn't find the right words. "Da Herr sei mit du," he murmured, and headed for the door. *The Lord be with you.*

He hit the steps at a run, crossed the yard, and threw himself into the buggy. Joss seemed to recognize the urgency, starting off instantly at a quick pace.

Concentrate. Think about what you must do, not about the past. Never about the past.

They reached the road and turned left, into the driving rain. Thank the gut Lord there weren't cars on the road, though if there had been, he might have flagged someone down, asked to use a cell phone.

Too much time explaining, probably. Get to the phone shanty, make the call. He knew just where it was, at the far end of Leah's parents' pasture, accessible by another narrow lane. After this, Daniel Glick would probably be putting one in considerably closer.

Unless he was mourning—

No. Don't think that, not now. Leah would be all right, her baby, too.

Rachel had been frightened. No one else would guess that, masked as it was behind the brisk command she'd taken of the situation. But he had known—had felt it in the grip of her hand, as if they were connected at a place deeper than words.

The rain drove in his face, stinging like ice. Joss plunged sturdily on.

Gideon narrowed his eyes. They'd passed the lane that led to the Beiler farmhouse. The one to the phone shanty would be coming up pretty quick.

With a blare of a horn, a car swept past him, sending up a sheet of water that nearly blinded him. He clenched his jaw to keep from saying something he shouldn't.

It had been raining that night, too. The road had been a black ribbon against the blacker fields, almost invisible in the downpour. Naomi had huddled, crying, on the seat, ducked down under the blanket. She wouldn't have seen the car coming at them, known it was going to hit them, known they were going to die—

His hands tightened on the lines, and Joss slowed. There was the lane. Do what he had to do. Forget the time when he'd done nothing but live.

The buggy jolted along the narrow lane, hardly more than a track in the field. Joss halted automatically at the shed, and Gideon jumped down and raced for it. Grabbed the phone, punched in 911. The operator answered immediately.

He stammered out the words, remembering what Rachel had said.

"We're sending a unit at once. If you stay on the line until they arrive—"

"I can't. I'm at a phone down the road. I must get back to them."

The words surprised him as he heard them come out of his mouth. He didn't want to go back.

But he would. Of course he would. Rachel and Leah and her baby needed him.

Once Gideon had gone, Rachel felt more alone than she ever had, even in the dark days after Ezra's death. Alone—with Leah and her unborn child depending on her.

She took a deep breath, giving herself a shake. Foolish, so foolish she was being. They weren't alone. God was with them. Leah and the baby were in His hands, not just hers.

"Now, then." She bent over Leah, trying to sound calm. "This baby is going to be fine, and you, too."

Leah's head moved restlessly on the pillow. "Are you sure? What if . . ."

She couldn't let Leah's mind travel down the path of all the things that could go wrong. "Trust, Leah. Just trust."

"I do, but—" Leah shook her head, managing a slight smile. "You're sure you know what to do?"

"Well, I did have three babies." She stroked her friend's belly. "That was a bit different from delivering someone else's, for sure, but at least I know what to expect."

Again she felt the contraction almost as soon as Leah did. Again they rode it out together.

When the contraction receded, Leah sank back against the pillow, face white.

"Rest now, just rest while I get things ready."

Thank the gut Lord Leah had planned on a home birth. Everything the midwife might need was ready at hand. Rachel moved quickly between the bed and the chest, busying her hands while trying to calm her mind. She'd told Leah she knew what to expect, but she didn't.

She stood still for a moment, a folded sheet in her hands, picturing herself at this point when Mary was born. Of course she'd had the midwife there and her own mother, too.

Gideon would bring help. She focused on that. He would.

And if the boppli arrived before the help did? *The Lord is my strength and stay.* Her heart spoke the words, and it seemed to fill with peace. *A very present help in time of trouble.*

Leah gasped, and Rachel hurried to help her through the contraction. Somehow, the peace didn't leave. She could feel it steadying her hands, calming her voice. God's peace flowed through her on a tide of love to Leah and the boppli, and she knew God would give her whatever strength she needed.

CHAPTER NINETEEN

It seemed an eternity until Rachel heard the thud of boots on the back porch and knew that Gideon was back. The back door swung open.

"Rachel?" He called her name, his voice strained. "The paramedics are on their way."

"Gut." She smiled down at Leah, cradling her babe in her arms, and went to the door so she could see his face when she said the news. "They will be just in time to check out Leah's baby girl."

"The babe . . . it's here already?"

"A beautiful little girl." Joy filled her heart, bubbling through her until she wanted to laugh with the sheer happiness of it. "She and Leah are both fine, thank the gut Lord. Do you want to see them?"

"I'd best go down to the end of the lane. Tell the emergency crew where to turn in." He swung around and bolted back out the door.

Was he uncomfortable about being with a woman who'd just given birth? Was this too vivid a reminder of the way his wife had died?

Rachel hadn't even thought of that when she'd pressed him into service. She'd needed someone, and he was there. Even if she had remembered, there would have been no other solution.

"Rachel? Is there any sign of Daniel yet?"

Leah's voice sounded stronger by the minute. She was eager to show off her daughter, obviously.

As for Rachel—well, she'd rather see the paramedics at this point. She thought the birth had gone well, and everything seemed as it should be, but she wasn't a midwife. Having three babies of her own didn't make her an expert on all the things that could go wrong.

She went to peer through the kitchen window at the lane, but saw no one except Gideon. She hurried back to Leah, carrying the towels she'd had warming next to the stove.

"Not yet, but I'm sure he'll be along soon. Let's wrap this around your little girl to be sure she's snug enough." She tucked the soft, warm towel around the tiny bundle in Leah's arms.

"She's so perfect," Leah crooned, touching one small pink hand. "I can't take my eyes off her."

"I know." She remembered those first moments of bonding—that sense of absolute wonderment that so perfect a creature could have come from her.

Leah's mouth crumpled suddenly.

"What is it? Are you in pain?" If something went wrong . . .

"No." Leah wiped tears away with the back of her hand, laughing shakily. "I'm being silly. Just—I'm so glad you were here today. If you hadn't been—"

"But I was, so don't think that. And I'm glad, too."

She wrapped her arms around Leah in a loving hug. They had gone through so much together, she and Leah. And now she'd been here to experience the wondrous gift of helping Leah give birth to her first child. As terrifying as it had been at times, she would never forget this as long as she lived.

"Did Gideon leave?" Leah brushed a strand of hair off her face.

Rachel smoothed the hair back and secured it with a hairpin. "He's watching for the paramedics." Even as she said the words, she heard the sound of tires on the gravel. "Here they are. I'll go and let them in."

In minutes the house seemed overly full of the emergency workers— three of them, but one a woman, to Leah's obvious relief. She checked out Leah while another looked over the baby and the third filled in forms.

Pushed out of the room where she'd been indispensable, Rachel had busied herself with making coffee. She could use a cup herself, and she didn't doubt that someone else would. She glanced up to see Gideon lingering on the threshold.

"Is everything all right? Leah and the baby?"

"They seem to be fine, as far as I can tell. The emergency workers are with them now. They'll know better. I—"

Without warning, her knees seemed to buckle. She sat down abruptly in the nearest chair.

Gideon was with her in two quick strides. "Was ist letz?" He knelt next to her.

"Nothing. I mean, I'm all right." She pressed her hand against her cheek and blinked to keep the tears away. "I'm being silly, that's what. Anyone would think I had that baby."

He reached toward her and then seemed to change his mind. Instead he filled a mug with coffee, added sugar, and brought it to her.

"Drink this." He wrapped her hands around the warm mug. "You delivered the boppli. Seems to me you have a right to be a little shaky after that."

"Ja. Shaky is right." She sipped cautiously at the scalding brew, feeling its heat all the way to her stomach. "I was too busy to think about what could go wrong. Now that it's over—"

"Now that it's over, it would be ferhoodled to fret about things that didn't happen."

"Or things that happened in the past?"

She studied his face, so dear to her now. It was a dangerous question, but somehow the events of the last hour had pushed her beyond her usual caution. Gideon could be angry with her if he wanted, but this once she would try to probe past the guilt he kept like armor around him.

He took a step back, his face tightening. "Some things you can't help but remember."

"Remember, ja. But you didn't let the memories keep you from doing what had to be done." That was important. She sensed it but didn't have the words to explain why.

He grasped the back of a chair, his big hands dwarfing the slat. "Leave it, Rachel."

"I can't." Her throat was tight, but she forced herself to go on. "I can't let you hide yourself away behind guilt that wasn't yours to begin with. You didn't choose to have an accident."

"No." His face twisted. "But that doesn't matter. At least today Leah and her baby lived. I'm glad of that, but if you imagine it evens things up, you're wrong."

"Of course I don't think that." She'd get up, but she didn't trust her legs to hold her. "There's nothing to even up, nothing to repay, don't you see that?"

He didn't. That was written in the tense lines of his face. And before she could find any other words, footsteps thudded on the back porch and Daniel burst into the room, his eyes wide with fear.

"Leah . . ."

"Leah is fine." Strength surged through Rachel, and she went to him, clasping his hands in hers. "You have a beautiful daughter."

The fear dissolved into incredible joy. "A little girl? You're sure they're all right?"

"Go and see for yourself." She pushed him toward the door. "They're waiting for you."

He paused for an instant on the threshold, and she doubted that he even saw the three Englischers in the room. Then he ran toward his wife and baby.

She was crying again. She mopped at her face with her hands. This was a day for tears as well as joy, it seemed.

She turned to say something of the kind to Gideon, but it was too late. He was gone.

Much as she might want to, Rachel had no time to think about Gideon. Drawn by the emergency vehicle, Leah's parents hurried in with the children, who'd apparently gone home from the sale with them.

"Leah? The baby?" Mattie Beiler clutched Elizabeth's shoulders, keeping her from rushing into the room.

"All well." Rachel's eyes filled again at the words. "The paramedics are still in there. Maybe best if only Leah's mamm goes in at the moment."

"Ja, that's right." Elias, Leah's father, caught young Jonah and put his hand on Matthew's shoulder. "We will wait a moment."

Elizabeth came to Rachel as soon as her grossmutter disappeared, seeming to need the security of another woman. "The boppli is all right? You're sure?"

"I'm sure." Rachel hugged her. "A little sister for you."

"A girl?" Elizabeth's face lit, the anxiety vanishing from her eyes. "I'm glad. I mean, a boy would have been nice, too," she added, always eager to do and say the right thing. "But I already have a little brother."

"Becky is going to be jealous of you, I'm afraid. She would love to have another baby around to help with and to hold."

Rachel's heart seemed to wince as she said the words. She would love that, too, but it was unlikely ever to happen now.

The paramedics came out, ready to leave after failing to convince Leah to go to the hospital. She would stay at home, she insisted, just as they had planned.

People started arriving, worried and eager to help. Some were satisfied with a brief explanation and headed off home to prepare food to bring. Others started for the barn to take over Daniel's chores, needing no explanation of what had to be done. One of Leah's brothers went to contact the midwife. It was her community at its best, but Rachel could have done with a little more quiet.

Probably Leah, in the room adjoining the kitchen, felt the same. When she'd planned to stay downstairs for a few days with the new boppli, maybe she hadn't anticipated the noise problem.

When the rush finally died down, Rachel tiptoed to the doorway to take a peek inside. Leah slept, the babe dozing in her arms. Daniel sat on the edge of the bed, one hand over hers, the other touching his new child.

Blinking back tears, Rachel beckoned to the children. They slipped out quietly. "We should let your mamm sleep now, ain't so?"

They nodded, maybe a little reluctant. Then Matthew clapped Jonah on the shoulder. "We'll go do our chores. No sense letting other folks do what we should do."

The boys went out, and Elizabeth tugged at Rachel's sleeve. "About what you said before—about Becky, I mean." Her small face was very serious. "Tell her that she can love my new baby sister, too. All right?"

"Ja. Ser gut." Rachel hugged the child, touched by her thoughtfulness. "I think your grossmutter went upstairs to get some blankets and diapers for the boppli. Maybe you can help her."

Elizabeth nodded and scurried off toward the steps, skipping a little in her happiness.

Everyone was happy, it seemed. Everyone but Gideon.

Rachel's heart ached so much that she put her hand on her chest. Gideon was a prisoner of his own guilt, and he wasn't the only person who hurt as a result.

She loved him. The feeling had crept up so gradually that she hadn't even noticed it until it was too late to stop it. Not like she'd loved Ezra—not more or less. Just different. This love wasn't the same, but it still could be full and complete. They could have been happy together.

Gideon had helped her in so many ways, even with things they hadn't spoken of. He'd helped her heal from her grief. He'd helped her gain the confidence that she could manage on her own. And now, with God's help, she'd do exactly that.

But they could have been happy.

Daniel came into the kitchen, a contented smile still lurking in his eyes. "I know you must be getting back to your own family, but Leah is awake and wants to see you before you go."

"Gut. Then I can see that sweet babe again."

She started into the room, and as she passed him, he touched her arm lightly.

"Denke, Rachel," he whispered. "Denke."

She nodded, heart full, and went to Leah.

Leah leaned back on pillows propped against the headboard, still cradling her sleeping daughter in her arms. Rachel sat down gingerly on the bed, careful not to jostle them.

"You know, you really can put her down in her bassinet."

Leah's lips curved. "No, I can't. Not yet." She traced her finger along the baby's soft cheek. "I'm too busy marveling at her."

"I know." Rachel said the words softly, content just to watch Leah with her babe.

Their friendship had lasted for her entire life, but it wasn't the same as it had been. That was gut. With each new challenge met, with each grief they endured, they grew, and so did their bond.

She didn't have to say that to Leah. Some things went too deep for words.

"Daniel and I have been talking for months about the name for the boppli. Funny, but we could never decide on a girl's name." Leah dropped a feather-light kiss on the baby's head. "Now that we have seen her, we know exactly what it should be."

"And what is it?" A family name, most likely.

Leah smiled, but it was tinged with just a little sorrow. "I want you to meet Rachel Anna Glick. Named for the sister I lost, and for the friend who is closer than a sister."

Tears filled Rachel's eyes again. For a moment she couldn't speak. Then she managed a whisper.

"Denke, Leah." She touched her friend's hand. "Perhaps one day Anna will return."

"I never stop praying for that. I never will."

"I, too," she whispered, her heart full.

Gideon tightened the screw and stood back to study his handiwork. It was odd. This idea had been in his mind for a long time. Today, he felt driven to turn it into reality.

The model windmill was an exact copy of the real thing, but it stood only five feet high. Just the right size, he'd think, to go into someone's garden.

He picked up the next crosspiece. Maybe he'd been figuring that working on something new would keep his mind off Rachel. If so, he'd been wrong. She drifted through his thoughts, distracting him, making him feel things he'd put away long ago.

"What do you have there, Gideon? Something new to sell?"

The voice startled him. He turned to see Bishop Mose pausing in the doorway as if waiting for an invitation to enter.

"Komm in." He put down his tools. "What brings you out our way today?"

"Ach, if I'd use my head, I wouldn't have to put so many miles on my buggy." The bishop rounded the worktable and stood surveying the miniature windmill. "I had to speak to Aaron about trading his date for the worship schedule. So I thought I'd step out here to see what you are working on."

"Something new. You're right about that." An object that was just "for pretty" as the people said. Would the bishop question that? "As for selling—well, I haven't got that far yet."

Mose walked all around the windmill. "Just like a real one, ain't so?"

Gideon nodded, waiting.

Mose stroked his beard, seeming to consider. "A gut idea, I'd say. Englischers will want one of those to put in their gardens. Some of our own people, too, I don't doubt. You should put one on display."

"Maybe."

He'd said once, half-joking, that he'd make them for Rachel to sell alongside her plants. But going into partnership with Rachel suddenly seemed a dangerous business—dangerous to both his heart and his peace of mind.

Mose didn't prompt him for more of an answer. That wasn't his way. He just looked at him for a long moment, wise eyes seeming to see further into a person's heart than was comfortable.

"I stopped by the Glick farm on my way here. Baby and Mammi are both doing fine. Thanks to you."

Gideon picked up the crosspiece and began fitting it into place. "Not me. I did nothing but make a phone call. Rachel is the one who did the hard part."

"Ja. Leah and Daniel are mighty thankful that she was there. But you arrived at just the right time, I hear. The gut Lord's doing, no doubt. Rachel and Leah both would have been frightened if they hadn't known they could count on you to get help."

"It was only what anyone would do." He tapped the screw to start it and began to screw it in. "I'm thankful Leah and the boppli are both doing well."

And he'd be even more thankful if he could stop talking about it. Thinking about it. Remembering Rachel's courage and her confidence in him.

Bishop Mose showed no inclination to leave. He propped himself against the workbench as if he had all day to talk. "Did you hear what they named the boppli?"

"No."

"Rachel Anna."

Gideon had to swallow the lump in his throat. "That's fitting, isn't it? Since Rachel brought her into this world."

"Ja. She's a fine woman, Rachel is."

"Nobody knows that better than I do." Where was this going?

"I guess that's true enough. You've spent plenty of time over at Rachel's place this spring. I don't know how she'd have gotten along without you."

Bishop Mose was clearly hinting, and maybe he'd best deflect him from his matchmaking.

"Just doing the work I promised is all. Guess I won't be seeing as much of her and the kinder now that it's done. I'll be starting on a new job next week."

"I see." Bishop Mose blew out a long breath. "So you made gut on your promise to Ezra and that's an end of it, is it?"

Gideon focused on the work so he didn't have to look at the bishop's face. "I'll still help as they need me. I'm not going to leave Ezra's family on their own."

Mose took a step forward, so that he stood next to Gideon. He touched the blade of the model. "I'll be honest with you. I had hoped for more than friendship for you and Rachel."

Gideon's fingers tightened on the crosspiece. If he gripped it any harder, he'd probably break it right off.

"I know what you're saying, but I'm not the man for her. She deserves more than I can give."

"Ach, that's nonsense, that is. You'd be a fine husband to her, and a fine father to those children. Why does everyone see it but you?"

He swung to face the bishop, feeling the dark emotions roil like thunderclouds. "You're wrong. They're wrong. I can't."

"Gideon, Gideon." Mose's voice was gently chiding. "What happened to Naomi and the babe was tragic, but it was a long time ago. You can't mourn forever."

"I can feel guilty forever." His voice cracked. "I can't forgive myself."

"That is wrong, Gideon, and I speak as your bishop as well as your friend." The old man's eyes turned to steel, and the steel filled his voice, too. "Failing to forgive yourself is failing to accept God's forgiveness. You're saying you know more than your Creator. You're wrong, and it's time you faced the truth. You are turning away from God's plan for your life, and that's the most tragic thing anyone can do."

He turned and walked out of the workshop, leaving Gideon stunned and speechless.

CHAPTER TWENTY

*S*he was always up early, even on Saturday, but Rachel didn't remember a time when she'd felt so nervous about what the day would bring. The eastern sky had begun to brighten when she heard the *clop-clop* of horse's hooves in the lane. She peeked out the kitchen window to see Daad helping Mamm down from the buggy seat. Her mother started toward the house, while he drove the buggy on toward the barn.

She hurried to open the door. Her mother's hug dispelled some of the jitters.

"I'm happy to see you. I didn't expect you to be here this early."

Mamm set a pan of still-warm sticky buns on the counter next to the coffeepot and hung up her bonnet. "Ach, you know how your daadi is. He's not happy unless he gets places before everyone else."

"That's if anyone else comes." Rachel poured a mug of coffee for her mother.

"Of course folks will come. Your ad looked real nice in the paper. Georgia Randall from down the road brought it to us. She'll be coming by, I know. Said she wanted to get some snapdragons in. I told her you'd put some back for her."

"I'll be glad to." Rachel didn't expect that much of a rush on any of her flowers, but Mamm would worry she'd run out before her English neighbor arrived. "I'll be glad to sell even a few things today. Hopefully then folks will tell others, and I'll get some steady business from it."

Her father appeared at the door just then, stomping his feet on the mat.

"Ready for some coffee, Daad?"

"Ready for you to tell me what needs doing," he answered. "Got to be set for business when the customers get here."

She couldn't help it—her eyes filled with tears. "Denke. It means so much that you came."

Her father brushed that away with a sweep of his hand. The thunder of children's feet on the stairs said that the young ones had heard their grandparents' voices, and Rachel banished the emotional response. This was her day to behave like a businesswoman, and that didn't include any crying.

"I'll see to the children's breakfast," Mamm said. "You go on out with your daad and get organized."

"Ja, I will." She gave the children a smile. "You be wonderful gut for your grossmutter, now. It will be a busy day."

She hoped.

"What first?" Daad said the moment they were outside. "You're wanting to put some tables up so you can have plants outside the greenhouse, aren't you?"

"Ja." But she didn't want her father to be doing any heavy lifting. "Let's check on the number of seedlings I have potted, first. See if you think it's enough to start with." She headed for the greenhouse. "Komm."

If she waited until the children came out, she could enlist them to help carry the planks for the tables. Daad would insist he could do it, as he always did. He hated admitting that the doctor had cautioned him to slow down.

By the time they emerged from the greenhouse, the sun had struggled above the trees, and a wagon came lumbering down the lane. Rachel stared, holding her breath. It wasn't—ja, it was. Isaac and William sat side by side on the wagon seat.

Isaac drew to a stop near her, inclining his head to her and to her father. Daad nodded in return, not speaking. Was he holding on to a grudge against Isaac? She prayed not. It would be far better to let go. Whether or not Isaac had done wrong in going to the elders about her was of less importance than restoring family relationships.

"We brought some sawhorses and planks to set up tables for your plants. Just tell us where you want them."

"That's wonderful gut of you both." She smiled at William, but he was carefully avoiding her gaze. "Right here near the drive will be perfect. Denke."

"About the farm—" Isaac looked as if he were shoving the words out. "We'll keep going the way we have been. No need to make any changes that I can see, ain't so?"

It was as close to an apology as Isaac was ever likely to come. She nodded, thankful. "Ser gut."

Isaac slid down, and in a moment William followed suit. They began unloading the materials for tables. Daad watched, frowning a bit. Finally his face eased, and he caught the end of a plank as Isaac slid it off the wagon.

Now, if only she could get William to speak to her, perhaps one of the thorns would be removed from her heart.

The tables began to take shape. She carried a flat of snapdragons out, veering so that her path led her close to William.

"William, will you put these on the table for me?"

He started like a deer at the sound of her voice. Nodding, his eyes still not meeting hers, he reached for the flat.

She seized the moment to pat his hand. "Denke, William. It's kind of you."

Color flooded his face. "I—I'm sorry. I'm s-s-so ashamed."

"It's over," she said quietly. "You'll confess. God and the people will forgive."

"But I—"

"No, William." Her fingers tightened on his. "Forgiveness is a precious gift. Don't push it away with your guilt." Pain gripped her heart at the reminder of Gideon. "That hurts too many people. Promise me."

His eyes were dark with questions, but he nodded. "I promise."

"Gut." She turned away, trying to quell the memories of Gideon that flooded her. For today, at least, she must keep reminders of him at bay so that she could do the work that was before her. She'd have plenty of time to think of him. To regret.

Another buggy appeared in the lane. She started toward it. Surely everyone she'd expect to help was here already.

The buggy pulled to a halt. She could not, after all, keep away from reminders of Gideon, since it was Lovina, his sister-in-law, who smiled at her a little uncertainly.

"Lovina, it's so gut of you to come." She would not let Lovina feel that anything that happened between her and Gideon affected their friendship.

"I wouldn't miss your opening. I brought some things." She gestured to the floor of the buggy, stacked with trays. Several gallon jugs of lemonade nestled against the seat.

"What is all this? You didn't need to bring food."

Lovina slid down from the seat and began pulling trays out, handing them to Rachel. They were filled with dozens of cookies. "I noticed that whenever stores have their grand openings, they always have refreshments for folks. So I thought you could, too."

Rachel's throat tightened. Lovina's expression suggested that she was trying to make up for something. It could only be that she knew or guessed what had happened between Rachel and Gideon and was trying, in her own way, to express sympathy.

"You are so kind. If Gideon—" She stopped. That sentence couldn't go anywhere happy. "Denke."

"Gideon is an idiot, and I'd like to tell him so." Lovina snorted, grabbing a jug of lemonade. "But Aaron says we must be patient. Patient! What do men know about it anyway?"

Rachel actually managed a weak laugh at Lovina's words. "I'm not upset." Grieved and pained, but not upset. "It is in God's hands."

Lovina looked as if she thought the Lord could use a little help, but she kept the words in. "Let's get these inside until opening time, ja?"

"Ja." Rachel led the way toward the kitchen. Odd, to feel so heartened by Lovina's support.

She'd like to believe that patience was the answer, but she couldn't. She feared all the patience in the world wouldn't bring Gideon to the place where he could love again.

There was still a half hour to go before the opening time, but a car came down the lane already. Rachel assessed the situation, nerves jumping. Were they ready?

The refreshments weren't out yet. Everything else looked fine. The potted marigolds glowed yellow and orange along one end of the table, while snapdragons formed a rainbow at the other end. Between them were waves of cosmos and zinnias, ready to take off in someone's garden.

A second long table held the perennials Rachel had potted up. Not so many of those, but she could always do more if there was a demand. They were ready.

She took a deep breath and turned to greet her first customer. But it wasn't a customer. It was Johnny.

Any concern she felt at having him come when so many Amish were around was supplanted by pure gratitude. He'd supported her throughout, believing in her idea when others didn't. Without his help and encouragement, her dream might not have become a reality.

"Johnny. You're here." She hugged him hard. "I'm so glad."

"I'd have come earlier, but I stopped to put up a few directional signs. Wouldn't want your customers getting lost on these back roads, would we?"

Probably no one else would notice the nervousness shown by the way he shifted his weight and ran his hand through his hair. But she knew him too well to be fooled by the casual expression he'd put on.

"You are so kind. I'd never have thought of that." She squeezed his arm. "I just hope I have some customers to follow the signs."

"That's a sure thing." He patted her arm. His gaze wandered past her, scanning the display of flowers ready for sale. Then he froze.

"Guess I should have known Daad would be here." He moved back a step, his jaw hardening. "I don't want to cause trouble, Rach. I'll leave."

"No." Sharp and hard as an axe, the word stopped him. "Don't you dare go."

"I'm thinking of you . . ."

"If you are, then think of this—I can't stand to keep losing people I love. You and Daad are just alike. Do you know that? You're both letting your stubbornness keep you apart."

Emotions warred on his face. She could almost feel the desire to leave, but to his credit he fought it.

"I don't want to hurt you." He stopped, as if he struggled to get the words out. "But if Daad won't change, there's nothing I can do."

"There's always something you can do." She said the words fiercely, unable to keep Gideon out of her mind. "You don't just give up."

"But—"

"You don't have to apologize for what you believe. Don't expect Daad to apologize for what he believes, either. Just take a step toward him. Give him a chance."

Johnny stood there a moment longer, fists clenched. Slowly, as if he were wading through a muddy field, he started across the lawn to where William was helping Daad set up a table for the refreshments.

A step sounded on the porch behind her. Mamm stood close, hands folded under her apron.

"You heard?" Rachel whispered.

"Ja." Mamm's hands seemed to grip tighter, and Rachel knew she was praying.

Please, Father. Please. Don't let them shut each other out.

Johnny reached, grabbing the end of the board Daad was trying to put onto the sawhorses. Daad froze. They stared at each other, the length of the board between them.

Daad gave the smallest of nods. Together, they put the board into place. Together, they lifted the next one.

Thank You, Father. Rachel felt the tears Mamm was stifling, felt her own eyes prick. *Thank You.*

A few hours later, Rachel knew that her opening was a success. She'd been steadily busy, selling to English and Amish alike.

She knew, well enough, that the Amish had turned out to support her and might not prove to be continuing customers, but that didn't matter. Plenty of English had come, praised the quality of her offerings, and promised to tell others.

Everyone had come—everyone except Gideon. Rachel tried telling herself that she was foolish. She had every reason to be happy today. Her business was booming, her friends had turned out to support her, the breach with Isaac and William was well on its way to being healed.

Best of all, her father and brother were working their way toward a new relationship. God had answered her prayers in an amazing way, and she was truly grateful.

Yet each time she looked at the greenhouse, overflowing with plants, each time she saw the windmill, its blades circling gracefully, each time she let her mind stray to Gideon, her heart grew heavier.

Nodding and smiling as she waited on a customer, she tried to be sensible. Gideon had done what he'd set out to do. He'd fulfilled his promise to Ezra, and thanks to him, she would become self-sufficient.

She still had to make a decision about the farm, but with Isaac no longer pressuring her and some money coming in, she could take her time. She would listen for God's leading and trust that He would show her the right decision at the right time.

And then she saw him. Gideon worked his way through the crowd toward her. He carried a windmill—the model windmill he'd shown her the plans for, that day when she'd begun to feel she knew him.

She took a deep breath and forced a smile. "You've made the model windmill you talked about. It turned out so well. You must be pleased with it."

"Ja." He set it at the edge of her flowerbed, twisting it to settle it firmly into the damp soil. "I made it for you. For the business, I mean." He was staring at the windmill instead of her. "Maybe folks will want to buy them for garden ornaments."

"Maybe they will." Was that the only reason he'd come? To try to give Ezra's widow another small source of income? She swallowed, trying to relieve the tension in her throat. "You're very kind."

For an instant something flared in his eyes at her words. It was gone so quickly that she couldn't identify the emotion.

He cleared his throat, as if his was as constricted as hers. "I wonder—" He glanced around, seeming to register the other people for the first time. "Could we—there's something in the greenhouse I want you to see. Can someone else take over here?"

Before Rachel could speak, someone bumped her elbow. Lovina had slipped behind the table where she kept the cash box.

"Let me handle the sales for a bit. You've been working all day."

"Denke, Lovina."

She wouldn't let herself imagine what this might mean. Instead, she walked steadily across the lawn to the greenhouse. Gideon came beside and a little behind her, not touching. He ducked his head to follow her into the greenhouse and closed the door behind him.

She'd forgotten how much he filled up the greenhouse when they were inside together. With plants hanging all around and filtering the sunlight, it was as if they'd sheltered inside a quiet cave.

Gideon took a breath so deep that his chest heaved. "This is not a gut time. Your opening—" He stopped, shook his head. "I know how William feels when he can't get the words out."

Somehow his awkwardness gave her courage. "Just say it, Gideon. Whatever it is. You can tell me anything. We're friends, ain't so?"

"Can I tell you that I love you?" His hands clenched. "Ach, I'm making a mess of it, but I want, I need for you to know my heart."

Love. She heard the word, and her own heart seemed to swell to meet his. She reached out her hands to him, hardly knowing that she was doing it, and he clasped them in his.

"I think I've loved you for a long time, but I couldn't accept it. How could I love you when Ezra was gone? How could I love you when Naomi was gone?"

"Having loved before shouldn't keep us from loving again."

"No. It shouldn't." His fingers moved caressingly on the backs of her hands, and the touch went straight to her heart. "But I was blind to that, tied up inside myself."

"What changed you?" She wanted to put her hands to his face but held back, almost afraid to believe this was happening. "At Leah's, you said—"

"I was stupid." His mouth curved just a little. "Lovina has been aching to tell me so. I don't know why she hasn't."

A bubble of happiness was rising in Rachel, filling her with warmth and light. "Because Aaron told her to be patient."

Gideon's chuckle was soft and deep. "Bishop Mose ran out of patience with me."

"Bishop Mose? What did he—how did he know—"

"He knows everything, I think. Especially the things we don't say."

His eyes darkened. "He told me that not forgiving myself was a sin. That it was refusing to accept God's forgiveness, thinking that I knew better than God."

"Gideon, I'm sorry." She wanted to comfort him, but she didn't know how.

"Don't be. At first I felt as if he'd hit me between the eyes with a two-by-four. It knocked me to my knees. And then I knew it was true. I'd shut myself away from the Lord with my stubbornness, and shut my heart away from loving, too."

"We make mistakes. It's only human." And how often those mistakes came down to forgiveness—forgiving yourself, forgiving others, even forgiving God for taking away someone you loved.

"Can you love someone so stubborn and foolish, Rachel?" He raised her hands to his lips, and his breath crossed her skin in a promise.

She seemed to see Ezra's face in her heart. He would always be there, but he wouldn't regret the happiness she and the children would find with Gideon.

"I can," she whispered, lifting her face for his kiss. God had brought them both through the darkness to new life. They would cherish every day, in His name.

Anna's Return

*This story is dedicated to the treasured friends
whose unfailing encouragement and support helped to
make it possible—you know who you are!
And, as always, to my husband, Brian,
who always believes in me.*

CHAPTER ONE

She was beginning to fear that the prodigal daughter wouldn't make it home after all. Anna Beiler pressed on the gas pedal. "Come on, you can do it." The old car responded with nothing more than a shudder.

Daad would probably say that this was what she got for depending on something so English as a car to get her home, and maybe he'd be right. Just the thought of seeing her father made her stomach queasy. How would he, how would any of the family, react to Anna's turning up at her Amish home three years after she'd given up all they believed in to disappear into the English world?

The car gave an ominous sputter. It might be her prized possession, but she didn't know much about its inner workings. Still, that noise and the shaking couldn't be good signs.

She gripped the steering wheel tighter, biting her lip, and faced the truth. She wasn't going to make it to the Beiler farm, the place where she'd been born, the place she'd left in rebellion and disgrace. She'd been almost nineteen then, sure she knew all about the world. Now, at twenty-two, she felt a decade older than the girl she'd been.

But there, just ahead, she spotted the turnoff to Mill Race Road. Two miles down Mill Race was the home of her brother and sister-in-law. Joseph and Myra would welcome her, wouldn't they?

Forced into a decision, she'd have to take that chance. She turned onto the narrow road, earning another protesting groan from the car. Her fingers tensed so much that she'd have to peel them from the steering wheel. Worse, now that she was so close, all the arguments for and against coming here pummeled her mind.

Was this the right choice? Her stomach clenched again. She didn't know. She just knew returning was her only option.

It was strange that things looked the same after three years. Pleasant Valley, Pennsylvania, didn't change, or at least not quickly. Maybe there'd been a little more traffic on the main road, but now that she was off that, not a car was in sight.

The fields on either side of the road overflowed with pumpkins, cabbage, and field corn that had yet to be cut. Neat barns and silos, farmhouse gardens filled with chrysanthemums, sumac topped with the dark red plumes that made them look like flaming torches—this was September in Pennsylvania Dutch country, and she was coming home.

Maybe she should have written, but when had there been time? There'd been no time for anything but to get out of Chicago as quickly as possible. And there was no way she could explain the unexplainable.

She glanced into the backseat, and her heart expanded with love. Gracie slept in her car seat, good as gold, just as she'd been throughout the long trip. At not quite a year old, she could hardly have understood her mother's fear, but she'd cooperated.

The neat white sign for Joseph's machine shop stood where it always had. Anna turned into the narrow gravel lane, determination settling over her. It was far too late to worry if her decision would work. She had to make it work, for Gracie's sake.

Joseph and Myra's place was a hundred-year-old white frame farmhouse, identifiable as Amish only by the fact that no electric lines ran to the house. They owned only a few acres, not enough to farm but plenty for the machine shop that her mechanically minded brother ran.

In the pasture to the right of the lane a bay horse lifted his head, eyeing her curiously, probably wondering what a car was doing here. Tossing his mane, he trotted a few feet beside her along the fence.

If Gracie were awake, she would point out the horsey, something that up until now Gracie had seen only in her picture books. Everything about this place would be strange and new to her.

Not to Anna. For her, it all had an almost heartless familiarity. The very sameness made it seem to her that Pleasant Valley had gotten along quite nicely without her, thank you very much, and could continue to do so.

Joseph's shop was in the large outbuilding at the end of the lane, while off to the left beyond it stood the horse barn. Surely there'd be room in one of them to store the car.

Get it out of sight—that was all she could think. Get the car out of sight, and then they'd be safe.

Maybe she ought to drive straight to the shop. She could park behind it, if nothing else. As if it had read her mind, the car gave one last sputter, a cough, and died, just short of the house.

"No, don't do this," she muttered. She switched the key off and then turned it on again, touching the gas pedal gently.

Nothing. The car seemed to sink down on its wheels, like a horse sagging into clean straw after a hard day's work.

She pounded the steering wheel with the heel of her hand. Still, at least she was here. Joseph would help her, wouldn't he? He'd always had a tender spot for his baby sister.

Mindful that Gracie still slept, Anna slid out of the car, leaving the door open for air, and straightened, groaning a little. Her muscles protested after all those hours in the car, to say nothing of the tension that had ridden with her.

She glanced down at the faded blue jeans, sneakers, and wrinkled shirt she wore. It might be less harrowing for Joseph and Myra if she'd arrived in conventional Amish clothes, but she'd certainly have drawn attention to herself driving a car that way.

Not giving herself time to think about their reaction, she walked quickly to the back door.

She knocked on the screen door, paused, and then knocked again, louder. Nothing. The inner door was closed—odd on a pleasant September day. She opened the screen door, tried the knob, and the realization seeped into her. The luck that had gotten her all the way here from Chicago had run out. No one was home.

She stood on the back step, biting her lip, frowning at the car. The dark blue compact, liberally streaked with rust, had been her friend

Jannie's, and now it was hers, the only car she'd ever owned. Pete knew it well, too well. If he'd followed her—

That was ridiculous. Pete couldn't possibly have known where she was going. She had to stop jumping at shadows.

But her common sense seemed to have fled. All she could think was to get the car out of sight and submerge herself and Gracie in the protective camouflage of the Amish community as quickly as possible.

Joseph and Myra were away, but one of their horses might still be in the barn. If she could hitch it to the car, she could tow the vehicle out of sight. Hurrying, she checked the sleeping baby. Gracie still slept soundly, her head turned to one side in the car seat, a small hand unfurling like a leaf next to her face.

Gracie was all right. She just had to keep her that way. Anna turned and jogged toward the barn, urged on by the fear that had pursued her all the way from Chicago.

She slid the heavy door open and blinked at the dimness, inhaling the familiar scents of fresh straw, hay, and animals. From one of the stalls came a soft snort and the thud of hooves as the animal moved. *Thank heaven*. If the horse had been turned out in the field for the day, she might never have caught it.

The bay mare came willingly to her, nosing over the stall boards. It was Myra's buggy horse, most likely. Wherever they were today, they'd taken the one Joseph drove. Did he still have that big roan?

Lifting a lead line from the hook, Anna started to open the stall door.

A board creaked behind her, and she whirled toward the sound, her breath catching.

"What are you doing with that horse?"

A man stood in the open doorway, silhouetted against the light behind him. Not Joseph, for sure, but Amish, to judge by the outline of him and the cadence of the words he'd spoken in English.

Well, of course he'd spoken English. That was what he thought she was, standing there in her jeans and T-shirt—an English woman. A horse thief, maybe.

He moved toward her before she could find the words for an explanation, and she could see him better. Could recognize him.

"It's . . . Samuel Fisher, ain't so?" The Amish phrase she hadn't used in three years came readily to her lips. Samuel was her sister-in-law Myra's brother. Maybe Joseph and Myra had asked him to look after things while they were gone today.

He stopped a few feet from her, assessing her with a slow, steady gaze. Slow, she thought. Yes, that was Samuel. Maybe *deliberate* would be a kinder word. Samuel had never been one to rush into anything.

"So. Anna Beiler. You've come home, then."

He'd switched to Pennsylvania Dutch, and it took her a moment to make the mental change. After so much time away, she even thought in English.

"As you can see."

"It's been a long time."

"Three years." She shifted her weight impatiently from one foot to the other. She didn't have time to stand here chatting with Samuel. The baby could wake—someone could spot the car. "Do you know where Joseph and Myra are?"

He took his time about the answer, seeming to register every detail of her appearance as he did. "They've gone over to Fostertown for the day. Joseph didn't say anything to me about you coming."

"Why should he?" The words snapped out before she could moderate them.

Samuel's strong, stolid face didn't register much change—but then, it never had. His already-square jaw might have gotten a little squarer, his hazel eyes might have turned a bit cold, but that was all.

As for the rest—black suspenders crossed strong shoulders over a light blue work shirt, and a summer straw hat sat squarely on sun-streaked brown hair. He seemed taller and broader than he had when she'd last seen him. Well, they were both older. He'd be twenty-six, now, the same as Joseph.

"Joseph and I are partners in the business, besides him being my brother-in-law," Samuel said, voice mild. "Usually he tells me if he expects somebody, 'specially if he's going to be away."

"Sorry," she muttered. "I didn't mean to be rude. Joseph didn't know I was coming."

"Ja, I see. And you thought you'd take Betsy to go and look for them?"

"No, of course not." Her fingers tightened on the lead rope. "Look, Samuel, I need . . ." How to explain? There wasn't any way. "I need to put my car in the barn or the shop, but the engine died. I thought I could pull it with Betsy. Will you help me?"

He kept her waiting again, studying her with that unhurried stare. Her nerves twitched.

"Well?" she demanded.

Samuel's firm mouth softened in a slow grin. "I see you're as impatient as ever, Anna Beiler. Ja, I will help you." He took the rope from her, his callused fingers brushing hers. "But I wish I knew what you are up to, I do."

She stepped out of his way as he opened the stall door, talking softly to the animal. He didn't seem to expect any answer to his comment, and she couldn't give one.

What could she say? She could hardly tell him that she'd come home because she had no place else to go—and that she was only staying as long as she had to. Little though she wanted to deceive anyone, she had no choice. Gracie's future depended on it.

Samuel looped the lead rope through the ring in the upright and went to get the harness. The deliberate movements gave him a few moments to consider. Was he doing as Joseph would want?

Well, Joseph might not be happy to have a car stowed in his barn, but he would be wonderful glad to see his little sister home again. Samuel knew him well enough to be sure of that.

He lifted the harness from its rack and carried it to where the mare stood patiently waiting. Anna was not quite so patient, moving back and forth like a nervous animal pacing in its stall.

"I'll harness her up and use a chain to attach her to the car. That should be plenty gut enough to move it, long as we're not going uphill."

She caught the harness strap on the other side of the mare as Samuel tossed it over, pulling it into place. "Where should we take the car, do you think? The barn or the shop?"

He considered. "Joseph might not want it in the shop, where people are in and out every day. Let's put it in the back of the barn for now."

If she was home to stay, she'd be getting rid of the car first thing, he supposed, so what difference did it make? When he'd first spotted the car, and then seen the woman going into the barn, he'd thought it was someone looking for the English couple who lived down the road. Anna Beiler had never entered his mind.

Anna ran her hand down the mare's shoulder, crooning to her, and then reached underneath to fasten a strap.

"Seems like you remember how to do this," he said. "I thought you might have forgotten, after living as an Englischer so long."

"It's coming back to me." Her voice was dry and clipped, all her softness saved for the animal.

Anna had changed, no doubt about that. Those jeans and shirt didn't leave a lot to the imagination. She'd always been slim, but now she was almost skinny.

The blond hair he'd always seen braided neatly back under her prayer covering was now pulled into an untidy knot at the back of her neck. Her slim shoulders were stiff, as if she couldn't let herself relax.

The strain showed in her face, too, in small lines around her blue eyes and in the tight way she held her mouth. He remembered a rosy face always alive with feeling—either passionately happy or sad or angry. Anna had never done anything by halves. She'd always felt everything more intensely, it had seemed, than anyone else.

Now—well, she looked as if the outside world had knocked all that youthful spirit out of her. The English world could do that. His own experience had taught him well.

He veered away from that thought. What had happened to him outside had nothing to do with Anna.

"What took Joseph and Myra to Fostertown?" She asked the question as if tired of the silence rather than from any need to know. Or maybe she was trying to ease her own tension with talk.

"Myra's expecting again. I suppose you know that." He raised an eyebrow in her direction, not sure how closely in touch she'd stayed with the family.

"No." A faint flush stained her cheeks. "I didn't know."

"The doctor wanted her to have some special blood tests done at the clinic over in Fostertown, so naturally Joseph wanted to go with her. Your sister Leah is watching little Sarah."

"There's nothing wrong with Myra or the baby, is there?"

"Nothing I know about."

He'd seen the worry on Joseph's face lately when he looked at his wife, but if there was a problem, it would be Joseph's decision whether to tell his sister or not.

"How is Leah? And her family?" Anna put the question carefully, not meeting his eyes.

"They're well, as far as I know." He hesitated. How much had Anna been in contact during these past three years? "Your mamm . . ."

She stiffened. "I know about my mother's death."

"I wasn't sure." He picked up the chain and slung it over his shoulder.

"Because I didn't come back for the funeral?" She shot the question at him, hands on her hips.

Defensive, that's what she was.

"It's not my business," he said quietly, and began to lead the mare out of the barn, leaving her to follow.

Anna caught up with him in a few steps. "I'm sorry." She bit off the words.

He shrugged, a little uncomfortable. "It makes no matter. I'm sorry for your loss."

They headed for the car parked in the lane by the kitchen door. "I'm sure Joseph wouldn't mind if you left the car where it is for a bit," he ventured.

"I can't. I don't want to."

Which is it, Anna? Can't or don't want to?

He wouldn't ask the question, because it wasn't his business and she wouldn't tell him, but he did wonder. Something was going on here besides the obvious fact of Anna's return.

"What about you?" Anna glanced at him, maybe wanting to change the subject. "You fence-jumped before I left. When did you come back?"

"I wasn't gone long. Less than a year."

He had a feeling she wouldn't press him on it, not that he couldn't have evaded questions if he'd had to. He'd had plenty of practice.

But Anna wasn't really interested in him—not in what had taken him away or in what had driven him back. She was preoccupied with her own worries, only talking to fill the silence.

"You work with Joseph, you said?" She made it a question.

"Ja, he took me on as partner two years ago. That's my place over there." He jerked his head toward the neighboring house, surrounded by fenced pastures for his horses.

She followed the direction of his nod, staring at the two-story frame house. "That place was owned by an English couple, I thought."

"They sold up and moved south, to get away from the winters, they said. I'm still taking out the electric and such."

It was a big job, but he could take his time about doing it. He had only himself to please. He could do it as he wanted.

Anna shot another glance at him, maybe wondering why he was clean-shaven like a boy. "You're not married?"

"No." It was his turn to be short. He'd had practice evading that question, too, and it surely wasn't Anna's business.

They'd reached the car, and he spoke soothingly to the mare as he backed her up. Betsy was inclined to be a little skittish about anything strange, but he could talk her into doing this.

"Wait a second."

He stopped the horse where she was. Anna darted to the back door of the car and ducked inside. He heard the soft murmur of her voice.

And then she was out again, holding a baby in her arms.

He took his time absorbing that. Anna wouldn't be surprised that he didn't immediately respond. After all, she'd always thought him tediously slow, maybe even stupid, as he recalled.

So, Anna had come back with a child. The little girl looked to be about a year old, with rosy cheeks that hinted she'd just woken up.

Anna had no husband, it seemed. Her ring finger was bare.

Ach, this would set folks talking, for sure, the news flying around the valley faster than fast. As to how her family would take it—well, that he couldn't guess.

"This is my daughter. Her name is Grace. Gracie." Her chin lifted as she spoke, and he saw in her blue eyes a spark of the defiance that the old Anna had had in such abundance.

The child had blue eyes, too, round and wondering as he approached and held out his hand to her. Her hair was silky and as white-blond as corn silk. She considered him for a long moment, her face solemn, and then grabbed at his fingers and giggled.

He broke into a smile. "You're a fine little girl, you are, Gracie." He glanced at Anna and found her looking at the child, her face alight with a fierce, possessive love. "You look a bit like your mammi."

Anna's eyes met his then, wide and unguarded just for a moment. That look, with all her defenses down, went straight to his heart and stuck there like an axe biting into wood.

"Denke," she said softly. "Thank you. Just let me find a safe place to put her, and I'll help you move the car. Gracie crawls like greased lightning."

"Ach, you don't need to be helping me. I'll take care of it." He jerked a nod toward the back door of the house. "The key is on top of the door frame. Go on inside with the boppli."

She looked as if she'd like to argue the point. Probably didn't want to be beholden to him if she could help it. But instead she nodded, took a bag from the car, and headed for the house.

He watched as she disappeared inside. Then he turned to the horse, patting her absently, his mind struggling to absorb everything that had just happened. Little Anna was back, and she had a boppli.

Small wonder she wore that look of strain. Her situation was difficult for sure. As for her future—that was beyond his imagination.

Relief swept over Anna when she closed the door behind her. At least now she was safe from the chance of being seen, to say nothing of getting away from Samuel's cool gaze.

Had he been judging her? She couldn't be sure, but the idea made her seethe. She'd thought she'd wiped out her quick temper during the difficult years away. Maybe she'd been wrong.

Or maybe it was being back that had her reverting to the old, rebellious Anna. That wasn't a pleasant thought. She'd need all the maturity she'd gained to negotiate the coming weeks, maybe months.

How long? How long until she felt it was safe to stop hiding?

Grace wiggled, fussing a little and reaching toward the floor.

"Down?" She took a quick glance around the kitchen, but of course Myra's kitchen, including the floor, was spotless.

She put Gracie down, smiling as she crawled quickly to the table and, using its leg for support, pulled to her feet, wobbling there. Gracie seemed ready to take a step, but she wasn't quite brave enough yet.

The smile faded quickly. In her bright pink romper and tiny sneakers, Gracie could not be mistaken for an Amish child, any more than anyone would think Anna Amish in her jeans. If she were to succeed in blending in here, that was the first thing that had to change.

"We'll make it," she promised, scooping Gracie up again and kissing the downy hair that curled around her ears. "We will. I promise. I love you, little girl."

Gracie giggled at the kiss and squirmed to be set down again.

"In a minute you can crawl. Right now, let's find something suitable to wear, for both of us."

She walked through the hallway, memory coming back as she did so. Joseph and Myra had been fortunate to be able to buy this house when they first married, thanks to the success of Joseph's machine shop. Her brother was clever with machines, adapting English technology to work in ways the Amish could accept. She felt a familiar impatience with the endless adjustments Amish people made to live in a modern world.

Upstairs, she found Joseph and Myra's bedroom without difficulty but hesitated, not liking to touch Myra's things without permission.

Still, if she knew her sweet, shy sister-in-law as well as she thought she did, Myra would be delighted to lend anything she owned. She'd also probably be vastly relieved to see Anna in traditional garb rather than English clothes.

Anna put Gracie down on the rag rug beside the bed and rummaged in the diaper bag for her favorite ball. "There you are. Be good while Mammi gets dressed."

Quickly, before her qualms overcame her, she looked through Myra's things. Luckily they were about the same size, so that shouldn't be much of a problem.

She found a dress and apron combination in a deep forest green hanging from a hook.

"This will work," she said to Gracie, who was picking at a dark red color in the rug with one tiny finger. "You'll be surprised when you see how I look."

She peeled off her jeans and T-shirt and pulled on a plain white slip. Next she slid the dress over her head. Funny, to feel it flutter around her legs. She frowned for a moment, trying to remember the knack of fastening the bodice with the seven straight pins, but it came back to her almost at once.

Now the apron, and the black stockings. Her sneakers would be acceptable, so she wouldn't have to raid Myra's shoes.

She stood for a moment when she'd finished, rubbing her palms on the skirt of the dress, until she realized that her hair was still pulled back in an elastic.

Again, her fingers seemed to remember what to do as she twisted her hair into a bun. She had cut her hair first thing when she'd decided to leave, as a gesture of independence, but she'd soon found it hard to deal with and let it grow again. It wasn't as long as most Amish women's, but the bun and kapp would hide that. She settled one of Myra's white prayer kapps into place.

Prayer. She'd done a great deal of that in the past year, struggling to find her way, struggling to hear God's comfort and guidance.

But often her frantic pleadings seemed to fall on deaf ears. Maybe she'd neglected God for so long that He had forgotten her.

She looked at Gracie. No, she hadn't been forgotten, or she wouldn't have this beautiful, precious child.

Denke, she whispered silently. *Thank You.*

It took her a few more minutes to find something of her little niece's that Gracie could wear, but finally she was satisfied. They would pass for any Amish mother and daughter. She could probably walk right past someone who'd known her in Chicago. Most of them would only turn to stare at the clothing, not noticing the woman who wore it.

That was the idea, she reminded herself, carrying Gracie back down to the kitchen. Dress humbly, modestly, so that you don't stand out or draw attention to yourself. It was the community of believers that was important, not any single individual.

She'd rejected that when she left, but now she needed it, would rely on it.

Once in the kitchen she put Gracie in the wooden high chair next to the table. "Let's find you something to eat. You must be hungry, ain't so?"

She blinked, a little surprised at herself. Would it be that easy for her to go back to talking Amish, thinking Amish?

And being Amish? The voice of her conscience questioned. *Are you ready for that? Or are you playing a part?*

She pushed the thought away. Get something for Gracie to eat—

The back door opened. Samuel stood there, filling the doorway, his mouth agape. This must be the first time she'd actually disturbed that stolid countenance of his.

"Do I look Amish again?" Sure of herself on this, at least, she watched him.

He lifted those level eyebrows that gave him such a serious expression. "You forgot something."

"What?"

He pulled a paper towel from the rack and handed it to her. "Amish women don't wear stuff on their lips."

The lack of mirrors had done her in. She'd forgotten the lipstick. Quickly she scrubbed her lips with the towel until it no longer came away with the slightest tinge of color.

"Better?"

"Ja. You don't need that stuff anyway."

"That might almost be a compliment, Samuel. If it weren't for your disapproving frown." She let her irritation show in her voice. "I should think you'd be a little more understanding than most people."

Her tart words didn't make a dent in his composure.

"Ja, I was a fence-jumper, too." The words seemed heavy, as if laden with something. Guilt, maybe? "That's how I know it's not easy to come back. Do you think you can be again the girl you were?"

"I don't want to be." The words came out quickly, before she had a chance to think that she didn't want to have this conversation with him. She shrugged. "I'm three years older. Maybe a little wiser, I hope."

"And you're certain-sure you're ready to be Amish again?"

The question pricked at her, sending her tension soaring. Did he see through her so easily? No, he couldn't possibly know why she'd returned. No one could.

She squared her shoulders, facing him. "My readiness will be a question for my family to answer." *Not you.*

"True enough." He glanced out the door at the sound of buggy wheels. "I suppose you'll know that soon. Here they are."

CHAPTER TWO

*M*yra passed another plate for Anna to dry. She gave her a shy smile, as if still getting used to having this unexpected guest in her house.

"You didn't have to help. I'm used to doing the supper dishes by myself, I am."

"I'm glad to do it." Besides, it might keep her from thinking too much.

Myra glanced across the kitchen to where almost-three-year-old Sarah played on the floor with her new little cousin, as if checking to be sure they were all right. So far, at least, the girls seemed happy to share the blocks, but who knew how long that would last?

Myra turned back to the sink, plunging her hands into the sudsy water. "It's wonderful gut to have someone to talk to over the dishes. To tell the truth, I missed this time with my sister once I was married." She flushed a little. "Not that I'd want Joseph to think I had any regrets. But we used to have the best talks while we were doing the dishes. I'll bet you and Leah did, too."

"Ja, that we did."

At the thought of her older sister, Anna's throat muscles contracted. Even with the ten years' difference in their ages, she and Leah had always been close. When she left, Leah had been the only one who seemed to understand.

She'd promised Leah that she'd stay in touch. She hadn't kept that promise. She hadn't been here for Leah's wedding or the birth of her little girl or when Mamm had died. Could Leah forgive that?

She cleared her throat, trying to evade those thoughts. Things she'd been able to banish to the back of her mind when she was far away were loud and insistent here, demanding answers.

"I want to thank you again for the use of the clothes." She brushed at a tiny soap bubble that had landed on her sleeve. "It's kind of you."

"Ach, it's nothing at all." Myra might not know just how to react to her sister-in-law's return, but she followed her generous heart. "I'm happy to share them. I'm not sure I have the black covering for church for a single woman . . ." She stopped, a flush mounting her cheeks. "I mean . . ."

"I'm not married." Anna pushed the words out, steeling herself for the response. This was how it would be, trying to explain herself to the family and the community. She'd better get used to saying those words. "But the white one is fine."

After all, how silly would that feel, to be wearing the single woman's black kapp with a baby sitting on her lap? She hadn't even thought of what it would be like to go to worship here again, to feel all those people watching her.

Myra, at least, had no condemnation in her eyes. "I'll get out another dress or two for you," she said, avoiding the subject of whether Anna would wear the black kapp expected of a single woman at worship.

"Denke," she said softly. Unexpected tears stung her eyes, and she blinked them away. She must be tired. She never cried.

It had been a very long day. She could only be thankful that Gracie had slept so much in the car. Of course that meant that now she was full of energy. The baby banged a block on the floor, getting a quick smile from Myra.

"Ach, your Gracie is such a bright little one. So active, too. She must keep you busy."

"She does that." Of course, back in Chicago, other people had cared for Gracie while she worked double shifts, trying to bring in enough money to support the two of them. That would seem strange to someone like Myra.

It wouldn't be necessary here, she realized. At least, not if the family welcomed her back.

She concentrated on the plate she was drying. If she looked at Myra, Myra might see the fear in her eyes.

Her heart filled with a longing she hadn't anticipated. If only the others reacted as Joseph had . . . with concern, yes, but also with immediate love and support.

It all depended on Daadi; all three of them realized that. Even as they'd talked over the supper table, she'd known that was what lurked in Joseph's mind, behind his words.

Samuel hadn't been there, though he apparently usually took his lunch and supper with Joseph and Myra. He'd made an excuse to leave so that they could talk, showing more consideration than she'd expected.

The moment the meal was over and the silent prayer after the meal had been said, Joseph had pushed back his chair.

"I'll go over and tell Daad you're here." His smile had tried to reassure her. "That's the first thing, ain't so?"

It was what she had intended, if only the car had cooperated. Instead she'd landed here, putting her problems onto Joseph and Myra.

She rubbed the plate with the towel, trying not to think beyond the action of the moment, but she couldn't stop her churning thoughts.

"Joseph should be back soon." Myra probably meant the words to be reassuring.

She nodded. What was happening with Daadi? How was he reacting?

He'd always been fair. That was the first thing people said about Elias Beiler; he was fair.

But he'd babied her, just a bit, she saw now. The last of the family, the girl who'd finally come along nearly ten years after Leah—yes, Daadi had been easier on her, and she'd tried his patience sorely.

And now she was doing it again. Returning after all these years without a word, an unmarried woman with a baby . . .

She hadn't even come when Mamm died. It was all very well to justify it in her mind—happening as it did just when Gracie was born, when Jannie was dying. But Daad might not . . .

Myra touched her hand gently. "Don't worry so."

She tried to smile, but the effort failed. "I can't help it. If only Daad will see me, I'll tell him how sorry I am. I'll tell him—"

But what could she say? Back in Chicago, coming here had seemed a simple solution to the nightmare that surrounded her. She would come home and disappear into the tightly knit Amish community where Gracie would be safe. She hadn't thought enough about what it would mean both to her and to the family.

"Joseph will do a gut job of telling him." Myra patted her hand. "You can count on him."

Myra had always thought the sun rose and set on her young husband. Anna loved him, too, but she had a more realistic picture of Joseph's ability to communicate such difficult news.

She heard the clop of the horse's hooves in the lane, the creak of the buggy. Drying her hands twice over, she tried to swallow the lump in her throat. Joseph would have done his best, but what if it wasn't enough? What if Daad wouldn't see her?

The door opened. Joseph came in, his face impassive, and she took an impulsive step toward him.

"What did he say?" Her heart was in her throat.

"Ask him yourself." He stepped aside, and she saw that Daadi was behind him.

"Daadi . . ." Her voice caught on the words, her mouth dry. "I'm sorry . . ."

Before she could get anything else out, her father had crossed the kitchen in a few long strides and swept her into his arms.

She couldn't have spoken then, not for anything. Her tears spilled over, wetting the soft cotton of his shirt, and she let them fall.

Strong arms around her, comforting her, just as Daadi had held her the time she'd fallen from the apple tree when one of the boys had dared her to climb higher. She'd broken her arm, and her next older brother, Mahlon, had earned a whipping for such a foolish dare.

Daadi had held her then, letting her cry, while Mammi ran for something to immobilize the arm. His shirt had felt as it did now—soft and warm against her cheek, smelling of the clean fresh air that had dried it.

She wasn't six any longer. She shouldn't weep on her father's chest. But it was so comforting to feel the safety and security of that embrace that she didn't want to let go.

"Ach, it's all right." His voice was husky. "Don't cry anymore, little one. It's wonderful gut to have you here again at last."

The love and forgiveness in his voice threatened to bring on another bout of crying, but she stifled it. She drew back, wiping her eyes with her hands.

"I'm sorry—" she began again, but he silenced her with a shake of his head.

"Enough of that," he said. "I must meet my new little grandchild."

Fighting for control, she nodded to where Gracie sat on the floor. Daad's eyes misted, his mouth trembling just a little above the beard that was nearly all white now. He moved to the children, squatted down.

Sarah threw herself at him, of course, and he hugged and kissed her, greeting her gently.

"So," he said, once Sarah was satisfied with her share of attention. He extended a hand to Gracie. "This is little Gracie, ja? Wie bist du heit. It's gut to meet you."

Gracie stared at him for a moment, her blue eyes round. She reached a chubby baby hand and grasped his white beard.

He chuckled. "Ja, that is real, it is." He held out his hands to her. "Will you come to me, Gracie?"

She studied him for another moment, as if trying to make a decision. Then she smiled and reached for him. Murmuring something so soft only the baby could hear, Daadi lifted her in his arms, holding her as close as he'd held Anna.

Anna blinked back tears that threatened to overflow again. *Now was the moment.* She should tell Daadi the whole story now. She should trust that when he knew, he'd help her.

But he was bouncing Gracie in his arms, his face filled with love. Joseph and Myra were smiling, arms around each other's waist as if they had to touch at this moment, too. And emotion she hadn't anticipated had a stranglehold on her throat.

"We must have some cake and coffee, for soon it will be time to put these little ones to bed." Myra wiped away a tear and hustled to the stove, lifting the coffeepot. "Komm, Joseph, fetch the applesauce cake from the pantry for me."

Joseph, with a quick wink at Anna, did as he was told. The moment when she might have spoken was gone.

Maybe that was just as well. She took the plates and forks Myra handed her and began to put them on the table, as swift and smooth as if she were back working in the restaurant again. Sooner or later she must tell Daadi, at least, everything about Gracie.

But later would be better, wouldn't it, when he'd had a chance to get used to having her here again?

And could she—should she—really tell him everything? Gracie was the important thing. Anna had to be sure of keeping Gracie safe above all, even if it meant putting a barrier between herself and her family.

"Now," her father said a few minutes later, feeding Gracie a small crumb of applesauce cake, "we must decide where you and the little one are going to live. Joseph, what do you think?"

He was consulting her brother, not her, and making the decision for her as automatically as he'd always done. Once that would have provoked an angry outburst. But she'd learned control during her time away. She couldn't afford to indulge in emotion now.

Joseph folded his hands and looked at Myra, and she gave a tiny nod. "Anna can stay here."

"That's gut of you both." Daad nodded, as if it was no more than he'd expected. "But Anna and her baby should have the right to move back into her old room at the farm, if she wants."

Now it was her turn to exchange glances with Joseph. Levi, their oldest brother, and his wife, Barbara, ran the farm with their growing family, while Daadi had moved into the small daadi haus. Living with Levi and Barbara would be like stepping onto a whirling carousel. Dizzying at best, even if she could contrive to keep from getting annoyed with Barbara's well-meant meddling twenty-five times a day.

"Denke, Daadi, but I think that would make things too crowded for Levi and Barbara." She glanced at Myra. "If you're sure . . . With another baby on the way, you might rather have your privacy."

Something, some faint shadow, crossed Myra's face, but then she was smiling. "Ja, we're sure. We have plenty of room." She reached across the table to squeeze Anna's hand. "And besides, it will be gut to have a sister in the house again."

Anna couldn't speak for the emotion that welled in her. She could only look at the faces around the table, reflected in the mellow glow of the gas lamp above them. Plain faces, filled with love for her.

And she sat here accepting their love, their help, and all the while she was hiding the truth from them.

The sun had barely finished drying the grass, but Samuel wanted to get in a few minutes' worth of working the new bay gelding on the lunge line before he started at the machine shop. With the line in one hand and a buggy whip in the other, he started the animal trotting in a wide circle around him.

The field next to the lane gave him a near view of Joseph's house, making it impossible not to think about Anna's arrival. And to wonder what had happened when the family found out.

The young horse, distracted by a car going past out on the blacktop road, broke gait, and began to canter. Samuel stopped it and started it again. Patience and repetition—that was what it took to make a gut driving horse.

The screen door banged as Joseph came out on the back porch, saw him, and waved. With both hands occupied, all Samuel could do was nod.

Joseph had certainly been wonderful happy to see his baby sister again. He wasn't one to hold grudges or dwell on problems. Quick to forgive, forget, and move on. He was sometimes too quick to want unpleasantness over, maybe. Joseph would sure never be the one to ask hard questions.

Forgiveness was part and parcel of Amish life, and usually in a case like this, families welcomed the penitent home with joy. Anna's situation was more complicated than most, though. She'd come home with a baby.

He frowned, narrowing his eyes against the sun. Something else bothered him about Anna's attitude. He couldn't quite put his finger on it, but he'd sensed something. If you'd been through a challenging situation yourself, it seemed to give you an extra measure of understanding and maybe an obligation to help someone else going through it.

He backed away from that unwelcome thought. Anna had plenty of family to assist her through this difficult time, to say nothing of Bishop Mose and the rest of the community.

Elias Beiler had come to the house last night with Joseph, not that Samuel had been spying on his neighbors. He'd been in the midst of scraping tractor-patterned wallpaper off the walls of the bedroom that faced Joseph's place, and the windows had given him a clear view.

He'd just been thinking it was a bit of a shame he'd had to get rid of those tractors, put up by the elderly couple who'd sold him the house. They'd wanted to make the room special when their grandsons came to stay. He'd glanced out the window and seen Joseph's buggy pull up the lane, and recognized Elias sitting next to him.

So that was all right. If the head of the family accepted Anna and her babe, the rest would as well.

For some reason, the thought of Anna was like a splinter under his skin. He couldn't forget how she'd looked yesterday—drained and exhausted, with all that sassy cheerfulness wiped off her face.

He knew from his own experience that people didn't find it easy to shed the outside world. Anna had been gone three years. She'd had a child. That was very different from the usual young Amish male taking off for a few months or a year, with the thought always in the back of his mind that he'd come home when he was ready to be baptized, join the church, and marry an Amish girl.

Anna's experience was not like that, and more different still from his own.

Turning as he gave the command to walk, he saw her. He hadn't heard her come out, but Anna stood by the fence, the little girl in her arms. She was obviously talking to the child about the horse—something maybe little Grace hadn't seen in her young life.

He let the gelding walk for another moment or so, gradually drawing in the line so that the circle grew smaller. Finally he stopped him, rubbing his neck and murmuring words of praise in his ear. The bay pricked his ear to listen.

He turned. Anna was still there. Leading the horse, he walked over to her.

"Anna." He nodded. "Do you think the boppli would like to see the horse up close?"

"What do you think, Gracie?" Her voice was soft with love when she spoke to the child. "Look at the horsey. Do you want to touch him?"

Gracie babbled something that might have been approval, and he moved the horse a bit closer to the fence so that her small hand could touch its mane. The bay gave a little shiver of the skin, as if he'd been brushed by a butterfly.

"You look better today. Not so tired," he added quickly, thinking Anna might take offense at the comment sounding so personal.

She did stare at him for a second, but then she smiled, a little quirk of the lips that wasn't very convincing. "I did sleep well last night. And Gracie slept soundly in her borrowed crib, didn't you, love?"

She tickled the baby, and when Gracie chortled, Anna's face lit with pleasure, too. For a moment he seemed to see the girl she had been—always alive with emotion, ready to plunge headlong into anything.

"I'd think you could take it easy for a few days, now that you've got through the hard part of telling the folks you're here."

Her gaze evaded his. "I made peace with Daad, if that's what you mean. I haven't seen any of the others yet, except Joseph and Myra."

"As long as you're settled with your daad, they'll all fall in line. You'll see."

She lifted her brows, blue eyes sparking a bit. "Is that the voice of experience speaking?"

"I guess it is." Maybe it was as well to change the subject before she got riled. "Was Joseph all right with where I put the car?"

She nodded. "You know how he is about machinery. He'll probably be taking it apart before long, just to see if he can figure out what's wrong."

"Ja, that's for sure. Joseph never met a machine he didn't like."

"I see you're still as attached to horses as you used to be." She patted the gelding's neck. "I thought you said you were working with Joseph in the shop."

"I am. The horses are just a little sideline. Somehow folks got the idea that I have a gift with unruly beasts. So they bring all their troublesome ones to me."

"You always had that talent. You helped my daad with that mare that tried to kick the buggy to pieces, and you were probably only about fourteen at the time."

He grinned, surprised she remembered. That day was still clear in his own thoughts, because it was the day he'd recognized his gift.

He'd been over at the Beiler place for some reason, had seen Elias putting the new horse between the shafts, Anna watching him. No sooner had Elias turned his head than the silly beast went crazy, rearing and kicking so fierce no one could get near him.

He hadn't stopped to think, just grabbed the horse's head and held on, talking softly all the time. He'd gotten a few bruised ribs for his trouble, but he'd calmed the animal down. He could still see Anna's shocked, scared face.

"I think that was the day I figured out soft words worked on horses, especially when they're trouble."

"This one doesn't look like trouble. He's a beauty." She rubbed the gelding's face, and he blew gently at her hand, accepting the praise.

"He's okay. This one I picked up for myself, off the harness track. He's a bit flighty, but he'll settle down in time."

There might have been a touch of pridefulness in the words, he warned himself. If he was gut with horses, it was because the Lord had given the gift, and no praise to himself for it.

The baby, maybe feeling left out, waved her hand at the horse, who jerked his head back, startled.

"There, now, silly beast." He spoke in the animal's ear. "You don't need to be afraid of a beautiful little girl like Gracie."

Anna caught the baby's hand, holding it still in hers. "Denke, Samuel. Of course I think she's beautiful, but I still like to hear other people say it."

"You're a proud mamm, is all. You're fortunate to have her, even if . . ." He let that trail off, since there was no gut way that he could see for that sentence to end.

"Even if I don't have a husband?" She said the words quietly, but her lips had tensed. "Husband or not, I am fortunate to have her, and I wouldn't trade that for anything."

It didn't come easy to him to talk about it, but he couldn't leave it at that, or Anna would think he was passing judgment on her.

"I should have just said that you're fortunate to have her, Anna. I don't know that I'll ever . . ."

He stopped, wanting to bite his tongue. That slip proved that he was better off as he was—deliberate in thought, slow to speak—because anything else got him in trouble.

"Don't you want to have a family?" Anna, of course, was on it in a second.

"Ja, sure I do." He turned to the horse, using that as an excuse not to meet her gaze. "I didn't mean anything else."

Anna was curious—he could feel it flowing from her. A few years ago, if she had been curious, she'd have fired questions until she got the answers she wanted. Now, it seemed, she'd gained a little control over her tongue.

He had to be grateful for that, because he wasn't going to show his feelings, not to her or to anyone else. It was enough that he knew for himself what his limitations were. He'd never take on anything that he couldn't be sure of carrying through. And marriage—how could he chance that? How could he know he wouldn't turn out just like his father?

CHAPTER THREE

Anna's stomach churned so badly that it would be a wonder if she could swallow a thing at the family picnic they were headed toward the next day. It didn't help that Joseph had suggested she and the baby ride with Samuel, since the larger buggy Joseph envisioned for his growing family was yet to be built.

Samuel's buggy rolled down the road at a steady rate, and thank goodness he didn't seem inclined to chat. She alternated between feeling that the buggy was getting her there before she was ready and thinking how slow it was in comparison to a car.

At least the horse wouldn't break down. She gave a fleeting thought to her own car, still safely hidden in the back of Joseph's barn. He hadn't mentioned it, and she wouldn't.

As for Daadi, he hadn't questioned how his erring daughter had gotten back to the fold. He'd just been happy to welcome her home.

Would the rest of them act as generously? She had no idea.

She glanced at Samuel, his big hands steady on the lines, and looked away as quickly. It seemed that as Joseph's partner and Myra's brother, Samuel was automatically included in family events. She'd feel a bit less stressed about this meeting if he weren't there looking on.

Or maybe she wouldn't. Maybe there was nothing that would lower her tension except getting this over with.

She cradled Gracie in her arms. The baby had been lulled to sleep by the movement of the buggy within minutes of starting the trip.

Samuel tilted his head to smile at Gracie. "Sarah always used to fall asleep like that in the buggy. I guess little ones like the rocking."

"I just hope Gracie doesn't wake up cross. She has a lot of relatives to meet. I want her to make a good impression." She touched a small, relaxed hand with her fingertip.

"Cranky? Myra says she's the best behaved boppli she's seen, including her own."

So he and Myra had been talking about Gracie, and, by extension, about her probably. Her cheeks warmed. She'd better get used to that. Her return would be the source of plenty of gossip in the valley, just as her leaving had been.

Then she'd just gone away, slamming the door on Pleasant Valley and its opinions. Now she had to find a way to bear the results of her actions.

"You should have been around when she was teething." It took an effort to sound relaxed. "We were both up most of the night, and me struggling to stay awake at work the next day."

"You had a hard time of it." He said it matter-of-factly, but she thought she caught an undertone of pity in his deep voice.

She shrugged, the sense of his pity making her want to squirm. But she wouldn't let him know that. "Not worse than a lot of other people, I guess."

She'd made her choices. She would live with the consequences.

The buggy slowed as Samuel followed Joseph into the lane at the farm. Now memories crowded in upon her, whispering relentlessly in her ear. There was the apple tree and the little seat hanging from a low branch that Daadi had fixed for her. Levi and Barbara's children probably used it these days.

Her gaze went to the window of her bedroom on the second floor of the neat white farmhouse. Who slept there now?

She'd been lucky, her brothers had always said, getting a room of her own. But Mamm had declared that with ten years between her and Leah, they shouldn't have to share.

Her stomach tightened even more at the thought of her sister. What was Leah thinking about her return? Anna hadn't been kind to her that last summer, yet Leah had been the only one who'd seemed to understand. Even when Anna lay in the hospital, to blame for the accident that had put her there, Leah had been by her side.

Anna cleared her throat. "How are they— What is everyone saying about my coming back, do you know?"

Samuel's broad shoulders moved slightly, as if he started to shrug but thought better of it. "There hasn't been much time for me to hear anything, now has there?"

"That sounds pretty evasive. You may as well tell me, whatever it is."

"Your brother Mahlon's eager to see you," he offered, as if that might make up for something. "You know he and Esther Miller married, don't you?"

"Ja." Thanks to Myra, she did. That had happened after she'd lost touch with Leah.

Not lost touch. The voice of her conscience was stern. *You broke off contact, because you didn't want to tell her what was going on in your life. Be honest with yourself, at least.*

"What about Levi?"

Her oldest brother had taken over the farm when it got to be too much for Daadi after Mamm's first bout with cancer. Levi was close to Daad—would that make his attitude toward her better or worse?

Now Samuel did shrug. "I haven't talked to him. No point crossing bridges before you get to them, is there?"

"This bridge is only a few feet away," she said. "If you've heard he's angry with me, I'd rather know."

"I see you still want to have all the answers, Anna. Just like you did when you were little." His lips curved slightly.

"Actually, I thought I had all the answers, as I recall." She'd been so sure of herself once.

Samuel gave a small sound that might have been a chuckle. "Ja, I thought I knew a bit about life before I jumped the fence. It didn't take long out there to show me how dumb that was."

"I know the feeling." She made the admission before she stopped to think that she didn't want to confide in Samuel. Or anyone else, if she could help it. "But about Levi—"

"You're as persistent as a horsefly, Anna. I don't know, but surely Levi and Barbara wouldn't be having everyone here to greet you if they were mad at you, ain't so?" Samuel's reasonable tone began to sound a bit strained.

"They would if Daadi wanted it." They'd respect his judgment outwardly, even if they disagreed. "Let me guess. It's Barbara, isn't it? She never liked me."

Samuel glanced at her face. "You didn't give her a lot of reason to like you, now did you?"

"Maybe not."

She'd been a rebellious teenager then. Barbara had been only too ready to give advice, and she'd been just as ready to resent it. Just as she resented the fact that Samuel seemed able to see right through her.

"Leave it," Samuel said, his voice gentling. "We're here. Everyone will get used to having you back. Things will be just like they were before."

He pulled up to the hitching rail, and the buggy stopped.

Samuel was right. They were here, and it was time to stop worrying and face everyone.

But he was wrong, too. Because things would never go back to being the same. They couldn't.

Samuel dropped to the ground before she could move. He took her arm in support as she stepped down, Gracie in her arms.

"It will be all right," he said, his hand warm and strong against her sleeve. "You'll see. They're your family. You can trust them, if you can trust anyone in this world."

Before she could respond to his unexpected support, she was swamped by a crowd of young nieces and nephews, all clamoring to see their new cousin. Head spinning, Anna tried to sort them all out. The children, at least, were glad to see them.

"Ach, what a noisy bunch of kinder." Daadi waded through the flock of grandchildren. "The boppli is sleeping. Can you not see that?"

But even as he spoke, Gracie stirred, lashes fluttering, and opened her eyes. She looked around wonderingly. With her cheeks rosy from sleep and her blond hair curling damply against her neck, she looked like a baby doll.

"She's near as pretty as my baby sister."

It took a moment for Anna to count up ages and realize that this tall young girl was Elizabeth, Leah's stepdaughter.

"Elizabeth, you're nearly a grown-up woman now, aren't you?"

Elizabeth's naturally serious expression relaxed in a smile. "I was eleven my last birthday, Aunt Anna. Can I carry Gracie? I help my mammi with Rachel all the time."

At a slight nod from Daad, Anna passed Gracie over. "She might be a little cross," she warned. "She just woke up."

But Gracie seemed entranced with her big cousin. She caught hold of the string of Elizabeth's prayer cap, and the girl grinned. "That's just what Rachel used to do when I held her. She's two now, so she doesn't like to be held so much, you know."

"Come along," Daad said. "No need to stand here when there's folks waiting to greet you."

Anna took a breath and hoped she didn't look as nervous as she felt. "I guess not."

They started toward the house, Elizabeth bearing the baby proudly. Her younger brother had Myra's Sarah by the hand, chattering away to her, and Levi's two boys were already racing each other to the porch, their little sister trotting after them.

The porch, and the waiting cluster of people. For a moment no one else moved. Anna's eyes seemed to see them as an outsider would, as a group of solemn, archaically dressed strangers. Then one figure started toward them, running a few steps, and Leah threw her arms around her.

"Anna. You're home at last." Leah pressed her cheek against Anna's, and Anna wasn't sure whether the tears came from her or her sister.

"Ja, I am." But even as she said the words, guilt pricked at her. Home? It was home, but not in the sense that Leah meant. Leah thought she was here to stay.

She'd given this life up three years ago. She belonged to the outside world now. This place was only a refuge, until she felt it was safe to leave.

Leah drew back, studying her face, her green eyes intent and serious. In spite of all the times they'd quarreled, Leah had been the one to understand her the most. She'd even understood why, after the accident, Anna had had to leave.

For an instant, panic edged through her. It was as if Leah looked right into her and saw all that she was trying to hide.

Anna turned away, hoping she'd done it quickly enough to mask her feelings, and returned her brother Mahlon's warm hug. She stood back, gazing up at him. "You can't still be growing, can you? You seem bigger to me."

"That's my Esther's fine cooking," he said, his ruddy face flushing with pleasure. He reached out and drew his bride to him. "You remember Esther, ja?"

"That I do." She hesitated a moment, not sure how to greet the girl who'd married her brother a year ago last November in a wedding she'd missed.

But Esther seemed to have no qualms about following her husband's lead. She pressed her cheek against Anna's. "Wilkom, Anna. Wilkom home."

Over her shoulder, Anna saw Leah picking Gracie up, holding her in a close embrace. Something that had been tense inside her seemed to ease. It was going to be all right, wasn't it?

Barbara marched off the porch, managing not to look at Anna. She clapped her hands. "The food is ready. Komm, we must eat while it is hot."

A moment of silence followed, and then came Daadi's voice. "We will all greet Anna first. Then it will be time enough to eat." He fixed Barbara with a firm stare.

A flush mottled Barbara's round cheeks. "Ja, ja," she said quickly. "I didn't mean anything else."

But she had. And maybe, despite the hugs and the welcomes, there were others who weren't best pleased to see Anna again.

By the time supper was over, Samuel realized he'd started to relax. Funny, that he hadn't recognized how tense he felt. Not for himself. For Anna.

They sat around the picnic table, all the adults. The children had gone off to play, the older ones watching the younger, except for Gracie, who sat on Anna's lap, chewing contentedly on a wooden rattle Leah had given her.

So things were all right between Anna and her older sister? He wasn't sure. On the surface, Leah had welcomed her warmly, but an outside observer like he was could see the awkwardness that still lay between them.

"More pie, Samuel?" Barbara held a slice of apple crumb pie out temptingly, but he shook his head.

"It's wonderful gut, but I couldn't find a place to put it. Give it to your husband, won't you?"

"Ach, Levi will be having it for a bedtime snack, like as not." She moved around the table, but getting no takers for the pie, she slid back into her seat next to Levi. And fixed her gaze on Anna.

As if aware of that stare, Anna moved slightly. She was feeling uncomfortable, that was certain-sure. He remembered that feeling from his own return, even though the circumstances had been different. It was a sense of being caught between two worlds and belonging to neither.

She'd get over it. Even now she was joining in the easy talk from time to time. With the baby to consider, she had every reason to sink back into the life she'd left with no second thoughts.

Unlike him. She'd come back, he supposed, because she wanted to raise her child here. He'd come back because he had to.

That was the difference between them. He'd never know, not for certain-sure, whether his commitment was solid. Or whether, like his father, he had it in him to let everyone down.

"So, Anna." Barbara broke into a conversation about the right time for harvesting the pumpkins. "Why didn't you marry the boppli's father?"

Silence fell around the table, broken only by an indrawn breath or two. Barbara had the reputation of saying things other people didn't dare, but this time she'd outdone herself.

Anna had paled. A ridiculous longing to protect her swept through Samuel. She wouldn't want to answer a question like that here, in front of everyone. But wouldn't it be better to get it out, once and for all?

Please, Lord . . .

"Barbara, I thought better of you than to ask that. Anna's reasons are between her and God. The bishop will speak to her about it, not you."

Elias's voice was as severe as he'd ever heard it. Even Levi, who usually went along with his brash wife, seemed to shrink away from her.

It was true enough, what Elias said. But . . .

Trust them, Anna. Trust. I didn't, and I've grieved ever since.

"I . . . I didn't mean . . ." Barbara had turned brick red at the rebuke.

"It's all right." Anna seemed to straighten where she sat, as if preparing herself for a trial. Her hand caressed the boppli's head. She shot Samuel a glance. "Samuel reminded me that I should trust you. And I do."

She sucked in a breath. "There was never a question of marrying the baby's father. Gracie is mine—has been since her birth mother put her into my arms, but I didn't bear her. Gracie's mother was my dearest friend. I made a promise to her when she was dying that Gracie would be my daughter. She is, and she always will be."

CHAPTER FOUR

*A*nna held her breath, looking at the faces around the table. She shouldn't have blurted it out that way. What had happened to her resolve to let them believe Gracie had been born to her?

She couldn't do it. When it came right down to it, she couldn't lie to them. Ironic, after all the lying she'd managed to do during her rebellious rumspringa. That girl seemed pretty far away now.

Still no one spoke. They were waiting for Daadi, she knew. She couldn't read anything from his expression, and her heart grew cold. The others—well, there she saw doubt and questions.

Her gaze collided with Samuel's, and she looked away quickly. He shouldn't be here for this. It was private, between her and her family.

Except that maybe they weren't her family any longer. If they couldn't accept that Gracie was her child, she'd have to leave.

The thought was there, in her mind, when her father finally spoke. "You must tell us more, Anna. Help us to understand."

Convince you I'm telling the truth, you mean? The quick, defensive words were there in her mind. A few years ago they'd have spilled out of her mouth, but she wasn't that headstrong teenager any longer. She needed their help, and she'd have to submit to whatever they asked.

Submission. The word left a bitter taste in her mouth. That was the core of Amish life she'd always found impossible to accept.

Times change, so the saying went. More likely, time had changed her. She could accept anything for Gracie's sake. She wrapped her arms around her daughter, feeling Gracie's head pressing against her heart.

"I was going to school in Chicago and working as a waitress to pay my way." She chose her words carefully, needing to make them understand a world they'd never known. "Another of the girls working there needed a roommate, so I moved in with her."

They wouldn't be able to picture the run-down, dirty building or the cluttered apartment. Or imagine the triple locks on the door.

She took a breath. "Jannie, my roommate, had a boyfriend. Pete, his name is. He was in and out of trouble all the time, mostly for selling drugs."

Daad shook his head slowly, not in disbelief but in sorrow, it seemed. "That is a bad thing, it is."

"Jannie got pregnant, and I could see something wasn't right." That was one benefit of growing up Amish. She'd been around enough pregnant females, animal and human, to know what was normal. "I got her to go to the clinic. They found she had leukemia."

Someone around the table sucked in a breath. Leah. "Poor thing."

"Ja," Myra said softly.

"When she told Pete, he couldn't handle it. He just wanted out." She was consolidating into a few sentences the weeks of anguish, of comforting Jannie and trying to see the path ahead.

"Jannie . . ." How could she make them understand a waif like Jannie, rootless in an uncaring world? "She didn't have anyone. No family, no one who could help. When she lost Pete, she was desperate."

"So you helped her."

If there was a trace of surprise in Daadi's voice, she decided to ignore it.

"I was all she had." She took a shaky breath. "When she realized she wasn't going to live, all she wanted was to know that her baby would be safe." Jannie, who'd never seemed to have a mind of her own about anything, had proved unexpectedly strong when it came to her baby. "She asked me to raise her child, and I promised that I would. The nurse put Gracie into my arms minutes after she was born." She dropped a kiss on Gracie's hair, inhaling the sweet baby scent. "I knew she was mine in that moment."

A faint murmur of understanding came from the other women. Barbara nodded. They knew that moment.

Daadi was frowning, though. "What about the father? He has the right to his own child."

She bit back angry words. They wouldn't help. Daadi could never really understand a man who would put his next fix ahead of his child. Daadi would always try to be fair, even to someone like Pete.

"He didn't want her." She cradled Gracie in her arms. That was true. Pete hadn't wanted the baby. "He signed the papers giving her away. She's my child, both in law and in my heart."

Her words seemed to linger in the silence that greeted them. She pressed one hand against the rough wood of the picnic table, willing someone to speak. No one did.

Rebellion rose in her. "You'd be happier if I came back an unwed mother," she snapped. "Would that be easier to forgive?"

"Don't, Anna." Leah might have been chiding a fifteen-year-old Anna for hiding English clothes in the barn. "You know that's not so. We're just trying to understand, ain't so?" Leah glanced around the table, seeking agreement.

Several heads nodded. Mahlon, her next-older brother, usually so happy-go-lucky, still looked faintly shocked, but he nodded, too.

To her surprise, it was Barbara who reached over to pat her hand. "You love her, whether she came from your body or not."

"Ja," she said softly. "Denke, Barbara." Too often her annoyance with Barbara's nosiness made her overlook the woman's warm heart.

"The Stoltzfus family, over by Big Creek, they adopted three English kinder," Samuel said, dropping the words in quietly.

"Ja, but they are a married couple." Mahlon glanced at his young wife, as if trying to gauge her opinion.

"You've all accepted my three young ones as family," Daniel, Leah's husband, said, wrapping his hand around hers. A blind person could see how much those two loved each other. To think she'd once been furious with Leah for considering marriage to Daniel.

"If the law agrees the baby is Anna's," Joseph said, "then we'll have no quarrel with the English over it."

Anna should have been grateful for their support. She was, for Gracie's sake. But still her rebellious spirit rose. They all thought they had a share and a say in her life. That was what she'd jumped the fence to escape.

"I will talk to Bishop Mose," Daadi said at last. "No one else needs to know anything but that our Anna is back with her child." He looked at her, and his face softened. "You are here, where you belong. You'll talk to Bishop Mose, kneel before the church, and be accepted back. It is what we've all prayed for, and we are thankful."

She nodded, lowering her face so that she didn't have to meet his gaze. How could she kneel before the church and ask them to accept her back when she didn't intend to stay? How could she hide among her own family without telling them the whole story about Pete?

A shiver ran through her. She seemed to see again the twisted anger on Pete's face, the maudlin tears he'd shed when he'd shown up at her door, demanding to see his baby, dismissing the papers he'd signed. Saying little Gracie belonged to him.

The baby's safety came first, no matter the cost.

"Ja, Daadi," she said softly. "Denke."

She looked up then. The others appeared happy, or at least relieved.

But Samuel—Samuel looked as if he saw right into her heart and knew what she was hiding.

"*Hand* me that wrench, will you?"

Samuel passed the tool to Joseph, smiling a little. There was nothing Joseph enjoyed more than a challenge like the one posed by the balky baler. "You won't be content until you've fixed it, will you?"

"Course not." Joseph looked up at him, grinning. "Converting tractor-drawn machinery to horse-drawn might seem like a step backward to the outside world, but to me, it is fun. Any real mechanic would feel the same."

The Amish ban on connecting to the power grid meant plenty of work for someone like Joseph, who could use a portable electric generator, powered by a gasoline engine, to run a welder. And because the end purpose was to keep horse-drawn equipment in the field, the bishops agreed to it.

"I guess I'm not a real mechanic." Samuel didn't need to be embarrassed about admitting it to Joseph. Joseph knew it as well as anyone, but said they made a gut team anyway.

Samuel could only hope that was true. Joseph's offer to go into business with him had come at a time when he'd desperately needed it. It had made him feel like a useful part of the community again. He wouldn't soon forget what he owed Joseph.

Which maybe partly accounted for how troubled he felt over Anna. Joseph cared so much about his little sister. It would be a shame if he ended up getting hurt.

Joseph gave the baler a frustrated tap with the wrench. "So tell me something."

"Ja, what? If it's something about the machine, you know it better than I do."

Joseph shook his head, concern slipping into his eyes. "What are people saying about Anna coming back? And the boppli?"

"I haven't said a word to anyone." That wasn't really an answer to the question, but maybe Joseph would let it slide. "Your daad didn't want us to talk about it." He shrugged, rising from where he'd been squatting next to Joseph on the rough floor of the shop. "I wouldn't, anyway. I remember how it felt, coming back, figuring every blabber-maul in the valley was gossiping about me."

"I know you wouldn't say anything, but I bet you hear plenty. I saw how everyone shut up fast when I stopped at the feed mill. They had to be talking about Anna."

"Ja, well, you know how folks are." Samuel shifted his weight from one foot to the other. "They're bound to talk, but soon as they see that things are all right with the family, they'll settle down."

At least, he hoped so. Anna's situation was a bit different from his. He hadn't come home with a baby.

"Little Gracie makes a difference," Joseph said, echoing Samuel's thoughts. Hands on his hips, he stared out the open shop door toward the house. "It's not like the usual."

No, it wasn't. The usual was a young man like he'd been, who, at the end of his rumspringa, decided to taste the outside world instead of getting married and settling down as people expected. Most of them came back, convinced they belonged here.

He'd come back. But the conviction—that was what he was missing.

That was why he hadn't found a bride, despite the broad hints of his friends.

How could he, when he didn't know his own mind? When he didn't know how much of his father was in him, ready to burst out and bring the world crashing in on people he was supposed to love?

Joseph sighed, and Samuel knew his thoughts were still on Anna. "I guess we just have to ride it out until somebody else does something to get folks talking. It'll be better once Anna has seen Bishop Mose."

"Ja." If anyone could help ease Anna and her babe back into the church, it would be Bishop Mose. Samuel just wished he felt sure that was what Anna really wanted.

"Somebody's coming." Joseph stepped out into the sunshine, and Samuel followed him. "A car."

"Maybe the English are starting to hear how gut you are with the machines," he said, nudging Joseph.

"Not likely. If a thing doesn't run on the electric, they're not interested."

It was a pickup truck, not a car, bright red and shiny as could be. Samuel made a quick comparison to the run-down vehicle Anna had arrived in. This glossy piece of metal wouldn't want to be in the same garage as Anna's heap.

The Englischer got out, tugging his ball cap into place. With his jeans and flannel shirt, he looked like most of the English farmers in the valley, but most of them wouldn't be driving such an expensive rig. Farmers put their money into stock or equipment, not something fancy to ride around in.

"Good day." The man nodded, looking from one to the other of them. "I'm looking for Samuel Fisher."

"I am Samuel Fisher." Making the switch to English was easy enough. Dealing with reminders of the outside world was not. "How can I help you?"

"I'm Jase Bartlett." The man thrust out his hand. "Have a place over on Shady Point Road."

Samuel shook hands. The name was familiar, even if the face wasn't. "You have the horse farm, ain't so?"

"That's me." Bartlett didn't seem surprised that he was known. He'd come to the valley more than a year ago and snatched up a farm that several Amish had had an eye on. He'd torn down the old farmhouse and put up something new, torn down the barns and sheds as well, putting in new stables and what seemed like miles of rail fences around acres of pastures.

"I've been hearing about you, Fisher. People say you're pretty good at training difficult horses. That true?"

Samuel kept his face expressionless. "I like to train horses, ja."

Bartlett raised his eyebrows. "The way I heard it, you're some kind of horse whisperer, able to get through to any animal."

The man seemed intent on making Samuel brag about himself. "Are you wanting some work done with one of your horses, Mr. Bartlett?"

Bartlett's face seemed to darken. "I've got a new gelding that's proving troublesome. Good breeding, and I paid a fancy enough price for him, but he's a mean one. Not that I couldn't break him of his bad habits myself, but I just haven't got the time right now. So, what do you say? You interested?"

Somehow Samuel thought that if Bartlett were able to train this expensive animal himself, he wouldn't be here. His instincts were telling him that both the man and the horse might be more trouble than they were worth.

"I am sorry, Mr. Bartlett, but working with horses is a sideline for me. We have much to do in the shop right now, and I don't think I'll have time to take on a raw animal now."

Bartlett's flush deepened. It seemed he wasn't one to take no easily. But before he could speak, Joseph clapped Samuel on the back.

"Ach, it sounds like a job made for you. Don't worry about the shop. We're not so busy right now that we can't spare you." Joseph switched to Pennsylvania Dutch to add, "Besides, a man like this will pay well."

"Sounds like your friend can spare you," Bartlett said quickly. "What do you say? If you do a good job, there's more work I can throw your way."

Samuel glanced at Joseph, who nodded encouragement. "Well, I guess I could give it a try. When did you want to bring the gelding over?"

The slam of the back door punctuated the question, the screen probably caught by the breeze. Anna stood on the back porch, seemingly frozen in place by the sight of the Englischer.

Then, before Jase Bartlett could turn to look that way, she whisked back into the house, closing the door behind her.

Bartlett rattled on, talking about the arrangements, and Samuel nodded and responded. But inside, he was back to wondering and worrying about Anna's return. Did he think she was telling the truth? That had been what Joseph really wanted to know, even if he hadn't come right out and said it.

The answer wasn't a simple one. Samuel did believe that what Anna had said was true. He just didn't believe she had told them everything.

The Englischer was gone. Anna pressed her hand against the screen door, surprised that her thoughts had taken that form.

Her alarm really had nothing to do with the fact that the man was different from the Amish, but only with the reminder of the outside world, where Pete might be looking for her.

That was foolish. The fear that curdled her stomach was irrational. She had to believe that.

But could she? Probably not as long as her memory of the last time she'd seen him was so vivid. He'd been high—she'd realized that the moment she'd opened the door.

Her fingers tightened on the handle she held now, as if she could go back, relive that moment, and not open the door.

That's what she should have done, but she hadn't. How was she to know? She hadn't seen or heard from Pete since long before Gracie was born. She'd hardly expected him to decide, after all that time, that he wanted to see the baby.

Not just see. Take. Her skin crawled with the memory. He'd gone from tears to fury and back again, talking wildly about running off with Gracie. He'd go to Mexico, or Canada, where no one would look for them. He'd be a good father to his little girl.

She's not yours. That's what she'd screamed at him. *She's not yours.*

He'd come after her then, tossing her out of his way as if she were a rag doll. Her ribs still hurt from where she'd hit the floor.

That was what her neighbors had heard. Two college boys, who hadn't seemed interested in anything more serious than girls and games, had rushed to the rescue, hustled Pete out, and told her to call the police.

She hadn't. Maybe she'd still been more Amish than she thought. The Amish didn't turn to the law to settle their problems.

Instead she'd packed up everything she could carry, put Gracie in the car seat, and fled.

She shook her head, trying to make the memory go away. Pete had never known anything about her background, so even if he wanted to come after her, he couldn't. The Amish, living off the grid, possessing no computers or cell phones or credit cards, could not easily be traced. They were safe here.

That should make her feel better, but she knew she wasn't going to be content until she was sure that visitor had nothing to do with her.

She went out onto the porch, picking up the basket she'd dropped when she'd seen the truck, and glanced across the yard. Joseph had disappeared, probably into the shop. Samuel stood where he'd been, watching her, as if he knew she would come and speak to him.

Swinging the basket as if the garden were the only thing on her mind, she went across the yard, the grass whispering under her feet. The walnut tree was heavy with nuts, the green pods starting to fall and blacken.

Mamm had always said the black walnuts were the most delicious— that they had to be because they were so difficult to harvest. She could help Myra with that, if she was still here. Samuel watched her, his face unreadable. She gestured with the basket.

"I'm going to get some peppers to roast. Myra wants to put some up."

He nodded, looking at her as if knowing that wasn't all that was on her mind.

Annoyance pricked at her. "Who was the Englischer?"

"His name is Bartlett."

He was telling her as little as possible. Why?

"Did he say anything about me?"

Now something did flicker in Samuel's eyes—surprise, maybe. "Mr. Bartlett has a troublesome horse he wants me to work with. That's why he came here, to ask me about the animal."

"I see." She tried to smile. "I'm glad you're getting some more business." She hitched up the basket. "I'd better get on with the peppers."

She started to turn away. Samuel reached out, his hand clasping her wrist. She stopped, startled, feeling the warmth of his grip.

"Why would you think the Englischer had come about you, Anna?"

"I . . . I don't." She'd been an idiot, asking him that. "I just wondered. I mean, I suppose my coming back made a lot of talk."

"Among the Leit." The Amish. "Why would the English know? Or care?"

"They wouldn't." She tugged at his hand, feeling the strength of his grip. "What are the Amish saying, then? You're in a position to tell them plenty, aren't you?"

His face tightened, making him look far older than she knew him to be. "I would not do that, and I think you know it."

She'd rather hang on to her anger, but he was right. That didn't make her feel any more kindly toward him. She took a breath. "Sorry." The apology was ungracious, but it was the best she could do. "I don't believe you'd gossip about me."

He let her hand go, a smile flickering across his face. "I'm the last person who'd do that. I remember too well what it was like when I came back."

"Plenty of talk, I suppose."

"Ach, it soon died down. They found something else to talk about."

"*Someone* else, more likely." Her shoulders moved, as if to shake off the sense of people watching. Commenting. "That was one of the reasons I left. I hated everyone thinking they had the right to talk about what I was doing."

"Even when it was kindly meant?"

"That was the worst." He wouldn't understand. How could he?

Samuel's hazel eyes were serious, intent on her face. "You don't like people taking an interest in you."

"Not when it means they think they have the right to judge." Her temper flared again in an instant. "I didn't like it then, and I don't like it now."

He continued to stare at her without a visible reaction, his face impassive. "That might make it a little hard to go before the congregation with a humble heart, don't you think?"

How did he know to press on exactly the point that bothered her most? She fought down the surge of temper that only he seemed able to unleash in her.

"That's between Bishop Mose and me, Samuel. Or are you wanting to be chosen for a minister the next time it comes around?"

"I could not do that." He pushed that idea away with a quick, instinctive movement of his hands. "But I do know what it's like to come back after living English. I can see that something is wrong, Anna. If there's anything you want to talk about, anything you think maybe the others wouldn't understand—"

"There's nothing!" She snapped the words, not sure whether anger or fear predominated in her heart. "There's nothing wrong, and I'd be pleased if you'd mind your own business."

Clutching the basket, she brushed past him and hurried to the garden.

CHAPTER FIVE

*A*nna slid the skin from one of the peaches Myra had scalded, the fruit smooth and heavy in her hand. She hadn't done this in a long while, but the technique came back to her, as if her fingers remembered what her mind had forgotten. The aroma of the peaches, rich and sweet, filled her head, carrying her back to her mother's kitchen and the easy chatter of women working together.

Helping Myra can peaches kept her hands busy, but it left her mind free to worry about what the evening held. Bishop Mose would be stopping by after supper to talk with her. Daadi had sent word over this morning, which must mean he'd already spoken to the bishop about her.

What would Bishop Mose ask her? And how would she explain herself to him? She needed his acceptance if she was to stay here. She forced herself to loosen her grip on the peach before she bruised it with her worry.

Myra sliced peaches quickly into a bowl of water treated with a pectin solution to keep them from darkening. "The Elbertas are the best ever this year, I think." She darted a glance at Anna. "But you are not thinking about peaches just now. You are fretting about the bishop's visit, ja?"

"How did you know?" In the week she'd been here, Anna had begun to discover that for all her outward shyness, Myra could go straight to the heart of the matter.

"Ach, it's only natural, ain't so?" Myra's hands stilled on the peaches for a second, and then she clasped Anna's hand in a brief, wet squeeze. "It will be all right. You'll see. Bishop Mose will understand."

"I hope so."

But did she hope that, really? As she recalled, their district's bishop, wise with years, had a way of knowing what was in your heart. She wasn't sure she wanted him looking that closely into hers.

"I'm certain-sure," Myra said, her voice warm with affection.

"Denke, Myra." Anna's heart filled with gratitude for her sister-in-law's caring. "I appreciate your saying so."

Myra took the next peach. "Ach, I just thought maybe you wanted to talk to someone about it, and I'm the only one here. Or you could run over to Leah's, if you want. I can handle the canning myself."

"That's all right. I don't need to see Leah."

A chill settled on her heart. That was just as well, since it seemed Leah didn't want to see her. For all her words of welcome and her warm hug, Leah had made no effort to seek her out for a private talk since her return. It looked as if Leah wasn't ready yet to go back to being sisters.

She should try to look on the bright side of it. At least this way when she left, she wouldn't be hurting Leah again.

Her heart twisted. She didn't want to hurt anyone. If she could have found another place where Gracie would be safe, she wouldn't have come here.

She had to protect Gracie, no matter what, so she'd do what was necessary. She would submerge herself and her daughter into the Amish world until it was safe to come out.

And then what? How many people would she hurt when she went away again? If she could stay here while keeping her distance from the others . . . Well, that wasn't worth thinking about. It was next to impossible in a community like this. Nobody kept any distance, it seemed.

Myra lifted clean jars from the hot water bath, and together they began to fill them. The amber slices slid into the glass jars easily, making the glass seem to glow from within.

"Looks nice," Myra said. "Satisfying."

Anna nodded. "It does. I don't know why I used to try so hard to get out of helping with the canning."

Myra chuckled, smoothing a strand of hair back from her damp forehead with the back of her hand. "Ach, I was the same. Always thinking that Samuel had it better, because he got to work outside with Daadi."

"I'm afraid I just wanted to get out of the work, period." Her thoughts had always been drifting off far from the farm, as she recalled.

"It's different now that the work is for my own family," Myra said. "I like to see the jars all lined up on their shelves and know that we'll be eating well all winter. And you, too. Your Gracie loves fruit as much as my Sarah does."

Myra's calm assumption that they'd be here for the winter to eat the peaches shook Anna, and it took a moment to reply. "She does enjoy her food."

Gracie seemed to have blossomed in the time they'd been here, her cheeks rounding, her chubby little legs getting sturdier. Maybe she was just thriving on all the attention she was getting and from being encouraged to try new things by her two-years-older cousin.

Where would she and Gracie be, come winter? She didn't know. Not here. By then Pete would have lost interest, or else he'd be back in jail.

She couldn't go back to living Amish, not after having been in the world for so long. Not after being free to make decisions for herself.

"I'm glad you're here." Again, Myra seemed to respond to her thoughts. "It's gut to have another woman in the house."

"You're nice to say that, but I'm sure you'd rather be alone with Joseph and your little Sarah."

She glanced out the window over the sink. The shop was clearly visible, and even now she could see Samuel's tall figure move past the open door.

She'd talked to Samuel at meals, of course, in the two days since she'd accused him of nosiness, but she'd been careful not to venture near the shop while he was there working. She didn't want another private conversation with him, maybe because her conscience was telling her that she owed him an apology. He'd been trying to help, and she had slapped the offer away as if it were an insult.

"With my mamm gone and my sister living clear out in Indiana, I've missed having a woman around to talk to, and that's the truth," Myra said. "Especially now." She rested her palm on the small bump under her apron, smoothing it protectively.

Anna had seen Jannie do the same thing, time after time. Unease shivered along her nerves as she thought of that trip Myra had made to the clinic the day she'd arrived.

"Myra, is something wrong?" The question was out before she could tell herself it was intrusive—as intrusive as Samuel's offer of advice.

Myra set down the jar she'd been wiping and stared at it for a long moment. "The doctor is concerned about the baby."

The words cut straight to Anna's heart. "Myra, I'm so sorry." She fought to keep her voice level. "You must be worried. What does the doctor say?"

"Just that I must have more tests. That the tests will show if the baby has problems." She pressed her hands against the edge of the sink, as if she needed to hang on to something, and then she turned a fear-filled gaze on Anna. "I try to have faith that it will be as God wills, but I . . . Oh, Anna, what if something is wrong with the boppli? What if I am not strong enough to handle it?"

Anna's throat was too tight to answer, her mind a jumble of images in which Jannie and Myra seemed to mix. She wrapped her arms around Myra. Myra clung to her tightly, her tear-wet cheek pressed against Anna's shoulder.

"It will be all right," she said, her voice soothing once she could speak. "It will."

But what if it wasn't? Things didn't always turn out for the best. Anna knew that only too well. How could sweet, sensitive Myra handle it if her baby had a serious medical problem?

Myra pulled back, grabbing a dish towel to blot her eyes. "I'm sorry. I shouldn't act so weak. It's just that sometimes I feel I must let it out, and I can't cry in front of Joseph. He doesn't know what to do when I cry, and it upsets him so."

Anna patted her arm. "You can cry in front of me anytime you want."

For as long as I am here. The words clung in her mind like a bramble caught on her skin.

"I wondered . . . I wanted to ask you . . ." Whatever it was, Myra seemed to have trouble getting the words out. She stopped, took a deep breath. "Anna, would you go with me when I have the tests? I don't want to keep taking Joseph away from the shop, and besides, it just makes him worry more. I'd go by myself, but I guess I'm just not brave enough."

"Of course I will go with you." What else could Anna say?

She was digging herself deeper and deeper into life here with every word, every deed. Caring too much. Letting people count on her. But she didn't seem to have any other choice.

Samuel had put in a busy day in the machine shop until late afternoon, when Joseph had chased him out, saying he knew full well that what Samuel really wanted to be doing was taking a look at Mr. Bartlett's horse.

They both knew that was true. So here he was, leaning on the fence of the training ring next to the lane and enjoying the slant of late afternoon sunshine, watching the animal.

Just watching. According to Bartlett, who'd driven the truck and horse trailer over early in the morning, the gelding was Star's Midnight Dream, but his barn name was simply Star, for the small white patch on his forehead. Otherwise he was a sleek, glossy black, well-fed, and shining animal, but with a nervous toss of the head and a leery roll of the eye that would make any horseman immediately wary.

So for today, Samuel was just watching.

Watching the horse, ja, but very aware of Anna, who'd just come out of the house with the baby on her hip. She seemed to bring little Gracie out every afternoon at this time, probably when the child got up from her nap.

Also part of Anna's routine, at least for the past few days, was ignoring him. Since the day she felt he'd spoken out of turn, that was.

Well, maybe he'd been wrong to speak. But he'd been in her place himself, teetering precariously on the fence between Amish and English, and when he saw someone else there, he couldn't help but reach out a hand. Speaking so to Anna had taken him beyond what was comfortable for him, but he'd done it. She hadn't been grateful.

The animal's ears flicked back, as if he heard something, and he rolled his eyes toward the house. Samuel took a quick glance over his shoulder. Anna and Gracie were coming toward him.

"Anna. And little Gracie." He held out his hand to the baby as he would to a wary animal.

There was nothing wary about Gracie. She'd obviously gotten used to seeing him, maybe connecting him in her mind with the horses she loved to watch. She grabbed his fingers, clutching tightly and grinning, showing off her two bottom teeth. She babbled something that might have been a greeting.

"Ach, I'm such a dummy that I don't understand. Is she speaking English or Pennsylvania Dutch?"

"It's getting hard to tell. Maybe she's already bilingual." There was a little strain in Anna's manner, but her words were friendly enough. "She and Sarah chatter away to each other, and they seem to know what they're saying, if no one else does."

"Sure they do. Just like the horses make their thoughts known, even if we don't understand them much of the time."

"I see you have a new addition." She nodded to the gelding, who threw up his head as if he knew she was talking about him.

"Ja, this is the horse belonging to Mr. Bartlett. Star, his name is, but I'm thinking Trouble would be more accurate."

"That's why Bartlett picked you. He thinks you can do what he can't."

"I'm not sure Mr. Bartlett would say that he can't." He couldn't stop a smile. "It's only that he doesn't have time, you see."

"I see. Aren't you going to start working with him today?" Her eyebrows lifted a little, so maybe that was a criticism.

"Are you still on English time, Anna Beiler? Still rushing to do things by the clock?"

"No." She looked a bit nettled. "I just thought, from what Joseph was saying about it, that this was a chance to take a step that could mean success for you."

"Success?" It was his turn to raise an eyebrow. She'd moved in the world's direction, for sure.

"Well, you know what I mean. If you're as good a horse trainer as Joseph says, maybe that's what you ought to be doing."

"What I'm doing is working in the machine shop with Joseph," he said flatly. "That is what I do, and I'm content."

Even as he said the word, he wondered. Was he content? He'd made his decision, and he'd abide by it. But whether it had been made with the heart or the head, he still wasn't sure.

Star, taking exception to a barn swallow that swooped low over the fence, tossed his head and trotted to the far end of the field, where he pawed at the ground a few times before dropping his head to the grass.

Anna watched him. "You'll have your hands full with this one, I think."

"Ja, you're right about that." He tickled Gracie's chin. "Gracie won't be petting Star for a while, that's certain-sure." He glanced from the baby's face to her mother's. "Are things going all right for you, Anna?"

"Fine," she said, clipping off the word. "Don't I look all right?"

"You're looking more Amish every day." He leaned back against the fence to study her. "I could say you still look a little nervous, but if I did, you might bite my head off."

Her lips pressed together for an instant. "Again, you mean. I should apologize for what I said the other day. I was rude. I know you were just trying to help."

"It's not a problem."

"You're kind to say so." She disentangled Gracie's fingers from her kapp strings, patting the chubby hand. "Maybe I am a little nervous. Bishop Mose is coming by to talk to me tonight."

So. Anna would face the bishop, and it bothered her. "Well, that's not so bad, is it? You've known him since you were born."

She nodded, but her gaze slipped away from his. "I guess that's so." She was silent for a moment, but her forehead was knotted. "When you came back, what did he say to you?"

He didn't especially want to remember that time, but he would, if it helped Anna.

"We talked. About why I'd left, and what it had been like out there." He jerked his head, but Anna would know he wasn't meaning the distant line of trees, but what lay beyond. "He talked about what it meant to come back. Asked me to be sure I was ready before I made the commitment to be baptized."

Anna nodded. She didn't look as if she relished that prospect. "You went before the congregation then."

"Ja. Bishop Mose said I could wait for a bit if I wanted, but my mamm was sick, so it was important to do it right away." His throat thickened. His mother had been dying; they'd all known that. But she'd seen her son restored to the fellowship before she passed.

"Myra told me about her death. I'm sorry."

He nodded, not able to say more. Anna was pushing him down some roads he'd just as soon not take.

"You've seen the rest of it with others. I knelt before the congregation, confessed, was forgiven. And everything was like it had been before."

"Like it had been before." She repeated the words, but they didn't seem to give her much comfort.

"Don't look that way, Anna." Impulsively he reached out to her, wanting to wipe away that expression. "I came back because I had to, you see. Because of my mamm. It will be easier for you. I'm sure of it. After all, you came back because you wanted to."

For a long moment she stared at him, her blue eyes wide with some emotion he couldn't name. And then her lashes swept down, hiding it from him.

"Ja," she said, her voice flat. "I'm sure you're right."

"*After* supper" could mean most anytime, Anna decided as she and Myra washed up the dishes. Bishop Mose could show up soon, and she had to be ready.

Unfortunately, her mind was a blank.

Samuel had reminded her that she'd known Bishop Mose from her earliest memories, which was certainly true. She'd loved going to his harness shop with Daadi, and he'd always had a gentle word and a twinkle in his eyes for her. But that had been long ago, and this was now.

Myra, maybe sensing her discomfort, kept up a gentle flow of chatter that allowed Anna to simply smile and nod from time to time. Behind them, Joseph sat on the floor, playing with the two little girls as naturally as if Gracie had always been a part of their lives.

Funny, how that thought gave her pause. If she'd come back here with Gracie right after Jannie's death, how different would the situation have been?

She didn't want to think about the answer to that question. She hadn't wanted to come back then, didn't really want it now. Her life was out there, in the world, where she could make up her own mind about things.

You came back because you wanted to, Samuel had said. *That will make it easier.*

Her stomach cramped. She hadn't wanted to. Everyone here seemed to accept that without question, but it wasn't true. And if Bishop Mose asked her point-blank, how would she answer?

She looked across the room, her gaze seeking her child. Gracie stood, balanced uncertainly, holding a block in each hand, waving them and laughing at something Joseph said to her.

Anna's heart turned over. She would kneel in front of the congregation, beg forgiveness, all to keep Gracie safe. The girl she'd been three years ago wouldn't have been able to humble herself in that way, but then she hadn't known what it was to have a child. For Gracie, she would do anything.

The clop of a horse's hooves came almost as punctuation to her thought. Bishop Mose must be arriving already.

He entered smiling, little Sarah running to meet him as if he were another grossdaadi. He scooped her up in his arms and spoke to her in a low voice. Gracie, following her cousin's lead, looked for a moment as if she'd let go and toddle toward him. Then she plopped down on her bottom and crawled across the floor. She grabbed his pant leg, and he stooped down and picked her up, too.

"There, little Gracie. What a fine girl you are, and almost about to walk already."

Gracie babbled something incomprehensible and patted his snowy beard. Anna's heart lurched. If only . . .

She let the thought trail away, not sure what it was she hoped. Just to get through this, maybe.

"Bishop Mose, you'll have coffee and peach cobbler, ja?" Myra was already pouring the coffee into a thick white mug.

"Ach, Myra, you know my weakness." He sat down at the table, a child in each arm. "Now, what shall I do with these two sweet girls?"

"Best let me take them, or they'll be spilling your coffee for you." Joseph lifted the kinder off Bishop Mose's lap, plopping them down with their toys. "Komm now," he said. "A few more minutes to play before bedtime."

"Joseph, you'll have cobbler now, won't you? And Anna?"

"I don't know—" she began, not sure how to respond. She'd expected the bishop to want to talk with her privately, and the living room was tidy as ever, with two chairs pulled together for a quiet talk.

"Komm, fress." Bishop Mose waved her to the table, seeming to read her thoughts. "Sit, eat. We can talk together while we have some of Myra's wonderful-gut cobbler, can't we?"

Nodding, she went to take her seat at the table. She probably wouldn't be able to choke down a bite, but if this was what he wanted . . .

Apparently it was. He dug into the cobbler with obvious pleasure, all the while sharing the latest news from town and comparing opinions with Joseph on how long the fine fall weather would hold. Myra perched on her chair, one wary eye on the kinder, and Anna knew that at the first sign of fussiness, she'd sweep them away to bed.

Anna toyed with her cobbler and waited for the moment when she'd have to answer the bishop's questions.

When he finally turned to her, his expression was as kindly as ever. "So, Anna, you've come back to us. You want to be accepted as part of the community again."

She nodded, discovering that her throat was tight. "Ja, I do." She tried not to think about how soon she might be going away again.

"And why did you decide to come back?"

That was the question she feared. She'd made up an elaborate answer she'd thought would convince him without telling any outright lies. And now she couldn't seem to say any of it.

She tried to imagine how her friends in the city would react to her fear of trying to deceive him. Classmates in her college seminar would no doubt mutter about outdated superstitions. The other servers at the restaurant would expect her to stand up for herself. If you don't take care of yourself, who will, they'd wonder.

Nothing either group thought had anything to do with life as it was lived in an Amish community.

"I . . . I needed to be home," she said, staring at the tabletop, her voice choking on the words.

"Ja," he said. "Then that is gut."

The silence grew between them, and after a moment she raised her eyes to his. "What do I have to do? Will I go before the church then?"

Her mind filled with the act of kneeling before the congregation to confess. Her wayward imagination presented her with an image of her sociology professor making notes on that, eyebrows raised in disbelief.

"Ach, we don't have to rush." The bishop held out his mug to Myra for a refill.

She lifted the pot from the stove, filling his mug and topping off Joseph's.

"Denke, Myra." Bishop Mose blew on his coffee and then took a sip before returning his gaze to Anna. "You ask what you should do, Anna, but you are already doing what I would advise, I think. You must sink yourself back into being Amish again. Help Myra and Joseph, come to worship, be a part of the community. Embrace with a whole heart what you rejected when you left. Can you do that?"

"Ja." She felt almost let down, as if she'd been prepared to make a grand sacrifice and then was told it wasn't necessary. "I can." Although as she thought of it, the "whole heart" part might be a little difficult. "Is that all?"

He smiled, maybe a little sadly. "Is there nothing you yourself think that you should do, Anna?"

She blinked, her mind scrambling. Had she forgotten something important?

"Any wrongs left over from your fence-jumping that need to be righted?" he probed, and she heard a trace of steel in his voice.

Wrongs she'd committed, in other words, in the passionate desire of her eighteen-year-old self to live her own life.

Her father, her sister, pained by her actions. Her mother dying while she was gone, and her not even here to say a last good-bye. The family whose buggy she'd hit while driving a car belonging to her English friends. More, probably, that she hadn't even thought of. She found she was pressing her hand against her heart.

"Ja," he said gently. "I see. You might want to do something about that, Anna."

She nodded, not able to speak. She'd been intent on hiding the truth from him, thinking herself a hero for being willing to humble herself outwardly before the congregation in order to keep her daughter safe.

Instead, Bishop Mose had turned her inside out. *What does the Lord require of you but a humble and contrite heart?* The scripture floated up from her subconscious. Bishop Mose had set her a task far harder than kneeling and confessing.

CHAPTER SIX

Samuel swept the floor of the shop, finding the routine chore relaxing. Anna's arrival had introduced a new element into the flow of their days—not unwelcome, but a bit disturbing, even so. He was one who liked knowing what was coming from one moment to the next, not that anyone but the gut Lord knew that for certain.

Finishing, he propped the broom in the corner, stepped outside, and pulled the door shut behind him, taking a moment to lock it. Once people in the valley, Amish and English alike, hadn't bothered to lock anything, but times had changed. He wasn't as much concerned about thieving as he was that some foolish kid would get into the shop and hurt himself.

Samuel stood in the afternoon sunshine for a moment, deliberately turning over in his mind his approach to the new horse. Star would be a challenge, no doubt about that. Someone had made the animal wary and defensive where humans were concerned, and it would take time and patience to overcome that.

And while he was thinking of wary creatures, Anna was in the yard, taking sheets down from the clothesline.

How had her meeting with Bishop Mose gone? He'd seen the bishop's buggy arrive last night, and he'd seen it leave again an hour or so later.

While he hesitated, wondering whether to approach her or not, she turned, caught sight of him, and nodded. He walked over to her, catching the end of a sheet that had drooped close to the grass.

"Denke." She took it, shaking the sheet out with a quick flip of her wrists, and started to fold it. "You're done for the day, are you? Or is my brother still tinkering with a job?"

"Tinkering, yes, but not on a job." He couldn't suppress a grin, knowing how predictable Joseph was on this subject. "Can't you guess where he is?"

She blinked, and then glanced toward the barn. "He's working on my car, isn't he? I guess it was only a matter of time."

"Joseph never met a machine he didn't want to take apart." He studied Anna's face. Was she content over Bishop Mose's counsel? He couldn't tell from her expression. "Still, when you sell the car, it would be as well to have it working."

"Sell the car." She stopped, turning her face away from him as she took a white pillowcase from the line. "Ja, I guess you are right."

Her reaction raised a few more questions in his mind, in addition to the ones that had been there since the day he'd found her in the barn.

"How did it go with Bishop Mose?" he asked abruptly. Maybe she'd tell him to mind his own business again.

Her hands stilled on the fabric for a moment. Then she folded the pillowcase and dropped it into the basket at her feet. "All right, I guess. Not exactly what I expected."

"The bishop can be a bit surprising at times." He waited.

For a moment it seemed she wouldn't speak. Then she gave her head a frustrated little shake. "I thought he'd say I must kneel and confess to the church. I'd do it, and then it would be over."

"He doesn't want you to do that?"

"He says there's time enough later for that. That I should get used to living Amish again, make things right . . ." She stopped, turning to a row of small sheets that must be from the kinders' beds.

Make what things right? "Bishop Mose cares more about what's in the heart than on outward forms, ain't so?"

"I guess so." She was frowning, her fingers toying with a clothespin. "Kneeling and confessing wouldn't be easy, but I'd do it."

Most folks came to that, sooner or later, when they'd transgressed. The difficult moments were soon past, and the relief at being restored to full fellowship was worth almost anything. But was that driving Anna? He wasn't sure.

"People think being Amish is about clothes and electricity. They see only the outside and judge by that. We know it's more about having a humble and obedient heart."

Her mouth tightened at that. "They wouldn't understand, even if you told them. The people I knew out in the English world didn't see much value in being humble. You must know that. You lived out there."

"Ja." He didn't want to talk about his time out among the English.

She seemed to sense that, looking at him with a question in her eyes. "I couldn't believe it when I heard you'd gone. You were the last one I'd expect to jump the fence. Why did you?"

"Not for the cars and the clothes, any more than you did." He tried to turn it back on her.

"I wanted freedom. I wanted to make decisions for myself, not just accept what other people told me." She tilted her head to the side, looking like the girl she'd been, full of questions and curiosity. "That wouldn't be what drove you."

"No." He'd walk away from Anna, but that wouldn't be fair. He'd been the one to start this conversation. "I went away because of my father."

He saw her process that, remembering probably the talk it had caused when a middle-aged man with a growing family had jumped the fence, disappearing into the English world without a word of explanation.

"You wanted to find him?"

"Ja, but . . . not only that." His hands closed into fists, pressing against his legs. He wasn't ready to go further than that.

Her blue eyes filled with sudden sympathy. "You wanted to understand."

"Ja." *Coward,* he told himself. *You're not facing the truth.*

He didn't want to. And he certainly didn't want to talk to Anna about his reasons for leaving. Or his reasons for coming back.

It wasn't her fault that her return made him think too much about that time in his own life. Made him question too much.

He cleared his throat. "My daad—"

A bird cried harshly. He stopped, spinning to look toward the barn. That noise . . . Then he heard it again, and he started running. It wasn't a bird. It was Joseph, calling for help.

Anna raced toward the barn, a few steps behind Samuel, fear running with her. Her heart stuttered in an effort to pray.

Please, God, please, God. The words kept time to her pounding feet. Joseph wouldn't cry out like that unless it was bad.

She plunged through the barn doorway behind Samuel and stopped, struggling to see in the gloom after the bright sunlight. Dust motes swam in a shaft of light disturbed by something.

By the car falling from a jack. She rushed forward, breath catching in her throat. Joseph lay trapped under her vehicle.

Samuel dropped to his knees next to her brother, not touching him.

"Hurry! Get him out! Why aren't you moving?" She shoved Samuel's shoulder and plunged past him, reaching for Joseph. She'd get him out herself if Samuel was too slow to do it.

Samuel grabbed her arm, yanking her back. "Don't touch him."

"We have to help him!" she blazed at him. She couldn't see Joseph's face, just his legs. He could be dead—

His legs moved, just a little. She could breathe again. "Joseph, can you hear me?"

The only answer was a low groan.

"Anna, listen to me. We can't pull at him. That would only make it worse." Samuel caught her by the arms, shaking her a little. "Are you listening?"

She stifled a sob and nodded.

"We need jacks to get it off him. Run. Ring the bell first—if the neighbors hear, they'll come. Then go to the shop. There's a jack on the bottom shelf to the right of the door. Bring it. Got that?"

She jerked a nod. Samuel was right. They needed help. She ran from the barn.

Sunlight stabbed at her eyes as she raced across the yard. She stumbled onto the porch, breathing hard, trying to form the words to pray.

Help Joseph, Lord. Please help Joseph. She reached, groping for the bell rope, caught it, and pulled hard and fast. The bell pealed out, its clamor alerting anyone within hearing distance to come.

Myra pushed through the door, eyes wide in a pale face. "Who?"

No time to break it gently. "It's Joseph. He's in the barn, trapped under the car. Samuel is with him. I've got to get a jack." She grasped Myra's arm. "He's going to be all right."

No time for more. She turned and ran toward the shop. Behind her she heard the bell ringing again, sending its call across the quiet fields as Myra pulled and pulled on the rope.

The jack was right where Samuel had said it would be. Anna grabbed it and ran again, pain stabbing into her side. Even as she hurried toward the barn she could see men coming, running from the field beyond Samuel's where they'd been harvesting.

A cloud of dust on the lane from an approaching vehicle meant one of the English neighbors had heard, too. They'd bring a phone, maybe had already called 911.

For an instant she was one of them, furious at being without a phone in an emergency. Who lived this way? What if someday something happened to her baby and she couldn't get help?

She stumbled into the barn, clutching the jack. Samuel had already replaced the jack Joseph must have been using, and he had rigged up a lever with a heavy anvil and a barn post.

He grabbed the jack she carried.

"Has he said anything?" she asked.

"No." He tried to maneuver the jack into place. "It's better this way, Anna. Best if he's unconscious while we're getting the car off him."

How could he sound so calm? She clutched her hands together. But panic wouldn't help.

Myra ran into the barn, white-faced but tearless. "They are here—"

Others brushed by her then, men all alike to her dazed vision with their black pants and beards, hurrying to Samuel's side. Myra made an instinctive move, and Anna caught her before she could go closer.

"Wait, stay here. Give them room to work."

"Ja." Catching back a sob, Myra nodded.

A woman bolted into the barn—English, with a cell phone in her hand. "I've called nine-one-one. They'll be here soon." She put her arm around Myra, exchanging glances with Anna. "How bad . . . ?"

"Joseph is trapped under the car." The car. Her car, which shouldn't even be here.

"I'm Rosemary Welch." The woman was slim, in her early thirties, probably, wearing jeans and a flannel shirt over a white tee. She ran a hand through curly dark hair. "I'm sorry my husband wasn't home to help. What can I do? I've got my car. Do you want me to go for anyone?"

Myra didn't seem able to answer. She could only stare at the car, her whole being straining toward her husband's motionless body.

"I don't think so, thank you," Anna answered for her. "Thank you so much for coming and for calling the paramedics. We are grateful."

"No problem." The woman glanced toward the car, as if wondering what it was doing in an Amish barn, but she didn't ask. "I'll wait. I can drive Myra to the hospital if need be."

"Thank you," Anna said again. "Maybe the children . . ."

Myra seemed to rouse herself. "They were still sleeping when I heard the bell. Someone should go to them . . ." Her voice trailed away, as if she couldn't complete the thought.

Again Rosemary and Anna exchanged glances. "I'll look after them, Myra," Rosemary said quickly. "You stay with your . . ." She stopped, apparently not knowing who Anna was.

"I'm Anna Beiler, Joseph's sister. Some of the other women will come soon, I'm sure. If you could stay with the little ones until they get here?"

The woman nodded, already moving to the door. "Call me if you need me."

When she'd gone, Anna put her arm around Myra's waist. "You have gut neighbors."

"Ja." Myra seemed to rouse herself. "Do you think— Can't we go a little closer?"

Nodding, Anna led her around the side of the car, safely out of the men's way.

"They'll have him out in a moment. It will be all right," she murmured.

She didn't know that it would, and the fact that Joseph was still unconscious seemed bad to her, but Myra needed hope to cling to. They both did.

Samuel was directing the operation, the other men moving without question to follow his lead. He was calm and steady despite his anxiety for his friend.

The anger Anna had felt at him for not moving more quickly drained away, leaving her cold inside.

"Now," Samuel said.

She saw what they intended. The men were levering the car up, shoving jacks into place as it lifted. She held her breath. If it slipped . . .

It didn't. Samuel dropped to the floor, peering beneath the car. "Once more," he said.

Again they levered the car up, muscles straining, shirts darkening with sweat. The instant the jacks were in place, Samuel snaked his body under the car next to Joseph. She held her breath, praying, knowing Myra was praying, too.

She saw Samuel's hand gesture, and the men bent as one to slide Joseph gently out.

"He's alive," someone said, and Myra seemed to sag against her.

Thank you, Lord. Thank you.

Figures darkened the rectangle of sunlight in the open doorway. The paramedics had arrived and were moving quickly to Joseph, kneeling next to him in the center of a circle of Amish figures.

"You'll go with me to the hospital," Myra said, clutching Anna's hand.

"Ja, of course I will," she soothed.

But all the time her thoughts spun in a wheel of blame. This was her fault. She had brought the car to this place where cars were forbidden. If not for her, Joseph wouldn't be lying there, bloody and motionless. She should never have come home.

How much longer would they have to wait for word? Anna moved to the window of the waiting room, trying not to fidget, and stared out over the flat roof of the adjoining hospital wing. It had been hours, surely, since Joseph had been taken to surgery.

Please, Lord. Be with my brother. She fought to compose her mind to prayer, but her thoughts skittered helplessly in every direction. Now they fled to Gracie, and she yearned to be sitting with her at the kitchen table right now, spooning cereal into her mouth.

"You're not worrying about Gracie, are you?" Mahlon moved to her side, a cup of coffee looking too small in his big hand.

She tried to manage a smile for the gawky teenage brother who'd turned into a responsible married man while she was gone. "How did you guess that?"

"Wasn't hard. You'd either be thinking about her or about Joseph."

"I'm doing plenty of thinking about him. And praying, too. If only . . ."

"Ja," Mahlon said. "He shouldn't have tried to do that by himself, for sure. But he's strong. He'll come through this fine, ain't so?"

He was asking for reassurance, she realized. Beyond his height and beard and outward maturity, she glimpsed the boy he'd been—a year older than she, but always seeming younger, the happy-go-lucky boy who'd tumbled into mischief without thinking.

"That's right," she said, trying to sound confident. "Nothing can keep Joseph down for long."

He nodded, pressing his lips together as if to keep them from trembling. "You don't need to worry about your boppli, either. My Esther will take gut care of her and little Sarah, too, for sure."

"I know she will." Mahlon's young bride had come straight to the house to take over the babies, while Levi's wife, Barbara, organized the folks who kept showing up to help.

Those who weren't taking over duties at home were here, it seemed. The waiting room had slowly filled up as word had spread through the Amish community.

She turned back to the room. Daad was talking to Bishop Mose in one corner, a few older men forming a supporting circle around them. With their dark clothes and white beards they looked like a cluster of Old Testament patriarchs.

Leah sat on one side of Myra, clasping her hand. Samuel was on the other, supporting his sister. Other Amish, their faces as somber as their clothes, waited with them, murmuring softly now and then.

Suddenly Anna saw them as her sociology professor would have . . . a strange, anachronistic group with their old-fashioned clothes and their identical hairstyles, talking in their own version of Low German interspersed with English words.

Different. Odd. He wouldn't have used those value-laden words, but that's what he'd have meant. She stared at them, feeling as if she were looking at an illustration in a textbook.

She blinked, trying to shake off the sense that she saw them from both inside and outside the group. Coffee, that was what she needed.

She skirted a small group of men and headed for the coffee urn. As she passed, a word from their conversation reached her. *Car*. They were talking about the car, of course, the cause of this tragedy. Her car, which never should have been in Joseph's barn to lure him to disaster.

Her hands weren't quite steady as she lifted the lever on the coffee urn, filling the cup. Naturally they'd be talking about it, even as they prayed for Joseph. She glanced again at Myra, her face tense with strain, and at the supporting figures on either side of her, hiding their own pain to comfort her.

Was this what it had been like the night she'd landed in this same hospital after the borrowed car she'd been driving had hit an Amish buggy? Had Daadi and Mammi grieved and been comforted by the community?

She didn't know. She hadn't even thought of it as she'd come out of the daze of medication, aware only of her own misery. Mammi, Daad, Leah—one of them, patient and loving, had always been next to her when she woke.

She'd repaid them with impatient words and stony silences, so obsessed with her own concerns that she hadn't even thought about what they were going through.

She spotted Bishop Mose coming toward her. She took a hurried gulp of the coffee, trying to wash away the shame that had hit so unexpectedly.

"Some coffee for you?" She reached for a cup, trusting that the movement hid her face for a moment.

At his nod, she filled the cup, adding the sugar she knew he used.

"Denke, Anna." He took the cup in a work-worn hand that was stained by the oils he used in his harness shop.

"People out there," she said, jerking her head toward the window, "they couldn't imagine a bishop who has to do his own job as well as his ministry."

Bishop Mose didn't seem surprised by a comment that had to sound odd under the circumstances. But then, it would take a lot to startle him.

"I guess that's true. But Paul still made tents when he was an apostle, ain't so?" He didn't seem to expect an answer. "How are you, Anna?"

She clenched her teeth, determined not to say what she was thinking. But the words slipped past her guard and came out anyway.

"It's my fault. If I hadn't brought the car here, none of this would have happened."

For a moment those wise old eyes surveyed her. "Joseph had nothing to say about what he did, then?"

"I didn't mean that." She fumbled for a way to express what she felt. "Everyone knows how fascinated Joseph is with machinery. I should have realized that if the car was there he'd start tinkering with it. I should have gotten rid of it."

"And Joseph should have known better than to crawl under a car supported by one old jack, ja? And all alone, besides, with no one there to help him. Ain't so?"

Somehow she'd rather cling to her guilt. Was that just another way of being self-centered?

Bishop Mose patted her hand. "We've all got plenty of real things to feel guilty about in this life, without taking on burdens that don't belong to us." He squeezed her hand briefly. Without waiting for a response, he moved off toward Myra.

Things to feel guilty about—she had those, all right. They'd been slapping her in the face ever since she'd returned. Her friends in Chicago would reassure her that she hadn't done anything wrong, that she'd just been trying to find herself, that she deserved to be free.

She didn't. The conviction landed on her. She didn't deserve that freedom she longed for so much. Not until she'd made things right with the people she'd hurt.

Chapter Seven

Samuel held Myra's hand in his, heart aching for his little sister.

Dear Father, give her strength. She will need it.

Strong wasn't a word he'd ever used to describe Myra. Their sister, Elizabeth, on the other hand—no one ever doubted Elizabeth's powers. Even though she came between Samuel and Myra in age, she'd bossed them all around from the cradle, and no doubt was doing the same for her husband and kinder out in Indiana.

Myra was the gentle, easily wounded one, and maybe closer to his heart for that reason. He'd always thought he had to protect Myra. Until she married, of course. Then she'd found her strength in Joseph. It was a knife in his heart to think she might lose that, all from a moment's thoughtlessness.

He should have insisted on going with Joseph. He might have known Joseph wouldn't be content to tinker around with the car's insides. No, he'd have to test out every bit of it, because that was the kind of mind he had, endlessly curious about every piece of machinery he saw.

"Samuel."

He jerked his mind back to the present, realizing his name had been spoken more than once, and stood to greet Daniel Glick, Leah's husband.

"I just came from your place," Daniel said, turning his straw hat in his hands. "Everything is fine there. The kinder are happy and the animals fed. I locked up your house and saw to the horses myself."

"Denke, Daniel." He'd known, of course, that everything would be taken care of. That was their way in times of trouble.

"Is there any news?" Daniel lowered his voice, glancing at Myra.

"Not yet." Samuel realized he was clenching his hands and deliberately relaxed them. "All we can do is wait. And pray."

"Ja. I am doing that, for sure." Daniel hesitated. He glanced at Leah, and it seemed a silent communication passed between them. "I was thinking that my oldest boy, Matthew, might be some help to you in the machine shop if Joseph is laid up for a while. He seems to have a gift for machinery."

"He does that." Samuel had seen enough of young Matthew to be aware of the boy's interest. It was a sacrifice for Daniel to be offering him, both because Daniel could use the boy's help on his own farm and because it was well known that Daniel would rather see the boy a farmer. "Let's talk to Joseph about it, soon as he's able," he said.

Please, Lord . . .

"Things will change with Joseph laid up." Myra looked up at them suddenly, her face pinched. "I don't know how we'll manage."

"You mustn't worry about that now." Samuel bent to pat her clasped hands. "It will be all right. Joseph will be fine." She needed to believe that.

Daniel moved off to a group of men. Leah stood, stretching a little, and Anna came to take her place on the plastic chair next to Myra. Someone offered coffee. Samuel waited. Prayed.

Finally the door opened. This time it was a doctor, a surgical mask hanging loose around his neck. He looked a bit startled by all the people there, gazing from one to the other.

Myra rose, Samuel and Anna standing with her. "My husband . . ." she began, and her voice wavered.

"Mrs. Beiler." The doctor looked relieved to have her identified. "Perhaps you should come out into the hall to talk."

"Komm, Myra." Samuel reached for her, but Anna already had her arm around Myra's waist. Together they walked through the door with her, Elias Beiler following them.

The door swung shut, cutting them off from their people, but not from their support. He could still feel them there, hoping and praying. Myra clutched Anna's hand. They'd grown close in the short time since Anna had returned.

"He's come through the surgery very well," the doctor said quickly, as if not wanting them to imagine anything else. "His vital signs are good, and he should be regaining consciousness soon."

"Can we see him now?" Elias asked, as if he couldn't believe his son was all right until he saw for himself.

"He's still in recovery now, but I'll have a nurse come for you as soon as you can see him."

Myra nodded, tears welling in her eyes. Samuel could tell that she hadn't caught much more than that Joseph was alive.

The doctor started to turn away. Surely there was more they should know . . .

"How extensive was the surgery?" Anna's crisp voice had the doctor turning back to them. "What exactly are his injuries?"

Again surprise marked the doctor's face. Had he not expected intelligent questions from them?

"The head injuries aren't severe. He has a concussion. There's some damage to his left eye, but we believe it will heal in time. He's very bruised, so don't be alarmed by that when you see him."

Anna nodded. "What else?" She clearly didn't intend to let him get away until they'd heard everything. Her years in the English world had taught her something of persistence, it seemed.

"The injuries to his chest were more serious. Several broken ribs, a punctured lung."

Myra sagged a bit at that, leaning against Anna's shoulder.

"He will be all right in time?" Samuel put the question he knew was in Myra's mind.

"He has a long recuperation in front of him, but he's young and strong. I don't see any reason why he shouldn't get back to normal, given time."

Elias put his hand against the wall, relief coming over his face.

"Denke." Myra's voice was little more than a faint murmur.

The doctor nodded. Then he walked briskly away.

Myra wiped at her tears with the palm of her hand, the way she had as a tiny child, and the gesture tugged at Samuel's heart.

"He's going to be fine," Anna said. "You see, Myra. Everything will be all right."

All right, in time. Samuel's mind spun with the changes it would mean for all of them until Joseph was well again. The shop, the horses, Myra's pregnancy . . .

Myra murmured something to Anna, their heads close together. She'd grown to depend on Anna so quickly, he thought again. It was gut, surely, to have Anna there at the house with all that the future held.

Except that Anna might not be the best person to depend upon. She might do exactly what she'd done before—she might run away.

Anna slipped out of Joseph's hospital room. With all the rejoicing going on, she wouldn't be missed. After nearly a week's stay in the hospital, Joseph would be coming home tomorrow.

Myra had seemed a different person when she heard the news. She couldn't be happy until she had him home with her, to spoil and care for.

Thank you, Lord. Anna murmured the silent prayer as she hurried into the elevator and pushed the button for the lobby.

For days she'd been looking for an opportunity to call her friend Liz in Chicago, but that normally simple task had proved unexpectedly difficult. Phone booths seemed to be a thing of the past now that everyone had cell phones. Everyone but the Amish, of course.

However, she'd spotted a lone pay phone in a hall off the hospital lobby. She could call her friend, find out what she needed to know, and be done in time to meet Rosemary, Myra's English neighbor, in the lobby for the ride home.

Rosemary had been a huge help with rides over the past week. The church members had taken over everything else that needed to be done, but that they couldn't do.

The woman intrigued Anna. Childless, with a husband who traveled for work much of the time, Rosemary nevertheless didn't have a job. That fact had certainly worked out to the family's benefit this week.

Anna started down the hall at a quick pace, saw the woman at the reception desk glance up at her in surprise, and slowed down. That was something else to get used to. There was seldom a reason to hurry in Amish life, unlike the frantic pace of her routine in Chicago.

Her luck was in—the pay phone wasn't in use. She dug out a huge handful of coins and stacked them on the ledge. Now, if only Liz wasn't working the lunch shift . . .

The phone rang four times, and then the machine picked up. Anna bit her lip in frustration. When would she have another opportunity to call?

"Liz, this is Anna. Annie. I'm sorry to miss you—"

"Annie!" Liz picked up, cutting off her message. "Is it really you? Girl, I've been worried. Why haven't you called? Is Gracie all right? Where are you?"

It took a second to get back into the rhythm of Liz's rapid-fire questions. The last one Anna certainly didn't intend to answer.

"I'm fine. Gracie's fine. I'm sorry I didn't call sooner, but there hasn't been a chance."

"Nonsense."

Liz's sharp-tongued retort was typical. When Anna had first gone to work at the restaurant, she'd been more than a little scared of the woman. Liz had been a server at Antonio's for as long as the restaurant had been in business, and she didn't put up with slackers or sass.

Since Anna had worked hard and kept her mouth shut, Liz had had no complaint. She'd proved herself to be a true friend during the rough times.

"I've thought about you often, but things have been complicated."

Liz couldn't know how complicated. How good it would be to sit in Liz's cozy living room right now, feet up, eating popcorn and watching an old movie on television. That had been their favorite evening in, since Anna couldn't afford a babysitter and a trip to the movie theater.

"You can always find time to pick up the phone," Liz said, but there was affection under the tart words. "You sure that baby's okay?"

"She's doing great. Trying to walk, babbling all the time. She likes it here."

"So where is here? You haven't told me yet where you are."

Liz always came to the point. Anna didn't want to lie—probably couldn't lie. Liz knew her about as well as Leah did. Maybe better, in some ways.

"It's best if you don't know. Then you won't have to lie if Pete asks you."

"I don't mind lying to Pete," Liz said easily. "But maybe you're right, at that. If I don't know, I can't make a slip. And Pete's been making a pest of himself."

Anna's stomach tightened. She'd been telling herself that Pete would have given up by now, but she knew that underneath, she'd been afraid of this. "What did he do? He didn't hurt you, did he?"

"He did not. He knows I'd see his sorry self in jail before he could count to three if he laid a finger on me. Honest, sweetie, that's what you should have done instead of running away."

"Maybe so." But she wasn't like Liz. For all the bravado she'd shown when she left home, she had an innate reluctance to make a fuss, to draw attention to herself, and above all, to go to the law.

Amish didn't go to the law to solve their problems. If they were harassed too much to ignore, they'd move on rather than fight.

"Well, it was your choice. If you need money—"

"No, nothing like that." Anna knew perfectly well that Liz had little to spare. "I just want to know what Pete's been up to."

"Hanging out around the restaurant, 'til Antonio got fed up and threatened to call the cops. That made him back off, but he's talked to everyone you know, trying to find out where you've gone."

Her heart sank. "I hoped he'd forgotten about us. Maybe he really does care about Gracie."

"Well, he had a funny way of showing it if he did." Liz had a core of solid common sense, and it showed. "Knocking Jannie around the way he did, and then cutting out on her when she needed him the most. You take my word for it—this is just a whim. He thinks he wants the baby because he can't have her. That's Pete all over, always wanting what he can't have."

"I hope you're right." Prayed she was right.

Pete's sudden interest in Gracie was the one twist Anna had never expected. He'd signed the relinquishment papers giving up his parental rights before Gracie was born, doing it with a sneer and a cutting comment. Why did he have to come back?

Anna rubbed her forehead tiredly. She'd better wind this up before she ran out of coins.

"I wouldn't worry too much," Liz said. "He's either going to lose interest because it's too much work to go on looking, or he's going to end up in jail again for dealing. Either way, you don't need to be afraid of him."

"I'll try not to. Thanks, Liz. I hate to cut this short, but my ride's probably waiting for me."

"You kiss that baby for me, okay? And call me again when you can. And Annie? Don't worry. It's bad for you. Gives you wrinkles."

"Okay, okay," she said, laughing a little in spite of herself. "I'll call you again when I can."

She hung up but sat for a moment, pressing her fingers against her forehead, trying to swallow the lump in her throat. It had been so good to hear Liz's no-nonsense tones and even better to feel the sturdy affection that lay behind the words.

But the news Liz had delivered hadn't been what Anna had hoped. She'd longed to hear that Pete had disappeared back into the underworld he usually inhabited, and had lost interest as soon as she was gone, but apparently that wasn't the case.

She straightened, scolding herself. She couldn't give in to discouragement. She and Gracie were safe here. Besides, Myra and Joseph needed her. She couldn't desert them now.

The only trouble was that the longer she stayed, the harder it would be on everyone when she left.

Well, she'd deal with that when she had to. She rose, turned, and saw Samuel leaning against the wall opposite her.

Her temper flared. "Were you listening in on my phone call?"

He pushed himself away from the wall, no shadow of returning anger in his face. "It's not my business who you call, Anna. I was looking for you because Rosemary is waiting."

She'd almost rather he snapped back at her, instead of being so reasonable. "Sorry." She bit off the word and started back down the hall.

He fell into step beside her. "I tried to stay in touch with my English friends when I came back. But it just didn't work."

"Why not?"

He shrugged. "I guess we didn't understand each other's lives anymore. We didn't have anything to say to each other."

"That won't happen with Liz. We're too close for that."

He pushed the door open, holding it for her. "I hope you're right, if that's what you want. But maybe in the long run you'll drift apart. That doesn't mean the friendship wasn't strong, just that it was time for it to end."

In the long run she wouldn't be here. She might not be lying outright about that, but with every word, every thought, she was deceiving people. She'd thought it wouldn't matter, as long as Gracie was safe, but it did.

"I just want to go over the records for the shop." Joseph tried to push himself up from the rocking chair in which he'd been settled. He grimaced in pain, and Anna helped Myra ease him gently back down.

"I'll get the books, all right?" That was the last thing Anna thought Joseph should be doing after the exhausting day he'd had coming home from the hospital, but he'd reached the point of irrationality.

She exchanged glances with Myra and saw that her sister-in-law was thinking exactly what she was. If Joseph were a cranky toddler, they'd put him to bed no matter how he objected.

Daadi, sitting in the rocker across the room, cleared his throat. When Anna looked at him, he nodded slightly.

All right, she'd get the books. She headed out the back door, pausing on the porch step to listen to the stillness.

Dusk had settled over the farm, easing away the day's work, telling them it was time for rest. It reminded her of the storybook she'd read to Sarah and Gracie when she'd settled them in bed, all about the mother creatures of the farm putting their babies to sleep.

Thank goodness the rest of the family, except for Daadi, had finally gone home. They'd meant well, she supposed, gathering around to share the happiness that Joseph had left the hospital at last. But she'd seen the pain and exhaustion on his face.

She walked across the lawn, frowning when she realized that the shop door stood open, framing a rectangle of light from a lamp.

Samuel must still be there.

She stopped in the doorway. "Samuel, you are working late."

"Ach, not working exactly." His hand was arrested on the point of extinguishing the battery-powered lamp that stood on the workbench. "Just clearing up a little. What brings you out here?"

"Joseph. He won't settle down and go to bed. He wants to look at the records."

"He thinks I won't keep up with the paperwork, that's all." Samuel grinned, shaking his head. "And he'd be right about that. But should Joseph be taxing his eyes with figures?"

"Probably not, but he's past being sensible. Maybe if he sees for himself, he'll be content to go to bed where he belongs."

"Stubborn, that's what he is." Samuel pulled a dark green ledger from a shelf. "I will go in with you, if that is all right, and tell him everything is under control. He might believe it."

"I hope so." She waited in the doorway while he turned off the lantern and joined her. "*Is* everything under control?"

Samuel didn't speak for a moment, his face somber in the dimming light. "I'm not so gut as Joseph is at the work. Nor so fast. I'm thinking I should maybe send the gelding back to Mr. Bartlett. I'm not going to have time for him and the shop as well."

"You can't do that." The words were out before Anna thought about them. "The horses mean so much to you. You can't give that up. I mean, I'm sure Joseph wouldn't want you to do that," she added hastily.

"Denke, Anna." He stared across the fields toward his barn, as if longing to be there now. "But I can't let Joseph down when he needs me."

"I guess not." She couldn't argue with that. "Why not wait a few days before you do anything? Let things settle down a little before you make a decision."

"You give gut advice," Samuel said, smiling. "I'll think on that. Wait and see how Joseph is after he's had some rest."

"Rest is exactly what he needs. Even the trip home tired him. He should have been in bed hours ago, but he wouldn't go while people were here."

"Maybe he enjoyed the company after a week in the hospital."

"If it were me, I'd rather be alone."

He tilted his head, eyes crinkling. "Myra had a cat when she was little. Foolish creature tangled with a groundhog and came out the worse. The cat crawled under the barn to nurse its wounds, and Myra cried herself sick until I went in after it. I was bleeding worse than the cat by the time I got it out."

Anna found she was laughing as they reached the porch. "That's me, all right. Don't come near if you don't want to be scratched."

"I'll keep it in mind." He took a step toward the porch.

Anna caught his arm to stop him, and he instantly turned to her.

"Just one thing before we go in . . ." She should mind her own business, but she couldn't stop herself. "Remember what I said. Don't give up on the horse unless there's no other way."

He stood still, his gaze fixed on her face. "Denke, Anna." His voice was soft, his head tilting so that they were very close in the quiet evening. She felt the corded muscles of his arm, strong under her hand, his skin warm against her palm.

Her breath caught. His eyes seemed to darken, but maybe that was a trick of the light. The moment stretched between them, as fragile as glass.

Then he was turning to the house. "Maybe we'd best go in."

She nodded, moving quickly up the three steps to the porch and across it to the door. They'd better, before she let herself be so silly as to imagine she felt something for Samuel.

He followed her into the living room. Myra stood next to Joseph, her hand on his arm. "Komm now, to bed. The books will wait until tomorrow, ain't so?"

"Ja," Samuel said quickly. "There's nothing here for you to do tonight. Get some rest, and we'll talk in the morning."

Joseph shook off his wife's hand, frowning either from headache or frustration. "Everyone should just stop telling me what to do. I'm fine."

Myra looked at Anna—the wordless exchange of mothers who know the signs of overtiredness in young children. The sensation of understanding and being understood jolted her, coming so close on that moment outside with Samuel. A flicker of panic went through her. She didn't want to be fitting in here. She didn't belong here any longer.

Without a word, Samuel handed Joseph the ledger. Joseph opened it, stared at the page for a moment, and then slammed it shut, pressing a hand to his forehead.

"Useless," he muttered. "I'm useless. I can't even see the page to keep the books for you. What gut am I like this?"

Samuel's face tightened, a muscle twitching next to his lips. Anna knew what he was going to say, and she was helpless to stop him.

"I can handle the business until you are well. You must not fret over it. I'll send the gelding back to the Englischer so I can concentrate on the shop."

A protest rose to her lips, but she stifled it. This wasn't her business, remember?

"Oh, Samuel, you mustn't do that." Myra's face puckered. Poor Myra was on the verge of tears, worn out by her worries for Joseph and her fears about her pregnancy.

"Myra . . ." Anna wasn't sure what she intended to say, but she didn't get a chance.

"That is enough." Daad's voice was quiet, but it carried a firmness that wouldn't be denied, reminding them that he was the authority in the family. He rose from the rocking chair where he'd been sitting, watching them all. "Joseph, you are too tired to be thinking about the business. Your job now is to rest and get well so that you can care for your wife and family."

For an instant Joseph looked mulish, but then his gaze fell, and he nodded. "Ja, Daadi."

"There is no need for Samuel to give up his work with the horses. I have spoken to Daniel and Leah. Their boy Matthew will come every day, starting tomorrow, to work in the shop. I also will help. If more is needed, Mahlon can come in the evenings. Anna can take over the book work. She is gut with that."

He was telling them what to do without the least doubt that they would obey. For an instant the old rebellion flared in her.

She slammed the door on it. She was a woman grown, not a heedless teenager. If she expected the family to take her and Gracie in, she had to do her part.

"Ja, Daadi," she said.

"Komm now." Daadi took Joseph's arm, and Samuel moved quickly to his other side. "It is past time you were in bed."

CHAPTER EIGHT

Samuel led Bartlett's gelding toward the ring he used for training. He hadn't expected to have time to work with the animal today, sure that despite what Elias Beiler said, he'd have to give up training the animal until Joseph was well again.

That would mean giving up entirely, he was sure. The little he'd seen of Bartlett had suggested the man wasn't endowed with much patience. If Samuel couldn't do the work on his timetable, he'd find someone else.

But to Samuel's surprise, by three in the afternoon he and young Matthew had gotten through the day's work, and with a bit of assistance from Elias, they'd begun to catch up on tasks that he'd let slide while Joseph had been in the hospital.

Matthew was keen on anything mechanical—that was certain-sure. Daniel was going to end up being disappointed in his wish to see the boy a farmer. There wasn't much point in arguing with a God-given gift. Probably the younger son would be the farmer in the family.

So the burden of the shop had eased, but another had come to take its place. Samuel couldn't stop thinking about those moments with Anna last night.

They'd been talking, that was all, just being friendly. He'd even been thinking what a relief it was that Anna was talking to him as she might to a brother, instead of an enemy.

Then she had put her hand on his arm, and he'd looked into her eyes, and he'd felt as if the world were not steady under his feet. He'd gone on one of those carnival rides once, when he was a teenager, where the floor suddenly went out from under you. It had been like that—confusing and exciting all at the same time.

His life wasn't a carnival ride, and he wasn't looking to make a commitment to anyone. Maybe he never would be. The thought of his father sent coldness through him. So he had to show Anna that he wanted to be her friend. Nothing less, but nothing more, either.

It was about time to show Star that he wanted to be friends, too. He led the animal to the center of the ring and stopped, unclipping the lead line and holding him by the halter. Star was getting to know him now, and he consented to having his forehead rubbed.

Talking softly all the while, he let go of the halter and walked around the animal. Star's ears moved toward him, his eyes watching Samuel warily.

When he'd gotten behind him, he flicked the line lightly toward Star's rump. The gelding's head jerked up, the whites of his eyes showing, and he trotted toward the fence. Another flick of the rope sent him cantering around the ring.

Samuel kept his gaze on the horse, turning to face him as Star circled, flicking the rope occasionally to keep him moving. The animal had beautiful conformation and a smooth, fluid gait. Mr. Bartlett had chosen well when he bought him.

But something or someone had made the horse cautious, even afraid of humans. Samuel had asked around, knowing the interest horsemen had in other people's animals. Word was that Bartlett had been ready to give up on the animal before he'd shown up here. A pity that would have been to let one person's mistake ruin such a fine animal.

Samuel was barely aware of time passing as he worked the horse, first in one direction, then in the other. When Star finally began showing signs that he wanted to stop, Samuel coiled up the line, turning away from the horse as if losing interest.

His senses alert, he waited to see what the animal would do. Was he ready to extend some trust? Star took a few steps toward him, head down. Then a few more. Finally he nudged Samuel's shoulder with his nose.

Pleasure welled up in Samuel as he turned toward the horse, giving him a strong rub on the forehead. "You are a fine boy, you are."

He walked away a few steps. Sure enough, the gelding followed him. He circled to the right, letting Star follow, until he was facing Joseph and Myra's place. And stopped. Anna stood there, watching him.

The surge of pleasure he felt at seeing her was even stronger than his pleasure with the horse—strong enough to remind him of his decision. He must show Anna that he wanted to be her friend, nothing else. He couldn't let her feel awkward with him because of a moment's unguarded attraction. He also couldn't let her think there was anything more between them.

He walked toward her, the gelding following him. "I'm sorry," he said as he reached the fence. "I did not realize you were here."

"I didn't want to interrupt you when you were working." She was staring at Star, who had stopped a few feet away from the fence, eyeing Anna much as she did him. "Is this the same animal that was so skittish the last time I saw him?"

"He's settled down."

"You mean *you've* settled him down. I watched you working with him. That's amazing."

He shrugged. "Nothing so special about it—it just takes patience and gentleness."

"If that was all, anyone could do it. I've never seen a horse bond with a person so fast."

"Horses are herd animals, and he's missing his herd. I just helped get him wanting to be a part of my herd."

She looked unconvinced. "How can you possibly know what he wants? Honestly, Samuel, it's as if you can read his mind."

"Not his mind." He smiled at the idea. "But since the horse can't say what he's thinking or feeling, you have to learn to read his movements and reactions to understand him."

She thought that over, nodding slowly. "That's exactly what a mother does with a baby. Those first weeks are so scary, because you haven't a clue to what they want. And then, when you're ready to tear your hair out, you realize you've figured out what every cry and every movement is saying."

"It's much the same, I'd say." Her comments had set him wondering. "You had little Gracie from the time she was born?"

"Ja. Jannie never came out of the hospital after her birth." Anna's eyes clouded with the words. "She was able to hold the baby once, but that was all. Then she just slipped away from us."

He'd never met Jannie, but he could picture the scene just the same. "I'm sorry for your loss. It must have been ser hard for you."

"I loved her like she was my own sister. I guess I felt responsible for her, too, because she didn't have anyone."

Neither did you, Anna, he thought but didn't say. "Couldn't the doctors do anything for her?"

She shook her head. "They said Jannie might have lived a little longer if not for the stress of the pregnancy, but I know she never regretted having the baby."

"And you've never regretted taking her, that's clear."

"Not for a minute." Anna's lips curved in the way they did whenever she mentioned Gracie. "Even when she kept me up all night when I had to go to work early. Even when she scared me half to death running a fever."

What must it have been like for Anna, raised in a family and community that supported each member, to have dealt with such a life-changing experience all alone? He couldn't imagine.

"Gracie is lucky to have you."

Her eyes shone with unshed tears. "I'm the lucky one. She's exactly what I wanted most in the world, but I never knew that until I held her in my arms."

He hesitated. "Gracie's birth father—he doesn't want her at all?"

Tension tightened Anna's mouth. "He signed the legal papers giving up all his rights to her months before she was born. He just walked away."

The words set up an echo in Samuel's heart. His father had walked away, too. He'd thought that once he found his father, maybe he could understand his leaving, but he hadn't understood. He never would.

When he was growing up, folks had always said how much he was like his daadi. He'd thought then that nothing could be any better than that.

Anna was looking at him, maybe wondering why he was quiet for so long. Pain gripped his heart, and he tried to shove it away. Anna seemed to have the power to bring out all the thoughts and feelings he tried to forget, and for an instant that angered him.

"Did you want to see me about something?" The question was too sharp, honed by the unsettling memories of his father.

Anna blinked a little, her face tightening at his abrupt tone. She took a step back from the fence, as if she shouldn't be there.

"It's not urgent. I've put together a simple way for us to keep track of the income and expenses, that's all. I'm sure you want to work with the horse now, so I'll show it to you later."

She turned, walking away with her head erect.

He'd upset her. They'd been talking like friends about something that was painful to her, and he'd cut her off as if he didn't care. He didn't like himself much at that moment.

But maybe her anger with him was all for the best. He couldn't let Anna start to depend on him, because he didn't trust himself enough for that.

This was right, he reminded himself firmly. So why did it make him feel so bad?

People were staring at them. Anna sat next to Myra in the waiting room at the medical clinic. She clasped her hands together in her lap, staring down at them, and willed herself not to mind.

She'd forgotten what it was like to be the object of that rude gawking. In the city, she'd been one of thousands of people, all busy with their own concerns, not so much as making eye contact with those they passed in the street.

Here, in these clothes, she was an object of curiosity. She'd always hated that. She hated it now.

She glanced at Myra and gave herself a mental kick. She should be comforting Myra at this moment, not absorbed in her own feelings.

She touched Myra's sleeve. "Maybe it won't be much longer."

At least she didn't have to be concerned that anyone else in the waiting room would understand the dialect. That was one advantage of their differences.

"Ja." Myra grabbed her hand and clung. "This test—do you know anything about it?"

"Didn't the doctor tell you what to expect?"

Myra shook her head. "He told us all the risks of the test, and that I should have it anyway." Her fingers clutched and strained. "Anna, what if it hurts the baby?"

Anna wrapped the straining fingers in hers. "Listen, it's going to be all right. I remember when my friend Jannie had to have so many different tests, and she came through them fine."

"Did she have this amniocentesis?" Myra said the word carefully in English, there being no equivalent in Pennsylvania Dutch.

"Ja, she did." Anna had gone straight to the computer on campus then and looked it up, so that she and Jannie would be ready. "Why did the doctor say you had to have this test? Was it because of something that showed up on a blood test?"

Myra nodded. "The doctor said so. He has many Amish patients, so he knows about the inherited diseases."

That was one of the perils of being Amish. With most of the community descended from the same small group of ancestors, the chance of genetic abnormalities showing up was greater. Anna's heart twisted as she thought of her own healthy child.

"What will they do to me?" Myra's eyes clouded with worry.

"I'm sure the nurse will describe it to you." It might have saved Myra some apprehension if the doctor had explained when he'd ordered the test. "They'll do an ultrasound to see exactly where the baby is. Then the doctor will put in a long needle and take out a tiny amount of the fluid around the baby to test."

Myra closed her eyes for a moment. Anna seemed to see Jannie, face pale, closing her eyes at the prospect of yet another test, trying to shut out the bad things.

"Denke," Myra murmured, opening her eyes. "I feel better when I know what to expect." She patted Anna's hand and released it. "Let's talk of something else."

"All right. What?" She was willing to cooperate, although she suspected Myra wouldn't be diverted so easily.

"Are you sure you are willing to take care of the books for the business?"

"It's no trouble at all. I'm happy to help with the shop."

Except for the fact that Samuel seemed to be avoiding her these days. He still hadn't managed to find time to talk with her about the simple system she was trying to set up to keep track of expenses.

"You mustn't take notice if Joseph fusses at you about it. He thinks no one can do it but him."

"I won't let Joseph worry me."

As for Samuel—well, obviously he had been embarrassed by the foolish little surge of attraction between them. Maybe he'd thought she was growing too attached to him. Warmth came up in her cheeks at the thought.

"Something is wrong between you and Samuel," Myra said, again seeming to read Anna's thoughts.

Was she so transparent? Her first instinct was to deny it. "What makes you say that?"

Myra shook her head. "I know my brother too well. I can see what's happening. He likes you, and that makes him nervous."

"It's nothing—I mean, he doesn't like me that way. We're old friends, that's all."

Myra seemed to catch back a sigh. "He likes you," she repeated. "I saw it, and I hoped . . . Well, I know I shouldn't matchmake."

"No, you shouldn't." Anna's stomach twisted at the thought that people might have been talking about her and Samuel.

"He's never been exactly outgoing with girls. Slow and steady, that's our Samuel." Myra's smile had a tinge of sadness. "But after our daad left, it seemed like he turned inward. Mammi tried to get us to talk about it, but Samuel never would."

"He was about sixteen, wasn't he, when your daad jumped the fence?"

"Ja. We were all sad and hurt, but Samuel took it the hardest. He and Daadi were always so close, you see. Samuel just couldn't understand it. He couldn't talk about it, either."

Anna remembered when Ezra Fisher left. The valley had buzzed with little else for a couple of weeks. It wasn't unusual for a teenage boy to take off, but for a man in his forties with a wife and family—that was practically unheard of.

And then a few years later, Samuel had gone, too.

She hesitated, but the pressure to ask was too strong to ignore. "Was that why Samuel jumped the fence?"

Myra's face clouded. "I don't know, not for certain-sure. He never talks about it. But I think he wanted to find Daadi. To find out why he left."

"Did he?"

Myra shrugged. "He doesn't say. He came back when Mammi got so sick. He tries to act as if everything is the same as before, but it's not. I just wish he could be happy again."

Anna's throat was tight, and she couldn't seem to come up with anything reassuring to say. Whatever was going on with Samuel, it was all tied up with his father's desertion. She couldn't begin to understand him, but she knew enough to be sure that giving in to their mutual attraction would be a big mistake for both of them.

"Mrs. Beiler?" A nurse, clipboard in hand, looked inquiringly at them. "We're ready for you now."

Myra stood, her face white and set, and walked toward the woman.

Apprehension shivered through Anna, and she murmured a silent prayer as she followed them. If this was bad news, how would sweet, gentle Myra find the strength to cope with it?

Anna took a deep breath and slid down from Daad's buggy, reaching up to take Gracie as Daad handed her down. Already, a boy in his early teens was running up to take the horse and buggy and lead them off— that would be his duty at the worship service this morning. The buggies would be parked in neat rows, while the horses were tethered in the shade, content to stand there for as long as it took.

If she could have found any excuse to avoid attending church this morning, she'd have grabbed it. She'd suggested that she stay home to take care of Joseph, allowing Myra to go to worship, but Myra wouldn't hear of it.

Probably Myra was happy for some time alone with her family. She'd been unusually quiet in the two days since her amniocentesis, taking a nap Friday afternoon at Anna's urging and spending most of yesterday making a new dress at the treadle sewing machine.

Worrying, most likely. Anna dropped a light kiss on Gracie's forehead. Gracie smiled and patted her face in return.

The loving exchange heartened Anna. She glanced at her father. "I'll join Leah, Daadi. We'll be fine."

At least, she hoped they would. Sitting with a baby through a three-hour worship service could be a challenge, to say nothing of the fact that this was her first appearance at church since she'd returned.

"I'll walk over to her with you." Daadi held out his hands to Gracie, and the baby lunged toward him, smiling, already delighted with her grossdaadi after such a short acquaintance.

Daad must know Anna was apprehensive. Carrying Gracie, walking with her to where the women assembled before the worship service . . . that was a gesture of his support. Some of the tension eased out of her.

The service today was being held at the Stoltzfus barn. During the week, the family would have spent hours sweeping and scrubbing until it was as clean as any church building.

Anna still had vivid memories of how much work that preparation had entailed when they hosted church at the farm. Mammi had enjoyed it, though, almost as if all the preparation was a part of worship.

The benches would have come by wagon from the last host family. They'd be arranged in rows in the barn, along with copies of the Ausbund, the hymnal, even though most people knew the hymns by heart.

The white barn gleamed in the September sunshine. Beyond it, in the hedgerow, spires of sumac had already turned color, looking like so many flames.

Men stood in quiet groups or shook hands soberly, their white shirts, black pants and vests, and straw hats setting them apart from the world. When the weather grew colder, they'd add black jackets, and the straw hats would give way to black felt.

Daadi marched across the stubble of grass toward where the women were gathering, grouping themselves by age. Fortunately, Anna would be seated with other young mothers who'd probably be sympathetic if Gracie started to fuss.

She hoped so, anyway.

Heads turned to watch them as they passed. Probably her cheeks were pink. She kept her gaze down, trying to ignore their interest. It would be a poor repayment for Daadi's thoughtfulness if she gave in to the desire to glare at people.

Her story would have spread throughout the church district by now. Did they believe it? Or were they thinking, whispering, that Gracie was probably her out-of-wedlock child?

"Here is Leah." Daadi greeted Leah and her little daughter, Rachel, before handing Gracie back to her, kissing the baby's soft cheek as he did. "I will see you after worship."

"Denke, Daadi," Anna said, but he was already moving off toward the group of older men.

"Wilkom to worship." Leah touched her sleeve lightly. "It's gut that you are here."

"Brave, don't you think?" Anna lifted her eyebrows in a question.

"Ach, don't say that," Leah said. "Folks are just happy to see you back, that's all."

"I hope they'll still be happy after they see how Gracie is during the service."

Anna bounced the baby in her arms. She wiggled, reaching toward the ground, reminding Anna of how Samuel read the body language of the horse. Gracie was certainly making her wants known.

"You can let her down now, if you want," Leah said, glancing down at her two-year-old, Rachel, who was busy pulling up blades of grass.

"If I do, I'm afraid she'll scream when I pick her up again."

Leah smiled. "We've all heard that before. If you need to bring her out during the service, Mary Stoltzfus has a bedroom ready on the ground floor for changing and feeding."

"We'll probably have to use it."

The commonplace exchanges made Anna feel better. Leah was talking to her easily now, more like her old self again. Maybe all it would take to relax the constraint between them was time.

Leah had understood, at least a little, when she had left. Would Leah understand why Anna had come back?

Her mind backed away from that thought. She couldn't tell Leah all of it, any more than she could tell anyone else. If the community knew that Gracie's father was after her, what would they do?

She glanced at the sober faces around her, at the quaint, old-fashioned clothes, at the barn where they would worship. They wouldn't understand. How could they? They didn't have experience with anyone like Pete, and couldn't envision the ugly underbelly of society where he lived. They might think that as Gracie's father, he had a right to take her, no matter what papers he had signed. Even Daadi, with his innate fairness, might think that.

Anna's arms tightened around Gracie, and she recognized the truth. She'd been thinking that Leah was putting barriers between them, but she was just as guilty of that herself.

Anna was the one who didn't dare cross the boundaries. She couldn't trust Leah or anyone else with the truth about Pete, because she didn't know what they might do.

However she might wish it otherwise, the chasm between her and Leah could not be mended. Not now, at least, and maybe not ever.

CHAPTER NINE

racie slept on Anna's lap, lulled into an early nap by the long, slow unison hymns that had opened the service. The first time Anna had attended an English service, a praise band had led the congregation in music so loud and fast that it had made her head spin.

She'd come to appreciate the lively songs in time, and now the long, slow, quavering notes of an Amish hymn sounded almost like bagpipe music. She patted the sleeping baby gently. Gracie appreciated Amish hymns, it seemed, just as she did buggy rides.

Next to Anna, Leah sat with her head bowed. On her lap, Rachel folded and refolded a handkerchief, totally absorbed in the task. For just an instant Anna could feel herself at that age, sitting on Mammi's lap, doing the same thing.

On the other side of Leah her dearest friend, Rachel, for whom Leah's daughter was named, sat with her little ones close to her side. Anna had been cautious, seeing Rachel again, knowing that if Leah had talked to anyone about her rebellious sister, it would be Rachel. But Rachel had greeted her with a smile and a kiss.

Anna had never been quite so content as the teenagers here seemed to be. She glanced toward the section of benches where teenage girls sat, their dark dresses neat, white aprons pinned over them, heads bowed. Behind all that conformity, someone must feel as restless and rebellious as she had at that age.

And now here she was again, not restless or rebellious, just out of place. She was as separated from everyone else here as she was from Leah.

She bit her lip, staring down at her shoes. Maybe she was wrong about Leah. Maybe she could trust Leah with her fears about Pete. And even if she didn't, why did that have to keep them from being close? Everyone had secrets they didn't want to share.

And if you do, what then? her conscience asked. *Someday, when it's safe, you'll leave, going back to raise Gracie in the English world.*

When she did, she would break her sister's heart again. It would be even worse than the first time, worse than not being here when Mammi died. Grief took hold of her throat, so sharp and hard she could barely breathe.

Bishop Mose stood to deliver the long sermon. She tried to focus on his words, blocking out every disturbing thought.

The bishop began to speak about forgiveness, that cornerstone of Amish faith. Forgive as you would be forgiven. His voice was firm, but gentle and compassionate as always.

She hadn't expected to be bothered by the service today, beyond a little awkwardness. She'd assumed she could sit through it, saying her own prayers, thinking her own thoughts.

She couldn't. The detachment with which she'd been able to view the singing had vanished. Bishop Mose seemed to be speaking directly to her, and when he mentioned the Prodigal Son, she felt as if she'd been dipped in boiling water.

She tried to shut out his message. She couldn't. Her emotions battled, tearing at her, and she had to fight to keep back tears.

Gracie jerked awake on her lap, probably sensing her emotions, and started to cry. Anna cradled her, patting her, but it was no use. Gracie wailed, and Anna wanted to wail with her.

Murmuring an excuse to Leah, she slid out of the row, carrying Gracie quickly toward the door and out into the sunshine.

The moment they were outside, Gracie stopped crying as abruptly as if Anna had thrown a switch. She inhaled deeply, feeling her own anguish subside—still raw, but eased.

She jumped when Leah slipped an arm around her waist.

"Are you all right?"

"Ja. We're fine." She bounced Gracie in her arms as she started walking toward the farmhouse, pretending that Leah's concern was for the baby, not for her. "She stopped crying as soon as we came out."

"Gut." Leah walked beside her, holding little Rachel's hand. "But it was not Gracie I was worrying about. It was you."

Apparently Leah wouldn't let her get away with evading the question. Anna took another deep breath, trying to compose herself. She mustn't say anything, not when her emotions were so raw. It would be too easy to say more than she should.

She shouldn't, but the words burst out of her anyway. "I'm sorry." Her voice choked. "I wasn't here for Mammi. I'm so sorry."

"Oh, Anna." Leah's arms went around her, warm and strong and comforting, as they'd always been. "I know you must grieve over Mammi, but she loved you. She didn't blame you."

"I should have been here. I don't even know how—" She stopped, not sure she wanted to hear details.

Leah drew back so that she could see Anna's face. "Mamm was very peaceful at the end. I think maybe she always knew the cancer would come back, and she'd accepted it. She died at home, with Daadi holding her hand. She just seemed to slip away between one breath and the next, like stepping through a doorway."

Anna felt as if her heart were breaking. "I should have been here. How could she forgive me for not being here?"

Leah wiped the tears from Anna's cheeks. "You know the answer to that question, now that you have a child of your own. You never stop loving. Never stop forgiving."

"Ja, I guess so." She glanced at Gracie, who was staring at them with wondering eyes. "I just wish I had been here to say good-bye."

Leah patted her arm. "You're here now," she said simply. "That's enough."

She should say now that she'd be leaving. Say it quickly, before she hurt Leah again. But she couldn't. Gracie's safety was at stake.

You could stay. The voice spoke quietly in her heart, startling her with a possibility she hadn't even considered. *You could stay.*

No, she couldn't. She fell into step with Leah, moving toward the house.

She couldn't go back to living this way. Her independence was too important to her. She couldn't give that up.

But they love you here. They love Gracie. You could be safe.

They mounted the steps toward the porch. The scent of coffee floated out of the open door, announcing that someone was anticipating the end of the worship service. Voices came with the aroma, clearer as they moved into the house.

"... should be on her knees before the congregation, she should, not sitting there as if she's done nothing wrong—"

The speaker, realizing she had company, cut off her words.

Too late. Anna stopped, vaguely aware of Leah's arm going around her.

She couldn't deal with this. Clutching Gracie, Anna pulled free, turning to flee across the yard, stopping only when she realized that there was nowhere to go.

Leah reached her a second later, taking her hand. "Anna, it's all right. Don't listen to them. They don't know—"

Anna shook her head violently. "Don't. They only said what everyone else is thinking. I don't belong here anymore."

"Wait, here is another handful of receipts." Samuel passed the papers over to Anna, who sat next to him at Joseph's desk in the shop, trying to make sense of their bookkeeping.

She took the receipts, raising her eyebrows a little. "Are you sure that's all?" She obviously wasn't impressed with their system.

"I hope so." He hitched his chair a little closer to the desk, frowning at the stacks of papers. "I did tell you that I'm no gut at the paperwork, ain't so?"

"You did." She sorted through receipts, her face intent on organizing. "But you're not the only one. Some of these date from before Joseph was hurt."

"We get so involved in the work, you see." That wasn't much of an excuse, but Anna nodded.

"I didn't realize how busy the shop was. You have almost more work than you can handle," she said.

"Ja. Between the needs of dairy farmers to use machinery to meet government regulations and all the small businesses our people now run, it's commonplace to use hydraulic and air pumps powered by diesel engines. So that means more machines to be repaired or converted all the time."

"So Joseph's love of tinkering has paid off, I guess." But her face was shadowed when she said the words, and he suspected she was thinking of the accident. She didn't speak of it, though, just focused more intently on the receipts.

The activity did give him a chance to study her face and wonder how much she was hiding behind her concentration on the work. Myra had told him about Anna overhearing Mary Stoltzfus's unkind words, having heard about it in her turn from Leah. If Anna had thought to keep it quiet, she'd be disappointed.

Myra had been near tears when she told him. With all her tender heart, she wanted to see Anna settle down and be happy here.

Anna will not talk about it, she'd said. *She should. You try to get her to speak, Samuel. You've been through it, so you know.*

Ja, he knew. And he cared, but it was dangerous, talking to Anna about his time away. Talking would reveal his own still-raw places. And whether Anna would be helped if he did—that he didn't know.

Anna tapped a stack of receipts into neatness and fastened them with a paper clip. "You've got to do better," she said, frowning sternly at him. "You and Joseph both. These tax records have to be in order for the quarterly payment."

"Ja, I know." He ran his fingers around his collar. He had a healthy respect for the IRS, and he didn't want to make any mistakes, especially with Joseph laid up. "You tell me what to do, and I'll try to do it."

"I think the simplest thing would be for you to put every scrap of paper for the business into the boxes at the end of every day." She gestured to the small cardboard boxes she'd placed on the desk, one marked for income and one for expenses. "Don't try to enter them into the ledger. I'll take care of that."

"Gut, gut. Nothing would make me happier."

"I hope Joseph feels that way." A faint line appeared between her brows. "I wouldn't want him to think I'm interfering."

"He'll not think that. And even if he does . . ." Samuel hesitated. "You'd know it was just the pain and frustration speaking, ain't so?"

She nodded. "It's hard for him to be laid up this way, I know."

"He should be happy you understand so much about keeping the books. I'd be lost in a blizzard of paper if I tried."

A smile chased the worried look from her eyes. "My boss used to say that. The owner of the restaurant where I worked. He was a wonderful chef, but he couldn't keep track of finances at all, so I helped him with that. He liked to say that was why he gave me time off for my college classes."

"It sounds as if he was a gut friend," Samuel said, wondering how he could possibly lead the conversation into what had happened at worship. Myra was counting on him to do it.

"Antonio always said the people who worked at his restaurant were like family, and that's how he treated us. Jannie worked there, too. That's how we became close."

"I'm glad you had friends there," he said. "It can be lonely out there among the English."

She nodded, her eyes darkening, and he thought she'd experienced that loneliness, too.

"But you decided to come back," he ventured. "I guess, with the boppli, you wanted to raise her with your real family."

For a moment something a little startled showed in her eyes and was quickly hidden. Then she nodded. "Gracie has loved it here."

She almost sounded as if she were saying good-bye. Maybe he'd just have to be blunt about it.

"I heard what happened with Mary Stoltzfus yesterday. You are upset."

She pressed her lips together. "It was nothing. Do you have a copy of the last quarterly tax form?"

He passed the form over. "Ironic, that was. Seems to me Mary Stoltzfus would have been better off in the barn hearing Bishop Mose talk about forgiveness. Maybe she'd have learned something."

Anna's hands stopped moving on the ledger. She pressed them flat against the pages, staring down. He heard the soft inhalation of her breath.

"It's not easy to forgive," she murmured. "Or to be forgiven."

"No. It's not." He thought about his own return. Forgiveness was never easy, especially when it was yourself you had to forgive.

"When you came back . . ." she began, but then stopped, shaking her head. "Never mind. It doesn't matter."

"It does matter." He startled himself, as much as her, when he put his hand over hers on the ledger. He could feel her tension in the taut muscles. "I don't know that it helps you, but when I came back, I had doubts about belonging again. Fears about how other people would accept me, but mostly doubts about why I came back."

She looked up then, eyes surprised and intent. "You doubted yourself?"

He wanted to back away from it, deny that he doubted, then or now. It seemed a weakness, admitting it. But how could he help Anna's struggles if he didn't?

"I came back because my mamm was sick. I had to, and I wanted to. My family needed me." He paused, not wanting to put it into words. "I came back for gut reasons, but not because of faith. When I knelt before the congregation, I knew they forgave me, but I felt like a fraud." His voice thickened. "Sometimes I still do."

It was very quiet in the shop, so quiet that all he could hear was the sound of his own breathing.

Then Anna gave a little sigh. "Denke, Samuel. Thank you for telling me. For being my friend."

Friend. The word echoed in his mind. He had thought he wanted to be Anna's friend, but all at once he knew he wanted to be more than that. And the idea scared him half to death.

"*No,* no, Sarah." Anna gently removed the toddler, who was trying to reach the squeezer they'd set up on the picnic table in the yard, ready to do a big batch of tomatoes. "That's not for little ones. You and Gracie play with your ball."

She tossed the ball across the lawn and watched Sarah run after it, her sturdy little legs pumping. Gracie stood, waving both hands in the air as if she'd fly. Apparently deciding she could go faster crawling, she plopped onto her bottom and sped after her cousin.

"These tomatoes probably look like a bucketful of red balls to them," Myra said, pouring a pail of tomatoes into the hopper.

Anna shoved the wooden plunger down and began turning the crank. "Wouldn't they have a grand time with them? We once went to a tomato battle . . ." She let that sentence die out.

"You and your friend?" Myra didn't seem bothered by the mention of Anna's life in the English world.

Anna nodded, watching the tomato juice pour out of the squeezer into a bowl. "Jannie and some other friends. It was a tomato festival at the county fairgrounds."

Liz had gone. And Carl, the boy Anna had dated for a month or two before realizing they had nothing in common other than sitting beside each other in class. Pete had been there for a while, grumbling and complaining.

Then he'd disappeared for an hour and come back, bright and talkative. She should have realized what that meant, but she'd been too naive, and was just glad that Pete wasn't making Jannie miserable any longer.

"And they threw tomatoes at each other?" Myra cleaned the next batch, hands moving quickly as she cut out any bad spots.

"Ja." Anna smiled, forcing thoughts of Pete and his drug use out of her mind. "Picture a game of eck ball, only with tomatoes."

Myra giggled. "That sounds like fun. Nobody seems to play eck ball much anymore."

Eck ball, or corner ball, was a uniquely Amish sport. "Maybe boys don't like getting clobbered with that hard ball."

"You'd never get me doing it, that's for certain-sure," Myra said. She glanced at the tomato juice, seeming to measure the amount. "I was thinking I could cook down some sauce and make spaghetti when the family comes on Friday."

"I seem to recall everyone telling you that you weren't supposed to fix a thing," Anna said. "This is to be a chance for everyone to visit with Joseph, not to give you extra work."

"Ach, spaghetti is easy enough, and I know the children like it. Besides, it is Gracie's first birthday we're celebrating, so we have to make cake, too, ja?"

Gracie's birthday. Anna's heart clutched at the thought. "I can't believe she'll be a year old already."

"I know what you mean. When Sarah turned one—" She stopped, swinging around as the back door opened. Daad appeared, supporting Joseph as he made his way slowly out onto the porch.

"We thought we'd come out and watch you work," Daadi said.

Joseph nodded, pressing one hand against his ribs. "Got to make sure you're doing it right."

"You'd best be careful, or I might come after you with these tomatoes." Anna held up red-splashed hands.

Joseph chuckled and then groaned, clutching his ribs tighter. "Ach, don't make me laugh. It hurts too much."

"Then you'd best stay away from these two little girls." She nodded to Sarah and Gracie, who were rolling across the grass like a pair of puppies. "They're being a circus."

He smiled, his face looking less drawn every day, it seemed. "They make me feel gut." He settled in the chair Myra held for him, looking up into her face and saying something soft that made her smile and touch his cheek despite the tomato stains on her hand.

Anna's heart squeezed. The love between Myra and Joseph seemed to grow stronger with this adversity over Joseph's accident and with the waiting to hear the results of Myra's amniocentesis.

She had been waiting these past few days, too, and she wasn't sure what she was waiting for. A sign, maybe. Stay? Or go?

Her emotions had been all over the place. She hadn't even realized until she sat in worship on Sunday morning that she'd been considering staying. Thinking about being Amish again, forever. Committing herself to bringing Gracie up Amish.

Then had come that overheard nastiness, and she'd found it impossible to hang on to her emotions. Luckily no one had been there to see but Leah.

Of course they'd all found out anyway. If you wanted to keep anything to yourself, you'd better not belong to an Amish family, where one person's trouble or joy belonged to everyone.

She should have been annoyed that Samuel, of all people, had been the one to speak to her about it. Should have been, but wasn't. Samuel had been through this situation, so he knew. And he cared—cared enough to talk about his own deepest feelings to her.

Since then, they hadn't had a private conversation. They'd both been busy, constantly surrounded by other people. Still, if he'd wanted to, he could have found some excuse to be alone with her.

She glanced across the lawn. With the workday over, Samuel had gone on to his second job, working the big gelding. They were in the ring now. By this time, the horse was following him around like a puppy dog.

Daad gave her the next pail of tomatoes. "I thought I'd help you and let Myra have a break."

She nodded, watching as Joseph held out his arms to his small daughter. Myra bent over them, her hand moving, probably unconsciously, to stroke her belly.

"Are they going to be all right?" Anna asked the question softly, turning to her father as if she were a small child again.

"It will be as God wills." Daad's fingers closed over hers on the handle. "They will deal with whatever comes, with His help."

She nodded, tears stinging her eyes. Her emotions were just too close to the surface for comfort.

Daadi busied himself with cleaning the next batch. "Little Gracie likes to watch Samuel with the horses, doesn't she?"

Anna nodded, a little surprised by the change of subject. "Samuel certainly has a gift for training horses. I never thought he'd have that skittish animal practically eating out of his hand."

"Samuel knows how to be slow and patient. The creatures sense that. After all the troubles with his daad running away and his mamm dying, he's turned into a gut man." Daadi glanced at her, his eyes bright with curiosity.

She saw instantly what he was thinking, and she took a mental step back. Daadi would be only too ready to jump into pairing them up, just like everyone else in the community. Matchmaking was their favorite sport, far more popular than eck ball had ever been.

"Daadi, there's something I've been wanting to talk to you about." Something she should have done before this, probably. "About the family . . ." She paused, surprised that her throat had tightened up . . . "The family that I hit with the car."

That had been the determining factor that finally sent her over the fence. Driving an English friend's car, coming upon the Amish buggy on the dark road . . . For months she hadn't been able to remember any of it, and even now she remembered very little. But it had been the final straw in her rebellion, the thing that sent her careening into a world she had been ill-prepared for, for all her eighteen-year-old bravado.

"Aaron Esch and his wife and kinder," Daad said, seeming unsurprised. "Ja, what about them? They were shaken up, bruised a bit, but no one was seriously hurt. You knew that then."

She had known it, but only because Leah had told her. That should have been her first thought upon awakening in the hospital. Instead, she'd been wrapped up in her own concerns.

Glancing at Gracie leaning against Joseph's knee, Anna realized that even though the past years had been difficult, maybe they'd knocked the selfishness out of her.

"I never talked to them. I never told them how sorry I was. There must have been a lot of damage to their buggy, too." She had just walked away, taking refuge with her English friends, and leaving her family to deal with the consequences.

"I took care of having their buggy repaired. That was only right." Daadi's face was grave, not minimizing what had happened, but not accusing her either. "Those Englischers, the ones that owned the car, I heard they wanted to give Aaron money so he wouldn't go to court, but naturally he wouldn't take it."

Naturally. That wasn't the Amish way, and they wouldn't take money for following the Ordnung, the unwritten rules by which all the Amish agreed to live.

"I wish I could repay you for that. It must have been a lot—"

Daadi stopped her with a hand on her arm. "There's to be no talk of repaying between family, Anna. You are my child. Would you want little Gracie to repay you?"

"Gracie hasn't broken the law. Or broken her mother's heart." Her throat choked on the words.

"Perhaps a mother's heart is made to be broken, over and over," he said gently. "That seems to make it stronger. As for the Esch family, if you want to ask their forgiveness, you can. Why don't you mention it to Esther? They're her second or third cousins, so she'd know how to talk to them."

"I will." She'd forgotten that Mahlon's wife was kin to the family. Asking their forgiveness wasn't much, but it would go a little way toward clearing up the mess she'd made before she left.

"And while we're talking about cars . . ." Daad paused, studying her face. "I'm thinking it might be time for you to get rid of the car of yours that's sitting in Joseph's barn."

She could only stare at him, astonished at the strength of the negative feelings that rose in her at the words.

She'd been thinking about staying, true. But to get rid of the car . . . maybe her reaction was telling her that she wasn't ready for that at all.

CHAPTER TEN

*A*nna walked along the road toward Rosemary's house, two loaves of pumpkin bread in the basket on her arm, with a sense almost of having escaped. She ought to feel guilty for thinking that, but it had been so long since she'd been alone that she couldn't seem to help it. She loved her family. She was grateful to them for taking her and Gracie in. Still, she couldn't help the feeling of being slowly smothered.

That was what she missed most about life in the English world. Not the presence of electricity at the flick of a switch or the ability to flip on the television and see what was happening in the world.

No, what she missed was more basic than that. Independence. The ability to live her own life and think her own thoughts. Most of all, sometimes just to be alone.

She turned in at Rosemary's mailbox, walking down the gravel driveway toward the house. The loaves of pumpkin bread she carried were a thank-you from Myra, who'd been fretting that she hadn't done anything to repay Rosemary for all the rides she'd given while Joseph was in the hospital.

The drive rounded a stand of hemlocks and the house came into view. A long, stone one-story, it sat in an L-shape around a fieldstone courtyard furnished with a loveseat, chairs, and an umbrella-topped table. A gas grill snuggled against one of the walls, looking far more elaborate than most people's stoves.

When Anna reached the door, Rosemary pulled it open before she could ring the bell.

"Anna, how nice! It's good to see you. How's Joseph doing? And

Myra? Is the business going okay without him?" She took Anna's arm, practically hauling her into the house.

Smiling at the enthusiasm, Anna handed Rosemary the basket. "Some pumpkin bread from Myra, with all her gratitude for your kindness. And they're well." It took a moment to adjust to speaking English again, but then it seemed the most natural thing in the world. "Joseph is pretty antsy at not being able to do things, of course."

"Of course. Men are always terrible patients." Rosemary headed for the back of the house, beckoning her. "Come into the family room and have some coffee. I'm dying to talk to you."

Anna followed her past a formal dining room and equally formal living room. "You have a lovely home."

Lovely, but the rooms were so perfect they didn't look as if anyone used them.

"It's all right." Rosemary seemed to dismiss the space. "We really live back here."

The hallway opened into a large family room where sunshine streamed through a skylight. The kitchen was in one corner, separated from the rest of the room by a counter. White leather couches formed a semicircle in front of a stone fireplace. The glass panels of French doors gave a view of a landscaped garden with a decorative pond in the center.

Rosemary was in the kitchen, already pouring coffee into two mugs. "You will have coffee, won't you? You just have to stay and visit."

"Yes, thank you." Whether you were English or Amish, a cup of coffee was always a good excuse to sit and talk.

"Over here." Rosemary, carrying the mugs, led the way to a round table next to the doors.

Anna joined her, inhaling the scent of the flavored coffee. "What a lovely garden."

"Not bad," Rosemary said. "But it doesn't really fit here." She shrugged. "We thought we wanted to live in the country, but then we built a house and put in a garden you could find in the suburbs of any big city. Weird, isn't it?"

"Maybe so." Anna hadn't been thinking that, but now that Rosemary had pointed it out, she realized that what she said was true. The house and garden were a contradiction in the middle of farmland.

"So tell me." Rosemary leaned toward her across the table. "I've been hearing about you coming back after, what was it . . . three years away?"

"About that." Apparently it was too much to hope that the English, at least, wouldn't be interested.

"Why come back after that long? Because of the baby, I suppose." She answered her own question.

"Yes, because of Gracie." That was true, though not for the reason most people seemed to think.

"So this story that the baby is actually the child of a friend—is that true?"

Anna felt reasonably sure her mouth was agape.

Rosemary laughed. "That's me, tactless to the end. Sorry about that, but I figure if you want to know something, you ought to come right out and ask."

Anna found she was returning the smile. The words had been said in such a friendly tone that it was impossible to take offense. Rosemary reminded her of Liz . . . forthright and honest.

"I don't mind telling you. Yes, Gracie really is the daughter of a close friend who died shortly after she was born. There wasn't any other family."

"Sad. But the baby has ended up with plenty of relatives now, right?"

"Right."

"We built this big house thinking we'd have babies to fill it." Rosemary's eyes were shadowed. "It hasn't happened. Not yet, anyway."

"I'm sorry." She wanted to ask what the doctors said about Rosemary's chances of getting pregnant, since she wanted it so much, but she barely knew Rosemary, despite the woman's quick friendliness.

"No sense in brooding about it. That's what my husband says." She waved her hand, as if trying to dismiss the subject. "You must have found it tough, getting used to the real world after growing up Amish. How on earth did you manage all alone?"

"I had some English friends who helped at first." They'd soon fallen away, though. They weren't family. "Even so, I wasn't nearly as prepared as I thought I was. Getting a job, finding a place to live, getting my GED—all of it was new."

Funny, that no one else had asked that. Her family seemed to consider her life out there a blank page. Samuel, who knew what it was like more than anyone, had only talked about the adjustment of returning.

"Rough." Rosemary took a gulp of her coffee. "Was any of it what you expected? Was it worth it?"

She considered. "The independence was great. Just being able to decide things for myself was so different from anything I was used to."

"Yeah, but there are downsides to that—like not having anyone care if something happens to you." Rosemary sounded as if she understood that personally.

Anna nodded. That had been the worst of it. "I made friends, eventually. People who became like family to me." She shook her head. "I'm sorry. I'm talking too much about myself. Tell me about you. Where are you from?"

That was always a safe question in the outside world. People always seemed to be from someplace other than where they were. If you asked an Amishman that question, he'd look at you blankly.

"Originally Los Angeles." She shrugged. "My husband changed jobs a lot at first. Always onward and upward. You know how that is. We saw this area when we were driving to Pittsburgh for a job interview. He had this vision that we'd settle down in the country, live close to nature, and he'd quit working so hard, but he never will." She lifted her hands in a giving-up gesture. "He's gone most of the time. Truth is, I'm bored."

That was how Anna had always felt as a teenager, bored out of her mind by the sameness of life here. Now—well, now she didn't have time to be bored. Amish or English, she didn't have time for that, not with a child to raise.

"So tell me." Rosemary's curiosity apparently wasn't slaked yet. "Are you really going to stay?"

The blunt question gave her pause. She thought about her reaction to Daad's comment about getting rid of the car.

"I don't know," she said honestly. She glanced at the clock. "I should be getting back."

"Do you have to?" Rosemary shook her head. "Well, sure, you've got stuff to do, I know. That's the Amish. Always busy. Maybe if I didn't have electricity, I wouldn't be bored." She smiled, standing when Anna did. "Listen, come back any time. Whenever you want to feel like an Englischer again."

"Okay, I will." Funny, how easy it was to fall back into an English way of speaking.

"Great." Rosemary gave her a quick hug. "See you later."

Maybe Rosemary just wanted someone to talk to, but that didn't really matter. Anna had found a friend, and she hadn't even realized that she needed one.

Anna stood on the back porch, Gracie in her arms, watching the family gathered in the backyard for the picnic. With the meal over, adults settled in their seats to talk, while the children, too restless to wait for the cake and ice cream, chased each other around the yard or lined up for turns at cranking the handle of the ice cream maker.

Once again Anna had that dizzying sensation of seeing them as an outsider did. Who were they, these people who dressed so strangely and spoke a different language? That was what an outsider would see.

An outsider would see her as one of them. Same clothes, same language, same mannerisms—quiet, unassuming, humble. No outsider could look at her heart and know what was happening there. Sometimes even she couldn't.

Gracie tugged at Anna's kapp string, one of her favorite occupations. Anna caught the chubby little hand and kissed it, making Gracie laugh. Certainty settled in her.

What she felt or didn't feel at this moment didn't matter. The only important consideration was keeping Gracie safe.

"Anna, you're keeping that beautiful boppli to yourself, ain't so?" Mahlon's Esther hurried up the porch steps, Mahlon close behind her. "Let me put these dishes in the kitchen, and then I want to take her."

She paused to coo at Gracie. "She remembers Aunt Esther, don't you, little schnickelfritz?"

Gracie babbled something incomprehensible, clasping her hands and then stretching them up, as if ready to fly out of Anna's arms.

Anna was swept with the need to hold her close. *Don't be so eager to fly away, little bird. You need your mammi still.*

Would she ever feel ready to let Gracie go? Somehow she doubted it.

Mahlon held out his hands to Gracie. "Come and see me, little one."

Gracie hesitated for a moment, giving him a coy smile. Then she lunged into his arms. Laughing, he lifted her over his head, making her shriek with glee.

"Careful," Anna warned. "She just had her supper. You don't want applesauce and mashed potatoes all over you. Maybe I should take her."

Mahlon settled Gracie high in his arms. "You're just jealous because she wants Uncle Mahlon now. I'll look after her." Before Anna could answer, he marched off the porch with the baby.

Gracie would be fine with him. Maybe Mahlon didn't know a lot about babies yet, but he wasn't the careless boy he'd been. He was a grown man, perfectly capable of watching Gracie. Probably he and Esther would be starting a family of their own before long.

Anna should be helping Myra bring out the birthday cake instead of standing here worrying. She headed for the kitchen, her thoughts flickering to the girl she'd been. That girl had never taken responsibility for a thing, if she could help it. She couldn't have imagined how she'd feel as a parent.

"Anna, look at the cake Leah brought." Myra was cutting thick slabs of chocolate cake. "Barbara brought snitz pies. Maybe get that cream out to go with. And the birthday cake is all ready except for lighting the candle."

Nodding, Anna went to the propane refrigerator for the whipped cream. She had made the cake herself that morning, yellow cake with white frosting, trimmed with pink icing. She wasn't good enough with icing to write Gracie's name, but Gracie wouldn't know.

There would be no photos to hold the memory. The ban on cameras irked her, but then, she wasn't likely to forget this day. "Shall I take coffee out then?"

"Ja, that would be fine." Myra looked up, her cheeks flushed. "Joseph looks gut tonight, ain't so?" Her eyes grew concerned. "I was afraid he'd be too tired for this. You don't think it's too much for him, do you?"

Anna glanced out the kitchen window. Joseph sat in the rocking chair they'd carried out for him, a pillow at his back to cushion the sore ribs and a footstool under his feet. He was deep in conversation with Samuel and Leah's Daniel, young Matthew nearby listening in respectfully to his elders.

"Joseph looks fine right now," she said. "We can keep a close eye on him in case he starts getting tired."

"Ja, you're right." Myra shook her head. "I worry too much, but . . ." She hesitated, and Anna knew without more being said that she was thinking about the babe she was carrying and the test results she was still waiting for. "I'm glad you're here, Anna. I don't know what we'd do without you just now."

"I'm glad, too," she said, picking up the coffeepot.

To her surprise, that was true. The trouble with the car that had landed her at Joseph and Myra's door seemed to have brought her to the right place at the right time. Whatever the future, she was here with them now.

The future. She carried a tray with cups and coffeepot to the door, pushing the screen open with her hip. Let her mind go there, and it would start spinning again. With no money and no viable transportation, she couldn't leave now if she wanted to.

Samuel saw her coming. He jumped up to take the heavy tray from her, his fingers brushing hers. "I'll carry that for you."

"Denke, Samuel." She withdrew her hands quickly, afraid someone might see. Might comment.

"He just wants you to hurry back for the cake and pies," Joseph said, smiling. "He's still hungry."

"I think you're talking about yourself, Joseph," Daniel put in. "A man needs plenty to eat when he's recovering, ain't so?"

Joseph patted his lean stomach. "Wouldn't hurt, I guess."

"There's a piece of cake and pie with your name on them," Anna assured him.

She glanced around for Gracie, and found her sitting in the grass with Sarah. They both had small wooden toys their grossdaadi had carved for them—a duck for Sarah and a dog for Gracie. The end of the picnic table held a stack of other gifts for the birthday girl.

Sarah held up the duck in front of Gracie's face. "Quack, quack, duck."

"Quack," Gracie parroted. Everyone laughed, and Daadi bent to pat her head.

Heart full, Anna turned back to the kitchen for the birthday cake.

When she came back out, the mood had changed. She sensed it the moment she approached the adults, reading it in the lowered voices and troubled faces.

"What is it?" She put the tray of cake down.

"Nothing," Mahlon said quickly. "It's nothing."

"Barbara was just telling us the gossip that's going around," Samuel said evenly, his gaze meeting hers.

A surge of gratitude went through her. Samuel understood better than anyone that she'd rather know than guess.

"What are they saying?" She stood stiffly at the end of the picnic table, feeling like the accused.

Barbara's normally ruddy cheeks were flushed even more. "Levi says I should have kept my mouth shut, and maybe he's right. But that Mary Stoltzfus is just plain mean-spirited."

"Barbara . . ." Levi said.

"Well, she is." Barbara glanced at her boys, chasing each other around the oak tree. "Maybe because she had no kinder of her own, she always thinks she knows more than anyone. Well, she was wrong about our Anna, and I told her so right to her face, right there in Mueller's store."

A mix of feelings roiled in Anna—surprise that Barbara had stood up for her mingled with annoyance that she'd done it in so public a place, along with anger at Mary Stoltzfus and her interfering.

"What is she saying?" She managed to say the words evenly.

Barbara's color deepened to a dull brick shade. "That little Gracie is really your child, and that the rest of the story is a pack of lies. And I said to her, 'Mary Stoltzfus, you should be ashamed and on your knees in front of the congregation yourself. Elias Beiler himself saw the papers making Gracie our Anna's adopted child, and the bishop is the one to know Anna's heart, not you.' That's what I said, and I'd say it again." She looked around, as if wanting someone to argue with her.

Anna couldn't say a thing. That Barbara, of all people, should be the one to spring to her defense—well, as Samuel had once pointed out to her, she'd never given Barbara much cause to like her. Her throat was almost too tight to speak, but she had to.

"Denke, Barbara. Denke."

She'd have tried to say more, but Gracie picked that moment to take two wavering steps. Even before Anna could exclaim about it, Gracie suddenly seemed to realize what she was doing, wobbled, and fell onto her hands and knees. More surprised than hurt, she burst into tears.

Daadi reached her before anyone else could. "There, there, little one." He scooped her up in his arms, cradling her against his chest. "You're all right, ain't so? You're just learning to walk. It takes a few tumbles to learn something new."

Gracie sniffled a time or two and smiled, with an effect like the sun coming from behind the clouds. She patted his beard. "Ga-da," she announced proudly.

"Ach, she's trying to say grossdaadi, the little dear," Esther said.

Murmurs of agreement, of love, sounded. Daadi's eyes were bright with tears as he smiled and kissed Gracie.

Anna tried to swallow the lump in her throat. She wanted Gracie to be safe, and so she was. The family would give Gracie more than Anna ever could alone.

And if, in the end, she decided they should leave, at least Gracie would have known their love.

Longing welled up in her. Anna wanted to say something, do something, that would show what her heart couldn't express.

She thought of the car—two cars, really. A car had taken her away from them, and another had brought her back again. That was the car that was parked in the barn, mute cause of Joseph's pain.

She patted Gracie, secure in her grossdaadi's arms. "Daadi, I think it's time to get rid of the car. Do you know someone who would haul it away?"

He nodded, his eyes bright, his expression telling her that he knew exactly what she was saying.

"Ja, Anna. I will take care of it for you." He clapped his hands, getting everyone's attention. "Komm, it's time we lit the candle on that birthday cake."

Anna slipped out the back door into the dusk, much as she had when she'd been a teenager. Back then, she'd have been planning to hitch up Mamm's buggy and go off to meet her friends, sometimes Amish but more often English.

Now, she simply wanted a few minutes to herself—that, and to find the toy dog Daadi had carved for Gracie. Somehow in the midst of all the cleaning up, the toy hadn't made it back into the house.

She stepped down off the porch and switched on the flashlight she carried. She'd never find the small object in the grass without it. If the house had electric lights on the outside, as so many English farmhouses did, she could throw a switch and illuminate the whole area.

The Amish dictum had usually been that if it runs on batteries and doesn't depend on a connection to the power grid, it's acceptable. With the advent of so many other battery-operated gadgets, from boom boxes to cell phones and iPods, the lines had to be drawn over and over again.

She swept the flashlight beam across the yard in an arc. Could she get used to this way of life again?

She could give up electric lights, she supposed. But could she give up her independence after all she had gone through to get it?

The flashlight beam picked up a glimmer of white, and she stooped, but it was only a paper napkin, probably blown off the table.

She wanted to give Gracie the best life possible. Was an Amish life the best for her? What about college, a profession, all the things that the outside world considered important? The more she thought about it, the more she felt as if her head would explode.

"Have you lost something, Anna?" Samuel's voice came out of the dark beyond the range of her light. She swung around, the beam striking his blue shirt, his tanned face.

He put up a hand to shield his eyes from the glare, and she lowered the torch immediately.

"I'm sorry. You startled me. I didn't realize anyone was out here."

"Just making the rounds of the barn and henhouse," he said, moving closer.

"Don't you need a light for that?"

He gave a low chuckle. "It's not dark out yet, Anna. Switch that off and let your eyes get used to it. You'll see."

When she didn't move, he put his hand over hers on the flashlight and turned it off. She began to protest, and he held up his hand.

"Just wait."

They stood, not speaking. The rhythm of the evening settled over her—the rustle of the breeze among the tall sunflowers along the fence, the chirp of crickets, the lonely call of some night bird, answered by the whoo-whoo of an owl.

Her tumbling mind seemed to still along with her body. She inhaled. Exhaled. Saw the rhythmic flashes of the lightning bugs rising from the grass.

Gradually, as if the lights went up slowly in a theater, she realized she could see. Her eyes picked out the picnic table, the chairs, even a ball one of the children had forgotten. And there, in the grass almost at her feet, the small carved dog.

She bent and picked it up, closing her fingers around the smooth wood. "This is what I was looking for. Daadi made it for Gracie. I must have dropped it when I was taking her in."

"Ja?" He took the dog from her, turning it over in his hand. "I saw her playing with it, but I didn't realize Elias made it. He's a gut grandfather, he is."

"And father." Daadi understood so much, it seemed. All the things she didn't say.

"Ja." The word came out a little rough, and she remembered about his own father, who'd lost himself voluntarily in the English world, leaving his family to fend for themselves.

"I heard what you said to him about the car," Samuel said. "It's ser hatt for you, giving that up."

So hard. She nodded. "That car was the first one I ever owned. The only one, maybe. I guess it meant freedom to me."

"Ja, I know. I wanted a car first thing when I jumped the fence."

She should go in, but it sounded as if Samuel wanted to talk. Given Myra's worries about him keeping everything to himself, she couldn't discourage him. She sat on the picnic bench and patted the space next to her.

"Komm, sit for a minute. Tell me about it."

He folded his long frame onto the bench, propping one elbow on the table behind them. "Not much to tell. I found out that it's not so easy to get a car when you don't have a job or a credit card or even a telephone." He shook his head. "I was so green. Totally not ready for what it was like out there."

She studied his face in the dim light. "Why did you go, then? It seems so out of character for you. You were never a rebel."

"Like you," he said, his teeth flashing in a smile.

"Like me," she agreed, not even sure now what had been so important about that rebellion of hers.

Samuel looked down, his face growing serious. "It was my daad's leaving, first off. It unsettled all of us. I kept trying to fill his shoes, thinking I'd be able to go on without him."

"But you couldn't," she finished for him.

"I tried. I got baptized into the church, I courted Rebecca Miller, and we talked about marrying. But the closer it came, the more doubts I had. Mamm was still grieving about Daad, and I couldn't seem to feel right about anything, not knowing why he'd left. I got it into my head to go after him."

It made sense, and it also made her reasons for leaving seem frivolous in comparison. "You risked so much."

"I did. The church doesn't look lightly on baptized members leaving. I could have talked to Bishop Mose, explained what was in my mind. That's what I should have done. Instead I went running off, not telling anyone what I intended, hurting my family even worse."

His voice roughened, and the sound hurt her heart.

She touched his hand lightly, wanting to comfort him. "I'm sure your mamm understood."

"I hope so. But it pained her. It made it seem like I was siding with him." His fingers curled around hers, as if he needed something to hang on to.

"Did you find him?"

He was still for so long that she thought he wouldn't answer. Then he took a ragged breath.

"I found him. You know, I pictured him living in a shack someplace, maybe drinking himself to death, ashamed of what he'd done." His fingers clutched tighter and he stopped, as if he couldn't go on.

"It wasn't like that," she guessed, trying to help him along.

"No. Instead I found he had a whole different life, living with a woman who had a farm outside Columbus, Ohio. He looked prosperous and happy. He was so at ease that you'd think he'd never lived any other way, even though it was her money that put the clothes on his back and the car in his driveway, I'd guess." His words were heavy with bitterness.

"I'm sorry." Anna tried to imagine it and couldn't.

"I felt like I'd never known him. Like maybe he didn't even know himself."

Through the bitterness, she sensed what it was that Samuel feared. She longed to comfort him as she would Gracie.

"You're not like him. You're not."

"I hope I'm not. But how would I know for sure? When I came back, Rebecca wanted to pretend my leaving had never happened, but I couldn't. I couldn't marry her, not knowing if I wouldn't suddenly make up my mind to walk away."

"You wouldn't," Anna said again, searching for a way to convince him of what she saw so clearly. "You're not someone who gives up once you've set your hand to something."

Surely his endless patience with the horses, his steadfast determination to run the shop for Joseph, proved that.

He was shaking his head, and she put her hand to his cheek, wanting to stop him. To comfort him. But his skin was warm against her hand, and the touch sent that warmth shimmering along her skin.

He looked at her, something startled and aware visible in his eyes even in the dim light. The breath caught in her throat.

Then his head came down, and their lips met. She ought to pull away, but she couldn't. She caressed his cheek, felt his arms go around her, drawing her close, and lost herself in his kiss.

After a long, dizzying moment he drew his lips away slowly. Reluctantly, it seemed. He brushed a trail of kisses across her cheek before he pulled back and looked at her.

"I didn't mean for that to happen," he said gravely.

"Neither did I." She could only be surprised that her voice sounded so calm.

"But I'm not sorry." A smile lit his face with tenderness. "I'm not sure what it means, but I'm not sorry."

He rose, clasped her hands for an instant and then let them go. "Good night, Anna. I'll see you tomorrow."

She put her fingers to her lips, watching him stride off toward his place until the gathering dusk hid him from view. She didn't know what it meant either, but for once, she wasn't running away.

CHAPTER ELEVEN

*A*re you still working on that old corn binder?"

Samuel looked up at the sound of Joseph's voice to see him leaning in the shop doorway. "As you can see. This time I'm going to get it working if I have to rebuild it from scratch. Should you be out here?"

Joseph moved a few more steps, listing a bit, and lowered himself to the wooden chair next to the desk. He was still hurting, clearly.

"Not according to your sister. She put me in a chair in the yard like she was putting a puppy in a pen and told me to stay there."

Samuel grinned. "Myra's getting a bit bossy, I'd say. Still, maybe you ought to go back out there and behave before she catches you. She might blame me."

Although truth to tell, he was glad to have some company about now. It might keep him from reliving over and over those moments with Anna last evening. He kept catching himself staring into space with a silly grin on his face.

"Ach, it's not going to hurt me to sit here a bit instead of out there in the yard. I'll take the blame if Myra catches me."

"That you will." Samuel tinkered with a stiff bolt, finding that his stubborn imagination still refused to be diverted from the image of Anna's face in the moonlight.

The why of it was simple, wasn't it? Anna had been a lovely girl, one anybody would want to kiss. When she'd come back, a grown woman, he'd thought at first that she looked hard, with her English clothes and her tight, wary expression.

Changing to Amish dress had made her fit in, but it had taken time for the wariness to fade. She probably hadn't even realized how her expression had countered her clothing.

Now it seemed that the bright, sassy manner and pert look of her teenage years had mellowed into a very appealing maturity.

Joseph's chair squeaked as he moved. "Do you think Anna is settling down all right?"

The question, coming out of the blue, made Samuel instantly guilty. Did Joseph know about last night? How could he? Anna wouldn't have gone in the house and said she'd been kissing him—that was certain-sure.

Samuel cleared his throat. "She seems contented enough."

At least he thought that was true. They had all been too busy since the accident to do much sitting around and thinking, except for Joseph, who probably had too much time for that.

"Ja, she does," Joseph agreed. "And she's keeping busy, what with helping Myra and taking care of the boppli."

"Then what has you so worried?" A thread of uneasiness went through Samuel.

"I guess I was just thinking about the girl she used to be, always running from one thing to the next, always so enthusiastic. She's changed."

Samuel sat back on his heels. Joseph's thoughts were following the same trail as his, though not for the same reason.

"She's grown up, is all. She probably took some hard knocks out there in the English world. That would change anyone." It had changed him.

"I guess." Joseph's gaze seemed to look into the past. "When I think about how she used to be, I remember that we all wished she'd settle down, especially when every boy in the district was looking at her." He smiled. "You, too, as I recall."

"Ach, no, not me." Samuel studied the bolt he'd just detached. "Well, maybe I looked at her from time to time. Such a pretty girl, who wouldn't look?"

"Well, then," Joseph began.

"I knew she'd never have time for someone like me," he added quickly. "I was too much a stick-in-the-mud for Anna."

He hadn't been last night, though. He wasn't the only one enjoying that kiss. They'd both grown and changed in the past three years.

"That Anna never wanted to take responsibility for anything." Joseph stretched a bit and then winced, putting his hand to his side. "Then the baby was dropped in her lap. Nothing takes more responsibility than being a parent does."

"True." Samuel gave Joseph a questioning look. "But I'm thinking you surely didn't come out here to talk about how your sister has changed. What is worrying you about her?"

"Not worrying, exactly." Joseph linked his hands together. "Just thinking about Myra and the new boppli. Myra's getting so she depends on Anna a lot."

Samuel mulled that over for a moment. "You're afraid Anna might go off and leave Myra flat, is that it?"

He had to admit that the thought had crossed his own mind a time or two. The longer someone spent in the English world, the less likely it was that he or she would ever come back to stay.

"It could happen. I don't want to think that, either for Anna's sake or ours." Joseph's forehead furrowed, the lines of his face deepening. "Myra needs all the support she can get right now. This worrying about the boppli . . ." He let that trail off.

"I know," Samuel said softly. "I am praying about it, too."

Joseph nodded, the corners of his mouth pinching in. "If only there was something I could do to make this waiting easier for Myra. Whenever she sees me looking at her, she puts on this smile like everything is fine. It near to breaks my heart."

If Joseph could do something, anything, he probably wouldn't fret so much. It was the inactivity that was eating at him, as much as anything, Samuel guessed. Joseph was used to working hard, dawn to dusk, not sitting in a chair, waiting to heal.

He gestured toward the corn binder's innards, knowing they made more sense to Joseph than to him. "Can you take a little look at this? Would it do any gut to tear this down already?"

Bending forward, Joseph peered at the machine, but he quickly sat back with a muttered exclamation. "Ach, I can't get my eyes to focus enough even to see. What if I never do? What will happen then?"

"Your eyes will heal," Samuel said quickly, regretting that he'd said anything about the binder.

"How do you know?" It was nearly a snarl.

"They will." He tried to sound sure. "You just have to give it time, like the doctor said."

Joseph nodded, but Samuel didn't think he was convinced.

Nor was he himself convinced. He'd been hoping that in a week or two, Joseph would be able to come back to the shop. If he couldn't . . .

Well, if he couldn't, then Samuel would carry on, even though he was beginning to think he might want to work at something other than the machine shop for the rest of his life.

Maybe he'd have begun to think that anyway, once he'd started working with that horse of Mr. Bartlett's. But Anna had something to do with the turn his thoughts had been taking lately. She'd stirred him up, making him think of possibilities. Maybe he'd been too mired in routine since he'd come back.

That was one characteristic that hadn't changed about Anna. She'd always come into any group and sparked it up. She might have grown up in many ways, but she still seemed to have that effect on people.

On him.

If any of her friends from Chicago could see her, they wouldn't believe their eyes. Anna knelt in the garden, picking the last of the peppers for the relish she'd told Myra she'd make.

She held a bell pepper in her hand, feeling the weight of it, then lifted it to her nose to inhale its freshness. Her city friends thought relish was something you bought at the grocery store.

She knew perfectly well what she was doing. She was keeping her mind occupied and her hands busy so she wouldn't think about those moments with Samuel. Those kisses.

It was funny, how she'd ignored him when she was a teenager. He was Joseph's friend, nothing else. She'd thought him slow and maybe not too bright.

But there'd been nothing slow about those kisses. And Samuel was bright enough when it came to the horses he trained, to say nothing of how he kept the shop going and supported Myra and Joseph.

Standing, Anna stretched her back and glanced over at the cucumber vines to see if any cukes remained, but the vines were brown and withering.

A movement caught her eye. Samuel came out of the shop and started for the house. Then he spotted her. He veered off the straight course and headed for the garden. A flutter of excitement in the pit of her stomach made her feel as if she were sixteen again.

"Anna." A smile teased the corners of his mouth. "Busy, I see."

"I told Myra I'd make some end-of-the-garden relish this afternoon. If I haven't forgotten how to do it, that is."

"It'll come back to you." He pushed his straw hat back on his head, glancing at the farmhouse, his brows drawing down. "Myra chased Joseph back into the house a bit ago. I hope he didn't overdo it, coming out to the shop."

"You didn't have him hauling any machinery, did you?" She tilted her head back to smile at him, her instinctive reaction startling her a little. Was she actually flirting with him?

It had been so long, she wasn't quite sure. For the past year she'd been so busy and burdened just struggling to survive that she hadn't even thought about men.

"No, I didn't." His smile flickered. "He's not getting better as fast as he thinks he should. He wants to be back at work in the shop. I think he's secretly convinced that nobody can do it as well as he can."

"I don't believe that. He was just saying this morning what a great job you and Matthew and Daadi are doing. He feels bad that you can't spend more time with the horses, I know."

Samuel's broad shoulders moved in a shrug. "It makes no matter."

"But it's important to you. Working with Mr. Bartlett's animals could open new doors for you." She was probably saying too much, but wanted him to have his chance.

"Ach, I can be patient about that. It will work out as God wills."

Anna picked up the basket. "I've never been especially patient."

The fine sun lines around his eyes crinkled. "I remember that about you, Anna. You always had to push things along to make them happen faster."

"I guess so." Memories pricked at her. "Sometimes that didn't work out so well."

"Was it better, out among the English? Did things go fast enough for you there?"

He stood there as patient as if he had all day to talk to her. Maybe it was that patience that had tricked her into thinking him slow.

"Things were always happening out there, I guess. The months went by so quickly. It was all I could do to get by, especially after Gracie was born. I didn't have time to think about whether I was bored or not."

He nodded. "I found it hard to keep up out there. Even knowing English, it was still like they were all talking a different language. And so fast. I'd be sorting out one thing and they were on to something else."

She remembered that feeling. "Once all I heard was English around me, I found I started to get better."

"Maybe you were more ready for it than I was," Samuel said.

She considered that. "When I left, I thought I was prepared because I had English friends. I wasn't."

Those first months had been indescribably difficult. A dozen times she'd been ready to come home, but something—pride, maybe, or stubbornness—had kept her going.

"We weren't intended to be prepared for English life," Samuel said. His eyes seemed to warm as they rested on her face. "Now that you're back, you're living a life you're prepared for. Even down to remembering how to make garden relish."

She laughed. "That's yet to be seen. But I'd best get going on it."

"One thing, first." He paused, as if not sure how to say it. "The county fair opens on Wednesday."

He stopped, and she waited. "Ja?" she said finally, when it seemed he was stuck.

He cleared his throat. "Joseph wants me to go and look over the equipment displays. I thought . . . well, maybe you would want to go with me."

For a moment she could only stare at him. Her instinctive reaction was to pull back. It had been too long. She wasn't ready.

"That . . . that would be nice, but I can't leave Gracie with Myra. She has enough to do."

"We can take Gracie along. She will like to see all the animals."

Anna had a sudden image of the three of them walking around the fair, looking like a family. "Samuel, I can't. People would say that we are courting."

He lifted an eyebrow. "Is that such a bad thing? Anyway, I thought Anna Beiler didn't care what folks thought about her. Ain't so?"

That had been the old Anna Beiler, the one who was careless with the people she loved. Now she knew better. If you lived in a community, you had to care what people thought.

But she also knew she wanted to go. She wanted to have a day with Samuel and the baby, to see how they were together.

It meant stepping into deep water, didn't it? Did she have the courage?

She took a breath. "Ja, Samuel. Gracie and I would like to go to the fair with you."

The house hadn't been this quiet since the day she and Gracie had arrived. Anna washed vegetables in the sink, trusting that neither of the two little girls would wake from her nap when she was in the midst of making the relish.

It was certain-sure that if one woke, the other would, too. Already Sarah and Gracie were more like sisters than cousins, looking for each other first thing every day.

She paused, staring down at the pepper in her hand. It was irrational, wasn't it, to feel almost . . . well, jealous that Gracie had so many other people in her life now. But for all these months, she'd been everything to Gracie. And Gracie to her.

If that changed . . . well, it should, shouldn't it? Amish or English, children grew, and their worlds grew, too, becoming larger than just mommy and baby. Maybe the question she was really skirting around was whether she ought to be moving into a relationship with Samuel.

What relationship? She called on the skeptical part of her mind. A few kisses, a single outing together . . . that didn't make a relationship. In modern society—but she wasn't in modern society, was she?

She got out the wooden chopping board, as comfortable now in Myra's kitchen as she'd been in her own tiny nook of a kitchenette back in Chicago. It had been a relief to come in from the garden and find that Joseph was taking a nap, apparently tired out from walking this morning, and Myra had gone to the store for groceries. That had put off the moment when Anna would have to tell them that she and Gracie were going to the fair with Samuel.

Not that Joseph and Myra would raise any objection. Quite the contrary. They'd have trouble hiding their elation, probably, and that would be enough to make Anna want to back out.

Maybe she should anyway. Maybe . . . The sound of a car in the driveway cut short that line of thought. She leaned over to look out the window over the sink, to see Rosemary sliding out of her late-model SUV.

Anna dried her hands on the dish towel and went to the door. She hadn't expected to see the English neighbor again so soon. She'd enjoyed their conversation and the taste Rosemary had given her of the world she still missed, but she suspected none of the family would smile upon her developing a friendship with an Englischer, thinking it too tempting. Which it probably was.

"Rosemary, how nice to see you." She reached the door before the woman could knock. "Myra is out now. She'll be so sorry she missed you."

"No problem." Rosemary took the open door as an invitation and walked into the kitchen, her glance sweeping over the peppers, onions, and cauliflower on the counter. "Looks busy in here. I was hoping you'd have time for a cup of coffee."

"There's a pot on the stove," Anna assured her. "I'd love your company, as long as you don't mind if I keep on with this. I'm afraid the girls will be up from their naps before I've finished."

"Always busy," Rosemary commented, making herself at home

and pouring her own mug of coffee. "I never saw anybody who liked work as much as the Amish."

"Oh, I don't know. I saw some pretty fierce workaholics when I lived in Chicago."

"Was that where you were?" Rosemary came to lean on the counter next to her, carrying the mug, obviously ready for a chat.

Anna nodded, sorry she'd let that slip. She'd be better off to keep that part of her life private. Still, what could it hurt for Rosemary to know she'd lived in Chicago?

"Maybe you're right." Rosemary shrugged her shoulders, staring a bit glumly into her coffee mug. "Here's my husband rushing off on another business trip just a day after he got home. Apparently the company can't get along without him for more than twenty-four hours."

"I'm sorry." Anna responded to the note of disappointment in Rosemary's voice. The woman was lonely, that was all, with her husband away again and apparently no prospects of the child she longed for.

"Oh, well, that's life, right? At least when he's not here I can eat a frozen dinner and snuggle up in front of the television with an old movie."

"*It Happened One Night*?" Anna suggested.

"*Casablanca*," Rosemary said. "If you want a good cry, you have to watch Humphrey Bogart giving up the woman he loves for the greater good. Hey, I thought Amish didn't watch movies."

"They don't." We don't, she corrected herself. "I had a friend in Chicago who loved all the old Clark Gable and Humphrey Bogart movies. We'd get together on a Sunday afternoon and watch them."

For a moment Anna longed to be in Liz's small apartment. The sensation was so strong that it was almost a pain. She was swept with that sense of being two different people—of English Annie looking contemptuously at Amish Anna.

"So what exactly are you making?" Rosemary left the subject of old movies abruptly.

"Relish. My mother used to call it end-of-the-garden relish because you put in whatever's left in the garden. It's delicious." She gestured with her paring knife at the array of vegetables on the counter.

"Hmm. I guess, if you say so." Rosemary sounded doubtful. "It seems like an awful lot of work just to use up leftover veggies. I'll bet I don't go through more than a jar of relish in a year."

"We do eat a lot of relishes. Haven't you heard of the Pennsylvania Dutch seven sweets and seven sours?"

"I guess I've seen it on restaurant signs, but I didn't know you had to make it from scratch. Don't Amish believe in buying food at the grocery store?"

Anna had to smile. Rosemary was obviously intrigued by her Amish neighbors.

"The Amish shop in stores. That's where Myra is now, at the grocery store."

"Well, then." Rosemary tapped a manicured fingertip on her mug. "Why bother to go to all this work just for a jar of relish? Or is it religious? Do you believe that God wants you to work this hard?"

Anna tried to sort out her thoughts, knowing she wasn't the person best suited to be explaining Amish beliefs to anyone.

"I don't know that any Amish person would put it that way, exactly. Most Amish want to work the land if they can. They take pleasure in raising the food their families will eat, and it does taste better than something that's been processed to death."

"Maybe so." Rosemary sounded doubtful. "I guess I don't get this whole living close to the land thing. Richard—that's my husband—he seemed to think he'd be happy puttering around the garden, but now that he has one, he doesn't have the time anyway."

"Everyone isn't suited to country life." That was the most noncommittal response she could think of. She certainly didn't want to discuss Rosemary's husband with her.

"That's me," Rosemary declared. "In fact, I'd think that was you, too."

Anna's knife slipped, barely missing her finger. "What do you mean?"

"Well, just that you were away for what—three years? Is it really possible for somebody to come back and be Amish again after that?"

Anna's jaw clenched. It was a question she'd asked herself, but she decided she didn't care to hear it from someone else.

Rosemary's expression said she knew she'd gone too far. "Listen, I shouldn't have said that. My trouble is that I'm alone so much, when I do have somebody to talk to, stuff just falls out of my mouth."

"It's all right." It wasn't, but the woman had apologized.

Rosemary set her mug in the sink. "I really did have a reason for coming today, besides being nosy. I wanted to ask if you'd like to work for me a few hours a week. That big house gets to be too much for me to keep clean. You could set your hours whenever you want."

A refusal hovered on her lips. She had so many responsibilities here, with Joseph still not working. But a job would put some money in her pocket, money she wouldn't have to account to anyone for.

"Say twelve dollars an hour?" Rosemary asked, rushing the words. "That sound about right?"

If she had even a little coming in, she wouldn't have to feel so dependent on the family. And if she needed to leave . . .

She shut that thought off quickly. Hadn't she been telling herself that maybe this was the right life for her and Gracie? If she were really sure of that, she wouldn't be thinking that way.

So maybe she wasn't convinced. Maybe she didn't know her own mind at all. And Rosemary was still waiting for an answer.

"Thank you, Rosemary. I'd like to do some work for you."

Chapter Twelve

*A*s soon as they walked through the gates at the county fair-grounds, Anna knew she'd made a mistake in coming with Samuel. What had she been thinking?

The crowds flowed good-naturedly along the rows of stalls, aromas of a dozen different foods filled the air, and from the distance came the shriek of the rides. It was familiar, and at the same time it scared her.

It was one thing to be Amish again at home, among people who loved her. But when she'd ventured out, even in the church, her acceptance hadn't been complete. The memory left a bitter taste in her mouth.

And here she was back in the English world again, as an Amish woman.

"What is troubling you, Anna?" Samuel seemed to have an uncanny knack for reading her moods.

"Maybe it would have been better if I hadn't come." She glanced down at Gracie, asleep in the stroller Samuel was pushing. "If *we* hadn't come. It feels odd, being here like this."

"Because people are staring at us?"

"I hadn't even noticed that, but now you've given me something else to worry about."

He smiled at her tart tone. It was oddly freeing, knowing she could talk openly to Samuel in a crowd and no one would understand them.

"It hasn't been that long since I was one of them." She nodded toward the nearest clump of English who passed.

"Anna, you were never like them."

"Not those people in particular," she said. Maybe she shouldn't have picked a group of Goth teenagers, all in black, as an example. She shot a sideways glance at the piercings and dyed hair. "And they think we look odd."

"So we do, to them." Samuel was unaffected, no matter how people gawked. "You are Amish again now, Anna. That's how it is for us."

Her eyebrows lifted. "Is this a test?"

"Only if you see it that way. Only for your own sake, not anyone else's."

"I don't understand."

He gave a quick glance at the kids. "Those teenagers dress as they do because they want to be looked at. We dress as we do in obedience to God and the church, to remind us that we are to be separate."

A group of preteen kids in jeans and T-shirts, out of school for the first day of the fair, raced around them, jostling the stroller just enough to stir Gracie. She gave a startled cry.

"Ach, little girl." Samuel bent over the stroller before Anna could move. Unfastening the harness, he picked her up. "There, now. It's all right. There's nothing to be scared about. I have you."

He spoke in Pennsylvania Dutch, and Gracie quieted almost at once, as if she understood every word. Or maybe it was the slow, calm way he spoke that made the difference. Gracie, like the skittish horse, responded to his tone.

If they stayed, Gracie would grow up knowing the dialect, not even learning English until she went to school. If. Anna wanted to give her unruly mind a shake. It wasn't like her not to know what she wanted.

"Let's get a funnel cake and sit down for a few minutes until she feels like going back into the stroller," Samuel suggested. He nodded at a stand with long wooden picnic tables and benches under a blue-and-white canopy.

"Ser gut." Anna pulled the diaper bag from the stroller. "I'll give her something to drink while you get the funnel cakes."

By the time Anna had settled on a bench with Gracie chugging from a sippy cup, Samuel returned. He was balancing two paper plates filled with the powdered-sugar-coated treats.

"We could have shared one," she said as he sat down next to her.

"Speak for yourself." He grinned, holding a small piece out to

Gracie. "Gracie and I will eat one ourselves, we will. Funnel cakes are wonderful gut, Gracie."

Gracie took the fried treat from his hand and lifted it tentatively toward her mouth. She stuck out the tip of her pink tongue and touched the sugar. Suddenly her dimples showed, and she crammed the whole thing into her mouth, then reached eagerly toward the plate.

Anna laughed at Gracie's delight, giving her a squeeze. "Just a little more. Too much funnel cake can upset a tiny tummy."

"It tastes like the fair, that's what it is," Samuel said. "They never taste quite the same when we make them at home."

"Better not let Myra hear that." Myra had decided to make funnel cakes yesterday as a treat for Joseph, since he wouldn't be going to the fair this year.

"I didn't say they were better," Samuel protested. "You know, that's my first memory of the fair. Sitting on my daad's knee eating funnel cake." For an instant, sorrow shadowed his eyes.

"For me it was caramel apples," she confessed, memory taking her back to that childhood taste. "Mahlon and Joseph always had to have their cotton candy, but I wanted a caramel apple. When we were little, we couldn't wait for September so we could go to the fair. It was even more exciting than school starting."

Samuel nodded, understanding, and gave Gracie another small piece of funnel cake.

"It wore off when I was a teenager," Anna said. "Then I just wanted to be like my English friends."

"Plenty of us are that way during our rumspringa. You weren't the only one who hid jeans and T-shirts in the hay mow and learned to drive in some English friend's borrowed car."

"I didn't want them to see me as Amish. I thought I could keep that part of my life separate."

"Ja, kids are still trying that. Look at the haircuts on some of the teenage boys in service on Sunday morning. They didn't get those cuts in the kitchen with their mother's scissors."

If he was trying to make her laugh, he succeeded. "I know. I noticed. If they want to hide it, they need to be a bit more subtle."

"Annie!"

The exclamation had her turning toward the sound. The next thing she knew, she was being enveloped in a hug.

"You're back. I never thought I'd see you again. Where'd you disappear to? Don't you remember me? It's me, Shelley."

Anna disengaged herself. "Of course I remember you, Shelley." The hair that had once been brown and curling was now blond, done in a sleek, smooth style that just brushed Shelley's shoulders. Instead of the usual teen uniform of jeans and T-shirt she'd worn in the days before the accident, Shelley wore a pair of slacks and a bright, silky top.

"Never mind me," she exclaimed. Apparently she still talked in exclamation points. "I want to hear all about you. Look at you, with a husband and baby!"

"I don't . . ." Anna could feel herself blushing, but before she could think up an explanation, Shelley grabbed her arm.

"Let's sit down and have a cup of coffee together, okay? I want to catch up on everything."

"I don't know . . ." She glanced at Samuel. He waited, his face impassive.

"Oh, come on. It'll be fun."

"I would like to find out what happened to all of them." She said the words quickly in Pennsylvania Dutch to Samuel. "Do you mind?"

He stood, giving Gracie a little pat. "I will go and check out the farm machinery. I'll meet you back here in about half an hour. All right?"

She nodded. Of course it was. She had every right to catch up with her old friends. But as Samuel turned away, she caught the disappointment in his eyes. If this outing had been a test, it seemed that she'd failed.

"Not bad," Shelley said, sliding onto the bench opposite Anna and watching Samuel walk away. "If you like them solid and disapproving."

"Samuel didn't disapprove of you. He just didn't want me . . ." She let that trail off, since the thought didn't help.

"He doesn't want you hanging around with your old teenage friends," Shelley said. "I get that. How long have you two been together?"

"We're not. I mean, we're just friends."

This was more complicated than she'd expected. She wanted to make contact with Shelley again—to feel that their friendship had been real. She'd left so soon after the accident that she hadn't had a chance to talk with her.

"So, friends. Tell me more." Shelley's bright eyes flicked to the baby. "What about the baby's father? I thought you Amish didn't believe in divorce."

"We weren't married." She hesitated. If she didn't want to tell Shelley everything, it would be better not to say anything.

We're friends, aren't we? Her younger self seemed to be protesting. *We tell each other everything.*

"Wow," Shelley said. "And you went through with having the baby? But I guess you people wouldn't go for any other option."

Other option. Anna's arms tightened protectively around Gracie. "No," she said, her voice strangled.

"Well, looks like it all ended up okay," Shelley said cheerfully. "I sure wouldn't want to be settled down with a family right now, though. Just getting through school is hard enough."

It was probably safer to talk about Shelley's life than hers. "You're still in college?"

"Still." She sighed. "I'm just home now because my mom got all nostalgic about having everyone here for my dad's retirement party. I'm headed back to campus tomorrow."

"This must be your last year. Do you have any career plans?"

"No, I have another year. I changed majors too many times. It's accounting now, and I have to stick with it whether I like it or not. My dad says he's not going to pay good money for me to party and change my mind every five minutes."

That sounded exactly like the Shelley Anna used to know, and she smiled. "I'm sure there are plenty of good jobs for accountants."

"At least I'll be able to find a job in the city where something's happening." Shelley gave the fair a dismissive glance. "Did you hear about Casey? She got into UCLA, the lucky thing. Never comes home anymore."

"No, I didn't." Since she'd barely known Casey, it was tough to generate any interest.

"It's true. And Megan did get into Juilliard, but she dropped out her first semester. Couldn't stand the pressure."

"What about Jarrod?" Anna had been dating Jarrod that summer. She'd thought she was in love with him.

Their romance hadn't survived for more than a month or two after she'd left home. Still, she cared what happened to him.

"He's at Penn State. Runs track, got into a top fraternity."

Their lives seemed so different from hers that it was hard to find something in common. This was what Samuel had meant when he talked about drifting away from his English friends. Shelley seemed years younger than she was, even though Anna knew they were the same age.

"So you and Jarrod . . ." Shelley tipped her head to the side. "That didn't last long, did it?"

"No. After the accident we sort of went in different directions. But I'll always be grateful for the way his family helped me then."

"Well, they owed it to you," Shelley said. "Jarrod never should have let you drive their car. Naturally his folks wanted it settled quickly and quietly, before somebody got the bright idea of suing them for damages."

Anna took a moment to absorb that. It had never occurred to her that there was any reason other than kindness for their help.

"Nobody would have sued them," she said finally. "The other family was Amish. They wouldn't go to court any more than mine would."

"Other family?" Shelley looked blank.

"The family in the buggy we hit. Don't you remember?"

Shelley had been sitting next to her in the car that night. How could she have forgotten those terrifying moments—the lights striking the orange triangle on the back of the buggy, the realization that they were going too fast . . .

Gracie fidgeted in her lap, as if sensing her discomfort, and made a little sound of distress. Anna bent over her, soothing her, trying to get control of herself.

Anna didn't remember. She hadn't, in all these years, remembered anything about the accident. Those fragments that had flashed into her mind—she didn't want them there.

"Sure, I remember now." Shelley shook her head. "Sorry. It's been a long time since I thought about that. Anyway, at least nobody got hurt."

Anna could only stare at her. "I did."

"Oh, yes, well, I guess I forgot that you were in the hospital afterwards. But you're okay, right?"

Shelley had forgotten. She hadn't come to see Anna in the hospital, hadn't gotten in touch.

Anna looked back at her teenage self with a sense of surprise. Had she really thought that Shelley was her friend?

Anna had known true friendship from both Amish and English people, but what she'd had with those kids wasn't it. She seemed to be seeing that whole time more clearly now.

They . . . Shelley, Jarrod, the rest of them . . . they'd been into the novelty of introducing an Amish girl to the wild side of life.

And she'd been no better. She'd welcomed their company because they were the perfect means of rebellion, not because she cared about them. It wasn't very pretty, but it was true.

Anna cleared her throat, trying to think of something to say. There wasn't anything, it seemed.

"It has been so nice to see you, Shelley." Anna rose, putting the diaper bag in the stroller basket. "I must go now."

"Right, sure." Shelley glanced at her watch and gave a little shriek. "I've got to go, too. Listen, stay in touch, okay?"

Anna nodded. But she wouldn't. Neither of them would. She understood that now.

Samuel barely needed to touch the lines to convince Blackie to turn onto the county road. The old horse knew the way home as well as he did, maybe better. He'd chosen to drive old Blackie today, not wanting to trust one of the younger animals in fair traffic. Even Blackie had been a bit twitchy from time to time with all the excitement.

They could both relax now. There'd be little enough traffic on this back road.

He glanced at Anna. She'd been quiet while he'd negotiated the busy road around the fairground, but he'd caught a glimpse of her hand gripping the side rail. Now she patted the sleeping baby in her lap, her face tilted down.

"Did you enjoy the fair?" he asked, wanting to break the silence.

She nodded. "Gracie loved seeing all the animals up close. And that sausage sandwich we had was definitely overload."

He grinned, relieved to hear her sounding normal. "Too bad you didn't have room for one more caramel apple."

"Ach, don't remind me." She patted her stomach.

"Well, you have to eat the thing that means fair to you."

She sobered, glancing at him. "It bothered you when I wanted to talk with Shelley. I'm sorry."

That was a little more plain speaking than he'd expected from her, and it took him a moment to reply. "It wasn't exactly how I'd pictured our day at the fair together. For a second I wondered if you'd set that up."

She looked up at him, eyes wide. "I didn't."

"No, I know that. I could tell you were surprised to see an old friend there."

But her eagerness to talk to the English woman had made him stop and think about where he was going with this interest in Anna. Since his own return, he'd avoided showing attention to any woman, fearing his own character.

And if he did think about committing to someone, it needed to be an Amish woman who was strong in her own faith. He could hardly say that about Anna.

She pressed her lips together, making him wonder what she was thinking.

"Shelley and I are not friends anymore," she said finally.

He nodded. "That happens." He'd predicted that, in fact, but he didn't think she'd believed him.

She shook her head. "She and the others . . . it seems as if they're just kids playing at being grown-ups. Waiting to start their real lives. I can't believe I wanted to be like them."

He clucked to Blackie, who had taken advantage of his distraction to slow down. "It's not so odd. Most of us go through a time of wanting the freedom our English friends have." He suspected that her concern ran deeper than that, though.

Her eyes were shadowed. "I'm not sure that they ever were my friends." A car went by, sending out a spray of loose gravel, and she seemed to wince.

"Maybe, maybe not." He wouldn't say things just to make her feel better. "Sometimes English kids want to hang around with the Amish just for kicks. To make fun of them, like. But I'm thinking you had other English friends who were real, like Gracie's birth mammi."

Anna's smile flickered, chasing some of the shadows from her eyes. "That's true enough, but I didn't think to hear you say it."

"Ach, I don't discount the value of friends, even with folks who are very different. Take that horse of Mr. Bartlett's, for instance."

"The horse?" Her eyebrows lifted. "Now you're comparing me to a horse?"

He grinned, glad to see the liveliness coming back into her face. "Now, just hear me out. That animal was nervous as a cat at first, kicking at the stall bars, knocking over his water pail, making a nuisance of himself every time he was in the barn. So I got the loan of a goat from Aaron Zook."

"A goat." Her lips were twitching.

"Ja, a goat. Don't you make fun of me now, Anna Beiler. Those two animals got to be friends in no time at all, though they're as different as can be. Calmed that nervy horse down in no time flat, that goat did."

"So I get to be either a horse or a goat, do I?"

"Ach, you're definitely the horse, if you must be one or the other. Strong and high-spirited, but a mite uneasy in a new place."

"This isn't a new place—" She stopped, her head swiveling as a car roared up behind them.

He didn't bother to look around, concentrating on keeping his hands steady on the lines. The driver gave a loud blast on the horn, and the car swerved around them. Blackie, used to motor vehicles, flicked an ear at it, nothing more.

Samuel turned to Anna, but a casual comment died on his lips. Her face was dead white, her lips trembling, and she clutched the child fiercely against her breast.

"Stop—please stop. I have to get down. I have to!"

The hysteria in her voice sent a shock through him. "It's all right, Anna. They didn't hit us."

A farm lane led off to the right through a grove of trees. He turned Blackie into it and off onto the grass, then brought the buggy to a halt. He let the lines drop, knowing Blackie would be content to stand there indefinitely.

"Anna—" But before he could get out more than her name, she slid down from the buggy, carrying the baby. She rushed a few steps away and stopped, her shoulders shaking.

He jumped to the ground and went to her, approaching as slow and easy as if she were a wild creature. "Anna?" He reached out gently to touch her arm. "Was ist letz? What's wrong?"

She was trembling. A wave of caring had him putting his arm around her before he thought that she might not like it. But she didn't pull away.

"Was ist letz?" he said again. "That car passing so close—did that frighten you? Blackie is used to traffic."

She shook her head. "The accident." Her voice choked on the words.

Easy, he cautioned himself. Take it slow. "The accident," he repeated. "The one you were in with those English kids."

She nodded, head down, pressing her cheek against the head of the sleeping child. "I know what happened. They told me when I woke up in the hospital. But I never really remembered it."

"You had a head injury." He'd gone to the hospital once, like most of the community. And he'd helped out with Joseph's work, freeing him to see to his family. "Sometimes people don't remember."

"That's what the doctors said. That probably I'd never remember. But today, when I was talking to Shelley, a little of it flashed into my mind. And just now . . ." She stopped, as if she couldn't go on.

"When that car raced around us, it made you remember." He patted her shoulder, wishing he could take the pain away.

"I was driving. Jarrod said he'd teach me. They kept telling me to go faster, laughing, saying there was nothing on the road."

Her words seemed to gain momentum as she spoke, as if she couldn't get them out fast enough.

"It was exciting, racing through the dark, seeing the road curving ahead in the headlights. When I saw the orange triangle, the buggy, I was going too fast. I tried to swerve, tried to brake, but it was too late. I hit them."

"Ja." What could he do but agree? "Thank the gut Lord no one was badly hurt."

"It was my fault. I did it." Her eyes darkened with pain. "There was a family in that buggy. A mother holding her child." She held Gracie even closer. "I could have killed them. They must have been so afraid. How could I not remember that?"

"Maybe God knew that you needed time before you remembered," he said gently. "We can't understand His ways."

"I did that to them," she said again. "Afterward, when Leah tried to talk to me about it, all I found to say was that it wasn't so bad. That other people had done worse. How could I have dismissed it like that? What kind of person am I?"

"Anna, stop." He put his hands on her shoulders and turned her to face him. "If you see now that you did wrong, then that needs confessing and mending. But you're not that heedless girl anymore, are you?"

She took a breath, and it seemed to him that she steadied under his hands.

"No," she said softly. "I'm not."

"You're not," he agreed. "You're a woman grown, and you've had your share of pain. It's made you strong—strong enough to handle this, too."

Her eyes filled with tears, but they didn't spill over. She nodded.

His own heart was full, and he knew that he was past the point of choosing whether he had feelings for Anna. Wise or not, he did.

CHAPTER THIRTEEN

Anna could only be thankful that the trip to the medical clinic was by car, not by horse and buggy. Daad had arranged for Ben Morgan, an elderly Englischer who enjoyed driving the Amish, to take her and Myra today.

Not that she wouldn't eventually have to get back on the road in a buggy, but after what had happened the day before on the way home from the fair, she was glad it didn't have to be today.

How had that happened? She still didn't quite understand how she could suddenly remember so vividly after all that time had passed. It was as if a closed door in her mind opened, and the memories and emotions had come exploding out.

Samuel had been unfortunate enough to be in the way.

She had been the lucky one—lucky that he was there. For someone who didn't talk a great deal, Samuel had a gift for saying the right thing.

She glanced at Myra. Her sister-in-law sat quietly, hands folded in her lap, looking down. She was apprehensive, of course, about what awaited them at the clinic.

Doubt assailed her. Maybe Myra would be better off to have someone else with her. Leah had volunteered at the clinic, after all. She knew the people there, knew far more than Anna about genetic diseases.

But Myra had asked her, and so she was here, praying she could be what Myra needed today.

Praying even more fervently that all she'd have to do was help Myra celebrate good news.

Still, the very fact that Myra had to go in for an appointment seemed ominous to her. Good news might easily have come in a letter. It was usually bad news that had to be delivered in person.

"Here we are, ladies," Ben said, with a cheerfulness that didn't quite ring true. He'd undoubtedly figured out that this wasn't a routine visit. He drew the car up under a tree on the edge of the gravel parking lot. "I'll sit here in the shade. I brought my book, and I'm in no hurry at all."

"Denke, Ben." Anna slid out of the car and then realized that Myra hadn't moved. She sat frozen, staring at the front door of the clinic.

Anna's heart missed a beat. *Please, Father, guide me. Help her.*

She walked quickly around the car, opened the door, and took Myra's hand. "Komm, Myra. It's time for your appointment."

Myra just gazed at her for a moment, her eyes wide and frightened. Then she got out, moving as stiffly as a very old woman, and let Anna lead her up the front steps.

Once in the center hall, she guided Myra to a seat in the waiting room. The clinic, she knew, was on the right side of the building, while the labs and research facilities were on the left.

Leah had talked about the volunteer work she did for the researchers, helping to record the family trees of Amish families affected by genetic diseases. Would Joseph and Myra be joining that list?

"Sit down, Myra." Anna settled her on one of the plastic chairs that lined the wall. "I will tell them you're here."

The woman behind the reception desk heard the name and checked it off on the form. "If you'll have a seat, Dr. Brandenmyer will see you in a few minutes."

Anna nodded and returned to Myra, taking the seat next to her. She put her hand over Myra's clasped ones.

"It will be all right," she said softly. "You'll know soon."

Myra let out a soft moan. "If something is wrong with the baby, what will we do?"

If Anna closed her eyes, she could hear Jannie asking the same question. But it hadn't been the baby with a problem. It had been Jannie.

She took a shaky breath. She'd been worrying about how Myra would cope if the news was bad. Maybe she should be concerned about herself, too. Could she be strong in a similar situation yet again?

"Mrs. Beiler?" The door beside the reception desk had opened. The man who stood there was tall and lean, with graying hair and an eager, youthful smile. He approached them, holding out his hand. "I'm Dr. Brandenmyer. You're Leah Glick's sister-in-law, I understand."

"Ja." Myra seemed to thaw under his friendly smile. "This is Leah's sister, Anna Beiler."

The smile was turned on her. "It's so nice to meet you. We think very highly of Leah around here."

"It is good to meet you, Dr. Brandenmyer." That friendly smile had been accompanied by a look so piercing that it seemed he could see right through her.

"Just come along with me, will you please?" He went striding back through the door, and they had to hurry to keep up with him.

He led the way to a room that looked more like someone's private study than an exam room. He gestured them to a pair of padded chairs, picked up a folder from the desk, and then drew up a chair facing them.

He didn't put the desk between them, she noticed. Some of Jannie's doctors had seemed to take refuge doing that.

"You've come here for the results of your amnio, so I won't keep you waiting." His hand rested on the manila folder on his lap, but he didn't open it.

Myra nodded. Her hand went out to clasp Anna's, and Anna held on tight.

"I'm sorry to have to tell you that it looks as if your baby has Down's syndrome."

Myra sucked in a strangled breath. "Are you sure?"

"We can't tell one hundred percent, of course, but yes, I'm sure. I'm very sorry."

"Denke," Myra whispered.

Anna put her arm around Myra's shoulders, pain like a knot in her chest. "I'm sorry," she murmured. "So sorry."

Myra nodded, her grip on Anna's hand wrenching.

"This is never good news, of course," Dr. Brandenmyer said. "We're more fortunate now than we used to be, because we're able to detect it early. It is a little unusual in a woman as young as you are."

Anna realized he was studying Myra's face as he talked, gauging how she was dealing with the news. He'd probably been in this situation more times than he could count, but there was no mistaking the compassion in his eyes.

"I have some reading material for you that will help you understand." He flipped open the folder and took out several small booklets, which he held out. Myra didn't move, so Anna took them.

"Thank you, Dr. Brandenmyer."

"It will be difficult to tell your husband, I know. I hope he's recovering all right from his accident?"

Myra nodded. "He is much better, ja."

"There is one thing you and he might want to discuss." His tone was cautious, as if he tiptoed into the subject. "A fairly high percentage of women who get this news decide to terminate the pregnancy. You can—"

"No." Myra seemed to come back to life. She put her hand protectively over her belly. "No, we will not do that. Our baby will be as God plans."

He reached out to pat her hand. "I didn't really expect anything else, but it's my job to tell you all your options. We know that about fifty percent of Down's syndrome babies also have heart defects, so that's another factor to consider."

Myra closed her eyes, as if she couldn't look at his sympathetic face any longer. Or as if she needed to hide.

"We understand," Anna said. She wasn't sure Myra could handle any more information right now.

Dr. Brandenmyer's gaze met Anna's, and she felt he understood all that she was thinking. He nodded.

"Maybe it will be as well if we leave it at that for now. Go home, talk with your husband, be sure you know what you want to do. You'll be seeing your regular doctor for appointments, but coming here for tests from time to time, so we'll talk again."

With her arm around Myra, Anna helped her to rise. She could understand now why Leah thought so highly of this man. No one could have been kinder.

But now she needed to get Myra home to Joseph. They'd have to figure out how to face this sorrow together.

. . .

"Is Myra doing any better today?"

Leah looked down at Anna from the stool on which she stood, wiping down an already clean wall at Mahlon and Esther's house in preparation for worship services on Sunday. The work frolic was in full swing, with every available person from the family pressed into service.

"I'm not sure." Anna rinsed out the cloth she was using to wipe down the baseboards. "I thought so yesterday, but she really didn't want to come today, and I thought I shouldn't force her."

"She's helping by watching the kinder. The work goes faster without them, for sure."

"Ja, that's true enough. If we had your Rachel, plus Sarah and my Gracie and Barbara's two youngest running around, the house would be getting dirty instead of clean. Not that it isn't perfectly clean to start with," she added hastily. Esther's house had, as always, been spotless when they'd arrived this morning.

Leah chuckled. "For sure. I don't know how Rachel does it, but she can create more chaos in five minutes than the other children do all day."

"Maybe she takes after her naughty aunt." Anna said the words without thinking and then wished she hadn't. Her relationship with Leah was mending, but maybe it wasn't as strong as all that yet.

But Leah was smiling. "Ach, don't you talk that way about my baby sister. You weren't naughty, only spirited."

"And spoiled," Anna added.

"Maybe a little bit," Leah said. "But I'm as much to blame for that as anyone. Mammi and I were so happy for another girl after all those boys." She paused, looking down at Anna, her hand resting on the wall. "Maybe we made it harder for you in the long run. I'm sorry."

"Goodness, Leah, you've nothing to be sorry about." Anna blinked away the tears that had sprung to her eyes at her sister's words. "You were always the best big sister, even when I drove you crazy." She could think of a number of things her younger self had blurted out that she wished unsaid. "That's why I'm feeling that you'd be the better person for Myra to lean on now, not me."

Leah climbed down from the stool and moved it over, frowning a little. "I think you're wrong about that. Myra probably feels more connected to you. You're much closer in age, after all."

"Maybe that's so, but your work at the clinic makes you much better prepared than I am to help her."

The sense of helplessness she'd felt sitting with Myra in Dr. Brandenmyer's office swept over her again. Leah would know better what to say.

"Your friend must have gone through difficult times when she was pregnant, ain't so?"

"Ja, of course. But it's not the same. Jannie knew she was dying."

Leah's eyes clouded with pity. "Poor girl. But even though the cause was different, the grieving process is the same. Myra is grieving the loss of the child she expected to have, and she's adjusting to the one she will have."

Anna nodded, considering that. She'd read everything she could find on the stages of grief when Jannie had learned what she was facing. She just hadn't thought about how that applied to Myra.

"I see why everyone turns to Teacher Leah with their problems," she said. "Even if you're no longer the community's schoolteacher, you still have all the answers."

"Not all," Leah said, turning back to the work. "After all, you're the one who went to college, ain't so?"

The edge in Leah's voice startled Anna so much that for a moment she just stood, staring at her sister. Then she put out her hand to stop Leah's brisk movements with the sponge.

"Leah? Does it make you angry that I took college classes?"

Leah kept her face averted. "Why would that make me angry? We'd best get to work, or Esther will think she has slackers for sisters-in-law."

Anna was tempted to let it go. But if she and Leah were going to repair their relationship, surely it was better to get all the sore spots out in the open.

"Talk to me, Leah. I can see that it bothers you. I know the church frowns on higher education, but I was living in the world then."

Leah stared down at the sponge in her hand. She turned slowly, still not quite facing Anna.

"I have a wise friend at the clinic," she said slowly. "An Amish woman who jumped the fence for the sake of an education. She told me once that people leave for all sorts of reasons—some for conveniences like electricity and airplanes, some for opportunities, like education. If I had ever left, it would have been for that. For learning."

"And I was the one who had that chance." Anna's mouth twisted with the irony of it. "I'm sorry, Leah. I didn't think. Do you still—"

"Ach, no," Leah said quickly, turning to her fully and clasping her hands. "I am in the right place for me. I know that for certain-sure. Our kinder are mine to teach and help, and I can learn all I want from reading. Sometimes I just wonder what college is like, that's all."

"And I was the one who got to find out, when I never cared a thing for learning. Your friend was right. I left for the freedom I thought I'd find there."

"Did you?"

Anna considered. Had she found the freedom she'd wanted so badly?

"Not so much as I imagined. I was still tied down, but by different things—the need for a job, for an education. And then by my love for Jannie and for Gracie."

"Would you change, if you could? The life you imagined for the one you have?"

"Never," she said instantly. "I have Gracie. Loving her is more important than anything."

Leah smiled gently. "Then you know how I feel, too."

Anna clasped Leah's hand and felt the warmth of her sister's grip. They had crossed a bridge in the past few minutes, she and her sister, and it was one that brought them closer at last.

You will have another sandwich, ja?" Esther passed the platter of cold meat sandwiches around the table again, determined to feed her helpers.

That was part of the routine, almost a ritual that Anna remembered from her earliest childhood. Whenever one family was hosting church, all the women would gather early in the morning to clean, then share a simple lunch together before returning home.

She'd never really thought about it before. As a small child, she'd found it a happy break in the routine; as a teenager, she had usually complained beforehand, no matter how much she enjoyed the gathering once she actually got there.

The work frolic was comforting in its own way, a time for women's voices and women's work and women's laughter. If the men and the children had been here to share the meal, the talk wouldn't turn to matters of pregnancy, childbirth, and mothering.

"You're fortunate, you are, Esther." Barbara helped herself to a slab of applesauce cake. "When we host church, it must be in the barn. The way your living room and dining room join makes it easier to have it in the house already."

"I hope folks will not feel too crowded." Esther cast an anxious glance toward the front of the new house she and Mahlon had moved into in the spring. "We'll have to do the gathering with women in the kitchen and men on the front porch, I think."

"Ja, that will work best," Barbara agreed.

The gathering before the service allowed worshippers to file into the house in the traditional order . . . older women first, then younger, followed by children and teenage girls. Then the men, with the teenage boys bringing up the rear.

Anna found she was visualizing the silent procession, feeling the spirit of solemnity it added in preparation for worship. They didn't enter worship individually, chattering about the week's events or laughing with friends. Even if the place of worship was a barn, it was entered with reverence.

Esther poured coffee into thick white mugs. "I wish Myra had come today. Anna, you must take some applesauce cake home to her. Is she eating all right?"

"I don't think she's had much appetite the past couple of days, but she's making an effort."

"Gut, gut." Barbara heaved a sigh, her usually happy face solemn. Barbara had popped out five healthy kinder with little fuss and bother, and she was obviously hurting for Myra. "I wish we could do something. Leah, do you think this doctor can really be sure?"

As always, the family turned to Leah, the teacher, for answers.

"Not one hundred percent, as Dr. Brandenmyer told Myra, but the test she had is nearly always right. He's very gut at what he does. We're fortunate to have him in the area."

"The Amish are the reason he came here," Esther pointed out. "For the genetics, Mahlon tells me."

Anna had to contain a smile at hearing her scatterbrained brother held up as an authority. She could tell that Leah had the same impulse, and it reminded her of all the times Leah had nudged her to keep an unwise word to herself, as if she saw the thought forming in a balloon over Anna's head.

"All we can do is give them our support and pray that the boppli is born healthy," Leah said.

"Dr. Brandenmyer said that fifty percent of Down's syndrome children have heart defects." Anna's heart ached as she said the words.

"Well, and that means fifty percent don't. We will pray for that, and for strength and wisdom for Myra and Joseph." Leah's tone was soft but firm. "Such children can sometimes go to school, like the Esch boy and Ezra Miller's two youngest."

"Ja, that's true."

Anna realized that Leah wanted to keep them focused on the positive, and she was right. Myra didn't need gloomy faces around her.

And Esther, who was still childless, didn't need to be frightened by a situation she might never have to deal with. Esther probably already worried about all the cases of Crigler-Najjar syndrome in the Miller family tree.

Esther's family included her distant cousins, who had been coming home from a visit to relatives when they'd had the misfortune to meet up with Anna Beiler behind the wheel of a car.

If she could find a chance to talk to Esther alone, she would ask about them. She'd never understood what the family had gone through until those moments coming home from the fair, when she'd held Gracie close to her body, terrified that she wouldn't be able to protect the baby if the worst happened.

She'd never be able to find peace until she could make amends. The thoughts she'd been having about staying—how could she do that if she were not forgiven?

The others began getting up from the table, gathering their belongings together, and she saw her chance.

"Let me help you clean up the kitchen, Esther." She seized a stack of plates and carried them to the sink. "I don't have to be home right away."

Esther protested, of course, but in a few minutes the others were gone, and they were alone together in the kitchen.

Esther rinsed soap from a plate and handed it to her to dry. "You really didn't need to stay," she said.

"Actually, I wanted to talk with you."

"With me?" The whites of Esther's eyes showed, as if she were afraid of what Mahlon's fence-jumping sister might want of her.

"About your cousins who live out on the Fisherdale Road. Aaron Esch and his family." She sucked in a breath. "The people I hit with the car that night."

"Oh." Esther's apprehension didn't ease. "What about them?"

"I would like to go and see them." She chose her words carefully. "So that I can tell them how sorry I am. But I don't want to go there if they would rather I didn't."

That sounded as if she was trying to protect herself, wanting only to go if she could be assured of a welcome. Was that really what was behind her thoughts?

"Do you think they might be willing to talk with me?"

Esther washed a cup with unnecessary vigor. "I'm not sure that's a gut idea."

Anna felt as if she'd taken a punch to the stomach. "You mean they haven't forgiven me."

She hadn't truly anticipated that, she realized. Forgiveness was a basic tenet of Amish faith. She'd always thought, deep in her heart, that they would forgive.

"I don't know," Esther said, taking Anna's hand in her wet, soapy one. "Really, Anna, I don't. I mean, they wouldn't say much to me, being married to your brother. I just remember talk about how the little girl cried every time she had to get in a buggy afterward, and well . . ."

"I see." Where did she go from here? Anna wondered. If forgiveness wasn't possible, what then?

CHAPTER FOURTEEN

Samuel patted the big gelding, murmuring soothingly as he lifted the front hoof to finish the shoeing job. He had the animal in cross ties in the barn, but still, he was cautious, as always, working around a creature that outweighed him by so much.

Concentrating on the job at hand usually wasn't hard for him, but today too many other thoughts distracted him. Like Myra's unborn baby. Like Anna, and his feelings for her.

With Mamm gone, and Joseph's mamm passed as well, he'd thought maybe Myra would want their sister to come from Indiana at this difficult time, but she'd rejected that when he suggested it. She had her sisters-in-law, she'd said. She had Anna right here every day.

He began pulling off the old shoe. It had worn a bit unevenly, he noticed. He'd have to check the other shoes for that. A quiver went over the horse's skin, and he leaned against the animal's shoulder, comforting it.

Anna was here, ja, she was. He couldn't think about her without going right back to their trip to the fair. To what had happened on the way home.

The lack of knowledge that made a driver blow a horn in the horse's ears didn't surprise him—that sort of thing happened often enough that he didn't give it a second thought any longer, especially when he was driving an animal as well-mannered as Blackie. But Anna's reaction had startled him.

It had startled her, too, he figured. Her memories and grief had overwhelmed her without warning. She'd clutched Gracie as if she'd never let go.

As for him, he hadn't been much help to her in that crisis, now had he? Afterward, when it was too late, he'd thought of a dozen things he should have said to her. Maybe he really was as slow as Anna had always thought him.

Putting the hoof down, he straightened, stretching his back. Farriers who did this all day long often ended up bent over nearly double. He took the new horseshoe from the box.

"Komm now," he said, running his hand down the leg, pinching the cannon bone to get the animal to lift his hoof. "Almost done."

Ja, his day at the fair with Anna and Gracie had turned out different from what he'd expected. He'd thought they would have a pleasant day out, a chance for both of them to see how well they fit together, with no commitment on either side. Instead, a car full of careless teenagers had pushed them too far, too fast.

Well, him at least. He'd recognized, standing there feeling helpless when Anna needed him, that he'd gone beyond friendship, like it or not.

As for Anna—who knew what she felt? They hadn't been alone together since, so maybe that in itself was an answer.

He started to clinch the nails when the barn door rattled.

"Samuel?"

The gelding snorted, jerking against the cross ties. Off balance, Samuel tumbled backward.

"Samuel!" Anna arrived at his side a second later, before he could get himself up off the floor.

"I'm so sorry." She reached for him, her face filled with worry. "I shouldn't have come in without checking to see what you were doing."

She slid her arm around his waist to help him to his feet, and for a moment he let himself enjoy her embrace. Then he straightened.

"It's nothing. I am fine." He flexed his wrist, wincing a little. Maybe not so fine.

"You're hurt." Anna took his wrist in her hands, feeling it gently.

"It's nothing. Just a little bruise." He pushed away the temptation to let her keep fussing over him.

"I'll get some cold water." Before he could protest, she'd grabbed a bucket and hurried to the barn pump. She pumped furiously, filling the bucket.

In a moment she was back. She grabbed his hand and thrust his fist into the bucket. "This will help stop the swelling."

Suppressing a smile, he sat down on a straw bale, bucket and all. "Ja, Dr. Anna."

"Don't laugh," she protested, and he saw how seriously she was taking it. "I've caused enough trouble for people already. I don't want to add you to my list. Especially not now."

"It was Star's fault, not yours." He nodded to the gelding, now watching them as calm as he could be. "If I'd had my mind on my work, he wouldn't have gotten away with it."

Samuel certain-sure wasn't going to tell her why his mind had been straying, not with her sitting next to him on the straw bale, looking at him with such concern in those blue eyes.

He forced himself to stop drowning in those eyes and concentrated on what she'd said. "What did you mean, 'especially now'?"

"That's what I came to tell you. One of Bartlett's workers stopped by the house. Mr. Bartlett is coming this evening to see how the horse is coming along. If your wrist is bad, you won't be able to show him what you've done with Star." She sounded ready to weep at the thought.

"Ach, it's okay." He lifted his hand, dripping, from the water and flexed his fist. "See? And the gelding will do fine." He smiled. "As long as you promise not to scare him."

"Maybe I'd better stay far away." She gave a mock shudder. "I wouldn't want to jinx you."

"You couldn't do that." He saw the concern that lingered in her face, and he longed to wipe it away, longed to see her smile.

"I told Myra I would bring Bartlett's message over because I wanted to see you." She was looking down, so that all he could see of her face was the curve of her cheek. "I haven't properly thanked you for your kindness the other day."

"You do not need to thank me, Anna. You were hurting. I wish I could have found the right words to make it easier for you. But I'm not so gut at that."

"What you said was true, and I'd always rather hear truth than pleasant lies."

Who had told her pleasant lies? he wondered. Someone out in the English world? A man she cared for?

"I'm sorry that you were frightened."

He didn't dare raise the question of who had told her pleasant lies. If he asked, if she answered, it would be yet another step deeper into a relationship he wasn't sure could work for either of them.

Anna shook her head. "Maybe what happened was for the best. It made me feel how much hurt I caused when I went away. If I'm going to stay here, I have to make amends for that."

If. The word chilled him. "Are you putting conditions on being here, Anna?"

She looked at him then. "I don't want to, but you're the one who said I must make amends."

"I don't think that's exactly what I said—"

She shook her head, cutting him off. "Close enough, and it's what I feel, too. Now that I know what that family went through because of me, I have to find a way to make things right with them."

"Your father already took care of the buggy. By this time, they will surely have forgotten about it."

Her eyes darkened. "Esther thinks they wouldn't want to see me, so I've written them a letter, saying how sorry I am." She gave a shaky little laugh. "Who would guess it could take three hours to write a single page?"

"It's not easy to express what's in your heart."

Who knew that better than he did? Right now his own heart filled with caring for her, but he couldn't find the words to express any of it.

And even if he could, should he? Anna had the baby to consider. She couldn't take a chance on a man who might let her down.

Anna sat still a moment longer, looking at him as if waiting for something. Then she rose.

"Denke, Samuel. Thank you for listening. I should go. I hope it goes well with Mr. Bartlett."

He should stop her. He should tell her what he felt. But doubt kept him silent.

"*I* heard a truck," Myra said, glancing toward the side window that overlooked the lane and the ring where Samuel worked the horses. "It must be that Englischer, come to see Samuel about the horse."

Anna dried the dish she was holding and detoured past the window to put it away. "It is. He's standing by the fence, talking to Samuel."

She forced herself to move away again. It wouldn't help Samuel's confidence if he thought they were spying on him.

"Ach, I pray it will go well for him." Myra's voice filled with concern. "Samuel was so nervous he hardly touched his supper, did you notice?"

Anna nodded. She'd noticed. She'd seen his big hands crumbling his roll instead of lifting it to his mouth. She'd begun to notice too much about Samuel for her own peace of mind.

"Samuel has such a gift with the horses," Myra went on, apparently determined to talk about her brother. "I think it could be a business for him, don't you?"

Anna did, but she wasn't sure whether to say so or not. She glanced at the living room, where Joseph was sitting on the floor, playing with Sarah and Gracie.

"He wouldn't do that as long as Joseph needs him," she said, lowering her voice to speak under the clatter of dishes. "You know that."

"Ja, but Joseph is better." Myra was sounding more like her normally optimistic self tonight. "Look at him, playing in there with the little girls. He hasn't done that since the accident."

"We'll probably have to help him up off the floor when he's done."

Myra giggled. "You're right. And he won't like it, ain't so?"

That little giggle did Anna's heart good. "We'll make him behave, the two of us."

Myra nodded, her hand stilling on the cloth. "He's been so worried about me he's practically ferhoodled these days. But that must stop. I'm fine now."

Myra could hardly be fine, but if she was adjusting to the news, that was a relief. She'd seemed so quiet and stunned at first that they hadn't known what to do. "I'm glad you're feeling better."

"Ja." Myra ran her hand over her belly, smiling a little. "It's so foolish to worry. God will take care of our little boppli, I know."

Anna wasn't sure how to respond to that. Was Myra trying to convince herself that the test had been wrong? Surely not.

"I'm sure God will be with you and the boppli," she said finally.

Myra put another dish in the drainer, her lips still curving in a smile. "I love him already, you know. I feel as if my love protects him."

"Ja, I know."

This was bringing back memories. Jannie, convincing herself that all the tests were wrong, that she would be well and healthy, that Pete would give up his drugs, that they'd live happily ever after.

"You feel that way about your Gracie," Myra said. "At first I didn't know what to think when you told us she'd been born to your friend, but now I see that you love her just as much as if you'd carried her, like I am carrying my little boy."

"Did the doctor say the baby is a boy?" Anna didn't remember anyone saying the baby's sex. In fact, she'd thought Myra and Joseph didn't want to know.

"No, but I can tell." Myra caressed her stomach again. "I know."

Alarms went off in Anna's head. Myra's grief would be all the worse if she convinced herself of things that weren't true.

"You know, in those booklets the doctor gave us, it mentions a woman at the clinic who counsels patients." Now that Anna thought about it, that was probably the woman Leah had mentioned. "Maybe it would be a gut idea to go and talk with her a time or two."

"Ach, I don't need that. I have you to talk to, and Joseph. I'm fine."

"Myra . . ."

But Myra had walked over to the window. "Look, Anna. Samuel is working the horse now. Oh, he looks fine. You'd never know that gelding was the same skittish animal, would you?"

Anna joined Myra, standing back from the window so that Samuel would not catch their faces pressed against the glass. She could see

Samuel perfectly well from here—his shoulders broad under his blue shirt, his black suspenders crossing them. He wore his straw hat, but even with the shade it cast she could see the intent look on his face as he worked the horse.

"He's done such a professional job with the gelding. I hope Mr. Bartlett appreciates it."

Myra clutched Anna's hand, as if that would make the watching easier. "I know I'm prejudiced because he's my brother, but Samuel really is a fine-looking man, don't you think?"

Since that was just what she'd been thinking, she could hardly argue, so she nodded. "He has a lot of character in his face."

"Everyone sees that, I think. Everyone but him." Myra's eyes misted over. "When our father left, it seemed like he took all of Samuel's confidence with him. I'm afraid Samuel fears he's like Daadi. Unreliable."

Everything in Anna rose to deny that. "That's just nonsense. Everyone knows how responsible he is. Why, look how he's taking care of the business. He'll even give up working with the horses if Joseph needs him."

She was giving away feelings she hadn't even known she had, speaking so heatedly in Samuel's defense. But surely anyone who knew Samuel well would say the same.

Who was she kidding? She had feelings for him. If she were free to follow her instincts . . .

But she wasn't. She glanced into the living room. Gracie stood, a red ball in one hand, attempting to throw it toward Joseph. Instead it slipped from her grasp when she flung her arm up, falling behind her. She spun around, wobbling a little, looking at the ball with round-eyed surprise.

Anna's heart clenched with love. She couldn't follow her instincts where Samuel or any other man was concerned, because her daughter came first. Maybe she understood, better than she had thought at first, Myra's frantic need to believe her baby was all right. The love of mother for child was elemental.

If she stayed, if Samuel was interested and willing to commit . . . Well, those were all huge ifs. How could she be sure that this life was right for her baby? And how could she be sure that her own rebellious spirit wouldn't wake and demand freedom again?

As for Samuel, he seemed to have backed away from the feelings he'd shown the night he kissed her and from the intent she'd sensed when he'd asked her to go to the fair. She'd thought then that he was imagining them as a family. She'd thought that a relationship was there if she wanted it.

Since then, her sense had been that he'd backed away. Even today, in the barn, she'd thought he was going to express his feelings, but he'd fallen silent.

Maybe he felt that was for the best. Maybe neither of them was ready for anything more than friendship.

Celebration seemed to hang in the evening air, mingled with the spicy scent of the marigolds planted along the edge of the back porch. Anna glanced at Joseph and Myra, sitting side by side on the porch swing. They looked . . . contented, that was the word. Despite all the trials of the past weeks, at the moment they were simply thinking of Samuel.

"So the Englischer, he was pleased," Myra prompted Samuel, sounding like a child who wants to hear a favorite story again.

Samuel leaned back against the porch post from his perch on the top step, setting aside the plate that had contained a slice of apple crumb pie. He glanced at Anna, as if inviting her to smile with him at Myra's moment of happiness.

"Ja, Myra, he was most pleased. He said he would recommend me to his friends."

"And he paid well," she prompted.

"He paid well." He grinned. "He paid well enough to make up for any customers I lost us in the shop while Joseph was out."

"Don't be ferhoodled," Joseph said. "You've done fine, you have."

"With Matthew's help, and your daad's. That boy has a gift for mechanics. He fixed that automated sander from the carpentry shop without advice from anyone. I'd have been asking Joseph, if it was me."

Anna leaned back in the rocker. She ought to gather up the dessert dishes and coffee cups, but she lingered, listening to the soft voices and watching the lightning bugs rise from the grass.

"Bartlett wants me to go along to the auction at New Holland with him. Help him pick out a young horse to train for driving. He has a fancy to get a buggy." Samuel paused, frowning a little. "I'm not sure if I should. It takes a lot of time to school a young horse."

Was he thinking again that he had to give up what he wanted for others? Surely not. "It must not take more than retraining one that's already been spoiled, like Star. You did wonderful gut with him," Myra said.

"That's right." Joseph jumped in on her words. "You'll take the time you need for it. It's important. And besides, I'm doing better every day, ain't so, Myra?"

She nodded, patting his knee. "You'll soon be all well."

It was what Myra would say to Sarah if she bumped her head, but Joseph didn't seem to notice. For that matter, Joseph and Samuel also didn't seem to notice that there was anything wrong with Myra's sudden cheerfulness. They both loved her and wanted so much to see her happy that they didn't look beyond the surface.

Anna would like to believe it, but she couldn't. She studied Myra, who was talking now with animation about something Sarah had said that day. All that easy chatter . . . that wasn't Myra.

Anna would have to do something. Talk to Joseph. Or maybe Samuel would be better. He was her brother, after all. Yes, Samuel was the one. She didn't want to worry Joseph if there was no need. Surely together she and Samuel would be able to convince Myra to talk to the counselor.

Joseph stretched, yawning. "I'm ready to go in, I think."

"I'll go with you," Myra said, standing. When Anna started to move, she waved her back to her seat. "Stay, no need to go in yet. Talk to Samuel."

Once the door closed behind them, Samuel gave a soft chuckle. "My sister, the matchmaker. Just ignore her. You don't have to stay out here if you have something else to do."

Anna shook her head. "It's a beautiful evening. I hate to go in."

"Ja." Samuel glanced out across the darkening fields. "We won't have too many more warm evenings like this to enjoy sitting out."

She tilted her head back to look up at the half-full moon. "It reminds me of when I was little. Everyone would gather on the back porch in the evening after chores, and I'd beg to be allowed to stay up later. 'Just five more minutes, Mammi.'"

"And she let you." His voice was warm, as if he had memories like those, too.

"Ja. I'd be so sure I could stay awake, but of course I couldn't. I'd drift off to sleep with their sweet voices in my ears."

She wasn't sure how it happened. One moment she was fine, and the next her voice choked and tears threatened to spill over.

Samuel swiveled toward her. Without saying anything, he reached out and took her hand. His was work-hardened and warm, but so very gentle. His fingers moved on the back of her hand, caressing it, sending waves of comfort through her.

"You are missing your mamm," he said finally. "I know. I feel that, too."

She nodded, not sure she could trust her voice to speak. She just held on to him, letting his strength and comfort flow through her, until the tightness in her throat eased and she could speak.

"She was so patient, always. She took such joy in every little moment with each of us."

He clasped her hand gently. "That's the kind of mother you want to be, ain't so? The life you want for your daughter, too."

"I guess so." What he said was true, wasn't it? Certainly that she wanted to be at least half the mother Mammi had been.

Exasperation with herself welled in her. Why couldn't she just decide, once and for all, that this was the life she wanted for herself and her daughter?

Samuel's fingers tightened on her hand. "Anna . . ." He hesitated, as if searching for words.

She had to stop him before he said something that would change things irrevocably between them. "Myra," she blurted out the name. "We have to talk about Myra."

She felt the surprise that went through him at the abrupt change. Felt him hold back for an instant and then accept.

"What about Myra? She seems better today, ja? I am so relieved that she's adjusting."

"Adjusting? She's not adjusting at all. Don't you see that?"

He let go of her hand then, frowning. "But she seems happier, more like her old self."

"That's just it." Anna leaned toward him, willing him to believe her. "That's not normal. She can't simply get over news like this all in a moment."

He mulled that over, not responding right away, his face in the dim light giving nothing away. Finally he shook his head.

"I don't know, Anna. Don't you think it's possible that she's prayed and has come to some peace about the boppli's condition?"

If only that were true. "But she hasn't. When we talked, she as gut as told me that the doctor is wrong. She said she's sure that the baby is a boy, and that he'll be fine."

She saw Samuel absorb the impact of her words. His face tightened, the skin seeming to draw against the bones. "Have you told Joseph?"

"Not yet." She shook her head. "I hate to upset him just when he's starting to improve. But I think she needs to talk to someone about it. There's a counselor at the clinic, a woman Leah knows. But Myra insists she doesn't need to see her."

Again he was silent. She expected herself to be impatient with him, but she wasn't. His lack of reaction didn't mean that he didn't understand or that he didn't care. It was simply Samuel's way.

"I'm not convinced you're right," he said slowly. "But I know we can't take a chance. We must all help her. Joseph, Leah, you, and me. But mostly you, I think."

"Me? Why me?" Did Samuel really want to trust his sister to her?

He took her hand again, holding it in a warm, insistent clasp. "You're the woman who is closest to her right now. She counts on you. I know you will help her. Ain't so?"

She nodded slowly, but somewhere deep inside a seed of doubt began to open. How could she help Myra face the truth? She had enough trouble doing that herself.

CHAPTER FIFTEEN

I'll let you get started on the dining room cleaning, first." Rosemary set a cleaning caddy filled with supplies on the oval table. "Just let me know if you need anything else."

Anna nodded, picking up a bottle of furniture polish. There had been a subtle change in Rosemary's manner since Anna had arrived as a household helper rather than a neighbor. Subtle, but there. Obviously they were now employer and employee.

That was fine. After working in a restaurant for three years, Anna knew it was best to just smile and get on with it. Whether a customer shouted at you for something that was the cook's mistake or stiffed you on the tip, that was just the way things were.

Besides, being Amish was good training in humility. She started polishing the mahogany breakfront. All that was really important was that she'd found a way to earn a little money.

And why is that important? the little voice at the back of her mind asked. *Because you're not really committed to staying here, that's why. Because you think someday you're going to want to run again, and the money will be needed.*

She'd saved up before she left the last time, squirreling away most of the money she'd earned working at Paula Schatz's bakery in town. But then the accident had happened, and she'd had to leave much more quickly than she'd intended.

The money hadn't gone far . . . just about enough for the bus that had taken her to Chicago, with very little left over.

Jarrod's mother had offered her money when she'd learned Anna was leaving. Anna had turned her down, of course. They'd done enough for her, hiring a lawyer to defend her against the driving charge. She couldn't take anything else from them.

In retrospect, Mrs. Wells had probably been so happy to see the Amish girl out of her son's life that she'd have gladly paid anything, not that Anna would have taken money for that.

Not very pleasant thoughts, she decided. She concentrated on the polishing, liking the way the liquid made the rich color of the wood come out.

Rosemary wandered back in while she was working on the table legs. "That looks great." She ran a finger along the top of the breakfront. "I just love this piece, don't you?"

"It's very nice," Anna said, starting on the chair legs while she was down on the floor.

Rosemary picked up the window cleaner and a paper towel. "I'll do the glass on the doors."

Anna glanced up, a little surprised. "You're paying me to do the work."

"I know." Rosemary grimaced slightly. "I was trying to be the boss, because that's what my husband told me to do. 'Tell the girl what to do and let her get on with it,' he said. But I'm not very good at that. I'd rather work along with you."

Anna had to laugh. So the change in Rosemary hadn't gone very deep. "I would like that better, too."

Rosemary sprayed the pane of glass and began polishing energetically. "It's pretty boring, doing the cleaning by myself. I guess it's different in an Amish family, with so many people around to help. You always have company."

"Ja, I guess so." Anna remembered what Myra had said about doing dishes with her sister when she'd first arrived. "Working together can be a time for talking and joking, too."

"That's the thing," Rosemary said. "Having someone to talk to."

Anna could hear the yearning for connection in Rosemary's voice. She knew the feeling. She'd certainly felt that way herself, when she first went to Chicago. She'd been out of place there, and apparently Rosemary felt out of place here.

"I was often lonely when I went out in the English world," she confessed, wondering if it would help. "I was independent, but lonely."

"I'm not . . ." Rosemary stopped, shrugged. "Well, I guess I do get lonely, with my husband gone so much of the time."

"Why did you move here? I'd think you'd be happier in town, where you'd have near neighbors." Joseph and Myra's place was the closest house, and that was a good half mile down the road.

"Oh, we thought it would be fun. Picking out the land, deciding on the house plans, and then decorating the place." Rosemary stood back from the breakfront to see the effect of the shiny glass doors. "I did enjoy that. I picked out everything in the house myself, and Richard gave me free rein. Whatever I wanted, I could have."

"Generous," Anna said. Richard must do very well if he could afford that.

"Richard is always generous. He's just not here very much to enjoy the place now that we have it." Rosemary leaned on the back of a chair, the paper towel idle in her hand. "Once the house was finished, I realized there wasn't much to do here."

"What did you do before you got married?" Anna reminded herself that Rosemary was paying her well for her time. If she wanted to use that time to talk, she'd listen.

"I was a secretary. Richard's secretary, to be exact. I worked my way up from receptionist to the boss's secretary." She made a little face. "That's a pretty tacky story, isn't it? But I do love him."

"I can see that." There was a softness in Rosemary's eyes whenever she mentioned her husband. "It's a shame you can't have more time together."

"I guess it's not like that for you Amish. Myra and Joseph are together all the time, I see."

"Just about. That's the Amish way. They started out being farmers, with the whole family working together to run the farm. But it's hard to find enough good farmland, even here in the valley, so people have to turn to something else. They still try to keep the work as close to home as possible."

"Joseph could probably make a lot more money if he went to work in a factory."

"That isn't the most important thing to us."

Us, she'd said. But here was another place where she felt like two different people. The Annie who'd worked for tips in the restaurant so she could take college classes—that Annie would have done almost anything to make more money. She had known only too well that it meant the difference between having a decent place to live and being out on the street.

And she was still doing it, in a way. Hedging her bets. Working for Rosemary to have the money she'd need if she left.

"Do you miss it?" Rosemary asked. "Your life in Chicago, I mean."

"Sometimes," Anna said, trying to be honest.

"Gracie's real mother—birth mother, I mean. She wasn't Amish, was she?"

The question startled Anna. "No, she wasn't."

Jannie hadn't been anything definite, it seemed. Just another of the lost kids who ended up in one big city or another.

"It makes me wonder." Rosemary tilted her head to the side, watching Anna's face. "I wonder if you're doing the right thing, trying to bring up an English child in the Amish world."

For a moment Anna couldn't speak. The blow had been unexpected. Finally, she fell back on words that weren't her own.

"Her mother wanted me to raise her right. That's what I'm trying to do."

"Sure, I know you have Gracie's best interest at heart. I just wonder if bringing her up Amish is what her mother had in mind."

Anna took a breath, tamping down her anger. Rosemary seemed to be one of those people who blurted out what was in her head, even when it wasn't really any of her business.

"Gracie is my child," Anna said. "I must make the decision about what is the right life for her."

It was what she believed with all her heart. She just wasn't sure she knew what that right life was.

Anna shook out the damp sheet and pinned the corner to the clothesline Joseph had put up for Myra in the backyard. The breeze caught the sheet, billowing it out like a sail. Anna lifted her face.

It felt like fall suddenly, with a crispness in the wind that hadn't been there the previous day. The calendar was turning to October, and this long September warm spell was coming to an end.

Anna clipped the sheet to the line, trying to concentrate on the simple task. Trying not to let her mind spin back to that conversation with Rosemary yesterday.

Was it right, to consider bringing Gracie up as Amish? Was that what Jannie would have wanted?

When she and Gracie had arrived, all she'd been able to think about was safety. Like a rabbit diving into its hole at the approach of the fox, she'd bolted home, knowing they'd take her in.

Knowing, too, that she could disappear into the community. The outside world would look only at the dress and think Amish, without peering any more closely at the individual behind the prayer kapp.

The panic that had driven Anna had vanished quickly, but it had taken weeks to make her feel safe. Now she did. Now she seriously considered staying.

And that brought her full circle back to the question she would like to avoid. Was it right to bring Gracie up here?

She reached automatically for the basket to pick up the next piece of laundry and found it empty. She'd hung the entire line full with sheets and pillowcases without even noticing.

She stood for a moment, frowning as she watched them flap in the breeze. She wanted to talk to someone. If she could lay out all her doubts, maybe her course would become clear.

As a child, she'd always turned to Leah, the big sister who could solve every problem, but she couldn't talk to Leah, of all people, now. She would be so hurt if she knew Anna had doubts.

All of them would, if they knew. The whole family had enough to worry about, what with Joseph's slow recovery and Myra's cheerful pretense that nothing was wrong.

As Anna picked up the basket, she saw movement out by the barn. It was Samuel, leading one of the horses. Over his shoulder was the chain he'd used to move her car that first day.

Anna dropped the basket and scurried toward him, telling herself it was none of her business what he was doing, but compelled to go anyway.

By the time she reached the barn, he'd already disappeared inside. She hurried in. Samuel was harnessing the horse to her car.

"What are you doing?" she said.

Samuel looked up. He was probably startled, but his stolid face didn't reveal it. He patted the horse's shoulder.

"I asked you that the day you came back, when I found you in here harnessing up Joseph's buggy horse."

"I know. I remember." She crossed the barn floor toward him. "What's going on, Samuel? Where are you taking my car?"

His eyebrows lifted slightly. "Your daad sent word over by Matthew. He's arranged for the junkyard man to come for it today. He asked if I'd haul it out of the barn for them, not wanting the tow truck to come in here."

"Today." She'd been expecting it, but still it seemed to catch her by surprise.

"Ja, today. You did tell him to get rid of the car, ain't so?"

"I did." She hesitated, but after everything else she'd said to Samuel, she could say this. "I just didn't think it would bother me so much when the time came." She moved closer, patting the dusty fender much as Samuel had patted the horse. "This was Jannie's car. I couldn't afford one. As you can see, she couldn't afford much of a car."

The tension in his expression eased. "Your friend left it to you."

"I hadn't driven since the accident, just used public transportation, but she insisted I had to try. In case I needed to get the baby to the hospital or anything."

"So she cared about the baby's future, even knowing she wouldn't be there."

Anna ran her finger along the side mirror, her thoughts drifting into the past. "We drove out of the city one day, when she felt well enough. She wanted to see the country, she said. To see trees and grass again before she . . ." Her voice failed her.

"I'm sorry." His voice was a low rumble. "It's brought up sad memories."

Anna shook her head. "Bittersweet, maybe. Not entirely sad. She was happy that day."

"If you don't want to get rid of the car, you can tell your daad why. He'd understand."

"No point in that. It's so far gone it's of no use anyway, I guess."

For a moment Samuel stared at her, as if absorbing her words. Then something flared in his eyes. "Were you planning to make a quick getaway, Anna?"

The edge of anger in his voice caught her on the raw, startling her. Samuel, who never lost his temper, was furious with her.

Her own temper rose in an instant. "If you're thinking I'd run off and leave Myra when she needs me, you don't understand me as well as you think, Samuel Fisher."

He seemed taken aback by the direct attack. He took a step toward her, the anger fading from his face, and something solemn taking its place.

"If you left, I would be sorry on my own account, not just on my sister's. I would be disappointed in you, as well."

The mood had changed so quickly she felt oddly off balance. Everything that might be between them seemed to hover in the air, unspoken. She wanted to touch him, to assure him that she was here forever, that it was safe for them to love each other. But how could she? The doubts still clung.

She shook her head, trying to swallow the lump that had formed in her throat. "I don't want to disappoint you. Or anyone else. I just . . ."

It was hopeless. He wouldn't understand. He'd have only the simple answer that she belonged here, so her child did, too.

"Tell me." He caught her hand in his. "What is troubling you so?"

Anna couldn't seem to turn away from his intent gaze. Finally she shook her head.

"It's foolish to let it trouble me, maybe. But when I was working at Rosemary's yesterday, she said something that . . . well, it raised a question in my mind." She stopped, not sure she should continue.

"What did she ask?" Samuel obviously wouldn't let it go.

Anna took a breath. "She asked whether it was right, to raise a child born English as Amish."

Samuel was quiet for a long moment. She had the sense that beneath his calm surface, tension roiled.

"I shouldn't have said anything," she said quickly. "Just forget it."
She tried to smile, but it probably wasn't very convincing. "I've gotten
into the habit of confiding in you, and that isn't fair."

His hand tightened on hers. "We are friends. We should be able to
say the difficult words, ja?"

She nodded, her throat tight.

"So tell me what it was your friend Jannie expected from you."

She took a shaky breath. "At first, she counted on me as you would
on any friend. She thought she was going to be all right. She floated
along on that belief for months, it seemed, ignoring what the doctors
told her."

Her throat thickened still more, so that it was an effort to get the
words out.

"When she finally accepted that she wasn't going to survive, all her
strength went to the baby."

"It's what a mother does," he said quietly.

She nodded, tears pricking her eyes. "Jannie had always been so
timid. Malleable. She never seemed to have a thought of her own, just
went along with what everyone else wanted. Suddenly she was a mother
lion. She decided what she wanted to do and pushed everyone into line.
Got the lawyer, got Pete to sign the papers, arranged for me to adopt.
The lawyer was doubtful about me. He tried to get her to give the baby
to an agency for adoption, but she was determined that I would be
Gracie's mother."

"Did she tell you why?"

"She said she could count on me to raise Jannie right."

"If she thought that, it was because of the person you are, ja?" His
voice was gentle.

"Of course."

"And you are who you are because of how you were raised. How
could she trust you with her baby without trusting what you come
from?"

His words seemed to sink into a place deep in her heart, easing and
soothing. They rang true, and she knew he was right about what Jannie
had intended.

"Jannie knew I was Amish," she said slowly. "She was the only one out there who did know. She must have realized, must have thought all along that coming home was what I would do."

"That is what I would think, from what you've said about her."

"Denke, Samuel." She looked into his face, gratitude welling in her. "Thank you."

"There is something else I must say. Something you might not want to hear." His voice was very grave. "Your friendship with the English woman . . . I don't think it is a gut thing."

She could only stare at him. "Rosemary? Why would you say that? True, she did raise doubts in my mind, but that's just because she didn't understand. I'm sure she meant well."

"When you are with her, you start to think like an Englischer again, ain't so?"

Think like an Englischer. The words echoed. Maybe they were true. Maybe that's why they stung so much.

She straightened. Grateful as she was to Samuel, she wouldn't let him dictate who her friends were.

She managed a smile. "I appreciate your help. Now I had better let you get back to your work, and I'll get back to mine."

She turned and walked quickly out of the barn.

"*Komm,* komm." Myra's hands fluttered as she gestured Samuel toward the bedroom. "The boppli's crib must go in the corner of our room, where I can get to it easily."

Samuel carried the crib mattress through the doorway, his misgivings growing. "Myra, you have months to get the crib ready for the boppli. Why must we do it today?"

"Over here." Myra ignored his question. "The crib must be here." She sketched the shape of the crib with her hands against the wall.

He set the mattress down. "I will go and get the tools and the other pieces."

"Ja, ja," Myra said absently. She stared at the spot where the crib would go, smiling.

He hurried out of the room and back down the stairs, wishing he knew what was going on in his sister's mind. She had taken a sudden fancy to set up the crib she had borrowed from Barbara, since little Gracie now occupied the one that had been Sarah's. She didn't want Joseph doing all that bending, so she'd decided that Samuel must do it.

He glanced into the living room, where Joseph was keeping the two little girls occupied. Joseph met his eyes and gave a helpless shrug. He didn't know what to do, either.

If Anna were here, she might be better equipped to handle Myra's sudden whim, but Anna had gone over to Leah's house this morning to help her prepare for a party at the school.

Anna was never far from his thoughts these days. He sorted through the crib components, which Levi had stacked on the back porch, making sure all the bolts and nuts were there.

He'd gone over and over the conversation he and Anna had had in the barn yesterday, trying to assure himself that he'd said the right words. He could understand her worries about what the English woman had said. It was no simple matter, bringing up an English child to be Amish.

But Gracie had been Anna's child since she was born, and Anna had never stopped being Amish, despite her attempt to live in the English world. He believed with all his heart that what he'd told Anna was true. Her friend must have known that the way Anna was raised made her the person she was.

He carried an armload of crib bars up the stairs and into the bedroom. Myra still stood where he'd left her, looking with dreamy eyes at the place where the crib would go. Concern edged its way to worry.

"I'll get the rest of it," he said, and escaped.

Coward, he accused himself as he hurried down the steps. If Anna were here, she'd know what to do. He felt a flare of resentment that he knew was totally unreasonable. Anna had every right to go to Leah's or anywhere else this morning. He should just be relieved she wasn't back at Rosemary's again.

He wasn't wrong, was he, thinking that the Englischer's friendship wasn't best for Anna right now? Most Amish had some English friends, but for Anna, so recently returned, he feared the lure of that other life might be too great.

Anna hadn't liked it when he'd said so. He'd seen the flare of resentment, quickly suppressed, in her eyes.

In the old days, Anna wouldn't have bothered to suppress it. Maybe that wouldn't have been so bad. At least then she wouldn't have been treating him with such cool politeness.

That bothered him more than he'd like to admit. Worse, it made him wonder whether his concern over that friendship was for Anna, or for himself.

He carted the rest of the crib pieces upstairs. He'd best concentrate on the job at hand. Worrying about Anna didn't get him any further, did it?

But he couldn't shake her from his mind so easily. He squatted, pulling the crib pieces together under Myra's watchful eyes.

"I will put Sarah's quilt on it for now," she said. "But I'm going to make a new one, just for him. He'll like that, don't you think?"

"Ja." Samuel's voice sounded strangled, and he cleared his throat. "When do you think Anna will be back?"

"Sometime this afternoon." The faraway look faded from Myra's face, thank the gut Lord. She smiled. "You like our Anna, don't you?"

"I like her fine. Don't you go matchmaking, now."

"Why not? Who else will say it to you, if not your own sister? You and Anna would make a fine pair."

"Why?" He attached the side rail to the headboard. "Just because Anna needs a daadi for Gracie and I'm past the age of courting a teenager doesn't mean we're right for each other."

"Don't be ferhoodled. Because you two fit together perfectly, that's why. I wouldn't have thought that three years ago, but you've both changed. You've grown into yourselves, in a way."

"Maybe. Anna has grown and changed, that's certain-sure." He stared at the screwdriver in his hand, wondering why he'd picked it up. "But I don't think the changes in me have made me any more suited to marriage. Maybe less, if anything."

"Ach, Samuel, you must not think that." Myra dropped to her knees next to him, startling him. "This is because of Daad, ja?"

He shrugged. "Maybe." He tried not to say more, but the words seemed to press at his lips, wanting to come out. "You know what it did to us, him leaving like he did. What if I did that?"

"You wouldn't."

The total confidence in her voice comforted him, but he couldn't let go of his fears so easily.

"Nobody would have thought that about Daad, either, but he did."

Myra was silent for a moment. "Didn't anyone?"

That brought Samuel's startled glance to hers. "What do you mean?"

Her gaze slid away from his. "I . . . nothing. I shouldn't have said that."

He took her chin in his hand, turning her face toward his. "Tell me. Did you know Daad was thinking about leaving?" It seemed incredible that little Myra would know something like that.

"Not know, exactly." Her eyes darkened with the memory. "But sometimes when he was away from home working with the carpentry crews . . . well, when he came back, he talked differently. Like that other place out there was his real home." She shook her head, as if bothered by her inability to explain it all. "And he wasn't so very gut at keeping his word, Samuel. We all knew that, even you."

He opened his mouth to speak and closed it again. He didn't know what surprised him more, the fact that such words were coming from little Myra or that they rang so true.

"Daadi . . . maybe it's true that he didn't always do what he said he would." His memory provided him with too many examples of that. "But there was always a gut reason. And he'd make it up afterward."

Just saying the words made him see how lame they were. Could a man ever make up for not keeping his word?

"You see," Myra said, as if she knew what he was thinking. "I loved Daadi, but I guess I always knew I couldn't count on him." She put her hand on Samuel's arm. "It's harder for you. You were his favorite, and you'd have done anything to please him."

Samuel wanted to deny it, but he couldn't. "If that's true . . ." His voice sounded like someone else's. He cleared his throat. "If that's true, it makes it even worse. I always wanted to be like him. What if I am?"

"Ach, don't be so foolish." Her tone scolded lovingly. "Look at yourself. You've never broken your word one single time in your whole life. Everyone knows that about you, except maybe you."

He shook his head. He couldn't sort it out. He needed time to get his mind around it.

"I'm not telling you what to do." Myra patted his arm. "I just want you to be as happy as I am." She reached out to touch the crib with a gentle caress. "I have Joseph, and Sarah, and a fine home. And now the new baby. My perfect little boy."

Her words stabbed Samuel, chasing away every other preoccupation. "Myra, the doctor said—"

"Ach, don't even think about that. The doctor was wrong, that's all. I'm sure of it."

"But Myra . . ."

She rose, hand cradling her belly. "Komm, get working on that crib so I can see how it looks. I will get the bedding for it." She hurried from the room before he could say another word.

He sat down on the floor, feeling as if gentle Myra had just taken his heart and shaken it. First the revelation about his father, and now this . . .

He'd misjudged the situation with Myra, dismissing Anna's concerns. He should have listened to her. She'd been right.

They had to persuade Myra to get help, but how? His heart quailed at the thought of arguing with her about her baby.

He had to talk to Anna the minute she got back. Anna would know what to do.

Chapter Sixteen

Anna clucked at Myra's buggy horse, and the animal obediently picked up speed along the narrow road. It was surprising, really, how quickly she'd felt familiar with the horse and buggy again. After not driving a buggy in three years, the lines had felt odd in her hands at first, but now it was as if she'd never been away from it. The tension she'd felt after the near-miss coming home from the fair was still there, but it was under control.

She had to admit there was at least one advantage to driving a horse instead of a car. The horse had instincts a car never could. Myra's buggy horse was on her way home, and if she didn't stop her, the mare would keep going until she got there.

She had a stop to make, now that she'd delivered the baked goods to Leah for the school sale. She'd picked up a phone card the last time she went to the grocery store for Myra, so she could finally make a long distance call to Liz in Chicago.

A phone shanty stood at the intersection of two farm fields. She checked the horse and turned into the dirt lane that led to the shanty.

The idea of putting a telephone in a shed far from the house was so foreign to the English world that she was glad she didn't have to try to explain it to anyone. People out there made being constantly connected a necessity, as if they couldn't survive for even a few hours without cell phones and e-mail. She'd seen people in the restaurant trying to eat and talk on the phone at the same time, and ignoring the human being sitting across the table, like as not.

To the Amish, a telephone in the house would encourage idle chatter with others instead of concentration on the family. Still, they recognized that a telephone was necessary for emergencies and sometimes for businesses. So the answer was simple—put the phone far enough away from the house so that one wouldn't be tempted to idle talk but near enough to be reached when needed.

Betsy, apparently deciding that the phone shanty was Anna's only possible destination, came to a stop next to it without being asked. Anna got down quickly, pulling the phone card from her pocket.

At last she could talk to Liz. Maybe hearing her friend's voice would erase the unsettled feeling that had haunted her lately.

Not lately. She ought to be honest with herself, at least. She'd been unsettled since the car had been hauled away, to be exact. It had taken her last illusion, irrational as it had been, that she still controlled her ability to come and go. And that conversation with Samuel certainly hadn't helped, either.

He had been so kind, so reassuring when she told him about what Rosemary had said. His calm, reasonable approach had comforted her. More, it had restored her faith in her own judgment.

Then he'd as much as told her she should drop her friendship with Rosemary, as if Anna were a child who needed his guidance. Or more likely from his viewpoint, a slightly defective Amish woman who couldn't be trusted to have an English friend without being lured back to that world.

Anna had thought they understood each other. She'd thought he was the one person she could count on for support. Well, she'd been wrong.

Irritation made her yank open the door to the phone shanty. She stepped inside. A plain black phone sat on a rough wooden shelf, a basic answering machine next to it. A blinking light suggested that the owner hadn't been by to check messages recently.

There was not even a stool to encourage anyone to stay and chat. She put the plastic card on the shelf next to the phone and breathed a silent prayer.

Please, let Liz be there. I need to talk to someone who will understand.

The good Lord must have been listening, because Liz picked up on the second ring. Longing swept through Anna at the sound of her voice. If she could see her right now, sit and talk . . .

"Liz. It's Annie. I'm so glad you're home." Just saying the words made her feel like Annie again.

"Annie, thank goodness." Liz's voice fairly leaped through the telephone receiver. "I've been going crazy wanting to talk to you. Why haven't you called?"

Anna skipped over the question, knowing she couldn't answer it in any way that Liz could understand. "What is it? What's wrong?" Her heart seemed to pick up speed at the urgency in Liz's words.

"It's Pete." Liz's voice was controlled, but an effort. "He's been around again, trying to find out about you and the baby."

Anna's heart thudded to her shoes. "Did you talk to him? What has he done?"

"Don't get excited. Honestly, I thought by this time he'd be long gone, but it hasn't worked out that way."

"Liz, I'm so sorry—"

"Now you stop that." Liz was brisk. "It's not your fault that idiot has slid over the edge into crazy. If he'd stop pickling his brain with drugs, maybe he could see sense for once."

Anna found she was pushing the receiver against her head so hard that it hurt. "Did you talk to him? Did he threaten you?"

Liz snorted. "He tried. I'm not scared of a nutcase like him."

Anna took a breath, trying to focus. Liz wasn't letting Pete scare her, and she couldn't either. "What exactly did he say?"

"Just the same as before. He kept saying Gracie was his baby and he wanted her." Liz snorted again, expressing her opinion of Pete. "I told him he didn't know a thing about bringing up a baby and never would. I told him he didn't have a legal leg to stand on."

"What did he say to that?" The walls of the shanty seemed to be closing in on her, and Anna had to force herself to breathe.

"That he wasn't counting on the law to get her back. That's why I had to talk to you, Annie. I had to tell you. I'm afraid that if he finds that baby, he's going to grab her and take off."

"He's not going to find her." Anna had to be sure of that. She had to. She closed her eyes, searching for the calm that eluded her.

"Annie, listen. When Pete realized he wasn't going to get anything out of me, he said he didn't need me anyway. That he'd figured out how to find you without help from anybody."

An icy hand closed around Anna's heart. For a moment she couldn't speak. Gracie . . . She wanted to drop the phone, race home, grab the baby. Run. Run.

She couldn't. What good would that do, to run mindlessly? *Please, Lord. Help me to think.*

"Annie? Are you there? I tried to get him to tell me what he meant, but he wouldn't."

"Yes. I'm here." She took a breath. "He was bluffing. He had to be. There's no possible way he could guess where I am."

No one in Chicago knew about her past. She'd told no one, just Jannie. Jannie wouldn't have said anything. If she had told Pete where Anna was from, surely he'd have come after her before this.

"Well, that's good. But regardless, you need to go to the cops."

"I don't think . . ."

"Never mind thinking, just listen to me. Pete's a convicted felon who signed away his rights to the baby before she was even born. The police will help you. They'll give you some protection."

Anna tried to imagine the reaction should an Amish woman go walking into the local police station. This wasn't an ordinary situation, but if she went to the police, she'd have to tell them everything about Jannie and Pete.

Anna had the legal papers. She could convince them, eventually, but how long would that take? If they made inquiries in Chicago, which they were bound to, her location might slip out.

And sooner or later it would leak out here. How could that help but happen? And her family would know all that she hadn't told them.

"I can't." The words burst out. "I mean, it would just make things worse if people knew. Besides, I'm sure Pete couldn't know how to find me. We're safe here."

Please, Lord, let me be right.

"I still think the cops—"

"I can't, really."

Liz was silent for a long moment. Then she sighed. "Well, as long as Pete is wandering around the neighborhood here bothering people, we know he can't be coming after you. I can try to keep tabs on him, so we'll know if he sets out on any long trips. But you've got to give me a phone number where I can call you if anything happens."

That was the one thing Anna couldn't do. "I can't. I mean, I don't have a phone."

"Come on, Annie." Liz's voice was laden with disbelief. "What are you doing, living in the dark ages? Everyone has a phone."

"I don't. I'm sorry." She rubbed her temple with the heel of her hand, trying to think.

"You don't want to give me an address, I suppose. But what about a neighbor? There must be somebody who could pass along a message to you. Don't you have a landlady or a super?"

There was Rosemary. She could give Liz Rosemary's number. But if she did, she'd have to tell Rosemary at least something of the truth.

For a second, Samuel's face formed in Anna's mind. What did it say about their relationship, if she confided in Rosemary and not in him? Maybe it said he was right in what he feared about her.

Gracie. She had to keep her mind on Gracie, no one else. She took a breath.

"I'll give you the number of a neighbor. You can trust her with a message for me."

The ban on telephones, annoying enough when she was a teenager and longed to be in touch with her friends, now seemed monumental. Anna turned the buggy into Joseph's lane. The horse, knowing the terrain as well as she did, picked up speed as she sensed her barn.

If Anna had called Liz sooner . . .

Still, what good would that have done? It wouldn't change the facts. Whatever was going on in the recesses of Pete's mind, he'd apparently become obsessed with the baby he'd never wanted.

Anna had had to give Liz Rosemary's number, no matter what Samuel thought of her relationship with the neighbor. Rosemary's telephone represented her only lifeline to Liz. If Pete really did know something about where Anna was, she had to have warning.

She'd intended to stop at Rosemary's on her way home, but Rosemary hadn't been there. It was unreasonable to feel so annoyed over that fact. Rosemary couldn't have known that Anna would need her.

Her hands were cold on the lines, despite the warmth of the day. What had she been thinking, trying to hide Gracie in a place where she couldn't even call for help in an emergency?

The horse slowed as the buggy neared the end of the lane. Samuel and Matthew appeared in the shop door. The boy ran to the horse's head while Samuel approached the buggy, looking up at Anna, his face tight.

"Matthew will take care of the horse and buggy for you." His tone was abrupt. "Komm, please. I need to talk with you." He held out a hand to help her down.

She had to yank her thoughts away from Gracie to concentrate on his words.

"In a bit, ja? I must go and check on Gracie first." She needed to hold her daughter in her arms and feel that she was safe. The need was a physical ache.

"Gracie is napping." He took her arm, urging her toward the shop. "Myra put her down not half an hour ago. This is important."

Important. Her mind skittered from one thought to another as she let him lead her to the shop. What would Samuel consider important at this point? Had he glimpsed her buggy approaching Rosemary's house and decided to lecture her again?

The shop was dim after the bright sunshine outside. Before her eyes could adjust, Samuel turned to her, his figure no more than a dark bulk against the rectangle of light from the doorway.

She took a quick breath. If he thought he could dictate who she saw, he'd better think again.

"It's Myra." His voice roughened with emotion. "Anna, you were right about her. We must do something."

Now Anna saw what was in his face. *Fear.* He was afraid for Myra.

She reached out, touching his arm. It was like iron under her fingers. His control was holding, but she had a sense that it wasn't going to last for long.

"All right, tell me. Tell me what happened."

He sucked in a breath. "She wanted me to put up that crib for her, so I was doing it."

"Already?" Levi had brought the crib yesterday, but what was the hurry?

"She insisted. She started talking about the baby." His eyes were dark with misery, and the look tugged at her heart. "Anna, I should have listened to you. I didn't. I thought I knew better."

"That doesn't matter." She shoved her own worries to the back of her mind. "Tell me what she said. She didn't try to hurt herself, did she?"

His face went white. "No!" A shudder went through him. "You don't think she would do that!"

"I don't, but we have to think of every possibility."

"There was nothing like that. She seemed happy. Too happy, I thought. And then she started talking about how the doctor was wrong. How she was going to have a perfect baby boy."

"Ja," Anna said, her heart sinking. "I was afraid that's what she was thinking."

"She's not accepting it. I thought she was coming to see that whatever happened, it was God's will. I thought that was why she seemed so calm now." He sounded as miserable as Anna had ever heard him. "And all the while she was just convincing herself that it wasn't real."

"Samuel, you have to understand. This news is just too hard to accept, so she has to make herself believe it isn't true." Again Anna thought of Jannie's pretense that everything was all right.

Samuel shoved his hand through his hair and rubbed the back of his neck. "I should have seen it. I know Myra better than anyone. Why didn't I see it?"

"You can't blame yourself."

She'd wanted him to understand, but she hated seeing the pain in his face, hearing the blame in his voice. Samuel would fault himself—that was inevitable. He always held himself to a higher standard than anyone else.

"If I had listened to you . . ."

"It wouldn't have made a bit of difference as far as I can see." She forced herself to sound brisk. "We have to get Myra to agree to see the counselor. Ja?"

Her attitude seemed to steady him. He took a deep breath, his gaze focusing on her face. "Are you sure this woman can help her?"

"I don't know, but if she can't, she'll work with the doctor to find the answers for Myra. Leah knows this woman. She has every confidence in her."

"Ja, that's gut." The haunted look slid off his face. Given practical steps to take, Samuel would have the strength for it.

"Did you talk to Joseph about what Myra said?"

He shook his head. "He did seem to think something was wrong with her insisting on putting up the crib right away. As for the rest, I waited for you. I thought . . . well, you were the one who saw it first. I thought you would know what to do."

She nodded, trying to focus on how to handle the situation. "Maybe it would be best if you talked to Joseph about what Myra said to you. I'll check on her. Then I think I should tell Leah. She might come over and speak to Myra."

If Anna went to get Leah, she could stop and see Rosemary on the way. That sounded so selfish, but she had to deal with the pressure of her problems, too. The sooner she made arrangements about Liz calling, the better.

"That is the right plan. I'll see what Joseph thinks. Surely, if we all show Myra how worried we are, she'll go to see the counselor, even if she thinks she doesn't need it for herself."

"Ja. Myra would do anything to keep the people she loves from worrying."

That was true, wasn't it? Anna's thoughts jumped back to her own worries. Not even Myra's love and caring could help with that.

Fear rushed through her again. Pete. She had to keep Gracie safe. She realized that her fingers were digging into Samuel's arm.

She let go quickly, pressing her hands together. She had to concentrate on the problem at hand. One thing at a time.

"This is going to be all right, Samuel. Have faith." She started to turn away.

Samuel took both her hands in a warm, firm grip, preventing her from moving. "Something else is troubling you, Anna. Was ist letz? How can I help?"

"I . . . It is nothing." Tears stung her eyes. She wouldn't cry.

His hands enclosed hers, not letting go, and his intent gaze held hers. "It is not nothing, I think. You were already upset when you got home, but I was too caught up in my own worries to see it. Did something happen while you were out?"

"Not exactly." Her lips were trembling. She clamped them together. She couldn't break down, not now, not in front of Samuel. "It's nothing." She should pull her hands away from his, but she couldn't. She found too much comfort in his grip.

He lifted her hands, holding them close against his chest. She could feel the beating of his heart.

"I know better, Anna." He shook his head, his eyes never leaving hers. "Maybe neither of us was ready for this to happen, but it has. We are too close now for you to lie to me. Tell me what is wrong. Let me help you."

Tears welled in her eyes. "I want to, but I can't," she whispered.

"Ja, you can. Whatever it is, I will try to understand."

The need to speak flooded through her. "I can't . . ."

He waited. Just waited, his hands pressing hers against his solid chest.

She choked back the tears. "You can't help. No one can." She sucked in a ragged breath. "It's Gracie's father. He's looking for us. He wants to take her away from me."

Samuel stood motionless as he struggled to accept and understand Anna's words. He should respond quickly, but he couldn't. That was not his way.

He focused on her face, seeing the mixture of torment and rebellion in her eyes. "I don't understand. You told us the father didn't want the baby."

"He didn't." She almost spat out the words. "He couldn't wait to sign the papers giving up his rights. She wasn't even born yet, and he already knew he didn't want her."

"Then what has happened?" Samuel felt the impatience running through her, and he held her hands firmly in his, sensing that if he didn't, she would run away. "Help me to understand."

"How can I, when I don't understand it myself? He didn't contact Jannie when the baby was born. He didn't come to Jannie's funeral. Then he turned up a year later, suddenly deciding he wanted the baby." The anger in her voice slid away to a tremor. "It was as if Gracie was a toy he'd forgotten about for a while and then remembered."

"I'm sorry. So sorry." Whatever the right or wrong of it, Anna was hurting, and Samuel longed to make that better. "What kind of man could not want his own child?"

But even as he said the words they were bitter on his tongue. His own father had been able to walk away from his children without a backward glance.

Anna turned away from him, as if he'd said the wrong thing, rubbing her hands on her arms as if she were cold. "I'm sure there are plenty of men who don't want to be fathers. And Pete has been scrambling his brains with drugs for years. I doubt he could form a thought about what it means to be a father."

"Poor man."

She spun, anger flaring in her eyes. "Poor man? What about all the people he's hurt? He doesn't just use drugs himself. He sells them. He knocked Jannie around for as long as they were together. The night he came and tried to take Gracie—" She stopped abruptly, wrapping her arms around herself.

"He tried to take her away from you?" Samuel's blood chilled at the thought. "Anna, what happened? You weren't hurt?"

She took an audible breath, pressing her fingers tight against her arms. "I didn't have any warning. Just opened the door and there he was. He barged in before I could react, yelling, demanding that I produce the baby. Thank heaven she was asleep." Her voice trembled a little on the words.

"You had no one to help you?" His heart pained him at the thought of her facing that alone.

She shook her head. "I tried to talk sense to him, reminding him that he'd signed away his rights to her, but I don't think he even heard me. He was high on something, his eyes wild. When I wouldn't produce Gracie, he tried to go after her. We struggled. He hit me, knocked me down." She spread her fingers against her ribs, as if remembering the pain. "I couldn't have stopped him."

Samuel's own hands clenched into fists. He couldn't raise them against another human being, but for the first time in his life, he wanted to. *Forgive me, Father.*

"What happened? How did you get away?"

"The neighbors heard what was going on. They rushed in, hustled him out. They called the police." A tremor went through her. "They said I should go in the next day and file a complaint against him, but I didn't. I packed our things and ran."

"You came home," he said. That, at least, he understood, that longing to be home.

"I came home. But he's still after us." She pressed her fingers to her temples, turning to face him. "I was so sure he'd forget about it. Either that, or be arrested again for dealing. But Liz says—"

"Liz. That is the friend you called, that day at the hospital."

"I talked to her then and again today." Her breath seemed to catch, and her blue eyes grew dark. "She said he hasn't given up. He's questioning my friends about me. He even told her that he had a way of finding me without her help."

"Anna, I'm sorry. If I had known . . ."

If he had, would it have changed anything between them? The longing to protect her was stronger than Samuel could have imagined possible.

"You couldn't have done anything," Anna said. "I have to see Rosemary. Liz will call her if anything changes."

For a moment Samuel tried to reason away the hurt that brought. "You would trust a stranger when you won't trust your family?" *Or me.* That was what he really wanted to say. "Anna, you must talk with your father about this."

"I can't. Don't you see that?" She turned on him, anger bringing a flush to her cheeks. "You heard what he said that day at Barbara's picnic. You know how fair he always is. If he thought the father wanted Gracie, what would he do?"

"Anna, listen. If your father understood all of it, if he knew everything you've told me, I'm sure he would stand by you."

"And what if he didn't? What if he said that a legal paper doesn't make Gracie mine? I can't risk it. I can't tell him. Once it's said, it can't be unsaid."

"But—" Samuel thought she was wrong, but her quick mind ran circles around his. He couldn't find the argument that would convince her.

"Samuel, you can't tell anyone." Fear made her voice urgent. "You must promise me that you won't tell anyone what I've told you." She grabbed his arms, her grip fierce. "Promise me."

"Ja, Anna, I promise." Whether it was right or wrong, he could do nothing else. "I won't tell. And I will help you."

She let go of him, stepping back, her face changing as if she had turned into someone he didn't know.

"Help? If Pete came and tried to take the baby, what could you do? You wouldn't take up a weapon against him. You wouldn't call the police."

"Anna—"

She shook her head, eyes filling with tears. "Don't you see? I can't keep Gracie safe here. I should never have come home."

CHAPTER SEVENTEEN

Anna's throat was still tight with unshed tears from that painful scene with Samuel when she reached Leah's house. No matter how frightened she was about Pete, Myra's problems were more immediate.

Reason told her that chances were very small Pete could find her, even if he'd somehow learned where she came from. Amish society was one of the few places in America that was off the communication network. No search of phone records or Internet sites would tell him anything.

"Ach, Anna, it's wonderful gut to see you." Leah turned away from the kitchen sink, drying her hands as she hurried to embrace Anna. "I didn't expect you to come back again today, or I wouldn't be in the midst of doing the dishes."

That was the flip side to Amish isolation. She hadn't been able to call and tell Leah about the trouble. She'd had to come and hope Leah was here.

"It doesn't matter at all," she said quickly. The stacks of baked goods Leah had been collecting this morning must all have been delivered. With its warm wood cabinets and sparkling countertops, Leah's kitchen looked like any English kitchen, except that the appliances ran on propane and there was a gas lamp over the pine table.

"I had to talk to you—"

Anna's words were arrested when two-year-old Rachel came rushing across the kitchen to throw herself at Anna's legs. "Gently, Rachel," Leah chided.

Anna scooped the little girl up in her arms to plant a kiss on her chubby cheek.

"Gracie," Rachel demanded, patting Anna's face.

"Gracie couldn't come this time. Next time, all right?"

Losing interest since her cousin wasn't there, Rachel wiggled. "Down."

Anna couldn't help but chuckle as she lowered her niece to the floor. "She does know what she wants, doesn't she?"

"She's spoiled, that's what, with Daniel and the older children fussing over her since the day she was born."

Given the indulgent smile on Leah's face, Anna thought they weren't the only ones doing the spoiling. Rachel was the boppli Leah had never expected to have, until Daniel came to the valley.

And if Rachel was a little indulged, was that so bad? She was also greatly loved, not just by her parents but by her extended family, indeed, her whole community.

Anna's heart clenched. If she had to leave, Gracie would never know that love.

"Sit, now, and I'll fix some tea." Leah waved her dish towel toward the nearest chair.

"Not now, denke." She had to get to her reason for coming. The memory of Myra's bright, unnerving smile pushed at her. "I have to talk to you about Myra."

Leah's eyes filled with concern. "What has happened?"

"She's not adjusting at all to the situation. She's convinced herself that the doctor is wrong. I'm afraid, when the reality finally hits, it will devastate her."

"Ach, I was afraid of that."

"I hoped we could get her to meet with your friend at the clinic, but I'm afraid she won't agree."

"Lydia Weaver. Lydia is just the person to help her. I've never met anyone more compassionate." Leah's own face shone with caring.

She tossed the dishtowel she was holding onto the rack and went to the door. "Elizabeth?" she called up the stairs.

"Ja, Mammi." Footsteps thudded on the steps, and Leah's stepdaughter appeared. "Aunt Anna." She smiled. "It is gut to see you."

"Elizabeth, I need you to watch Rachel. Aunt Anna and I must go out for a few minutes."

Curiosity filled Elizabeth's eyes, but she didn't ask questions. She just nodded and went quickly to the living room where Rachel was playing.

"Now." Leah took Anna's hand in a firm grip. "We will go to the telephone shanty to make an appointment for Myra right away."

Anna felt the burden she'd been carrying grow suddenly lighter as they hurried out to the buggy. Leah could be counted on.

She climbed up, and Leah got quickly into the seat next to her.

"The closest phone is just across the field, but we can go by the lane." Leah pointed out the route. "Daniel had the phone shanty put in after little Rachel arrived so soon and Rachel Brand had to deliver her."

"I'm sorry." Anna's words came without planning. "I wish I'd been here."

"I know." Leah clasped her hand.

"If I hadn't stopped writing, it wouldn't have been so hard for you to find me."

"When you left, you promised you'd stay in touch." Leah said the words slowly, as if they were heavy. "Why, Anna? Why didn't you?"

Tears blinded her eyes. "I thought it would all be easy." She looked back in wonderment at the foolish girl she'd been. "When it wasn't, when it was a struggle just to survive, I felt I couldn't tell you that. And I couldn't lie, so I just stopped writing."

Leah clasped her hand firmly for a moment. "You can tell me anything."

Anything? Pain struck Anna's heart.

She'd thought that once she told Samuel about the troubles with Pete, she'd be free of the compulsion to tell someone, but instead the need was even stronger. She longed to spill out the whole story to Leah. Leah, more familiar with the world than most Amish through her work at the clinic, would probably understand.

But what if she told Daadi, and what if he thought Pete should be given a chance? How could she risk it?

She couldn't. Anna wiped away a tear with the back of her hand and saw that tears filled Leah's eyes, too. "Look at us, riding along and crying. What would people think if they saw us?

"They might think it is gut that I have my sister back," Leah said.

Anna's heart clenched, and again she felt the pressure to tell Leah. But she couldn't.

"What if Myra refuses to go?" She asked it abruptly, because it seemed easier to focus on that.

Leah patted her shoulder. "I think when the two Beiler sisters are determined, no one will stand in their way for long. We'll get her there."

"Samuel will help. We talked about it, and he'll convince Joseph."

"Ja, that's gut. Myra needs everyone in agreement on this."

Leah gestured toward the grassy lane that led to the shed, and Anna turned in. Betsy probably wondered why she was making two trips to a phone shanty in one day, but she plodded along obediently.

"So you and Samuel are getting close, ain't so?" Leah said.

A few days ago Anna would have been able to turn the question away with a laughing response. Now she couldn't. Now her throat clogged with tears at the thought of how she'd left things with Samuel.

If she could change what she'd said to him—no, she probably wouldn't if she could. What she'd said was true. She dare not risk doing what he wanted. And if Pete came . . .

If Pete came, all she could do was what she'd done before. Run. As far and as fast as she could.

Joseph was getting stronger—there was no doubt about that in Samuel's mind. He'd come out to the shop when Anna left for Leah's again, obviously curious.

Not having figured out how to tell him about Myra, Samuel had taken the cowardly way and shown him the machine he was working on. The result was predictable. At the moment, Joseph was seated on a chair next to the workbench, tinkering with the portable generator that had been acting up.

Joseph's improvement was a relief to Samuel's mind, but in a way he almost wished it weren't so, since that might give him an excuse not to have the conversation he knew he must have.

He'd promised Anna he'd talk with Joseph, and so he would, as soon as he finished welding the broken harrow. He slid his goggles into place and started the torch.

Unfortunately, even that didn't keep him from thinking of what Anna had said, standing in this very spot.

She'd been upset, that was all. She hadn't meant it about leaving.

But he was afraid she did, and after hearing her story, he couldn't bring himself to blame her for anything she'd said. Thinking of her confronting a dangerous addict on her own tied his stomach in knots. He could only thank God she hadn't been hurt.

Still, she'd lied. She continued to lie to her family by what she didn't say, and now she'd brought him into the lie, too.

If she let her fear of that man push her into running again, what chance was there that they'd ever see her again?

She'd leave pain behind for all of them, but he couldn't pretend he was thinking of the others. It was the possibility of his own loss that tortured him. He loved her.

He'd never intended to let that happen. Hadn't thought it could. But it had. And now, just when he'd begun to believe he could trust himself to love someone, she might disappear.

He switched off the torch and bent to have a look at the harrow. Anna wouldn't leave. She and Gracie were happy here. He had to believe that.

Satisfied that his work, at least, was under control, he tossed the goggles aside. Enough of these thoughts. He had to talk to Joseph, and the sooner the better.

Joseph looked up at his approach and put down his screwdriver, stretching cautiously. "I'm thinking maybe that's enough for today. I should go in and make sure Myra's all right. Did you know Anna went off to see Leah again this afternoon?"

Samuel didn't miss the critical note in Joseph's voice. He leaned against the end of the workbench, trying to decide how to respond. Ordinarily Joseph was the most easygoing of men, but his slow recovery had put an edge on his temper.

"It's gut to see Anna and Leah being friends again, ain't so?" he said mildly.

Joseph pressed one hand on his ribs as he levered himself to stand. "That's fine enough, but Anna left Gracie for Myra to mind. She should be helping Myra, not giving her extra work to do."

Samuel had the sense that Joseph was probably talking out of his own frustration at not being able to do what he should. Still, Samuel couldn't let a rift start between Joseph and Anna if he could help it.

"Anna went to see Leah today because she's worried about Myra. As I am. We hope that Leah will be able to help."

"What do you mean? Worried about what?" Joseph straightened to his full height, supporting himself with a hand on the bench. "Myra's fine and healthy. The doctor said so."

Did Joseph really not suspect anything? "Ja, her body is all right. But her mind—"

"There's nothing wrong with my Myra's mind. I am her husband. If something was wrong, I would know."

"Joseph, have you heard the way she talks about the baby? It's like she didn't hear anything the doctor said. Anna thinks—"

"Ach, Anna. I love my sister, but she always brings too much drama to everything. You know what she was like when she was a teenager. She's making a mountain out of a molehill, that's all."

"Anna isn't the person she was when she went away. She's a grown woman now, and she's worried about Myra. So am I. It is not gut for Myra to refuse to accept the truth."

"There is nothing wrong with Myra." Joseph's face reddened. "It is a difficult time for her. You should be supporting her, not criticizing her."

Samuel had gone about this all wrong, it seemed. "I am not criticizing. I just want her to get the help she needs."

"Myra is fine." Joseph turned away, probably too fast, because he sucked in a breath and put his hand to his ribs. "Just leave it alone. Both of you leave it alone."

He walked stiffly out of the shop. Usually Samuel would have given him an arm to help him into the house, but he didn't think Joseph would appreciate that right now.

Samuel ran a hand through his hair. Anna had trusted him to gain Joseph's support, and he'd failed.

Anna checked the chicken potpie that simmered on the stove. Almost done. Maybe supper would improve the atmosphere in the house. Everyone, even Sarah and Gracie, seemed a bit out of sorts since she got home.

Her own thoughts had been chaotic. Leah's call to her friend at the clinic had resulted in an appointment for Myra tomorrow. Now, somehow, they had to convince her to keep it.

And Anna had stopped at Rosemary's on the way home. She'd tried to explain as little as possible, but Rosemary had jumped to so many conclusions that maybe it would have been better to tell her everything.

Rosemary had agreed to come right over if Liz called. That was the important thing. But she'd gone further than that. She'd offered Anna a loan to leave now—today, in fact.

Anna ladled potpie, made the traditional Amish way with square, puffy noodles, into Myra's biggest earthenware bowl. She didn't want to take Rosemary's money. She didn't want to leave now, maybe not ever. But it might be better, at that. If she were to leave, the longer she put it off, the harder it became on everyone, including herself. At least now she knew someone would support her, if it came to that.

She'd told Samuel she wouldn't leave while Myra needed her. The promise stuck in her heart.

She headed for the door to call everyone for supper, only to find them already coming in from the backyard, Myra holding Sarah's hand, while Samuel carried a wiggling Gracie.

"Supper is on."

"Ja, we smelled it." Samuel's smile seemed a bit strained.

Anna pulled the highchair close to the table. The bustle of getting everyone settled created a cover for her question to Samuel. "How did it go?" she murmured.

"Not gut." Concern darkened his eyes.

There wasn't time for more, but she thought she could guess the rest. Joseph was refusing to face the truth.

She slid into her seat, clasping her hands for the silent prayer that began the meal.

Dear Father, help us. Are we doing the right thing? Help Myra.

She sent a covert glance at Gracie, to find her sitting quietly, small hands linked as she concentrated on mimicking the others. Anna's heart seemed to turn over. Gracie was at home here. How could she think of taking her away?

Joseph nodded to Samuel, who lifted the heavy bowl of potpie and started it around the table. What had happened between the two of them, then? Samuel had said it was not gut.

Anna tried to concentrate on cutting up the puffy square of potpie dough for Gracie, who was already making a fine mess with her apple-sauce.

"Gracie, not with your fingers." She put a spoon into her daughter's hand. "Use the spoon."

"Sarah would still rather use her fingers than a spoon," Myra said. "I must work on that before the boppli comes."

Anna nodded. If Myra was talking naturally about the baby, that was what they wanted, wasn't it?

Myra ran her hand across her belly, lips curving. "I will feel him kicking soon, ja? I remember from Sarah. That is such a joy, to feel that. Remember the first time you felt that, Joseph? Remember?"

Anna's heart sank. Myra was talking too fast, her eyes too bright, her cheeks flushed like someone with a fever.

"I'm sure you will," she said, hoping to soothe her.

Joseph clasped Myra's hand in his. "I remember. We are all right about this boppli." He shot a glance at Samuel. "Myra and me, we accept God's will for this child. We will love and care for it, no matter what."

"He." Myra's voice emphasized the word, and she snatched her hand away. "Our baby is a little boy, I know it. He is our perfect little son."

"I know you would like a son this time." Joseph spoke carefully, as if any word might cause hurt.

"It is a boy. I know it. I don't need any tests to tell me. The boppli feels different this time, and everyone says that's a sure sign."

Alarm shivered through Anna. She had to find something to say to defuse the situation. Myra seemed to be teetering on the edge of an explosion.

"We could start a crib quilt for the boppli," she said. "Wouldn't that be nice?"

The words, meant to comfort, seemed to have the opposite effect.

"Don't talk as if I were a child myself." Myra's voice rose. "You think there is something wrong. There's not! Nothing is wrong with my baby!"

They were all stunned into silence, to hear gentle Myra shout at them. Then Sarah, never having heard that tone from her mother, burst into tears. Gracie's face puckered, and in an instant she was crying, too.

Myra's chair scraped as she shoved it back. Anna expected her to go to Sarah. Instead, she turned and hurried from the room, shoulders stiff. They heard the thump of her feet on the stairs, followed by the slam of the bedroom door.

Anna leaned over Gracie, trying to comfort her. "Hush, hush, little one. It's all right."

Moving stiffly, Joseph lifted Sarah from her chair, cuddling her in his lap. He looked at Samuel, his eyes dark with misery.

"I'm sorry. You tried to tell me, but I wouldn't listen. I'm sorry." He glanced at Anna, as if to include her in the apology.

"It's forgotten," Samuel said quickly. "Myra is all that's important now."

Joseph nodded, his eyes suspiciously bright. "Ja." He cleared his throat. "Anna, you and Leah, you will help, ja?"

"Of course we will." Pain clenched her heart to see her big brother look so hurt and bewildered. She would do anything she could to make this better.

And what if she had to leave? What would she do then?

CHAPTER EIGHTEEN

After nicking himself with the screwdriver twice in ten minutes and coming within an inch of slicing Matthew's hand, Samuel had decided that he was a danger in the shop. Leaving Matthew to carry on, he'd brought Mr. Bartlett's new young horse to the ring to work him for a bit. That, at least, he could do without danger to anyone else.

His problem wasn't hard to figure out. His heart was with Myra at the clinic, and his mind busy with prayers for her.

Be with her now, dear Lord. Open her to hear the counselor's words.

The two-year-old gelding, apparently sensing his lack of concentration, dropped to a walk. Samuel flicked the lunge whip in his general direction to get him moving again.

After Myra's outburst at supper last night, he'd thought it would be impossible to get her to the appointment, but it hadn't turned out that way. Maybe she'd actually frightened herself as much as she had them.

In any event, when Joseph had gone up to the bedroom to talk to her once the children were settled, she'd been so passive that that seemed to frighten him, too. Convinced this was for the best, bolstered by Anna's conviction, he'd finally gotten her agreement to see the counselor.

This morning she'd clung to Anna, so it had been decided that Anna would go with Joseph and Myra while Leah stayed with the children. Samuel didn't doubt that Leah had spent the time praying, just as he had.

When he spotted the car turning into the lane, he slowed the horse, bringing him in smaller and smaller circles until the animal stood next to him. He stroked the strong neck, murmuring quietly for a few minutes before turning the colt into the adjacent pasture.

Common sense told him that they could hardly expect a miracle from one session. Even so, he wanted to rush into the house, needing assurance that his little sister was better.

He contented himself with strolling toward the back porch, wondering whether it would be too obvious if he went inside for a drink of water. Maybe so. Instead he used the pump by the porch, lingering over filling the tin cup, pushing his straw hat back on his head, drinking. He was about ready to repeat the process when Anna came out of the house.

He waited until she neared him, reading the tension in the fine lines around her eyes. "How did it go?"

"Not here."

Anna took a quick glance around. She nodded toward the grape arbor and led him quickly to the slight privacy it provided. Then she turned toward him, and what she saw in his face must have telegraphed how worried he was.

"I'm sorry, I didn't mean to alarm you. It's nothing bad. The counselor was very encouraging."

"But you're still concerned." He could read her feelings so easily, even as relief flooded through him at the counselor's confidence.

"I'm just not sure." She bit her lip for an instant. "Myra was so quiet when she came out of the office. I thought— I hoped and prayed we'd see . . . well, some sign that she's coming to grips with the situation." Anna looked up at his face. "I pushed this, I know. Have we done the right thing? What if . . ."

"Now stop." He took hold of her arms, feeling the tension in her. "Anna, you must not think that way. You saw how Myra was last night. You know we had to make this decision for her, out of love."

"It's so difficult. I keep thinking of Jannie, of how I questioned myself every day. Was I doing the right thing for her? I'd never been responsible for anyone before. Never wanted to, never thought I could be."

Her uncertainty took hold of Samuel's heart and squeezed. "Was that why you ran away from us?"

"I don't know. Maybe." She shook her head. "It didn't work, if that was why. I took responsibility for Jannie and then Gracie. And now Myra." Her voice trembled. "What if I'm wrong?"

"I told you. You're not wrong." He drew her closer, uncertain if this was what she needed, but longing to comfort her.

With a sigh, Anna leaned against his chest. He wrapped his arms around her. *Comforting,* he told himself. *That's all she needs right now.*

"This time you're not alone." He said the words softly, his breath stirring the hair at her temples. "We're all taking responsibility for our Myra. We all love her, and the boppli."

Anna nodded, and he felt the movement. His heart was so full it seemed it would burst out of his chest. He longed to tell her what he felt, but this . . . this was like walking on ice. The smallest misstep could send him plunging to the depths.

So he stood, holding her, sensing the tension ebb slowly from her body. Loving her.

How foolish he had been, to think he couldn't love anyone for fear he was like his father. When true love came, it wiped away every doubt. If he told her . . .

No, not now. Not when she was so worried. He rested his cheek against her hair and was content.

"Anna?" Leah's voice accompanied the slam of the screen door. "Are you out here?"

Anna pulled back, wiping her face with her palms. "I'm here." She walked quickly out of the arbor, and Samuel followed.

Leah stood at the bottom of the porch steps, looking a little flushed when she saw them. "I'm sorry. I didn't know—"

"I was just filling Samuel in on what happened," Anna said quietly.

"Gut." If Leah thought anything else, she was wise enough not to say. "I'm heading home now. I'll stop over sometime tomorrow."

"That would be a help," Samuel said. "You understand this better than we do."

Leah shook her head. "You're both doing fine." She patted his hand, and then seemed to realize that she was holding an envelope. "I nearly forgot. Matthew brought the mail in. There was a letter for you." She handed the envelope to Anna and hugged her. "Don't worry too much, the pair of you. Myra will be well."

Anna gave her a quick squeeze. "Denke, Leah. Da Herr sie mit du."

May God be with you. It was the first time Samuel had heard Anna use the loving response since her return. Leah's eyes sparkled, and she walked quickly toward the buggy as Matthew drove it up.

Anna stood for a moment, holding the envelope in her hand. She looked a bit frightened. "Samuel, it is from Aaron Esch. The family . . ."

"Ja, I know." The family whose buggy she had hit. "Aren't you going to open it?"

She took a deep breath and then ripped the envelope open. A single sheet of paper fell out. "It is from Aaron's wife."

She bent her head to the words, and he murmured a quick, silent prayer. Anna was dealing with enough just now. Let the letter not make things worse.

She looked up at him, pressing her lips together as if to keep them from trembling. "She says they will see me, if that is what I want."

"Is it?"

She hesitated for a moment, then nodded. "I think so. It's time I took responsibility for what I did."

"It's a long drive to the Esch farm. I will take you there, if you like."

Her fingers closed over his. "Denke, Samuel."

Giggling, Sarah sent a spray of bathwater onto Gracie's round tummy. Gracie responded by waving both hands, splashing herself in the face and dampening the front of Anna's dress. She looked so startled at what she'd done that Anna was surprised into a laugh.

"Two little fishes swimming in the creek." Anna grabbed the towels she had waiting. "The big bird swoops down and snatches them up."

She scooped Gracie up with one towel and then quickly grabbed Sarah with the other, leaving no time for wails about leaving the bath.

"Bird, bird," Sarah cried, entranced with the new game. "Dry me, bird."

"I will, I will." Anna pulled them both into her arms, rubbing their pink bodies with the towels. She was getting herself nearly as wet as they were, but holding them so close made it worthwhile. Their innocent laughter was an antidote to the day's worries.

They were probably making more noise than they should, since Myra was supposedly asleep in the bedroom across the hall. Myra had spent the afternoon there, come down and picked at her supper without speaking, then gone back up again, saying she was tired.

It was so unusual for Myra to sleep during the day that Joseph's stress had shot up again. Maybe it would have been better to let Myra come to terms with the baby's problems on her own. Maybe . . .

Since Anna had the same worries, she could hardly argue. She'd chased him and Samuel off to keep Sarah and Gracie occupied while she did the dishes. A half hour in Samuel's calm, steady presence would be better for Joseph than a half hour of asking questions to which they had no answers.

Anna popped nightgowns on the two squirming children, thinking that she could have used a quiet half hour with Samuel herself. For an instant she was back in his arms again, feeling the steady beat of his heart against her cheek.

Gracie wiggled free of her and made a dash for the bath, clearly intending to climb back in.

"No, you don't." Anna snatched her up, nuzzling her soft, damp cheek until Gracie giggled. "Time for two little girls to have their stories."

"Sarah pick," Sarah declared, and darted for the bedroom.

Gracie twisted to join her cousin, so Anna put her down and followed the two of them into their bedroom. Gracie grabbed a book as well, and Anna sat on Sarah's bed, drawing Gracie onto her lap and snuggling Sarah against her.

The orange reflection of the setting sun suffused the room with a gentle glow, and the soft sounds of evening filtered in—the whoo of an owl, the distant clop of a horse's hoof, the continuous cricket chirping.

Anna pressed a kiss on Gracie's damp curls as she opened the book of nursery rhymes. If they left, Gracie would lose this peaceful setting, the stable upbringing, the love of a large family.

But if they stayed, she would lose everything the world valued—higher education, the latest technology, clothes and cars and all the rest of it.

The choice might not be Anna's to make. The thought lay under the tale of Jack and Jill as she read.

There had been no news from Liz. She clung to that as she read a Bible story, said prayers, and tucked them into their beds with hugs and kisses. Gracie was already half-asleep, and she curled under her blanket without a fuss.

Sarah took a few minutes to arrange her rag doll just so, but her eyes were drooping, too. With a last kiss, Anna went quietly out.

Myra stood in the hallway, looking heavy-eyed. "I fell asleep." She sounded surprised. "Did you put Sarah to bed already? I should have."

"You needed the rest. She went down fine for me, but she's not asleep yet. Why don't you go in and snuggle with her for a minute?"

Myra brushed her forehead with her hand, as if wiping away the wisps of sleep, and tiptoed into the room.

Through the half-open door, Anna could see that Gracie didn't stir. Sarah sat up, holding out her arms to her mother, and Myra sank down on the bed, hugging her. Myra's shoulders shook, and Anna tensed. Maybe it hadn't been such a good idea for Myra to go in, not if she was going to let Sarah see her crying.

Perhaps Myra thought the same, because she straightened, talking softly to her daughter. She kissed her, tucking her in, and came out quickly.

"All right?" Anna closed the door.

"Ja." Myra blinked, as if trying to focus. "I was just—" She stopped, hand on the door, and then leaned her head against it.

"Myra—" Anna wasn't sure what to say. If only Mamm were here. Mammi would know what to say. The thought was like a sharp stone in her chest.

"Remember what it is like when they're tiny babies?" Myra said, drawing away, still touching the door with her fingertips. "Remember how you could never stop worrying about the baby, even when she was sleeping, so you'd keep checking on her?"

"I remember." Anna put her arm around Myra's waist, urging her gently toward the stairs. "Sometimes I couldn't hear her breathing, so I'd put my hand on her, just to feel the movement of her chest. It's a wonder I didn't wake her up every ten minutes, doing that."

She could laugh at herself, looking back at it now, but at the time it had been terrifying to have that small life in her care.

Myra actually smiled. "Ach, I was the same. Maybe every mother is."

Myra's response sent a wave of relief through Anna. It was Myra's own sweet smile. "Maybe so, but I didn't have anyone to ask."

"I'll know better this time." To Anna's dismay, Myra's face assumed that mask that declared everything was fine, but she thought she detected a few cracks in the facade.

"I think maybe we'd be a bit that way with every boppli, no matter how many we have," Anna said carefully. "Loving each one as if he or she is the only one, a little like God loves us."

"Of course we do. I will. My boppli is fine, he's fine, he . . ." She stopped short, her lips trembling. "I can't." Her voice choked, and tears flowed down her face like a sudden downpour.

"It's all right," Anna murmured, and then was disgusted with herself. It wasn't all right. Why couldn't she think of something useful to say?

"What if I can't do it?" Myra spoke through the tears, and the mask was gone for sure now. "What if I can't take care of the boppli? What if I can't love this one like I love Sarah?"

There it was, Anna realized as she put her arms around Myra. That was the fear at the center, the one Myra hadn't been able to express.

"You will," she murmured. "Some days you might feel as if you can't, but when that happens, we'll be there to help you. The family won't let you down. God won't let you down. You're not alone. You know that, don't you?"

For a long moment Myra didn't respond. She just clung to Anna. Then, slowly, she nodded. "Ja," she whispered, and the fierce grip of her hands eased. "Ja. I know that."

The tension in Anna ebbed as well. Myra had taken the first step on a long, difficult road.

The closer the buggy got to the Esch home, the more Anna wanted to run in the other direction. Coward, she chided herself, but it didn't seem to do much good.

She glanced at Samuel. His strong face was shielded by the brim of his straw hat so that she couldn't see his eyes, but she imagined that his tension had increased as well.

They had talked during the long ride, mostly about how Myra had been over the past few days. She had seen the counselor again yesterday, and again had come home quiet and withdrawn, but overall she seemed better. She talked rationally now about the baby, without the frantic optimism she'd displayed before, and she'd expressed a desire to talk to Bishop Mose.

Anna found she was watching Samuel's sure hands on the lines. Other than expressing his deep concern for Myra, he'd kept their conversation casual, a far cry from the moments they'd shared that day in the arbor. Either Samuel didn't feel comfortable pushing too close when she was preoccupied with this visit, or he regretted what had happened between them.

Either way, she should be glad of his retreat. She'd grown to care for Samuel, and she recognized the desire to let that caring ripen into something stronger. But she couldn't do that, not when the future was so uncertain.

Samuel slowed the horse and made the turn into a farm lane. Her throat tightened, and she gripped the seat with both hands.

"Is it too late to change my mind about this?" She was only half-joking.

His gaze assessed her. "It's natural to be nervous."

"What if they don't forgive me?" She asked the question, but she was afraid to hear the answer.

"If they refuse forgiveness, then the burden of that failure is on them." He said the words as if no doubt existed in his mind.

"Don't you think that quick forgiveness lets the sinner off too easily?"

"Easily?" He came to a stop some distance from the front porch but didn't move immediately, seeming to ponder the word. "You have suffered for what you did, I think. Maybe you will continue to suffer. It is up to God. All we can do is follow His direction. Forgive, if we wish to be forgiven." He jumped down and held out his hand to her. "Komm. They're waiting for us."

He was right—a man and woman stood on the porch.

"Aaron, Elizabeth." Samuel took over, nodding gravely to them. "This is Anna Beiler."

Anna's voice seemed to have disappeared. She nodded, taking in the expressions on their faces. The man, his dark hair cut short in a bowl style, his beard wiry, looked at her with what seemed to be curiosity. But the woman—when Anna met her gaze, she felt as if she'd received a blow.

"Komm." Aaron Esch spoke as he opened the door. "Wilkom to our home."

They filed into the living room and took seats as solemnly as if they were going to church. And waited. Obviously Anna was supposed to speak first.

She cleared her throat. "Denke." Her mouth was dry, so dry she didn't know how she was going to get the words out. "I asked to come because I wanted to see you in person to ask for your forgiveness. I regret, so much, that my actions harmed your family."

They looked back at her, their faces impassive. It was only now, when she thought it might not be granted, that she realized how important their forgiveness had become to her.

Finally Aaron nodded with deliberation. "It is gut that you feel so, but not necessary to ask. We forgave you long ago, as Christ commands."

Something flickered in the woman's eyes as he said the words, something hidden so quickly that Anna almost missed it. Maybe she only saw the feeling because she was sensitive to everything they did and said. And so she knew. Aaron might have forgiven her, as he said, but Elizabeth had not.

Anna's heart seemed to wince. Was that so surprising? Would she forgive so easily if someone put Gracie in danger?

"Denke. I . . ."

A little girl ran into the room and stopped, obviously taken aback at the presence of strangers. She must have been about five or six, with big brown eyes that studied them curiously.

"Mary, komm, schnell." The woman rapped out the words and reached for the child. The little girl's face puckered, and she ran to her mother, burying her face in her mamm's apron.

Another blow to her heart. That Elizabeth felt the need to protect her child from Anna—it was almost too painful to bear.

But she had to. That was why she was here.

"I have a daughter of my own now." She centered her heart on Gracie, searching for the strength to go on. "I didn't understand until I was a mother how terrifying it is when your child is in danger." Her voice choked in her throat. Tears welled in her eyes. "I know now. You would suffer anything to spare your child."

She wanted to say more, but the words failed her. She put up a shaking hand to wipe away her tears. Tried to speak again, but could only shake her head, covering her face with her hands.

"Don't be sad."

Anna was so sunk in her own guilt that she didn't realize at first that it was the little girl who spoke. The child tugged at Anna's hands, pulling them away from her face.

"Don't cry. It'll be all right. My mammi can make it better."

Anna looked from the child's sweet face to the mother, to see Elizabeth's face crumple. Elizabeth held out her hand, and Anna took it.

CHAPTER NINETEEN

*A*nna walked down Main Street, remembering to adjust her stride to the casual stroll of an Amish woman instead of the fast pace of a city dweller. Samuel had wanted to pick up something from the hardware store on their way home, so they'd made a stop in town. Remembering that she was nearly out of Gracie's vitamins, she'd decided to walk the two blocks to the pharmacy.

The maples that lined the town square were already changing color, and a crispness in the air declared that fall was really coming.

Despite her concerns about Myra and her fears of Pete's actions, at this moment she felt only a strong sense of relief. It surprised her, in a way. She hadn't fully realized how much her unpaid debt to the Esch family had weighed on her.

Had Bishop Mose understood that when she'd first come back? Maybe that had been behind his reluctance to let her kneel before the congregation to confess.

If she had confessed then, she'd have been faking it; she knew that now. She'd thought that would be the utmost in humiliation, but really, she'd have been trying to take the easy way out. Bishop Mose hadn't let her go through the motions, and whatever happened to her in the future, she'd be forever grateful.

She pushed open the glass door of the pharmacy, catching a glimpse of herself as she did. To dress Amish meant to be stared at when you went into the English world, but it also gave her a pleasant sense of anonymity. She was any Amish woman, her hair and face half-hidden by the bonnet.

She dawdled in the baby supplies aisle, knowing she didn't have to hurry. Samuel would dally over his transaction, getting all the news of town while he was at the hardware store.

Thinking about him gave her an odd little flutter in the region of her heart. He had understood, without question, her need to see the Esch family. He'd been confident she could do it—more confident in her than she'd been in herself. She wasn't sure how it had happened, but he'd become so important in her life that it was hard to imagine doing without him.

She carried the vitamins to the counter, exchanging the usual comments about the weather with the clerk as she paid. She would go back to where they'd left the buggy, and Samuel would be waiting. They'd have another half hour or so alone together on the way home. Maybe she could find the words to tell him how much she appreciated his support.

She walked toward the door. Just as she reached it, a rack of newspapers caught her eye. She turned aside to read the headlines, and then glanced through the plate glass window at the street beyond.

Her breath stuck in her throat. Pete—that was Pete, walking across the street toward the square, peering around as if looking for someone. Looking for her.

She recoiled, grabbing the paper rack to steady herself. He couldn't see her, surely he couldn't. She stood safely away from the window. But if she hadn't stopped at the last moment to look at the papers, she'd have walked out onto the street within twenty feet of him. Her heart thudded in her ears, nearly deafening her.

How could he be here? She moved carefully to the other side of the rack, peering toward the small park at the heart of the square. Pete sat down on one of the green benches, glancing up and down the street. He'd picked the perfect location to watch for her, able to see anyone going into or out of the Main Street shops.

Calm down. Think. He wouldn't be doing that if he knew exactly where she was. That gave her a chance.

But why hadn't Liz called? Her mind skittered off in that direction. Liz must not have realized he'd left Chicago. She'd find out, probably, but by then it would be too late.

Please, Lord, help me think this through. Help me to make the right decision. If I don't—

No, she wouldn't let herself veer down that road. If she let panic take over, she'd lose. She pressed her fingers to her temple, a wordless prayer rising in her heart.

She had to get home, grab Gracie, and get out of here before Pete started working his way through the Beilers in the community. At least he wouldn't find them conveniently listed in the telephone book. That would delay him for a while.

She could go to Rosemary. Rosemary would drive them to Mifflinburg, where they could get a bus to somewhere, anywhere.

She took a breath. She had time. Pete operated on brute force, not brainpower.

Still, sooner or later it would occur to him to start asking around. People, even English people, knew the Beilers.

She couldn't go out on the street. He'd see her for sure if she did that. Wheeling, she hurried to the back of the store.

"Is there a rear door I can use? Please, it's important."

Maybe it was the quaver in her voice that convinced him. The pharmacist gave her an odd look, but he led her back through the pharmacy shelves to a door that opened onto the alley.

With a quick look in both directions she slipped out, murmuring her thanks. The alley was empty, and she scurried along toward the hardware store, thoughts tumbling even faster than her rushing feet.

Samuel would help her. She just had to get to Samuel. Did Pete know he was looking for an Amish family? Maybe, maybe not, but she couldn't take a risk that he might. Jannie had known.

Oh, Jannie, did you tell him? I trusted you to keep my secret.

Only another block to the hardware store, but now her luck ran out. The alley ended abruptly at a fenced-in lot. She had no choice but to go back to Main Street.

She stopped at the corner, taking advantage of the cover provided by some passing shoppers to peer down the street. Pete was still sitting on the bench, a block down.

She had to get to Samuel. She'd have to pray Pete didn't know he was looking for someone in Amish dress. She waited for the next passersby and then slipped onto the sidewalk just ahead of them, hoping they screened her from view. Her stomach twisted, and she held her breath, waiting for the sound of running feet, of Pete shouting her name.

Nothing. And there was the hardware store, with its hitching rail along the side for Amish buggies. Samuel stood next to his buggy, lifting a box in.

She couldn't contain herself any longer. She rushed to him, grabbed his arm. "We have to go. Now!"

The surprise on his face gave way to a startled comprehension. Without a word, he grasped her arm and helped her up to the buggy seat. He released the line and swung himself up, clucking to the horse to back him away from the rail.

"Not by way of the square," she said, urgency filling her voice. "We can't go that way."

He nodded, turning in the opposite direction, and in a moment they were heading down the side street, away from danger.

Samuel kept his tension in check as they wound through several back streets to get clear of town. Obviously something had happened in the few minutes they'd been apart—something that had frightened Anna badly. The baby's birth father. What else could it be?

He turned onto the road that led home. Anna kept swiveling, staring behind them, her hand up to shield her face.

If she wouldn't break the silence, he would.

"Is anyone following us?"

She turned around, hands grasping the seat as if to force the buggy to go faster. "It doesn't look like it. I can't see anyone."

He waited, but she didn't go on. Apparently he'd have to pry the words out of her.

"What is wrong? Was it him . . . Pete?"

She nodded, fingers tightening on the seat until her knuckles were white. "I was about to come out of the pharmacy when I saw him crossing the street to the square." Her voice quavered. "If I'd walked out a minute sooner, I'd have walked right into him."

"But you didn't." Samuel put his hand over hers where it gripped the seat. Her tension was so strong that her skin seemed to spark. "God was watching out for you."

She bit her lip. "I hope so."

"I know it," he said, hoping that gave her strength.

"I couldn't go out the front of the store. He'd have seen me. He sat down on a bench in the square where he could watch the whole area. The pharmacist let me go out the back way."

Samuel considered. "So he doesn't know exactly where you are."

"If he knew that . . ." She sucked in a breath. "If he knew that, it would already be too late."

He tried to think it through, tried to put himself in the mind of the man. He couldn't do it. It was too great a stretch.

"All right, then. If all he knows is that you're from this area, then he's just guessing that you're here. He can't be sure you'd come home, because you didn't tell anyone. You can lie low until he gets tired and goes away again."

She was already shaking her head. "I can't. He's bound to ask around. Sooner or later, he'll find someone who knows me."

"Amish are ser gut at playing dumb in the face of nosy questions. No one will give you away."

Her mouth twisted. "I wish I could believe that. But even if no Amish would tell, there are plenty of English who know where the Beiler family lives."

"Anna . . ."

"It's over, Samuel." Her voice was filled with anguish. "I don't have a choice. Gracie and I have to leave. We can lose ourselves in some big city where he'll never find us."

Never. Now, when he was about to lose her, he knew how much he loved her.

"Don't, Anna. You can't just leave." *I love you.* "We'll take care of you and Gracie."

"I can't stay." Her fear was so strong it was like a third person sitting on the buggy seat between them. "I have to keep my daughter safe."

Samuel fought to keep his feelings in check. It wouldn't do, when she was terrified for her child, to put the burden of his love on her.

"Anna, I understand that you must protect Gracie. But this man—surely he will listen to reason. He has no right to the baby, and he's not able to take care of her. Why would he want to take her away from people who love her?"

Anna stared at him, her face bleak. "Did you never run into someone like him when you were out in the world? Someone with such a skewed view of reality that they were lost to good reason and common sense?"

"If that's the case, I wonder that the baby means anything at all to him."

"He's not thinking straight." Her lips pressed together as if to hold back the pain. "Liz had it right. She says Pete always wants most what he can't have. Right now, that's Gracie."

"But if we all talk to him . . ."

"Don't, Samuel." All her pent-up grief seemed to fill the word. "This does no good at all. If Pete finds me, he's going to try to take Gracie. If he does . . . if he does, it's not just that I'll never see her again. I'm afraid that if he takes her, she won't survive."

Her voice shook on the final word, and Samuel's heart seemed to tremble in his chest.

"Anna, listen to me. You must tell your daad and Bishop Mose."

"No, they—"

"When they understand what is at stake, they'll help. They'll even go to the police, little though they'll like it. I'm certain-sure of that."

She threw up her hands in a gesture of helplessness. "Maybe you're right. I hope so. But don't you see? It might be too late. Pete isn't counting on the law to get Gracie back. He's going to grab her and run."

"We won't let that happen." He had to make her believe that, and she was already shaking her head.

"Pete is the kind of man who settles conflict with his fists. He's dangerous, and I've put all of you in danger by hiding here. All I can do is get out of his way. Once he sees I'm gone and no one knows where I went, he'll leave the rest of you alone."

It stabbed him to the heart that she thought she had to protect them.

"Anna, you must trust in the people who love you. Trust in God to deliver us from this evil."

But he saw in her eyes that she had gone far away from him already. She shook her head again.

His heart was breaking for her. Knowing what it would cost, still he had to say what he would do. "You must tell them. If you don't, I will."

She turned on him then. "You have no right to interfere."

"I love you, Anna. I believe that gives me the right to take care of you and Gracie."

Pain drew her skin tight against the bone. "If you do that, I will never forgive you. Never."

The instant Samuel stopped at the house, Anna jumped down from the buggy. She couldn't say anything—there was nothing to say.

Samuel had said he loved her. That was a separate pain that she couldn't begin to deal with now, so she closed it away. Now all she could do was get Gracie someplace safe.

She hurried into the house, registering that Samuel had driven off toward his barn. She had until he'd dealt with his horse and buggy and come back to the shop before he'd tell Daadi. By then, she had to be gone.

No time to pack their clothes—she could only stuff as much as possible into Gracie's diaper bag.

She barreled into the kitchen. Myra, coming in from the living room, gave her a startled look.

"Anna, I didn't realize you were back. Is something wrong?"

"No, nothing." *Everything.* But she couldn't tell Myra. She couldn't burden Myra with her troubles, and she certainly couldn't say she was leaving. "Is Gracie napping?"

"Ja, they both are." Myra smiled. "She was a little lamb while you were gone."

Myra always thought that. She was as gentle and loving with Gracie as she was with her own Sarah.

"I'll go take a peek at her." Anna hurried up the stairs, not letting herself think about all that Gracie would lose by leaving here. There were too many things she couldn't think about now.

She slipped into the children's bedroom. Sarah slept as intently as she did everything, her arm around her rag doll.

In the crib, Gracie lay on her stomach, thumb in her mouth, eyelashes forming perfect crescents on her rosy cheeks. She stirred a little as Anna pulled out the diaper bag and began to fill it.

She would take the essentials. There was no time for more. Pete could be on his way here right now. Her vivid imagination gave her too clear a picture of him rushing down the country road in a fast car, sweeping into the house, snatching Gracie. Disappearing with her.

Law-abiding people were always at a disadvantage when it came to defending themselves against the people who didn't go by the community's rules. The Amish were among the most law-abiding people anywhere, and so maybe the most vulnerable.

Anna swept the room with a quick glance to be sure she hadn't missed anything crucial, and then touched Gracie's cheek lightly.

"Komm, Gracie. We have to go now."

The child's eyelids fluttered. She looked at Anna and gave a sleepy smile. "Mammi," she murmured.

Anna's heart clenched. She lifted Gracie into her arms and took the blanket that lay over the end of the crib. She might need that tonight. Who knew where she'd be by then?

God knew. Samuel's voice echoed in her mind. *Trust God, Anna. Trust the people who love you.*

She couldn't. Not because she doubted their love, but because they had no idea what they were up against. Confronted with Pete, Daadi would make allowances for him, thinking him a father who surely had some right to his daughter, no matter what papers he'd signed.

Samuel, a little wiser in the ways of the world, would still try to reason with Pete. He wouldn't fight back—that would violate his most deeply held beliefs.

Hoisting the diaper bag to her shoulder, Anna took a last look around the bedroom. They had been happy here. They'd been safe and loved. But the safety had disappeared now, and she couldn't believe that love alone would keep them safe.

Myra stood at the bottom of the stairs. She watched as Anna came down, frowning a little. "Anna, what is this? Where are you going?"

She forced herself to smile, hoping she could look and sound natural. It hurt to deceive Myra, who was as dear to her as a sister.

"I need to run over to Rosemary's for a bit." That part of it was true enough. "I thought I'd take Gracie along. May I use your horse and buggy?"

"Ja, of course." Myra didn't lose her puzzled look, but she agreed without hesitation. "We'll talk later then, ain't so?"

Anna nodded. Later. Later, maybe, she could write to Myra, try to explain. Try to tell her how much she regretted this step.

She hurried away before she could say more. The image of Pete rushing down the road filled her mind.

She sped toward the barn. Thank heaven no one was in sight. No one stopped to ask her what she was doing or where she was going.

By the time she reached the barn, panic had a grip on her throat. *Run, run.* The words pounded in her mind. Run, just as she'd run when she left Chicago. Just as she'd run when she left here the first time.

Myra's mare poked her head over her stall door and whickered a welcome. Anna set Gracie down in the pen that was sometimes used for young animals, clean and empty now. The baby would be safe there while Anna harnessed the horse.

Go to Rosemary's. That was the first step. Rosemary would lend her English clothes, surely, and drive her to Mifflinburg. Once there, she could get a bus to Harrisburg, maybe change there and go on to Baltimore. Baltimore was a big enough city for one woman and a small child to get lost in.

She had to hurry. Samuel could be telling Daad even now. Pete could be driving up the lane.

The mare, maybe affected by Anna's fear, began dancing, her hooves thudding against the wooden floor. Perhaps even Betsy knew Anna was crying inside at the thought of leaving.

"Hush, now, Betsy. Steady." The mare quieted at her voice, tossing her head a bit.

The barn door scraped. Anna spun toward the sound, and her breath caught. Pete stood there, fists clenched, eyes dark.

"Where is my baby? Where is she?"

CHAPTER TWENTY

$\mathcal{S}$amuel had told them, and Anna would never forgive him. He walked out of the shop, giving Elias and Joseph the space they needed to discuss what they would do.

As for him—well, he already knew what he had lost, didn't he? He'd had no choice. All Anna could think was to run, as she had run before.

God had used her running then to bring her home again, where she belonged. Surely He couldn't mean for her to leave again.

He walked away from the shop and stopped in the yard, not sure what to do. Maybe he ought to try talking to Anna again. He half-turned toward the house, but his eye was caught by the glitter of sunlight reflecting off something metal.

A car, parked up the rutted track that led from the road to the barn. The barn door, standing open. An icy hand seemed to grip his heart. Anna—

He began to run, his heart thudding. The man she feared must be there. Had he followed them after all? Anna and Gracie were in danger.

He reached the barn door, thrusting it wider as he went in. The man who stood facing Anna didn't even seem to notice.

"Give me that baby!" He punctuated the words with a violent gesture of his clenched fist.

Anna stood between the stalls, and beyond her Samuel spotted Gracie pulling herself up on the small pen. Anna held Myra's buggy horse by the halter. The mare shifted nervously at the unusual sounds.

"Anna. Are you all right?"

She looked at Samuel, her eyes wide and dark.

He took a step toward her, his gaze focused on hers as he spoke in the dialect the stranger wouldn't know. "Listen to me. Chase Betsy toward him, and then run and get the baby. Try to get over here to me."

She gave a faint nod.

"What're you saying?" Pete swiveled toward him, and any hope Samuel had of reasoning with the man vanished. Pete's thin face was distorted with anger, his eyes wild and dangerous.

Samuel held out a hand, as he would to a skittish horse, automatically trying to calm him. But all his attention was on Anna.

"Anna, schnell."

Anna let go of the halter and slapped Betsy's rump, giving a wordless shout. Betty's hooves scrabbled on the wooden floor, and she lunged toward the open door, baring her teeth at the unaccustomed treatment.

Samuel held his ground, knowing the mare was too smart to run into him. Pete shied away like a frightened animal himself, throwing up his hands to shield his face.

Anna snatched Gracie into her arms and whirled, but there wasn't time. She couldn't make it to the door before Pete recovered.

The distraction let Samuel move. He put himself between Anna and the stranger.

"Watch for a chance to run. It will be all right." *Please, God, let that be true.*

"Talk English, I said!" Pete took a step toward him and seemed to gain some marginal control of himself. "Found yourself a boyfriend, Annie? He can't help you. You just walk over here and give me that baby."

Samuel kept his gaze fixed on the man as he would on a copperhead in the woods. From the corner of his eye he could see the shake of her head.

"Gracie is my daughter, Pete." Her voice was calm, even reasonable, but Samuel heard the terror beneath the words. "You know that. You signed the papers. You told Jannie you didn't want anything to do with a baby. Remember?"

"Yeah, well, I changed my mind. She's my kid. I want her."

"The law says Gracie is my daughter." The edge of desperation was more noticeable.

"I don't see any law around. Just farm boy here." Pete jerked his head toward Samuel. "You think you could hide from me in that costume, Annie? You always thought you were smarter than everybody. Always telling Jannie she could do better'n me. Well, I found you, didn't I?"

"How did you do that? I covered my tracks pretty well."

Samuel knew what Anna was doing—stalling for time, trying to keep him talking. But time for what? Who would come to help? He should have gone for someone instead of racing in here.

"Your friend at the restaurant kept chasing me away. I went back one night, figuring I'd bust up his office. Then I saw his file cabinets. Guess whose job application form was in there. Yours, with the name of some bakery where you worked before, right here in the middle of nowhere."

Anna's lips pressed together. She'd said her friends wouldn't give her away, but she obviously hadn't thought of that application. She seemed to take a breath, as if to rally herself. "So you came here. I saw you in town."

Pete grinned. "I saw you, too. Didn't want to start a fuss out in public, so I just thought I'd follow along at a safe distance. See, the guy at the gas station already told me where the Beilers lived, so I didn't have to get too close." His face darkened suddenly. "Enough of that. Give me the baby."

"Why? You don't love her. You don't even know her."

"She's mine. I'm taking her." He flexed his fists. "You think farm boy here is going to stop me?"

"I will not fight you." Samuel said the words slowly in English. "But I will not let you take Gracie."

Pete didn't respond. Maybe his words hadn't even penetrated. Instead, he charged toward Anna.

Samuel stepped between them. He could not hit the man, but he could put his body between Anna and danger, and he would.

Pete jerked back, anger flaring in his face. Then he swung.

Samuel made no effort to deflect the blow. Planting his feet, he took it, hands at his sides, like being hit full in the stomach by a horse's kick.

"You think I'll back off because you won't fight? You're wrong."

Pete swung again, this time catching Samuel on the jaw, snapping his head back.

"Stop it!" Anguish colored Anna's voice. "He won't hit you because it is against our faith. Please, Pete. Give Gracie a chance to have a decent life. That's what Jannie wanted for her."

"*My* kid," Pete muttered, shaking his head. "Mine." He feinted, trying to get around Samuel. Samuel stepped into his path again. How long? How long could he do this?

Pete charged him, his fists connecting viciously. Samuel's head spun, and he staggered back a step.

Had to stay on his feet. Had to. If he didn't, there'd be nothing protecting Anna and the baby. Couldn't let go, couldn't . . .

His feet went out from under him. He struggled, trying to get up. Pete kicked him, sending him back down again.

Red haze threatened to envelop him. He fought it, hearing Anna cry out. Blinking, he tried to focus, saw Pete grab Gracie and send Anna to the floor with a blow.

Gracie gave a frightened scream. Samuel struggled to get his knees under him, push himself up. Pete was going. He was heading toward the door with Gracie . . .

"Stop!" Elias's voice sounded like a clap of thunder. "Stop now!"

Anna had never heard anything more welcome than her father's voice. She rolled to her side, pushing herself up, trying to clear her head. Daadi was there. Daadi would make it right.

In an instant, sense came rushing in. What could Daadi do? Pete would not let one old man stop him.

"Daadi, don't . . ."

"You think you can stop me, old man? You want to fight?"

"I will not fight you," Daadi said evenly. "But I will not let you take my grandchild."

"We also."

Joseph was there, clinging to the door to stay upright until Myra slid her arm around him. Matthew pressed close to Daadi's side, his young face filled with determination. The four of them filled the doorway. Her people.

"You can't stop me."

But for the first time, she heard doubt in Pete's voice. She forced herself onto her knees.

"Pete, stop and think. You don't want to do this. You can't take care of a baby. What kind of life will you give her? How can you travel and hang out with your friends when you have to watch a baby?"

Pete shook his head, his face twisting. "Tell her to quit the screaming. I can't think with all this screaming going on."

"She won't stop just because I say so. She needs comforting. She needs her mother. Please, give her to me, Pete."

"No!" His face contorted. "I'll take care of her. She's my kid."

"How will you care for her?" Daadi's voice was stern. "You have beaten an innocent man who would not raise a hand against you. You have hit a woman who loves the child. Is that how you will take care of her?"

"I wouldn't hurt the kid. Just make her stop crying." Pete's voice rose. He shook Gracie. Her crying lifted to a frightened shriek.

A fresh jolt of terror went through Anna. "Is that what you told Jannie? That you wouldn't hurt her?" Her heart was beating so hard that it drummed in her ears. Was he hearing any of this? "How long do you think it will be before you strike out at Gracie?"

"I wouldn't."

But she thought there was hesitation in his tone, and her heart leaped with hope.

"A father wants what is best for his children," Daadi said. "No matter how much it hurts him, he does what is best for them."

He didn't press. He just stood there, looking at Pete, his face grave. Waiting.

Please, God. Please, God.

Pete's expression hardened, as if he'd made a decision. He strode toward the four who stood in the doorway, and her heart seemed to stop.

He thrust Gracie into Daadi's arms. Gracie buried her face in her grossdaadi's shoulder, her shrieks fading away into sobs as he cradled her in his arms.

Joseph and Myra moved back, clearing a path. Without a word, Pete walked away.

A sob shook Anna. She managed to crawl the few feet to Samuel even as the others hurried toward them.

"Samuel! Are you all right?" Stupid. Of course he wasn't all right. He had let Pete beat him. For her and Gracie.

His smile was the slightest twitch of his lips. "We are all right now." Then his eyes glazed, and he slumped into her arms.

Anna bent over Gracie's crib. She winced a little as the bar brushed her ribs. Once again, she had Pete to thank for a set of bruises, but this was the last time.

Oddly enough, she had no doubts about that. God had delivered them today. He wouldn't let them down in the days and years to come.

She stroked Gracie's hair, crooning to her. Gracie's eyes drifted closed as sleep claimed her. Anna lingered, reluctant to leave the room. Though she didn't doubt God's care, it might take a while before she felt easy when Gracie was out of her sight.

She kissed her fingertips and touched them lightly to Gracie's forehead. "Sleep well, my sweet girl," she whispered.

She tiptoed from the room. Judging by the sounds coming from downstairs, most of the family was still here. They'd begun arriving within an hour of Pete's departure, summoned by that mysterious Amish grapevine that seemed to work better than any telephone. Even Bishop Mose had heard and had come.

Anna started down the stairs, listening to the hum of voices in the kitchen. The women were there, it seemed, while the men had taken over the front porch.

Bishop Mose saying thanksgiving had, she thought, short-circuited all the wondering and questioning. The right reaction to such unprecedented events, his attitude seemed to say, was to praise God for His deliverance.

She reached the bottom of the stairs and hesitated. She wanted, no, needed, to see Samuel. To assure herself that he was all right.

He'd refused to let the paramedics take him to the hospital, insisting that his bruises would heal and nothing was broken. Maybe so, but the need to see for herself drove her to find him. A glance through the window told her he wasn't on the porch with the other men.

She went back to the kitchen, to be greeted by the smiling faces and loving voices of the women. Rosemary, who'd arrived with a message from Liz moments after Pete had left, had gone home finally, saying she'd call Liz back.

Everyone else was here, waiting. Leah, sitting on the bench with little Rachel asleep in her lap and her stepdaughter leaning against her shoulder. Myra, her face filled with a peace Anna hadn't seen there in what seemed a long time. Barbara, cutting slabs of apple walnut cake that Esther was passing around.

Her people, Anna thought again, as she'd thought when they'd put themselves between Gracie and danger. Not saints, just ordinary people who loved her. Her family.

"Did she go to sleep all right, poor lamb?" Barbara asked. "She wasn't still upset, was she?"

"No, she is fine." Anna hesitated, feeling as if she should say something to them, something of how she felt, of how dear they were to her.

"Ser gut," Leah said softly, her face communicating she knew exactly what Anna was thinking. "Everything is gut now."

Anna nodded, sure that if she did try to speak, she would burst into tears.

"Samuel insisted on going out to check on the horses," Myra said, her voice casual. "If you wanted to go out for a breath of air, you might tell him there's cake and coffee ready anytime he wants."

Anna's heart filled. "Ja. I will." She went quickly out the back door.

They would talk about her and Samuel once she'd gone, but that didn't bother her as it once had. She understood now that it was all in love.

Their voices faded as she walked out into the cool evening. She stepped off the porch and paused. Would Samuel have gone over to his barn?

But there he was, leaning on the fence, watching the young colt grazing in the ring. Like a bird heading for its nest, she went to him.

He shifted toward her as she walked across the grass and joined him at the fence. His face was so battered that she grew in a shaken breath at the sight, but his eyes were peaceful.

"How are you?" She touched his hand where it lay on the rail, and he clasped hers instantly.

"I am well." He smiled. "Contented, I think, is the right word. Do you know what I realized today, when I was lying on the barn floor?"

"That you should never have gotten involved in my troubles?"

"No. Never that." Gentle humor edged the words. "I realized how foolish I'd been, with all my worries about whether I would make the same mistakes my father did." He turned to face her, clasping her hand in both of his. "I knew then that I was ready to die for you and Gracie. If I would die for you, how can I doubt that I would live for you, always?"

He'd stolen her breath away. "Are you so sure of me?" she said when she could finally speak. "I have a bad history of running away when things are difficult."

"I'm not worried." His eyes were tranquil. "You will not run anymore. I love you, Anna, but I won't rush you. Take as much time as you want to answer."

She realized the answer didn't require any time at all. It was already there, in her heart. She'd come home in desperation, but it was God leading her to the place where she needed to be. The only place where she could be the person she really was in her heart.

She smiled, looking at him. "November is not so far off," she said. "If Bishop Mose thinks I'm ready to be baptized into the church, we can be married then. I have a feeling I would like to follow tradition in that."

"Anna Beiler, following tradition," Samuel said. "Think of that. Are you sure?"

"I'm sure." She lifted her face for his kiss. "The prodigal is home to stay."

EPILOGUE

Anna took the black prayer kapp from her head and set it carefully on top of the bureau. She picked up the white one that sat waiting and placed it on her head.

The act seemed almost as solemn as the vows she and Samuel had taken moments earlier before Bishop Mose and the gathered community. She and Samuel were husband and wife. In a moment she'd meet him to go back downstairs to take part in the wedding meal—their first appearance together as a married couple.

"Anna, do you need any help?" Leah paused in the bedroom doorway, smiling at her. "You are a bride, little sister. I am so happy to see this day."

"Denke." Anna blinked back the tears that sprang to her eyes. "I wish Mammi—"

Leah came quickly to hug her. "I know she would be very happy. She always liked Samuel so much."

"She did, didn't she?" Even when Samuel had been just Joseph's friend, Mammi seemed to have a soft spot in her heart for him. Now he was her daughter's husband. Leah was right; Mammi would be pleased.

"The food is ready to start serving." Myra came in, her eyes growing moist as she looked at Anna. "But first I had to come and see my sister."

"Twice your sister," Anna said, her heart filling with love.

Myra was rounder now, though it didn't show so much when she wore the cape, as she did today in honor of the occasion. She and Joseph had moved past the difficult adjustment they'd had to make into a state of serenity about the baby. The shadows were gone from Myra's eyes, and she seemed to look ahead with joy.

"Your friend from the city didn't know what to think of the wedding." Myra's eyes twinkled. "She asked if you were forbidden to wear a bridal gown because of the baby. I told her this is your bridal gown, but I don't think she understood."

Anna smoothed her hand down the skirt of the deep blue dress she wore, made by her own hands with a little help from Myra. And the white apron, which would be kept to be put on over her dress when she was buried. She wouldn't tell Liz that—it would be too much culture shock.

"No, Liz wouldn't understand, but I think she is happy for me." Liz had gotten over her initial surprise at learning Anna was Amish. She'd probably been a little hurt, too, that Anna had kept that from her, but she seemed to understand. And she had traveled all the way from Chicago to sit on a backless bench in a barn for three hours to see her friend married.

"Rosemary has taken her in hand," Leah said. "She'll explain it all."

Anna nodded. Rosemary had proved to be a staunch friend to the Amish. She'd begun volunteering at the medical clinic, filling her days with work that was valuable to the whole community.

"I have gut friends and family. I owe you all so much . . ." She couldn't find the words.

"Ach, enough," Leah said. "There's no talk of owing among family."

"Besides, your groom is here, waiting to take you downstairs." Myra gave her a little shove toward the bedroom door.

There in the hallway, Samuel stood waiting, holding Gracie in his arms. He'd been solemn for the ceremony, but now his lips curved with pleasure at the sight of her.

She went to him quickly. "I thought Elizabeth was watching the little ones."

"Ach, how could our Gracie not sit with us at the eck table for our wedding?" Samuel cuddled her close. "She is our daughter, so she must share the joy of this day."

"Until she starts to fuss at being still for so long," Anna said, but her heart was touched by his gesture.

No, not a gesture. Samuel really did feel that way. He had been willing to lay down his life for Gracie. No one could love more than that.

She reached toward him, and Samuel drew her immediately into the loving circle of his arm for a warm, strong hug.

"So," he said, dropping a kiss lightly on her lips, "are you ready to go downstairs and greet our friends as husband and wife, Anna Fisher?"

"I am." She said the words like a vow. She linked her arm with Samuel's, and they started down the stairs toward the waiting crowd.

Below, she saw the happy faces of those who waited for them—the dear, familiar faces of all who loved and supported them. Her family, her church, her friends. They would stand by this new family through all the years ahead, God willing, and she would be forever grateful that God had brought her home.

Chicken Potpie

For noodles: Mix together 1 tablespoon butter, ¹/₂ teaspoon salt, and 2 cups flour. Add 2 beaten eggs and 2 tablespoons milk. Mix together until a firm dough forms, then turn onto a floured board and roll out in a thin layer. Let stand for 30 minutes. Cut into 2-inch squares.

2 potatoes
2 onions, sliced thin
3 cups cooked chicken, cut into bite-sized pieces
2 cups hot chicken stock
salt
pepper
parsley, chopped

Slice potatoes ¼-inch thick. Line the bottom of a heavy kettle with potato slices. Add a layer of noodles, then a layer of onions, and sprinkle with salt, pepper, and parsley. Add a layer of chicken. Repeat all layers, including potatoes, using up all the ingredients. Pour boiling chicken stock over all. Cover tightly and simmer on the stove top for 20 to 30 minutes, until potatoes are tender.

Funnel Cakes

3 eggs
2 cups milk
¾ cup sugar
3–4 cups flour
½ teaspoon salt
2 teaspoons baking powder
vegetable oil
confectioners' sugar

Beat eggs in a small mixing bowl, then add milk and sugar. In a separate large bowl, sift together half the flour with the salt and baking powder. Add the milk and egg mixture. Beat batter until it is smooth. Add only as much more flour as is needed to make a batter just thin enough to run through a funnel. To a large, heavy skillet add vegetable oil until it is two inches deep. Heat oil until hot. Drop dough through the funnel into hot oil, twisting the funnel as the batter falls to make swirled shapes, each one seven to eight inches round. Cook until the bottom is light brown, then turn and cook the other side until it is also light brown. Remove with a slotted spoon and drain on paper or linen towels. While still warm but not hot, dust with confectioners' sugar.

End-of-the-Garden Relish

12 large green peppers
12 sweet red peppers
12 large onions
1 small head cauliflower
1 stalk celery
3 cups sugar
3 tablespoons salt
2 tablespoons mustard seed
1 quart apple cider vinegar

Substitute cucumbers or other types of peppers as desired. Core and remove seeds from peppers. Remove ends and outside layers from onions and the ends from the celery. Remove stem and any leaves from cauliflower. Chop the vegetables to a fine dice and combine them in a large stockpot. Add the sugar, salt, mustard seed, and apple cider vinegar (white vinegar can also be used). Cook over high heat for about 15 minutes. While still boiling, ladle into hot, sterilized canning jars and cap.

Dear Reader,

I hope you've enjoyed meeting the people of Pleasant Valley. Although the place doesn't actually exist, it seems very real to me, as it is based on the Amish settlements here in my area of central Pennsylvania.

I would love to hear your thoughts on my book. If you'd care to write to me, I'd be happy to reply with a signed bookmark or bookplate and my brochure of Pennsylvania Dutch recipes. You can find me on the Web at martaperry.com, follow me on Facebook at facebook.com/MartaPerryBooks, e-mail me at marta@martaperry.com, or write to me in care of Berkley Publicity Department, Penguin Random House, 375 Hudson Street, New York, NY 10014.

Blessings,
Marta Perry

Photo by Lorie Johnson Photography

A lifetime spent in rural Pennsylvania and her own Pennsylvania Dutch roots led **Marta Perry** to write about the Plain People who add to the rich heritage of her home state. She is the author of more than fifty inspirational romance novels and lives with her husband in a century-old farmhouse.

Visit the author online
at martaperry.com
and facebook.com/MartaPerryBooks.